To Kirk

Stu Plu

Note for Librarians: A cataloguing record for this book is available from Library and Archives
Canada at www.collectionscanada.ca/amicus/index-e.html
ISBN 1-4251-0934-9

Printed in Victoria, BC, Canada. Printed on paper with minimum 30% recycled fibre.
Trafford's print shop runs on "green energy" from solar, wind and other environmentally-friendly power sources.

TRAFFORD
PUBLISHING™
Offices in Canada, USA, Ireland and UK

Book sales for North America and international:
Trafford Publishing, 6E–2333 Government St.,
Victoria, BC V8T 4P4 CANADA
phone 250 383 6864 (toll-free 1 888 232 4444)
fax 250 383 6804; email to orders@trafford.com
Book sales in Europe:
Trafford Publishing (UK) Limited, 9 Park End Street, 2nd Floor
Oxford, UK OX1 1HH UNITED KINGDOM
phone +44 (0)1865 722 113 (local rate 0845 230 9601)
facsimile +44 (0)1865 722 868; info.uk@trafford.com
Order online at:
trafford.com/06-2692

10 9 8 7 6 5 4 3 2

It was a place cloaked in serenity, surrounded by tall spruce with wind whispering through the tops.

His father had taught him trapping and survival skills and told him of how he had proposed to his mother on the shore of this small, secret lake. Since his mother had died, he had often accompanied his father on his trapline and fishing expeditions. During the late autumn, they stopped with the canoe to harvest the wild rice which grew like a delicate sand-coloured forest around the shoreline. He had watched his father's gaze toward one rocky shoreline, sheltered by the spruce and learned it had been there that he had proposed to his mother.

The young woman in the bow of the canoe turned and smiled. "It's beautiful. How come you never brought me here before?"

He smiled back as the canoe coasted gently toward the shore. "I wanted it to be a surprise."

"Just having a honeymoon is a surprise. I wish your dad was alive to know we were carrying on the tradition. I think he'd be happy." They watched the treetops nod in what seemed approval as they moved with the wind.

That evening under darkening sky and the rumble of an approaching storm, they huddled together under the canvas lean-to. They had eaten, made love, then made love again. It was the first time for both of them and they were imbued with a sense of awe at the mutual discovery of each other's body. They heard the gutteral croak of a raven and saw it land in a tall tree on the far side of the pond. Raucous cries came from the tree as three young ravens on adjacent branches vied for the food their mother had brought. Each one flapped its wings, strengthening them for flight. A bolt of lightning crashed down nearby, accompanied by a chorus of wind which rippled the water's surface.

Startled, one young raven flapped with fright and uncertainty in panicked flight, low above the water toward the campsite. It landed with a soft crash onto a low branch and looked at the campers with alarm. It croaked in frustration to its mother who continued to feed its siblings on the branch it had just left. Another bolt of lightning hit the tree with a blinding flash and a deafening explosion.

The young trapper and his new wife jumped in alarm, their hands over their ears. They looked to see the tall spruce now entirely naked of its bark, standing white and ghostly before them. The top smouldered from the heat of the bolt, the smoke wafting away in the wind as the rain began. Cold drops the size of marbles punished the ground around them as the spruce boughs above them shredded the drops into a cold mist.

From one of the branches of the ghostly tree hung three inverted black bundles of smouldering feathers, their claws gripping the branch in a final agonizing spasm of death.

The young raven looked without comprehension toward the remains of its two siblings and mother. It croaked once, then eyed the remains of the young couple's meal. It landed awkwardly beside the remains of the pickerel near the fire pit and began plucking the eyes from the fish heads. It glanced warily at the trapper and his wife as it ate. The trapper smiled and the raven cocked its head to one side, studying his features. The raven had never seen a human before, but immediately associated them with food. It watched the humans warily at first as it gorged itself, then, sensing no danger, turned its full attention to the meal. Once sated, the young raven regarded the two with a calm gaze, cocking its head from one to the other, but its black eyes lingered on the trapper. With a papery rustle of its feathers, it departed.

"I think you've found a friend," said his wife. It wasn't afraid of you. It almost looked as though it knew you."

He watched where the bird had flown into the darkness of the branches, wondering what had made the bird watch him with such intensity.

When they went to sleep that evening he had a dream that he was flying, seeing the treetops from far above. That was the day the dreams really began.

CHAPTER 1

Pilson mumbled to himself as he watched the taut cables slide past each other like greased, black snakes. His magnified eyes behind the thick lenses watched the dark entrance to the mine shaft of Q-1, oblivious of the other bodies gathering near him with their aromas of grease and sweat of unwashed shirts and yellow slickers.

The mouth of the shaft issued a cold sigh of subterranean breath as the air was forced up by the quickly rising cage and its human cargo. The cage slowed silently and came gradually into view, the hat lamps of the miners glowing like dim yellow disks in the semi-darkness of early morning.

"Merde, anudder new topman, "cursed Frenchy Rivest. The voice sounded as though it came from Pilson's armpit. Rivest had sidled in close to his work partner. He was nearly two heads shorter and fifty pounds wider. A dozen others gathered near them, waiting to start their shift, their breaths wisping around them as white vapour in the sub-zero air which blew in from the open door of the headframe. The residual dampness of their clothing made them shiver.

The floor of the cage stopped uncertainly, moved up slightly, then down, to stop finally nearly a foot below the ramp. Cursing under their breaths the huddled mass of bodies in the cage oozed ponderously up out the cage and onto the surface. Wreathed in their odours of sweat and grease, they moved slowly like blackened zombies from some nether-world toward the showers where they would slowly and luxuriously convert back to human form.

"De last time we 'ave new topman , 'e bounce dat cage two feet at de bottom." said Rivest, taking a long drag on his cigarette, causing him to double over with a coughing spasm. "One guy 'e barf all over me from behind, so I barf on de guy in front. Merde what a mess." His eyes were watering from the coughing spasm.

Pilson watched his partner wordlessly with an unblinking stare but not without affection, thinking that he looked like a miniature version of a lumberjack.

Standing together, Pilson and Rivest looked like a hard-hatted version of Mutt and Jeff, Pilson being tall and slightly anorexic in appearance, a visage that deceived others to the actual strength he possessed resulting from the daily regimen of lifting drill rods from the bore hole. Each thirty foot section of rod weighed nearly seventy pounds and with a hole over a thousand feet deep, the effort to draw the full length of the rods was considerable. Peering myopically through spectacles with lenses that magnified his eyes to such an enormity that he resembled a slightly panicked owl, his expression never seemed to change...not even when someone made the mistake of ruffling his feathers in the bar. Then, it was a rather demented looking owl that bludgeoned into insensibility a very surprised and drunk patron. The onlookers and staff had been equally surprised at this rare but vicious response, seldom intervening, for the young man's eyes held a coldness that prevented intervention. He had then returned to his table where he was often the only one drinking, and with huge eyes blinking in apparent disappointment, delicately sipped his beer with the unconcern of one who had simply flicked a dead fly from the table.

Rivest on the other hand was a short, stocky plug of a man with a flattened face and heavy dark eyebrows that knitted together above his nose. His wide-set eyes had a tendency to diverge, often causing him to walk into light standards following a bout of drinking in the local inn, which was usually six of the seven nights of the week. On Sundays he went faithfully to mass where the congregation thought he was truly devout since he honestly appeared to be repentant, due to the pained expression in his reddened eyes. His wife, who walked arm in arm with him, usually did so simply to keep him upright.

"Make way for the Tar-Baby Team," said a voice from the back of the cage as they crammed themselves into the damp confines. The clothing of Pilson and Rivest were liberally coated with hardened layers of drilling grease from the rods of their diamond drill rig. The grease had cracked into patterns that resembled that of a crocodile skin. These particular clothes they never washed because they were more effective for repelling water than the new yellow slickers. To stay dry was to stay warm, and with a drill rig that sprayed icy water under high pressure from every available opening, the greasy layer was a blessing.

No one spoke as the cage-tender rapped out the signals on the bell-chain to the topman, who controlled their descent from the top of the headframe. As the clangingr ended, the huge winches unwound the cable and cage slowly began its descent. The last vestiges of a slate grey dawn disappeared. The cage began to plummet and within seconds the six-hundred and nine-hundred foot levels flashed past. At each level, segments of square fluorescent light flashed past dark images of men frozen like blurred shadows against the cold light, waiting for their ride to surface on the upward trip. The cold air from the bowels of the mine rushed through the lattice-work of the cage, producing a low moaning sound. It reflected the thoughts of many of the men who would rather be going anywhere to make a living than their daily plummet to the dark and damp.

A snap and rumble in quick succession came through the rock, making Pilson flinch and peer upward, toward the cable attachments on the overhead section of the cage. "Dose 'ighballers workin' overtime again," said Frenchy, referring to the mining contracting company that was doing much of the drilling and blasting in the producing sections of the mines' upper levels. The fact that the blasting was taking place on the level immediately above the two-thousand foot level of their drill site was cause for more unease.

As the cage slowed for the last level, twelve sets of eyes watched in wonderment as the track floor stopped at nearly chest height. Muttered oaths came from several of the men as the cage-tender rapped out corrections to the new topman. The cage jerked upward to stop abruptly two feet too high. The oaths of the miners were energetically joined by those of the cage tender. The obviously rattled topman finally eased the cage to a level where the miners could off-load.

The miners muttered their way off the cage, leaving Pilson and Rivest, to walk to their diamond drill site where their sat, its drill bits imbedded with tiny shards of black African diamonds to allow the it to slice through the rock of the Precambrian shield.

It was quiet in the underground cavern next to the main shaft, except for the hissing of airlines and a huge fluorescent light fixture that buzzed and blinked.

The cage-tender quickly lit a cigarette and pulled down the steel mesh door that covered the cage-front. "You guys are going to have company down here the next few days." he said, pointing to a small flatcar sitting on the rail siding near the cavern wall.

Pilson and Rivest could see it was stacked with bags of explosives called Amex, boxes of Cil-Gel and Pentomex primers. The fifty pound bags of orange coloured Amex gave off a slight petroleum aroma.

"The Highballers are going to be down here with you for the next couple of weeks and I'm sure as hell glad I'm not here with you." He gave an evil smile and a wink as he rapped out the signal on his lanyard to ascend. Within seconds the cage had risen silently up out of sight, leaving the two of them together to ponder the arrival of a mining company whose workers had a reputation for putting bonus pay before their and anyone else's safety. Their job involved the use of large amounts of high explosives, packed into hurriedly-drilled holes at the rock face and detonated. The promise of bonus footage was the only motivation and it overrode all other concerns, safety included.

"I hope someone told those crazy bastards that we have a station down here," said Pilson in a high strangled voice, his eyes seeming to grow even larger behind his spectacles as his Adam's apple working frantically. He stared at the explosives car where one of the bags of Amex trickled a fine stream of orange coloured granular explosive onto the track floor. The tiny particles called prills were forming a mound a couple of inches deep from a corner of a plastic bag where it had been ripped open, possibly during manual unloading.

"Merde, I took 'oliday two week ago, should 'ave take anodder week," replied Frenchy with a look of disgust at the flatcar.

Without another word they each shouldered a couple of empty wooden core boxes waiting on the track floor which had been left there by the previous shift. With their lunch boxes in one hand, they shuffled toward the huge swinging blast doors. The huge doors opened to the drift, where their drill sat nearly a kilometre away. Shouldering the doors open, they turned on their hat lights and set them on narrow beam so they could see further into the darkness of the drift in front of them. The walk to the site was without conversation, each immersed in his own thoughts, interrupted only by the hissing of the high pressure airline along the top of the drift wall and the swishing sound of their greasy slickers.

Near the end of the drift sat the drill, squatting like a huge metal mosquito, its drill rods ready to bore into the hard rock with the ease of the insect it resembled in its quest for rich seams of nickel. The drill seemed to suck its life from the rock, its only reason for existence being to probe the vast dark regions below. It squatted in what was known as a pillar raise, a vertical column which had been blasted out of the rock adjacent to the drift, with its roof dome ending about fifty feet above the drill site. The roof was of concern to the drillers because of tiny cracks that had developed near the rock bolts and the heavy metal mesh attached to it to prevent pieces of the rock ceiling from falling on them from above. A scaffolding was constructed in the raise, reaching into the darkness toward the roof, interspersed with three wooden platforms, all connected by ladders.

It was Pilson's job to stand on the uppermost staging while Rivest hauled the lengths of drill rod out of the hole with the air-powered winch. The winch cable was looped around a pulley or sheave wheel, mounted by rock bolts into the rock ceiling. Pilson disliked this part of the job, hearing the cable straining under the tension of pulling tons of weight from the hole, humming like a softly plucked guitar string as the sheave wheel pulled at its rock bolt anchors in the rock with the sound of a reluctant wisdom tooth being extracted. It was part of his job to unscrew the threaded metal plug which fit into one end of the rod lengths once they were pulled from the hole. Frenchy held the rods below with locking jaws connected to a long steel handle to prevent the whole length from slipping back into the depths. When tension was let off the winch so the rods could be broken at the joins and unscrewed, the plug at Pilson's level spun with blurring speed in response to the relaxed tension on the cable. To try and complete the release of the plug by hand before it stopped spinning was to invite a couple of amputated fingers. Through it all he never lost his glassy-eyed owlish appearance, but his Adam's apple seemed to grow in proportion with his eyes and bobbed up and down with its own nervous cadence.

By the time they reached the air-driven drill known as a twin, with its four air-powered pistons, Pilson's throat was in full motion like that of a great heron trying to swallow an uncooperative frog.

"Eh, what luck partner," said Frenchy, "graveyard shift 'ave pulled 'an put de rods back down for us." It was one of the few times he smiled at work. There was the prospect of making some bonus footage at the beginning of the shift.

Pilson's throat stopped bobbing and he smiled with relief because all they had to do was pour oil into the reservoirs and grease all the nipples on the drill head before starting the next run. They felt like they had won the lottery...so many other times they had needed to pull up to a thousand feet of drill rod before being able to earn any footage from the next run.

Frenchy turned on the air for the drill and that of the water pump which rattled like a lawnmower engine. The water was pumped through the hollow centre of the drill rod to cool the tip and prevent it from becoming overheated deep in the hard rock. He cranked open the air valve and started to drill, pausing only briefly to read the note from the previous shift concerning the depth of the hole. The drill howled in a mournful voice, the fog of its cold exhaust venting into the damp air of the confined space, lit with the baleful light of an air-driven mercury vapour bulb and generator.

The site was rocked by a sudden concussion. The force of the explosion knocked the hats and lights from their heads, completely drowning out the howl of the drill with a sharp, cracking blast. Rock dust and particles hurtled past the pillar raise, some fragments ricocheting off the drill and into the dark. With their lights knocked from their hats and swinging at knee-level, Pilson and Rivest stood, mouths open in stunned surprise.

"Merde, tabarnac! What de fuck was dat!" said Rivest, his ears ringing, reminiscent of the time his wife had hit him with a frying pan. To

Frenchy it had been a minor misunderstanding. To his wife Francine there was nothing minor about the smell of another woman's perfume mingled with his beer breath. She decided her technique lacked follow-through. He decidd to duck next time.

Pilson's Adam's apple moved furiously but he said nothing, staring toward the drift face a hundred yards from their site. He finally spoke in a whisper: "Those asshole Highballers had a round ready to go and never warned us. Shit, they aren't even supposed to be down here until tomorrow," he added in a whisper, clipping his light back onto his hat.

"Listen," said Frenchy in a hoarse whisper, as he leaned slowly from the pillar raise into the drift, half expecting another explosion. All he could hear was a faint roar like water going over a waterfall. " Dey open de airline at de rock face to blow out de fumes."

Pilson leaned out and shone his light down the length of the drift from the direction of the blast, his eyes wide and magnified and his throat beginning to get very sore from the fine rock dust and fumes. He heard nothing from the other end of the drift other than the throaty roar of the air from the high pressure line.

Brady Bardman had just lowered his four rolls of thirty-five millimetre film into the fixer solution when the darkroom phone rang. In complete darkness he reached out with one wet hand, feeling for the receiver on the wall and answered. On the other end was the voice of a man who had a habit of ruining his day. He had a premonition that he should have called in sick today.

"Brady, you have to go back underground for some quick shots on the two-thousand foot level of Q-1," said Zenon Mikeluk, editor of the company newsletter. "Come and see me in my office, we have to talk about what we need."

"I'm in the fix." he said, barely concealing the frustration from his voice at being sent back into the hole. He had spent most of the day before, waiting for a drill crew to repair their new rig so he could get some shots of them working. It had been Mikeluk's order to stay until the shoot was finished...even if it took all day. "I'll be up in fifteen minutes,"he said, agitating the film to hurry the fixing process.

"Make it ten," snapped the voice from the other end. "The boss will be here too."

He snapped the white lights on in the darkroom and agitated the film even faster in the vain hope it would clear more quickly.

8

In his late twenties and only in his present job for the past three months, Bardman was still on three months probation. He knew he had to be on his best behaviour since being fired from his previous job as a staff photographer with a daily newspaper. His dismissal was the result of his tendency to speak his mind about editors with no photography training and their warped ideas on what constituted a good photograph. He came to the conclusion that most of the editors were kissing the butt of the publisher and assigning photographers to do grip-and-grins of the publisher shaking the hand of some witless politician or major advertiser. He kept saying to himself that he had three more months of butt-kissing and shoe-licking to make it off probation here. It didn't mean he would change his attitude about doing the best job possible, but he knew Mikeluk was going to push him just for the fun of seeing him fly off the handle and jeopardize his chances of staying. *Probably has a relative who wants the job,* he thought to himself. He wasn't going to give him the satisfaction of a knee-jerk reaction to the persistent verbal digs he received regularly from him.

He quickly transferred the film to the wash tank and propelled his stocky two hundred pound frame toward the editors' office. At only five foot four, he walked with a swagger to prevent his thick thighs from rubbing together. His belt had a tenuous hold on his pants below an evolving beer belly, and his shirt appeared ready to split and reveal his hairy girth in all its corpulent glory. His outward appearance of fat hid considerable physical strength, like that of a weight lifter going soft. Others of the staff often watched with trepidation for a sign that his pants were about to succumb to gravity.

"Aw damn," he muttered under his breath, suddenly realizing his tie had been dangling in the fix while on the phone. It was soaking wet with the fixer chemical and the vinegar-like smell emanated from him as he fumbled with the knot, looking for a place to discard it before entering Mikeluks' office. With his right hand he shoved the freshly-folded tie into his pant pocket and entered the editors' office. He immediately saw the editor deep in conversation with an immaculately attired man in his fifties. Their appearance was conspiratorial and their stance made him uncomfortable.

"Ah Brady there you are. This is Roger Jenkins, *our president,*" said Mikeluk saying the last words as though he was going to pull the company flag out and start waving it around in a fit of company patriotism, perhaps even sing a few bars of the company song. He sincerely hoped one didn't exist or it might be his next duty to learn and perform it on demand.

He extended his hand toward Jenkins. Too late, he realized it was still soaked with the chemical fixer from his tie which he had jammed into his pocket. Their hands came together with the sound of two pieces of raw meat slapping together.

Jenkins' attempt at an intimidating power handshake had been thwarted by the moisture. While trying unsuccessfully to maintain some kind of grip on the chubby photographer's hand, he looked him in the face with the uncomfortable expression of someone reading the fine print on a tube of hemorrhoid medication.

"Sorry," said Bardman, blushing furiously. "Sometimes I literally get immersed in my work." He could feel the moisture from the tie soaking through the fabric of his pants near his groin, and a distinct chemical-induced itch was developing in the area of his genitalia. His initial apprehensions about this meeting were quickly being realized, and all he wanted to do at the moment was scratch himself and run with abandon back to the soothing confines of the darkroom.

Mikeluk rolled his eyes at him while the president sniffed daintily at the fingers of his right hand. He reached into his trouser pocket for a hanky with the other.

"We need some colour shots taken at the two-thousand foot level, where you sat on your butt most of yesterday to get one shot. The accusatory tone put the hair up on the back of Bardman's neck. There's been an incident near the diamond drill site on that level."

"An accident?"

"No, an *incident*." Zenon Mikeluk had a self-satisfied smirk on his freckled face. It was a twelve year old face on a thirty year old marshmallow-like body. His pants were too short and it was obvious he wasn't wearing socks. Acne pimples blotted his pasty complexion, topped by a full head of curly brown hair which was rumoured to be driving the president's daughter wild.

It didn't surprise Bardman to see the two conversing like family, if the rumours were true that Mikeluk had in fact deflowered the president's homely daughter. Sometimes the price of advancement is just too high he thought.

"If there are bodies and gore all over the place, I suppose you'll want colour shots. I hate blood and gore, all I did was chase ambulances on night shift at the newspaper."

Mikeluk said, "Sorry to disappoint you old fellow," with a fake British accent and an equally fake smile. "Just a bunch of loose rubble and rock where an explosion went off. We don't even know how much explosives but it was enough to rupture an airline at the face of the drift and nearly concuss the two diamond drillers working nearby." He was pacing back and forth,

10

back arched, moist red lips pouting, his voice taking on a distinctive Churchill-like tone. His hands deep in his pants pockets worked furiously at something newly discovered there. For a moment he studied the squashed remains of a fly on the ceiling directly above him., wondering how anyone could have swatted it that high up.

Roger Jenkins had not added to the conversation, instead he busied himself with his freshly wetted hand, alternately wiping it with obvious distaste and sniffing it, causing his dark eyebrows to wriggle like a couple of hyperactive caterpillars. Finally, pursing his lips as though having sucked on a sour lemon, he jammed his hands deep into his pockets and began working frenziedly with whatever he could also find down there. His face shone as though just having had a facial treatment, and his hands, the rare times they were out of his pockets were immaculately manicured. In contrast to this and his expensive suit, was the Mickey Mouse watch on his left wrist. It had been a gift from his pimply but much-loved daughter, and he refused to remove it, much to the frustration of his gargantuan wife whom he referred to with his drinking cronies as the sofa that walks. "We want you to go down alone because the less people that know about this the better," said Jenkins, the interior of each pant pocket beginning to jump as though a rodent was trapped there. "We've talked to the two drillers who were near the explosion and asked them to keep quiet. You probably remember them; you photographed them about a week ago."

Jenkins realized that Bardman had his gaze fixed on his hyperactive pant pockets and quickly removed his hands. "Don't disturb anything at the site, just take every angle you can, and then rush the film through this evening so we can see contacts in the morning."

Mikeluk watched without speaking, smirking at Bardman as Jenkins took his leave with a flourish of both hands in the air in an effort to rid them of their stink as though conducting an orchestra through the 1812 Overture at double time

"You might consider changing your pants before coming in to work tomorrow, Bardman. Quite frankly you stink," whined Mikeluk still smirking, amused at the photographer's discomfort, enjoying a sense of his own personal superiority. It was something he seldom experienced with any of the other staff.

With a cold knot of anger in his guts, Bardman left without replying. He shot a glance at his editor which would have peeled paint. Mikeluk caught his expression and the smirk faded as quickly as a politicians promise.

Back in the photography department, Bardman quickly packed his two Quantum battery packs for the Vivitar flashes. With them went slave cells to trigger a flash at a distance from the main one. He would need the other flashes to light an area as large and dark as the drift face, without running cords that people could trip over. Into the bag also went two Olympus OM-1's with power-winders, a 24mm, 35mm, and 58mm lens. He would avoid using the 24mm because it distorted the image at the edges, and scale would be important when it came to gathering evidence.

Fully decked out in his yellow slickers, hard-hat, and safety glasses, his size fourteen steel-toed rubber boots, made a 'galumphing' sound on the way down the hall, tripod under one arm, and camera bag over his shoulder.

Picking up his hat light and battery at the charging station, he headed once again to the cage area where he could hear the soft moan of the skip tram hauling ore from the depths to the surface in its high speed bucket.

It was a silent trip with only the cage-tender for company. He hated the constant popping of his ears as they tried to adjust to the changes in pressure caused by dropping quickly the two thousand feet to the bottom of Q-1. He could almost taste the grease, its stench so strong, hanging in the air like smog. The grease covered the floor of the cage, and smeared the lattice work of the sliding door, forcing him to stand in the centre of the cage to avoid soiling his camera bag. A chill crept over him and slid down the neck of his open collar like a serpent seeking warmth.

"Fancy camera ya got there," said the cage-tender leaning against one grimy corner.

Bardman only nodded in reply, He preferred to remain wrapped in his own murky thoughts and not really care if the other man was offended or not. He could feel the others hat light shining inquiringly into his face but decided not to look up at it.

The cage quickly slowed and eased to a stop. The cage-tender lifted the two outer doors and even before Bardman had fully exited, the man swiftly yanked on the signal handle to return to the top, where he could finish his coffee and get back to his western novel.

Bardman wheeled suddenly and yelled, "Hey, come back for me in about an hour." The two steel-toed boots rising toward the surface gave no indication they had heard as they disappeared quietly from sight.

Bardman stood alone and silent under the harsh glare of the florescent lights hanging from the ceiling of the drift. One of them buzzed and flickered. It was the only area equipped with electric lights on each of the levels. The need to see well was paramount where the off-loading of equipment and explosives took place. It was also the area where ore cars dumped their loads into the gaping maw of the primary crusher along one wall of the cavernous area. The cars were tipped automatically by a steel inclined wall, as the cars passed. The crusher opening was crossed by a series of steel rails called grizzly bars to prevent oversized ore from crashing down onto the huge chains that began the crushing process before sending it to a secondary crusher on the surface. Pieces too large to drop through the grizzly bars were dealt with by an unfortunate soul with a sledge hammer, tethered to a safety line in the event he lost his footing. The metal mouth was silent, waiting with infinite patience for its next meal. A small flatcar sat on the rail siding just inside the huge orange blast doors that swung out to the drift.

Thankful for the opportunity to take the weight from his shoulders, he put his load of equipment on the car and pushed open the swinging blast doors with it into the darkness of the drift. From what seemed a long way off he could hear the banshee howl of an air-driven diamond drill, echoing ghost-like, rising and falling in pitch. He turned and went the other way into the darkness, his hat light illuminating a tiny part of the track ahead of him as he bent over the car, listening to its wheels rumble against the walls of the drift. During the twenty minute journey he could hear the occasional snap and rumble of explosives being set off at other levels as the rock transmitted the sound through the rock and then through the air of the network of tunnels. He realized Teresa was going to be really pissed off if he was late for dinner, but at the moment other, more troublesome thoughts were forming in his mind.

CHAPTER 2

The Kenworth, with its elongated hood eased up the incline of a small hill, its empty forty- foot trailer swaying slightly on the uneven gravel road. Teresa D'Amico shifted down into third overdrive on the fifteen speed transmission and watched the tachometer drop toward the 1300 rpm mark. Cresting the rise, she was able to shift up again into top gear. The Cummins diesel engine gave a rattle of contentment as the load eased on the transmission. It had been a gruelling trip north with 40,000 pounds of high explosives. The hydro-electric project to the north was damming off the Blackwood River and diverting other lesser rivers to produce power for a perceived power shortage in the near future. At least that was what the politicians said on the news. She gave them about as much credence as the average used car salesman. She and her partner, Joe McKay had left the explosives depot the night before with their load of Amex and Cil-Gel and without their knowledge, an illegal inclusion of Pentomex primers and a small wooden barrel of caps and fuses. She glanced over at McKay in the jump seat. His eyes were half open under the peak of his cap perched on a mane of shoulder length black hair. She was always amazed at how he could sleep quietly sitting bolt upright. The sun was rising above the horizon ahead of them like a frozen orange adorned with ice crystals suspended in the -50 degree air of a January morning.

McKay opened his eyes and squinted, leaning slowly toward the partly frosted windshield. "Raven farts," he said quietly.

"What the hell are you taking about?" she replied, her eyes beginning to water from the intensity of the light blazing through the frosted windshield.

"Right there on the horizon. See them?"

" You mean those little clouds over the trees, the ones that look like little cotton balls?"

"Yeah, " he said. "Raven farts. When the raven finds a fresh meal in the morning, you know, something that's died. They eat so much they can hardly fly. When they finally take off, they get gas and start to fart."

"What a bunch of crap," she said with a disbelieving smile.

"No, that comes next. We call those birdy-bombs." His broad native face turned toward her, his intelligent eyes sparkling with mischief. He took in the tall lithe form of his partner, admired her muscularity that didn't overcome the obvious feminine qualities. With the heater turned up full in the cab, she had stripped down to a T-shirt revealing the corded muscles of her arms as they guided the eighteen wheeler toward home.

She looked furtively back at him, unsettled by his appraising glance. When she had first started with North Haul Trucking, she had no idea who her partner would be but only having earned her class 1 and air brake endorsements in the past three months, she really had no choice. She soon learned she was fortunate to be teamed with one of the best drivers in the company, known to be level-headed and unexcitable. She learned a lot in the three months they had worked together at North Haul Transport, but it had taken almost a month before their conversations had progressed past the morning salutations and muttered instructions. He enjoyed ragging her with descriptions of the bodily functions of various animals of the wild which usually resulted in her rolling her eyes or shaking her head quietly in dismay."Now what are you looking at?"

"You ever wear dresses?" said McKay his eyes crinkled around the edges as he smiled, revealing wide white teeth with a gap in the front through which he spit frequently and sometimes whistled tunelessly.

"No, you?"

He gave an audible grunt and smiled to himself, realizing he was beginning to lose these verbal jousts with her. He was a little intimidated by her attributes of brains, body and abilities, so decided to change the subject. "Time for a kick and pee," he said, stretching his arms over his head to touch the back of the cab with his hands. His back arched and his mouth opened in a yawn that appeared to unhinge like a snake swallowing prey. He slumped loosely back to the jump seat and pointed to the side of the road where it seemed wide enough for her to pull over without obstructing other traffic.

Without a word she pulled to the side and stopped, pulling the large, coloured airbrake parking buttons for the tractor and trailer. They made a pop and whoosh sound as the parking brakes engaged. "One of these days, you're going to throw your back out stretching like that and I'll be stuck driving all the way home," she said, reaching behind the seat for her jacket.

"It's something my old man showed me. I'll show it to you sometime when my wife is out of town visiting my fat sister-in-law."

She didn't respond to the little wink he gave as he exited from his door, other than a sour little smile, the type she reserved for puppies that pee on the carpet. She knew he was happily married and had no in-laws. Sometimes the best response was no response.
Her driver's door suddenly opened and he was staring up at her, not smiling and his face devoid of the usual healthy colour.

"Come and look at somethin'," he said, motioning sideways with his head.

"She climbed down, happy to stretch her legs as the frigid air almost immediately began to cause a burning sensation to her nose and ears. She quickly zipped up her jacket and reached for her mitts behind the seat, already starting to shiver.

"Need more body fat," mumbled McKay to himself.

"Stop comparing me to your sister-in-law. If this is a flat tire, you can fix it yourself, 'cause you found it."

Clouds of vapour came from their mouths as they exhaled and her eyes were beginning to water from the cold air, forming tiny rivulets down her cheeks to end in a tiny frozen icicle at the tip of her chin. Their boots crunched audibly on the frost-impregnated road as they walked toward the middle of the 40 foot trailer.

McKay raised a mitted hand to the side of the trailer, pointing to a hole, and then another several feet toward the rear. "Somebody's shootin' at us," he said quietly, turning to look at her with a seriousness she had never seen before. They walked to the other side and saw one exit hole with its metal edges curving outward.

"One must be still in there," she said, walking to the rear swing-out doors to open them.

He grabbed her hand before she could lift the latching handle and said: "This is cop's business. We call 'em as soon as we get back."

She relented as he pulled a metal seal from his parka pocket and looped it through the locking holes of the latch mechanism. "Did this happen going up or coming back empty?" she said, beginning to shiver almost uncontrollably.

McKay shrugged. "Dunno...this hole's too high to hit the powder, but the other one might have hit somethin'" he said wiping his nose on the back of his sleeve. "Might have hit the Amex...it's stable, but the other stuff would have turned us into a big hole in the road." He leaned forward, taking a closer look at her face. "I'm drivin'...you don't look that great." She offered no argument, silently glad she could be passenger for a while and walked silently to the other side of the tractor. The engine rattling in the sub-zero air seemed very loud compared to the still, silent forest on either side of the road, blanketed by the pristine white mantle of new snow. Five minutes later while shifting up to overdrive, he popped the gearshift into neutral with a pained expression and eased the rig to the side of the road once again.

She looked over at him with concern.

"Forgot to take my pee." he said, hurriedly climbing from the cab.

She smiled to herself and settled her head against the jacket now acting as a pillow against the frost-covered window, and closed her eyes, hoping she could catch at least an hour of uninterrupted sleep.

The old trapper sat on a piece of deadfall, his two 'bear paw' snowshoes leaning beside him in the deep snow. As he munched his moose meat sandwich his eyes took in the vacant trap before him. At one time this area had regularly offered up beaver, mink and bobcat that he had skinned, stretched and cured for the prime prices paid by the buyers from the south. He didn't understand the intricacies of the fur market, nor those who came to haggle over the pelts that he and the other trappers had brought in but he could begin to understand the scope of the white man's stupidity and greed when they began damming up rivers and diverting others for their hydro-electric projects.

On this small unnamed tributary of the Black Wood River system, the water had risen over the past year until the beaver had abandoned the area and gone elsewhere for more stable water level to make their homes. In the toboggan hooked to the rear of his snowmobile there was a large canvas sack containing the hard-frozen carcasses of a mink and two bobcats. The contortions of their bodies bespoke the possibility that the leg-hold traps may not be as humane as the public was led to believe. He felt an affinity to all the creatures he trapped and he respected their environment with a reverence that was part of his spiritual upbringing. He hated to see anything suffer. His deep-set eyes surrounded by the tough leathery skin of his face were still sharp despite his seventy years. His large hands with fingers the shape of sausages were as strong and muscular as they had been in his youth, but the legs of his short stocky body were beginning to fail due to osteoarthritis in his knees. The once simple, joyful act of rising on a clear cold morning had become agony and it seemed hours before his joints would begin to loosen. The snowmobile, a gift from his son who lived in the white man's world, had done much to take the burden from his legs.

He refused to give up the bear-paw snowshoes. They allowed him to leave the contaminating noise and stink of the machine to examine his traps amongst the comforting silence of the forest. In the pristine snow he could read the activities of the citizens of the forest. The deer often stayed to well-travelled paths and left their body outlines where they had bedded for the night. The occasional track of a bobcat was seen, sometimes punctuated by the blood and feathers where they had found an unwary ptarmigan or grouse hiding in the snow. Cow moose with their yearling calves made double prints while the bulls went their solitary ways until rutting time urged them back. The snowshoe hare left its distinctive over-sized prints, but his favourite creature could be heard frequently chortling in the distance, its' song echoing amongst the trees.

The large raven watched from a distance, hoping the old trapper would leave an offering as he had so often done in the past.

"Old black one you follow me like I was prey," said the old trapper to the silence around him. He sat still with the remnants of his sandwich in one hand and pulled back the hood of his parka to listen. The occasional crack of wood could be heard as the sap froze in a tree trunk, splitting it. The new snow from the night before lay in a white blanket covering the bases of the trees as well as heaped upon the boughs in sparkling white mounds. Occasionally the snow slid from the boughs to the ground with the sound of a cold whisper.

A black shape took form barely within the periphery of the old trapper's eyesight and sat without moving. The trapper slowly held out his arm full length, his palm up with a piece of moose meat in plain view. The raven moved gingerly to a closer branch, swivelling its head around, its' intelligent eyes watching for danger. The large black beak and those two shining eyes made it the comedian of the bird world. Finally the raven moved to within mere feet of the offering being held out. It peered intently from its perch over the shoulder of the old trapper who had not moved. With a final leap and thrashing of wings the raven snatched the meat from the trapper's hand and fled in full flight to the surrounding spruce trees. From the concealment of the foliage, the raven emitted a chortling croak as it downed the meat in one gulp.

Slowly, the trapper rose and stepped into his snowshoes. The sun was getting lower and in December the dark came very early in the northern latitudes. Reaching the snowmobile he pulled a large canvas tarp from the rear and quickly erected it into a lean-to into which he put his heavy sleeping bag. A bed of spruce boughs made soft mattress under the sleeping bag and before long, a comforting fire warmed the old trapper as he prepared a meal of bannock and hot, sweet tea. In the distance he could hear the howl of a lone wolf as the shroud of darkness and the stillness of the forest descended around him.

Sam Pilson and Frenchy Rivest were well into their third beer when the waitress arrived at their table with two more bottles of lager. "Eh Dorothy, free beer now eh?" said Rivest, his black hair standing in spikes from his head as he eyed her full breasts. Across the table, Pilson reached for one of the beers without the slightest curiosity as to who had sent them. He thought he might even have ordered them, but couldn't recall. He reached for his wallet.

Dorothy stopped him in mid-reach."Toothless Jake and Big Don are payin' this round," she said with a wave of her thumb in their approximate direction a couple of tables away. "They said to tell ya it works better'n Aspirin."

Through the smoke and crowd, Pilson could make out Toothless Jake Smiley and Big Don Bunkerfort watching them, smiling in a conspiratorial manner. Pilson motioned them over with his hand rather than compete verbally with Hank Williams Junior wailing rom the juke box about tears in his beer. He still had a ringing in his ears that overrode all the sounds of hooting, hollering and clashing of musical tastes from two different juke boxes at opposing ends of the bar. The juke boxes faced each other, looking like multi-coloured refrigerators, their contents of terrible country-western music assaulting everyone in the bar. He grinned drunkenly at them, his throat bobbing with anticipation.

Toothless Jake grinned hugely back with pink gums, a featureless cavern with only a pink tongue darting out like a tiny snake seeking out the next drink. Jake's squinty eyes and his cap in permanent lock position with the peak to the side showed he had been here for some time and was planning to stay longer.

Big Don in contrast to Jake's elfin grin and build was a study in latent power. At six feet, four and 250 pounds, he slumped in his chair, legs splayed out in front of him, his enormous chin resting on his chest, and his too small baseball cap perched on the back of his head. His fingers played with the puddles of beer on the table in an attempt to draw a likeness of Dorothy's bosom. The art kept running onto the floor and Big Don was becoming a frustrated artist. He turned and gave a slow wink to the two diamond drillers along with a dainty wave from his pinky finger. As if by telepathy, Toothless Jake and Big Don rose simultaneously from their chairs with beers in hand and made their way over to them.

"I t'ink I ask Dorothy out tonight," said Frenchy, his chin resting in his hands, both elbows soaking up spilled beer from the table top. With his short stature he looked like a drunken ten year old barely able to see over the table's edge.

"Fee wouldn't go out wif you, your hairf a meff," said Jake from between his gums.

"Oh sure, all womens like Frenchmens eh? All my 'air need is a little somet'ing to 'old it down," he said while splashing his hands on the beer-sodden table and then slicking his hair down with them. His hair was straight back as though he had broken the sound barrier headfirst.

"You look like a drunken paintbrush," said Big Don now tipped back in his new chair which creaked under his weight. He watched Rivest and Pilson with amusement. "You'd be a real catch for some girl who likes hair soaked in beer. All she'd have to do is lick your hair once in a while."

" Eh, great idea," said Rivest sitting up straighter. " Dorothy would love dat. I even pour my beer down my pant for 'er."

Pilson leaned forward and looked at Frenchy's already soaked crotch and smiled wordlessly at him with his magnified eyes behind the thick lenses. Except for the corners of his mouth, his facial expression was like that of a reptile about to eat a rat.

"Aw tabarnouche, 'ow I do dat?" declared Frenchy now peering with great interest at his own crotch area. He could feel his amorous possibilities slipping away.

"You havin' another wet dream about me?' chided Dorothy from over Frenchy's shoulder.

He leaned back in his chair, his mouth open in wonder at the apparition presented by her bosom as he stared from beneath at those marvellous protuberances. She leaned over and seemed to peer down his throat while he saw the two objects of his drunken desire come within grabbing distance. He lunged as best he could, already being in a rather compromised position...and missed as Dorothy nimbly stepped back. His chair began to topple and Big Don reached out a huge arm to stop it in mid-fall. Frenchy sensed some extra weight in his crotch area and looked down to see the cloth deposited there by Dorothy who was now turning away toward the bar. "You 'it my love spot wit dat clot Dorot'y. Will you marry me?" The expression on his face indicated that he was either thoroughly drunk or thoroughly in love. To Frenchy there was little difference

"Sufferin' from a little headache there Frenchy?" said Big Don with an expression of new interest on his face.

"It almost pinned us to the wall like moths." replied Pilson in a high gargling voice. His hearing was beginning to improve despite the sounds of Dolly Parton in the distance, shrieking something about working nine to five. The other juke box countered with the moans of Randy Travis, something about bones.

It was obvious to Big Don that the overly magnified eyes were due to more than just the eyeglasses that appeared to have been cut from the bottoms of Coke bottles. He could see they were both scared silly and the beer was only a temporary relief.

"Duh docteur, 'e check us out," said Frenchy, with beer dribbling down his chin. "'E 'old up 'is fingers an' say, 'ow many? I say quatre, an 'e say this ain't no damn cat. Damn English, don' no 'ow to say four, make me wanna puke."

"Fure, four. It comef right after free," said Jake with his hat now turned completely around to the rear.

"Doc said we don't have concussions. Just headaches that'll last a couple of days with ringin' ears," said Pilson industriously peeling the label from his beer bottle. His hands shook. "We have to go back down tomorrow to check and see if the staging is still safe for pulling our rods, but they better sure as hell make sure there's nothin' else down there to go boom or someone's going to be wearing a drill-rod suppository. It was the longest sentence any of the group had ever heard him speak, and Pilson himself appeared to blink his huge eyes in surprise at the precedent he had set.

"Oh mon Dieu, my poor 'emmorhoid." moaned Frenchy, his hair standing once again at attention.

"Did you smell anything strange before the explosion?" asked Big Don, slouched forward, huge arms on the table and looking intently at his partner. His stare made Pilson's throat come alive with nervous energy.

"Just Frenchy's socks but the whole shift knows that smell." He didn't know why he said that, suspecting his new-found verbosity might be caused by the beer.

"D'ats because dey 'ave h'adverse reaction wit Docteur Scholls. said Frenchy who was now stuffing Dorothy's table rag down the front of his pants, giggling and drooling simultaneously.

"The blast came from the end of the drift and we never go there unless we have to go to the John," answered Pilson who was becoming uncomfortable with the direction of the conversation as well as the location of Dorothy's bar rag. "Besides, the boss told us to say nothing to anybody until they had somebody investigate the place."

"Well we have an interest in what happened too," said Big Don leaning even more over the table toward Pilson, whose reaction was to lean further back in his chair and make threatening gestures back with his throat. "We either supply or make all the explosives that are used down there," he continued, his face now tense, even threatening. "If it was our powder that blew up in your face we want to know about it and how it got there."

Toothless Jake only nodded silent assent to the two drillers who had suddenly become considerably more sober in the past five seconds. They sat in silent thought for a moment while the stench of smoke, stale beer, and

Frenchy's socks permeated their nostrils. Suddenly they both got up from their chairs and left without a word.

It became obvious to Rivest and Pilson that they had been interrogated with the help of a couple of beers. They looked at each other silently. Frenchy started to giggle. Pilson stared glassily at his partner in consternation.

The last thing the two explosives men saw as they left the Stag Inn was Frenchy standing on his chair, hands down by his groin, waving something at Dorothy who was doubled over in laughter. Pilson had a look of general disbelief on his bespectacled face while his throat bobbed spasnodically.

Joe McKay wheeled the Kenworth into the North Haul yard as the sun set. It had been an eight hour drive back despite pulling an empty trailer. While D'Amico slept with her head against her coat, his thoughts kept returning to the bullet holes. There had been no answers, only more questions as to their origin. He knew full well that the hydro projects were destroying peoples lives, those people who relied on hunting, trapping and fishing simply to subsist. He hoped they wouldn't resort to such a response, but he could understand their frustration at not knowing how or to whom to express their justifiable anger. As he backed the trailer into a space between two others, his partner stirred and yawned, uncoiling from her curled up position like a boa constrictor. The interior of the cab was coated with a fine veneer of dust, blackened by grease. There was the pungent aroma of diesel fumes, armpits and sweaty clothing.

D'Amico was glad that the explosives act dictated that the drivers be nonsmokers, because the added stench of the ash tray would have been enough to force her to look for another job. "Here we are," she said while trying to moisten her mouth which had hung open while she had slept. Eyes bleary from fatigue she climbed to the ground with her jacket as McKay exited from the driver's side of the cab.

A shrieking of metal ensued as McKay cranked the trailer dollies down by hand to allow the trailer to be unhooked from the tractor. He muttered the occasional curse under his breath as he had to shift the crank shaft into the lower gear due to the lack of grease. There seemed to be grease everywhere except where it was most needed, namely on the moving parts.

The sound sent shivers up D'Amico's spine as she stood on the flat deck of the rear of the tractor, unhooking the twin air hoses that supplied air from the compressor to the trailer brakes. The frigid metal fittings drained the warmth from her hands despite her heavy mitts as the exhaust from the idling diesel engine snapped into the air from the vertical exhaust stack next to her. The vapour trail from the stack went straight up into the still night air where a vivid display of green aurora borealis writhed ghost-like across the sky, obstructing even the sharp dots of the stars. She could make out a well-defined halo of rainbow colours around the full moon, a sure sign that the frost causing such refraction would promise even more cold weather for the days to come. A final metallic groan emanated from the trailer dollies as they settled firmly onto the frozen ground, lifting the trailer slightly above the level of the fifth wheel attachment which connected the two units together. She jumped to the ground and reached under the trailer near the fifth wheel, found the length of chain connected to the release mechanism and yanked mightily on it. The dogging pin released with an audible click. The units were now unlocked and ready to be separated.

McKay climbed behind the wheel, released the parking brakes and slowly eased the tractor from beneath the trailer while she drained the air from the air reservoir at the rear of the trailer to prevent the condensation built up in the brake drums from 'dynamiting', or seizing them up. It had taken only one experience of releasing brakes with a steel bar to never forget the process.

"What do you say we park this thing and go for a beer?" said D'Amico, her throat dry from the dust in the cab.

He smiled and nodded agreement as the tractor now unencumbered from the trailer bounced or 'bob-tailed' its way, chains rattling like a metallic symphony from behind the cab along the rough street toward the company garage. The hard suspension without the extra weight jolted them both wide awake.

"Does your wife think I'm a bad influence on you Joe?" she said, making her voice sound sweet and musical in a mocking Barbi-doll way.

"I told my wife that some woman with more muscles than me shouldn't worry her. You know what she did? She went into the bathroom and looked at her muscles in the mirror. Now she's planning to take up weight-lifting at the high school gym," he said with mock seriousness. "Because of you, I'm going to be with two women who are stronger than me. My son will think I'm a wimp."

She smiled while listening to his complaints that were no doubt fictional to get some kind of response from her. "Just teach him how to cook and let us women do all the hard work," she chided.

He leaned closer to the windshield and scraped some frost from where his breath had been freezing on the interior surface.

When they finally arrived at the Stag Inn, the neon sign on the outside was liberally coated with hoar frost from the warm, moist air leaking in visible streams of vapour from around the door. They side-stepped quickly as a small compact body hurtled uncontrollably into the cold night, followed by a flurry of mitts, parka and toque.

"Aw Dorothy, don' be mad. I h'am only a Frenchman in love. Merde, tabarnac," slurred the tiny patron, still on his hands and knees, his recovered toque pulled down over his eyes. Thus encumbered, he proceeded to grope for his mitts and parka while pushing his toque above one eye which was now beginning to swell shut and darken.

D'Amico bent and picked up the mitts, handing them to the diminutive drunk who managed to get them backwards on his hands. Mckay handed him his parka while she held him upright and helped him stuff his mitted hands down the sleeves only to become stuck short of actually coming out the ends of the sleeves. McKay did up the zipper of the ejected patron to the top so that all that showed was his nose which was also beginning to swell to an unhealthy size and colour. Looking like an over-sized pre-schooler on a binge, the former patron staggered into the night.

"Think he'll make it home alive?" said she to Joe as they watched the diminutive figure stagger along the sidewalk and stop for a serious conversation with a fire hydrant.

"Thanks to the Stagger Inn. Who knows?" He spoke with a hint of sadness in his voice.

"Stagger Inn...crawl out. Isn't that their motto?" she added as they entered the bar and were assaulted with a cacophony of shouting, clinking beer glasses, stench of stale beer, and cigarette smoke. Don William's voice could barely be heard over the insane din as he moaned something about learning to read the six o'clock news.

"Damn! I forgot I'm cooking dinner tonight for Brady in a half-hour," she said, taking in with distaste the scene of debauchery before her. She realised she was only one of two women in the establishment, the other being the waitress who was attempting to straighten her blouse and button it high enough to hide what appeared to be tooth marks above the bra line of the left breast. An ice pack was wrapped to the knuckles of her still balled left fist.

"Don't worry, we'll drink quick and stagger quicker, 'cause if I'm late for supper, my wife starts to throw things. You know how women are," he said with his familiar wink.

She elbowed him in the ribs roughly enough to make him flinch. Despite his chauvinistic comment, she had to admit she enjoyed cooking for

Brady Bardman. He ate everything without complaint, often asking for seconds, glad to get a meal someone else had cooked. His only obligation being to help with the washing up afterwards. He knew a good thing when he saw it.

Nearly one hour later, Bardman sat back in the kitchen chair with his legs stretched out, feet resting on the other chair, cradling a can of beer on his stomach with both large hands. A head of Romaine lettuce whistled past his head, hitting the micro-wave behind him with a solid THUNK. It lay beside him on the table, dripping water onto the surface. " Tossed salad again tonight?" he quipped, admiring D'Amico's shapely derriere in the tight jeans as she bent into the refrigerator looking for more ammunition.

"Flying Caesar salad and Fettuccine Alfredo," came her voice from the refrigerator interior, as she launched a bundle of carrots from between her legs. He caught them with one hand, the other hand still on his beer and placed them next to the lettuce. He prepared for the next projectile. Green onions and zucchini followed in quick succession as though fired from some highly specialized female organ. "And how was your day?" she giggled, her head down, watching him from between her legs.

"Went for a beer in that alcohol cess-pool did you?" he said with mock severity.

"You can tell?" came her reply from the still-inverted head.

"Yeah, but you know it's nearly impossible to drink in that position."

"What else have you tried from this position?" she replied, beginning to giggle and hic-up in rapid sequence.

He cranked an imaginary hand camera from an inverted position. "I do the occasional nature shot, but they all turn out upside down."

"Great, nature-porn! My favourite subject." she giggled, laying on the floor, still fighting the hic-ups. She began to crawl on all fours toward the chair where Bardman's feet rested.

"Can I be a nature-porn star too?

"You mean with your clothes on?" he said with mock incredulity.

"Of course I wouldn't take them off for just anybody." She sat semi-upright in the chair, and pushed Bardman's feet unceremoniously to the kitchen floor with a resounding thump. She wiped tears from her eyes with a Kleenex which she then used to blow her nose with a resounding honk. She could hear Bardman's stomach begin to gurgle hungrily like faulty bathroom plumbing.

With the giggling spasm over, they prepared the meal together. She prepared the sauce while he chopped the vegetables. Both being very hungry and slightly giddy, the meal was consumed with little conversation.

He never ceased to be amazed at the quantity of food she could put into that slim, athletic body. They had met several months ago in the Produce Section of the supermarket. She had mistakenly thrown an egg plant into his adjacent shopping cart. He had promptly thrown it back into hers. They related the episode to friends as their first food fight and his tentative first steps toward vegetarianism. While standing in the express line behind her, he had plotted to find out more about the tall woman with short dark hair and tight jeans. Mostly his eyes concentrated on the tight jeans which brought scowls of disapproval from the matronly check-out woman.

"What do you do with those things?" he had asked as she placed the egg plant on the counter.

"Usually I use it for self-defence in the produce section," she replied warily, eliciting a smirk from the check-out spinster.

"I prefer cucumbers myself, you can use both hands."

"That sounds dreadfully obscene," she replied with a fake English accent as she hunted through her trucker wallet for money.

The check-out woman was beginning to blush and scowl directly at Bardman as though he were to blame for her spinster-hood.

"Wanna go for coffee?" he blurted, causing the store employee to nearly slam her fingers in the cash register.

She turned demurely and said: " Are you buying sir?"

He smiled in affirmation, then turned and stuck his tongue out at the woman at the express counter. She, in response turned her back to him and gave him the finger.

"You have an interesting diet," she said, eyeing his bags containing a variety of junk food, sanitary napkins, foot products from the pharmacy section and a large can of weed killer. All of them items he had thrown at random into his cart as he had followed her around the store.
Introductions were done over coffee at the lunch counter, and despite their earlier kibitzing at the check-out counter, each had an invisible protective armour that manifested itself in subtle evasiveness during their conversation. Over the months, the armour gradually dropped when each realised the other was not a clinger and their mutually independent attitudes posed no threat to each other. As they came to trust each other more, he learned that she had previously been married. She never offered details and he never pressed due to the occasional look in her eyes that said this was off-bounds. They were

26

nearly the same age, late twenties he surmised, but she was secretive of that also.

To D'Amico, Bardman resembled an over-sized teddy bear with curly hair framing wide expressive eyes with intelligence and humour in them. It was the eyes that caught her attention. For a man could be a perfect specimen but if his eyes were not up to her standard he soon became non-existent. She didn't mind the evolving beer-belly because her culinary plans were in motion to deal with it. And despite his obvious bulkiness, he was active, being an avid kayaker in the summer but had taken a hiatus from downhill skiing which he loved and at one time had been an active member of the Canadian Ski Patrol. He had scoffed with derision when he learned she loved to cross-country ski, or what she called Nordic skiing. His derision became louder when she announced her intentions to join the local zones' Nordic section of the Canadian Ski Patrol. To him that wasn't skiing, but rather sweating in the cold with funny looking things on the feet. She had waxed poetically about the skate-ski technique, its speed and sense of freedom, not to mention its ability to reduce over-sized waistlines. He had listened in a condescending manner, trying not to offend her. However in the back of his mind there was the rare thought that would surface sometimes when he watched her slim figure, that all she spoke was not nonsense.

"So what were you taking pictures of down there?" she asked as she headed toward the sink with the dishes.

"I'm not supposed to say much about it but something exploded on the two-thousand foot level near a diamond drill site...knocked the drillers around pretty good I guess. The company president wanted some shots of the area for the investigator coming in tomorrow. It was a nice break from those damn grip and grins," he said referring to the many presentation shots of awards made by the administration.

"So what was powder doing down there?" she said, shooting detergent into the sink. "That isn't a producing level of the mine is it?"

"The other end is going to be next week. The highballers are setting up there now. I saw one of their powder cars on the track leaking Amex all over the track floor today."

She made a face at his last comment. "That company has the worst safety record in the whole mine, it's no wonder they manage to kill a couple of guys each year, just blow them to pieces, kablooey...gone."

She turned and watched the water run into the sink with the dishes, then said: "Somebody's been taking shots at us. We found two bullet holes in the trailer today."

Bardman watched her with concern, saying nothing, but with obvious questions.

"We don't know if they shot at us while we were loaded or coming back empty. I've never seen Joe look scared before, but today he was so pale he could have passed for a white man."

"Have you called the cops?" said Bardman now sitting straighter in his chair, his eyes watching her intently for any sign she may start to show the delayed stress that could manifest itself hours after a traumatic event. She seemed to show none, other than an inability to stand still.   The dish towel landed squarely on his head, looking like some askew Arab headwear.

"Gonna help me with these dishes Lawrence of Arabia, or are you planning on cooking next time?" she said, reaching for the dish cloth now soaking in the sink.

He pulled the towel slowly from his face, rolled it into a tube and whipped it against her jeans where the fabric was tightest.

She yelped with surprise and in one fluid motion flung the wet, soapy dish cloth to land solidly against his face. The ensuing battle over domination of the dishes resulted in the kitchen floor being washed. Bardman resolved to use more discretion with his retaliatory actions, because they always seemed to make more work in the end.

CHAPTER 3

The old trapper woke before dawn. The frost of his breath had formed an icy rim around the edges of his sleeping bag. Around him the forest was still silent within its mantle of yesterday's snowfall, the dark trees standing like sentinels with supreme patience, waiting for the sun to awaken their world. He rolled slowly onto his side and retrieved the frayed parka which he had slipped under his sleeping bag to keep warm. It had provided more cushioning along with the spruce boughs for an old body which was becoming more sensitive to the creeping cold. Each year he had become more aware of the deterioration of his body, the many aches and pains that spread with greater intensity, especially in the mornings. His lungs over the years had breathed in the smoke of thousands of camp fires, and it was with a hacking and gurgling, culminating in an explosive burst of air that sent a brown, glistening projectile of phlegm beyond the confines of his lean-to. It landed on the branch of a shrub and quickly froze, resembling some tiny frigid rodent, suspended over the snow. He wiped his mouth with the back of his hand, and farted mightily. With a groan he opened the sleeping bag to allow the frosty air to invade its warm womb-like depths. He could smell the patent aroma of his feet as though some small animal had died there and never been disposed of. It mingled with the pungent remainder of his flatulence. The moving of his body, along with the cold air sent a message to his bladder that refused to be ignored. During the night he had fought a battle of wills with this organ which had become more antagonistic with age. The only thing worse than arising in the middle of a bitterly cold night to relieve himself was to fall prey to incontinence within the confines of the bag. He knew of old friends, trappers like himself who had nearly died of this affliction while deep in the forest on their traplines, wetting the bag and then having to change their clothing while covered with urine that froze almost instantly on their bodies like a hard yellow skin.

Once out of the bag, he slipped into his high-topped Sorels and with his parka still unzipped, he walked to a nearby tree where he marked his boundaries.

"Brother wolf, this is my territory today," he said, knowing that once he had moved on, the tree would likely be re-anointed by pungent wolf urine from a member of one of the packs that hunted in the area. He had heard their howls during the night and seen their tracks following those of the deer. He estimated two packs were hunting on the boundary of each others' territory, but not crossing over with respect for the other. He knew he had been watched by them, probably just out of sight of the light of his fire. He wasn't afraid of them but he remained wary. He had learned early in his boyhood the lessons of his father regarding their admirable qualities as parents and loyal mates. He also knew they preyed on those which were weak, keeping a species strong with the surviving fittest animals. In the back of his mind doubts were forming of his ability to fend off the wolves if they perceived him to be prey, should he show any signs of weakness.

"I hope you're catchin' lots of deer," he said toward the base of the tree where he realised with some amusement that he had unconsciously written his initials with his own urine. He smiled inwardly, remembering days as a young man when he and some of his friends had placed bets about who had the capacity to write their full name in the snow. Capital letters earned a premium, and poor Jonathan Athapaposkow, one of his best friends never had a chance. From the low-hanging boughs of the spruce he picked clumps of light green filaments of moss to use as tinder for his cooking fire. With it he gathered small pieces of birch bark from dead fall and some larger branches. Within minutes he had a fire going next to the log reflector and began melting snow in a blackened cooking pot. Once the water boiled he poured some of it into a tin mug for his tea and mixed the rest with oatmeal porridge mix. A handful of raisins was added to the mixture and within minutes his breakfast, looking slightly like house stucco was beginning to stick to his ribs as well as certain parts of his clothing.

He had once, years ago been instructed on table manners but out here he gave them no import as he deftly scraped the remnants of the porridge from his jacket front with his spoon and into his mouth. He cleaned his pots and utensils then walked about five minutes east of the campsite, following the footprints from the day before. Dangling at almost eye level was a rabbit hanging by its throat by a fine piece of copper snare wire. He had placed the roller-type spring snare along a much used rabbit trail. The snare was a simple device, using the loop of fine wire attached to a horizontal stick which had been wedged into two larger stakes with pre-cut notches. The horizontal stick with the wire loop had been fitted into the notches, but loosely enough that a struggling rabbit would dislodge it. A sapling had been bent over, and connected to the horizontal stick by thin nylon cord. The struggling rabbit had dislodged the stick, allowing the sapling to suddenly snap upright, yanking the rabbit with it and quickly strangling it. Thus it hung, stiffened by cold and death, a furry white offering of dull staring eyes slightly bulged by the tightened brass wire.

The old trapper smiled at his next meal and thanked its spirit for being generous enough to offer itself. He left an offering of tobacco near the

30

spot, hoping that the spirits of the forest would know of his appreciation and continue to be on good terms with him. He picked up the rabbit and the two stakes as well as all the nylon cord and headed back to the campsite. As he approached the site he could see between the trees, a raven sitting patiently on the lean-to, eyeing the remnants of his breakfast.

"You're late old black one," he said to the raven which turned its head and watched him warily." If you're with me at lunch you can have some of this." He held the dead rabbit aloft.   The raven gazed sideways at the offering, then intently at the old trapper. With a dry rustling like that of ancient fabric, the raven spread its wings and flew into the darkness of the surrounding trees. While breaking camp the old trapper heard the sound one guttural warble drifting from the beyond the trees.

Teresa D'Amico was jolted out of a sound sleep by the electronic shriek of the telephone next to her bed. She and Bardman had stayed up until nearly midnight listening to music and talking. The conversation had come easily between them because there was no sexual tension, at least none was evident on the surface of their budding friendship. She still didn't know how to regard their interaction or what lay ahead. She was reluctant to delve too deeply. He was probably sound asleep in what he called his 'hovel'. She sat upright, still fumbling for the phone.

On the other end of the phone was the voice of the North Haul terminal manager with the unlikely moniker of Walter Winkwell, usually referred to as Winky, much to his displeasure. Winky had been nearly as fat in childhood as he was in adulthood. He carried the pained expression of one who had suffered the inevitable persecutions and a litany of nicknames dreamed up by friends and foe alike. He was sometimes called 'the pear that walks', Other names pasted to his sorry persona were Winky, Inky, or Inkwell due to his habit of carrying leaky ball-point pens around in his shirt pocket. To have been called a nerd, would have been considered by him a promotion in the hierarchy of his personal little lagoon of life. His saving grace was a driving ambition, but not necessarily an ambition to drive that landed him a job with North Haul Trucking. Despite the rumours, he adamantly refuted the story that he got the job because he had caught his uncle, the owner of the company, making overtures to his equally large mother. These stories were met with some scepticism because the consensus was that his mother would have been hard-pressed to attract the flu, and consensus amongst the male population of the town was that the flu was a preferable alternative.

"Teri sweety," came the wheezy voice from the receiver of the phone. "The local constabulary would like a word with you down at the detachment this ack-emma."

"Oh piss off Winky and stop trying to talk like the bloody Queen of England, for shit sake," said D'Amico, realizing it was five in the morning. Being called sweety by Winky reminded her too much of the condescending tone of her former husband.

"Hey, don't you forget I'm your boss and I don't have to take this crap from you D'Amico. Just get your cute little behind down to the cop shop by seven this morning or I'll give constable Pusch your address and he can talk to you while you're still in your nighty." His voice slipped into a gurgle as he tried to hack up a cough candy that had become stuck in his throat.

She threw the phone across the room, chipping the plaster off the far wall, to land with a clatter on the floor.

"I heard that," came the tinny voice from the ear piece in the corner of the room. The handset was covered in dust bunnies where she had neglected to sweep since moving into the small apartment. She picked the phone up on its long cord, walked to the bathroom where she held the mouthpiece down inside the toilet bowl and flushed. After a couple more angry gurgling sounds from the other end the line went dead and she sat on the throne with a self-satisfied grin, voiding her bladder and trying to imagine the expression on Winky's face. The image made her burst into a fit of laughter which surprised her because she never laughed at five o'clock in the morning, and seldom on the john.

Constable Hans Pusch of the Royal Canadian Mounted Police had earned the nickname 'Broom' due to his moustache which fought for domination of his face with his nose.. To be called Pusch-Broom was only a natural progression of the minds trying to deal with the effects of isolation of that northern posting. In fact anyone in the detachment without a nickname was probably disliked, and his colleagues were considering retracting his because he was becoming one very insufferable human being.

"Well Miss D'Amico, what a nice way to start the day," he ejaculated in a voice that sounded as though he was in training for the local hog-calling contest. "A little statement perhaps concerning a couple of perforations to your vehicle?" He was looking down his large red nose at her with close-set eyes like twin black tacks which perched in perfect alignment with the bridge of his nose. Pressuring the eyes from above was the Neanderthal-like forehead, but the piece de resistance was the shrubbery inhabiting the space

32

between his nose and upper lip. The impression was one of nostril hairs growing rampant, the hairs protruding from under his nose in all directions. The creases in his uniform were sharp enough to be life threatening to anyone getting too close, and his chin was pressed into his tie, his back ramrod straight in what is known as the 'brace' position often forced on officer cadets in the armed forces.

"You saw the holes?" Her voice came from within the confines of her parka hood which was still cinched tight, leaving only a fur-lined dark tunnel into which Pusch peered without success..

"Yes, only this morning, but we couldn't find the projectile."

"You mean the bullet?"

"Mmm, yes, that. Any idea where they might have come from?"

"A gun maybe?"

"Oh, haw, haw. Let us dispense with the obvious my dear and do this in a serious manner," he said, his moustache now wriggling as though trying to escape from his lip. His forced smile showed only the tips of his upper teeth. "Wasn't a very good shot was he? I mean if he had been you would be little bits scattered all over a big hole in the ground by now wouldn't you?" he said, obviously warming to the subject.

"There's hundreds of miles of bush between here and Moose Falls where we were going. It could have come from anywhere. Why don't you tell me what you've found out instead of asking all these stupid questions? And I'm not your dear, dammit," shouted her voice from the dark tunnel.

He took a step back, unleashing an official looking glance in her general direction of her still upraised hood. "Step into my office and we'll fill out a report."

"This going to take long? I have to go to the John."

Pusch rolled his eyes, pointing toward the bathroom.

D'Amico, hood still up and Sorels dripping melted snow much to the dismay of the rest of the detachment headed for her relief. She had been given the rest of the day off by Winky, partly in consideration of the events of the past trip, but she suspected her reaction with the phone and her toilet had upset him to the extent that he didn't want to see her face around the office. At this moment she didn't want to see Pusch's either. The bathroom was one of the few places she could escape the cloying ways of the constable. His nasal whining voice could be heard on the other side of the door. She suspected he was trying to peek through the keyhole.

It had been an excruciating morning for Frenchy Rivest. When he woke his mouth tasted as though he had been sucking on one of his long-unwashed work socks. He knew this to be unlikely since they were still at work, hanging wreathed in their ghastly odours from the hook and bucket like those of hundreds of other miners, high in the cavern-like change room known as 'the dry'.

Now at the drill station, Pilson looked at his partners' swollen and discoloured eye with silent, magnified glances of disapproval. He said nothing while servicing the drill head with the grease gun.

Rivest's wife had been equally silent but the disappointment showed on her face, making him consider doubling his amount in the offering plate at church this Sunday.

It was going to be a rough day. The drill rods from the previous shift were still in the hole, the core barrel full and waiting to be pulled and emptied so that the previous crew got the bonus footage and not themselves. It was going to take two hours to pull the more than one-thousand feet of rods and then lower them again to begin their own drill run for the bonus they so badly needed.

Pilson had screwed the plug with the winch cable to the upper end of the rods extending from the drill head and began climbing the ladder of the scaffolding to be able to remove the plug once the rods were pulled to his height. Rivest turned on the air to the air-powered winch and began pulling the rods past the locking jaws that prevented them from sliding back into the depths, while they were being disconnected. The four-cylinder, air-powered engine gave a groan, tightening the winch cable until it was vibrating with tension, emitting a low hum. At the base of the drill rig, large railway ties to which the drill was anchored began to rise several inches from the rocky floor. It appeared as though the drill was attempting to get up and walk out of there, much to the surprise and consternation of Rivest who was still trying to deal with the foul taste in his mouth.

From his high vantage point, Pilson knew immediately what was wrong and screamed down, "Turn it off, the rods are stuck in the hole!"

Rivest reached quickly for the control, turning the air off. The drill rig slammed to earth with enough force to make the staging rattle and sway. Pieces of loose rock pattered down from the pulley anchored in the rock ceiling.

Pilson gazed wordlessly up at the rock ceiling, mouth agape, Adam's apple contorting his throat with spasms of unspoken panic.

"Dos bastard got de rods stuck in de 'ole," screamed Frenchy. His shout was followed by a string of invective that lasted several minutes and made Pilson wish he had something to write them down on for the sake of posterity Some he had never heard before, and the French words sounded exceptionally effective. Pilson watched his partner from above as Frenchy danced a demented polka, throwing wrenches and any other tools at hand against the drift wall. With some trepidation he climbed down to console his tiny partner, hopefully without risk to his own life.

The two of them viewed the jammed drill in mutual silence, illuminated by the overhead air-powered light. It emitted a high-pitched whine as it gave off its blue glow from the mercury vapour bulb. They both turned their heads as they perceived a dull rumble coming from the dark drift. Two small lights could be seen wavering in the distance, slowly growing larger as they approached. The rumbling increased until they could barely make out the outline of a small red electric locomotive with an equally small and red-suited figure swaying in the seat as it approached. They turned to each other and spoke the same words simultaneously: "Oh fuck, it's Wild Bill."

The tiny foreman, Wild Bill Hendrickson was less than five feet tall, garbed totally in red coveralls and topped by a red hard hat. The face beneath the hard hat was also red with a delicate lattice of delicate blue veins on his bulbous nose. Wild Bill was a drinker and at that moment he was obviously very drunk. Pale blue eyes reduced to reddened slits squinted at the two men. An equally tiny mouth smiled maliciously, showing a row of small rotting teeth like raisins glued to his gums. He was known as a mean drunk and since Frenchy was the only man in his employ whom he wasn't forced to look up at, often became the object of his vicious nature.

The two drillers watched in fascination as their foreman slowly climbed down and fixed them with a baleful stare fighting back an obvious case of gastric distress. Wild Bill belched and staggered forward in a pair of rubber boots that came well above his knees. His hard hat was askew, the light pointing at the top of the drift and on his tiny hands was a pair of green rubberized gauntlets of elbow length giving him the appearance of a slightly insane proctologist with an anal fixation. His closely cropped hair was so light that he looked bald beneath the hard hat, the skin glowing pink whenever he was angry or drunk, which was most of the time. His elfin appearance was deceiving because in reality he was one malignant little man who could make any drillers life miserable.

"Got a ph-one call from day shift. Said the hole was stuck here," he said, his voice like fingernails scratching a blackboard. He lurched across the track floor toward the two wary drillers.

"You mean the rods are stuck," said Pilson, correcting him, hoping Wild Bill would trip and knock himself out on the drill.

"S'what I said. You tryin' t'be some kind of smart-ass?" said Wild Bill, fixing him with his squinty blue eyes and looking up in the approximate direction of Pilson's nostrils. He then directed his gaze to the quiet drill and shuffled over to it. "Tried raisin' 'em?"

The two drillers nodded in silence.

"Tried the jackin' handle?"

They both shook their heads.

"Get it."

The jacking handle was a small wrench shaped like the letter C. It attached to the upper head of the drill, enabling the drill head to be turned counter-clockwise by hand with the aid of a long metal hollow handle, in this case a piece of drill rod, to give it extra leverage.

With much straining and sweating, Pilson and Rivest turned the handle while Wild Bill leaned against the wall of the raise trying with moderate success to light a cigarette. Finally he moved over to the drill and climbed onto the metal tractor seat atop the unit where it was possible to operate the air winch.

"Jam that handle against the frame 'n stan' back," he ordered Frenchy who complied with a sense of foreboding. There was silence for a few seconds and then: "Gimme some fuckin' air." he screamed at Pilson, near the shut-off valve. Wild Bill reached down and moved the shift knobs on the drill head to put it in reverse and cranked open the hand control to start the drill head rotating in reverse. Because the rods were still jammed in the hole, the drill head didn't want to turn at all, but the in response to the tremendous torque exerted by the drill head, the whole machine began to lift by itself

She wished she could get Brady hooked on the sport. It was not only a lot cheaper than downhill skiing but a lot more beneficial aerobically. Topping the crest of one long uphill she came to the half-way point warming hut where she built a fire in the wood-burning stove and sat on the bench in the glow of its warmth, drinking hot chocolate spiked with peppermint schnapps She munched on a sandwich, listening to the metal of the stovepipe tinkle from the heat. Near the sunny side of the cabin came the repetitious call of chik-a-dees, feathers fluffed hugely against the cold, feeding from a bag of suet hung from the corner of the hut.

Her mind went back to the two bullet holes in the trailer. She recalled Constable Pusch saying they had retrieved the slug from inside the wooden lining of the trailer and that it was an uncommon calibre, seldom found anymore. The numbers 44-40 were easy to recall, the first two digits being the last two numbers of her telephone number. What had shaken her during the interview was the opinion by the investigators that the shots had been taken while the truck was loaded with explosives. There had been tiny amounts of Amex imbedded in the smashed bullet and the hole of the wooden interior from which it had been dug. That meant the bullet had actually hit the explosives on its passage through the trailer body. She realised the stability of the explosives had saved her life as well her partner, Joe McKay.

The logs in the stove were hissing and cracking, waking her from her thoughts and bringing her mind back to the more pleasant surroundings. She caught the barely audible sound of voices of someone climbing the hill she had recently ascended She dreaded the arrival of others on her privacy. Rather than meet them on the trail she decided to pack up her small backpack and move on before they arrived. It was while putting on her skis outside the hut that she heard the whiny voice she wanted least in the world to hear, that of Constable Pusch, desecrating the aura of quiet around her.

Walter Winkwell was having a rough day. To start it off had been the early morning snooping around by the RCMP officer who seemed to cultivate a moustache the way some would tend a garden. He was always preening it with one hand, twirling the tips as he spoke in that whining, metallic voice. Earlier it had been D'Amico flushing her toilet in his ear on the telephone. And finally, the call from head office and his uncle Heronious.

His uncle had wanted to know just what the hell was going on up there and why were people shooting at the trucks? It seemed the cops had also informed the Explosives Regulatory Commission of the incident, and they were sending a representative for a friendly chat. With all the drivers except D'Amico and McKay on the road somewhere, only the office staff of two secretaries and one warehouse foreman were in the vicinity. A refrigerator unit or 'reefer' parked at bay number three was badly needed at one of the supermarkets. There was no one around who knew how to drive the remaining tractor to hook up to the trailer and deliver it where needed.

"How difficult can this be?" thought Winky. If a woman like D'Amico can make it look easy, well it must be easy. "Hold all my calls," he said with as much authority as his gurgling voice would allow to one of the secretaries. He had always wanted to say that. He thought it made him sound like a real CEO. With his Canadian Tire toque over his ears and overcoat flapping on the borders of his bountiful stomach, he stalked with stiff-legged determination toward the Kenworth, trying to remember how he had seen her start the thing the night she had given him a ride home in it when his car wouldn't start. He had the key in his pudgy hand and with some difficulty pulled himself up and into the cab. He hadn't realised how much effort was required to climb to the seat. Breathing heavily and with some dread he suspected he might have ripped his pants in the process of entering. With the key in place he turned it to the 'ON' position. Nothing happened. Then he saw the white starter button on the dash and jabbed it with his finger. The engine gave a short growl, making the whole cab lurch momentarily. He jabbed it again but this time held his finger down. The engine started to crank, belching clouds of white smoke out the exhaust stack and finally caught with a roar that sounded like a load of gravel being poured into a metal drum next to his ear. A buzzer on the dash began to harass him and he looked frantically around for something to turn it off with. Finally it stopped by itself and the engine exhaust was becoming clearer as well as the engine rattle being less pronounced. He eyed the gearshift with suspicion, unable to fathom why it had the button on the side and the flat paddle beneath it. He could see that there were five gearshift positions and chose the first one. He held his breath and started to slowly let out the clutch. The tractor surged forward slightly, bucked and stalled into silence. He started the engine again and tried again to release the clutch with the same result. He cursed under his breath as he tried once more, this time revving the engine higher as he once again eased the clutch out. A strong smell like that of burning rubber drifted up to him in the cab. "C'mon you mother, move it!" he bellowed, as the tractor began to move sluggishly forward. He pounded the dashboard in jubilation, enjoying the feeling of asserting himself, and catching a glimpse of the secretaries and foreman with their noses pressed against the frosted window of the office. The last pound on the dash did the trick. He had inadvertently hit the parking brake release button. The results were immediate and profound. The tractor, still at high revs, brakes unlocked and transmission in direct range, shot across the terminal yard toward the office window.

The three employees with their noses pressed against the glass let out a collective gasp which fogged the glass with their panicky breaths.

Winky screamed, his hands frozen in horror to the steering wheel. The tractor collided with the refrigerator unit, shifting it sideways from the loading dock.

The warehouse foreman leaned from the newly exposed loading bay and yelled, "Jeez Winky,.you should be fuckin' instructor.

Bardman hated grip-and-grins. He had been called to the President's office where Roger Jenkins was to give the monthly performance award to the graveyard shift of Q-1. The recipient, a stope miner still adorned in greasy clothing, hard hat and light, stood on the plush pile carpet of the office in his steel-toed rubber boots. He appeared distinctly ill-at-ease, nearly as ill-at-ease as Jenkins, who cast furtive glances at Bardman as he arranged his flash equipment for the shot.

"Mr. Bardman, can you hurry this along a bit? I have a meeting with some environmental people here in five minutes." The voice seemed to come from his nostrils as much as his mouth. He cast a glance at the miner who seemed not to understand or care about the proceedings. He smiled a plastic, toothy grin at the miner, who grimaced back at him from a grease-smeared face. It was obvious neither of them wanted to be there and the miner emanated a distinct odour of sweat and grease which filled the confines of the office.

Bardman nodded his readiness to Jenkins who promptly reached for a wooden plaque with a small engraved plate set into it.

The miner turned with a look of anticipation and relief toward Jenkins who had the plaque close to his face, reading the inscription.

"Mr. Dobrohorskins it gives me pleasure to present this performance award to your shift in recognition of outstanding work in whatever it is you do down there." He flashed the plastic smile at everything except the miner who appeared very confused. Jenkins took the man's hand to shake it. "Look at the camera, not at me," urged Jenkins. "At the camera. No not at the plaque, *at the camera*. He has to take the picture you see."

The miner glanced up toward Bardman whose eye was beginning to cramp at the viewfinder. The flash nearly blinded him. He released Jenkins' hand and peered closely at the inscription on the plaque uttering something to the President in a language that sounded eastern European. With his voice rising in volume and the words strung together like sharp points on a barbed wire fence he stalked from the room, waving the plaque at the receptionist in the next room, uttering what sounded like Baltic threats of promised retaliation.

"I wonder what got into him?" said Bardman, shooting off one more shot of Jenkins who was staring at his grease-smeared hand and at the dark smears from the miner's boots on the light pile carpeting.

"I thought he would have at least showered before coming here," exclaimed Jenkins, working feverishly at his hand with a salmon-coloured hanky from his jacket pocket.

"Don't be too upset with him," said Sylvia Kriz the receptionist from the other room. "He was speaking Czechoslovakian and he thought he was getting a raise. That must be what the other guys told him to make him come up here. We also spelled his name wrong," she added, managing to type, chew gum and speak at the same time.

Zenon Mikeluk poked his head around the doorjamb, frizzy hair and pudgy, freckled cheeks quivering with excitement. "Sorry Bardman, you have to go back to that drift face you shot the other day. It seems someone barged in there and tore down all the barricade tape, pushing a bunch of debris around in the process. We think it was the drillers at the nearby site but we won't know until we talk to them so just go there do your job and don't say anything to them, okay? By the way," he added "I saw some miner kicking something that looked like one of our awards down the hall. We should recruit him for our soccer team, he has great follow-through."

As Bardman packed up his photography gear, he noticed the arrival of the local environmental action committee. They sat in the waiting room, stern-faced, eyeing the greasy smears left by the irate miner on the carpeting. Jenkins was going to have a bad day and Bardman was glad to be leaving. On the way out he gave a little wink to Sylvia, getting a little smile in return.

Joe McKay wasn't sure he was glad to have been given the day off by Winkwell. It meant he would be stuck home with his two year old son, Joshua while his wife, Sadie went to her nurses-aid job at the hospital. At least they were saving the daycare money, an amount they had been reluctant to pay except for the raise she had received, finally bringing her take-home pay barely above minimum wage. As it was with their combined wages they managed to put some money away each month. Joe hoped that Sadie wouldn't find out about the secret fund he had finally closed out when he bought his father the used snowmobile. He hadn't seen him in years since he been to school in the south but his instincts told him the gift would be appreciated. He couldn't understand their mutual reluctance to communicate. Perhaps each knew there was still time needed to heal on both their parts.

"Hang on Josh, breakfast is almost ready," he said to his son who was belted into the highchair banging on the tray with youthful exuberance with a large plastic spoon. Hewas turned toward the stove and stirring a pot of oatmeal porridge with little enthusiasm. The pot bubbled and made rude 'splutting' sounds like some geothermic mud puddle. As a child he had hated the stuff with a dislike which continued into adulthood. But Sadie's instructions were explicit. At the risk of suffering her wrath, he momentarily contemplated pouring the vulgar mass into the toilet but was afraid it might plug the pipes.

"Here ya go partner," he said, putting the steaming bowl before his fidgeting son. "Want some milk and sugar? You bet, hang on." He reached back to the counter. He heard Josh sneeze explosively while his back was turned.

Josh looked with curiosity at what he had ejected into his bowl with the sneeze, his young mind rationalized that the extra green-glutinous mass shouldn't be there in the bowl, nor did it look fit for consumption. "Da...uk." he said to his dad, pointing where the sugar and milk were quickly camouflaging the ugly manifestation of his current case of Rhinovirus.

"Yeah, good isn't it?" he said as he attempted to shovel the porridge into his sons less than enthusiastic face. "C'mon, open up. Look out teeth, look out gums, open up, here she comes. What's the matter? Mom says you like this stuff...although I can't imagine why."

Josh pointed to the bowl. "Uk." was all he said. Joe agreed, it was uk, but he had to eat his uk or there was going to be hell to pay.

"Here, you do it then." he said, handing Josh the plastic spoon. Josh gripped the spoon in both tiny hands, smiled benignly at his dad, and brought the spoon down onto the offensive mass. The porridge splattered to all point of the compass, Joe was within easy range and received at least one-quarter of the flying debris. "Okay., that's it for breakfast partner," he said, seeing the smile on his sons' face grow even wider. "I wish I had been as smart as you when I was your age." He unbuckled the straps and removed Josh from the highchair. While his head was about shoulder level with that of his dad, Josh sneezed again while in his arms, adorning his dad's left shoulder with more 'uk'. "Da, uk." said Josh to his dad who only nodded, and wished his son would soon begin to enlarge his vocabulary.

Joe McKay had been born thirty-one years ago in the northern reserve of Hudson House to his mother, Sarah, and his father, Abraham. The community was a mixture of ramshackle houses made of salvaged lumber, cardboard and tar-paper. During the bitterly cold winters, the only thing between survival and a frigid death was the ancient wood-burning stove which needed to be constantly replenished from the snow-covered wood pile at the side of the shack. At night the wind would blow snow between the cracks which Abe tried to repair with more layers of wood and tar-paper. It never worked for long.

His dad worked part time at the Hudson Bay store stocking shelves and helping unload the frequent trucks that arrived with goods he could only hope to buy on his meagre wage. There were many people who had no work and without the assistance of Social Services, many would have starved. There were some who said they would rather starve than take the aid. Abraham McKay was one of them, but he wasn't prepared to sacrifice his family to starvation for the sake of his own pride.

Joe had no clear recollection of his early childhood, but as he grew older, he learned that he had nearly died of double bronchial pneumonia at the age of six months. His face would also bear for the rest of his life the silent testimony of chicken-pox scars. The seemingly endless progression of childhood diseases came and went and still he survived, but the toll was greater on his mother, Sarah, who's health had become progressively fragile since giving birth to him. She persevered, showing young Joe how to use a small axe to make kindling at the woodpile and carry water from the icy hole chopped in the creek nearby. When he was six, his mother became pregnant again, only increasing the look of hopelessness on his father's' face. It was the spring of his seventh year when his mother died while in childbirth, attended by a local woman known for her midwifery skills. Unfortunately she couldn't cope with a breach birth, and by the time his little brother's head had come reverse into this world both mother and little brother were dead.

While young Joe was sent to the one-room school where he was taking second grade, his father began taking long solitary walks along the banks of the Muskrat River and sometimes into the bush where the solitude seemed his only salvation. His work at the store suffered and the manager, a white man who had been there for the past five years was understanding until Abe showed up drunk one day and became argumentative. The drinking and the arguments escalated to the point where Social Services, alerted by the primary school teacher, made a visit and saw the emaciated state of young Joe McKay.

Joe's school work had suffered, although he exhibited a quick mind. It was hard to learn when his stomach ached for food. The teacher always seemed to bring a little extra for him at lunch and gave it to him discreetly, not to embarrass him in front of the other children.

It had been a warm day in August and school had been out for nearly a week when Joe and his dad returned from a successful fishing trip at Moose Lake. They had several large coolers of fat succulent perch, sauger, and white fish which they would either smoke in the newly-built smokehouse or dry on open racks in the sun. Joe particularly loved the perch pan-fried, along with the wild rice collected each October from the shores of Long Island Lake.

An official-looking blue sedan stood in front of their shack alongside of which were two official-looking people, a man and a woman. The man carried a briefcase, and was dressed in shirt and tie. The woman also wore a suit-type jacket with skirt and impractical high heels. Their gaze was stern and Joe felt a sense of dread.

"You come for the boy?" said Abe quietly, drawing a look of shock from Joe. The two officials only nodded looking sadly at the father and son before them.

Young Joe felt a cold sensation in the pit of his stomach as they entered the shack. The officials identified themselves as Child and Family Services for Indian Affairs and looked around the uncleaned confines of the home. Dirty dishes were stacked on the counter around which flies buzzed and crawled at random. The fetid smell of un-disposed garbage hung in the air.

"Why dad? Why are they here?" he said looking up at his father who had difficulty meeting his gaze.

"Can't look after you no more boy," said his father, looking at the floor. "Not enough money for clothes, food in winter, an' I'm out of work. I'm gonna go trappin' this winter an' I can't look after you. Besides, you got school an' you can go to school where they want to take you."

"That's right Joseph." said the woman with forced joviality, squatting down to look directly at him, her perfume wafting over him like a sickening miasma of summer flowers. The flies were beginning to pay special attention to her perfume. She squatted down, placing both hands on his tiny shoulders and smiled a large white smile at him.

He hit her in the nose with his tiny fist as hard as he could and ran from the home, tears blurring his vision, toward the river where he and his father had walked many times.

His father found him crouched by the riverbank, drawing designs with a stick in the mud. He sat beside him and quietly put his arm around him to hug him close, something his father had never done before. His father's clothing smelled of wood smoke. Joe loved the smell of wood smoke.

It was years later that he learned the young, pretty teacher who had called the officials out of well-founded concern had been called before the band elders for a Band Council Resolution. They BCR'd her pretty young ass out of there quicker than you could swat a fly and for years afterward the band had a hard time finding teachers for the school.

Bardman was back underground, camera bag and tripod with lights hung around his neck and over his shoulders. He could taste the combination of rock dust and lubricants hanging in the air around him. The sounds echoing down the drift from either end competed with each other in volume and variety. The pneumatic jack-legs, drills that looked like jack hammers, rattled like machine guns in the distance, several blending the sound into one continuous roar of sound. The confined space vibrated with sound, the shock waves bouncing off his face like the flutter of moth wings. From the other end, the direction he was walking came the ululating howl of the air-driven diamond drill, like some tortured animal in agony.

God, what a horrible place. Right now I'd like nothing better than to be breathing clean air in the sunshine and I don't give a shit if it is twenty below out there. Maybe I'll take Teri up on her offer to teach me how to cross-country ski. He had become more aware of the stares at his broadening girth by Mikeluk and Jenkins.

It was during his dark walk along the drift that he made some resolutions to himself that he was going to change his lifestyle. He was becoming repulsed by his own image in the mirror after showering. He had relegated the weigh scales to a corner of the closet under a stack of old laundry that he could no longer categorize as white or coloured. As far as he was concerned it was all laundry and went together into the machine for the sake of spending less time in the laundromat.

The howling grew louder as he approached the blue illumination around the drill site. Silhouetted in the light was the figure of a driller standing next to the rotating drill-head, adjusting with delicate movements the controls that changed the rate of rpm and rate of advance of the drill bit.. To the side, barely visible was his partner, crouching over something not visible and appearing to chop at that something with a hatchet. Both wore yellow ear protectors against the exhaust screaming out of the port on the top of the drill. The port was curved at right angles toward the drift wall, blasting the cold exhaust in an icy white breath across the track floor. The exhaust port was also covered with a sheath of ice an inch thick, formed by condensation.

He saw the hatlight of the crouching driller turn toward him and then wave the light in the direction of his partner to catch his attention. The other driller turned and projected his light also down the drift toward him, two yellow baleful eyes watching him unwaveringly and with no hint of welcome.

God what a horrible place. He thought to himself again.

The drill slowed to a low moan, finally chugging to a stop as the two drillers stood, watching him approach. The water pump for the drill continued to run with its put- putting like a lawnmower, accompanied by the high-pitched whine of the air-driven light.

"Eh picture-man, you come take my picture again?" said Frenchy as his partner stood silently with his hatchet still in his boney hand, eyes magnified to the extent that it nearly gave Bardman eye-strain to look him in the face.

"Sorry guys, the boss wants shots of this mess at the end of the drift, You have any idea how this tape got pulled down?" he asked, referring to the barricade tape used to restrict access to the area.

Pilson and Rivest put their hands in their pockets and shuffled their feet, saying nothing, looking like a couple of recalcitrant kids who had been caught with their hands in the cooky jar.

"It was our boss. Had a problem with his motor yesterday," replied Pilson, his Adam's apple trying to escape its confines. "Is he in shit for this?" he added with a hopeful tone, his hand still holding the hatchet, the other hand holding a roll of rough burlap material.

"What does your boss look like?

"Short, red suit, red face." said Pilson.

"Sounds like Santa Clause. Does he drink too?

"Does de Pope wear 'igh 'at?" added Frenchy with a giggle, wiping the grease from his hands with a square piece of freshly cut burlap.

"He looks like an impaired fire hydrant," said Pilson, smiling at his own description. "In fact, two nights ago Frenchy thought a fire hydrant was the boss. Stood there talking at it, shakin' his finger at it, even pissed on it in thirty below 'til I took him home. Thought his little dick was gonna drop right off."

"What I'm doing? I don' do dat, bullshit." said Frenchy, pulling out a greasy hanky and blowing his nose with a honk that made the fabric flap in the wind.

Bardman shook his head as the two drillers launched into recriminations at each other, and walked the last hundred feet down the drift, their voices rising in accusation and counter accusation. As he was setting up the lights for the shot, he shone his hatlight up at the large high- pressure airline at the top of the drift wall and saw the reflection of an empty vodka bottle hidden on the upper side of the ten inch pipe. The thought of going skiing with Teri was looking more and more attractive the longer he stayed down there. He took the pictures quickly and left, followed by the on-going dispute between the two drillers. He came to the conclusion that working underground either made people crazy or it was a prerequisite for the job.

Later that evening in his bachelor basement apartment while preparing dinner, Bardman heard three loud knocks at his door. Opening it, he saw her standing in the doorway, clad in multi-coloured lycra tights and a red fleece jacket and windbreaker. He was amazed how someone could look so stylish in weather so cold.

"I saw your car so decided to invite myself for dinner," she said, her cheeks pink from the cold air and eyes starting to water from the wind. "You told me so much about your cooking that I thought I'd come over and see for myself. Do you think that was rude of me?"

He was still staring at her long legs in the lycra and finally shook himself awake, not realizing she was staring back at him, her eyes bright with humour and a result of the exercise.

"Come in, come in. Bring your appetite and those two gorgeous friends with you," he said gesturing to her legs with an exaggerated flourish of his hand. They went down the steps toward the steamy confines of his basement apartment.

She picked up a small bag beside the door, previously unseen by Bardman. "I brought a change of clothes. Can I use your shower?"

He found her a clean towel and tossed it to her while she hung her jacket on the back of a chair near the table, then directed his attention to the large pot boiling on the top of the stove.

"So, what's for dinner...or is it a secret?" she said leaning over his shoulder and peering into the bubbling mass.

He could tell she had worked up a sweat on the ski trail and he was attracted to the pungently feminine aromas coming from her closeness. He was actually wishing she wouldn't take a shower, enjoying the sight and smell of her just the way she was. "I hope you like Kraft Dinner with a difference," he said looking over his shoulder at her, taking in the curly strands of sweaty black hair plastered to her forehead.

"My favourite, but what's the difference?" she asked as she pulled clothing from her bag and heading for the bathroom.

He suddenly wished he had cleaned the bathroom as he had intended for the past two months and realised too late that Teri may well come from her shower with a complete loss of appetite.

"I mix in hot Spaghetti sauce with vegetables on the side," he said peering again doubtfully into the pot, his eyeglasses steaming up.

He could hear the shower running and D'Amico humming a little tune. He quickly tackled the dirty dishes accumulated in the sink, hoping she would take her time to allow him to clean up the area he had described to her as a perfect centre-spread for Better Homes and Hovels. He was still wearing his own work clothing but without the tie and calculated the risk of attempting to change into less formal clothes while she was in the shower. His decision was made for him when he heard the shower stop.

She came from the bathroom as he was setting the table with the newly washed cutlery and he offered her a beer from the refrigerator which she accepted and drank quickly from as only one who has sweated off several

46

litres of water could. She checked under the lid of each pot while sipping her beer, still humming tunelessly to herself.

He sat at the table and watched with amusement as she seemed to make herself at home with an ease that made him a little uncomfortable.

"Sorry," she said. "I just have this unnatural interest in cooking and I've never seen spaghetti sauce used this way. It smells good though."

"You're not just being polite are you?" He leaned back in his chair, cradling his beer on his lap. He admired the healthy complexion of her skin and clarity of her large brown eyes. He had regretted never inviting her for dinner and was glad she had invited herself. It was a nice change to have someone to listen to other than the blow-dried newsman reading the t.v. news.

"I'm never impolite to the cook, no matter how bad the cooking. If I was they might make me wash the dishes," she replied with a giggle. "You wouldn't do that would you?"

He returned to the stove and ladled out a glutinous, red-coloured mound of steaming matter into large bowls. He added a couple of branches of broccoli from the steamer. It smelled a lot better than it looked.

Teresa was truly thankful for that as she watched with an almost morbid curiosity as each spoonful of the mixture landed with an audible 'plop' in the bowl. "What do you call this mixture?" she said, her nose hovering just above the rim, watching Bardman's glasses turn opaque up from the steaming mass.

"I call it my WICC dish."

"WICC?"

"Yeah...Wish I Could Cook dish. Dig in, don't worry about saying Grace, I already said that when I said thank God there's someone here to do the dishes."

After having taken an exploratory nibble, she began shovelling it in, smacking her lips in unlady-like fashion, thoroughly enjoying the taste of spices and pasta.

"You like?" he said, leaning over the table toward her, awaiting her approval.

"Yeah, ishgood." she said between chews. "Really chewy."

"Chewy?" he repeated with concern.

She stopped chewing, a puzzled expression on her face as she reached into her mouth with one finger and rummaged around with the concerned expression of one who might have a loose tooth.

He watched with undisguised horror as she extracted a small red elastic band from her mouth and stretched it a couple of times between her fingers, testing its elasticity. "Oh shit, that's from the green onions I chopped up for the mixture; thought I got them all. Sorry."

"That's one snappy little recipe you got there Brady." She stretched the rubber band again and released it, hitting him between the eyes, leaving a small red smear of spaghetti sauce just above the bridge of his glasses. She hooted with delight at her aim, one hand over her mouth, expecting a retaliatory effort on his part. It didn't come.

He sat and inspected the elastic band as if it was a freshly killed cockroach. "Food that strikes back. My favourite kind of meal." He laughed, taking a long drink from his beer.   She joined him with her hooting laughter.

Her laugh sounded to Brady like that of a slightly unstable loon. "So...how was the skiing? he said, hoping to divert the subject away from his cooking.

She wiped tears from her eyes with the corner of the table cloth since there were no napkins handy and resumed giggling. "It was great, beautiful trail conditions," she said, getting herself under control. "You'll never guess who showed up. Good ol' constipatable Pusch Broom." She continued: "I had to go and fill out a report about those bullet holes this morning and he must have seen the skis on the car. The next thing I know here I am at the warming hut at the top of Cardiac Hill and I hear these voices outside on the trail. I hear his voice for sure and decide to get the hell out of there before he arrives but I was too late. He saw me trying to put on my skis and hollered at me. Well, I didn't want to be rude so I said hello back. Besides, I wanted to see how he skied. He had these old three-pin bindings and pine-tarred skis that looked like museum pieces from a ski chalet wall.

"Sounds like he was following you,"

"He said he was going off shift when he saw the skis on my car and thought it was a great idea and borrowed skis and boots from the evidence room at the detachment, where they keep stuff that has been stolen and never reclaimed. So there he was out there skiing on stolen skis, borrowed knickers, and boots two sizes too big for his huge feet. Didn't think they made 'em that big. He had on these pink earmuffs that were probably also stolen from the property room...God knows who would want to steal those. Anyway, he was by himself. I thought with all the noise he was with someone else but he was just talking to himself as he was struggling up the hill. His face was as red as your sauce."

"Please, don't compare him to my cooking." He prepared some coffee, giving a cursory sniff to the coffee-maker to see if it had been washed lately. "I'm beginning to wonder about his motives. Maybe this is his way of harassment."

"You can't harass what you can't catch. Besides, I think he has a crush on me. I don't know if I should be flattered or scared to death. At least he can't pull me over for speeding on the trail, his pursuit skis won't go that fast," she giggled.

"Can he ski?" He sniffed the coffee cups and dumped a dead insect from one into the sink.

"Not really, he does the buffalo-shuffle. No wonder his face was red, he must have had a bitch of a time getting up Cardiac Hill. It was kinda fun though, doing the rest of the trail with him. He said I had a nice herring-bone."

"What did you say to that?"

"I said he had a nice bone too. I heard this CLUNK behind me and there he was sitting in the middle of the trail, blushing pink as my auntie's underwear. At least he has a sense of humour because he laughed when he wiped out on a corner at the bottom of the 'Screamer' and I said he could be arrested for impaired skiing."

"So did he invite you out for dinner?

"No but I offered to give him skate-ski lessons if he got some good equipment. He said he would take me up on that."

Bardman became uncomfortable with the direction of the conversation and felt what he feared were the first pangs of jealousy, something he hadn't felt since he was a teenager.

"Maybe I'll take you up on that too, I've been a couch potato all winter."

"You should. Besides, you'd look cute in a pair of lycra tights." Her eyelashes fluttered in mock flirtation as he rolled his eyes to the fly-specked ceiling

He knew he may regret his decision and drew the line at wearing lycra.

"Anyway I came here for another reason other than eating your stretchy food. You working tomorrow?"

"Nope."

"Good. Want to come for a ride? I have a load of transformers to take to the hydro project and I could use some company."

He thought for a moment, realizing that if he said yes he wouldn't be able to sleep in as he so loved to do on a Saturday morning. "What time do you have to leave?"

"Oh about seven" she said watching him cringe at the thought of the earliness of the hour. "C'mo-o-o-n." she pleaded. "I'll do the dishes."

"Sold," he said, pleased with his negotiating skills.

"Jeez, how come I always end up doin' the dishes," she moaned on the way to the sink.

The next morning arrived too soon for Bardman. He had the vision of Teresa and her lycra tights replayed over in his mind as he tried unsuccessfully to get some sleep. He realised the tights had been a part of her persuasion along with the story of Constable Pusch, to get him into Nordic skiing. He was determined to draw the line at the possibility lycra tights of his own. Despite the darkness he was glad to see through the ground floor window a low cover of grey cloud in the sky. That meant the cold snap was coming to an end and was probably bringing with it more snow.

He was surprised how chipper he felt this early on a Saturday and realised it was because he was looking forward to seeing Teresa in her work environment. He revised his thoughts and realised he was simply looking forward to seeing her again. The sisterly kiss she had planted on his cheek in thanks for the dinner had affected him more profoundly than he was willing to admit and he couldn't get those damned lycra tights out of his mind.

As he pulled into the terminal yards of North Haul he could see the orange marker lights of one tractor glowing in the semi-dark, and her slim, dark figure cranking the trailer dollies off the ground. She waved toward him as he parked beside her car and reached for the thermos of coffee he had bought at Hazel's Hangout.

"Climb in and keep warm," she yelled over the rattle of the Kenworth's diesel engine.

He was surprised how high the cab was above the ground and the effort required to haul himself up to the door by way of the handrails. Once inside, the sweetish smell of the diesel and grease reminded him of the smells underground and he was beginning to have second thoughts about having agreed to come.

The driver's door opened and she climbed in bringing with her a gust of cold air from outside. "Well, you don't look any worse for wear. I'm glad to see you brought some lunch," she said with a cheerfulness that immediately brightened his outlook on the trip. "There aren't a lot of places to stop on the way for food and the ones that are available sell nothing but grease. That could mean trouble for someone with your diet of high rubber intake."

He realised he may never live down the elastic band episode, settling into his seat, accepting his fate at having to endure the coming diatribes about his culinary expertise.

She released the air brakes and eased the tractor-trailer forward in first gear across the terminal yard. Once on the street she began shifting up with a smoothness that surprised him.   "Why don't you use the clutch?" he said, watching her feet as she moved the shifter through its positions. As far as he could see she hadn't used the clutch pedal at all and had shifted several times.

"Don't have to except to put it in first gear," was her reply. "All I have to do is match the engine rpm with the gear I want to use. The truck has to be moving forward at the right speed or the transmission might not allow me to use that gear. For instance if we're doing 50 kph like we are right now and I want to shift back into second gear, the engine will say 'whoa, I can't make my engine rev high enough to match a gear that says I should be travelling six kilometres per hour instead of 50. Does that make sense?"

He looked at her with his mouth open, trying to comprehend what she had said, his eyes slightly glazed. "Not really. Maybe it's still too early in the morning for me."

She gave a quiet smile as she concentrated on the road ahead which was becoming more visible in the grey morning light.

The road was of crushed rock, just wide enough for two large trucks to pass with seemingly only inches to spare. On either side was frozen muskeg and Precambrian shield covered in a blanket of deep snow, extending from both sides of the road to the dark outline of the spruce trees that stood as they had for thousands of years. In more open parts where the trees thinned, it was possible to see the hard, bare rock which reflected light from tiny particles of embedded mica. Throughout the rock could be seen veins of white and pink quartz, and if one was very lucky, they might see the occasional speck of gold in the white quartz.

"Wow, take a look at this," she said pointing at a cloud of steam rising from around the first Bailey bridge over the Black Wood River. They approached at a slow speed. She gradually shifted down as they came down the incline, slowly applying trailer brakes with the handle on the steering column to prevent the tractor from spinning out on the icy surface. The steel beam framework of the military-type bridge was wreathed in the cold mist coming from open water below it and it was impossible to see what was on the other end. "They must have opened the diversion near Wapiti Lake," she said as she brought the truck to a halt at the end and slightly of to one end of the bridge. She set the parking brakes and leaned out her open drivers

51

window to listen. "I don't hear anything on the other end, it might be safe to cross but we'll have to be quick because someone might come over the crest of the hill on the other side. There's only room for one vehicle at a time."

Brady opened his passenger side window and listened. The only sounds they could hear were the rushing of the water beneath the bridge and the distant croak of a raven somewhere in the forest. From their end of the bridge it was possible to see the water had risen several feet and would be rising more.

She yanked the air horn cord above her left shoulder, creating a deafening blast of sound that bounced in echoes off the far river bank. No other sound came in reply, the silence so complete it was as though their heads were swathed in cotton...except for the unceasing roar of the river. She restarted the engine and eased onto the bridge and several seconds later they climbed the far incline and out of the mist-wreathed bridge as though exiting from another dimension. They climbed toward a brightened morning sky sunlight played like splotches of gold paint daubed onto the uppermost tips of the trees.

Bardman glanced in his side mirror and saw the orange ball of the sun climb slowly through the mists surrounding the bridge. The spans were nothing but thick dark lines, fading to the far side of the river mist.

"Can we stop so I can get a picture?" he said leaning closer to her so she could hear over the engine noise.

"Only when we get to the crest, otherwise we might not get going again," she replied. "I should have known there was more than lunch in that bag."

"I couldn't resist," he said apologetically. "It'll give me a chance to add to my photo stock of this area." He was reaching for the bag as the truck came to a stop and quickly climbed from the cab. Below and back-lit by the sun was the scene he had seen in the mirror. He raised the Olympus OM-1 with the 24mm lens and took a light reading on the sun so the bridge girders would be silhouetted, showing the sun as a bright spot through the clouds of the mist. The open water created tiny highlights, sparkling like individual diamonds from the water. He took several quick shots, bracketing the exposures and then switched to the 300mm lens. The viewfinder showed a compressed image, the sun was now a large yellow ball rising slowly above the mist, the bridge girders becoming a dark lattice work covered with hoar frost, looking like white icing on a cake. He knew he had to work fast before the sun rose too high and lost its warm colours, a contrast he was looking for with the snow and frost. As he watched through the viewfinder, a pair of headlights appeared on the crest of the far rise from where they had just come. Another truck painted its outline on the sun as it started down the slope toward the bridge. He took several quick shots using the motor drive to catch the truck against the sun and a couple more of the headlights and marker lights glowing through the mist on the bridge.

As the truck crossed the bridge, grinding in a lower gear, two shots rang out from upriver, spaced a heartbeat apart.

Bardman turned to where he thought the sound had come from and thought he could see movement among the trees. He quickly raised his camera and took a couple of exposures in the direction of the lone figure. He peered more intently through the telephoto lens, trying to find the movement he thought he had seen but saw nothing more.

The truck climbed the hill toward them, labouring to the top with a full load. The signs on the front bumper and the front of the trailer stood out in their vivid red on white letters, 'EXPLOSIVES'.

He tried to flag the truck down with a wave of his arm, but the driver merely waved back and moved past, accelerating on the more level road. He ran for the cab and climbed quickly in beside Teresa who had elected to stay warm and sip a cup of coffee from her thermos. The engine still idled, the heater fan on full and Luciano Pavarotti at full volume threatened to blow the windows out of the cab with Italian gusto.

"Did you hear the shots?" he shouted over the aria at D'Amico who had her head back on the headrest, eyes closed, still sipping the coffee.

She turned toward him while turning down the volume of the tape player. "Did you get your shots? Can we go Now? Why do you look so white?"

He stared in exasperation at her and finally said: "Someone just took a shot at that truck that came past and it was carrying explosives." His hands were beginning to shake and he was having difficulty catching his breath, his head feeling light and dizzy.

"Brady don't you go passing out on me. What shots?" She was alarmed at the pasty colour of his face. "Put your head between your knees and take deep breaths...not too fast. That's better, now tell me again what you heard."

He repeated in a more calm manner about the shots he had heard and soon Teresa also became pasty-faced.. She had not even opened her eyes as the truck passed, not realizing it was a North Haul truck with a new driver.

"We have to catch him," said Bardman, his voice rising in pitch.

"I don't think we can. We're heavier than he is and that's a faster truck, if it's the one I think it is. Besides, he has a long head-start on us and he can't legally stop anywhere until he's unloaded."

The truck that had passed them was out of sight as they began moving again, picking up speed painfully slow. They both willed the truck silently to go faster but the limitations of the engine and load refused to be influenced by anything other than the mechanical factors already in motion.

"We might not catch him until we reach the construction site, and then we'll have to wait for him to come out of the explosives storage area, because our load won't allow us in there," she said, her jaw muscles clenching as she put full weight on the accelerator. "We might have to wait and catch him as he comes out and then try to flag him down."

Their truck was bounced and jangled with every bump and depression in the road. The collection of tools and spare parts stored behind the seats shifted and rattled as the cab swayed at the higher than normal speed. Finally she slowed to a more sane speed, realizing that there was no point in putting their own lives in danger when they knew they would catch up to the other truck eventually. They were both silent for the next half hour when she finally slowed and pulled the truck to the side of the road.

"I have to pee," she said with a pained expression. "If you see traffic coming from up ahead, just give short honk on the horn and don't even think about looking in the side mirror because I'll be at the back end." There was no humour in her voice and Brady was learning that anyone who tempted fate with Teresa while she was in this state of mind, would pay a heavy price.

They had another four hours of travel time before reaching their destination and it gave him a chance to sit back and reflect on the circumstances that had brought him to these remote areas that attracted him so strongly.

He had been born thirty-three years ago in a small Manitoba farm house near a tiny village with the unlikely name of Quick Ville. There was nothing quick about the place and that was alright with the population of nearly 400 people who made their home in the picturesque river valley where the Little Saskatchewan River meandered into and out of their lives like some travelling salesman on his way somewhere no one cared about. Except for Brady Bardman, that is.

When the Bardman family moved from their ill-producing quarter-section of farmland into Quick Ville, Brady had his first taste of school in a building with more than one room and a post-menopausal, nearly retired teacher who had to teach four other grades besides his. The school room was chaos, usually with the teacher asleep at her desk, a result of the medicine for her bad nerves, her half-lens reading glasses sliding down her nose with each snore, jowls of her cheeks vibrating with each passage of noisy air. She suffered with an incurable flatulence that would make the windows rattle and young ears pop with the pressure change. The ensuing laughter usually woke her with a start and sometimes ended with the strapping of some poor student unfortunate enough to have been caught in her baleful glance and perceived by her to be not attending to the work at hand. A lot of tender young hands were abused over the course of the years. She remained, but the school board wouldn't replace her...it was just too hard to find a replacement.

He learned over the years to play hooky but just enough not get himself kicked out of school entirely. With an average just over the passing mark, he lived and breathed for summer holidays when playing hooky was in fact sanctioned. The summer he turned twelve was different He remembered that day as though it was yesterday.

His head was under the covers and he could hear the first chirping of the birds in the early morning. It had barely cooled off during the evening and the whirring of the fan set at the top of the landing by the stairs so it could swivel and direct the cooling draft into each open room had been punctuated with the distant muttering of a lightning storm to the south. He had got up sometime during the night and watched from the bedroom window, hoping the storm would come his way and cool the air in the stifling bedroom. His younger brother Billy tossed and turned in the bunk above his where the air was hotter still, near the ceiling. Finally he had gone back to bed and slept on top of the covers, a sheen of sweat covering him like slick, second skin. When he awoke again he was back under the sheets, the covers laying in a heap on the floor, the sun streamed through the window, turning the bedroom once again into a merciless oven. He could see a galaxy of dust particles suspended and floating lazily in the brilliant shaft of sunlight from his window. From below in the kitchen came the clanging of pots as his mother busied herself with breakfast.

"Brady," came his mothers voice up the staircase. "go and get a pail of water for breakfast."

He groaned and rolled over to face the bottom of the above bunk, seeing the depression made in the thin mattress by his nine year old brother. Still laying on his back he reached up with both feet to the mattress and pushed upward.

His brother yelped. "Mo-o-o-m, Brady's bouncing me again."

"Squealer." he said as he bounced him again, causing his brother to holler once more.

Billy leaned over the edge and stuck his tongue at him.

Brady replied by placing his hand under a sweaty armpit and forced his arm down suddenly.

"M-o-o-o-m, Brady's making arm-farts at me."

His mother called him once more with the tone of voice that made him move with alacrity. She had added threat of calling his dad from his sit-down in the outhouse. It was one of the few places his dad could escape the constant bickering between him and his brother. He had a suicidal urge to take up his sling-shot and bounce a few rocks off the wall of the dilapidated structure of the outhouse. The vision of his dad trying to catch him with his pants down around his ankles made him giggle as he rolled out from between the sheets. The smell of burnt toast came to his nostrils. Sitting on the edge of the bed he examined his socks and judged they could be worn for another day, maybe two, but to make them wearable he had to beat them against the bedpost to soften them up. The ensuing dust storm from the encrusted socks whirled through the shaft of sunlight from the window. An odour like a combination of three day old popcorn and rotten cabbage permeated the room. He looked with satisfaction at his handy-work and forced them on his feet, knowing they would eventually conform once again to the contours. He heard his mother yell once again and the outhouse door creak and slam shut as his father headed back to the house.

"I'm coming mom," he yelled from the confines of his T-shirt, half over his head He wondered what he could do today. Yesterday had been so hot that even moving from the shade of the old maple trees in the front yard had been enough to make him dizzy with the effort.   As he clattered to the bottom of the stairs, his mom handed him the shiny two-gallon pail and he ran out the front door to the pump in Rudniski's yard a block away. He was glad they had a friendly dog, but the white goose that patrolled the yard never failed to honk and hiss at him as he approached the pump.

"You get the hell back here with that water, pronto," yelled his dad from the front door.

His trot became a run with the pail banging painfully against his hip, and the trip back was as unpleasant, with the goose threatening him until he left with the full pail and he jogged back, slopping nearly half the contents on his dusty jeans and feet. He figured the water would render his socks wearable for an extra day.

The July sun was already beating down on his head and the cicadas were buzzing from the trees like tiny power-saws. The aroma of the goldenrod standing in bright yellow clumps in the roadside pervaded the air with a strong perfume that almost made him sneeze. Large red and yellow dragon-flies hovered than dashed across in front of him chasing their breakfast of mosquitoes like attack helicopters of the insect world. He prayed with all his might that they weren't having oatmeal porridge again this morning.

"It's about time." said his brother as he entered with the water. "Mom wants to make juice to go with the porridge." Billy was seated next to his dad who was watching Brady with disapproval, glancing at the pant legs of his jeans, dark and wet.

"Brady peed his pants." giggled Billy, shovelling sugar onto his porridge, then pouring on the milk.

With both hands he lifted the pail to the counter top, slopping a little on the floor and then sat down to his bowl of oatmeal which had cooled, forming a thick grey skin over the top. With his spoon he peeled the scum back and looked underneath as though searching for slugs under a rock, grimacing with distaste. His dads hairy hand appeared in front of him, finger extended downward and began thumping the one finger against the table surface next to his bowl.

"Eat, it'll put hair on your chest," said his dad with stern face, a brown-smeared, hand-rolled cigarette dangling from his upper lip as though secured there with glue. Each time he spoke, the remnant of cigarette flapped like a piece of dead skin. His finger was the colour of tobacco and still thumped the table in front of him. He was always given the same motivation by his dad to eat the prison-fare that was sometimes set before him. He didn't have the guts to say that he didn't care if he never had chest hair and he figured it would be worth a thoroughly tanned behind out by the woodpile to inquire as to the lack of hair on his own fathers chest. His mom sipped her coffee noisily, looked at him over the rim of the cup and finally said: "Auntie wants to go swimming today, so you go along and keep an eye on her okay?"

"Aw mom I was gonna go bike ridin' with the guys."

"Never mind, you just do what your mother asks," said his dad, waving the brown finger in his direction again. Billy was sitting hunched over his porridge, drawing designs in the top scum with his spoon, smirking at him from the other side of the round table, enjoying Brady's discomfort.

At that moment he had an overpowering urge to fling a spoonful of porridge at his brothers' grinning face. Before he had realised it, the thought had become a knee-jerk reaction, and his brother sat with one eye covered with oatmeal glop, mouth wide open in the beginnings of one of his patented wounded-howls.

His father's hairy, brown-fingered hand quickly reached across the table, grasping him by the T-shirt and lifted him from the table in the direction of the woodpile.

He knew he wasn't being asked to split more wood for the cook-stove and resigned himself to the laying-on of the wood to his backside. Biking wasn't going to be such a pleasure today after all.

By noon the dusty streets of Quick Ville were oven hot from the sun that appeared to be a molten mass soldered to the hard blue sky. The only movement was the occasional stray dog trying to find the cool shade of a tree to lay under.

Brady rode his Glider bicycle along the dusty main street, glad of the breeze he created as he passed the cool beckoning confines of Rumpole's Drug Store. He was tempted to retreat into the cool darkness where the whirring Coke machine with its cool, sweet treasures sat inside, next to the huge rack of comic books. He saw several other bicycles parked on the sidewalk, recognizing those of Duel, and Snake. If he didn't have to go and baby-sit his auntie at the river, he could be sitting there out of the midday heat, a cold Coke beside him and read comics for the rest of the day. Old Rumpole never seemed to mind that they never bought any. He probably realised they didn't have the money.

The old metal Coke sign next to the store hung silently, radiating the heat of the sun onto the street. A dried up tumble weed lay beneath the sign as though seeking refuge from the hot silent violence being done to the parched Manitoba town. Reluctantly he rode on toward the brackish water of the river and the manmade lake which had no name. He rode, partly standing on the pedals, his reddened and very sore posterior not touching the wide seat. He had suffered through the walloping at the woodpile, administered by his dad who punctuated each strong swing of the stick with muttered expletives. After four or five whacks he gave out with his obligatory wailing to signal he had received the message and was duly penitent. He knew he had the rest of the day to himself once his auntie had finished her swim and in the back of his mind was a seed of an idea of the tortures he could inflict on his brother. As he approached the bridge over the river, he heard a voice call.

"Hey you, yoo-hoo."

It was his auntie propelling herself on two crutches toward him from her small home next to the river, large floral pattern cotton dress flapping with the exertions and a fresh breeze now starting from the east. Her hair was white and spiky like that of an elderly porcupine, her eyes slits in a white, puffy face. Her bulk moving across the road toward him looked like a piece of garish furniture that had escaped from some decrepit showroom.

"Didja bring yer swim trunks?" she huffed at him as he straddled his bicycle, amazed at her mobility.

"Forgot em," he lied, not wanting to face the ignominy of having his friends see him swimming with her. Besides, he couldn't really swim, but dog-paddle and he usually swallowed enough water to satisfy the cravings of a camel.

"Yer mom wanted me to teach ya how ta swim," she called from the dry-rotted confines of the change house. "Can't go 'round splashin' like a little dog all yer life can ya now?"   "Naw guess not." he replied lethargically, fighting down the impulse to peek through one of the structure's many knotholes and satisfy his curiosity about the mysteries of the naked female form, a major topic of conversation amongst the guys. There was always speculation about which girl in class had begun to grow boobs and which were using Kleenex in the bra.

Auntie exited from the building into the bright sunshine, squinting, lunging on her crutches across the grass toward the water's edge, next to the bridge abutment, and an old plank raft anchored several metres from shore. The shoreline itself was of slimy mud except where the town had unceremoniously dumped a truckload of fine gravel which they passed off as sand and thus was born Quick Ville Beach, usually known as Quicksand beach, but sometimes more accurately, Leech Beach. The leeches proliferated under the old raft from which the swimmers dived and then sat, dangling their legs in the water. It was a matter of pride for a guy to have a dozen of the slimy, squirming creatures hanging from his legs and between his toes. Even better if it made the girls run shrieking away, the topic of their conversation the rest of the day. It was the only way the guys around there knew how to get their attention, short of taking a bath on a regular basis.

His auntie's breathing was laboured as she leaned her crutches against the bridge abutment and lowered herself into the tepid water, her black one-piece bathing suit forcing the white soft skin to roll in folds from its confines like un-baked bread dough.

He was glad he hadn't peeked.

"Now don't go away, "cause when I need to come out, you have to hand one end of one of my crutches for me to grab onto, ya hear?" bubbled his auntie as she side-stroked out into the midstream of the tepid river.

He nodded assent and ran onto the bridge walkway for a better view as she swam slowly through the brown water. He wondered if she would catch any leeches on her legs.

He finally sat on the bank next to the bridge and watched the barn swallows wheel and dart like tiny jet planes after insects, warbling and chortling to each other, then disappearing under the cool shade of the bridge to their mud nests. Occasionally the flapping and cooing of a disturbed pigeon echoed from the dark underside. About a quarter mile down river he could make out the forms of kids jumping from the railing of the dam into the side opposite the spillway. He could hear their laughter as huge geysers of water shot up when one of them did a cannonball off the high railing. From the distance they looked like a collection of albino monkeys skinny-legged, knobby shoulders and silly grins of summer that they hoped would never end. He looked where he had last seen auntie, and she was nowhere to be seen.

He ran to the walkway and looked out over the water on the side of the bridge where he had last seen her. Then he ran down to the waters edge and peered under the shade of the bridge but could only see as far as the nearest concrete abutment. She wasn't there. In the near distance he could hear the voices of his buddies on their bicycles coming down the paved hill toward the bridge. Old man Rumpole must have finally kicked them out he thought. He could hear them singing in unison one of their favourite riding tunes:

She was coming down the hill
doing ninety miles an hour
when the chain on her bicycle broke.
She went sprawling in the grass
with a sprocket up her ass
And her left tit was punctured by a spoke.

The song ended in a burst of raucous laughter as the three cyclists rounded the curve onto the bridge and saw him standing with his hand shading his eyes from the sun's glare off the river.

"Hey B.B. watcha doin'? Lookin' for yer virginity? said Duel Hancock as he stopped beside him. With him were Snake Jakeman and Baldy Headman.

They had all taken great pleasure in dreaming up nicknames for each other, preferably something that suited the last name. Brady felt short-changed to have been given B.B. as his nickname. It just didn't seem to have any imagination. They looked like three criminally intent Mouseketeers their ears appearing over-large due to the short haircuts their parents had dictated for summer. Each was scrawny with the beginnings of muscularity in contrast to his own chubbiness.

"I can't find auntie, she was swimming by the bridge here a minute ago and she just disappeared," he replied, still looking over the railing.

"Bardman did you lose your auntie again?" said Baldy Headman in a whiny voice, mimicking the tone of Brady's aunt.

The others giggled uncontrollably. Then tiny Snake Jakeman lost his balance while perched precariously over the crossbar of his bicycle. He clattered with his bicycle to the hot tarmac of the road, his hands stuffed between his thighs and appeared to be trying to lick the road's surface.

"Crushed gonads, crushed gonads," cried Duel Hancock as he watched his friend's agonized contortions.

The group cracked up at Snake's plight but soon realised B.B. was truly concerned with the whereabouts of his auntie. It just wouldn't set a pleasant conversational tone at supper to have to explain that he had lost her. Quietly the four sets of eyes scanned the water on either side of the bridge and then further out toward the dam downstream where the crowd of swimmers seemed to have diminished.

"Hoo boy, B.B. lost his auntie," said little Snake with a strangled voice, barely recovered from his injured privates. "I wish I could do that with mine. Could she come swimmin' with you next time?" he continued.

"Shut up and look for her you little shithead," scolded Baldy looking down on him from an extra head and shoulders height. He was big for his age and with jagged front teeth to go with a permanent scowl.

"What's that white thing over by the other side of the river?" said Duel, pointing with one hand, the other shading his eyes. All eyes turned in that direction and saw a white mass slowly moving downstream in the main current toward the spillway of the dam.

"Oh shit, it's her!" cried Brady as he grabbed his bike and took off for the far side of the river.

The others followed now giggling with excitement of the chase. They threw the bicycles down on the opposite bank and ran along the shoreline to overtake the gently bobbing white mass.

He called her name as he drew even with her, surprised at how far the deceptively fast current had carried her.

"She looks like a huge marshmallow." cried out Snake as he jumped gingerly from one rock to the next in his bare feet. "How can she sleep like that? I sink like a rock."

"You ever hear her talk? All she is is hot air. It's a wonder she doesn't fly away like a balloon," replied Baldy, measuring the distance left to the dam and its one open spillway.

The roar of the water was growing in volume and they could see the spray of the spillway where it crashed down on the huge rocks on the other side. They had all heard stories of one swimmer or another being swept over and mauled by the rocks and current. As far as they knew no one had drowned but there had been close calls, a fact their parents used to dissuade them, unsuccessfully from swimming above the dam.

In desperation he picked up a rock and threw it at the slumbering form of his auntie.

"Hey great idea." yelled Snake. "If we can't wake her up maybe we can sink her." As he threw a rock he began singing verses of the old tune 'Sink the Bismark'.

A volley of rocks bracketed the target, for that's what she had become now to them, a target, a challenge for their marksmanship. The small geysers from the rocks came close as they got the range, but still she floated on, a human hazard to navigation which in most cases was nothing larger than a muskrat. The mass of swimmers on the bridge railing stopped cavorting and watched their efforts as the target drew closer. A couple of girls had their hands to their mouths in horror while some of the boys giggled with a combination of fear and excitement. They were practically looking down on her inert form, her mouth wide open, snoring in her blissful sleep. A rock bounced off her forehead, an example of marksmanship that was denied by all participating, but it popped her eyes open in time to see a crowd of young faces peering down at her, yelling something she couldn't understand because of the roaring in her ears. Then she went over the spillway.

For months afterward it had been the talk of the town how Brady's auntie fetched up on the rocks below the dam, no real harm done except for a black and blue goose-egg sized lump on her forehead. Few of the townspeople believed the story of her being hit by a thrown rock. Rather it was believed the injury was received upon landing in the spillway. Whatever the consensus and considerable discussion, Brady's father tended to treat him more kindly after that, even at times volunteering to show him how to throw rocks with a large sling made of two leather thongs and a pouch. Fortunately for Brady, his auntie never volunteered teach him to swim after that.

CHAPTER 4

Bardman bounced awake amidst the sound of jangling of steel bars and tools from behind his seat as the tractor-trailer went over a large pothole. He had a strange taste of stale metal and dust in his mouth and his neck was stiff from slouching while asleep in the jump seat.

"Sorry about that, I couldn't avoid it," said Teresa with a smile from the drivers side. "You were really sawing logs there for a while. In fact you were talking in your sleep."

"What did I say?" he asked, rubbing sleep from his eyes, stretching his arms in front of him to relieve the kinks in his neck.

"I don't know, you kept saying something like swim, swim."

"Oh God ...it was a nightmare. I had a dream about when I was a kid and my aunt got washed over the dam back home."

"She drown?"

"No, she washed up on the rocks below the dam, looking like a bloated mermaid and accused me of trying to kill her. It's really weird though, ever since that happened, my dad treated me a whole lot better. He was almost civil in fact."

She shifted her gaze to him momentarily, remembering her own upbringing with a domineering father. Her only escape at that time from a strict Italian family was through marriage. She really didn't care what her new husband's ancestry was. If it wasn't Italian it didn't matter. What did matter to her soon after was her new husband's lethargic approach to married life; a chauvinistic attitude of feeling entitled to a maid service with sex on the side. It didn't last long. The separation and divorce were almost as disruptive to her family as the marriage. Now on her own, she realised her real potential lay in the freedom to make decisions for herself.

"We're almost at the Muskrat River diversion project. See the crane above the trees?"

He blinked his bleary eyes and leaned forward for a better view. Along the side of the road were huge ruts gouged out by road construction equipment and rows of trees laying like silent victims of a massacre. This is a mess, he thought to himself as he saw the once pristine forest being desecrated. As they drew closer he could see discarded equipment and heavy steel cable curling like long, rusted brown worms protruding from the ripped up earth.

The shoreline of the Muskrat River had also been denuded of trees above the control structure which was obviously completed and in operation where it diverted water into the Black Wood River. He realised the high water they had seen at the bridge was a result of more water being held back at the control gates.

"I thought we were going to the dam site," There was obvious disappointment in his voice. He had never seen a hydro project up close and his curiosity was more from an environmentalist point of view than merely satisfying of curiosity. What he had seen so far at the control gates offered a foretaste of what he suspected he might see at the main dam site project. It brought a sense of revulsion to see the devastation to the surrounding natural areas.

"Sorry partner," replied Teresa, watching the tachometer. "We just have to drop these transformers here and then trade trailers for stuff going back south. The explosives truck made the turn off to the dam site thirty miles up ahead and if we're lucky we might catch him on the return trip.

They entered the camp area, the roadside lined with a series of Atco trailers used as bunkhouses for the employees. Between the structures were covered walkways to protect the workers from the bitter cold. Each structure looked like a large shoe box, flat on the sides, with triple pane windows at intervals. From a door in the centre of each connecting walkway extended a sidewalk of logs nailed together in sections to form what was called a corduroy road. It was on these corduroy roads the workers walked each day to the cookhouse where they were fed huge quantities of food, one of the few concessions they experienced for their isolation except a high hourly pay scale. For some it wasn't enough pay to endure the unending stench of unwashed bodies and clothing. The nearly total deprivation from female contact was another factor that sometimes cut a worker's employment short, because work in any labour environment could be isolated, mean-spirited and sometimes violent.

She brought the semi to a halt in front of the cook-shack. "This is where the receiving clerk usually hangs out this time of day," she said as she put on her parka and climbed from the cab.

Bardman caught a whiff of what smelled like fried chicken and followed enthusiastically.

The interior of the cook-shack was uncrowded but the aromas from the kitchen indicated they were ready for the hungry day shift who were expected soon. The few inhabitants, hunched over coffee turned their heads in unison and watched Teresa with interest as they walked to the coffee dispenser and helped themselves. The air was hot and humid from the huge steaming pots in the kitchen. Soon they felt sweat trickle down their backs. Brady felt the dirt-smeared floor would have prompted any food inspector to close the place down immediately if had it been in the city, but such action here would have endangered his life.

"Teri, git yer sweet buns over here," called a voice from the far side of the long narrow room. Seated at one of the long tables was a large man with long blonde hair and ruddy features. In front of him was a clipboard with what appeared to be a collection of shipping manifests with the North Haul logo on top. "Got our transformers?"

She approached, nodding, and sipping her coffee at the same time, spilling some down the front of her shirt. She didn't enjoy the chauvinistic comments that always seemed to come her way, but over the months they had decreased when they realised she was as competent at her job as they at theirs.

"Good, just sit there and enjoy your coffee and I'll have the forklift come over and take 'em off. We have a traffic jam at the loading dock so you're just as well off here. I got a call from your boss; he wants you to bobtail over to the project and pick up an empty trailer there to take back. Here's the number of the trailer," he said shoving a sheet of paper toward her with a five digit number written on it. "We usually send stuff back in these trailers but they warned us not to, in fact they had us put a seal on the door. Somethin' about the cops wantin' to have look at some holes in the side."

Brady and Teresa stopped drinking their coffee and looked at each other in silence.

"You two look like you've just seen a ghost," said the shipper / receiver as he prepared to leave.

It took the forklift operator nearly a half-hour to off-load the transformers, enough time for them to sample some of the fried chicken. Both agreed it was better than either had tasted in town. Freshly fed and watered they left the campsite after dropping the flatbed trailer where it was and headed for the intersection thirty miles to the north and another hour of driving to the hydro project. The ride was an uncomfortable one without the extra weight of the trailer to dampen the stiff shock absorbers of the tractor. Each small rock or pothole in the road made the rig bounce and jangle. The chains and binders that had secured the transformers on their pallets hung from the exterior rear of the cab only added to the racket. The term bobtail was appropriate because they seemed to be bobbing all over the road and Brady's kidneys were starting to ache with a dull pain that increased with each bounce.

"Well you got your wish, you're going to see the project, but it'll make us late getting back. Damn that Winky, why didn't he just have the other truck bring the trailer back if it's all that important?"

"More bullet holes by the sound of it," replied Bardman. "Maybe he felt you had more experience with shot-up trailers." He had tried to add some levity to the now sombre atmosphere, immediately regretting the attempt.

There was no reply from her as she hunched over the wheel. Suddenly she began pounding on the wheel with one fist. "We forgot to call the office about hearing those shots. Damn, we'll have to wait until we get to the project."

"Why don't they put CB radios in these trucks?" asked Bardman attempting to unscrew the top from his thermos bottle.

"Winky's decision. He said that with all the radio-detonated explosive caps around these sites he didn't want to be responsible for one of our trucks blowing one to smithereens by blabbing on the radio at the wrong time. Didn't you see the sign as we came in that said turn off all radio transmitters?"

He recalled seeing the sign. While he sipped the remains of his coffee, remnants of his dream filtered through his mind. Parts of it had been more vivid than he had ever experienced before. He felt a finger tap him on the shoulder.

"What ever happened to that sharing personality of yours?"

He handed her the cup as she drove with one hand on the wheel and asked: "Have you ever thought about what all this is doing to the environment?"

She looked suspiciously at the up of coffee. "You're right, it is pretty crappy coffee isn't it? Where do you suggest I throw it?"

"No, I mean all the construction and what it's doing to the wildlife. How can something so destructive be called progress?"

She drove in silent thought for a moment, nodding to herself, aware that Brady was watching her reaction. "It provides a lot of work for people like me and Joe Would you rather see us on welfare?"

"What about all the natives on welfare because their hunting and fishing has been ruined? he countered. "Are their needs any less important than ours? They lived here for hundreds of years without ruining the environment and all it's taken us is a couple of generations to turn them into wards of the state."

"Are you getting radical on me Brady? 'Cause if you are, keep your opinions to yourself around these sites or we may both find ourselves out of a job. But...if it's any consolation to you, yes, I do think about what I see here, and it bothers me. I just don't know what to do about it because I don't want to lose my job." She handed the empty cup back to Bardman. "Go to sleep; it'll be nearly dark before we get to the project and there's not much to see on the way.

He sat back and closed his eyes but couldn't sleep. The images of the rusty coils of cable amongst the fallen trees were clear in his mind, as was the image of the rising water on the Black Wood River. "Did that water we saw at the bridge come from the control station we were just at?"

She thought for a moment. "Nope, the water flows the other way. That water came from Lake Winnipeg and what you saw was the effect of the control gates being raised to hold the water back and diverted around the project until they need the water there to make electricity. When they're ready to start producing, then they open the gates and let the water fill up the reservoir in front of the dam."

"So what happens to all the rivers they divert into? Don't they get flooded?" He sat upright again as though it would help his brain understand the complexities of shunting such huge masses of water around without creating environmental havoc.

"I guess so, but I think they can control it with the gates," she replied, a note of doubt in her voice.

"Until they need the water, then they drain the areas they've recently flooded. Right?"

She nodded, biting her lower lip in thought. She was beginning to regret having brought him along because her head was starting to ache with all his questions. "That sounds about right, but maybe they need to keep the water levels high to make sure they have enough to generate power. I mean what if there's a drought?"

"Sounds completely wrong to me," said Bardman now looking straight at her, eyes wide with the reality of how her job was contributing to the environmental mess he was seeing all around him.

"It's a damn job, so will you just get off my case?" she yelled, beginning to feel he was blaming her for what he saw. She was beginning to wish she had left him at home.

"Ya know li'l missy, ya shur are perty when ya git angry." he drawled in his John Wayne imitation. He saw her smile and realised he had been treading on thin ice with the conversation, but his thoughts to himself would have frightened her.

Beyond the trees they could see the bluish glow of the high power sodium vapour lights which lit the hydro project, reflecting off the low cloud cover. It was an alien sight to him, almost surrealistic to see the tiny figures of workers, dwarfed by the immense scale of the project. High intensity lights lit areas along the top of the dam where continuous pouring of concrete was taking place and he rolled down his window as they descended into this seemingly chaotic scene He could hear the unending rattle of the huge vibrators that settled the wet concrete firmly into the wooden forms, eliminating any chance of bubbles. He could see the pouring was nearly completed, comparing it with another section that had been finished. Everywhere were huge rock-wagons, hauling pieces of newly excavated rock the size of automobiles. They rolled on tires three times the height of a man. Scores of pneumatic rock drills, each powered by its own diesel air compressor bored holes which would later be filled with explosives. The sound was deafening, making him wish he had brought his ear protectors. As they approached along a side road, he could see a line of trailers, some with the North Haul logo.

D'Amico tried to read the numbers on each to see which one they were to return with. Sitting at the end of the line with only its marker lights on was another North Haul tractor, still running and its driver slumped over in his seat, head resting on the steering wheel. She flicked her bright beams at him but his head remained where it was on the wheel. Climbing from the cab she ran to other tractor where the driver was passed out, sound asleep.

Bardman watched her open the door of the tractor and shake the man awake. He woke with a startled expression and climbed down from his cab to accompany her to their own tractor. Finally, he also climbed down to join them, thankful to stretch his legs. D'Amico walked toward him, illuminated by the yellow and blue lights from the project nearly a quarter mile away. The earth vibrated and he could smell the smoke of the many arc welding units connecting the reinforcing bar together, to be later covered with concrete. It was a hard metallic smell of ozone that filled his sinuses and made him want to sneeze.

"Brady, this is Eric. He just hired on with us a few days ago. We have to adjust the brakes on his trailer and someone swiped his tools from the cab. He had to wait for us to borrow tools, so I'm going to help him, then we can hook up to our trailer and go back together" She reached behind the truck seat and extracted a red tool kit. From it she took a nine-sixteenth inch box end wrench and a hammer.

With the other tractor's lights on high beams, they were able to adjust the slack arms of the spring-loaded air brakes with a minimum of cursing and pounding with the hammer to unlock the locking ring on the adjusting nut of each brake pot. With that completed, she backed their tractor under their assigned trailer and soon had the airlines and electrical cord hooked up. Within minutes the two tractor trailer units were heading back toward town, away from the deafening sound and dazzling light of the project.

"Eric said some worker was lost in the concrete tonight." She was hunched over the wheel, her eyes beginning to show fatigue. "Fell off the scaffolding right into where they were pouring and got sucked down by the vibrators. Heard it from one of the guys helping unload the explosives. Said it was a buddy of his. He said they tried to reach him but he sank so fast it would have been impossible to find him The tried grappling hooks but came up with nothing. God, what horrible way to go."

Bardman could hear the sadness and fatigue in the monotone of her voice and tried to envision what a horrible end it must have been for the worker and those who watched helplessly as their friend was sucked to oblivion. He was to be entombed for what could be eternity. *So it eats people too, not just lively-hoods and the environment. How many people have to die or have their lives ruined by that obscenity out there?* His thoughts began to frighten him and he opened his eyes to look at D'Amico, her tired features illuminated by the baleful glow of the dashboard instrument lights. He realised her job was a difficult one and more so because she was a woman and had to deal with the attitudes of the guys she worked with. She had earned the respect of the new driver quickly because she not only had the right tools to adjust the air brakes, she knew how to do it quickly.

She turned and looked back at him. "What the hell are you grinning at?"

"You ever wear dresses?"

"What is it with men? Does a woman have to wear a dress to be a woman? You're the second person to ask me that."

"No, you're just an enigma, you seem able to do a lot more than just drive a truck. Do you ever feel you want to do more with your life?"

She was quiet in thought for a few moments, reluctant to share too many personal secrets. "My ex-husband used to own a construction company and I worked in the office. That's where we met. I did the typing, receptionist crap, the books, and all the go-fering I could handle for the rest of my life, and got paid minimum wage for it," she said, bitterness in her voice. "When we got married he expected me to keep working and wait on him hand and foot at home too, still at minimum wage. Less if you count all the housework. So, while he was away on some of his business trips I talked one of the company drivers into showing me how to drive the big trucks. I used to wheel them around the yard and practice backing them up to the loading docks. The other guys also showed me how to drive the forklifts and front-end loaders. It got so I was wearing coveralls more in the office than my skirt, and I liked it. I also liked the physical side of it and I think the guys got a real kick out of it. I swore them never to tell my husband."

"Obviously he found out about it."

"Oh yeah...about the same time I found out about the bimbo he was boffing while he was away on one of his business trips. So I threw all his stuff in the street, moved out and went to work for his competition, driving truck and doing their books on a contract basis. My poor husband had to hire someone for my job, pay three times the wages and has to do his own cooking and housework."

"I guess you could call that poetic justice." He resolved to clean his apartment more frequently and read a few more recipes other than those on the back of the Kraft Dinner boxes.

She nodded and looked at her watch. It was nearly 7 pm and they had another three hours before home. The moon was beginning to rise from behind the dark edge of the forest, a full silver ball with the dark splotches of the craters, smiling balefully at them over the treetops. The spruce trees along the side of the road were barely distinguishable by the lights of the truck At times it seemed that they were sitting still and the trees on either side moved past them like two endless dark trains to nowhere.

"Don't go to sleep on me Brady, I'll need your help to keep me awake." She rubbed her eyes with the palm of one hand and yawned hugely. She rolled her window down a crack to let in the cold outside air. The thermostatically controlled flaps in front of the engine radiator opened occasionally to allow cooling, accompanied by the sound of rushing air, then as quickly closed down to allow the engine to retain its proper heat level. The sound was soothing and had a tendency to put drivers to sleep.

He hunted through the collection of tapes in a greasy box on the floor and selected one at random. He popped it into the overhead tape player. George Jones' twangy voice harangued them from the overhead speakers. The frequent hard bumps turned his lyrics into an electronic squeal, reminiscent of Dolly Parton in full verbal flight.

"I said wake me, not the dead." She was relieved he hadn't played the classical tape, it would have put her to sleep in an instant. Her eyeballs felt as though coated in sand and blinking only produced a few paltry tears to lubricate their movement.   At this point she figured the only tape that would keep her awake would be the 1812 Overture, and she had an aversion to the sound of things exploding. Suddenly she leaned forward over the wheel, peering through the partially frosted windshield, the cold light of the moon bathing her face in its pale light. "What the hell is that?" she said barely audible over the sounds coming from the speakers. She turned the tape off and looked out the windshield. Ahead of them on the road, silhouetted against the moonlight were two figures, one much smaller than the other, walking hand in hand. Around them were the sparkles of frost, like tiny diamonds brushed on to the pristine whiteness of the snow. Their breaths could be seen rising from them in white clouds and drifting away ghost-like straight up into the quiet air and then toward the tree line as though seeking refuge in its darkness.

She began down-shifting the transmission as they approached the walking figures and finally stopped. The two ghostly figures had also stopped and turned in their direction, their faces illuminated by the headlights.

It was an old native woman with a young boy. The boy, about three years old, wore a toque that nearly covered his eyes. It was a Montreal Canadians toque. The old woman had a tattered babushka over her head, grey strands of hair protruding from the sides like old pieces of twine, frosty from her breath. Both wore mukluk-style footwear, heavy parkas and leather mitts on their hands. They stood expectantly in front of the lights, their brown eyes squinting from the glare.

D'Amico and Bardman climbed down and it was then that she realised the little boy was crying quietly, and his nose was running, mingling his tears. The snot streamed down to freeze in a multi-coloured amalgam in the form of an ice-sickle on the end of his chin.

They helped them both into the cab of the truck, Bardman setting the little boy on his lap and the old woman sat on a filthy soft-drink box near the gearshift, between the two seats. It had suddenly become very crowded and he could feel the little boy shivering violently on his lap. The extreme cold of the little boy's body drew the warmth from his own. His hair smelled of sweat and wood smoke. The old woman had her mitts off and her hands over the vents of the windshield defrost section. Neither had said anything, their mouths too stiff from the cold to utter any words.

Teresa started the truck forward again, alternately shifting and blowing her warm breath on her hands. They were both surprised how cold it had become, with the return of the clear skies.

"Thank you," said the old woman in a near whisper, almost like a prayer. "We had to leave; they were drinkin' an' startin' to fight."

"Who was fighting?" asked Bardman.

"Some of the men. We went into the bush for a wiener roast an' somebody brought booze. A couple of guys pulled knives an' were goin' at it. We had to get out...it was gettin' bad, an' they were all drunk."

Bardman could feel the hands of the little boy in his own. The hands felt like two frozen pieces of meat, so cold it was painful to touch them. He opened his parka zipper, turned the little boy around and inserted the two, tiny cold hands under his own armpits. The little boy whimpered quietly, leaned his head against his chest and went to sleep. He realised the mess on the cold little boys' chin was thawing and creating a slippery wetness down the front of his shirt. Oh well it had to be washed anyway, he said to himself.

The old woman looked up at him and gently smiled a toothless grin at him. "My grandson. We got friends in town. We'll stay there." Soon the old woman was also asleep, sitting completely upright on the plastic carton, swaying as if in a trance with every motion of the truck. The only sounds were the rattle of the engine and the frequent hiss of the air as the radiator dampers opened and closed.

Despite the sounds, Bardman remained wide awake the rest of the way home. Once or twice he saw Teresa steal a glance in his direction and thought he saw her smile at the little boy who was asleep and clung to his chest, drool and snot rolling down the front of his shirt.

The old trapper sat close to the fire, watching the deer meat suspended on a sharp stick as it roasted over the hot coals. Through the trees he could see the full moon slowly rising, casting the shadows of the trees onto the pale light of the snow that sparkled with the frost. He could hear the howls of a wolf pack in the distance but didn't feel threatened by them. What he did feel threatened by was the smell of another fire, somewhere to the north. He had smelled it before. He had made camp with the still-warm carcass of the deer tied to the toboggan of the snowmobile. The warm blanket of air provided by his fire made him secure, its light illuminating the closer trees with an orange glow. Finally, with the warm meat resting in his belly, he prepared for bed in his lean-to, his body fortified by a large cup of hot sweetened tea. As he was crawling into the heavy sleeping bag he thought he could hear the distant sound of snowmobiles, interspersed with the howls of the wolves. He was surprised at how human-like the howls were and as he lay on his side finishing a last pipe of tobacco, he came to the troubling conclusion that the howls were indeed human, and even more troubling, they were coming closer. He heard a shot, like a large branch snapping in the distance. They're hunting the wolves! As he lay in the lean-to, listening to the crackling of the dying fire, the sounds of the snowmobiles and the human howling gradually receded. He slept fitfully, once awakening to the sounds of the wolves drifting in a wild choir through the forest, singing the trees to sleep with a melody that had been heard over countless ages. Laying on his back he could see above, through a break in the trees, the brilliant stars of the Milky Way. Points of light like diamond dust sprinkled on a black cloth. As he watched the heavens, a ghostly green light insinuated itself across the stars in wavering sheets, condensing, then stretching and writhing in spasms that stopped suddenly, then began somewhere else in the sky. The air was still, as though the very forest was holding its breath to watch nature's light show of the Aurora Borealis. In the blink of an eye, a meteor painted a white streak across the face of the Aurora.

The old trapper smiled and was glad the heavens were in such an amicable mood. Soon he slept and with the sleep, his inner eye opened to its own universe of perceived reality.

The sun shone with a golden light through the trees, painting the snow yellow between the thick trunks, their dark shadows like bars across the snow. He could see movement beyond the trees. Dark ghostly shapes with glowing eyes, pacing back and forth, looking at him and then turning away as though waiting for some kind of silent signal to approach. His feet were extended in front of him, his bare toes wriggling like baby mice. He didn't feel the cold, almost as though the warm light provided him shelter. His back was against a tree, his arms resting at his side as he looked slowly down the length of his body. He was naked. He could hear the shuffling of bodies and low growls as the shadows beyond the trees moved with more impatience, the eyes watching him more intently.

The shadows moved warily toward him from the yellow-hued ice fog. With ears erect, heads down to sniff the snow, they came, finally to sniff at his feet, then his crotch, and finally his head.

He could smell their musky scent and hot breath He could feel the heavy fur brush his face as each passed to make an inspection. He had no will to move, nor could he had he wanted to. Finally they moved back toward the bright yellow light beyond the trees and out of sight. A dry rustling sound made him slowly turn his head and look above him. Looking down at him from a tree limb was the raven. It was strange, he thought to himself, he had never seen a raven smile before. Ravens weren't supposed to smile.

When the old trapper woke, his bladder cried for relief. He rolled onto his side and looked about the campsite. The remnants of the dream faded like an old photograph in some forgotten dresser drawer. He wished the dream would remain with him because he knew it held some importance for him, as did the display in the night skies. As he pulled himself from the sleeping bag, he could see numerous wolf prints surrounding his lean-to, and even up to the edge of his sleeping bag. From beyond the trees came the chortle of the raven, waiting for its breakfast offering.

Joe McKay had an uneasy feeling in the pit of his stomach as he eased the truck onto the road to Hudson House Reserve. He had tried to avoid making the run with groceries and dry goods to the Hudson Bay store. It had been years since he had left there with the social workers, watching from the back window of their car, seeing the sadness and guilt in the face of his father. It was an image that haunted him, hoping he could make his father understand that his resentment as a child had diminished with the years.

On the crest of a hill he could see the church spire pointing toward the heavens like an accusing finger for those who had left its fold. Further along and on the other side of the snow-rutted road was the small one room school where he remembered being more interested in watching flies copulate on the window sill during spring, rather than the intricacies of Arithmetic and English grammar. To his left and right were the derelict bodies of discarded automobiles, rusting in brown-splotched manufacturers colours, hoods raised, headlights staring lifelessly ahead. Objects discarded by a discarded people.

Down one barely visible track toward the Muskrat River, past the garbage site, and near a copse of aspen, was the shack he had known as a boy. From the look of the road, no one had been down there for days if not weeks. Beyond the aspens near the river was the spot he had sat where his father had put his arm around him, shown some affection toward him for the first and last time he could remember. He remembered the drive to the south with the two social workers had been silent, feeling a sense of betrayal by his father. The woman in the front still nursed her red and swollen nose, no doubt surprised what his small fist could inflict. He wanted to say he was sorry but his pride wouldn't let him.

His father had pre-packed a bag of clothing and personal items for him, including school notebooks from his previous classes. His senses felt numb and the passing of the trees along the roadside was dream-like. He hardly remembered stopping for lunch at the truck stop, but could recall the sweet stench of the diesel fumes from the huge trucks. Next to wood smoke, he liked that smell best.

Eight hours later, he had seen the countryside change from the evergreens, birch and aspen of the Precambrian Shield, to tree-lined lakes. Finally came the expanse of the prairies with fields of wheat, flax, and canola shimmering like painted squares of their fall colours of brown and variations of gold, encompassed by an electric blue sky. Occasional vagrant white clouds, wandered with the winds. The aromas overwhelmed him with their perfumes and the song of what he would later learn was the meadowlark, would startle him with its bell-like sound from the tops of the power poles lining the roadside.

When his eyes became tired with the onslaught of new things, he drew designs with his finger in the fine dust coating the armrest of the back seat, listening to the crunch of the tires on gravel. He felt as though his head was stuffed with cotton. He fell asleep to a dream of wood smoke and goldenrod, and the sounds of the Muskrat River.

They arrived at what was known as the Indian Residential School, nestled in a picturesque valley, surrounded by towering elm trees whose leaves were beginning to turn yellow and rattle in the wind with each gust. The aroma of freshly cut hay and grass smoke hung heavily in the air as well as a smoky haze, like blue morning mist, suspended above the valley floor and the river that ran nearby.

In the early evening light Joe could see the yellow squares of the windows lit from within as they came up the tree-lined driveway. The sky had turned deep purple, shot through with streaks of pink from the last light of the high cirrus clouds catching the last of the sun. The planet Venus shone like a single bright diamond, unwaveringly in the western sky as the deep purple turned to black. He turned to admire the colours as they got from the car. He feared he might never see them again if he entered the brick monolith with its glowing yellow windows.

The social workers were in conversation with a staff member that had come down the steps to greet them. They spoke in low voices and cast furtive glances at him as he watched the sky. The woman was caressing her nose while the staff member listened intently, looking at Joe with a serious expression. Finally the staffer came over with a subtle smile on his lips, and eyes that were at once serious and amused.

"So, Joe...I hear you like to box," said the man. "We have a very good boxing program here, I'm sure we'll be able to work you in somewhere and give you an outlet for you energies."

Joe didn't meet his eyes, but looked at his feet and the gravel under them, shuffling a rock from one foot to the other.

"My name's Albert. I'm one of the room monitors and I'll show you where you'll be sleeping. There are lots of other boys here and you'll get to meet them all soon. Come with me now, it's supper time and we're having macaroni and cheese. I'll bet it's one of your favourites." The words flowed from him as smoothly as oil from a can. The voice smeared itself across his small body, accompanied by the piercing eyes of the man before him.

Albert laid one bony hand on Joe's black hair to guide him in the direction, carrying his small bag in the other. He was a cadaverous man with sallow skin and eyes sunken below dark heavy eyebrows. His thin lips still smiled at the corners but the rest of the face seemed to have no humour. His white shirt billowed out from the belt line of his dark pants which were too short for his legs, showing bare ankles.

He appeared to Joe like a scarecrow with oversized feet and hands. He hoped it wasn't a result of the food.

As they entered the building's large double doors he could smell an aroma of burnt food mingled with detergent. The hardwood floors creaked under his weight as they ascended a wide flight of stairs and came to the dormitory area. Two rows of iron framed cots with an aisle down the centre stretched into darkness at the end of the room, the only light being supplied presently from the landing where they stood.

Albert showed him his cot and a small foot locker under it where he could put his belongings. "You've almost missed supper... but I'm sure there's something left," said Albert leading their way to the dining room.

They went back down the wide staircase that creaked with each step and smelled of varnish. The glistening bannister made Joe's hand squeak as he ran it along the surface as he descended.

Albert turned suddenly and yanked Joe's hand from the bannister, looking straight into his eyes, causing Joe to suddenly avert his.

Albert held Joe's hand for several seconds before letting it go, smiling at him with knife-thin lips as he did so. His eyes were emotionless, like those of a reptile.

Joe shivered involuntarily, looking at his feet on the stairs, wishing he could wash his hands of this man's touch. His appetite had diminished and the thought of food was beginning to make his stomach churn.

When they entered the dining hall and the long, wooden tables placed end to end, all clanking of utensils stopped suddenly and one-hundred and fifty pairs of young eyes turned to stare. They were eyes without spirit to Joe, who reluctantly looked back as he slid onto a bench seat at the end of one table.

The boy next to him quickly reached over and removed the eating utensils from his spot, giggling as he did so.

A hand coming from behind with the quickness of a snake landed with a smacking sound against the other boy's ear, making him jump and cringe with pain. He slid the utensils back to Joe, tears beginning to glisten in his large dark eyes. They exchanged no words as a bowl of macaroni thumped down in front of Joe. The contents were a mixture of cold noodles invaded by shards of burnt material from the sides of the pot, that looked suspiciously like cheese. A crust of heavy brown bread came next, along with a glass of milk that retained a white scum around the rim where the powdered milk crystals had stuck. There were sizable white lumps still floating in the liquid. As he ate, the sounds of the hall became filled once again with the slurping and gulping that only hungry children seem able to produce. The occasional belch was met with nervous giggles around the table.

Later that night, when the lights were out and each boy was in his assigned cot, he could hear the alien sound of a siren through the opened window next to his cot. He slowly rolled out of bed and went to the window which was bathed in moonlight, and looked through the heavy metal screening at the twinkling lights of a city several miles away. It appeared to him as though part of the starry heavens had landed within his reach and he wanted to reach out and touch it. He could hear the slow sound of bedsprings squeaking at the far end of the double row of cots. Barely discernible from where he stood, he could see the moonlight on the form of a figure on hands and knees, kneeling over a smaller figure on the cot. The squeaks continued, increasing in rhythm. He remembered the boy beside him who had been slapped and thought the squeaking was coming from his bed. As he returned to his bed he heard a nervous giggle and saw the large eyes of the boy on the next cot looking at him, pointing at him, and then making a motion with his finger through his forefinger and thumb of the other hand. It was a gesture that was unmistakable and the tightness that had been in his stomach when Albert touched his hand, returned. He was a long time getting to sleep because the squeaking sound of the bedsprings went long into the night. When he finally slept, in his dream he could smell wood smoke and hear the wind whistling softly through the spruce trees around him.

He was jolted awake with a clanging that made his ears ache. Near his bed stood Albert with a large trash can, smiling down at him as he beat it with a piece of broomstick. He moved down the line, noisily assaulting the metal container.

"Up, up, you young buggers. Time to earn your keep, get your education and be useful to society." His voice was punctuated by the beating of the trash can as he marched up and down the line, watching the boys climb naked from their bunks and head groggily to the bathroom. "Breakfast in ten minutes, the last three boys do all the dishes."

There was a flurry of small feet slapping the hardwood floor and rustling of clothing.

"Make your beds first or you'll be hearing from me later," he shouted with a voice that echoed from the walls.

The boys glanced at each other with fear in their eyes, knowing that later meant during the night and the horrible singing of the bedsprings.

Joe glanced up from making his bed, his trousers still down around his ankles, the images of last night still clawing at his mind.

Albert was staring at him. He was no longer beating the can with the broomstick. Instead, he was caressing the length of wood up and down its length with one hand, smiling his thin-lipped smile at Joe, his sunken eyes staring blankly from their dark sockets.

78

Joe felt as though he was going to be sick to his stomach and headed with the other boys to breakfast.

In the dining area he looked for the boy that had sat beside him, but failed to see him as he stood in line while the staff examined their outstretched hands to check for cleanliness. They shuffled like tiny prisoners along the serving line with their heavy porcelain bowls before them to receive a mound of grey oatmeal porridge. From that day on, Joe, innocent, naive, and open to the experiences of a world he didn't understand, learned to fear and hate. First he learned to hate oatmeal porridge. Then he learned to hate the world. The rest of his hatreds grew with what he saw and experienced in the residential school, some to scar him deeply for the rest of his life. The scars remained hidden beneath a veneer of smiles and jokes, returning only in his nightmares, triggered by the simple squeaking of a bedspring.

CHAPTER 5

D'Amico and McKay sat watching with disbelief as Big Don and Toothless Jake used their feet to gouge a small trench out of the hard-packed snow of the loading area.

"These guys are really nuts," said D'Amico, munching on a lettuce and tomato sandwich, the red juice trickling down her chin. They were sitting on the edge of the loading dock basking in the early morning sun of what felt like the first day of spring. Their truck was parked to the side of the loading bays, waiting to be loaded while the two explosives men gently buried a segment of sandwich under the snow and connected two thin wires to it. They backed away from the buried sandwich as Toothless Jake trailed the wire placing a thin skim of snow over it as he moved backward toward the loading bay where D'Amico and McKay sat watching.

He gummed a smile of evil anticipation at them from his crouching position, his tongue flicking in and out with excitement at what was to come. Big Don spread a few more bits of food in the area of the buried offering, smiling to himself while humming a tune. "Here birdy, birdy, come 'n git yer din-din," murmured Big Don to a group of ravens perched and watching with interest from a copse of trees near the rail spur line that ran behind the blockhouse which contained thousands of pounds of high explosives.

The ravens gurgled a couple of notes to each other and exercised their wings, eyeing the offering.

"This ought ta ruffle a few feathers," said Big Don, slowly climbing onto the loading dock beside the two drivers while Toothless Jake giggled and positioned a large square flashlight battery on the ledge to which he was connecting one wire to a post.

McKay watched with disapproval, wishing they could just be loaded and out of there. "I think this job has been warping your sense of humour. What do you do for entertainment when you're at home? Blow up the kids?"

"We give 'em ekfploding thuckerth," chortled Toothless as he eyed the sandwich in the snow.

"You mean lollipops," corrected Big Don, hunched over his lunch box the size of a small suitcase.

"F'what I faid... thuckerth"

80

Big Don snorted and bit into what appeared to be a full loaf of bread split lengthwise, stuffed with eight different types of luncheon meats drooping out of the sides along with huge yellow dollops of mustard and mayonnaise. The liquids squirted out and rolled down his cheeks in a multi-coloured river. He wiped his mouth with the back of his parka sleeve, already greasy and slippery from the remnants of other culinary adventures. "Here birdy, birdy, birdy," he called between fist-sized bites. An involuntary offering of crumbs flew in a spray from his dripping mouth.

Toothless Jake molested an English cucumber with his mouth and when he couldn't make a dent in it, threw it against the wall where it broke into several smaller pieces. With satisfaction he picked up the now bite-sized pieces and mashed them with his gums, swallowing with audible gulping sounds as each went down. His throat made a spasm like a cormorant swallowing a fish.

"Here comes one of those suckers now." Big Don watched without moving as a raven swooped in and flew away with a piece of sandwich. Others quickly followed suit until all that remained was the partially buried segment in the snow. "Here birdy," hummed Big Don softly. "Come'n git yer feathers ruffled."

The four of them sat without speaking, holding their breath, watching the large, black raven cautiously strut toward the piece of sandwich. It came close and cocked its head to one side, aiming one wary eye toward the bait, then walked sideways around the object again, and stole a suspicious look at the quiet onlookers on the loading dock. Another raven flew overhead, eliciting a warning cry from the one on the ground. Several others sat waiting expectantly in the trees nearby. The hungry raven edged closer and suddenly hopped away, flapping its feathers in the process and looking once again at the humans. Then it hopped back and jabbed once at the object with its large beak, stopped and had another sideways glance at the progress being made.

"Here we go, that bird's in for the surprise of its' feathered life," said Big Don under his breath.

The raven made two quick jabs with its beak and had the food before anyone could react.

"Fer Christ sake Jake, trigger the sucker," yelled Big Don as he saw the raven hopping about with the bait in its beak, flapping its wings in an attempt to get airborne.

"Aw phit, the battery!" Toothless Jake was up and running toward the small battery a few paces away.

The slack in the wire ran out, yanking the food from the ravens' beak as it tried to fly. Another raven waiting for such an opportunity, swooped down from the other direction and caught the food as it hit the ground, flying in the opposite direction, directly toward the lunching foursome on the loading dock. More of the wire trailing behind it had been yanked free of the snow by the attempts of the first raven. Toothless Jake reached for the single wire to complete the circuit to the electric blasting cap hidden in the piece of bread.

"No wait, don't Jake, don't..shit!" came a chorus of shouts to his confused ears as he fumbled with the wire in his excitement.

The raven veered at the last instant, nearly colliding with Big Don who was waving his arms like a windmill. The excess wire came to an end, ripping the bait unceremoniously from the raven's beak to land at their feet.

At that same instant, Toothless Jake made contact with the battery post.

The blasting cap exploded like an oversized firecracker, making their ears ring and hurling Big Don backward onto the concrete floor. Parts of his own sandwich lay where he had flung them in panic to the ground outside.

D'Amico gave a little shriek and buried her head with her arms, drawing her knees up in front of her, while McKay sat with his mouth open in disbelief. To him it looked as though the raven knew exactly what it was doing and had vengeance on its mind.

Toothless Jake realised too late what had happened and in reflex, picked up the battery and threw it as though the act would somehow reverse the consequences. The battery, thrown in haste landed on Big Dons' groin causing a howl of pain from the huge, still supine figure on the floor. "Aw phit, what a fuckup." He looked with concern at his partner who was holding his groin, still writhing on the floor of the blockhouse and giving out with a stream of colourful metaphors. He tried to elaborate an apology but his acute toothlessness and hyperactive tongue only resulted in a stream of drool at the side of his mouth. He fought his immediate reaction to run and lock himself in the toilet, a reaction he had since his substandard potty-training as a child.

Big Don's pain had eased somewhat, enough to speak coherently. "I swear Jake, if brains were copper wire, you couldn't short out the ass end of a firefly."

Jake tried to look appropriately contrite, hands stuffed deep within his pockets, shuffling his feet while looking at the floor. "Aw phit," was all he could say.

"Stop playin' with yer balls an' let's go to work." Big Don brushed himself off and looked at the ground at the remains of his sandwich. "Next time let's try a stick of Cil-Gel, maybe we'll git the whole damn flock."

McKay and D'Amico headed for the truck to prepare to back it up to the loading dock, their ears still ringing from the blast.

"Be real gentle backin' up," called Big Don from the dock. "We got a pallet of stuff in here sweatin' nitroglycerin. Sure wouldn't want to disturb that stuff." He smiled broadly at them, enjoying the ashen colours their faces had become.

In the closed circle of friends that drove the explosives trucks and a few of the explosives employees, word got around of Big Dons' exploding sandwiches and it became a matter of habit that no one would sit near him during lunch. Joe was upset at what he had witnessed. It was a mindless attempt at cruelty toward innocent wildlife. D'Amico was also very quiet as they took the small load of powder to Q-3, a smaller headframe several miles away.

"I think those guys are crazier than shithouse rats," said McKay. "Hell they could've blown the whole damn place to pieces and us with'em. Must be all the chemicals they inhale when they make the Amex or just pure boredom...whatever it is, they scared the shit out of me. What scared me even more is, that raven looked like it knew exactly what it was doing. It almost looked like it was smiling, flying along with that little bomb in its' mouth." He waited for a reply from her but none came. She was sitting in the jump seat with her eyes closed, either asleep or deep in thought. When she finally did open her eyes he could see concern in them as she spoke.

"This job doesn't seem to be fun anymore. Do you ever think what the explosives are doing, you know, the ones we take north to the hydro project?"

He nodded, quiet for a minute. "I see the rivers risin', floodin' the good fishin' and trappin' lands. I see the people in the reserve where I used to live, on welfare more now than ever, no way to make a livin' and no pride left eh. I can also see food on my table each day for my wife and son. They might be starvin' if I wasn't doin' this, an' if I wasn't doin' it, somebody else would be.

"So is it worth it Joe? We save ourselves and destroy others as we do it. Does that make it right? Or is that just progress, something we sell to the power hungry United States with their electric society?"

He shrugged his shoulders as the five ton International Loadstar bounced on the rough road. Trying to reconcile support of his family with the obvious desecration of the natural beauty being caused by the project was giving him a headache. All he really wanted to do was go home and sleep, because he had been having strange dreams the past few nights, the sounds of bedsprings squeaking, becoming closer as he slept, and sometimes the image of Jimmy No-name. It was one of the reasons a chasm had opened up between him and Sadie. Every time they made love, their bedsprings squeaked and the memories came back, bringing with it a cold sweat and complete impotence. Despite her attempts, Sadie had never been able to understand his silence, nor get him to talk about it. Their bedroom had become a barren land of mutual recrimination, neither knowing the other's thoughts.

"There's the security gate. Lets get this unloaded and call it a day." He braked and came to a stop a hundred feet in front of the security shack where they had to show their manifest to the guard and wait for the explosives guide-vehicle. He set the mechanical parking brake as they climbed out and walked to a nearby wooden walkway, parallel with the roadway.

The security guard waved at them from the closed window as they approached. They waved back only to see the guard, an elderly man with thinning white hair wave even more frantically. They glanced to their left at the gently inclined roadway in time to see their quietly idling truck roll past them. Gradually picking up speed, the driverless truck approached the guard shack and the now thoroughly panicked guard. D'Amico ran for the passenger door and tried to open it. It had always been prone to sticking and at this instant it chose to do so. While she was still clinging to the running board and side mirror, the truck rammed the shack with a loud crunch, shifting the small structure off its foundation a couple of inches.

The elderly guard inside staggered back clutching his chest, face the colour of paste, thinking to himself that he was in the wrong business. It was exactly what McKay and D'Amico were thinking at the moment, dreading the pile of paperwork that would be needed to placate the people who dealt with the explosives act.

"This just hasn't been our day," said D'Amico quietly as she handed the shaking guard the manifest detailing the load. The guard took it shakily, glanced at it, no longer concerned with its contents and called for the guide-truck. "We should apologize for that truck," she continued. "We've complained till we were blue in the face about that brake letting go on its own but Winky won't do squat about it. You sure your okay?" She looked with concern at the guard who was still sitting, gasping like a fish out of water, but with little more colour in his face. She looked at McKay who was watching her with concern. "I think I'm going to go for a ski after work, all this stress is giving me bad bathroom habits." She giggled with her hand over her mouth and saw McKay smile. His smile masked the concern he felt for his partner but the next instant he began to laugh as the tension from the incident dissipated.

When the guide-truck arrived, the driver saw the two of them laughing with tears coming down their cheeks. The elderly guard looked at them as though they were crazy.

Bardman waited for D'Amico that afternoon at the trail head of the Nordic ski area. In front of him was a large map showing the ski trails with different colours allotted to each. At various places of the map were wedge shapes, indicating a down slope and the name of the hill. The names, Screamer, Widow Maker, and Cardiac Hill, put him ill at ease. He was at least thankful for the longer days of the early spring weather and the chance to give this sport a try. As he stood looking at the cartoons of a Canadian Ski Patrol Nordic safety poster, a couple of skiers in eye-straining coloured tights started down the trail. He was surprised at how quickly the skate-stride took them down the wide trail until they were out of sight. He was feeling self-conscious in his borrowed equipment, particularly the heavy woolen knickers that itched where they touched bare skin, which was considerable because his only set of long underwear was in the laundry hamper.

At the parking lot he could see Teresa locking her car and carrying her skis over her shoulder. She waved and smiled brightly to him, the stress of the workday began to leave him like stones being lifted from his shoulders. She was wearing her electric-blue tights again as he had hoped and if anything would motivate him to ski quickly it would be the simple act of trying to keep those tights in sight. "I feel under dressed when I see you in those things."

"You sir, are under dressed. Those things went out of style ten years ago. But at least you borrowed the right equipment for this trail." She smiled at his discomfort in the itchy wool breeches and thought he looked like an over-sized primary student from the 1930's. All that was

85

missing was the cheese-cutter hat and motoring goggles. "Well, shall we begin? This by the way, is the front end of the ski."

"Don't patronize me, I feel silly enough as it is."

"Okay, I'm sorry. Let's start over. I'm going to show you the proper weight transfer for the skate-ski technique.

During the rest of that afternoon they practised weight transfer and achieving a long glide at the beginning of the trail head where it was reasonably flat and sheltered amongst the trees.   He was surprised how difficult it was to maintain his balance on the thin skis, but pleasantly surprised how much control the Salomon boot and the Profil binding afforded. The extra lateral control was much improved from when he had first tried the sport with old three pin binding systems and wooden-based skis. After doing several exercises on the flat, they started down the trail on a gradual downhill that curved to the right at the bottom. The wideness at the bottom allowed him to snowplough around the curve but D'Amico did a quick step turn, never slowing down.

He became even more aware of his shortcomings when they came to their first uphill and as he herring-boned up the incline he could see her skating in long graceful strides up the hill. *Up the hill for God's sake!* He wondered how she managed it. There was obviously more to this than met the eye, not the least being the need for good physical conditioning.

"You're doing really well for your first time out. A little sweat never hurt anyone did it?" She had waited at the crest of one hill as he trudged up and he was thankful for her diplomacy.

He agreed, the sweat did feel good. He was warm despite the lowering sun, now an orange ball peeking through the spruce trees, the trail the colour of slate in the lowering light.

She peered past his shoulder at the hill they had just climbed. "Oh no, not *him* again."

He turned and saw a skier with a furry hat with flaps on the side and peak turned up at front, trudging up the hill toward them. The skier looked up briefly and smiled at them, or more specifically at Teresa. He was struck by the huge, icy moustache clinging to his upper lip and the large nose that seemed to fight with his moustache for domination of his face. His eyes appeared as close-set black buttons.

"Why Constable Pusch, I do believe you're following me."

"Not at all Miss D'Amico, but I did notice your car in the parking lot, had no idea which trail you'd take, made a lucky guess I suppose." He laughed hugely at his own joke, darting little questioning glances at

Bardman and back at her. He was puffing like a whale about to submerge, his face red either from the effort or the embarrassment of finding her with someone else. His ear flaps waggled like the droopy ears of a bloodhound.

"Constable, I'd like you to meet my husband, Brady."

Both men's mouths dropped open simultaneously and nearly fell over, their skis slid around on the hard snow as with a mind of their own while they each jammed their poles into the hard-packed snow to control themselves.

"*Husband?* Oh, um pleasure sir. Pardon my surprise. I always thought Miss D'Amico was simply a, a, er."

"A Miss?"

"Yes, that's it one of those. Well I wasn't really following her you know, just out for a ski. Beautiful day for it don't you think?" He took his fur hat off and exercised the floppy ear flaps with both hands as though giving it flying lessons before setting it free. He jammed it back on his head and it cocked slightly to one side with an expression of determination. With a flourish he turned and went the way he had come, down the hill, arms windmilling as he rounded the bend. Seconds after he disappeared from sight they heard a crash and the sound of branches breaking, followed by what sounded like muffled curses.

"Does he always try to talk like an Englishman, and just how long have we been married?"

"Sorry about that, I know he was following me and I wanted to put him right off the trail.   Don't go out and buy a ring. Okay? And, I think he talks like an Englishman because he might be constipated all the time. You know...constipatable Pusch?"

They both laughed at the thought of him extricating himself from the foliage, his self- confidence as skewed as the hat on his head. Their voices echoed from the surrounding hillside, the quiet broken only by the occasional call of a raven in the distance.

"What did you find out about those shots that were taken at the truck by the bridge?" He was trying to remember how to put his hands through the straps of the ski poles.

"I don't think they were aimed at us; the police searched the area and found remnants of a deer carcass along with snowmobile tracks next to a camp site. The lack of bullet holes in the trailer was puzzling, it would have to be a terrible shot to miss Eric's truck from that distance. It's too bad your photographs of the guy were so dark because of the trees, it might still offer a clue. By the way thank you for the beautiful print of the bridge at sunset, I've had it framed and it's on the kitchen wall."

"So the police don't have any other clues?" He gave up on the uncooperative ski pole strap.

"If they do they haven't told me and I don't think they really have any reason to tell me. Maybe it might put the investigation at risk or something like that. You're starting to shiver, Brady, let's start back. I think you've had enough skiing for the first time out."

"It's not everyone who gets to lose their bachelorhood the first time skiing. This is a potentially very dangerous sport...*Miss* D'Amico."

"Who knows, you might lose your virginity next," she giggled from the rear.

I'm not taking off my breeches out here," he mumbled from shivering lips.

When they reached the parking lot, their cars were the only two remaining. They changed footwear as quickly as possible while the cars were warming up. She came over to his car as he was getting in, leaned down and gave him a quick kiss on the lips. "Thanks for coming. let's do it again soon."

He was already planning to visit the local ski shop and see what kind of spring clearance deals he could negotiate. On the return to town he listened to the local radio station and its unending country music. He surprised himself by singing along with a song he had never liked. His voice sounded like a cross between an angry donkey and an electric drill. It was the best he had felt in a long time, and he knew it wasn't just the skiing.

Sam Pilson and Frenchy Rivest were wet and miserable. They had been working the last four shifts on an up-hole, one of the most unpleasant aspects of exploration drilling because the cold water for the drill-bit ran back out of the hole and onto them where they had to stand to monitor its progress. It was a constant cold shower for at least one of them, the water milky with rock dust, running down shirt collars, out sleeves or into their rubber boots. What was even more unpleasant was their proximity to the highballers, a hundred feet down the drift and around a short bend.

The mining contractors had left their powder car on a small siding carved into the rock wall, and it was from there that they prepared their explosive charges. the small flatcar was piled with several layers of bags of Amex, the granular explosive and off to one side was a small wooden cask of caps and fuses. Lying nearby were also several small metal spools of what appeared to be yellow or orange wire.

Frenchy recognized this as Prima-cord, or B-line, an explosive cord that was used to set off different charges nearly simultaneously, or at different times, depending on the length of cord used. It burned or rather exploded at the rate of 2500 feet per second, and could be ignited by a simple fuse. He had shuddered when he had seen some of the miners using it in place of shoelaces.   The howl of the drill made conversation impossible so he waved his headlamp at Pilson who was attending the drill. He made a slashing motion across his throat to indicate break time and saw Pilson turn the air control. The relative silence was as though they had both gone suddenly deaf.

"No more up-holes Frenchy, let's refuse to do anymore up-holes," he said, wiping his face and thick lensed glasses with a filthy handkerchief.

They sat down upon a large square of clean burlap sacking used to wipe grease from their hands with pieces the size of place mats cut from it. As they opened their lunch boxes they could hear the rattle of the jacklegs working at the drift face. The jacklegs were a combination of an air-powered jackhammer, and a drill. It hammered the rock with a hardened, hollow steel rod, through which cooling water pulsed under high pressure and rotated the drill bit simultaneously. Because the drill and drill rod could weigh 125 pounds or more, it had attached at the bottom, a pneumatic leg which could be extended and locked in an upraised position which could support the weight of the drill as high as a man's head. A half dozen men could work at the face of the drift, each with a jackleg, drilling holes up to thirty feet horizontally, in a specified pattern. These holes were then pumped full of the granular explosive called Amex, primed, and cap and fused to explode from the centre of the drill pattern outward to the edge. What sounded like a single huge blast was actually several quickly spaced blasts allowing the rock to be first removed from the centre of the pattern, then the rest in a quick sequence of explosions cutting layers of rock outward until a new, neatly formed extension of the drift remained. The loose rock was then 'mucked' out for processing. A rock face set for a 'shot' looked something like an electrician's nightmare with the yellow B-line coming from each hole with its' explosives and converging at a central point. It looked like a spider's web, the central point being a high-temperature igniter with a timed fuse attached. The varying lengths of this deadly web controlled the sequence of the explosions for each series of holes.

As they quietly ate their lunch, they glanced nervously down the drift, knowing that a long silence from that end of the drift could mean the holes were being charged with their explosives. With the highballer's reputation for disregard for safety, the two diamond drillers ate like two underground rodents, always wary, always listening. They chewed, listened, looked, chewed, then listened again.

"What is dat stuff?" said Frenchy, leaning over and looking at his myopic partner's lunch.

Pilson looked down at the plastic container in his greasy hands, his magnified eyes peering with wonder at the contents as though seeing them for the first time. "Brown beans and cheese," he said almost apologetically, his Adam's apple going up and down like a tiny freight elevator.

"Phew! No wonder h'it stink around 'ere sometime. Your wife make d'at for you every day, you should 'ave serious talk wit 'er."

"Not married," grunted Pilson, looking with renewed suspicion at the mixture. Some of it had managed to splash on his glasses in tiny brown dots.

"Got a girlfriend?"

"Nope."

"Almost impossible to get one 'ere eh? No womens, too many guy, too much competition eh? Better to be married or bring one from 'ome. You see d'at one in de Bank of Montreal?"

"The little redhead?"

"Oui, oo-la-la, not bad stuff eh? 'Er face 'er fortune, but 'er boob draw interest."

They both laughed, their voices echoing from the rock walls. Pilson had managed to spill his beans in his crotch, making them laugh even harder. As their jocularity tapered off they realised it was quiet at the end of the drift.

"Merde, boom time soon," said Rivest, wiping his mouth with the back of a greasy hand, then trying to wipe away the resulting smear with a piece of burlap. The burlap threads stuck to the sticky corners of his mouth and made him sneeze. "Why don' dos dumb bastard blast at de end of de shift. No bonus today partner, I t'ink we 'ave to clear out soon."

They stood, stretching tired muscles, glancing down the dark drift. They both heard the sound at once, and saw the light.

"Oh fuck, Wild Bill," they said in unison.

Their foreman, Wild Bill Hendrickson arrived on his personal red locomotive, in his coveralls, looking like a malignant elf, a reject from Santa's work benches, now out for mindless revenge. He stopped the motor and stood up from the seat, hands on hips like a tiny Mussolini. "You two yahoos never do any work anymore? All I see is you two sitting on your butts or filling your faces. Damn hole won't drill itself, git to work or I'll find someone who will." Wild Bill's tirade continued with expletives bouncing off the drillers as they started the drill back up. The foreman still stood on the red motor. He watched Pilson with simmering hostility. The very sight of Pilson had prejudiced him against him the very first time he had seen him. He had never seen a human being resemble a barnyard hen, with eyes that stared from between the long beak-like nose. the Adam's apple that never ceased moving. The very gangling, uncoordinated nature of the man with arms nearly down to the knees and shuffling walk made him want to give him a swift kick in the butt, but he knew his short legs would never allow him that satisfaction. Instead, he vented his venom by verbally tormenting the man who never seemed to react to the verbal abuse, other than a measurable acceleration in the movement of his Adam's apple. This lack of reaction drove Hendrickson nearly apoplectic with frustration. If there was one thing Wild Bill hated, it was to be ignored.

Having exhausted himself verbally, Wild Bill reversed the little red locomotive and with an electric hum, receded into the distance, but not before a pair of magnified eyes from behind thick eyeglasses focussed on his tiny red-suited figure. The stare would have frightened Wild Bill had he looked directly into those eyes, for it was a stare of naked hatred of a depth that even Hendrickson had no ability to comprehend.

Rivest saw the stare and decided his partner might be more than just a little crazy. There had been times he had seen expressions of near adoration from his partner, other times confusion, but mostly blank expressions. It was as though his mind had taken a holiday, allowing the body to move mechanically, doing its job, but seemingly disaffected by the world around it. On the rare occasions of the 'stare', he noticed Pilson's throat ceased moving, suspending itself like a lump of coal, half swallowed by a creature that didn't seem quite human at that particular instant of its existence. At that instant, he wished he was somewhere else. He had no idea Pilson was in love with him.

As their drill howled, they saw the beams of hat lights through the mist of the drill exhaust passing their station. One of them flashed towards them several times to gain their attention. Rivest shut down the drill and he and Pilson wordlessly walked with the rest of the highballers to the huge lunchroom near the main shaft to await the coming blast and venting of the fumes from the airline. The roar of the opened airline at the far end from whence they had come bellowed at their backs like some animal let loose in the drifts. they could feel the cold air on their sweaty backs.

Pilson walked wordlessly beside Frenchy, his head down in thought, his eyes staring at the beam of his hat light on the wooden railway ties under the rails. As they filed into the lunchroom with its cold flourescent lights and long tables, he saw a familiar face, camera bag beside him, reading a science fiction novel, the juice of an apple running down his chin.

"Eh Mr. photographer, you always seem to be where t'ings go boom."

Bardman looked up from the novel and saw the two diamond drillers he had photographed previously near the site where the explosion had nearly ruined their day. Neither appeared jovial, although they tried to make conversation. At least the short French-Canadian tried. The other sat morosely, hands clasped in front of him, lips moving as though talking to himself.

The room shook and their ears popped with the overpressure of the blast as the huge orange swinging blast doors directed most of the pressure down the drift to spend its energy in the maze of tunnels.

"I found out what caused that explosion near your drill last month," he said to the short Frenchman. "It was a bootleg hole near the track level. It had been covered with loose rock. I guess the muckers didn't get in close enough with their machine to uncover it.

"So what set it off?" said Pilson looking intently at the photographer with a stare that obviously made the man uneasy.

"They don't know. The investigator said the explosives still in the hole could have been set off by vibrations from your drill, maybe even by another shot going off on a different level. You know the sharp crack you hear through the rock before you hear the actual explosion on another level? He said that could have even set it off...at least the cap, that is.

"Fuckin' highballers, I seen em drill right next to a bootleg hole without flushin' out the old explosives, said Pilson, staring at Bardman with his huge eyes. "Last year one of 'em exploded right next to a guy who was drilling'. Drill rod went right into his mouth and out the back of his head." Pilson smiled a strange smile as though relishing the thought.

Bardman and Rivest slowly shifted themselves a little further away from the strange young man. Neither of them had ever seen him look so amused, and his lips continued to move as though talking to himself.

The all-clear horn sounded in the lunchroom and the miners began the walk back to their stations.

Bardman followed the two diamond drillers and the highballers where the blast had been. At the site where the small flatcar of explosives had been stored on the siding, all the explosives had been used except a small pile which had leaked from a bag onto the track floor along with several feet of unused detonating cord on its spool.

With some trepidation they began drilling again. Frenchy watched the reference mark made with chalk on the drill rod as it progressed through the drill head. When the mark reached the chuck at the bottom of the drill head he knew when the core barrel collecting the sample core would be full. If he was slow to stop the drill when the mark reached that spot, it was possible to jam the rods in the hole or burn out a diamond bit. He listened carefully as the chalk mark edged down, hearing the howl of the drill waver slightly, his hand on the control. For one instant, the sound of the drill hiccupped, a tiny pause in the sound. At that instant, he shut it down as well as the puttering water pump at the side of the drift. He was still wet with the water that had run down the drill head and under his shirt. He was shivering as much from the cold as the recollection of Pilson's eyes, magnified from behind those thick lenses. He wasn't aware that his partner beside him was staring in a malevolent trance, directly at the back of their foreman's head.

Pilson was a product of his environment. Born to parents that refused to believe he was theirs.   His father was a large hairy man who seldom shaved, washed or brushed his teeth. His favourite pastime was to sit and drink beer with his buddies in the small dingy pub of the small prairie town of Kneejerk. When political pundits coined the phrase 'knee-jerk' reaction, the tiny population of 179 adopted it with glee. The whole town had a reaction of one kind or another, usually in the bar bending an elbow, or simply the adverse reaction to being in close proximity with each other.

His mother, before she was married was the only girl in town with a moustache that needed shaving on a regular basis. She wore knee-high stockings down around her ankles because her calves were so thick the material cut off her circulation. Her skin refused to accept maturity,

93

keeping the pimples that had plagued her since puberty. A friend in her class had told her that sex was a sure way of ridding the face of acne, did something to the body chemistry so she was told. She was all for experimentation, and did so with any test subject she could find, behind the old brick school which had been built in 1902. She practised with anyone she could find in the high grass, in the back seats of cars, once even in an empty grain bin with only a blanket beneath them. The grain dust made her scratch for days afterwards. If it had been awarded, she could have won the Nobel prize for experimentation and innovation in sexual impropriety. She became the most popular fifteen year old in town but she never got rid of the pimples popping out all over her face. What did pop out instead was a shrivelled, red, howling Sam Pilson. Suddenly his mother's popularity plummeted and the prospective fathers made themselves very scarce as she tried to discern little Sam's lineage.

The patronage at the pub dropped off to near abandonment and the owner did everything he could, short of waving the shotgun at her from under the counter to prevent her from coming around, babe in arms, making physical comparisons with the nervous customers.

Eventually Sam's father Wendell, in a drunken stupor, proposed to her and she accepted. Unfortunately for Wendell, they weren't alone. There were witnesses and no matter how much Wendell attempted to retract his proposal, the others swore they would act as witnesses on her behalf. Hell they were relieved someone had come forward, otherwise it might have been them, and most of them were married.

Little Sam was two months old at his parent's wedding and managed to pee all over his mother's white wedding gown, leaving a vivid yellow stain down the front. She never forgave him for that. Young Sam grew...upwards but not outwards. He was like a weed reaching for height, swaying in the winds of adversity, but never quite breaking. His first day in grade one, he realised, or at least his teacher realised he was short-sighted in the extreme. She recommended in a note to his parents that they get glasses for him. Wendell, who had insisted that his son's full name was Sampson, was livid.

"God, they look like Austin headlights," said his father when he saw his son with his first glasses. "How the hell you gonna be a Sampson when you can't even see where the hell yer goin'?"

Sam merely shrugged his shoulders and wiped his runny nose with his sleeve, making small snuffling sounds.

Wendell reached out and cuffed him on the side of the head. "Don't you make no wimpy whining around here, *you hear?* I see you cryin' for no good reason, I'll give you good reason to cry."

Young Sam stifled the tears his father's swat had produced and went to his room knowing there would be no comfort from his mother. The more he developed the more both his parents were sure he wasn't the product of their frequent sweaty grapplings of seven years past.

In fact, Wendell thought he could see a striking resemblance with Sheldon Wankel, the owner of the hotel bar. "Damned if I'll tip that little jerk again," muttered Wendell under his breath as he watched the boy go up the stairs to his room. He could see his wife's ankles and the bottomed-out hosiery around them as she washed the dishes. Each time she dried something, her large behind wiggled back and forth with the effort under the flower print dress. He watched her with suspicion, wondering if she and Sheldon had rolled in the hay as often as with all the others who had the opportunity.

She turned and looked at him questioningly, as he picked up the paper, giving a loud belch and scratching his navel through the sleeveless undershirt. He was no catch she thought, but at least he provided.

Above their heads from young Sam's room they could hear a series of persistent thumps, one after the other, slowly, but with a determined cadence like the sound of a baseball bat against a soft object.

Young Sam had found release for his anger and his vivid imagination formed ideas that would have scared his parents silly had they been aware of them. Sam's progress through school was less than notable, with grades that barely gave him a pass, with the exception being art class, where his imagination took form in sketches first with crayon, then advanced to line drawing, and coloured pencil. He had an accurate eye for caricature which didn't amuse his teachers who were his main subjects and adorned the inside covers of many of his notebooks. He remembered Mr. Kroeker, the history teacher in grade 10. He had leaned down from behind while Pilson sketched and quietly said: "Not bad Sammy, but it won't get you a pass in any of the important subjects." His breath had been strong enough to practically curl the edges of the paper and he early gagged with the stench.

Mr. Kroeker's teeth were brown misaligned stumps, discoloured by years of abuse and two packs of cigarettes a day. The girls of the class particularly tried to not call on his help because he had a habit of putting his hand on their shoulders as he stood beside them. Invariably the hand slid near the front, just close enough for a fingertip to caress the beginning swell of a young breast. Combined with the debilitating breath, more than one girl had needed to go to the bathroom where they became sick, barely able to return to class.

Janice Brown sat one row over from Sam and a couple of seats forward where he could steal the occasional glance at her red hair, long legs and firmly developing breasts. Whenever she caught him looking at her, she would tilt her nose up a little, making a little sniffing sound of disapproval, and not glance back for the rest of the day.

Kroeker, with his rumpled suits and tobacco-stained fingers had also been watching the development of Janice Brown with undisguised appreciation. From his desk at the front of the room he could also see that the magnified eyes of young Sam Pilson also had interests in that direction, unaware that the gangly young student had taken to secretly sketching her figure frequently on separate pieces of paper, hidden inside his notebooks.

On this particular day Janice Brown had worn a tight red sweater and tight black mini-skirt, leaving nothing to the imagination of her continuing development.

At the age of 57, Kroeker was surprised to realize that he was developing an erection, the likes of which he had not achieved since he was a teenager. With some amusement he suspected that Sam Pilson was suffering the same anomaly, squirming in his seat, face red and sweaty, casting frequent glances towards Janice's pert breasts and her long legs extended into the aisle.

Pilson thought he was going to die. He had never seen Janice look so good, and when he considered her a goddess at the worst of times, the effect on his brain nearly short-circuited several thousand synapses. Had it not been for the prolific production of testosterone roaring through his gangly, pubescent body he might have had a meltdown right there in his seat. As it was, things began feeling a little wet and he was afraid someone next to him might discover his dilemma. He speculated as to whether hitting his engorged organ with his ruler might make it go down but thought the action might be considered bizarre by his classmates. He looked up and saw old man Kroeker watching him with a strange smile on his face.

"Sam, come up here to the blackboard and fill the answers to the questions six and seven of the history question please," he said with silky malevolence.

His heart sank, realising his erection was still trying to escape from the crotch of his pants. He knew he shouldn't have worn the loose slacks this morning, but he listened to his mother's lecture about how tight jeans cut off vital blood supply to parts of the body. Nothing would have made him happier now than to put a full tourniquet on his offending protuberance, cutting off all circulation to the lower part of the body if it would save him from the impending ordeal. But no such luck. He had worn the loose slacks. He cursed his mother's taste in clothing. But most of all he cursed Kroeker.

Kroeker was still smiling, watching Sam's magnified eyes grow larger behind the glasses and his face redden even more. "We don't have all day Sam. Why don't you also explain verbally to the class while you're up here, the cooperation between the natives and the loyalists during the war of 1812-14?"

Sam could see Kroeker was enjoying himself and felt a cold hatred develop for a man that he had previously felt only ambivalence toward despite his gut-wrenching breath. He rose from his desk and walked as quickly as possible to the front, trying to shake his erection from its saluting position to one of benign obedience. He walked with a strange sideways limp.

"Do you have stomach ache Sam? You seem to be walking all scrunched over."

That was it! He had a stomach ache! He waited for him to order him to sit down but the order didn't come. Instead he spent what felt like hours answering the questions on the board, the chalk making spine tingling scratching noises when impurities touched the board's surface.

"Do you have to go to the bathroom Sam? You seem to be dancing around a lot up there. Maybe if I hummed a little tune you could do the dance for the benefit of the whole class," said Kroeker, thoroughly enjoying himself.

Sam forced his crotch against the ledge of the blackboard hoping the pain would deflate the erection but without success. Instead the effort appeared to enhance its size even more much to Sam's horror and astonishment. His large Adam's apple began to move at an alarming rate as the sweat ran in rivulets down the side of his red face.

"Now face the class Sam and give us your version of the loyalist-native cooperation during the war please."

Sam turned slowly around, eyes turned to the ceiling, beginning to hyperventilate, his cheeks puffing out with each breath. There was complete silence in the classroom as he presented the front of his trousers to his classmates. He looked down and saw the bulge of his pants liberally adorned with fresh chalk dust from the ledge.

The rest of the class reacted in different ways to his state of public arousal. The girls, at least most of them pretended to be reading something on their desks, their hands shading their eyes, a couple of them quickly glancing up. A couple of girlish giggles mixed with gasps of either delight or horror made Pilson sweat from every pore. He produced an acrid smell of fear and that in turn produced more sweat.

The guys sat with mouths open, some blushing in sympathy, others stifling laughter. To his horror, Janice Brown was staring appraisingly as though preparing to write an essay on what she saw. The effect was magical. The erection deflated like a punctured balloon tire, leaving the white smudge of chalk and a small spot of slippery wetness which had seeped through from the inside of his trousers.

"You might as well sit down Sam," said Kroeker with a smirk. "Or would you like to go to the bathroom first?"

He left the room with a cold feeling in his guts, feeling self-revulsion and a hatred for Kroeker who had clearly seen his plight. *The bastard was ridiculing me. He'll pay by god. I'll make him sorry he ever moved to Kneejerk.*

Sam Pilson managed to scrape through high school with less than distinction except for this one episode in his repressed existence. No one ever knew that from that day on that he was never able to achieve an erection, the onset of one quickly bringing feelings of shame and uncleanliness. He was tormented unrelentingly by the guys in the school and even later of whispered innuendo by the women of the town. During a period of development when social skills are being learned, Sam suppressed his social education and spent a lot of time in his room alone. Two days before he was scheduled to travel by bus to his first job with the diamond drilling outfit in the north, Kroeker's mobile home on the outskirts of Kneejerk mysteriously burned to the ground, converting Mr. Kroeker to a carbonized smiling effigy, fused with the heat-warped springs of his mattress. No one seemed to react with surprise, because he was known to smoke in bed and someone once said that the old fool was bound to burn himself up someday.

CHAPTER 6

Spring came slowly to the north. The short days grew longer and the snow became soggy underfoot. The rivers heaved their ice off like a burdensome overcoat, creaking and groaning as the large pans of ice swept along with the current. The tracks of rodents became more evident as the warmer temperatures drew them out, as did the flooding of their small burrows with the beginnings of spring run-off. The heavy snow made travel by snowmobile more difficult, especially across the bodies of water where ice had thawed and re-frozen, creating frightening pockets of water between the layers to trap an unwary traveller.

The old trapper had already broken through a layer of crust into the frigid, shallow water beneath and he thought he was about to make a cold trip to the bottom until the snowmobile lurched to a stop in six-inch-deep water and slush which had been trapped above the thicker layer of ice. Grunting with the effort, he coaxed the snowmobile out of the frozen slush with deft use of the throttle and made his way toward Hudson House where he had stockpiled his inventory of skins. Because of the flooding of his usual trapping grounds, the results had been disappointing, but he planned to ship the skins to the buyer's market in the mining town to the south, where buyers from all over North America and sometimes Europe came to buy prime quality furs. He was looking forward to seeing what the town was like and meet some of his fellow trappers, some of whom he had grown up with but seldom saw because of the isolated nature of their work. On the final leg of his journey home along the banks of the Muskrat River, memories of his son leaving for residential school years before came back to him as if they were yesterday. His lips moved without making sound, mouthing the thoughts in his mind. *I could say I am sorry for the pain I caused. The pain would have been worse if you stayed, too much drinking, no work, no pride in who we are. To change the white man's ways, we have to understand them, like a hunter understands his prey. We are still the hunters. It's in our blood, our souls, and in the souls of our ancestors who are grieving the changing of our ways. If I could see you again I would say I'm sorry.*

"One of the girls at work said she saw you in the truck the other day, driving with a woman. Is that the D'Amico girl you told me about?"

Sadie McKay watched her husband for reaction as they returned from grocery shopping at the mall.

"Yeah, that was her. I suppose they have both ends of their tongues waggin' when they see a woman driver," said Joe, who knew it was only a matter of time before unsubstantiated gossip would start to fly.

"I hear she's really good lookin'."

"Yeah, I suppose she is if you like skinny, muscular women."

"Do you?"

"Do I what?"

"You know what I mean. Do you think she's attractive?"

"I guess she is but I'm not attracted to her. She's just someone I drive with sometimes. She's a friend but I don't intend to date her."

"You say that as if you could if you wanted to."

Joe turned to face his wife as they came to a stop sign. He could see she wasn't in a joking mood. "Where's this conversation goin'? Are you worried that I'm cheatin' on you?"

She could see the concern on his face and wasn't sure how to broach the subject of their dwindling sex life. She could understand the general cooling off from their hyperactive sex lives when they were first married, but now they sometimes went months without any sex. "I was thinking maybe I should be a truck driver too. Might put some spark back into our sex lives."

"Holy shit!" shouted McKay as he applied the car brakes, nearly skidding them out of control on the slushy street.

Sadie screamed in response, not knowing the reason for the panic in Joe's voice. Joshua in back in his child seat woke with a start and began crying in ever-rising pitch, a sure sign he was tired and irritable. "What's wrong with you? You're drivin' like some of the these white people with suits an' ties."

Joe look over his shoulder at the receding figure of an old man on the sidewalk. The old man was walking as though drunk or extremely confused, in the direction of the Stag Inn. "That was my old man," he said quietly, still looking at the weaving figure as it turned through the front door of the Stag Inn.

"You haven't seen him for years. Are you sure it was him?"

He nodded slowly in the direction which the receding figure had disappeared. He felt as though in a trance until a car behind theirs sounded its horn. He had been shocked at the changes to his father's face, but his glance had been fleeting. He realised it had been a long time

since he had seen him. Even the time he had the snowmobile delivered
to his father's shack a year ago. It had been done by another employee of
North Haul. The anger and resentment he felt but didn't understand
prevented him from seeing his father face to face. *It's been twenty years, he
probably wouldn't recognize me either. What would I say to him if I saw him? What
would he say to me? Do I even want to see him after what he put me through all those
years, things I haven't even been able to talk with Sadie about, or even think about
without wanting to kill somebody.*

Joe helped unload the car while Sadie carried a still-screaming and
squirming Joshua to the apartment. "I'm going to go find him," he said as
much to himself as to his wife.

"I know," she whispered with sadness in her voice. She knew
there was a lot of pain in her husband and hoped some kind of
reconciliation would help put a love of life back into her husband's heart.
She remembered the way she had felt the day her mother had died, never
having been able to tell her how much she loved her, despite having
rebelled all her life against her mother's wishes. *Perhaps with the easing of his
pain, mine will ease too.*

Joe entered the darkness of the Stag Inn from the brilliant
Saturday afternoon sunlight. The slush and grit from the street coated his
boots like wet cement, leaving mucky trails on the old carpet of the
entrance. He had to stand in the entrance for several seconds to allow
his eyes to adjust to the dimness of the smoke-shrouded bar. Crystal
Gayle was crooning about her brown eyes changing colour on the
jukebox while a game of spots and stripes was being played on the pool
table nearby. The sharp CLACK of the billiard balls was accompanied
with slurred expletives and laughter. The stench of urine from the toilets
mixed with sweat, smoke, and stale beer assaulted his nose, even made
his eyes water slightly, adding to the discomfort of the cigarette smoke.
Nearly every table was full to capacity with baseball-capped patrons, their
heavy parkas thrown carelessly over the backs of the chairs. Some wore
multi-coloured toques with coloured pom-poms on top. The babble of
voices shouted above the jukebox mixed with the occasional smashing of
an accidentally dropped beer glass. The waitresses looked haggard, their
trays loaded to capacity, their prodigious memories allowing them to
remember what each patron in their section drank. He saw a group of
people in one corner that seemed quieter than most and started in that
direction. He watched for a familiar face, not seeing any in the low light
as he approached. What am I going to say if I see him? He stood near
the table surveying the faces of four native men, each with a couple of

drinks in front of them. The three with their backs to the wall had brown, weather-worn faces like old leather, their thick hands, gnarled and muscular. Two of them looked up at Joe, then across the table at the man facing them. The man with his back to Joe turned slowly and looked up at him and gave a sad smile of recognition. Without speaking he reached over and pulled another chair between his own and his friends, motioning Joe to sit down. He sat, still watching his father's face, seeing sadness, happiness and confusion fight each other for dominance of the cratered features.

"Have a beer with your old man?" said Abe McKay over the noise of the room.

Joe nodded, watching him. His emotions boiled inside him as he remembered that last day with him by the side of the river, wishing he could now put his arm around his father's shoulder the way his father had done with him that day. "Bring your pelts to the auction?"

His father nodded, running one finger lightly around the edge of his beer glass, never taking his eyes from it. He spoke to the beer-stained table. "The buyers weren't in a buyin' mood. Guess all those protesters changed a lot of people's minds about wearin' furs."

Joe saw the others watching him with curiosity, saying nothing but very interested in the conversation. He surmised they were also trappers and from the unhappy expressions that they had suffered the same setbacks as his father.

"This is my boy. Long time since I seen him. Lot bigger'n me now eh?"

The three others nodded back at Joe, showing shy smiles and said something in Cree to his father which brought quiet laughter. It had been years since he had spoken Swampy Cree and he only picked up snatches of the exchange.

His father turned to him, smiling. "They said you must have got your good looks from your mother."

Joe smiled back but said nothing. He felt there was a close bond between the four men at the table and he had been accepted as a peer because of his father. "Would you like to come home and see your grandson?"

His father smiled sadly, nodding, not looking directly at him but rather at his feet. Then he looked up at Joe, and smiled again. "That would be real nice. Am I invited for a meal?"

Joe leaned back in his chair, watching the expressions of the other men. "I'll call Sadie and tell her to set another plate."

When they arrived at the apartment, the aroma of roast beef, potatoes and vegetables greeted them along with a hug from Sadie, and a drooling smile from little Joshua.

Abe squatted down and pulled a small carved wooden figurine from his pocket. It was a carving of a raven, blackened possibly with boot polish and lacquered. Joshua immediately tried to taste the figurine and removed it, screwing up his mouth in distaste.

"Ravens don't make good eatin', but they sure like to eat," said Abe to his still-drooling grandson who was watching his face with a mixture of awe and shyness. He turned suddenly from his grandfather and wrapped his arms around Joe's leg to peek shyly at this strange, quiet old man who had given him the gift.

"You carry toys for kids in your pocket all the time?" asked Joe.

"Nope. I had a dream that I was goin' to see you soon, so I made it for him."

Joe was surprised at his father's answer. "How did you know we even had a kid? It's been almost twenty years since we saw you."

"Manager of the Hudson Bay store sees you sometimes. Says someone brought up a snowmobile one time on the truck an' left it with him, with my name on it. Guess he was askin' the other drivers about you. He said there's one driver, a woman, knows a lot about you, an' every time she came with a load, he'd ask her how you were doin' That manager always was a snoopy bugger. He'll say anythin' to a pretty face"

"She's a spy, that woman. Gonna have to have talk with her," replied Joe, smiling at the thought of D'Amico becoming a domestic informant.

They moved into the living room of the modestly furnished two-bedroom apartment. They hung their parkas in the closet and as he did so, Joe could detect a faint smell of wood smoke on his father's parka. The aroma triggered his memories, and it was as though he had never been away from his father. A sense of belonging was returning, and from the kitchen he could hear his wife singing along with a country western tune on the radio. *She never sings with the radio, in fact she never sings at all!*

He watched his father settle gently onto the couch, feeling its texture with his hands, his eyes sweeping the room as though trying to find some clues about the life of a son who had become a stranger.

During supper the conversation had been sparse, as expected between virtual strangers, but Joshua added some levity by flinging a steamed pea down the front of his grandfather's shirt, who then made an exaggerated effort at retrieving it, finally finding it in his navel, along with some blue lint. Despite some finger-wagging from Joe at his son, the atmosphere brightened and over the remainder of the meal and until his father had to meet his ride back to Hudson House. To Joe, they began to feel like a complete family again.

When he left his son's home, there was a peacefulness in his heart that he realised had been missing all these years. His son had promised to visit more often during the coming summer, probably during one of the regular runs with the truck to the Hudson Bay store. When asked about the carving of the raven, he had neglected to say that he had dreamt of the carving several nights before. He also realised he had forgotten to thank his son for the snowmobile. Thank-you's and apologies were two of the hardest things for him to say, but he knew things would have to change within himself. He first resolved that he was going to stop drinking, even moderately. There always seemed to be a catalyst for change but he was getting too old to make the adjustments easily. My life is startin' over, and time is runnin' out.

Bardman was enjoying the light. It filtered through the trees, reflecting off a hummock of snow nearby, illuminating the feeding chick-a-dees with its' soft luminescence. The sunflower seeds he had spread on the snow had attracted nearly a dozen of the small, black and white birds that moved hyperactively over the seeds, while making sounds like a faulty electric alarm clock. He sat unmoving on a square of compressed blue foam called Insulite. The blue pad kept his behind from the cold snow. In front of him was his camera, mounted with a 400mm mirror lens, on a tripod. With the fixed aperture of the lens of f5.6, he had to compensate for the changing light by changing the shutter speed of the camera. He gently leaned forward and refocused, clicking off a couple of exposures, trying to anticipate the movements of the small birds. For Bardman, the act of nature and wildlife photography was therapeutic, removing the stresses of his job as if they were cold chunks of ice, melting away from the warm shafts of sun shining through the silent forest. His breathing became deep and slow, nearly trance-like in the soft quiet of the forest.

Jenkins had chewed his ass out over the 'grip and grin shot' with the irate miner. Not being able to blame the miner for not understanding English, the miner had been duped by his workmates to come in the first place for the award. Jenkins needed someone to kick over the fiasco and Bardman was the only stray dog on his immediate patch of ground. So

Jenkins verbally kicked Bardman's ass with every epithet he could recall. The greasy smears left on the office carpet by the miner hadn't helped things, nor had it impressed the environmental group who had since sent several letters threatening legal action over various infringements of the environmental act, possibly the carpet was one of them. Jenkins needed something to kick, he just didn't use good judgment in his choice. He should have kicked Mikeluk's ass, thought Bardman. It would have been good practice for Jenkins to get used to asserting himself over the guy who was going to be his son-in-law, and it had been Mikeluk who had set up the shoot in the first place.

A subtle movement caught his eye near the base of a tree. Looking closer, in the shadows he could barely make out the form of a ptarmigan in its white plumage, sitting patiently, watching him. It was within range of a possible shot and with painfully slow movements he swivelled the camera toward the stationary bird and took a couple more exposures. Nearby on the snow were fresh tracks where squirrels and rabbits had searched for new shoots of grass beneath the snow, the rabbits leaving their droppings in patterns of small brown spheres. Nothing marketable in these shots, just fun and relaxing to do them. He had on occasion sold some wildlife shots to a nature magazine, some of them being of moose feeding in a swamp off the Blackwood River. He had kayaked to the spot in his R-5 River Runner, a small backpack lashed behind the cockpit with bungy cords, and everything else stuffed down the rear of the hull. His tent, sleeping bag and extra clothing along with the food made it a tight fit, but the kayak gave him a lot more mobility in the water. His best shots of the moose were from the kayak, early in the morning while he was sitting quietly watching the mist rise from the water. He had been near the edge of the shore when he heard the moose breathing and saw it lift its massive head above the swamp grasses and stare at him. He had remained still, excited at being so close. The moose was silhouetted by the yellow sun beginning to rise over the trees, the mist rising like smoke around its huge form as it stood in the shallow water. He had been proud of those shots and had been paid well for them. He was planning on doing something with wolves but he had yet to find an area they frequented, and they were as difficult to photograph as the very mists off the water. One instant they appeared to be there... the next they were gone. Only their tracks and spots of urine marked their passage.

What has the rising water done to that wetland? Has it been flooded? It probably has, and along with it similar spots all along the river. The moose may be able to adapt, move on to better feeding grounds, but what of all the other animals that can't just pick up and leave? They'll die the deaths of the profoundly ignored, unmourned, unmissed except by the rest of nature around them, with a finite ability to cope.

Bardman shifted on the foam pad, feeling the heat of the sun on his face. He wondered how some of his friends were doing at the newspaper from which he had been fired. Mediocre work and a combative attitude were the reasons given for his dismissal. He had taken flak from people on the job, sometimes subjects who didn't want their picture taken and he usually respected their wishes unless it was a story that demanded the shot. He had been threatened, roughed up, pursued by car, and cursed at, all in the name of getting the picture. At accident scenes, the editors wanted lots of colour, usually meaning blood, and he loathed to insinuate himself into the lives of those who were suffering. He reconciled himself to that part of the job by convincing himself that his images might prevent another such occurrence, whether it be an accident, fire or violence. He found it to be a glib rationalization. An excuse to put his camera into other people's suffering. Subsequently the lack of 'colour' in his shots soon relegated him to 'grip and grins' and product shots of toothpaste tubes for the advertising department.

He had seen it coming, when a freelancer, a buddy of one of the editors began hanging around, shooting contrived stuff that made it onto the front page but would have been rejected by any responsible editor. Suddenly and unceremoniously he was fired. The freelancer got his job and the only option was to try freelancing also.

The grinding stress of no regular pay cheque, trying to collect from truant clients, and the prospect of being ejected from his apartment made for sleepless nights. The ad for the staff photographer job with Quesnel Minerals saved his life, professionally and literally, because the battle with depression over having his ass hung out to flap in the winds of a cold, merciless world, weighed him down with a burden of lethargy and a craving to stuff his face with junk food. As his weight went up, his self-esteem dropped to the level of the city sewer system. Ten months later he was beginning to feel the same stresses, a boss that needed a someone to kick, and the challenge of trying to make presentation shots creative. He actually liked the shot of Jenkins with the miner. The contrast between the two of them spoke volumes. Jenkins in his immaculate, striped three piece suit, gripping the hand of a miner who was still in harness, smeared in grease, stinking of sweat, with confusion painted greasily on his face. He had made a print for his wall because it showed the inequities of life, the roles played by two actors, one who didn't want to make an appearance; the other wanting to take a bow, circumstances not allowing either to fulfil their wishes.

He opened his eyes, not realizing he had closed them. A dark shape moved on one of the branches in a tree near him. He trained the telephoto lens in the direction of the movement and could make out the shape of a raven watching him from its perch. A shaft of sunlight came through the trees, illuminating the head of the raven like a spotlight The bird's eyes watched him with intelligence. The feathers on the back of its head stood in jagged peaks. The raven looked away for an instant, then back at Bardman, who was still looking through the camera lens. He took two shots at a slow shutter-speed, trying to compensate for the darkness of the bird's feathers. He hoped for some detail, rather than just a black mass with a large beak on the end. He looked back through the lens to refocus on the bird's beak. That was when the raven appeared to smile. Bardman thought he might be going a little bit crazy.

With the spring run-off, the level of the Blackwood River rose even more, within mere feet of the bridges that spanned it. Large pans of ice cruised with the current, colliding with each other and parts of the bank with the muted sound of crystal and wood being shattered. Old trees that had stood for years were uprooted and taken along by the current, unwilling travellers, refugees on a highway of quiet destruction. The swift current destroyed outright some of the life in its path, drowning others, dispossessing the rest. The wetlands where the moose had fed was inundated, leaving nothing edible for the huge animals to feed upon, drying up the udders of the cows, starving the new calves who suckled at the cow's teats with little grunts of frustration. Only those that could move quickly to other feeding areas previously unclaimed, continued to thrive.

The hydro project still consumed its huge amounts of concre steel and the occasional worker. It grew in immensity. Its overall len became two kilometres, including the spillway and powerhouse. Th huge multi-bladed rotors which would be connected to the water powered turbines were slowly lowered into position within thei housings. One of ten, each turbine could generate 98,000 kilow power that lit and heated homes across the North American g creating comfort for thousands of inhabitants who really did countless other citizens of the natural world perished for th were warm in their own little burrows, covered by an electric blanket of ignorance.   The river that ran through the area of the hydro dam had become nothing more than a mudflat, the water having been diverted to another river, flooding its banks, destroying its uncomprehending citizens. One day the waters would return to produce the power, but in doing so, it would destroy that which had survived the initial deprivation of water. Among the hardest hit were the countless fish with nowhere to spawn. So, bloated with eggs and sperm, they died in strange waters which they considered alien to their offspring. The fishermen of the river grieved as they lived, quietly, inwardly, and with an increasing frustration.

Teresa hated skinned knuckles. It was one of the hazards of adjusting the brakes on the tractor-trailer unit as she crawled under the frame to get at the adjusting nut with the nine sixteenths wrench. Joe had volunteered to do it while she sat in the cab and pumped the brake pedal, to test the travel distance of the slack arm. But for the sake of her own independence, she refused the offer.   Joe appeared to be happier than she had ever seen him. "You look like a teenager who has just lost his virginity," she said as he punched the time card in the office.

McKay merely smiled. "Don't know if I should tell you anythin' after findin' out you've been spyin' on me."

"What...what's this spying? she said, feigning innocence.

"I'll tell you about it later, but I guess I should thank you for informin' on me."

"You mean you're thanking me for getting a little last night?"

"Yeah, somethin' like that."

"Boy, I can hardly wait to get on the road and hear all about this ⸮, but first we've got to adjust those brakes again on the explosives   I don't know what's with those things, we've had to adjust them ⸮y trip, and now they're going out of wack halfway through a

⸮ looked thoughtful, concern showing as he watched her ⸮k up to date, sometimes referred to as Creative Writing

⸮heck'em again before the long hill down to the ⸮uldn't want to find oncoming traffic with no ⸮. You want me to do the adjustin' and you do

⸮ and bleeding knuckle, she wished she

"What's the hold-up, why can't you can't you get this thing on the road?" shouted Walter Winkwell, manager of North Haul. He stood in the middle of a large mud puddle, galoshes on his feet, dress pants tucked into the tops. His neck was still sore, even since the removal of the cervical collar he'd been fitted with, the result of his first attempt at driving a diesel tractor.

"Well, I tell ya Winky," came D'Amicos' muffled voice from under the trailer, "If you would spend some money on getting these brakes fixed rather than have us drive a potential bomb, you might see us on the road sooner. As it is, we're on the clock and we're not leaving until these brakes are right."

"Just cut the crap and get going. This trailer needs to be spotted before the Boom-boom Twins go home. If you can't do it, I'll find someone who will."

She crawled back out from under the trailer and faced Winky, actually looking down on him from her advantage of two extra inches. Her hands behind her back gripped the wrench, turning the knuckles white with anger. "The Department of Transport would be really interested in the condition of these brakes, Mr. boss man, and if you are referring to Toothless Jake and Big Don, I'll let Big Don know of his new nickname. He has some little exploding things that could your clear your hemorrhoids real quick."

Winky leaned forward and said, his voice rising to a squeak: "Are you threatening me girly? 'Cause if you are I'll have your little tush out of here in seconds."

D'Amico stood on her tiptoes, looking down on his reddening face and spoke quietly, but with a venomous quality that made Winky take a step back.

"You go right ahead Winky, and I'll go see constipatible Pusch and suggest that he come out on the road sometime and do a brake test on a trailer of explosives. Then we'll see whose ass gets in a sling. He'll come down so hard on you, you'll have to wear stilts just to pee in the John." She let the wrench she'd been holding behind her back, drop into the mud puddle which Winky stood in, splashing grey muddy water onto his dark slacks. "Oops, looks like more than the trailer will be spotted today."

He turned on his heels and stalked off through the puddles, looking a bit like an obese duck, open overcoat flapping like wings, quacking angrily over his shoulder.

McKay had been leaning out of the tractor cab, watching and listening with interest. "You really gonna see Pusch an tell him about these brakes?"

"Jeez no, I think I'd rather blow up than have his moustache within ten miles of me." She rubbed grease and mud from her hands onto the legs of her coveralls. "Let's go spot this thing and go home for some sleep. Midnight comes quick enough and I think I'd rather have a tooth pulled than do this trip tonight."

That afternoon at the explosives depot, they quickly dropped the trailer on its' dollies at the loading dock, wondering where toothless Jake and Big Don were. As they left in the tractor, D'Amico heard a sharp crack and as she glanced in her side mirror, a tree toppled over at the edge of a clearing, on the other side of the railway tracks. "My God, now they're blowing up trees."

McKay, glanced in his own passenger-side mirror. "At least a tree can't outsmart 'em like that raven."

"I wouldn't count on that," she countered. Have you ever wondered about the aptitude test they give to people who want to work in a place like this?"

They bob-tailed back to their cars at the terminal, and to their respective beds for some much-needed sleep before the trip.

She heard the honk of the tractor outside her apartment at 11:30 that night. She had been awake a half hour before, preparing her lunch and a thermos of coffee. As she stepped into the cold night air, she could see fluffy flakes of snow swirling around the street light where the Kenworth sat. Its engine rattled and orange marker lights painted dots of orange light on the crusty spring snow. The air pressure relief valve gave off frequent blasts of air, something else she intended to harass Winky about, because the valve obviously wasn't properly calibrated to control the air pressure to the brakes.

It was a jolting ride on the hard suspension of the tractor to the explosives depot. They let themselves through the main gate with a key given to them so neither Toothless or Big Don would have to come out at such an ungodly hour and let them in. The trailer waited, loaded, warning EXPLOSIVES placards in place with their high red letters on white. The hook-up went smoothly as McKay backed the tractor under the trailer, she started connecting all the air and electrical lines that gave the trailer life. As they pulled away from the depot, it was exactly midnight and the snow became heavier. It swirled past the headlights in a mesmerizing flurry of white slashes against the darkness.

110

They had to keep the headlight beams on low because the light reflecting off the snow blocked their night vision, making it impossible to see the road. McKay drove while D'Amico sat slumped in the jump-seat, contemplating opening the thermos. She was still not fully awake and probably wouldn't be for hours to come, her Circadian rhythm had been completely disrupted by the unusual hour of activity. The internal clock told her she should be asleep, and she agreed whole-heartedly, but the demands of the job dictated she disregard her biological workings and do the job as Winky decreed.

It had been considered necessary by Winky and the foremen at the Project to haul the explosives at a time when traffic on the road would be at a minimum, and the arrival time at the site would coincide with the day-shift workers getting out from breakfast. It was some of these workers who would help unload the explosives from the trailer into the blockhouse. They would be as bleary-eyed as the two drivers who brought the load and worked with an equal lack of enthusiasm, for they would not be allowed to have breakfast until the unloading was completed.

McKay leaned forward, hunched over the steering wheel, his face lit by the greenish glow of the gauges. His jaw muscles rippled with tension. She watched her partner and wished he would loosen up. Perhaps her comments concerning his apparent happiness and sexual rejuvenation had been indiscreet. "You look ready to bust Joe. Tell me your thoughts, or are you pissed-off at me for something?"

He continued staring ahead, his jaw muscles less active. "Why did you tell the manager of the store at Hudson House about me?"

"He asked me. I thought he was a friend and wanted to know how you were doing."

"I don't have any friends there, there's nobody there who needs to know anythin' about me."

"I'm sorry Joe, I just thought I was doing something that would be good. You never talk about your home or your childhood. When the manager asked about you, I thought he was a friend of yours."

"He was friend of my old man's. Used to sell supplies to him for the trapline. My old man used to be gone for weeks at a time. People used to think he was dead, he was gone so long. The people who ran the school thought I was going to be an orphan and actually started adoption procedures while I was there."

"But your dad kept coming back."

111

"Yeah, he came back alright. He came back to the Stagger-Inn yesterday. I saw him walkin' down the street while Sadie and Josh were in the car. Damn near wiped out a light post in shock, scared the shit out of Sadie. Scared the shit out of me too.

She sat quietly, watching him search for words. For someone who usually rationed words like water in the desert, he was visibly struggling with his emotions and his lack of ability to communicate them.

"I guess I should thank you for bein' my informer. I had a beer with my old man yesterday an' he had supper with us. He an' Josh took to each other like crayon to bare walls. The trapline is failin'. He barely has enough to get through the summer, an' the fishin' is gonna be bad too because of the high water. I want to help him but he's too proud to ask, an' the last people he wants to ask is the welfare people."

She was gratified to hear him say so much without interruption, convinced that just talking about his thoughts would be beneficial.

"So what else is new with your dad?", she said, sipping at her now-cold coffee.

"My dad...I've been callin' him my old man, but he is my dad I guess. He said he's been havin' strange dreams, all about wolves in the bush and this raven that keeps smilin' at him. He said there was a raven that followed him on the trapline, an' he'd feed it scraps. No matter how far he went, it was always there."

"That's strange, because Brady told me last night that he took a picture yesterday afternoon of a raven that smiled at him in the bush. I told him he was working too hard and needed time off.   "So did he get a picture of the bird smilin'?"

"No, that's the weird part. He said when he saw the negative of the branch where the raven was sitting, it was empty. He had a great shot of the branch, but no raven, gone... poof... nothing."

"Nothin'?"

"Nothing. What do you think of that?"

"I think he should stop smokin' carpet lint," said McKay, smiling now and motioning her to pour him some coffee.

The spring blizzard became heavier. It created a pattern of confusing white streaks in the headlight beams. The snow built up on the windshield where the wipers pushed it to one side. The defrost fan was on full to prevent the snow from freezing to a hard crust, which would make the wipers ineffective.

McKay saw a dull reddish glow but couldn't tell how far ahead it was of their truck. The snow thickened in front of them, white blobs of

112

snow hurtling out of the blackness. He eased up on the accelerator until they were travelling no more than thirty kilometers per hour. He rolled down his side window and peered out to watch the shoulder of the road. The dull red glow had grown larger but had not become discernibly brighter.

D'Amico gave a little shriek, bracing her hands against the panel in front of her.

Instinctively he applied the brakes, and as he did so, he could see directly in front of them, only inches in front of their bumper, a sign which said, THIS UNIT MAKES WIDE RIGHT TURNS. It was then that he realised the red glow in front of them was that of a snow-covered tail light of another truck its driver also half-blinded by the snow.

"Jeez, Joe, we damn near rear-ended him," she said under her breath.

He breathed deeply, eyes wide awake. The weakly-glowing taillight of the other truck gradually pull away from them. He realised the other driver was probably oblivious of their presence and how close they had come to a collision.

They were both awake now, smiling at each other, glad they were partners. Glad they were still alive. They always seemed to have close calls, but came out smelling like a rose. No damage done.

D'Amico wondered how long their luck would hold out, because without it, pulling forty-thousand pounds of explosives, luck was the glue that kept them bound to this earth. She had heard Winky talking about hauling mixed loads, two or three different classes of explosives in one trailer to save truck time. She knew it was illegal to haul caps and fuses with any other class of explosives, just as it to include oxygen or acetylene bottles and metal pallet jacks. She wondered how far Winky would go in trading safety for profit. It was something she and Joe would have to talk about if they were to stay alive.

Four hours later and half way through the trip, they came to the steep incline with a caution sign posted at its crest. Below and two kilometres away, was the Blackwood River control gate complex. The control gates were gradually building up the level of water behind them, diverting any overflow upstream, into the Muskrat River system. With spring run-off started, the overflow was becoming considerable, but the controllers had no choice but to lower the gates from their huge steel gantries, preventing the water from flooding into the project site. Thus more water backed up, swelling the water levels even more in the Muskrat River system.

113

As they approached the crest before the incline, McKay slowed the truck, gearing down to control their descent down the icy, inclined road. He knew that too much speed would be disastrous because braking under these conditions would likely send the tractor-trailer unit jack-knifing out of control to either crash into the control complex, or the rock strewn ditch. Through the blowing snow they could barely see the gantry lights of the complex, like soft orange orbs of light floating below them in the distance. There was no visible oncoming traffic approaching the one lane over the structure, a relief for McKay who preferred not to apply any more braking than he needed on the slippery surface. His right hand rested gently on the trailer brake lever that extended from below the steering wheel. He pulled it gently toward him every few seconds to apply the trailer brakes, leaving the brake pedal of the tractor alone for fear uneven braking would throw them out of control. Each application of the brakes produced a soft hissing noise in the system, as the air pressure built up again to 125 pounds.

They had both pleaded with Winkwell to have Jake Brake systems installed in the trucks, systems that used the back pressure of the engine to control the forward speed without having to apply the brakes.

Winkwell, in his warped logic, refused the request, saying the terrain was not hilly enough to justify the expense of an engine retarder system. He hadn't considered the cost of an eighteen- wheeled bomb out of control.

As they slowly crossed the single lane of the control gate structure, D'Amico looked out her side window at the water illuminated by the overhead lights.

"Brady says he's going to come kayaking here once the ice is off. I can't imagine what he sees attractive about this place, there are hundreds of prettier places to paddle than this gravel pit."

She had over the last few months become puzzled with Brady Bardman and his long silences. He had become almost secretive of what he intended to do during the summer. She had hoped she would be included in some of his plans, but his comments were ambiguous at best, mumbling something about some experimental conversion to his kayak. He had even mentioned ordering another kayak from the dealer in the south, and having it shipped up by North Haul. Since she had invited herself over for dinner after skiing, she had not been to his basement apartment since. Rather, he somehow either manipulated her into cooking dinner at her place, or they went out for dinner. She wondered

114

what kind of secret he had in the apartment. She mentally chastised herself for being such a snoop.

McKay slowed the truck, pulling to the side of the road, finally stopping. "Take over partner, I'm goin' outside to check the tires," was all he said.

D'Amico gave a sigh of resignation, not really feeling like driving, having ensconced herself warmly within her own thoughts, oblivious to everything around her. She had to shake her head a couple of times and breath the cold air from the open driver's door to wake herself up to the task. They had three hours more to go before unloading and another seven or eight hours to come back, depending on the condition of the road. Reluctantly, she slid over to the driver's seat and waited sleepily for her partner. He finally climbed into the jump seat, eyes heavy with fatigue. He said nothing.

As she shifted through the gears, she turned to McKay who was arranging his parka behind his head in preparation for sleep. "I used to think this job gave me some freedom, now I realize it's just as confining as when I was married. The edge of the road sets the boundaries, we have to follow the turns where they put them, we can't even go the speed we would like to."

He sat back in the seat with his hat partially down over his eyes. "If you want to make that next curve, you're going to have to slow down."

He slept fitfully as the truck bounced over the rough road, the dark gradually giving way to a slate grey sky in the east. He dreamed of Jimmy No-name.

Jimmy had been named thus because he refused to tell any of his fellow students his name, although the administration knew it but didn't divulge it. They felt it wasn't any concern of the others. Jimmy was eleven years old, small for his age and despite his appetite, so skinny his clothes hung on him like a scarecrow. His shiny black hair had been cut in the style of an inverted bowl, which in fact was the method used, an inverted kitchen bowl placed on his head and everything showing below had been unceremoniously sheared off. He fancied himself to be one of the Beatles, the British pop group that was recently sweeping the world with its music and pageboy-type haircuts. "He loves you, yeah, yeaah, yeaaaah," Jimmy would sing at the top of his lungs wherever he happened to be going at the time, usually at a dead run with disregard for corners. The forehead over his wide brown eyes showed multiple bumps and bruises from his frequent collisions with fixed objects and occasional students who couldn't avoid him in time.

"You an' me gonna be buds," he said to Joe, soon after he arrived at the residential school. "Gonna protect each others' bums an' beat up anybody who don't like us." Then he giggled at the thought of trying to beat up someone who was usually twice his size. They sat together at the long dining table, jostling with their elbows, giggling nervously, watching furtively for any staffer that might cuff them on the side of the head to settle them down. Whenever they were overheard speaking their native tongue, they were denied a meal for each infraction, which Joe surmised was why his friend was so skinny.

The brothers, Catholic priests taught them English with the aid of a long ruler to augment their expertise as teachers, laying the wood on with vigour anytime a student uttered something in anything other than English. It wasn't the fear of God that was being instilled, it was the fear of priests and anything connected with the church. And none of them learned much due to the beatings and duress inflicted upon them.

Within three years, they had become close as brothers, sharing all their thoughts, or so Joe had thought until one bitterly cold winter's day in January. Joe had been in the basement of the building, near the furnace room that stank of coal and ashes. He had been sent by a brother to fetch some cleaning fluids. He heard Jimmy's voice cry out in pain from a small room off to the side. He heard the sound of a hand striking flesh, another yell of pain mixed with anger. He stood still, wanting to go to the partly opened door and peek through, but not daring to.

"Dirty son'm bitch," came Jimmy's shrill voice, followed by mocking laughter of an adult.

The door flew open and Jimmy propelled himself across the cement floor toward Joe who stood completely still. In the semi-darkness of the basement, he recognized Jimmy, who was trying to pull his baggy pants around his waist, his striped suspenders flopping at the sides. He saw tears were rolling down his cheeks and one eye was puffy and discoloured.

Jimmy was very quiet that evening at dinner, his head down, his hair nearly in his bowl of soup. He refused to meet Joe's looks of concern. None of the other boys would look at him, knowing that to do so would bring the wooden stick down upon their shoulders.

Later in the bathroom Joe had heard his wrenching sobs coming from within one of the cubicles, sounding as though his heart was going to come out through his throat. The other boys listened with sadness in

116

their faces, understanding the sounds of inner torture, some of them having suffered similarly.

At night, Joe could still hear Jimmy sniffling under his blanket, interrupted only by the occasional squeaking of bedsprings in the middle of the night. No one dared peek from within the protective blankets to see who was being visited. No one wanted to know, and each dreaded the possibility of a visit from the faceless antagonist who stank of coal dust and bacon grease.

Two nights later, Jimmy No-name's body was found hanging by a piece of electrical cord, wrapped around old pipes in the basement ceiling. A toppled chair lay on its side nearby. There was no investigation nor any contacting of family members of his tragic passing. The funeral in the chapel was short, followed by his tiny body being interred in a frigid hole in a nearby cemetery as the wind blew gusts of snow amongst the headstones. A small wooden marker was later erected with the name of just Jimmy carved roughly on it. There was no date. The marker disappeared only a matter of weeks later.

The lurching of the truck woke him from his dreams as the chains behind the cab rattled like some ghost of Christmas past trying to rid the weight from its shoulders.

"Every time I drive my passengers fall asleep," complained D'Amico. "I guess it can't be my bubbly personality, but at least I haven't been completely alone."

"I don't see anyone else here."

She pointed out his passenger side window at the treeline nearby. "Maybe it sounds stupid, but I think that raven has been following us for the past hour."

McKay came wide awake, looking out the window at the raven flying effortlessly, skimming the tops of the trees, not stopping to rest, keeping pace with the truck. "Why is it that every time I see one of those birds I get nervous?"

"I don't know. Are you superstitious?"

"Not really, but my old man was. To him everything in nature had a purpose, especially the spirits of the animals. I think the raven was a messenger from spirits of our ancestors."

"I hope it isn't a collect call," she replied quietly.

CHAPTER 7

They felt as though they had been in this part of the mine an eternity. They had first drilled an up-hole to find out what seams of ore might be above them, then another down-hole. Through fifteen-hundred feet of hard granite they searched with the sightless probe of the diamond-encrusted drill bit. The company geologists analysed the cores of rock brought up in the flat core boxes, looking for tell-tale seams of uniform grey colouration which would indicate pure nickel. After each shift they loaded the long, flat core boxes on their shoulders, sometimes two or three at a time. On the shifts when there was no small flatcar to carry them, they suffered with the heavy burden to the main shaft where they were taken to surface in the cage. It was a usual unpleasant and painful end to a long shift.

The highballers had moved further down the drift from them. The progress of their drilling was made in thirty foot increments. They could hear the drills where the miners were preparing to carve another section of rock from the end of the drift. As the drill howled and blasted its cold breath into the confined area, Rivest could see the yellow beam of a solitary light move past their work station. It moved toward the sound of the highballer's site at the rock face at the end of the drift. He flashed his hat light toward the other in acknowledgment to the lone figure, receiving one in return. He watched the company photographer walk past, large camera bag over his shoulder, heading toward the sound of the jackleg drills hammering in the distance. He didn't think it was the walk of a happy man. He shrugged mentally. Not many people down here seemed happy of their existence. It was just another place to dig for a living. It just happened to be more dangerous than most.

Rivest watched the colour of the water surging from the metal casing through which the drill rods passed, noting the darkness of it, like used, grey dish water. The way the drill had been effortlessly chewing through the rock the last few minutes, indicated they were possibly in a vein of pure nickel or maybe graphite. The drill was working too hard for it to be graphite though. It was gratifying to hit ore, to see a solid core of nickel a couple of feet long laying in the core box. On the occasions when a geologist had been present and a nickel core was exposed, the geologist was like a little boy at Christmas under the tree with his presents. The presence of the ore justified the existence of the drillers and the geologist; without it, there would be no need for them to be there.

Pilson waved his light in Frenchy's eyes, rubbing his stomach to indicate lunch time. With the drill shut down, the silence descended over them like a dark blanket. There was also silence from the end of the drift. As they rummaged through their lunch buckets, Bardman walked around the corner of their pillar raise, camera bag still over his shoulder hard hat tilted back on his head.   "Hey partner, you out takin' pictures again? I dunno what you see down dere wit de 'ighballers, nuttin' but bunch a rock an' greasy driller," He stuffed a large sandwich into a small mouth which had to strain to accommodate it. His cheeks puffed out like a chipmunk which had stumbled on a treasure trove of nuts.

Pilson watched Bardman through his thick lenses with a reptilian intensity. He tore his sandwich into small pieces before eating them due to an abscessed tooth that was making any kind of movement of the jaw painful. The dark grease from his hands transferred itself to the white of the bread, leaving black smears. He ate it with an enforced delicacy, poking the bread in one side of the his mouth with a finger, chewing slowly wincing momentarily with the pain of chewing too hard on the rotten tooth.

Bardman stared back, fascinated by the procedure, equally fascinated by the quiet malevolence of the magnified eyes. "Just progress shots. The boss wants a visual representation of the work being done down there."

"Boring stuff," said Pilson with a muffled voice as he attempted to move a piece of sandwich from one side of his mouth to the other with a greasy finger.

Bardman shrugged, not wishing to invite the opinions of the two drillers. In the distance he could barely make out the sound of an electric locomotive approaching and noticed that the two drillers had also heard it. They stopped eating and glanced at each other with apprehension in their eyes. The yellow locomotive rumbled past them without slowing down, pulling a flatcar stacked high with bags of explosives and boxes of primers, heading for the end of the drift.

Frenchy watched its passage, his jaw suspended open in mid-chew. "Merde, dey gonna blast again soon. I can't wait to get outta 'ere, all dis boom-boom crap is givin' me a 'eadache." He was stretched out on the burlap sacking material, his back against the rock wall, his short legs stretched out in front of him. The effort to speak and eat simultaneously had ejected part of his sandwich from his mouth to the lap of his greasy slickers. He flicked the piece away like a freshly killed insect, then watched in amazement as Pilson reached over, retrieved the partially chewed food from the track floor and popped it into his own mouth.

Pilson sat beside him, hands contentedly in his lap and gummed the piece of sandwich like a cow chewing its cud. He stared without expression at the opposite wall of the drift.

Frenchy aimed his light at the photographer who had been watching Pilson with a similar expression of revulsion and curiosity. "Ay partner you should get some picture of de big bang, rock flyin' flames, lotsa action, eh?"

Bardman had risen from his crouching position to start back toward the end of the drift. "Gotta go, got work to do. You might want to know...I saw your boss at the lunchroom area kicking the shit out of his little red motor. Guess it wouldn't start. He's one mean little shit isn't he?"

The diamond drillers rolled their eyes in mutual, silent agreement. They watched Bardman move in his cumbersome manner, tripod bouncing against his leg, and accessory bag rattling with each laboured step.

Pilson tried to smile, wincing in pain with the effort, holding his palm to his cheek and emitted painful cooing sounds. He had tried to get time off to go to the dentist, but Wild Bill had denied the request with the threat of firing him if he failed to show up for work.

As Bardman walked down the track to follow the explosives car, he could hear another locomotive approaching from the direction he had just come. It made a high-pitched whining sound as the electric motor propelled it along the uneven track. *Sounds like that mean little shit finally kicked some life into his motor.* He felt fortunate not to be working for a man like that. He knew he himself had a volatile nature and knew he would have lost patience, and probably his temper if Wild Bill had been his boss. He had seen the type all too frequently on construction sites as a student trying to earn tuition. There was often no civility between workers, especially between foremen and labourers. Threats of violence made by the foreman were commonplace. He wasn't surprised at the shoddy workmanship on some projects due to workers having to endure such duress.

Wild Bill arrived in his usual style, jolting to a halt on the track near the drill site where Pilson and Rivest had renewed drilling. They tried to look as busy as possible for his benefit. He sat on the padded seat of the locomotive, watching the two drillers, then finally climbed down from the motor like a homicidal two year old from a highchair. His tiny feet felt for purchase as he eased himself from the vehicle. He stood steadily, not like the other time when he had been drunk, but it didn't improve his demeanour because he preferred to be drunk. It made working in this grease pit more endurable, and when he wanted to vent his frustrations. These were his two favourite targets: especially Pilson. He signalled Rivest to shut down the drill. "Who was that walking down the drift?" he yelled in a voice that sounded like gravel rattling in a metal bucket.

"Dat photographer from the de company, goin' down to take pictures of de 'ighballers.

"Seems everywhere I go I see him wandering around with that damn camera, but I never seen him take any pictures." Wild Bill stood on the track, peering into the darkness in the direction Bardman had walked, realizing that anywhere there was blasting about to be done he had often seen the photographer in the area. Sometimes he had seen him take pictures, usually not.

"What the hell you lookin' at you googly-eyed freak?" shouted Wild Bill at Pilson who had been silently watching him from behind the drill. "You chewin' tobacco now? Why the hell is your face puffed out like that?"

"D'at's 'is toothache boss, sore as 'ell; 'e can't 'ardly eat or talk."

"That's tough shit. This hole comes first," replied Wild Bill, walking closer to the drill. "Start this thing up if you want to keep your jobs, and you stop looking at me like that you chicken faced freak!"

Pilson averted his eyes, unable to reply due to the pain from his tooth. His large, bony right hand gripped a fourteen inch pipe wrench tightly enough to whiten his knuckles. His whole body quivered as he cast a glance toward Frenchy with the beginnings of pure rage in his eyes.

Frenchy looked back, seeing his partner's face white with suppressed anger. He subtly shook his head at him, trying to calm the pent-up anger which Wild Bill was either too stupid or too blind to see.

As they began drilling under the watchful eyes of the foreman, they saw the lone hat light of the photographer walking back along the track. He walked past their site toward the main shaft, toward the cage to the surface. Each of them, including Wild Bill had a desire to go with him to the sunny spring air of the surface, but their obligations to a single two inch diameter hole in the rock dictated that they stay. Like so many others of the working world, they were slaves of the environment of creditors and the only way they knew to make a living.

Abe McKay sat in his ramshackle hut on the outskirts of Hudson House, sipping a cup of tea. He watched the morning sun stream through a dusty window, throwing a bright yellow patch of sunlight on the table in front of him. Its reflected warmth felt good to his old bones, helping to remove some of the pain of the cold in his joints.

The snow was nearly gone, leaving large muddy puddles surrounded by tufts of brown grass with new green shoots developing at their base. The Muskrat River had risen high on its banks, higher than he had ever seen it before. It gave no indication of receding, due to the control gates further down-river. The wind rattled the branches of the aspen and birch trees near the shack, the strong south wind whistling the song of promised summer, the verses of which he had heard and loved for 75 years. He used to whistle the same sounds with his lips but they were no longer able to do it, likewise the call of the songbirds that returned with spring. The only singing was in his mind now and that was becoming more vague. The memories of childhood and young manhood were clear as crystal stream waters, but the mental pictures of more recent days or weeks ago becoming blurred around the edges. He wondered if these events had actually occurred, or were they just a part of his dreams. His bones told him there would be no more trapping and he quietly grieved for the loss of a greater part of his life. *It don't matter no more. Trappin' is dyin' too, like the rivers and lakes. I can hear the trees and the water cryin' with the changes. There's more for me to do, an' this summer is the last summer I'll have. My bones talk to me without mercy, all my teeth are gone, but I still get soft food from the store. Manager says I have credit for as long as I want, an' don't worry about the bill. I think my boy did that. Next time I see him... gotta say thank you.*

That afternoon on the rutted main street of the village, he had met Angus Spence, an elder of the band council, nearly as old as himself. They had talked about the old days the way old people usually do, bemoaning the changes they see around them and the plight of the young people of the reserve with no way of making a living, to succumbing to the mind-numbing fumes of gasoline and modelling glue to escape the hopelessness that stalked them through every day of their existence.

Angus had spoken of a new sweatlodge they had built not far

from the river and how refreshing it felt to sit for hours in the total darkness, the heat of the hot rocks flooding their pores with sweat, cleansing their bodies and souls, cracking open the door to inner peace and a sense of oneness with the earth and themselves. Abe promised to take part in the next one, rejuvenated simply by the memories of the sweatlodges he had taken part in years ago. Smiling inwardly he returned home with his bag of groceries, anticipating his meeting with the others, as he had anticipated his first hunt as a young boy. *It would be good if I could get my boy to come, we could be a family again.*

"Why do you need two of these things? There's only one of you." Teresa was staring at a brand-new River Runner R-5 kayak sitting on the new grass in front of Brady's apartment. It looked like a streamlined plastic torpedo. Its one-piece moulded plastic hull shone white like the skin of a Beluga whale, its plastic, internal structure appearing like soft green patches of colour where they met the outer hull.

"I thought it would be nice to teach you to kayak, sort of in return for you teaching me to ski this winter. So what do you say, want to come kayaking with me?"

"Won't I fall out? It looks really tipsy." She bent from the waist and peered down inside the cockpit. "And it looks tight... jeez I could get stuck in there if I turn upside down. I hate being upside down in the water. My nose fills up, my ears block up and my sinuses gurgle like an old coffee maker for days afterwards. And that's just when I take a bath."

He bent forward, flicking an imaginary cigar in his fingers like Groucho Marx and said, "Trust me, I am an ace instructor, haven't had a single person drown on me yet...couple of married ones maybe and a divorcee, but no single ones. Madam you are as safe with me as a babe in arms, and believe me I've seen a few babes."

She giggled at his Groucho Marx impersonation, thrilled that he had some plans that included her this summer. She silently cursed her reluctance to broach the subject but was glad her patience paid off. "So, show me how you get in this thing without falling in the water."

"My pleasure. This by the way, this will be the only time you will see me wearing a skirt," He first inserted one foot then another through the top of a blue neoprene spray skirt. "You pull it up tight around the waist, nearly up to the armpits and then you climb in like this." He leaned the double ended paddle across the back of the cockpit, one end resting on the ground and demonstrated the entry by putting all his weight on the paddle shaft while easing first one foot, then the other into the hull, finally resting on the adjustable plastic seat. He then snapped the shock-corded edge of the spray skirt around the mouldings of the cockpit, making himself virtually waterproof from the waist down. He reversed the process to exit and had her try it several times so that she could enter and exit with ease."This is a lot different than doing it in water for the first time, but it's good preparation."

She sat in the kayak with the new paddle in her hands, a puzzled expression on her face. "Why are the blades not in line with each other, are they supposed to be like this?"

He had her do some paddling movements explaining how one paddle was 'feathered' at right angles to the axis of the one on the other end so it would cut the wind while the other was in the water.

"This is fun, but I'm not going anywhere, I thought these things were supposed to be fast," she said, smiling innocently up at him as he admired the way her tight cotton T-shirt stretched across her breasts every time she made a practice paddle stroke. "Hey, there are little foot-rests down on the sides for my feet!" She rocked the kayak from side to side on the grass, enjoying the feeling, realizing that without even being in the water, she was hooked. "Hey, when do we go paddling? Today?"

"No it's too late to start today, but now that you're used to crawling in and out of the thing, how about tomorrow morning, or does Winky have you working Saturdays again?"

"Sounds great! And you know what I'm going to do? I'm going to take you out for dinner to show my appreciation. But really Brady, you didn't have to buy another one of these for my sake, I probably would have bought one for myself anyway."

"I thought of that, but somehow I had to introduce you to it. If you really like it I'll sell you this one for what it cost me, but first I wanted to see if you would like it."

She stood outside the kayak, paddle in one hand, the skirt hanging down around her knees like a blue rubberized kilt. "I know I'll like it. It looks so fast just sitting there on the grass." She smiled at him, then moved closer and gave him a quick hug. "Thank you, you big bear, you're determined to get me into this aren't you? I guess the way I got you started skiing, I deserve this eh?"

Brady felt a warmth inside and two delectable pressure points where her firm breasts had made indentations on his shirt-front. He Tingled in other places as well and began to blush. "Don't mention it, just consider my offer." He hated blushing, it was something he had never been able to control and it made his face look like a stop sign with black, curly hair around the fringes.

That evening they went to Antonio's, the only restaurant Teresa approved of, where she felt the pasta met her standards. The proprietor reminded her of her uncle Vito, with the same handlebar moustache, giving him the appearance of a benign walrus.

A bottle of French Claret was before them as they sipped delicately, awaiting the entree.

"You once said you were from a small town didn't you? Is it typical of what I've heard small towns are like on the prairies?" she asked as she shuffled her cutlery around on her place mat to make it more uniform, checking each piece for water marks and cleanliness.

He watched her inspection of the utensils with amusement. "One of the favourite sayings about my home town was that it was so small the local prostitute was still a virgin." He watched her smile, glad that he could produce a bit of natural blush in her cheeks.

"Obviously she didn't make a very good living at it. No self-promotional abilities? "

"*Nobody* made a very good living there, except maybe the farmers who had their farms paid off, but it isn't that way now, even the well established farmers are struggling to survive."

"Your family farmed?"

"We did until I was about seven years old, then we moved to town. I tell people about living in a house with no electricity or running water and they think I came from a third world country. It wasn't until I moved away after high school that I ever lived in a place with running water."

"God I can't imagine that either. It must have been really hard in the winter."

"We never really thought about it because it was the way we had lived all our lives, chopping wood, melting snow or ice from the river for wash water, hauling water for drinking. I used to dread winters when I was a kid because there was nothing to do except play hockey on the outdoor rink or curl."

"You *curled?* You threw those dumb rocks up and down the ice? It really looks like a ridiculous game, I've never seen the point in it."

"That's because you've never tried it. It's a bit like kinetic chess because you use strategy and even psychology on the opposition. I've seen family members curl against each other and nearly come to blows over using sneaky tactics to throw the others off their game."

"Brady that sounds so childish." It was just a game and people would almost fight over it?"   "Yeah, maybe it was childish but they were competitive and when they couldn't fight on the curling ice, they would play hockey. Hell, fighting there was almost encouraged, besides, it kept you warm on a minus thirty degree day in January."

"You played hockey?"

"Up until the end of high school. The toughest team I can remember playing against, the whole time I played in town was the team from the Indian Residential School. It was like each of those guys had a personal grudge against you. They were tougher than nails, even the ones who played pee-wee league. One team called themselves the Wagon-Burners, and if you found yourself surrounded, you were in for the big hurt."

She was amazed at how animated he had become. He was normally very reticent about discussing his life before moving north. The combination of the glow from the wine and the intimate atmosphere of the dimly lit restaurant relaxed them both and she was glad to have a chance to better know this man who appeared to consist of contradictions.

"Joe told me he went to a residential school."

"Your partner? I don't envy him. There were some pretty horrible stories that came out of there. Do you remember which one it was?

"Somewhere near the south of the province. He said it was in a big valley near a city of about thirty thousand people. He wouldn't say which city. I think he'd rather forget about the whole thing, let alone talk about it."

"I know the one," said Brady chewing thoughtfully on a bread stick. "It was one of the worst. I heard that one of the kids I played hockey against hanged himself because he was being sexually abused. He was one of the tough ones I told you about, small and wiry. He would smile at you straight in the face and then punch you in the guts. Laugh at you while you puked all over on the ice. I guess no matter how tough they were, they weren't always tough enough for what was forced on them there."

"I think Joe's got a lot bitterness that he's trying to hide and that might have something to do with it." She dipped her bread stick in her wine and twirled it with her fingers.

Brady gently reached over and lifted her hand from the wine glass. "Let's talk about something a little more pleasant while we're here."

126

She smiled shyly back at him, allowing him to hold her hand gently in his. "Yeah, let's talk about kayaking tomorrow."

Early the next morning, he loaded the two kayaks on top of the roof rack of his old Volkswagen diesel Rabbit, and rattled off, trailing a cloud of blue smoke and disturbed neighbours to pick up Teresa at her apartment. The mid-May sun was refracting from the early morning dew covering the grass like tiny diamonds and the air was crystal clear. A couple of blue jays were having an argument in a nearby tree.

The previous evening had been one of the most enjoyable he had experienced for a long time. He realised that their relationship had evolved to a sense of mutual trust, allowing them to speak freely of their private lives without feeling self-conscious.

She had looked fantastic to him last night, with her hip-hugging dark slacks and white blouse open at the throat. She didn't overdo the makeup or jewellery, using just enough to make it obvious that she had very feminine tastes despite her job as a truck driver. When he had driven her home, he felt like a teenager on his first date, not sure if he should kiss her goodnight or give her a heartfelt handshake. Luckily for him she took the initiative and planted an enthusiastic and slightly wet kiss on his mouth, then shook his hand like a politician and thanked him for a beautiful evening. He had walked back to his car with combined feelings of giddiness and confusion, not knowing if he had said goodnight to a girlfriend or someone trying for re-election. Next time I'm going to refuse the handshake.

She was sitting in the sun on the front step of her apartment building when he arrived, still followed by the blue smoke and rattle of the diesel engine.

"I could hear you coming for blocks, you sound like an airplane coming in for an emergency landing," she said as she climbed in the passenger door. "At least the mosquitoes won't come back for a while. Have you considered hiring this car out as part of the town's mosquito abatement program?"

Brady laughed. "Now don't be too hard on old Velma, we've gone through a lot together. If you hurt her feelings she might just strand us somewhere. "

She patted the dashboard gently as though trying to make amends for her comments. "So where are we going to go today? Some place where I won't drown I hope, because I don't have a life jacket."

He pointed to the back seat where he had the life jackets and spray skirts stowed, indicating he hadn't forgotten anything. "We're going to head out to Ghost Lake south of here, a few miles from where we put in is the mouth of the Pickerel River. The water is still high and there shouldn't be any danger of us hitting rocks, that is if you feel up to it. This paddling business can be more work for the first time than you realize.

"Hey I'm game, show me everything," she said bouncing up and down in the seat like a twelve year old. "I brought a change of clothes too, just like you suggested, wrapped them up in double garbage bags so they won't get wet. Does this mean I'm going to get wet? That water will be cold as my mother-in-laws heart, I don't want to get wet." She flashed him a smile of mock concern.

"Just a precaution. You never know what kind of weather you're going to run into, especially in the spring. Trust me, I won't let you get wet."

"Oh yeah? And what kind of guarantee is that? Are you going to look after me if I catch pneumonia?" she said, slugging him lightly on the shoulder.

"I'll do better than that, I'll cook dinner when we get back," he countered, realizing he had again not washed the floor in weeks and had eight days dishes still in the sink. "But if you fall in just to collect a meal ticket, the deal's off."

She made an exaggerated pout with her lips. "Do I look like the kind of girl who would take advantage of some poor bachelor who can only cook Kraft Dinner?"

"Come to think of it you look just like one of those."

"Damn right!" She slugged him on the shoulder again, hard enough to make him wince.

Ghost Lake was a cold deep lake surrounded by Precambrian shield. The multi-coloured granite sloped in some places to the water's edge and in others, rose up out of it in sheer cliffs, topped by small spruce and juniper trees. The roots of the stunted trees spread out across the rock which was covered with multi-coloured moss and lichen, finding purchase where they survived in a symbiotic existence. In the distance could be seen several small tree-covered islands. The water was a smooth, cold, dark green. At the edge where they had laid the kayaks side by side, the water was clear enough to see several feet down until the rock disappeared into the water which near the shoreline seemed a rusty colour from the iron-oxide which had leached into the frigid water. The cry of a loon echoed eerily across the water as they stood, drinking in the beauty. "I see it," said Teresa excitedly pointing toward one of the islands where the lone bird swam in the distance occasionally immersing its long-beaked head to search for fish.

They put on their spray skirts and the life jackets over top, then moved the plastic seats forward on the single plastic rail so they could stow their spare clothing and some food for lunch in the stern of the kayaks. Brady had planned to stop at one of the small islands on the way back for lunch. The sun would have baked the island's rocky shoreline to a comfortable temperature by then. The water was still too cold for swimming, in fact remained that way throughout most of the summer except around the rocky shorelines where the rock radiated the heat into the water close by. To tread deep water in this lake was to have numb toes in a matter of minutes. followed quickly by acute hypothermia.

"Jeez, this is tipsy," said Teresa as she snapped her spray skirt around the cockpit with one hand while trying to hold the paddle with the other.

"Make all your movements slow and deliberate until you feel more comfortable," offered Brady, sitting comfortably in his kayak, watching her efforts, but still close enough to help if it was needed. "Before we go far from shore, I'm going to show you some basic steering strokes so you can control your speed and direction." He paddled slowly in front of her, only a short distance from shore and began with the sweep stroke to turn the bow of the kayak without producing a lot of forward speed.

Teresa grinned from ear to ear, still slightly unsteady but gaining more confidence when she realised the inherent stability of the craft. "Neato! This is great! It's almost effortless, and so quiet! Show me more, show me more!"

He showed her the basic forward stroke, then combined a sweep stroke with its wide radius movement across the top of the water from the front of the kayak to the rear, and then quickly alternated with a reverse sweep stroke on the other side which turned the kayak nearly completely around in the water.

She made a few whooping sounds as she nearly tipped while trying the reverse sweep stroke. She giggled with relief that she hadn't. "You don't know how close you came to cooking dinner on that one," she laughed at Bardman, who was having as much fun watching her first attempts.

He said, "I think you're a natural, but don't shift your weight too quickly. Besides, I can't do any cooking yet I still have dirty dishes to do."

"That's what I thought, maybe we could just order out."

He smiled, indicating for her to follow him as he turned gently to follow the shoreline, giving her a chance to get used to paddling without being too far from shore.

She moved effortlessly up beside him, the plastic skeg, which looked like a rudder on the stern kept the kayak tracking straight in the water. Every couple of minutes she would have to use a correcting sweep stroke to prevent colliding with his boat, smiling broadly at him and the surrounding scenery as the kayaks sliced silently through the water, with only a slight gurgling sound coming from the skegs at the stern. The loon called to them and they both stopped paddling to listen, hearing its haunting call bouncing from the hard granite walls, echoing its' song across the cold, still water.

"I never heard that call until I moved from Toronto. It sends shivers down my spine every time I hear it." Her kayak had drifted over and gently bumped Brady's as though looking for comfort. She reached over and gripped the edge of his cockpit, keeping their kayaks together. The craft rocked in the gentle waves while they listened. She turned and smiled. "This is a completely different dimension of living up here. I'm so close to the water I feel like I'm part of it."

"It's nice to convert another person to the lifestyle," he replied, watching the muscularity of her long arms. Her whole body was slim and muscular. It was a body that some men might consider almost masculine except for her obvious feminine attributes which were usually hidden by her work clothes.

"You speak of it as though it's some kind of religion for you."

"Maybe it is in a way, because when I need to get away from the stresses of civilization, I get in the kayak and paddle for a few hours. Nothing else seems to matter out here except me and the boat... and nature around me."

"Usually you don't go anywhere without your camera. Did you bring it with you?"

He nodded, pointing to the area beneath his spray-skirt.

"Between your legs. Isn't that a little bit cold, or do you have special insulation?" she said smiling mischievously at him. "Is it true what they say about photographers?"

"And what is that?"

"That they're all over-exposed and under-developed?"

"Getting a little personal aren't we for the first time out?"

She giggled. "I think it's all this nature around me. It makes me want to throw off all my clothes and go running bare-ass through the grass."

"You would have livened up a few of our annual United Church picnics back home."

She laughed, gently pushing her kayak away from his, using her hand then her paddle end against his hull.

Before they continued, he felt it was a good time to demonstrate the draw-stroke, which would allow a paddler to move the kayak sideways by using gentle figure eight motions with the paddle in the water beside them, while exerting pulling force on the paddle. Teresa nearly lost it a couple of times by trying to counter-balance by leaning away from the direction she was trying to move, rather than pulling on the paddle and leaning toward the paddle at the same time. Over the next hour they gained speed as she gained confidence in keeping her balance and using more force of her shoulders and abdomen to propel herself through the water. By the time they reached the mouth of the Tipi River, he felt he didn't have to look over his shoulder to see if she was alright. It gave him a chance to watch the shoreline for any sign of wildlife and the potential of getting a wildlife shot. He knew the chances were slim this late in the morning. The deer and moose had probably come in the first light of morning to drink from the shoreline.

The Tipi River was narrow and winding with birch and spruce trees lining its banks, the vivid white of the paper birch like slashes of vertical white against the dark green. Along the bank, trees leaned over the water, their roots with barely enough purchase to prevent them falling in. Others had succumbed to the pull of gravity and the slow erosion of the riverbank from the spring run-off. The tall trees, called sweepers, which had fallen part way across the river, acted as obstacles to other trees and detritus that washed downstream by the melting snow in the bush. Sometimes piles of branches, trees and the occasional deer carcass that had tried unsuccessfully to swim the swollen river became entangled together against the sweeper.

As the river narrowed around one bend, the current pushed their kayaks from behind. he realised a large spruce tree had recently fallen from the bank. The current pushed them with increasing speed toward the fallen tree on the outside of the curve, where the current was fastest..

"Follow me, hurry!" he yelled over his shoulder, straining into a sweep turn to the right to avoid the sweeper.

Teresa saw the sweeper, but too late. Without the years of practice maneuvering a kayak, her attempts at the sweep stroke weren't enough to avoid the tree.

He heard her scream as he turned back upstream to watch her progress. From only a few kayak's length away, he saw her broach alongside the fallen tree and then flip over. With several strong strokes he surged around the end of the tree and accelerated toward her inverted kayak which was jammed against the large tree trunk by the current. He could see no sign of her other than a gush of bubbles from below the inverted craft. Then he saw her hand extend from below, fingers grasping, finding no purchase. He reached over with his paddle, bracing it against a partly submerged tree branch and the top of his kayak, allowing the current to force him against her still-inverted boat. Her hand appeared again and this time he was able to grasp it with his, while stabilizing himself with his paddle across his kayak and the tree. He guided her hand to the paddle shaft, and he could see the cords in her forearm stand out as she pulled her head clear of the water, as her legs exited from the kayak's cockpit.

Her face was ghostly white, hair dripping in dark strings, and her hands shook convulsively as she looked at him with intense fear in her eyes. "Son of a bitch, that's cold!"

"Climb onto the tree trunk and crawl to the shore, I'll be right there."

He pulled a section of rope with a metal clip from behind his seat and clipped it to the rescue ring at the end of her kayak. He played the rope out as he paddled along the tree trunk to shore and before he exited from his own kayak, tied the rope to a large branch of the tree. He watched as she made her way cautiously on all fours along the fallen tree. She moved stiffly, her lips blue and her shivering increasing. The wet sprayskirt hung wetly to her knees, an encumbrance to her movements.

He quickly pulled his kayak well up on the shoreline and helped her from the tree onto dry ground. "It's okay, I have you now," he said gently as she leaned against him for warmth. Her shivering had become near convulsive and he knew he had to work quickly to prevent the hypothermia from becoming worse. He ran to his kayak and extracted the bags of dry clothing from behind his seat, along with another yellow water-proof bag. From the other side of the rear hull he took a roll of blue insulite pad, the same he had sat upon while taking pictures in the snow. He quickly had her sit on the blue pad and then wrapped her in a heavy duty foil thermal blanket, with the reflecting side inside to reflect her body heat back toward her. Without speaking, he stripped her of the life jacket and the wet spray-skirt.

"Can you hear me alright?" he said looking with concern into her eyes. "Take those wet clothes off, I'm going to dig out your dry stuff to change into and find a towel. "This is no time for modesty," he added as he urgently dug other items from the yellow water-proof bag.

"Screw modesty, get me warm for God sake," she said from between blue lips that didn't want to form the words.

He gave her a towel as she sat, hugging the thermal blanket around her. "First strip off, then dry off. I promise I won't look, I'll be too busy building a fire.

As she took off her sopping wet clothing, he busied himself snapping small dead branches from the trunks of dead spruce trees and collecting larger dead trees that were on the ground and not damp with rot. When he returned a few minutes later, she was in dry clothes, wrapping herself again in the thermal blanket, sitting on the blue foam pad.

He built a small structure with the smallest dry branches and some birch bark. He tucked beneath it a piece of fire-starter made from recovered dryer lint and paraffin melted into a piece of cardboard egg carton. Inserted into the paraffin and wrapped in Saran Wrap were two wooden matches and a red waterproof match which acted as an accelerant. The home-made fire-starter caught quickly. In minutes he was putting heavier pieces of wood on the quickly building fire. He went to the kayak near the river, returning with a thermos of hot tea. He poured her a cup of tea.

She accepted the cup with shaking hands that could barely hold the container. She cautiously raised it to her lips and slurped noisily. She put the cup down and moved herself closer to the fire, rubbing her hands vigorously to increase the circulation, taking sips of tea between shivering spasms. As she put more wood on the fire, she realised Brady was not close by, but was instead climbing out on the same tree trunk which she had crawled along in her hypothermic stupor.

He untied a piece of coloured rope and brought the free end with him back to shore. The other end was still tied to her water-filled kayak which was forced against the tree by the strong current. From another small sack Brady took two blue pieces of nylon strapping. He used a water knot to connect their loose ends, forming two loops. Each of these he looped around the base of a different tree and connected the end loops with a locking carabiner. On the rope, near the kayak he tied a

133

smaller piece of coloured rope, using a prussic knot, which he connected to another carabiner. Another prussic knot was quickly tied further up the rope toward the anchoring trees, and this end loop was put through the carabiner at the tree. The first prussic was connected to another carabiner, and had the main rope running through it. Fully configured, the main rope took the shape of a Z, anchored to the two trees, and using one prussic knot to grip the main rope for pulling, while the other prussic acted as a safety to prevent the rope from being yanked out of his hands while trying to gain new purchase.

Teresa walked over, still covered by the thermal blanket. She was much warmer from the effects of the dry clothes, warm tea and the fire. Her shivering had diminished considerably as she said, "Brady if I can help, let me know."

He looked up at her from his squatting position, relieved to see she was recovering. "I was just going to come and see how you were doing once I got this thing hooked up. How are you feeling?"

"Like a newly landed fish, but otherwise okay. Thanks for pulling me out of there, I thought I was gone. You know the strange thing? I never had my life flash before my eyes like everyone says when you come close to death."

"Maybe you weren't that close to death."

"Jeez, I don't want to get any closer. Once is enough thank you very kindly."

"Here, I'll show you how this Z-belay works," he said, pulling the rope taught. "You might have to sit here and keep this prussic knot from locking up when it should be unlocking. I'll be pulling on this end of the rope, but it might be a lot harder than I expect with all the water in the kayak, so be prepared to come and pull with me."

As it happened, it was lot harder than either had expected, but with their combined efforts they managed to drag the kayak away from the tree trunk and bring it to shore. With more effort they rolled it over so some water could drain from the cockpit, eventually allowing them to combine their efforts to lift first one end of the boat, then the other to sluice the water back and forth over the inverted cockpit, draining even more water from it.

"God, I'm actually getting warm from all this effort, and hungry," she said, panting with the effort.

"Good, because this is where we're stopping for lunch,"

"No shit, I thought this was just a swim stop. Am I going to be the only one that's going to get wet? She looked at him with a mixture of mischief and revenge as he backed away from her toward the dying fire. She was in fact pissed-off to the degree that she was considering throwing him in the river in retaliation. Then as if a switch had been thrown, common sense prevailed. They moved to the fire, added more fuel, and dug out their lunches. While they ate, Brady busied himself re-stowing the rope and carabiners in the smaller bag.

"Where did you learn to do that?"

"Remember I told you I was with the ski patrol at one time? Well, that's one of the things we had to learn to do in case we had to take an injured person up or down a steep slope in a rescue toboggan."

"Brady you never tell me anything, at least not very much. Do you always take your lady-friends out and dump them in the water? Is this your way of breaking the ice with a new chick?" Her voice quivered slightly with anger and delayed reaction to her ordeal.

He looked and felt very sheepish, or at least as sheepish as someone who looked like a teddy bear could look.

"I'm really sorry Teri, I should have realised there would be new deadfall on this river because of all the high water. I put you in a situation you weren't ready to handle and it almost killed you."

She put her hand on his shoulder as they sat together near the fire. They watched the flames as they curled smokily around the still-damp wood.

"I chose to come along and I think I had an idea of the risks, but if you think this is any way to get a girl to undress in nature, try it somewhere dry. It's interesting isn't it?"

"What is... falling into the water and nearly drowning?"

"No," she said dreamily. "It really is true, the closer you come to death, the more intense life seems to become. When I was watching you setting up your ropes to pull the kayak to shore, it was like watching a fantastic colour film. The colours were so vivid! I could smell every scent there was in the air, almost like it was the first time I had used my nose for something other than sticking in other people's business."

He smiled at the awed expression on her face. "Let's not make a habit of falling out of the kayak to improve your sense of smell."

"You know what I mean, it was dangerous but it was also fun...surviving was fun, not surviving wouldn't have been any fun at all, especially for you because you would have had to do all the explaining."

"Where do you come up with all these reassuring thoughts?"

"Oh I read a lot."

"Well stop reading the obituaries in the daily rag and try the comics for a change. This talk of death is a bit troubling since it would be your picture in the paper." He stirred the fire with a stick, trying to coax it back to life without having to go for more firewood. He looked at the pile of soggy clothing she had discarded and emitted a huge sigh. "I'm going to string a line to hang these clothes to dry. Do you feel up to hunting for some more fire wood for the fire?

She jumped to her feet, the effects of the frigid dumping nearly gone except for some residual stiffness in her fingers. "Sure thing bwana, you shoot and I scoot, nothing I like better than gathering firewood as long as I don't have to do the cooking and cleaning." She ran from tree to tree yanking on protruding branches, giving up on the ones that refused to yield. She was thankful to keep moving to stay warm.

He sat momentarily, watching with amusement. "Try the *dead* branches, they might be a little more cooperative.

There was a pause as she stuck her tongue out at him and said: "I knew that." The sound of branches cracking could be heard as she continued her assault on the defenceless spruce trees.

It took nearly an hour of waving the damp clothing over the fire on the end of a couple of sticks before they could be stowed back in the double garbage bags. The sun climbing higher in the sky warmed them as they both recuperated from the close call.

He removed his camera from the waterproof bag and watched quietly for any signs of wildlife. He wasn't expecting any but was pleasantly surprised when a whiskey-jack boldly landed at Teresa's feet and began scavenging the crumbs dropped on the ground. He moved quietly away and with his telephoto lens, shot a couple of frames of her as she coaxed it eventually to her hand with a crumbled granola bar. He framed her between two large white paper birch trees, the sun lighting her from the far side, creating a halo effect around her as she sat on the soft carpet of evergreen needles. The bird flew to a low branch with its prize. Teresa turned slowly toward Brady, smiling with excitement.

He took several more shots of her with her hand still extended while back-lit by the light beyond the trees. The forest seemed to hold its breath, all sound was soaked up by the thick, gentle moss beneath them. The leaves on the far side of the river suddenly shook violently.

"The wind's getting up, I think we should start back soon," he said listening to the rising tune in the spruce trees. The tops of the trees began to shift and then bend slightly, swaying in unison to the music of the air. The wind was from the west and he could see some grey clouds scudding along the horizon, gradually replacing the blue sky with a layer of cold, grey slate.

The paddle back across the lake was against the wind, and both of them, buttoned into their kayaks by the spray-skirts, kept warm as the waves broke over the bows and splashed against their chests in a greenish cascade.

Teresa whooped with excitement, lifting her arms high to keep the paddle clear of the breaking waves, then paddled harder before the next one broke. Her kayak rode the crests like a cork, rolling the water off its' surface like off a duck's back. From her chest to her feet she was warm and dry, but her hands were beginning to get cold again, from the aluminum-shafted paddle.

The day had been exhilarating despite her near demise, and she promised not to tell everyone how Brady had nearly drowned her the first time out. For her, the kayak had introduced her to a sense of freedom and escape she had never experienced before, but she knew it came with a price. The price was that she had to play by the rules of nature because if she pressed the boundaries of her luck too often, then nature would exact her price as had nearly happened.

She remembered a segment of poem by Henry David Thoreau, not recalling the title, but the essence which was:

> *I went to the woods*
> *because I wished to live deliberately*
> *To front only the essential*
> *facts of life,*
> *And see if I could not learn*
> *What it had to teach,*
> *And not when it came time to die,*
> *Discover that I had not lived.*

CHAPTER 8

Abe McKay watched the men remove the hot stones from the fire pit. They used a shovel to lift them into the metal water pails. The pails were carried into the covered structure of the sweat lodge through the small, flapped opening where they had to bend nearly double to enter. The circular, domed structure was supported by saplings tied together at the top. It was lower than a man's head to help retain the intense, dry heat within. He could hear the rocks rattle like a small avalanche into the centre of the shallow pit which was dug in the centre of the dirt floor. Then the outer flap was replaced over the entrance to keep the heat in.

The seven band council elders disrobed, one of them making comments of how the women might be hiding in the nearby bushes, watching. The consensus among them was that none of them were physical specimens worth a second glance. The atmosphere was one of relaxed good humour. Naked, they entered without speaking, each taking a space around the perimeter of the small structure, facing the centre where the rocks were piled, their backs touching the rough spruce boughs of the inside wall. A large tarpaulin covered the outside, keeping the sauna-like heat inside, causing each of them to sweat nearly as soon as they sat down. The aroma of the fresh earth and the ashes from the fire hung in the air, enveloped by the heat, the only sounds being the breathing of the inhabitants and the subtle clicking of the rocks as they began to cool.

With legs folded in front of him, Abe McKay let his head droop, chin resting on his chest, eyes closed, breathing deeply. He was aware only of the heat and the smells. The sweat ran in small rivulets from his face and chest and into his lap. His skin tingled as though tiny ants were swarming over him. The darkness was nearly complete. All he could see of the others was a vague outline of bowed heads against the dark tarpaulin. In his ears he could hear a high-pitched whistle and the rush of blood through his head at each beat of his heart. There was a sense of dizziness, almost floating and he would have fallen sideways had there not been people seated either side of him. As his breathing and heartbeat slowed, he no longer felt as part of his own body.

The colours of the aspen and birch among the dark spruce were like splashes of yellow paint on the dark green. The vivid colours rolled beneath him as he effortlessly followed the contours of the treetops, first down into a valley, then up and

138

over a crest, sometimes following a snaking stream that disappeared beneath the foliage.

He could feel the wind against his face; the rush of it singing a song of freedom as he let the air current lift him into a climbing spiral to see the red and yellow leaves spread even further before him. The sun warmed him with its yellow rays. If he were to descend and touch those trees would he no longer be able to fly in the fresh spring air? Would the allure of the trees capture him within its autumn-like foliage, denying flight to one that existed for flight alone, removing his reason for existence? He flew over a lake, its water sparkling countless tiny diamond suns. Slowly the reflections disappeared, replaced with hard greyness and right angles. The stench of desecrated earth could be smelled along with the decaying bodies of the forest people, mixed with smells from hell itself, of man-made brimstone and dark smears and gouged wounds in the earth below. With a series of gutteral cries he turned from whence he had come, flew back to spaces he knew, but feared would never know be again.

The smells of hot earth and sweat enveloped him with a silent blanket of comfort as he became aware again of ground beneath him and the slow breathing of his companions.

The naked men emerged from the sweat lodge without speaking, shivering slightly in the cooler air. The others dried themselves, then dressed, casting strange glances at McKay, saying nothing as they walked away, allowing the stones and lodge to cool slowly.

Angus Spence walked with Abe along the grassy path toward the community a short distance away, watching his old friend deep in thought. "Do you remember the first times we used the lodge? Did it bring back memories?" he asked in a soft, toothless voice.

Abe was quiet for a moment, walking slowly, fingering the tall stalks of grass as he passed. "It was like no memories I have ever had." He looked at his wizened old friend of many years. Angus had shrunk, as had he, but their ability to communicate without words had never diminished.

Angus' words were apprehensive, tinged with awe. "Where did you learn to do that? It's something I've never heard you do before, not even when we were young."

"What do you mean?" said Abe, now looking at Angus, who appeared concerned, deep wrinkles furrowing his brow, traversing heavy grey eyebrows.

"You were warbling like a raven, the sound was echoing inside the sweat lodge as if it was the middle of the forest. You really freaked us out."

Abe chuckled softly, scanning the sky, his eyes trying to adjust to the harsh midday sun. "I think you watch too much television my old friend, you're startin' to talk like the young people."

Angus followed the gaze of his friend whose eyes were fixed on a lone raven soaring the current of air far above them. It chortled a cry from high above, raising the hairs on the back of Angus' neck. It was the exact cry he had heard from the throat of his friend.

Roger Jenkins read the report with obvious concern, wondering how anyone could possibly misplace almost two-hundred pounds of granular explosives. The report before him stated that over the period of six months, the eight different producing levels of the mine where drilling and blasting was occurring, there had been a consistent shortfall of the amount of Amex allotted to them by up to ten pounds on the days the shortfall was noted. This amount estimated was based on the fact that the consistent length of the holes drilled, and number of them in the pattern, required a consistent amount of the granular explosives to fill, taking into consideration the space needed for the primers.

He picked up his phone and dialled Hank Aikins, the day-shift boss for underground operations.

"Hank, this is Roger. Roger Jenkins. No, not that one, I'm the President, Hank. That's right, the head honcho, the chief, the head butt-kicker. Yes Hank, of the company. Yes this company. "Tiny beads of sweat were forming on his forehead. He leaned back in his chair, staring at the ceiling. *Who the hell hired this guy?* "Yes Hank I'm the one who signs the cheques, in fact I sign your cheque personally, and I'm beginning to wonder if we're not paying you too much Hank." There was a silence on the other end, other than the sound of deep ragged breathing.

"Hank can you tell me how in hell the highballers have managed to misplace two-hundred pounds of explosives over the past six months? Well I have the report right in front of me and I'm going to bring it down personally and let you read it. And then you know what we're going to do? No Hank, I'm not inclined to violence. However I do believe in action, and you and I are going to go underground today and take a look at a couple of these drill sites. You have a hat and light ready for me when I get there and you can read the report as we're going down. *Yes now dammit,* or do you have alternative employment possibilities elsewhere?"

He hung up the phone with a curse, slamming it into the cradle. His face was red and perspiring with frustration. Who hires these people?

140

he thought to himself again, only to remember that it had been he who had personally hired Aikins. After all his posturing against nepotism, he had gone and hired his wife's cousin entirely on the basis of his written resume and her reference that he would make a great foreman. He regretted that evening he had spent in his office with a bottle of scotch, dreading the thought of going home to his leviathan of a wife. She had badgered him for months to find a position as she put it for her unemployed cousin. He had been laid off from his mining job in northern Ontario and she just knew he would make an excellent foreman. While in his drunken stupor she had placed a letter offering employment under his alcohol-veined nose along with a pen and showed him where to sign. He barely remembered her guiding his hand with hers while he tried to scrawl his signature. He speculated it was probably more her signature than his, but the results were the same; the arrival of her obese cousin, jowls quivering with gratitude, his eyes moist with affection for this man he'd never met before. The affection didn't last long, and it was never mutual.

Aikins' office was in the main headframe of Q-1, within spitting distance of cage station for the shaft. For months he had sat in his office, seeing the miners go on and off shift, filthy, dishevelled and exhausted. Their eyes were dead, devoid of emotion or spirit whether coming or going. He knew one thing for certain, he didn't want to go down there, no damn way. As far as he was concerned he was hired as a foreman and he could do it from the sunny side. Let those other poor jerks toil in the dark, he could administer it from here, at least what little he knew of the goings-on down there. His desk surface was littered with papers, not the official kind, but editions of every tabloid newspaper available at the newsstands. One bleated a headline about a grandmother who claimed to have given birth to an alien child after being abducted by naked spacemen with four foot long male organs. She was quoted as being willing to go back again in the name of science. There were comic books stuffed into hastily slammed drawers and the garbage can was over-flowing with what appeared to be often-thumbed skin magazines.

He greeted Jenkins at the door with a sweaty handshake and a manner that barely fell short of genuflecting at each second word. He was the epitome of obesity, his coveralls bulged at the seams, the belt for his hatlight had an extension sewed to it to fit his girth. His face gleamed pinkish, like a raw porkchop, small watery eyes peering anxiously from behind black-rimmed safety glasses. "I have your hat and light here," he gushed with a high voice. "It's never been used, so it's clean as a whistle.

This is your hat, it's new too. And white!" He cowered slightly from Jenkins as the president tried the hat on for size, handling the edges of it with his finger tips, lowering it from above as though crowning himself.

"*Oh that looks fine, just fine,*" he wheezed, afraid to suggest that the internal plastic headband should be adjusted so it wouldn't rest on his ears. "With your permission, perhaps we could turn it around so the light will point forward. He flinched under Jenkins' glare as the hat was rotated 180 degrees to point in the right direction.

"Now for your feet."

"What the hell's wrong with my feet?"

"Oh, er nothing.I'm sure they're very nice, but you need safety boots. I didn't know your size so I brought four pair."

Jenkins removed his Italian dress shoes and daintily lowered himself into a pair of high, steel-toed rubber boots which caused his pinstriped suit pants to bunch up at the knees, appearing as though he was wearing hockey shin-pads underneath.

"Er, do you have coveralls?" squeaked Aikins halfway into a bow, hands clasped in front of him as though he had just trapped an insect and was afraid to let it go.

Jenkins shook his head and sighed with frustration as the foreman rushed to a small metal locker and extracted a pair of his own, holding them out by the shoulders and comparing their size to that of the man that signed his cheques. He realized Jenkins' entire body could fit into one leg of the coverall's legs. He blushed furiously and stuffed the offending garment back in the locker.

Jenkins leaned forward, hands deep in the pockets of his suit pants, hard hat still resting on his ears, nearly covering his eyes so that he had to crane his neck upwards to see from under the rim.
"You won't let your boss get dirty down there will you Hank?" He spoke in a malevolent whisper, his eyes locked on Aikins, whose heavy pink jowls quivered with apprehension in sympathetic vibration with the rest of his oversized body.

They walked unsteadily and obvious uncertainty to the vertical shaft where the cage-tender ordered the topman to bring the cage to their level. Signal bells jangled and finally the cage with its quivering and pin-striped human cargo dropped like a safe falling from a bank window.

The cage-tender looked at Jenkins' pinstriped pants and the bulging fabric at the knees. He smiled at Aikins who refused to meet his gaze. "'Lo Upchuck. Long time no-see. what's the occasion; goin' fer a look-see?"

"Upchuck?" asked Jenkins.

"My nickname...I tend to get a little motion sick from time to time," replied Aikins who was decidedly paler in the face.

"Like, how often?"

He looked very uncomfortable and said, "About every six months."

"That's not so bad. At least it doesn't happen every time you go down."

The cage-tender chuckled, saying, "It happens every time fer Upchuck."

Jenkins looked sharply at Aikins who was trying to pull his over-sized neck and head into his coveralls like a turtle retreating into its' shell. *"Every six months, you only go down every six months and you're the underground foreman for day-shift?"* He was nearly screaming at him as they descended. His voice was whisked upwards by the cold wind rushing past them through the plummeting lattice-work of the cage floor.

The cage-tender facing the doors, watched the rock flash past, picked his teeth and smiled to himself as listened to the exchange behind him.

Shakey Smith, the topman in the top of the headframe controlled the descent of the plummeting cage. His uncertain hands were being guided by a generally hung over brain. His red-rimmed eyes watched the huge winch drums for the colour change the on the thick cables, warning of the approach of the desired level. The footage counter in front of him allowed him to stop the cage within inches of its destination. The quickly changing numbers were too much for his rheumy eyes and queasy stomach. Typically, he misjudged by several seconds the amount of time needed to bring the cage to a smooth stop for perfect alignment with the track floor of the intended level. His first reaction was to pull on the braking lever to stop the drum as he would make a panic stop with a car. Unfortunately for the cage's occupants he was also lousy driver with the reaction time of a three-toed sloth.

The cage surged to a sudden stop at approximately the eight-hundred foot level, bouncing the occupants as though on a trampoline, accompanied by the groans of the thick cables being stressed to their limits.

'Upchuck' Aikins, lived up to his nickname on the first bounce and went to his knees on the second as though making a sudden switch to an eastern religion. He repeated with equal vigour the ejection of his stomach contents, all over Jenkins' safety boots which were attempting to scuttle out of the way. His porcine body, controlled by some unexplainable logic, crawled on all fours after the scuttling boots until he had them cornered, where he proceeded to adorn them with his vomitus once again.

Jenkins kicked at Aikins like a postman at an ill-tempered dog, making little desperate gurgling sounds in the back of his throat.

The cage-tender leaned his head against the roll-up door, stifling his laughter, promising himself to buy Shakey Smith a couple of rounds the next time he saw him in the Stagger-Inn, which was nearly every night of the week.

The two dishevelled passengers exited the cage. Aikins walked unsteadily like a sailor who had been at sea for months. Jenkins attempted to mop the mess from his newly anointed boots with anything he could find, finally resorted to using the pages of the written report concerning the explosives which Aikins had still not read.

As they climbed on a small red electric locomotive, Aikins considered mentioning that it belonged the foreman of the diamond drill crew, but decided against it, considering the state of mind his boss was in. He closed his eyes as they rolled from the siding onto the drift track, their way lit by the baleful glow of the headlight. Neither one had remembered to turn on their hat lights and Aikins, with his eyes still closed wasn't aware of it. He hoped Jenkins knew how to control the speed of the motor, trusting in divine intervention in the event that he didn't. At that moment he didn't have any desire other than to have the rocking motion of the motor stop. The gurgling and groaning issuing from his pallid lips was causing Jenkins considerable alarm.

They rumbled through the darkness, two well-shaken men clinging to an even shakier machine. The sound of blasting on levels above them could be heard. First came the hard snap as the sound of the explosion was transmitted through the dense rock and seconds later a low roar as the slower medium of the air brought the sounds to their ears. The steel wheels of the motor clacked on the track joints with a steady rhythm, the uneven rails making the vehicle lurch from side to side as it found pieces of uneven track. The smell of ozone was strong from the electric motor. Their heads swayed back and forth with each lurch, shifting their hard hats from one side then the other. Another snapping sound assailed them, like a bullet whipping past their faces, followed by huge crunching sound which shook the motor.

"What the hell was that?" said Jenkins, backing off on the throttle lever, searching for the brake handle.

Aikins had finally turned on his light and finding the brake lever, gave it a gentle pull, bringing them to a stop. He turned around in his seat, setting his light beam to narrow and looked back down the track from where they had come. "Holy shit, would ya look at that, we coulda been squashed flatter'n bugs on a sidewalk."

Jenkins turned, mouth open in surprise. He saw the pile of rock illuminated by the foreman's light. The rock slab nearly as long as their motor, and several feet thick, sat as a single unbroken mass upon the tracks they had just passed. A deep gouge could be seen in the ceiling of the drift under which they had passed seconds before as though carved out by a gigantic spoon.

"This place isn't safe," muttered Jenkins under his breath. He reached up and turned his own light on, shining it directly into the frightened face of the underground foreman. "Maybe coming down once every six months isn't such a bad idea after all," he said under his breath.

Aikins started to giggle, his jowls shaking in time with his huge shoulders, belly resting on his knees, barely confined by the buttons on his coveralls.

Part of Jenkins understood the urge to giggle in response to such a close call with disaster. He fought the urge. It just didn't seem appropriate for someone in a three piece suit to giggle.

"I think I wet my coveralls," said Aikins, attempting to peer over his protruding belly, eyes streaming tears. He didn't know if the tears were from fright or relief at being alive.

Jenkins raised one hand daintily to his mouth, smiling behind it, stifling the first giggle he could remember since his puberty when he would giggle uncontrollably while peeking through a hole into the girl's bathroom at school. "We're going to have to tell someone about this. That thing on the track is a hazard. For God's sake man, did you piss your pants?

Aikins looked up imploringly from the spreading stain at his crotch and said, "You won't tell them *everything* will you?"

"That depends on how much improvement I see in your performance of your duties." His face had quickly regained its cold composure.

Aikins gave a small groan as Jenkins re-started the motor. He could see Jenkins smiling to himself, realising he could now be coerced into coming down on a regular basis and the thought made his stomach rebel again. He also realized the rock-fall from the drift ceiling would mean they had to walk back to the main shaft because the motor wouldn't have the power to push it out of the way. It would have to be drilled and blasted before a mechanical scoop-tram could be brought in to cart it away.

He drove the motor with more confidence. Knowing where the brake handle was made him almost bold. Besides, he felt the faster he drove the less chance there was of 'loose' from above landing on them. They both watched the rock ceiling by the light of their lamps, mouths open in what appeared to be silent prayer.

In the darkness ahead a soft blue light could be seen on the left side of the drift as though a large door had suddenly been opened in the fabric of space and time. As they approached the eery light, a howling sound wavered in pitch to a high shriek then back down to a low growl like that of a large animal in horrible pain. They passed the site quickly and could see the surprised expressions of two open-mouthed diamond drillers at their machine. The drillers were illuminated by the air-driven mercury vapour lamp above them, enshrouded by the vapour of the cold exhaust. The icy cold blast of the drill's exhaust struck their faces like the devils' own breath, its' icy howl shook their unprotected eardrums.

"One of the Deep Core crews," yelled Aikins into Jenkins' ear as the sound of the drill mercifully faded behind them, leaving a persistent ringing in their ears.

He nodded in reply, watching the darkness ahead. He began to hear the machine-gun rattle of the jack-leg drills in the distance at the rock face. He didn't know what he was going to look for when they arrived, but he needed to see the site to assuage himself that the explanation was a simple one. *It must be a simple explanation, how could anyone lose two-hundred pounds of explosives?*

"Here, read this report right now," said Jenkins reaching into his suit and handing the vomit-stained report to Aikins. "I need answers on this and I need them fast; something like this can't be tolerated and if I find questionable practices being used, heads are going to roll. Do I make myself clear?" he said, shining his hat light directly into the eyes of the underground foreman who took the paper daintily in his hand and tried to read it while holding his breath.

The little red motor lurched to a stop, its rear wheels raising from the tracks and slamming back down, jarring the spines and necks of the two men. Jenkins shut the motor off with a slap of his hand on the lever and repositioned his hat and light which had been thrown forward over his eyes to illuminate his vomit-encrusted boots.

A stream of harsh words came at them from behind and to the side of the track where they had stopped. Their combined lights showed a miner waving his arms as though practising for flight, shouting in what sounded like a Slavic tongue. Spittle sprayed from the miner's mouth as he hurled uncomprehensible insults at them. The spots of moisture flecked the President's suit as the miner moved closer. Jenkins tried to wipe the spots of spittle away with one hand but the miner came even closer, nose to nose with him, causing him to lean backward in the seat of the locomotive. He had heard that voice somewhere before but was more concerned with the gusts of paint-thinner-like breath assailing him along with the accompanying precipitation. The miner pointed to the front of the offending motor.

Aikins inhaled a ragged gasp of air and choked as though he had inhaled a large insect. In front of them, illuminated by the motor's light was an explosives car partially laden with bags of explosives...the rest being thrown to the track floor, some broken open and spilled like coarse yellow sand over the tracks. Also in disarray were boxes of primers and several spools of detonating cord by the drift wall.

The Slovak expletives had attracted more hat lights from the drift face where the other miners had heard the collision. They approached, conversing in words neither Jenkins nor Aikins could understand. There was Portuguese, Spanish, French, and a couple of eastern European languages, all speaking at once.

"Sorry, sorry, didn't see you there. Just came to see how you were doing. Wanted to check on your explosive situation," said Jenkins nervously, climbing from the motor, extending an unaccepted hand in greeting.

"Iss even more explosive now," came the guttural reply from the irate miner. "Iss all over ground. You should be put away and door lock-ed. Drive like Bulgarian," snorted the voice from beneath the hat light. The half-dozen other lights nodded up and down in silent agreement.

Aikins manoeuvred himself ponderously to the track floor. "Is there a bathroom around here?" he squeaked in his nervous voice to the crowd of lights which had gathered around them.

"Not hotel here," came the voice of the spokesman from the other side of the motor. "Have award-winning shit bucket over there."

He followed the beam and saw an upright 5 gallon grease pail with a wooden lid leaning against the side of the drift. He made his way sideways in a crab-like walk, trying to avoid his wetness being exposed to the group of miners. He knew he was unsuccessful when a guttural laugh

147

went up from the congregation of lights, all seemingly focussed on his crotch. He could feel his face flush with embarrassment and the need to be sick again was fast approaching.

"You sell maybe pots and pans?" said the miner derisively, shining his light over Jenkins' now rumpled three piece suit.

"*I am the President!*" shrieked Jenkins, arms stiff at his sides, feet together, hat tilting down over his barely visible eyes.

"Pah! And I am Czar of Russia," replied the miner, throwing a mock salute with a greasy hand.

A metallic crash followed by a shout of surprise came from the drift wall where the toilet was located. The cluster of lights turned toward the sound to reveal Aikins on the ground, legs splayed apart, crushed pail on its' side surrounded by a reeking flood of excrement and urine.

Aikins looked at the lights, eyes wide, jowls quivering and his tiny mouth moving as though trying remove a piece of toffee from the roof of his mouth.

"Eh big butski, you squash award-winning toilet." yelled the angry Czar.

Jenkins walked daintily over to the mess, being careful not to trod in the foul swamp and studied the crumpled container. Nailed to the underside of the toilet seat was the award he had presented to the miner in his office, its plaque now tarnished and smeared, its true value recognized by the recipient. A cold anger swept over him as he stared at the shit-encrusted award adorning the underside of the lid. He turned slowly to the sounds of laughter from the collection of miners whose lights illuminated the foul scene.

The miner who had recently proclaimed himself leader of Russia smirked back at him, as though daring him to do something that would give him a reason to use a physical response. His hands were on his hips, legs spread wide apart in a stance like a third world dictator. "Foreman has new office, suits him good. Maybe one day you will have office like that, yes?"

"Get off your fat ass and let's get out of here," hissed Jenkins under his breath as Aikins continued to sit, immobile in the stinking mass, his arms outstretched from his shoulders as though preparing for a crucifixion. Seeing his foreman in such repose appealed to him.

Aikins looked about him, contemplating the problem of moving his bulk from the stinking pool surrounding him, without immersing his pudgy hands in it. In response to a more emphatic hiss from Jenkins, he rolled himself over until he was on all fours, appearing like a hog about to wallow, and levered himself upright while emitting grunts of exertion. The sound of a porcine squeal came from the watchful miners, eliciting more laughter. They climbed silently onto the red motor.

"I'm driving, said Jenkins. Don't touch anything, in fact don't sit on the seat. "But it was too late. Aikins had already sat upon the seat with his wide buttocks, smearing the cracked plastic seat cover with his offensive imprint. He heard Jenkins emit a loud sigh of frustration while he sat in silent embarrassment, his lips and jowls quivering like a young choirboy who had been compelled to confess to nocturnal self-abuse. With a lurch, the motor reversed in the direction they had come. They could see the lights of the miners recede into the distance as they accelerated along the track.

"Sir..."

"Shut up."

"But..."

Before he could turn to look in the direction of travel, the electric locomotive slammed to a halt once again. The force threw Aikins over the front of the vehicle and onto the track floor. Jenkins' hat flew from his head, stopped short by the electrical cord connected to his battery. They had hurtled into the huge chunk of rock that had fallen from the drift ceiling. He had completely forgotten being nearly flattened by the solid mass which had brought them once again to a sudden stop.

Once again the Underground Foreman of day-shift crawled around on all fours, whimpering like a beaten dog while searching for his displaced safety glasses.

Jenkins recovered his hat and climbed from the motor and walked toward Aikins who was still on his hands and knees, searching with out-stretched hands. With a swift kick to his wide posterior, he sent him sprawling. "God that felt good. I think I'll do it again. You don't mind do you? No? Good." Jenkins planted his boot once more with vigour on the man's wide bottom, revelling in the way he splayed out like a beached blowfish, sucking for air, making little sounds in the back of his throat. "Get up you fat smelly turd of a foreman and start walking, we have a half hour walk back to the cage and I'm going to boot your butt all the way there."

Aikins struggled up and trotted heavily along the side of the track.

Jenkins followed at a walk, amazed at the spectacle of someone so obese, straining to stay ahead of him.

As Aikins widened the distance gradually between them, he realised he couldn't see as well as before. It was then that he realised the battery on his belt which powered his light was running out of charge. The beam was a distinct yellow colour and was barely illuminating the track floor at his feet.

"Aikins, wait, slow down."

"Tried to warn you..."

Aikins had actually increased his pace and all Jenkins could see was a dull glow from his fast-disappearing light. A bolt of panic swept over him like ice water poured down his spine. Ever since he was a boy he had been terrified of the dark, and now his worst fear was coming true, hundreds of feet underground, with countless thousands of tons of rock poised over his head.. With a quavering voice he called outs again. As his voice echoed from the rock walls, his light blinked out like a candle snuffed by the wind. He thought he heard a high-pitched giggle in the inky blackness ahead of him. As he felt his way along the track he edged over to the left side to keep his left foot next to the rail so he knew where he was on the track. He heard the giggle again, slightly closer, but couldn't even see his own hand in front of his face. The stench of shit and urine became stronger as he shuffled along the tracks.

"Aikins, are you there?" said Jenkins almost under his breath. He was trying to hold his breath now, the stink was so powerful. It has to be Aikins, he thought only he could smell that bad. Suddenly Jenkins pitched forward with a squawk, landing on one knee and both hands in a soft pile of reeking fabric. He was aware of something soft and damp wrapped around his ankles. The stench nearly made him gag. He remembered his cigarette lighter in the pocket of his suit jacket, and lit it from a sitting position. He could see the discarded coveralls of Aikins wrapped around his ankles where they had been discarded on the tracks. He realised he was also sitting on his rejected long underwear. At one time the underwear had been red but now it had a marked brownish stain. He realised his own hands had the same hue as well as Aikins' distinct aroma clinging to them. He swore under his breath and extinguished the lighter, plunging the surroundings back into inky blackness. He had never before experienced such complete darkness. He held his stinking hand close to his face, hoping to see its outline. All his senses perceived was the smell of shit beneath his nostrils. He thought he was going to puke. Getting to his feet he could hear the air line above his head hissing and the occasional drip of water from the parallel water line. From ahead came a sound that made him stop in his tracks, a sound like tortured souls crying for release, rising first to a scream of agony and falling to a low moan. Around one bend he could barely discern a bluish light in the distance and began walking slowly toward it, wondering where the foreman had gone.

As he approached the diamond drilling station, he could see the silhouettes of the two drillers as they attended the demands of the drill. He hoped to pass the station without being seen, but such was not the case when one of the drillers looked up in surprise and attracted his partner's attention. The sounds of the drill stopped. He turned and looked at the two silent drillers who stared back.

"H'at least dis one is not naked, but 'e smell de same, just like shit."

Jenkins said nothing, noting the other driller. He stared at the speed which his Adam's apple was shifting up and down. The movement fascinated him. He had never seen an internal part of the human body move so quickly. The eyes of the driller watched him without expression from behind eyeglasses that magnified the eyes so they completely filled the lenses. The expression was cold, never blinking, similar to that of a snake. He hated and feared snakes almost as much as the dark. In the pool of harsh blue light he could at least see around him and was reluctant to continue along the tunnel.

"Do you fellows have a battery I can borrow from you? Mine has gone dead."

There was a moment of silence as though the two drillers hadn't expected him to speak, and finally the short one said, "Sorry partner, no more batteries 'ere. Where de motor you came on?"

Jenkins explained, "On the other side of some loose that came off the top of the drift... down that way. We borrowed it from the siding near the cage. Thought we'd have it back by now. Hope the owner won't be too upset." He shuffled from foot to foot, now conscious of his own aroma, realizing it was the reason the drillers hadn't moved closer. He could feel his face flush with embarrassment.

"H'it belong to Wild Bill. 'E our boss, an a mean little bast-ard. Only t'ing savin' you from havin' de shit kick out of you is de smell, maybe not even d'at."

"I'm Roger Jenkins, president of this company," he said, taking a step toward the men, extending his hand.

The two drillers stepped back in unison, avoiding the hand.

151

He paused, then sniffed his hand. "Oh that's terrible. I had a little mishap back there, or, at least the other guy did and I tripped over it. You said he was naked?"

"Yup, like 'ow you say...de jaybird?"

"More like a sow," said the tall gangly driller, finally speaking up. "Nothing on at all?"

"Battery 'n ard-at wit 'is light, an 'is boots. 'E look crazy too, laughin' an jigglin'"

He tried to imagine the sight of Aikins naked, laughing, smelling as though he had come from bathing in a hog barn.

"You sure you de president?" said the short driller suspiciously.

"*Are you implying that I'm lying?*" answered Jenkins, the hiss creeping back into his voice.

"Partner, you covered in shit. If you har president, I h'am Louise de fourteen."

His eyes glazed over with frustration. "First the Czar, now Louise the fourteenth. I suppose Hitler will meet me somewhere along the drift, maybe Genghis Kahn along with some of his Mongol hordes." His voice rose until he was shouting. The saliva flew from his mouth, compelling the two drillers to step back to avoid the spray.

"D'at not possible, h'immigration never h'allow d'at kind of crap. Besides, d'ey all dead now."

Jenkins sighed and stared down the track toward the main shaft and the cage back to sanity and the blessed sunshine. As he stared, he could barely make out a pinprick of light in the distance. His attention down the drift was matched by that of the drillers. They watched the light grow larger, swaying side to side as though the light was worn by a drunken sailor.

"Oh merde! Wild Bill," whispered the Frenchman.

What followed became one of several legends born in the depths of the mine. For years, miners told variations of how Wild Bill Hendrickson upon learning the president, or at least someone who claimed to be president confessed to stealing his precious little red motor, then stranded it between a rock-fall and a powder car. Wild Bill had accused the aromatic gentleman in the soiled pin-stripe suit of being the pedlar who had sold his wife a set of completely unneeded pots and pans, then proceeded to demand a refund. Not achieving satisfaction, Wild Bill chased the purported president down the drift to the cage station, kicking him in the behind as best his short legs would allow. In his drunken state he fell down several times but always managed to catch up and kick the suspected pot-pedlar again. For the last hundred yards the only illumination was from Wild Bill's hat light, was of Jenkins running in semi-darkness, shrilly voicing his displeasure over his shoulder at the tiny red-suited psychopath in pursuit. Only after promises in front of the cage tender to buy him a new little red motor from company funds and refund his money for the cost of the pots and pans, did Wild Bill retreat.

The cage tender knew he could probably drink for several months for free, simply relating the tale over and over to whomever would listen. Of course it was only natural that embellishment would occur, to the extent that the National Enquirer had called the company office some months later to get the full story of the haunted mine where the president was chased shit-covered and screaming through the tunnels by a demonic dwarf dressed in red.

As for Aikins the underground day-shift foreman; he kept his job, just barely, by being witness to the driving abilities of the president, and the subsequent collision with the explosives car.

CHAPTER 9

For Brady Bardman, the gradual approach of spring was one of his few reasons for optimism. It was while in his kayak that he seemed totally at peace with himself as well as the world around him. While working for the newspaper he had endured shift work which disrupted his sleep and eating patterns. There were frequent times when he barely slept after a shift of covering accidents, fires, shootings, and the everyday upheaval of peoples' lives. His work made him an observer, a chronicler using photographic images, and sometimes at the behest of his editors, an interloper. It was all for the sake of *getting the shot*, and his bosses didn't care about the combined stresses of his own life thrown into upheaval. Just get the shot, get the colour, get the blood. The days off when he could load the kayak onto the roof-rack of his car along with his camping gear and disappear for two or three days at a time helped keep him sane. His colleagues were derisive of his scenic shots, the sunsets, sunrises, dew on grass and spider webs. He really didn't care what they thought. The shots he was most proud of were the ones of the wildlife. He found he could approach very close to waterfowl because they didn't recognize him as a threat as he and his kayak, drifted within easy camera range. His shots of Great Herons, Western Grebes, and Double-breasted Cormorants were some of his favourites. He could recall how on one trip a loon hen had attempted to lure him away from her chick by thrashing about in front of his kayak as though with a broken wing. She would then dive out of sight when he came too close.

On this day he was preparing to spend a couple of days on a small unnamed tributary of the Black Wood River. He had camped on the bank last year and seen sign of moose all around his site but never actually saw them. Their splayed hoof prints in the mud of the shoreline gave away their presence, as did the way the tender young leaves were nipped off at the tops of the red willows. The wildlife magazine that had previously bought the shots of the water birds were interested in seeing his shots of moose, provided he was successful in approaching the shy animal.

During the ninety minute drive north to the bridge where he planned to put in, he was surprised at the density of truck traffic. It seemed he was always either following or being followed by a truck, heavily loaded with construction equipment, or another one empty coming back for another load. The trees along the roadside were coated with the light brown dust thrown up by the truck tires. It covered his car interior like talcum powder. When he arrived at the bridge, he realised as he turned off the road and down an embankment that the water levels of the river had risen even more. The track he followed was an old construction road now out of use but still open enough to allow the old Volkswagen diesel to pass between the trees to park near the edge of the river.

By eleven in the morning he had secured his pack to the outside of the kayak behind the cockpit with bunji-cords and stuffed the tubular waterproof bag containing food and sleeping bag along with extra clothing down inside the hull behind the seat. As he lowered himself into the kayak, using his paddle shaft for stability he could clearly hear the unending rumble of the traffic over the bridge and taste the dust as it drifted down over him. Deciding not to use the neoprene spray skirt, he turned the kayak upriver and quietly followed the shoreline, admiring the greening of new growth along the riverbank. Each paddle stroke produced a quiet gurgling sound from the plastic skeg at the stern. The current was stronger than expected. Occasionally small whirlpools of surface turbulence forced the bow of the boat to one side or the other as it passed over them. The water dripped from the paddle shaft onto his lap despite the drip-guards, but he didn't mind. The sun was warm on the back of his neck, a pleasant contrast to the cold of the water in his lap. Soon the sounds of traffic disappeared and a soft breeze form the south sprang up, carrying the ratcheting cry of a kingfisher as it flicked from branch to branch over the edge of the river, watching for small fish below the surface.

He drifted slowly toward the embankment, reaching slowly in front of him for the waterproof bag strapped on the front of the cockpit, containing his camera with the 400 millimetre mirror lens. He could see the kingfisher sitting on a branch surveying the water below. Its oversized beak and tufted head appeared too large for its body. A few slow paddle strokes brought him closer to the bird and he allowed the current to slide him stern first into the riverbank to stabilize the kayak. Slowly, almost painfully he lay the paddle across the cockpit in front of him and took the camera from its bag. He brought the viewfinder to his eye and focused on the still bird, setting the shutter speed at125th of a second. His finger felt for the shutter button, and at the instant he was about to press it... the kingfisher flew to another branch. It cackled again, as though mocking his efforts. He smiled, knowing the kingfisher had been watching him all along, choosing to fly only when he made the move to his camera. He continued upriver, skirting a couple of large sweepers similar to the one that had caught Teresa. There were more than he had expected, a probable result of the high water eroding away the river bank with the spring run-off. In some cases he had to avoid whole trees bearing down on him, riding the current with their branches reaching above as well as below the surface. The uprooted trees swept past majestically in silence, a mute testimony of their passing to those still clinging to life on the crumbling shoreline. Their destiny would be somewhere downstream wherever the whim of the current might decide to deliver them along the shore; or perhaps pressed like corpses frozen in rigour mortis against the cold steel of the control gates of the Black Wood River. He was careful to avoid the obstacle course of deadheads, trees which had been ripped from the shoreline and had buried one end in the river bottom. The other end protruded just above and sometimes just below the water's surface to spear any unsuspecting boater. He watched for any wildlife that may have become stranded on the constant parade of detritus moving with the current. On only one occasion did he see anything. A lone raven perched on a large branch. The raven watched him warily as he passed. It gave a squawk of displeasure and a curious look as they met going opposite directions. Bardman turned to look back at the tree after it had passed and saw the raven had also turned to watch him.

Three hours later, with arms aching from the upstream paddle, he found the small tributary. He made his way along the narrow passage, branches of willows and birch meshing above to form a lattice-work canopy. The buds of the willow had become mint-green leaves, still folded, ready to spread and welcome the warmth of the sun. He had found this spot on one of his first paddles along this part of the river. The entrance had been nearly obscured by overhanging growth from the willows. The opening had beckoned to him, almost whispering his name, or so he had imagined. It wasn't something he was about to admit to any of his friends. The first time he had eased the kayak through the tiny tributary into the small bay, he felt as though he had been there before, the way someone hears a conversation and knows exactly what's going to be said next. His campsite had been on a rock ledge of Precambrian shield, with a lower ledge barely above the water where he could disembark with ease from the kayak. It was at a point where the stream broadened out to form a small lake barely 100 metres across, surrounded with water lilies, bulrushes, and the beginnings of a new crop of wild rice. In the late fall the wild rice would tower over any paddler, and the simple passage of a boat through the swaying stalks would drop as much as a kilogram of the long kernels of wild rice into it.

The rock felt warm to his feet, protected by light rubber booties called Water Walkers. He dragged the kayak further up the rock shelf and tied the bow with a length of nylon rope to prevent the wind or water from sweeping it away from him, although the small expanse of water was so well sheltered by the towering trees that he doubted the water was ever disturbed by anything but the strongest of winds. Still, he was careful because he knew friends who had once lost their canoe while on the shores of Lake Winnipeg, one of the largest freshwater lakes in the world.. It had been swept away by wind while being unloaded. The expensive Kevlar canoe was never found, and they had to flag down a passing fishing boat hours later, thankful they had at least removed enough supplies to stay dry and fed.

He detached the small, aluminum-framed backpack from the rear of the cockpit. The tent and sleeping bag along with the food and stove were removed from the space in the hull behind the seat. The free-standing tent was quickly set up on a level spot under a large spruce tree with the lower branches providing extra protection from rain or direct sun. The Sierra tent resembled one-half of an over-sized football. Inside went a heavy duty thermal blanket on the floor with the shiny surface up to reflect body heat back into the tent. On top of that a thin, inflatable mattress along with an inflatable pillow which also doubled as a water bag. He could hear the wind increase, singing with a rushing sound through the treetops, making them sway.

The huge spruce trees seemed to bend over to study this strange organism at their splayed feet. In such a protected area the only other effect of the wind was ripples playing along the water surface of the small lake, chasing each other like young nature spirits playing tag.

In the shade he became chilly and put on a light polar fleece jacket and wind pants while packing the bulk of his food in a small red sack. He then walked around the rocky shoreline of the small lake with the sack and a length of rope. With several tries he was successful in throwing the rope over a large branch of a spruce tree, tied one end of the rope to the food sack and pulled the sack high into the air, hopefully out of the reach of hungry bears. The slack end of the rope was tied off around the trunk at a point above his head. He hoped this would be far enough away from the campsite to prevent attracting bears, but had heard stories from other experienced campers of bears working in cooperation, standing on another's shoulders to get at a sack of food.

157

With everything secured, he untied the kayak and began a slow, quiet observation of the lake shoreline, watching for any sign of wildlife. In a couple of places he could see where the tops of water plants had been neatly nipped off, an indication there were moose feeding in the area. Amongst the bulrushes and lily pads just under the surface of the lake was a slimy green material speckled with tiny, lighter dots. These were recently laid frogs eggs, many of which would become food for fish and some wading birds. A sudden explosion of sound came from the confines of the bulrushes as two mallard ducks erupted from their hidden nesting area. Their sounds of alarm served as notice to all wild creatures that there was an interloper among them.

He wished there was some way he could communicate that there was nothing to be feared from him, but knew that could only be achieved by being quiet and moving as little as possible. The sun began to drop behind the tree line and the air became decidedly chillier as he turned back toward camp. He looked forward to firing up the Peak-1 stove and re-hydrating some of his home-made chicken / almond stir-fry with rice. He didn't expect to see any wildlife at once, preferring to wait until early morning just before dawn to go hunting with his camera. The small stove, resembling a tiny lunar lander, hissed as the blue flame boiled the water in which his meal gradually began to take on edible form. Also in the boiling water were two portions of boil-in-a-bag rice.

The far shoreline was a murky collage of green and grey, the tops of the highest spruce trees catching the light of the last rays of sun, their tips appearing to have been dipped in gold. In seconds that colour was gone too, leaving only the delicate pink of high clouds smeared against the darkening blue above. In the east a full moon was rising slowly over the tops of the trees.

As he ate, a small pot of water nearby boiled quietly for tea. He sat on the inflated air mattress which he had pulled to the bare rock near the water's edge. The silence was almost complete as he watched high above the blinking navigation lights of a jet aircraft, so high that the sound hadn't reached him. Moving at right angles even faster was a satellite, a tiny unblinking point of light, a reminder that it was impossible to escape signs of civilization, no matter where you went.

After cleaning his dishes and disposing of any left-over materials into a sealed plastic bag for the return trip, he lay on his back in his sleeping bag inside the tent. The tent flap was completely open to the open sky and he watched the milky way with its countless stars. The wind whispered quietly through the treetops as bits of stray breeze cooled him through closed bug screen of the tent entrance. He was glad it was still too cold for mosquitoes. Before he fell asleep, he heard in the distance, a family of coyotes holding choir practice. It was the most beautiful music he had heard for a long time as he drifted into sleep; the cool breeze caressing his face. He dreamed.

The clack of the snooker balls sounded muffled against the soft green of the table felt. They caromed off each other before coming to rest, one or two having disappeared into the table pockets. The air was heavy with smoke and hung in a blue wreath around the single, shaded light bulb that hung over each table, each illuminated space above the able like its own galaxy in the dark universe of the snooker hall. The still air smelled of cue chalk, sweat and tobacco. The oiled hardwood floor creaked under their weight as each player moved cautiously around the table, surveying the lie of the balls for the next shot. Players leaned low, peering over the table edge, squinting silently, lining up the cue ball while muted conversation was carried on by seated onlookers, waiting for their chance to get into the game. Sometimes money was lost or won, but never very much. No one had very much money, except maybe one of the farmers who had a good harvest that year. They seldom played pool for money, rather opting for poker in a room somewhere where their wives couldn't find them, a bottle of whiskey on the table to loosen the purse strings.

The screen door creaked and slammed shut as Duel Hancock lined up his shot on the blue ball. The three banks to the side was one of his favourites, having practised it for hours. It slipped into the side hole without touching the edges. "Come to lose some hard earned money B.B ?" said Duel as he surveyed his next shot on the pink ball.

Bardman watched without speaking, listening to the muted conversations from corners of the hall, punctuated with curses and laughter as someone either failed or succeeded with a shot. With a sharp CLACK, the pink was sucked in by the corner pocket and the white shooter ball came off the rail in perfect alignment for the black into the side pocket. With customary recklessness, Duel pumped it home, resulting in a low groan from his opponent, who had been sitting on a wooden bench along the wall, sipping on a cold Coke. Snake Jakeman, his face slick with sweat from the airless confines of the pool room hung up his cue with a quiet curse. He hadn't won a game all night and MAN he was thirsty from the moist heat of the night.

Snake threw two quarters on the table and two more to Duel for his win. Duel pocketed them quickly and started for the door, reaching for a cigarette from the pack rolled in the short sleeve of his T-shirt. Without speaking Brady and Snake followed into the still night air.

Above them, large winged, hard-backed beetles clattered around the buzzing mercury vapour street light, their wings clattering against the glass of the lens. Quick, dark shadows blurred past them as small brown bats swept through and around the beetles like tiny, furred pursuit aircraft chasing and catching the myriad of winged insects. The still, dark air around them muttered, then shook as the western horizon lit up with a translucent flash. No one spoke as they walked three-abreast along the dark shoulder of the highway which led out of town, toward the Quick Ville cemetery which overlooked the river valley.

A gust of hot wind pushed them from the back, a dusty breath of the earth with its' aromas of goldenrod, fresh-cut hay, and the heavy dampness of an approaching storm.

The ground-keeper's metal equipment shed at the inner edge of the cemetery stood with the door open. Brady and Snake went cautiously into the darkness as Duel went to the perimeter of the cemetery grounds and began searching in the high grass near the base of the tallest spruce tree. Snake and Brady watched from their shelter as Duel held the case of beer aloft, deposited earlier by Axel Rodham the bootlegger for most the town's under-age drinkers. The three of them had cultivated a relationship with old Axel, buying him the occasional pack of cigarettes as a tip. Axel wouldn't buy beer for just anyone. They had to show some appreciation for the service. It was really the only thing Axel was appreciated for, and then only by the under-aged drinkers.

Duel walked toward them, holding the case of beer over his head like it was a trophy won in hard battle. He opened his mouth to give a rebel yell, the kind that got him kicked out of high school and put one teacher in the hospital with a heart attack. The air around him fluoresced in brilliant whiteness as his muscular body arched and his feet leapt from the ground . The nearby spruce tree shed every inch of bark, including that of the twigs as part of the lightning bolt which had branched away from the tree and passed through their friend and to the ground.

The ears of Snake and Brady felt numb with the blast. Their eyes swam with vivid purple dots from the intensity of the bolt. The air smelled of ozone, boiled tree sap and burnt flesh. Twenty paces from them lay the still, scorched body of Duel Hancock, surrounded by twenty-four unopened bottles of beer which had spilled onto the ground from the smouldering case. As they carefully made their way to the body, the rain began to pelt down in drops large enough to sound like rocks hitting the shed roof. As if in a dream, they stood over Duel, staring down at his scorched body, his mouth still twisted into a macabre grin. Still staring. They each picked up a bottle in each hand and went back to the shed. They opened and drank them in shocked silence, a stone's throw from their smouldering friend. The rain roared down upon the small town cemetery, bending the high grass and swaying the trees in a macabre dance. The stray dogs ran for shelter.

"Too damn wet to move him now," muttered Snake, sitting on an upturned five gallon pail."At least his shirt ain't burnin' no more. Thank Christ fer small mercies, Amen"

Brady turned toward him and saw Snake's face in another lightning flash. He noticed Snake was smiling as he drank. As the lightning crashed around them, bathing the cemetery in blue-white light, Snake began to laugh. the laughter changed to a harsh braying sound, like a donkey fighting for its breath. In another flash of light, he could see tears streaming down Snake's cheeks. The increasing volume of rain made the air cold and they began to shiver, sitting on their metal buckets. He looked out toward his burnt friend and saw that the corpse had sat up in the rain. The sightless eyes and burned features smiled back at him, illuminated by the next flash of lightning. He turned to speak to Snake. Snake was gone.

Bardman woke with a start, his hands clawing at the air. He thought he had screamed. At least he knew in his dream he had screamed. He always screamed when the dream came. It had been years since he had a recurrence and the fact it came now was confusing. His throat was sore and he coughed harshly and rolled onto his stomach. He realised he had fallen asleep with the front of the tent open. At least that explains the sore throat, he thought, reaching in the tent pocket for his glasses. They were covered with dew and he had to wipe them with a finger to see outside.

A heavy ground fog covered the area, the grass dripping with dew. On the far side of the lake, barely visible, a large dark shape moved slowly from the shoreline to the water's edge.

He quickly pulled himself from the sleeping bag, shivering in the clamminess of the morning air. He quickly dressed. He reached for the camera at the foot of the tent and quietly crept from the tent toward the shoreline. He slid the kayak silently into the water. With a quiet gurgle the kayak sliced toward the far shore as he watched intently where he had last seen the outline of the moose. The sky was a soft blue, the remnants of some of the brighter stars remaining as false dawn crept over the horizon. The water of the lake felt warm compared to the cool air. The droplets ran down the paddle shaft onto his fingers, then landed in his lap, soaking his crotch. He wished he had put on the spray-skirt because the water was landing on the waterproof bag containing the camera. He eased through the high reeds of the far shoreline, hoping for a glimpse or sound from the moose that had come to drink or feed. The plants made a quiet swishing sound as they brushed along the plastic hull, sometimes tickling his face as he passed. He allowed the kayak to drift to a halt and sat quietly among the reeds as he carefully pulled the camera from the plastic bag. The long clear song of a white-throated song sparrow drifted across the water, accompanied by the warble of a yellow-headed blackbird, perched and swaying on a cattail near the shore. The lake and its inhabitants were awaking, greeting the world with their territorial songs.

With a crash of wings, the same two mallard ducks ejected themselves from within the cover of the reeds. Their frenetic quacks broke the pristine silence and faded in the distance as they flew in formation out of sight over the treetops. Directly in front of him, a huge rack of antlers appeared above the reeds and turned his direction, accompanied by a startled grunt. The water thrashed as the bull moose lunged toward shore, looking once over its shoulder toward him, and with a final snort from its huge nostrils. It crashed into the tree line and disappeared.

He sat quietly, the unused camera cradled in his lap. The kayak shifted gently on the swell created by the moose exiting the water. It was quiet again. Not even the birds sang as they held their breath, shocked into silence by the noise of the frightened moose. Shit, was all he could think to himself. If he wanted to get a good shot of a moose here, he was going to have to take a lot more care by setting up a blind on the shore near where they came to drink. He turned the kayak slowly for the opposite shore, pushing the reeds aside as the bow swung around and paddled toward his campsite. A small jumping wolf spider had somehow landed on the boat immediately in front of the cockpit. It was observing him with its formation of forward-looking eyes, in a crouched position. He extended his hand toward the spider. It moved quickly back. As he retracted his hand, the spider resumed its' position with a short hop. They played this game for several minutes until the spider grew tired of it, turned and jumped from the kayak to a nearby lily pad. The squawk of a raven echoed over the water from the opposite shoreline. Bardman looked toward his tent, nestled in the dark overhang of the spruce tree. He was surprised to see the barely-discernible shape of someone sitting in front of his tent. As he drew closer to the campsite, the figure appeared to sit and watch him without moving There was still no sound from other wildlife as the sky brightened and allowed him to see the aged features of an old native man sitting with his legs crossed. The old man examined his small Peak-1 cook stove, prodding it first with a stick, then he picked it up and shook it.

"What the hell is this?" said the old man with a soft chuckle.

162

Bardman replied, "My stove, I call it the lunar lander. I'll show you how it works if you would like some tea while I make breakfast."

"What's for breakfast? The old man was smiling a toothless smile at him as he gently placed the stove to one side, giving it a gentle nudge to see how stable it was.

"Cow phlops, sort of a pancake made from scratch with apples and cinnamon."

"Umph, if you'll eat it, I'll eat it... maybe."

He watched the old man warily. He had still not moved from in front of his tent, still seated cross-legged, his buckskin jacket open at the throat, exposing a small leather bag suspended from a string of rawhide. His graying hair was cut short, topped by a peaked cap that said CAT on a yellow square on the front. The cap was darkened by grease around the edges, as were the tattered jeans he wore. Steel-toed work boots were on his feet. His large muscular hands rested on his thighs as Bardman realised he also was being scrutinized as closely. He noticed an alertness in the old man's eyes despite his advanced age. The texture of his face was like an old brown paper bag which had been crumpled many times, the lines criss-crossing in patterns of tiny triangles, and deep furrows. There was a sense of humour and intelligence in that face. No hint of malevolence. He soon felt at ease with the man as he prepared the concoction retrieved from the bag in the tree. The aroma of wood smoke was heavy around the campsite, and since he had not had an open fire, realised it came from the old man, who watched his culinary efforts with interest.

He vigorously pumped on the pressure handle of the stove and with a final twist, locked the pump knob into position. Into a small pan he poured the powdered mixture and added some water from a plastic bottle. "This has cornmeal, whole-wheat flour, powdered skim milk, nutmeg, powdered egg..."

"Don't try to talk me out of it. I'm hungry, I'll eat it if you will," replied the old man as he leaned forward for a closer look. "That dried apple?"

"Yep, that goes in too, gives it the lumpy texture. Also gives it its name." He handed the zip-lock bag of dried apple to him to sample. He lit the stove which ignited with a whoosh of yellow flame surging from its' small burner. The old man moved back a couple of feet gumming the apple as Bardman began pumping frenziedly on the pump knob once again. Gradually the yellow flames turned blue from the increased pressure as the tiny stove emitted a quiet roar from its vivid blue ring of flame. The mixture was poured into an oiled, frying pan with a folding handle where it immediately began to sizzle and thicken.

"It has to get almost black around the edges to be cooked inside,"

His guest was still pursuing the piece of apple around inside his mouth with his tongue.

"There's maple syrup, the real stuff, none of this Aunt Jemima crap full of chemicals and food colouring." He gingerly lifted the pancake with a small flipper and quickly turned it over to lay back in the pan.

The old man had moved closer, sniffing the air, smiling with anticipation. From somewhere he had extracted a tin plate and cup, which were now at the ready. "An all this time I been eatin' oatmeal porridge... hate the stuff."

They both laughed quietly as he slid half of the pancake into the old man's plate, the rest into his own. As they ate quietly, a pot of water sat upon the little roaring stove in preparation for the tea. The breakfast was eaten in silence. The particles that spilled onto the ground were hastily retrieved by a grey jay which sat upon a low branch, waiting for more opportunities. As they sipped their tea, the grey jay landed on the old man's boot and struggled with one of the laces, finally giving up and hopping to the ground. It scavenged around the site, jumping and fluttering away whenever someone moved too quickly. A chipmunk competed, scurrying from pot to pot, peeking over the edge, then scurried in short bursts of speed. Occasionally it stopped to nibble something from between its tiny paws while standing on its hind legs, its small pointy ears alert for danger. The old man laid one gnarly hand palm up, flat on the ground in front of him. The chipmunk scurried over onto the hand and allowed itself to be lifted to within inches of the old man's face. He whistled softly and the chipmunk sat up and chirped abruptly looking straight into the wizened eyes of the human. Faster than Brady could imagine, the old man closed his hand around the chipmunk, inverted the fist palm-down, and opened the fist. The chipmunk was gone.

"How the hell..."

"Old trick my grandpa taught me," said the old man, standing to his full height. "He knew all kinda tricks but wouldn't show 'em to anybody until they were ready to see' em."

Bardman was surprised at the diminutive stature of the man. He estimated he stood less than five feet, but while sitting, he exuded a sense of power and size. It was as though with some kind of sleight of hand, the old man could transform himself, inflate himself one moment, then shrink the next.

"Thanks for breakfast. Next time I cook. Hope you like oatmeal porridge." The old man walked quickly toward the dense brush without looking back and melted without a sound into the dark undergrowth.

Bardman had neglected to ask how he had come to be here. He realised that although they had spoken very little, there had been considerable communication in other ways. The smile of the old man was similar to the dream he had that morning. It flitted in and out of his consciousness, sometimes caressing the unconscious recesses of his mind where the dreams lived. *That smile was so familiar!*   He sat near the little stove, aware that neither the grey jay nor chipmunk were to be seen. It was as though they had come to see the old man, to say hello to an old friend. Without thinking, he reached for his camera and looked through the viewfinder. With the 400mm lens, the branches of the nearby trees were magnified. The dark shape of a raven took form. It sat quietly surveying the still lake. He took his eye away from the viewfinder to look toward the branch. He refocused through the lens on the raven which had shifted to another branch, further into the light. Before he could even think of releasing the shutter, the raven looked directly at the camera before flying into the forest. He blinked a couple of times as though blinded by a brilliant light. He recalled the first time when he had tried to photograph a raven during the spring. He thought it had been his imagination gone wild due to the stress of the job. As he bent to collect the dirty pots and pans, the familiar warble of the raven drifted through the forest. He could still detect the faint aroma of wood smoke. He looked around to see if he was alone.

The morning sun warmed the rock where the tent sat. He knew there wouldn't be another chance for a shot of the moose or any other large animal near the shore until dusk. Until then he prowled the edge of the lake on foot with the macro-lens on his camera, getting close-up shots of dew hanging from plants, even a spiders web, like a network of transparent pearls, each one showing an inverted view of the world through its' natural lens. *Maybe to really understand what I'm seeing, I have to focus through nature's lens, and not my own.* He wondered if what he had seen the old man do with the chipmunk was not really sleight of hand at all. Perhaps what he had seen was a small crack in the veneer of reality. What most humans saw as nature, but not really as it appears. Like seeing a fish under the surface of the water, the image rippled and distorted.

165

He was getting a headache. He had not slept well the night before, at least not during his seldom-recurrent dream. He had not considered it a recurring dream for years, ever since Duel Hancock had been fried before his and Snake's surprised eyes that night in the cemetery.

It had been considered the safest place to go drinking because no one expected kids to be there after dark. Over the years all kinds of ghost stories had been concocted about unusual sightings after dark there. He had felt among family, having a couple of uncles, and grandparents buried there, as well as several friends killed in car or farm accidents. For months afterward he wasn't sure if he had actually seen Duel sit up in the lightning blasted rain, or if it had begun with his dreams. He never asked Snake what he had seen because Snake was never the same after that night. For that matter, was he? Had Snake seen the same thing as he? Snake had bolted from the shed into the violent storm. Until Brady left Quick Ville, Snake refused to talk about that night. Nor, to the best of his knowledge had Snake ever visited the site of his former friend's grave.

His head felt as though a red hot spike was burrowing in from behind his left ear and his neck began to stiffen. With slow steps he went to the tent under its cool canopy of spruce boughs and lay down on his air mattress. He was soon asleep with only the song of the wind in the trees and the rustle of the reeds against each other at the shoreline. He didn't dream, at least didn't remember dreaming, although when he woke three hours later with a dry mouth and small puddle of drool on his inflatable pillow, the image of the raven came to him. At first he thought it had been a dream-remnant, clinging like old cobweb from the interior of his mind. He shook his head, thankful the headache was gone, realizing he was hungry again. He had a bizarre urge for oatmeal porridge.

CHAPTER 10

Joe McKay stood quietly in the open doorway of the shack where he had spent the first years of his childhood. He never thought of that period of his life in the residential school as being part of his childhood. Rather, it had been a period of mutation during which time his body and mind became something as alien as the environment he had been forced into. He couldn't reconcile the memories of serene happiness he had experienced in these surroundings to those later years of abuse and self-loathing. He was an end-result looking at a mental image of what should have been, an image distorted by time, a reflection in a dark window, showing only form but no real substance or detail.

He stepped cautiously into the kitchen, the floorboards creaking beneath him, leaving his footprints in a fine film of dust. A battered Coleman lantern hung from a rafter over the table where a plastic table cloth lay, curling at the corners like an old discarded newspaper, yellowing with age. He was surprised to see no dirty dishes in the metal tub on the counter. His father hated doing dishes, preferring to stack them until there was nothing else to eat from. From the wood-burning stove came the scent of rancid bacon. A large cast iron frying pan hung from a hook over the stove, its edges grey with congealed lard or bacon fat. From behind one leg of the stove which was shaped like a rear leg of a cat, a mouse fidgeted, casting a wary eye in his direction, while nibbling on some morsel of food found on the floor. Everything was so much smaller than he remembered it.

"You lookin' for your dad?" came the quiet voice behind him, near the doorway.

He turned and saw a small wiry man with huge hands protruding from shirt sleeves that were too short for his arms. A peaked cap rested on ears which stuck out at near right angles from his head. The front of the cap nearly obscured his eyes, causing him to tilt his head back to see from beneath the peak.

"Haven't seen him for some time. Came out to see how he was doin'."

"Sometimes he takes off for a week... maybe more," said the little man as he withdrew a pack of tobacco and papers from his shirt pocket. "He never says where he's goin' or when he's comin' back. He didn't take his boat or canoe so he must be walkin'."

Joe watched him quickly roll a cigarette, never spilling a drop of tobacco and then lick the tobacco paper with his tongue. In a fluid motion born of long practice the man flicked an old Zippo lighter which flared like a greasy torch and applied the flame to the contorted paper tube at the corner of his mouth. Grey bristles surrounded his lower face in stark contrast to the nut-brown of his skin. The blue smoke, back-lit from the light from the doorway rose in wreaths around his head, finally swirling away in the warm breeze from outside. Joe stood without speaking. The small man stood in the doorway, quietly observing from within the veneer of smoke. It had been the smell of the rancid bacon that brought the images back like a scuttling insect, creeping from between the folds of his memory.

For three years he had rebelled at being in the residential school with its prison-like walls and regular corporal punishment for the slightest infraction. Despite his rebellion he learned to read and write, aided by the occasional whistle and impact of the wooden yardstick. It had been wielded by a chubby, baby-faced Catholic brother who could stalk the aisles between the desks as silently as his father could walk the bush. Whenever his gaze wandered to the sunshine outside the barred windows, a new welt would develop across his back. He had learned to mentally distance the pain from his mind, erecting a mental block which numbed him from the world around him. To his own surprise, he began to love reading. It had become an escape to worlds he could only have dreamed of. He was surprised to see worlds open up to him from between dusty, dog-eared covers with their spines broken and covers scarred by neglect. His other escape was through sports, something the brothers encouraged because it diverted the energy built up by enduring the frustrations of his cloistered life. Hockey became a passion with him as well as many of his fellow students, and during one memorable evening game, he earned his nick-name as the 'Brother Bopper'. Some of those days seemed as if they had occurred only yesterday.

The skies finally cleared. The storm had dumped mounds of pristine snow over the fields and roads. There had been worry among the students that the game against the Quick Ville Crackers would be cancelled due to the state of the roads, but word came that the highway had been cleared and the game was on. The announcement made during dinner by one of the brothers resulted in loud cheers along the length of the tables and a small food fight developed at the end of one table. The normal consequences of the food fight would have been a swift reaction

168

by the brothers patrolling the ranks of diners, but the prospect of getting out of their repressive surroundings was a relief for all, including the staff. Those not on the team and trusted not to run away were brought along on the dilapidated school bus as a cheering section.

"All team members report to the basement to pick up your equipment," yelled brother Fred over the revelry. Brother Fred's eyebrows furrowed in frustration at not being heard, so he picked up an unwashed cooking pot and began beating it with an equally dirty ladle, holding the two-handled vessel in front of him and swung the long-handled ladle freely with the other hand. Between muted BONGS on the pot he yelled for quiet. "The game starts at 7:30 this evening and that means you have a half hour to clean up and be at the front for the bus. Don't move. Sit still. We're playing the Quick Ville Crackers and if we win tonight it means we are in the quarter finals for this division. It also means that if we win, the team can sleep in an extra hour tomorrow. Okay, go."

Pandemonium broke out as the boys rushed for the basement where the hockey equipment was stored near the furnace room. The halls thundered with the impact of young feet and echoed with the yells of excitement.

Joe felt a hand whack the back of his head during the stampede to the basement and turned to see Henry Tootootsits smiling gleefully back. Henry's large hands and heavy body made him an ideal defence man for the team known as the Wagon Burners. "Hey Two-tits we're gonna go beat on some white kids tonight," said Joe, noting remnants of macaroni around his friends mouth.

"Gonna kick 'em in the balls," replied Two-tits as they came into the darkened basement.

A hush fell over the twelve boys as someone hunted for the light switch on the dank, flaking cement wall which always left particles on the oiled wooden floor.

"Line up here for your bags of equipment and keep your mouths shut," said Albert, the staffer who over the past years had become nastier in his demeanour. He had also become pudgier from the high carbohydrate diet, so that his shirt was stretched between the buttons, showing expanses of rolling white skin. To many of the students he was known as 'fish belly', sometimes shortened to 'fish', due to similarity of his skin and the pale underside of a fish. Usually, his seldom washed body smelled of bacon fat combined with his own repugnant body odours and his hair was a greasy nest, a haven for wayward vermin and anything that happened to fall from the overhead wooden joists.

The bag with number three stencilled on its side landed with a dull thump at the feet of Henry Tootootsits. "Shit, nothin's washed, smells like a cat pissed in here," said Two-tits, his head stuffed inside the open end of the heavy canvas bag. He snorted like a dog trying to sniff a gopher out of its hole. Muffled curses could be heard as he surveyed the contents with his nose. Finally he withdrew his head and giggled. "Those quackers in Quick Ville are gonna have to play holdin' their noses."

By now everyone had their heads stuffed in their bags, resulting in a variety of muffled expletives coming from within the stench-ridden confines. The sharp crack of a hockey stick against the rafters brought their heads up collectively.

"Dress. Never mind the smell, just dress," said Albert, the hockey stick held in both hands.

Hurriedly they donned their uniforms, some using old Sear's catalogues for shin pads, some without shoulder pads. All had gloves, often mismatched, usually with large holes, gnawed by mice. The uniforms were of the Montreal Canadienne's colours, with a home made crest depicting a burning settler's wagon on the front. The skates were equally tattered, having been donated by the local junior 'B' team after considering them unworthy of their own team. The Wagon Burners took perverse pleasure in the realization they had whipped some of the better, more well-equipped teams in the league. They had in fact intimidated them with cold stares during face-offs and muttered threats, as well as out-checked and out-played them in the corners.

The half-hour ride with the team and cheering section was raucous despite efforts by Albert to control it. Sticks were thumped on the floorboards in unison as they emitted the sound that sometimes moved the Quick Ville Crackers and their supporters to more than a few nervous glances. "Quack,quack,quack," shouted the team in unison with the thumping sticks.

It had been speculated that the former coach of the Crackers had been run out of town due to his renaming of the team from the original moniker of Quick Ville Cranks. During that period it had been a local joke that the players had to be crank-started. There was much speculation by local detractors as to where the cranks were inserted and their manner of use.

As the pudgy brother pulled the school bus into the parking lot of the open air rink, they could hear music from the public address system echoing from the nearby walls of the Royal Bank building and grocery store on the other side of the wide street . The Beatles singing *I Wanna Hold Your Hand* reverberated through the frosty night air as lines of bare light bulbs glittered brightly over the ice surface. Heads could be seen silhouetted along the perimeter boards where snow was banked up on the outside, allowing spectators to stand at nearly the same level as the tops of the boards. The clouds of their breath in the bitter night air hung like grey patches of cotton. The onlookers voices of excited anticipation mingled with the music, a crackling menagerie of sound from an antiquated speaker.

The sharp snap of the puck could be heard bouncing off the boards as the Crackers warmed up. Their newly-sharpened skates carved the ice like large knives, whittling out particles of ice to tinkle like shards of glass. The rink manager and his assistant pushed wide shovels along the ice surface to remove the last snow from the storm. With cold-stiffened arms, they shovelled the snow over the endboards of the rink, where lines of spectators stood behind the protection of a wire screening. Despite the high barrier of chicken wire, it wasn't unusual for a puck to deflect over the barrier and be lost until spring in the deep snow.

The dressing room was an elongated building with a slanting roof and a series of windows facing the ice surface, also covered with wire mesh to protect them from flying pucks. Along each side of the interior were wooden benches, shredded along the front by countless skate blades, where skaters had removed metal burrs from the blades, the result of a recent sharpening. The interior was heated to tropical temperatures with a wood-burning stove which turned the stove pipes a cherry red, causing them to tinkle metallically from the extreme heat. It was nearly impossible to sit within three feet of the roaring stove without clothing or skin becoming singed. The heat only intensified the odours of sweat and unwashed hockey uniforms.

The Quick Ville volunteer fire fighters kept the door to the adjacent fire hall unlocked in the event of a mishap with the roaring stove which was frequently if not fanatically stoked by Tom Burnside, the rink manager. Speculation was that he had increased the fire insurance on the building by three-fold, but that had never been corroborated. Whenever Burnside, a large florid man with rheumy eyes and a saliva-soaked cigar stuffed in the side of his mouth studied the red-hot stove pipe, it appeared more with an expression of hope than alarm. As though to show his disappointment at the lack of trust from the insurance people, he spat a brown stream of liquid tobacco and saliva onto the stove-top where it danced like a rancid brown insect, finally disappearing with a hiss. He grunted in satisfaction at the heat which was blistering the paint on the adjacent wall. He hated the cold but was thankful for the chance to escape his shrill wife who always seemed to find his stash of bottles around the house. The dressing room afforded a myriad of hiding places for his ever-present mickey of Five Star whiskey, and he knew his wife hated the smell o f the place so never went there.

The Wagon Burners began to sweat as they laced up their skates. They wanted to be out on the ice, knowing they would be at a disadvantage due to the effects of the sweat cooling on their bodies. Those who warmed the outdoor bench on the opposite side of the rink would be most disadvantaged, waiting for their shift, thumping their skates on the shredded wooden floor to maintain circulation. It wasn't unusual to start a shift, unable to feel your toes in the skates.

Joe and Henry were first out, cutting large circles in their end, flipping a puck between them and finally into the open net. They eyed the other team, watching for weak skaters and under-equipped players lacking pads but found none. As more of their teammates joined them, they passed the puck around and once the goalie, McGoo, named after the short-sighted cartoon character took his place, he was bombarded with pucks. A single blast came from the referee's whistle, a grocery store owner with slightly frosted rimless eyeglasses, a look of constant surprise on his face.

McKay faced off against a heavy-set boy wearing dark framed eyeglasses kept on by a thick elastic band. His full head of dark curly hair framed a cherubic face on a pair of shoulders that seemed to have no neck. When the puck slapped to the ice in front of them, they spent seconds fighting each other, their sticks locked together, kicking with their skates at the puck, locked in a waltz to the music of knife-sharp blades scraping against each other. Finally the puck was kicked free and the play went from end to end, ice chips flying with the tight turns around the goalie nets. The boards groaned with the impact of players bodies as the spectators, young and old alike cheered the teams on. Muffled cries rose from faces swathed in scarves, riding on the still, frigid air like the white vapour that floated vertically from their mouths. Overhead, a bright full moon bathed the rest of the town in a bluish light, surrounded with a hazy, multi-coloured ring of pale light. Dogs howled in the distance, probably in response to the excited shouts of the spectators.

With his breath coming in ragged gasps, Joe skated toward the bench for a shift change. Henry Tootootsits sat beside him rubbing his ankle where he had been chopped by a stick, grimacing silently in pain.

"That centre is gonna taste my stick next time out," said Tootootsits, ducking as a puck whistled past his head, gouging chips of wood from the boards behind them. "Now they're shootin' the puck at us. Hey quacker, you can't hit the goal so you aim at us?" One of the opposing team raised the padded finger of one glove in response and was promptly flattened by a cross-check from behind. The whistle blew and the Wagon Burner was escorted to the penalty box by a linesman amid a chorus of boos from the dark, swaddled, steaming masses surrounding the rink.

The public address system crackled to life with the static-filled voice of Tom Burnside announcing slurpily around his soggy cigar, the name of the offending player. The announcement was followed by a belch over the speaker and terminated by a blast of static.

Mrs. Burnside in the house next door, probably realised she had missed at least one bottle of whiskey in her quest to destroy her husband's stash.

The volunteer fire department members in attendance watched with trepidation as the smoke and vapour billowed from the chimney of the warming shack to blot out the brilliant stars of the Milky Way. It looked like some evil genie, just released from its bottle, reaching and writhing into the black sky.

"Power play on," yelled the pudgy brother from the end of the bench.

Joe, Henry and a new boy climbed over the boards as the players of the second line took their place on the bench. Tootootsits chased the puck into his own zone when he felt a sharp tug at his groin area. Looking down he could see the blade of hockey stick protruding from between his legs, still held firmly by one of the Crackers from behind. The blade yanked against his groin again and he heard a metallic clank from beneath him. With horror he realised his metal cup from the jock strap, usually referred to as the 'can' had been pried loose and was spinning like a little bronze toy on the ice. He was vulnerable in the most vulnerable of places. Tootootsits protected his own net, screening McGoo, realizing with dread that he was the only one in position to block a shot from the point. He imagined a target painted on his groin area as the opposing player loosed a slap shot at him. He dropped his stick and stood his ground, knees and thighs pressed together, both

173

hockey gloves covering his precious balls. The puck passed between his skates, a frigid, black blur along the ice, unseen by McGoo the goalie, who was staring in disbelief at the stance of his defenceman. The puck clanged against the bottom metal support of the net, spun on edge, then lay flat. A cheer went up from the supporters of the Crackers, followed by a groan from the Wagon Burner's cheering section.

"You lost your can Two-tits," said Joe as he fired the metal cup with his hockey stick toward him.

Two-tits' hands dove once more for his groin in a spasm to preserve future generations of his bloodline. The metal cup whistled past him and with a resounding BONK caromed off the head of the pudgy brother standing behind the bench. The brother went down limp as a bag of sugar and draped over the boards, his outstretched hands nearly touching the ice surface.

None of the Wagon Burners attempted to pull him back onto the bench, electing instead to cheer the marksmanship of McKay who was also being cheered by the opposing cheering section.

"Helluva shot," cried Henry, attempting to recover the cup which had bounced back out onto the ice. The attention of the onlookers around the boards was diverted momentarily by two dogs which decided at that moment to copulate enthusiastically behind the boards, near the Crackers' blue line. A couple of mothers covered their young children's eyes, whose protests went unheard. Play was delayed as several players from both teams studied the amorous canines from the other side of the boards.

The cry "FIRE" went up and all eyes immediately went to the warming shack where flames could be seen licking around the metal chimney and the surrounding cedar shingles. Several men from the group of onlookers ran for the fire hall, one of them pulling the handle on the outside wall of the fire hall, to activate the siren mounted above the building. Others rushed into the dressing room to carry out a thoroughly drunk and unconscious Tom Burnside, cigar still dangling from the side of his mouth which now dripped a brown drool, like a car with a leaky transmission. The copulating dogs began to howl in unison with the fire siren, as did every dog in town and a couple from farms within earshot. People began throwing snow onto the roof of the building, to no avail as the flames grew. An additional groaning sound was heard as the fire truck, an air force war time crash-truck creeped arthritically from the fire hall. The truck's stiff canvas hose was unreeled as the water pump was brought up to speed. The volunteer firemen stood, watching expectantly for the stream of water, but all that came was a trickle, as though the old truck had developed a urinary-tract infection. Recriminations began to fly among those who had neglected to fill the truck's water tanks. By now the building was well involved. Kids gleefully tossed snowballs onto the blazing roof as many others moved closer simply to feel the warmth of the flames on their faces. The two dogs continued to copulate, thankful for the added warmth.

Mrs. Burnside arrived at her husband's side, listening to his semi-conscious, whiskey-laden explanations as to the cause of the fire. Soon she was part of a trio, howling in unison with the dogs as well as the siren which someone had neglected to turn off. Her howls were at her husband who was now trying to stand, without success.

The onlookers giggled and made note that she was dressed in a floral pattern house coat which opened at the rear, exposing her bare buttocks now quivering with dimpled rage. The male dog lost interest in the bitch in heat and put its nose where so many people were looking, soliciting a shriek from the irate Mrs. Burnside. She turned and upon seeing the dog sniffing her naked posterior, grabbed the first thing available to throw. Unfortunately it was the previously-dropped and half empty whiskey bottle which had fallen from her drunken husband's coat pocket. She went into a wind-up worthy of a major league pitcher and flung it at the dog. It missed the dog by yards but continued on to connect with the back of the Mayor's head who was berating the embarrassed fire fighters.

The fire fighters looked at Mrs. Burnside with gratitude and decided to go for a beer at the Queen's Hotel, leaving the Mayor where he had fallen, mouth open and finger still pointing at the huge billows of smoke in unconscious admonishment.

Through all this, the Wagon Burners watched with fascination, their coach still draped over the boards but now beginning to groan and twitch. The pudgy, semi-conscious brother slid backwards onto the bench. The players moved aside to make room for him between them. The brother rolled his head several times, mouth open, tongue hanging out, and watched the building across the expanse of ice burn. "We won, we won...didn't we?" was all he could say in a slurred voice. Then he puked over the boards onto the ice

"Helluva game," said Henry Tootootsits to no one in general, as he watched the fire.

"Yep, a real barn burner," replied Joe McKay, handing the metal cup to his friend who received it with a sigh of relief and discreetly inserted it in its rightful location.

The two teams decided to mover closer to the fire to stay warm while they removed their skates.

It was while they prepared to go home that McKay spoke with the opposing centre who had proved so tough. While sizing up the thick-set boy with the dark-rimmed eyeglasses, he introduced himself to Brady Bardman, promising he wouldn't under estimate him the next time he faced him in a game.

As a consequence of the fire, the fire chief was fired, the Mayor hospitalized, the rink manager enrolled in a drying-out program, Mrs. Burnside praised for her aim, and the name of the local team changed to the Barn Burners. A few months later, there were six mongrel puppies from which the team chose one as a mascot. They called it Butt-End, either in reference to the end of a hockey stick or, as speculation had it, to Mrs Burnside's most outstanding physical feature.

It was the beginning of Joe McKay's nickname, 'Bonk' due to his ability to shoot an athletic supporter.

Henry Tootootsits continued to be known as Two-tits by his friends and was grateful to be able to carry on the family lineage. His reaction on the ice to being personally protection-less was there-after known as the Defensive Groin-Grope.

Joe McKay sat at the old table, picking at the dried edges of the rubberized covering of the table cloth. The fabric showed through like old cheese cloth and below it, he could see the faded stain of the oak table. He could remember his father making him eat his oatmeal porridge without sugar and only a splash of milk before sending him off to school. His father was working at the Hudson Bay store at that time, still trying to deal with the loss of his wife. He was beginning to realise why he had been sent away to the residential school. There had been nothing here for him. In that way his father had been prescient in a myopic way, able to see what the future held, but with a lack of clarity like opening his eyes under water and seeing the distorted images swimming past. To continue in his father's footsteps would have destroyed him the way it had destroyed his father. Now he realised the reason for his father's return to the trapline. It was a last attempt at saving his own life by returning to the dignity of survival through the use of one's own abilities. Joe's journey to the residential school was his beginning on a long road crossed with many intersections to lure him away. But away from what?

As the sun warmed the interior of the cabin, his head grew heavy. He moved the old creaking chair with its flaking paint and legs wired together closer to the table and put his head upon his arms. He closed his eyes. He could hear the dry fluttering of wings as a raven landed on the rusted garbage barrel near the open window and began rummaging through the contents. It croaked twice, receiving an answer from another raven in the nearby trees. As the warm wind rustled the high grass near the door, he slept and dreamed. He dreamed he was sitting on the riverbank, drawing images with the stick in the mud as he had done so many years ago. The drawing was of a large bird with staring eyes and an impressive beak.

The creak of a chair woke him and he could smell the unmistakable aroma of wood smoke. He loved the smell of wood smoke. With his mouth dry and head aching, he opened his eyes, peering along the surface of the table. His father's face swam before him, his chin resting on the cracked linoleum table cloth as though having been dismantled from the rest of his body. The eyes peered unblinking back at him. A yellow peaked cap with the word CAT was tipped back on his head. Joe closed his eyes again, willing the dream to go away. He opened his eyes again and his father's face became clearer. This time the chin nestled on strong brown hands, one fist upon the other, resting on the table surface. The face smiled, all but two teeth gone, the wrinkles around the eyes deepening.

"You used to sleep like that in school," said his father's quiet voice, blending with that of the warm southerly wind which rattled the window.

CHAPTER 11

Teresa sat quietly at her small kitchen table, a cup of coffee in front of her. She carefully sorted through the eight-by-ten black and white prints arrayed on one side of the table. "Brady these are great. You say you shot colour too?"

Bardman nodded, sipping from his mug, leaning back in his chair. He watched her go through the prints. Her enthusiasm wasn't fake. She truly seemed to enjoy seeing his work and this was gratifying to him. His ego needed to be stroked once in a while to confirm that his stuff was worthwhile. He smiled as she held a print up at arm's length, turning it horizontally, then vertically, frowning in concentration.

"I love this one. Can I have it for my wall?" It was a print of a damsel fly early in the morning, resting on a stalk of grass near the shoreline. On the stalk were beads of dew above and below the delicate insect with the long slender tail and wings folded along its length. It looked like a small, streamlined version of its larger cousin the dragonfly. The background and foreground were out of focus, the only sharp areas being the long body and wings of the insect itself.

"That one was fun, I was laying on my stomach in the dew and had to crawl on all fours so I didn't scare it away. The macro lens let me get in close. You should try it sometime."

She looked at him over the rim of her cup, seeing new colour in his face and a renewal of energy in his eyes. She knew the work with the mining company was soul-destroying with its internal politics and subtle clashes of personality. Combined with the aesthetically unappealing drudgery of taking grip and grins, the acidic nature of the company president and the uncomfortable surroundings of grease and noise of the underground. She could understand the therapeutic value of the work before her.

"You're not very happy with your work at the company are you ?"

He shrugged, swirling the coffee around in the bottom of his mug. "It's a job, it pays the bills, but it isn't what I want to do. I guess I'm still looking for what I want to do, just like I think you are."

"Don't change the subject. Right now what I'm doing is a damn sight better than what I was doing. This is the happiest I've seen you in some time. It's because of these pictures isn't it?"

He studied the shot of the damselfly, turned it from the vertical to the horizontal, squinted as though looking for something that eluded him. "I guess they represent something that is endangered. Not just this insect, but the fundamental aspect of nature itself. I feel that in my job I'm helping destroy it by working for a company that doesn't seem to give a shit about what it's doing to the environment. All they care about is their public image and the bottom line."

"So why not quit?"

He chewed his lower lip in thought, still studying the contents of his cup. "And how would I pay the bills? This place isn't big enough to support a freelancer. I couldn't make a living shooting weddings and passports, and the last time I took baby pictures the kid puked on me."

"I know. There are critics everywhere," she said, smiling at him. Her toes touched his under the table. In silence they played footsy in their sock feet, each of them now studying the bottom of their coffee cups while relishing the warmth passing between them. She smiled inwardly, realizing their mutual feelings for each other had found a conduit through their toes. The barriers she had erected against another relationship were gradually dissolving with the presence of someone who not only had masculine qualities she admired, but a sensitivity she had rarely seen in other men.

"What about the possibility of selling your nature stuff? You've got some great stuff here, there must be a market for it."

He reluctantly withdrew his feet from hers and leaned forward. He was beginning to feel he was being interviewed by a job counsellor.

"There's a lot of competition out there and the only way to get into the market is to have it accepted by a stock photo agency. The agencies demand hundreds if not thousands of images before they even consider marketing your stuff. Believe me I've tried. It always comes back with a nice little note saying they like your stuff but it just doesn't meet their current needs, then you open a magazine and see ads or illustrations using shots that are inferior to your own. At least I think they're inferior, but I'm prejudiced."

"You ought to be." She leaned over the table toward him, her cup extended in her hands to the centre of the table. "If you stop believing in your own abilities just because some agency doesn't use your work, then you lose the confidence to try new things. Don't let them do that to you Brady, don't let them control your life. You express yourself better in your photography than most people could ever do with words. You know what one of my favourite shots is that you took at the mine?

"Which one?"

"The one with the greasy miner shaking the hand of the president of the company. You can't tell which one looks more confused. You showed the very essence of those guys in one shot, and that is that they are interchangeable. No wonder the boss was pissed-off at you. He realised the only difference between him and the miner was the fancy suit. In fact the miner looked a helluva lot more intelligent than the president." She giggled as she remembered the image.

"Jenkins said he would fire me if I took another grip and grin like that," said Bardman with a chuckle. "I told him I made copies and would paste them all over town if he fired me. I said it as a joke but I think he took me seriously because the next day I could tell someone had gone through my negative files looking for the original."

"Brady that's scary. The first rule of happy employment is not to threaten the boss, even as a joke. Obviously he didn't take it as a joke."

He nodded seriously, looking over her shoulder at a shelf lined with stoneware pottery. Among the matching mugs and pots was a clay frog reclining on its side with a ridiculous grin on its face.

"I've had the feeling I've been walking on eggs ever since that day, but have been reluctant to admit it. If I lost this job I don't know what I'd do. There's really nothing else I want to do."

"I could teach you to drive a truck, we could be a team."

"Naw, that looks too much like work to me. Besides, you have a partner. The hours would drive me nuts. I need my eight hours sleep at the right time or I just don't function. I'm surprised you considered the idea. Aren't you happy with your partner?"

"Joe's a really good guy, but he's been really quiet lately. I mean this guy hardly says two words an hour at the best of times and now he's clammed right up. I think it has something to do with his dad. Remember we talked about him over dinner that time? He said his dad visited him and his wife for the first time in twenty years. Now he sits in the truck while I drive and just looks out the window as if I'm not even there.

"What does his dad do?"

"He's a trapper in the winter and fishes in the summer, been doing it for a long time, at least as long as Joe was away.

"Interesting," he said, seeing the concern on her face. "When I was camping at the spot where I got these shots, I met an old guy or maybe I should say he introduced himself to me."

"What was his name?"

"That's also interesting. He never told me. I never even asked. Never even considered asking because it was as though I'd known him all my life. He stayed for breakfast and poked fun at my pancake mix, but he still ate it like he was starving." He sat still a moment, deep in thought as she waited for him to continue. "I don't even know how he got there, just appeared in front of the tent while I was on the water. Then there was the raven."

Teresa sat up abruptly, hitting her knees under the table, startling him. Do you see a lot of ravens?"

"All the time. But this one was different."

He told her of the attempt to take a photograph of the raven from the ski trail, then the one at the campsite where he met the old man. He didn't tell her how he had seen the raven smile, because it had been so fleeting that he wasn't sure he had seen it himself. Nor did he mention the strange dreams he was having. He would have been surprised to hear her confess to strange dreams as well as her knowledge that her partner, Joe was also suffering from a recurrent dream.

The phone rang, breaking the silence. She lurched to the counter to answer it, as though her legs had gone to sleep. She said "uh huh" a couple of times and "shit" at least once before hanging up and thumping down in her chair with a sigh of resignation.

"Bad news?"

"That was Winky from work. Joe hasn't clocked in at work and he was supposed to take a load of powder north tonight. Shit, I had a day off coming and now I have to take it alone. Damn him, it's like he's gone on walk-about or something. His wife called the office looking for him, he's been gone since early this morning without a word to anybody." She turned and looked at the wall-clock with the golden sweep hand. "It's four o'clock now and I'm going to need some sleep before I pick up the trailer tonight. Why don't you stay for dinner? Actually it's left-over lasagna, but it needs to be eaten, then I'll kick you out so I can catch my beauty sleep.

"You know me, I never turn down a free meal." He leaned back in the chair, patting his stomach. He welcomed the opportunity of not having to eat alone another night.

Seven hours later, with lasagna stains on the front of his shirt, he watched the eleven o'clock news on his own television. He thought of Teresa waking to go to work for the next sixteen hours. Alone through the night in a bouncing truck loaded with forty-thousand pounds of explosives. He wished he could have gone with her just to keep her

181

company and be sure she was alright. Although he knew she was more capable than he in many ways, he still felt protective of her but powerless to intervene on her behalf. He wasn't looking forward to his own day at work. The whole morning was to be taken up doing executive portraits of all middle and senior management people in the company to be used in the annual report. It meant scrambling from one office to the next with the studio lighting on a schedule that was so tight that he would only have time for several exposures of each subject before having to set up in the next office.   He knew he was being evaluated on his performance and the results. He didn't sleep well that night.

Teresa had made a thermos of coffee before the trip and had difficulty drinking from the cup as the Kenworth growled and bounced its way between the dark stands of spruce trees on either side of the gravel road. Without looking at the load manifest, she had hooked up the trailer and left as quickly as possible. She was having difficulty waking up after her sleep. She knew her sleep patterns were screwed up and it would take several days of regular nights to feel rested again. In the pale green light of the gauges she checked the bags under her eyes in the interior mirror. Her face was pale and drawn, the dark hair emphasising the lightness of her skin. A ground fog had developed and was resting in the gullies like clouds which had come to rest across the road. They engulfed the headlights as the truck dove beneath its surface like an eighteen-wheeled submarine. The orange marker lights on the edges of the cab and trailer reflected off the mist, giving an impression of a white wall within inches of the cab. The headlight beams cut twin cones of light to disappear into a murky greyness, then as the truck ascended an upgrade, the headlight beams climbed, painting their whiteness onto the underside of the fog. The truck surfaced from beneath the ground fog, the brilliant night sky sparkling above with stars while the mist swirled around the beams. She swore under her breath as she lost sight of the road. The lights illuminated the top of the fog but didn't show the road beneath. She was riding an explosive ship through the night on a shifting sea of mist. The dampness chilled her, making her shiver despite the heater blowing over the windshield. She reached over her head and pushed the play button of the tape player. A singing farmer by the name of Russ Gurr harangued her from the speakers, changing to a shriek whenever the truck hit a rough spot in the road. She punched the stop/eject button but the abuse went on. Within seconds she was slamming the tape player with one fist while driving with the other hand.

Her heartfelt cursing increased in volume when the machine refused to shut off. It was then she noticed the flashing lights in her side mirror. They were unmistakably those of a police car. She didn't know how long they had been there, but prepared to pullover, her curses grew more intense as the tape continued its shrill vocalizations.

"Well Miss D'Amico, what a pleasant surprise," said the whiny voice from below her driver's side window.

She squinted into the beam of his flashlight and with gritted teeth said, "Constable Pusch, you're all I need tonight." She was tempted to suddenly open the driver's door and knock him off the running board.

"All alone with your particular needs tonight are we?" said the voice from beside beam as it wavered past her head toward the jump seat.

"Wish it were so."

"Get out of the wrong side of the bed again?" purred the voice with a hint of hostility. "Mind if I take a look at your cargo? I've always been curious about what you carry back there."

"The trailer's sealed. You'll have to sign a form and write down the seal number." She reached for a form and carbon paper supplied by the company in accordance with the Explosives Act of Canada while Russ Gurr sang a romantic ballad about a tractor. The effect on his nasal passages must have been painful.

As Constable Pusch made his way to the back of the trailer, D'Amico reached behind the seat and extracted a Polaroid camera used to document damaged goods prior to offloading of general freight. Every truck had one and had been useful in settling insurance claims quickly. As she walked along the length of the trailer she could hear the RCMP officer using a tire iron to remove the soft strip of numbered metal which had been threaded through the eyelets for the locking system.
"Now if you don't mind unlocking it my dear, I'll just take a quick peek and be on my way." His hand extended into the beam of the taillight, which painted it blood-red.

She stepped forward and unlocked the heavy padlock, removing it from the hasp and opening the latch to swing one of the doors open.

He gingerly pulled himself into the rear of the trailer and with his flashlight, surveyed the stacked pallets of brown boxes and clear plastic bags of yellow Amex. There was barely enough room for his size fourteen shoes on the end of the trailer. With one hand he shoved open the remaining door to expose more pallets, some with large sections of cardboard between them. He hummed a little tune as he flashed the light around the interior.

"Smile," said D'Amico from behind and below him. He turned and at that instant she took his picture with the Polaroid. It whirred and slid the undeveloped print from a slot, and before he could recover she took another one.

He aimed a brittle smile back at her, his huge moustache twitching with surprise like some caterpillar which had been awakened from a deep sleep. "Taken up photography as a hobby have we Miss D'Amico? Hope you got my good side, otherwise I won't autograph it with my name and phone number for you."

"Oh you can sign it if you like constable," she said demurely, stuffing the prints into a shirt pocket. "It isn't for me, but the people who write the explosives act might be interested in seeing you in a trailer of explosives with your pistol still on."

His hand went reflexively to the sidearm and she snapped another one along with a look of near panic on his face. He climbed down much faster than he had gone up.

"I don't suppose you can be persuaded to hand those pictures over to me eh?" he said moving closer to her so he could smell the aroma of her bath soap. Involuntarily he began to get an erection as he stood close to her. He subtly used one hand to shove the errant erection to one side of his uniform pants.

She shot the next picture from the waist as his hand rested on his crotch. She jumped back, crowing, "That one's a keeper."

Pusch spun on his heels and stalked authoritavely back to the cruiser with its still-flashing lights. "By the way," he shouted from his window, "Your taste in music stinks."

She hooted with laughter as the cruiser raised clouds of dust and gravel in an ignominious retreat. As she climbed into the cab to get a new seal for the rear doors, she admired her photography and the dumb expression on the face of the RCMP officer. The upright sections of cardboard caught her eye and she decided to take a closer look before locking back up. Her mood of joviality quickly disappeared when she saw six large steel bottles of oxygen and acetylene within the cardboard bulkhead, between the pallets of explosives. It was a load which could have had her thrown in jail and could still turn her into tiny little pieces of flesh and bone borne on the winds of an explosion. Back in the cab, checking the manifest she saw the note from Winky, taped to the main sheet it explained the destination of the bottles. they were to go to the control gate project. To have included them on the manifest would have incriminated Winky, so this way the only one put at risk was D'Amico. With a final swing of her fist she silenced the singing farmer and the tape player forever. It was fifteen minutes before she became aware of her skinned and bloodied knuckles.

Pilson and Rivest were glad to have finished the series of up-holes at their last site. The drill rig was loaded on a flatcar along with the timbers it had been anchored to, ready to be moved to another location. On another flatcar lay the thirty-foot lengths of drill rod, stacked twenty across and five layers high. On top of that were empty core boxes which contained the core samples each time the drill core was emptied of its contents. Their next location was to be the rock face where the highballers had been drilling and blasting. The seam of ore had tapered off. It was up to the exploration drilling team to find where the seam had gone.

The work was gruelling, needing the help of a Come-Along winch with its ratchet handle, one hooked end secured to a rock bolt in the ceiling. Its job was to lift the heavy drill head, still on its frame, off the flatcar so it could be swung into its new position, onto the timbers. Because the site for the drill was to the side of the track, it meant the drill would be slid sideways from the flatcar, using the Come-Along. The risky part would come when the drill cleared the flatcar and began to pendulum as it hung suspended by the thin cable from the overhead rock.

Frenchy made little grunting sounds as he pulled on the ratchet handle, tightening the cable to the drill.

Pilson had secured a safety rope to the side of the drill rig and tied it off to an airline on the other side of the track floor in hopes of limiting the swing of the rig.

"Partner, you tie d'at t'ing off like your life depend on it, h' okay?

He nodded his hat light in Frenchy's direction in response, then studied the knot used to tie the rope to the airline. He didn't know much about knots, but it resembled something he recalled learning while in the boy scout troop back in his home town of Kneejerk. He had hated being a Boy Scout, it was one of the many things forced on him by his father. His thick eyeglasses had made him the immediate target of the others. He had been nicknamed 'owl' by the rest of the troop and when he came to each meeting, owl calls of 'hoo,hoo' would go up. Because he hated being a boy scout, his hatred of knots included the one he had just tied.

Each time Frenchy pulled on the handle of the Come-Along, his grunts got louder. The cable from the ceiling to the lifting eyelet welded to the drill head became taut. The drill rig started to shift slowly as its bulk lifted from the flatcar.

"Stand back partner, dis t'ing is gonna come off pretty quick. You got h'it tied to somet'ing?" With one more pull on the handle the rig tilted and began to slide from the flatcar. The steel frame gouged a jagged path of wood shavings from its deck as it moved.

Pilson stepped back, his magnified eyes locked on the knot, his throat pulsated up and down like a tiny freight elevator.

As the drill slid toward Frenchy, the safety rope took up the slack as the ton of dead weight became suspended inches above the car. "Okay, give me some slack an' let h'it come to me," he called, stepping away from his position, out of line in which the rig would swing.

"Slack?" said Pilson with a high nervous voice, looking with dread at the knot being reefed ever tighter by the force of pull. "You want me to loosen it?" he said with incredulity in his quavering voice.

A low groaning sound was heard from the airline and they both realised the weight of the drill had pulled the airline from its mounts on the drift wall. The six inch airline had a visible bend where the rope was tied and a sharp hiss of escaping air under high pressure could be heard.

"H'untie de knot, let h'it swing or I 'ave to let h'it down 'ere." Frenchy began jump up and down in excitement; his arms flapped at his sides in frustration at his partner, who still eyed the knot with trepidation. A mounting bolt holding the airline to the rock pulled loose with the sound of bone being crushed, allowing the drill rig to start sway. This caused more force on the line with each pendulum motion of the weight, causing the airline to bend more. The hiss of air increased from the damaged air line. The compressed cold air caressed their cheeks like a breath from the grave.

Pilson saw that anymore swinging would pull the line entirely from the side of the drift and crack the airline open. He knew the high pressure air could at least deafen them if not knock them off their feet. From the flatcar he retrieved the hatchet and began hacking at the hated knot. The blade missed with each second swing and created a shower of sparks from the pipe.

Frenchy stared in horror as his partner swung maniacally at the knot with the hatchet. He tried to yell at him to stop but the rush of air had become a roar and drowned out his voice. As though in slow motion he saw the line begin to unravel as the drill rig made a last swing toward the the side of the drift. For several seconds the massive drill hung from the single rock bolt as the Come-Along swung ponderously back and forth. Before he could move in to release the tension, the rock bolt tore from the ceiling, crashing the drill onto its side on the track floor where it blocked the path of their red locomotive. The roar of the escaping air made conversation impossible. Frenchy waved his hat light down the track toward the lift station, and Pilson acknowledged the signal and began to walk dejectedly in that direction.

Ten minutes later, their ears still ringing from the compressed air, Pilson turned to Frenchy and said, "Jeez I hated the Boy Scouts."

"Why you say d'at partner?"

"I never learned how to tie knots...I hate knots. And what kinda Boy Scout can't tie knots?" Frenchy surprised himself by putting his arm around Pilson's boney shoulder in commiseration. "You got no problem tying 'em, de h'untying need a little work tho'. I tell you what, you tell Wild Bill why we got no h'air to drill, an' if you still alive later, I buy you a beer after work."

In reply, Pilson reached down and pulled his partner's head onto his shoulder and they walked side by side along the rails like hard-hatted lovers. Frenchy's mouth opened in surprise and considered pulling away, but Pilson's grasp was like iron.

"You okay partner?" He wondered how he had gotten himself into this position.

"I am now."

There was a note of confidence Frenchy had never heard before. He wasn't sure, but he thought Pilson might have kissed him on the top of the hard hat. He really hoped not and gave a sigh of exasperation which Pilson interpreted as a sign of contentment. From a level above them, they could hear the snap and rumble of blasting, like a subterranean thunderstorm. Like two mis-matched and greasy lovers embraced in a one-sided affair, they strolled, one innocently elated, the other profoundly confused, listening to the underground storm raging in the distance.

Big Don and Toothless Jake quietly watched the inspector go through their records. He had asked for the documentation of their production of Amex for the last six months. There had been discrepancies between the amounts of explosives delivered to the mine and the amount recorded as being used for blasting. All parties involved had been shocked to learn that nearly five hundred pounds of Amex couldn't be accounted for.

The inspector, a bespectacled little man with thinning, sandy hair and with the annoying habit of sniffing noisily after speaking, had grilled the two explosives employees in a cold humourless voice. His small, cold, blue eyes intimidated them, and neither would have been surprised to hear him speak in an exaggerated German accent, like a movie version of the Gestapo. Instead, he had the soft, humourless voice of a doctor, saying "hmmmm" a lot and scribbled notes into a small black note pad.

"Do you gentlemen have any idea what could have become of such a large amount of material?"

The two employees looked first at the inspector, then at each other and shrugged. "Muffed be fumbody fmuggling it fwum the mine," replied Toothless Jake. Big Don, towering over both of them, peered down and, nodded benignly like a friendly giant.

The inspector flicked through some pages of their records without reading the figures. "The mine records match yours, so that's the only possibility I can see too gentlemen. Unfortunately with the security set-up there, someone could push a wheel-barrow of the stuff through the gate and not be stopped. So far it's only Amex missing, if things like primers or caps and fuse were unaccounted for it would be more cause for worry."

Big Don looked at his watch, hoping the inspector would realize quitting time had been fifteen minutes ago. He was relieved to see the inspector look at his own watch and begin stuffing his note pads and pens away into the inside pockets of his suit.

The little man gave a curt nod and walked out the door without speaking.

"Looks like school's out an' the kids can go for a beer," rumbled Big Don, smiling down at his toothless partner who was showed his gums gleefully back at him.

"That little prick oughta take the pickle out of hif bum," said Toothless as he turned out the lights in the Atco trailer that served as their office. He reached to the peak of his cap and turned it sideways to the 'off-duty' position. Thus prepared, they retired to the Stagger-Inn for their pre-meal libation.

The warm late spring weather had increased traffic to the Inn, to the point where extra chairs had been crammed around the tables in probable contravention of the liquor laws. The front door had been propped open to allow the clouds of cigarette smoke out and a modicum of fresh air in. The smell of the smoke and beer emanating from the premises offended the occasional abstainer walking past on the sidewalk, as did the raucous shouting and full volume wailing of country music. Men in work boots, plaid shirts with vests and baseball caps took their leisure, downing beer and liquor as though prohibition was coming next week.

Dorothy, the buxom waitress, wordlessly plunked down four glasses of draft beer at their table. They knew that if prompt service was required, uncomplicated drinks were the quickest.

"Holy fit! Dorofy, who'f the new waitreff?" asked Jake as he watched a slim blonde girl weaving her way between the tables, carrying a huge tray of drinks. She moved like a ballet dancer away from the occasional groping hand, still able to deliver the drinks and pick up her tips.

"That's Natasha, just started last week," she said over her shoulder, as she deposited a tip into the front of her bra. "She's a hell of a worker and a real good kid too."

Big Don's mouth hung open, his eyes glazed over as he watched the blondes girl's lithe form pirouette between the tables. "Kin ya send her with our next order Dorothy, she looks like a little flower in a cactus patch."

"My, aren't we getting poetic. What's the matter, you getting tired of staring at my boobs? Don't try nothin' stupid with her, cause she don't take no crap from nobody."

Jake had become so enamoured with the new waitress that he had turned his hat fully to the rear and was slurping loudly from his glass, the foam running down his chin, onto his shirtfront. His eyes followed her as though she was the only person in the room, unaware that nearly every other patron was watching with equal intensity. He turned to Big Don and said: "We need more good looking waitrffef in thith plaif."

Big Don smiled at his wizened partner, slumped in coveralls too large for his scrawny frame. "You're a married man. What do you think your wife would say if you came home drunk and with eyestrain to boot? This is the first place she'd come to see what you been lookin' at."

"Not enough good lookin' women in thith town," he muttered under his breath, still watching the new girl. "Natafa, Natafa, thath a nife name."

"Maybe you ought ta git yerself some new teeth before you introduce yerself to her, she might take umbrage with yer pronunciation."

"Wif my what? Fer Chrife fake, talk Englif. You been readin' thofe damn bookf again? Rot yer brain fer Chrife fake."

"Don't you worry about my brain my little toothless friend, you're the one who's married an' undressin' the waitress with yer squinty little eyes. Yer wife finds out, she'll be beatin' on your brain with a rollin' pin."

"Aw fit, that only happenf in the comic ftripf."

"You look like you stepped right of the comic strips. Look at ya, no teeth, hat on backwards, coveralls unzipped halfway to yer crotch with a ratty old T-shirt underneath. Ya don't bathe, yer drunk nearly every night. How does yer wife put up with it? Hell I think I been puttin' up with it longer than yer wife. Either you start bathin', or we're gittin' a dee-vorce little buddy".

Toothless Jake looked puzzled. He had never heard his friend criticize him in such a manner. He looked down his coveralls and pulled the zipper closer to the top and turned his hat back to the sideways drinking position. He could feel the beginnings of a tear in one eye and that surprised him. His wife had said the same things to him for years with no effect, but now his best friend was saying the same things and the effect was devastating.

Big Don had seen the effect his words had on his friend and began to feel terrible. "Cheer up little buddy, the next round's mine, and I'm gonna flag down Natasha."

Jake promptly turned his hat once again to the rear and regaled his friend with his hugest pink-gummed grin.

"You wave hand mebbe for beer?" said Natasha as she deposited four glasses of draft before them. "Three dollar fifty pliss."

Big Don looked intently at the petite waitress. He had no idea she was so small, but when she stood next to him, her head was barely above his, and he was still sitting. His mouth had fallen open again as he saw the bluest eyes he had ever seen. They were wide-set eyes atop a pert nose and wide mouth. She wore no makeup and there was a slight sheen of perspiration on her upper lip. He blinked twice, still unable to speak.

Natasha turned to Toothless Jake and said: "Iss too bad your big friend is deaf mute, iss kind of cute."

Big Don's mouth closed with an audible click, while Toothless flopped his own mouth open in surprise. "Aaah, Dorothy said you were new," he replied, finally finding his voice.

"Am still on warranty, low mileage, just need good mechanic to rotate tires on regular basis," she said with a wink.

Toothless missed his mouth entirely and poured his beer down the front of his coveralls. Big Don's mouth dropped open again.

"Dorothy tell me to say this, she think is real choke. I don' unnerstand, why you don't laugh? I am Natasha," she said, holding her hand out to be enfolded by Big Don's.

"You speak real nice Natasha. Where are you from?" replied big Don, his open mouth finally forming a smile.

"I am Czech," she replied, snapping to attention, the beer tray nearly tipping its contents to the floor.

In response, Big Don and Toothless Jake snapped to attention in their chairs, nearly capsizing the table. They expected her to start whistling the Czech national anthem and perhaps march around the room, waving the cloth she wiped tables with, as a flag.

"I escape across border, come here, democracy, no more communism, good capitalism...by the way, where is tip?"

Their hands dove for wallets and simultaneously they each thrust a five upon her. She quickly folded them and poked them down inside her bra. "I must get bigger bra like Dorothy, hold more tips."

"Herf holdf a lot more 'n that," countered Jake, eliciting a sharp laugh from Natasha as she strode away, giving a final wink to Big Don.

"I do believe I am smitten," he said quietly, almost to himself as he watched her compact form weave between the tables.

Toothless Jake sat back, smiling, observing his huge friend and the effect one small blonde woman could have on him. "I waf beginning to worry about you my friend. At leaft you're not like thofe two fitting in the corner."

Big Don followed the gaze of his partner to a darker corner of the bar where two men sat side by side, their backs to the wall. One was short with dark curly hair, the other tall, gangly, and with eyeglasses that magnified his eyes to fill the lenses to the edges of the frames. He squinted into the dark corner, and saw beneath the table of the two men. They were holding hands, the short one appearing distinctly uneasy, the tall one constantly smiling, his Adam's apple throbbing up and down to the rhythm of Patsy Cline on the Juke box singing about walkin' after midnight. The drinkers at the adjacent tables had either not seen or ignored the two men. He had noticed Dorothy serve them and walk away with a confused almost hurt expression. "I think this world is changin' a little too fast for me sometimes. I mean what would people say if they saw you and me holdin' hands?"

"Oh would you, you big ftud?" replied Jake, leaning forward smiling from ear to ear.

Big Don waved his comment away as though batting away a troublesome insect. He sat in thought for a few seconds then said: "Well what the hell, if it turns 'em on why not. Hell there aren't enough women up here anyway. Reminds me of the guy we heard about workin' underground who wears pantyhose all the time. Some guys in the change room made fun of him and he beat the crap out of 'em. Hell there's probably guys down there wearin' bra's too.

"Don't tell Dorofy, fe'll want to work there too," laughed Toothless Jake. Once again, he managed to miss his mouth with the beer.

CHAPTER 12

When Wild Bill Hendrickson heard the news that his crew had failed to get the drill rig up and running as well as pull the air line from its mounting on the drift wall, his face became the same colour as his crimson coveralls. When he heard that the drill had also tipped onto its side, his apoplexy grew exponentially. He became a frenzy of curses, charging around the confines of his equipment storage area, spittle flying from his mouth like foam from a rabid dog. He hurled every insult he had heard or imagined as he kicked the walls with his tiny steel-toed boots .

Pilson who stood on the other side of the counter was thankful for the barrier between them. His magnified eyes watched the rantings without blinking. The only sign he was even slightly intimidated was the movement of his Adam's apple, making its frequent trips to the upper and lower extremities of his throat. It seemed that each small convulsion of his throat only increased the wrath of his foreman.

"First you break the air line, put the rig on it's side, and...and, jeez what a couple of incompetents," screamed Wild Bill, tipping his hard hat to the back of his head, showing an expanse of reddening scalp from beneath his close-cropped, fair hair. He picked up a used diamond bit, turning it over in one small, pudgy hand. He eyed Pilson like a dog studying a postman's leg. "You and your partner be here first thing in the morning and we'll take the motor down with tools to fix that air line. Why are you waggin' your pimply head at me? "

Pilson's face had turned paper-white as he tried to speak in a high-pitched gargling voice. "Er...the motor boss, it's...er, stuck behind the drill, an' we can't, er...move it, y'know."

Wild Bill had pulled a chair to the other side of the counter and climbed onto it the way a child would, first one hand then a knee, then both knees, finally bringing him to near eye-level with the scrawny driller. "You sayin' the motor isn't there?"

Pilson nodded silently, his eyes growing impossibly large behind his lenses.

Wild Bill slowly climbed from the chair, across to the counter top, brushing aside grease-stained paperwork with a sweep of his arm. He was on all fours, his red face thrust forward, nearly touching the driller's, whose throat became a near-blur of motion.

"Where...is...my...red....motor?" Wild Bills' eyes were rimmed with red, a small stream of drool oozed from one side of his mouth.

Pilson wanted to take a step backward but was suddenly mesmerized by the foreman's maniacal eyes. Finally he said in a quavering voice: "Er, like I said...stuck behind the drill rig."

Wild Bill attempted to stand up on the counter, the drill bit held in his hand like a hand grenade..

Pilson retreated for the door. As he exited the door, the drill bit ricocheted off his hard hat, followed by squealing and crashing sounds from the equipment room like that of some wild animal caught in a leg-hold trap.

During his retreat back to the change room, he realized he was no longer quivering with fear in reaction to the display of violence. Instead, there was a cold sense of satisfaction. He surprised himself at feeling uncharacteristic pleasure in having provoked such a response. The change room was permeated with the stench of sweat and grease, mingled with that of soap and shampoo. He lowered his bucket connected to a light chain from the ceiling where his street clothes hung. He could hear laughter and running water from the communal shower. Naked except for wooden clogs on his oversized feet, he clip-clopped across the filthy floor, his hands full of containers of soap and shampoo toward the steam. Without his glasses, he squinted to find the showers and, appearing like some gulag inmate suffering from malnutrition, shuffled toward the sound. He could hear the metallic slam of locker doors echoing through the expanse of the building. Inside the shower room were two opposing walls with over a hundred shower heads. Most were occupied by a staggering variation of naked human forms, all soaping or shampooing their pink bodies, the grease running from them in rivulets to the drains in the centre of the room. Each body seemed to be bleeding rivulets of black blood. Without his glasses, the men were only pink forms in the steam. The forms traded jokes and lewd comments, their eyes shut from the soap-spray. Nearly everyone had a soap-on-a-rope around his neck. Experiencing the indignity of retrieving a dropped bar of soap amongst these men was to invite the lash of a wet cloth to the buttocks, or good natured jokes about advertising the wares. He never joined in the ribald discussions and laughter in the showers. To the other men, he suspected it was a macho way of dealing with being among so many other naked bodies of the same sex. To joke about something was to pretend it didn't exist, to not joke was to be held suspect by the others. He never joked about the subject and was glad for

194

the extra space he was afforded on either side of his shower stall. He would have been surprised at the feelings of inadequacy he elicited from the others in the shower, for Pilson was hung like a horse, a stark contrast from the emaciated appearance of his body. A chorus of laughter came from the far end of the shower stalls, followed by the unmistakable voice of his partner, Frenchy Rivest.

"H 'it my penis an' I wash h 'it as fast as I want."

He smiled as the laughter continued. Frenchy was a never-ending source of amusement with his ribald antics in the showers. He felt disappointed that he was always excluded from these on-going jokes. He simply didn't know how to reply to them, and with his extreme myopia, he didn't want to appear to be staring too hard at any one or any part of anyone. He couldn't see if anyone stared back, so he preferred to stare at the wall.

He felt he had been excluded from nearly everything in life except the early abuse from his father and uncle. His father had never failed to ridicule him in his efforts at sports, his gangly frame so uncoordinated in his attempts to run during track events at his high school. He resembled a scarecrow trying to escape the crows, his shirt flapping in the wind, pants barely suspended by a leather belt cinched so high up and tight on his tiny waist that it appeared to cut him in half. He ran with his chin thrust in front, teeth clenched as though bracing for a collision with some unseen barrier. No matter how he greased and combed his hair, it always grew at unusual tangents from his head in spiky clumps. Ungainly though he may have looked, the running gave him a sense of escape from the ridicule he faced from his father.

"Boy, you're homely as a hedge fence," his father used to say. He never called him by his name, but since his father was drunk most of the time it was easier to call him' boy'. His mother, a quiet, timid woman with muscular hands as large as his own would hug him from time to time out of sight of his father and whisper his given name, *Sampson*. It was as though his name was a secret between them, the thing that tied them together, a verbal umbilical cord, never broken, but sometimes strained to the limit by his father's verbal lances.

He knew his father's brother simply as 'uncle', his given name never divulged by either of his parents. He was a large heavy-set man with jowls like those of a bulldog, and smelled of tobacco and stale urine as though he had constantly peed his pants. His mother never smiled when 'uncle' was there, whether for a meal or a stay of several days. He always slept on the sofa in the dingy living room, snorting and snoring through the night, where young Sampson could hear him from his small bedroom. Occasionally he heard his uncle make his way heavily from the sofa up the creaking staircase to his room where the toilet was located. The indoor commode which shared one corner of his room was nothing more than a five gallon pale with a toilet lid on top, which was set inside a larger container. A small pipe from the outer shell, connected to the chimney from the wood stove in the kitchen below his room. In this way the foul stench of the shit can, sometimes referred to as the honey bucket was vented up the chimney and to the outside. Despite the venting, the stench from the commode in the corner of the bedroom was overpowering, and more so after use by 'uncle'.

The first time he had felt the man's hands along his body, he had been laying in his bed. It was Saturday morning and he thought he was dreaming. It was a half-awake dream with all the unpleasant smells he associated with his uncle and after the experience, felt as though the horrible odours had been smeared all over his body like a yellowish, oily film. No matter how hard he washed himself he never felt clean. Even more troubling was his involuntary reaction to the rough fondlings of his uncle. At the age of ten, he had never before experienced an erection, let alone an ejaculation, but in one stinking, sweaty shudder he smeared his own bodily juices onto his uncles hands as well as the sheets of the bed. His shame at seeing the leering smile on his uncle's unshaven face brought a cold knot to the pit of his stomach, forcing him to the toilet to retch into the horrible, brownish mass beneath him.

After that first experience and the subsequent frequent visits from 'uncle' he dreaded seeing his father and brother drinking together. Whenever possible he avoided being near the house so he wouldn't have to listen to the drunken laughter, some of which he knew was aimed at him. On the nights the partying went on until morning, he burrowed his way into the hay loft of a nearby barn on the outskirts of town. His was one of many dirty little secrets in the village of Kneejerk, never to see the light of public scrutiny, but one day to be manifested in the most horrific way.

Frenchy had been concerned for Pilson and his errand to Wild Bill concerning the mishap with the drill. He had been relieved and then amused at his partner's description of the diminutive foreman crawling onto the counter top so he could be nose to nose with him. He was also surprised at his poise while he told the story. The gyrations of his Adam's apple had slowed almost to the point where it resembled a normal swallow reflex. His eyes had a near serene quality, looking Frenchy full in the eye, whereas before, his partner was reluctant to meet anyone's gaze.

Now, sitting in the crowded bar, he was afraid to meet Pilson's eyes because ever since he had grabbed his hand under the table as they sat side by side in the bar, he had been unable to extricate it. His grip was like a vice, forcing him to drink without being able to wipe his chin with the other hand.

"You know partner, I h'am two-fisted drinker, 'ow I do dat wit you 'olding one of my 'and eh?"

"Don't want nobody to hurt you Frenchy. Don't want nobody to even look at you," said Pilson, his eyes fixed on the far wall. His own hand moved mechanically to his mouth with his beer, and every time Frenchy tried to remove his hand from his own, he applied more pressure.

"D'ose guy next to us, dey are lookin' at us real strange."

"Those guys are nothin' to worry about. They can't have you."

"I don't want 'em to 'ave me, my wife 'ave me. What she t'ink if she see me like dis?"

"You have a very understanding wife. Someone as good lookin' as her won't have trouble findin' another man." Pilson gazed coolly into his partner's troubled and slightly inebriated eyes. He noticed that when he applied pressure to Frenchy's hand, his partner's eyes began to cross.

"I don't want 'er to find anudder man, I h'am 'er man. Partner why are you doin' dis? Ow! Modzi, you make me see double when you do dat."

"Frenchy you're the only friend I ever had. You know that? I never even had a girlfriend all through school, and all the guys called me the beak. They weren't my friends, never even tried to be, especially that teacher, but I fixed him good." His eyes had grown cold and distant, his thin-lipped mouth was a horizontal slash. His eyes appeared even more magnified behind the thick eyeglasses, like limpid pools of ice water, devoid of feeling.

Frenchy shuddered and said: "What 'appen to de teacher?"

"Oh he's dead now," he replied in a near whisper, a small smile forming on his lips, eyes staring wistfully at the far wall. "Very dead."

A huge man sitting next to them was looking intently at their hands gripped in each other. Pilson turned slowly and stared at the giant who had hands the size of baseball gloves wrapped around a beer. He recognized him as one of the explosives crew. Pilson's gaze was unwavering, unblinking, like that of a reptile staring its prey in the face.

197

The huge man quickly downed his beer and left his table, the colour gone from his face.

"We're real good friends you and me. Right Frenchy? I mean, you wouldn't ever do anythin' to wrong me would you?"

Frenchy grimaced in pain as his partner clamped down even harder on his hand. He looked up at him over the rim of his glass as he slurped from the head of foam. A film of beer foam collected on his upper lip. He had to set his beer down to wipe the foam away with the sleeve of his shirt. Without considering the consequences he took the glass of beer and poured some onto Pilson's hand.

Pilson immediately loosened his grip to wipe away the beer and as he did so, Frenchy leapt from his seat and started for the door.

Pilson didn't attempt pursuit. He sat quietly with his back against the wall, his eyes locked on his large hands around the beer glass. He clenched his hands in silent frustration. The glass collapsed under his grip, slicing deeply into the palm of the right hand. There was surprisingly little blood from the four inch cut and the startled customers around him couldn't tell if he had been crying before or after the injury. In fact he couldn't even feel his hand. The pain from within overpowered that of his sliced hand, a pain he had endured all his life and for the first time thought he had found someone he could confide in, perhaps even one day understand him.

To the north, the huge hydro project continued to grow. When first begun, over 800,000 cubic metres of earth and rock had been excavated. The entire station was expected to consist of 544,000 tonnes of concrete and 20,000 tonnes of reinforcing steel. The ten propeller-type vertical shaft turbines had a rated capacity of 98,000 kilowatts, producing 980 megawatts.

Brady Bardman was thankful for the opportunity to photograph something other than the grip-and-grins at the Quesnel office. He had almost hugged his editor when he had handed him the assignment to shoot the site for a story the magazine was doing on the construction progress. His need to escape the pastel walls and florescent lighting of the plant office had peaked with the increase in tension between himself and the president. The four hour drive to the site had given him an opportunity to admire the natural beauty of the land and purge himself of the stress which had built up inside him. He knew this was going to be just another guided photo opportunity to help publicize the hydro project, but if he was being used in that way, he didn't care. There would be other media there. He was sure they would cut through some of the crap and get to the real issues.

There were five media people who had come up from the two Winnipeg newspapers. Their eyes collectively followed the pointing finger of their tour guide, one of the junior engineers who was obviously taking great pleasure in showing off the massive scale of the project.

"Yes sir, this station will provide low cost power to all of Manitoba, including the north, as well as some of the northern states in the U.S. Those propellers you see being lowered are called turbine runners. That's what the water turns, which operates the generators," said the engineer with his white hard hat perched on his head at a rakish angle. He smiled lengthily at he cameras, still pointing, and finally realized they weren't going to take his picture. He dropped his hand to his side, blushing slightly.

Bardman had the 24mm lens on the Olympus and was focussing on the workmen below. While its warning horn sounded, a huge overhead crane moved slowly along the gantries with the huge five bladed, 12.5 metre wide rotor suspended beneath it. He clicked off several frames, framing the rotor with the gantry, the remaining circular openings yawned below, still vacant of their rotors, like huge open, toothless mouths waiting for their high-tech meals.

The engineer continued to explain the fundamentals of power production to the media, his skinny bare arms protruding from his short-sleeved white shirt. The front pocket of his white shirt was strained by a supply of pens on clips and a pocket calculator which threatened to slide out with each wave of his arms.

"The rotor sits on top of the shaft, which is turned by the propeller below. The stator is around the outside of the rotor and it remains stationary, that's why they call it a stator." He smiled condescendingly to the reporters but had to stop suddenly and reach for his hard hat which was beginning to fall off, due to it's overly-rakish angle. He could see the other reporters and photographers were overwhelmed by the sheer scale of the project, their mouths open in wonder, necks swivelling to watch the huge machinery and ant-like humans moving with purpose.

"What is all this going to cost the taxpayer?" asked a young woman with short red hair and horn-rimmed glasses. She had been scribbling frantically in her notebook and was becoming flustered when she realized she couldn't read what she had previously written.

"The total cost will be over five-hundred million dollars, but a large amount of this will be covered by the government," said the young engineer, shooting his best smile at the attractive young reporter.

"Where do you think the government gets its money other than from the taxpayers?" replied the reporter.

The engineer's smile was quickly extinguished as he realized his faux pas, and began to blush again. Large sweat stains were developing under his armpits and he slowly flapped his arms up and down as though preparing to hover, to dry the fabric as he walked. He heard the click and whine of a motor-drive and realized he had been photographed by the stocky photographer.

Bardman smiled to himself as he saw the engineer look at him with a scowl. The guide looked flustered at having been photographed with his arms flapping. The rest of the entourage smiled at his obvious discomfort.

"What kind of environmental studies have been done prior to construction?" It was the young woman again, her voice taking on a whiny tone which served to further antagonize the engineer.

"Oh that was extensive, I mean there were hearings ongoing for several years with all the concerned groups. And, as you noticed in the public relations brief, this project is a 'run-of-river' design with the spillway adjacent to the powerhouse. In this way it takes advantage of the natural structure of the river banks as a forebay, so there's less impact on the environment."

"What's a forebay?"

"Oh, sorry, that's the reservoir where all the water is collected to produce power.

"What effect has this back-up of water had on the native populations who live along the river system and rely on fishing and trapping to make a living?" The young woman was now smiling her broadest smile at the sweating engineer who was beginning to feel he was wading with alligators in a shallow swamp.

"It's had a minor effect but we feel that once the water level stabilizes, the fishing and trapping will become even better at its higher level."

Bardman spoke, unable to restrain himself: "What consultant gave you that information?"

The engineer had his back to the railing, facing the reporters ringing him, beginning to wish he'd asked for a last cigarette and a blindfold.

The reporters scribbled furiously while others shot multiple frames of the guide with perspiration beginning to form on his forehead.

"Well, I'd have to consult the report to know specifically, but I'm sure it's in there." The young engineer began to curse the pointed questions. His boss had told him it would be a cakewalk, just show them the model in the Public Relations. room, give them the handouts, a tour, and later some coffee with doughnuts and they'd be happy as clams in mud. Now he was being quoted and he wasn't even sure if the quotes were true because he was simply mouthing what he had heard his superiors say.

A shrill scream and wet thud echoed faintly from the depths below their vantage point on the catwalk. The group of reporters moved to the railing to look where the engineer was staring, his mouth open in disbelief at the workers gathering around the perimeter of the opening for the rotor. The workmen were leaning carefully over the abyss, peering into the depths, one appeared to be sobbing, another on his hands and knees, vomited into the void where the man had fallen.

Bardman quickly installed the 300mm lens on the camera body and focused on the men as he heard the others gasp with the realization someone had fallen far to the bottom of the draft tube where the water would exit.

"No, not that, please have some common decency," said the engineer as he tried to cover the lens with his hand. He had heard Bardman take two quick shots before he turned to see who was using the camera. The other photographers were still gaping open-mouthed, unable to see who had fallen as they watched men hurriedly lower lines to the bottom. In the distance they could hear the sound of a siren.

"How many people have died on this project?" said the young woman, now with a hard edge to her voice.

The engineer looked at her without his customary smile, the muscles along his jaw line rippling with tension. His eyes no longer held any friendliness toward his charges. "I don't have those statistics at this moment, but let me assure you this project has set safety records for something of this scale. You have to realize that the work these men do is inherently dangerous, but accidents happen... usually due to human error." He looked back over the railing as a first-aid team was lowered using the huge crane into the opening along with a wooden backboard and scoop stretcher. None of the four man team seemed in a hurry as they descended. They probably knew it was too late to be of any help other than the unpleasant business of scooping up the remains.

The amiable atmosphere surrounding the media tour was gone as the engineer led them away, the eyes of the media casting furtive glances down from the catwalk to the dark opening.

"You get any shots of what happened down there?" The young woman reporter was walking next to him, speaking in a whisper so the others wouldn't hear, especially their tour guide. "I don't recognize you. Are with one of the papers here?"

"The answer is yes, no, and maybe," replied Bardman.

"I only asked two questions, why did I get three answers?"

"Because you want some shots for your paper don't you? How come your paper didn't send a shooter up with you, cutting corners on the budget?"

"They gave me this and said to come back with something interesting." She held up a small point and shoot Canon 35mm camera in one hand. "You know, budget constraints and all that crap. I saw you shooting with the long lens and figured you were getting some good stuff. So what are you shooting, colour or black and white?"

"Colour negative, but with all the sodium vapour lighting, there's going to be a lot of yellow cast in the shots."

"Does this mean you'll sell the paper some shots? This is front page stuff and I'm sure we could offer top dollar for one-time use."

"I'm shooting for Quesnel Minerals and it could also get me fired for flogging stuff to you while shooting for someone else."

They were nearing a section of stairs, their feet echoing metallically on the sections of ridged steel. As they started down in file she held him back with one hand on his shoulder to allow the others to get out of earshot.

"There are things going on here that the public have right to know and photographs are part of it. If you're afraid of a conflict with your work, we can run the shots without any credit and pay you under the table. No one has to know and it might even open up the chance of more freelance work."

He admired her tenacity as well as her perfume as she stood one step above, looking down at him. The rest of the group had reached a landing below them, their steps and voices diminishing. "Give me your card and I'll send a couple of prints by courier tomorrow. They'll have to be from negatives that I remove from our files entirely." He also gave her his home address and phone number without revealing he had once worked for their competition and had been subsequently fired.

A shout from the hard-hatted engineer hurried them down the stairs to where he met them with a suspicious glance. The rest of the group smiled in a conspiratorial manner, guessing that they were either arranging a liaison of a personal or professional nature. He knew there was honour among thieves but very little among competing journalists especially when there was a potential story for the front page. The young woman, Samantha, "call me Sammy" Paige had filed his address away in her purse while he still clutched her card in his hand.

It was this hand the engineer was looking at, having guessed the intent of the photographer and reporter before him.

"Miss Paige, mister Bardman, could I impress upon you the importance of accurate reporting of what you saw here today? I realize there was a mishap today but we don't know how serious it was so we would appreciate restraint until more information is available."

"Will you be making a public announcement tomorrow?" asked Sammy Paige, her hands stuck into the front pockets of her tight blue jeans.

"Only after we find out if there's a need to notify next of kin."

"I think there's a good chance that will be necessary. Don't you? Or are you simply trying to suppress negative press?"

The engineer, his face reddening, stepped closer to peer down at her but to his disappointment she held her ground. She matched his stare from below, and studied the rampant growth of hair in his nostrils, then gave a little giggle and leaned forward for a closer look, enjoying his look of consternation.

"Do you view these circumstances as funny miss Paige? Would you care to let the rest of the group in on your private little joke?"

She read his shirt name badge as though for the first time and said: "Boogers mister Wade, your nose is full of boogers."

Wade turned abruptly, failing to hear the quiet clicks of Bardman's camera recording his reaction. "This tour is over *right now*. Please follow me to the security shack where you will turn in your guest passes and hard hats. If you have any other questions please contact the public relations department at head office." He pointed them toward a window set in a wall near the main entrance and turned on his heels, flapping his arms to dry his chronically dampened armpits.

As they walked from the main gate to the parking lot, Paige caught up with Bardman on the hot asphalt. "Any chance of getting a print of that jerk's reaction in there? I could really use a copy for my personal scrapbook" She had opened the driver's door of her rental car to allow a hot gust of air to escape from the dusty interior. She turned to him with an embarrassed grin and said: "I don't want to sound forward but, would you mind following me back to the airport? This car has been acting wonky all day and I don't want to miss my plane back to Winnipeg if it breaks down. Besides, driving alone on these isolated roads makes me a little nervous."

An ambulance passed them, heading out of the construction site for the hospital, three hours to the south. It was in no hurry with its passenger and Bardman surmised the news for the next of kin would not be good.

"Why don't we just follow him?" he said pointing to the receding ambulance. "He doesn't seem to be in any hurry."

She fell into the driver's seat with a thump that raised a cloud of dust into the baking interior. She put both hands on the steering wheel and leaned her head forward onto her hands. "You know, sometimes I hate this job," she said, staring blankly at her feet.

Bardman nodded and thumped the roof of her car, leaving a small dent in the thin metal as a sign of agreement. He sought out his rusty Volkswagen in another part of the parking lot, his shoes beginning to sink into the hot, black asphalt. He wondered how much the man who had just died, had enjoyed his work.

On the return trip along the crushed rock highway, semi-trailer loads of hydro equipment came from the south, laden with huge transformers, sometimes room for only one per truck. Huge steel girders coloured with red lead paint to guard against corrosion, and the unceasing parade of explosives trucks rumbled past them, raising endless clouds of yellow dust. Because they were following the leisurely-driven ambulance, bearing the dead worker, the returning tractor-trailers dead-heading for home, overtook them and frequently gave an impatient blast on the air horn. He thought about the dead man in the vehicle ahead of them. There would probably be an inquiry which would eventually become buried along with the statistics of others who had died on the site. He was glad he had gotten a shot of the sanctimonious engineer being given a nasal inspection by the young woman reporter. He admired her poise while the guide tried to intimidated her. He had worked with other women reporters on assignment, some with those same qualities, some without. Those without never lasted long in the cynical environment of the newspaper world. A story was just a story and consequences of the reporting were sometimes not considered as long as it increased readership and advertising revenue. He realized he was glad he wasn't back in the newspaper work although the boot-licking he had to endure in his present job was small consolation.

The weekend was two days away and he looked forward to getting back out in the kayak with his camera. Teresa had expressed an interest in seeing his favourite estuary where he had met the old native man, and that thought alone cleared his head.

Nearly four hours later, the sun slowly sank into the western horizon like a large orange ball pasted on a curtain of brown dust hanging in the air. He saw a large brilliant star in the velvet blue sky, just above the dust. The light swung his direction and approach rapidly, its intensity making him squint. He stared at the light as it grew larger. The roar quickly grew to a crescendo and died away as the Boeing 737 from Winnipeg turned above him, on it's final approach to the airport.

The smell of the spruce and birch smoke was strong in Joe Mckay's nose and made him sneeze a couple of times. He could feel the hot rocks somewhere near his feet and sense the presence of his father along with old Angus Spence on the other side. He could hear their slow breathing within the sweat lodge, occasionally clearing their throats and spitting onto the tinkling rocks, resulted in short hissing explosions. They were only three in an area that could hold a dozen, the result of a request passed along by Angus to the band council for no others to be present other than Joe's father and himself.   The dry heat made Joe's naked skin itch as the pores opened and the sweat ran in rivulets down his ribs and spine. He thought his eyes would adapt to the low light but after nearly a half hour only tiny cracks of light showed through the walls of the structure. He could barely perceive two darker areas in the lodge, the forms of his father and Angus Spence where they sat cross-legged, their backs straight, eyes closed and minds opened with the clarity of the early morning air. The three of them were positioned as three points of an equilateral triangle, but in a spiritual sense they formed a circle, that structure whether physical or ethereal represented quiet power, having no beginning or ending. Someone coughed across from him, then began a soft humming which deepened to come from the chest rather than the throat. In the darkness, the deep humming sounded like approaching thunder, muttering, as he had heard it as a boy at the school on those hot summer nights when the darkness outside held its damp breath as the roiling, flickering clouds approached, their throats rumbling.

He remembered how the leaves of tall elm trees whispered together in anticipation of the coming rain, and the cooler air felt like a cold glass of water held against a heat-fevered forehead. The trees outside the residential school would bend and roar in the increasing wind, the flashes of harsh lightning painting the shadows of the window screens in a maddening matrix against the opposite, chipped plaster wall of the dormitory. A cold gust billowed the white cotton drapes over his bed like the cloak of a ghostly visitor, lit by the flashes. The air made him shiver and pull his blanket up to his chin. The coarse wool made his skin itch. He smelled bacon fat.

A sudden flash and crack of the nearby lightning painted Albert's form at the foot of his bed. He pulled the covers over his head, willing the apparition away, feigning sleep. A light tapping on his foot made his toes curl and he clenched his blanket in his fists as if it could have been his mother's skirt, but she wasn't there. She had never been there, and now the worst of his nightmares had arrived. You knew your time would come. *Why didn't the others warn you? Maybe they did with their nervous giggles and fear in their eyes as they avoided your own. Maybe the lightning will hit him. Maybe if I just kick him in the balls.* The thought made him giggle under the covers and Albert, encouraged by it moved to the side of the bed and took his hand. It had a greasy texture and the smell of bacon fat made him sick to his stomach. As if in a dream, Joe arose from the bed and naked, walked with Albert. The hardwood floors creaked slightly under their weight as they went to the basement where Albert's small room and cot kept reluctant company with the huge coal furnace.

The furnace stood idle, a squat, sooty behemoth, its metal duct work like the huge arms of an octopus, reaching out to each corner of the building. It was dark and stifling in the confines of the basement room. The sharp odour of coal dust was everywhere. It tasted like fear in Joe's mouth. The sharp buzz of a nighthawk could be heard from an open window. It swooped through the sky in search of insect prey. As they approached the lower landing and the complete darkness of the basement, Joe held back, straining against Albert's greasy grip.

"You make one sound and you'll never come out of here alive," hissed Albert, gripping tighter to Joe's hand.

Joe made a low moaning from his throat and Albert clamped his hand over his mouth, propelling him toward the dark opening. The rain began to pound on the walls of the school and Joe could taste the bacon fat from Albert's sweaty palm over his own mouth. He was pushed backward onto a cot that creaked noisily, the hand still over his mouth, then rolled over onto his stomach, his buttocks in the air. He could hear Albert opening a jar and a stronger stench of bacon fat as the employee lubricated himself with the leftover matter from the frying pans. The pain was intense but Albert's hand over his mouth as he was entered from behind, allowing only muffled gasps from his nostrils. He had no idea how long it had gone on because he forced his mind into some deep recess where all he was aware of was the roaring of water like that of a waterfall or a thunderstorm on a hot summer night.

He could taste the tears as they rolled down his cheeks to his lips, his sobs coming in soft gasps, his body shivering despite the heat.

"The healing has begun," said the soft voice of Angus Spence as he threw open the flap of the sweat lodge. A brilliant shaft of light swept the interior. Joe could see his father sitting quietly across from him, smiling sadly, tears in his eyes.

"I don't blame you," he said, seeing his father's tears. "You did what you had to and it wasn't your fault. You will always be my father and I will always be your son."

Abe McKay bent his head and wept quietly, but they were tears of joy which were soon joined by those of his son, who for the first time in his life, felt clean as though emerging from a deep quiet pool of cleansing water.

Bardman was bent over the light table peering through a viewing loupe, studying the colour negatives he had shot at the hydro project. He had shot six rolls of the interior and exterior of the site and was at that moment studying one frame of the opening into which the worker had fallen. One worker was obviously yelling or screaming something, anguish visible on his face. Another man beside him appeared dumbfounded, also looking into the hole where the turbine was to be installed. On the interior ledges where the huge stator was to be mounted, huge bolts protruded from the reinforced concrete. It was there where the worker had been occupied, and as he studied the image he realized there was nowhere for a worker to tie onto with a safety line. He whistled quietly to himself in dismay. He knew that if these shots were seen by the officers of Workplace Health and Safety, there would be hell to pay as well as a possible law suit. With a small hole-punch, he marked several negatives for printing so he could find them in the dark, and inserted a strip into the Durst colour enlarger. He adjusted the size and focus of the image on the paper easel and prepared to make a test print. While doing this he was debating with himself whether he should send a print to the reporter. There were other photographers there and if his shot was published without credit, he knew it couldn't be traced back to him.

Two hours later when the prints were dry, he put an extra print in a brown envelope and addressed it to Sammy Paige at the newspaper in Winnipeg, along with his card and a note to remind her that his name was not to be used with the picture.

The phone rang as he finished up and he jumped nervously at the sound. He answered, and stood quietly, making grunting noises of affirmation and then hung up without saying goodbye. At the equipment shelf he checked the level of charge in the Quantum flash batteries, putting one on charge and selecting a couple of flashes and cords. He hummed to himself as he set another equipment bag aside, laying inside, a couple of empty colour print-paper boxes, each with a heavy, black plastic bag fitting neatly inside. On the outside of each box which held 250 sheets of paper were the words 'Light sensitive materials, open only in total darkness.'

A knock came on the door and Bardman shouted come in.

The door opened and the frizzy haircut of Zenon Mikeluk, Magazine Editor insinuated itself around the door frame. The rest of his features followed, his mouth pursed as though having sucked on a lemon. He stood there, a talking frizzy head between the door and the door jamb. His dainty pink fingers of one hand appeared around the edge of the door, the nails manicured to perfection. "Brady, I wanted to talk to you about tomorrow for those shots we need underground. Roger got on my case this morning, it seems there's some problem with explosives not being accounted for on some of the producing levels down there."

He looked up impatiently at Mikeluk who flinched slightly when he saw the expression in his eyes. "Why don't you come in? You look like a vacuum-cleaner salesman anticipating rejection. So what about these explosives gone missing? Why do you think I can help?"

Mikeluk slid inside like a burglar and leaned against the door. His hands were clasped in front of him, the fingers entwined and sweaty. "You're one person who nearly everyone down there has seen and won't question your reason for being there. We want you to keep your eyes open, watch for anything you think might be used to carry the stuff out without raising suspicion. An investigator has been going around talking to the security guards on the surface and the explosives employees at the plant where the Amex is made.

"How much is missing?"

"Nearly 500 pounds."

Bardman whistled to himself again. "That's a lot of powder. Why do you figure anybody would want all that?"

"That's not all that worries us, we need to know where it is. Somewhere in this town there is a bomb, that is if it's stored all together. Think of the negative P.R. for the company if it blew up." Mikeluk's chubby cheeks quivered as he shook his head in contemplation. His whole body seemed to vibrate with tension and his high voice was becoming higher.

" I'm sure the P.R. would be very negative. So what do you want me to take pictures of?"

"Anything that looks suspicious."

"When's the last time you were down there? *Everybody* looks suspicious if you watch them long enough. Shit, there are guys using detonating cord for shoelaces. Do you want me to go around taking pictures of their shoes? If I started doing that you might never see me alive again. I've seen piles of Amex spilled on the track floor where bags have broken open and good old Roger the dodger must be under suspicion too because the way I heard it he spilled a couple of hundred pounds of the stuff on his last joyride down there when he smacked into a powder car with Wild Bill's little red motor. All this stuff gets around on the grapevine, so why don't I go get a picture of Jenkins to add to the file of suspicious people?" He was getting red faced from waving his arms around, forcing Mikeluk into the corner of the equipment room.

"Speaking of pictures of the boss, he wasn't too happy with the latest grip-and-grin you shot of him. Said you made him look like a fool." He wedged himself further into the corner, anticipating Bardman's response. To his surprise, Bardman smiled benignly, saying nothing as he rummaged through his equipment in preparation for the next morning. "I didn't like it either and I'm the one who has to justify the use of certain shots in the magazine, perhaps you could shoot more than one frame of a presentation so I could have a little choice," retorted Mikeluk, his voice gaining in confidence as he switched to a subject where he felt he had more expertise than Bardman. He moved toward the light table where the unfiled negatives of the hydro project shoot lay and began to inspect them with the magnifying loupe. "These aren't bad, I see you've already clipped some for printing."

Bardman watched him with concern, wishing he had filed them before his nemisis could snoop around them and see the frames of the accident which he had no intention of filing with the others.

He straightened, making strands of his frizzed hair sway like ferns in a wind. He turned on his heel like a soldier on parade, his hands in his pockets, the confidence back in his face. He was after all, the pudgy photographer's superior and why the hell should he feel the least bit uncomfortable in his presence? "Contacts tomorrow. Okay? On my desk so I can go through these and make a choice for the story about the project."

"How can you do a story on the project if you weren't there?"

"Oh I have all the public relations releases they sent and I talked to the project engineer by phone yesterday. I think I have all I need." He puffed his small body up with self pride, his chubby cheeks blushed with pleasure as his hands worked furiously, deep in the pockets of his baggy slacks.

"Your boss assigned me to go underground tomorrow morning, so the contacts will have to wait, unless you want to contradict his orders."

The air went abruptly from Mikeluk's cheeks as the colour faded from his face. He spun on his heels again to peer with suspicion at the negative strips on the light table, rocking back and forth on his heels. His shoes squeaked like mice caught in a trap.

Bardman watched him with amusement, more than happy to let the wind out of his sails every time he began feeling superior.

"Well, just get them done when you come back up, but I need them on my desk by the end of tomorrow." He stalked from the room as though he had gastric distress and slammed the door behind him.

Bardman quickly moved to the light table and began cutting the negatives into strips of five to insert into the negative storage pages. He took care to remove all shots of the accident which were all in sequence, hoping Mikeluk wouldn't see the omission. If asked, he would say the film had been poorly loaded on the developer reels in that section and had been trimmed away before they were hung to dry. A thin excuse he admitted to himself, but it would have to do. He surveyed his equipment before turning out the lights. As he left the company administration building with the envelope containing the photo for Samantha Paige under his arm, he noticed a long line of men at the security gate going off shift.

The Security people, usually referred to as rent-a-cops were methodically going through everyone's lunch kits and personal bags. The word had gotten out about the missing explosives and no one, including the security people appeared happy about the subsequent measures. He drove quickly to the airport on the outskirts of town and managed to find a friend who was a ticket agent. The agent gave the envelope to the flight attendant who promised to call the newspaper on arrival and have the envelope picked up. With luck, the shot would make the late deadline, but he decided to call Paige, collect from the airport pay phone so the call wouldn't be recorded on his bill. He wanted to give her forewarning of the film's arrival.

While Bardman sat on his ratty sofa, reading the day's newspaper, with a cold beer clutched between his thighs, someone pounded on the door at the top of his landing. With a groan he raised himself from the sofa, spilling some beer on its horrible floral pattern. He clomped up the narrow stairwell, beer in hand and was met by Teresa, still in her coveralls, hands and face smeared with grease, a grim set to her mouth.

She glanced at his beer and said: "You got another of those to help me drown my sorrows?" She followed him down the dark stairwell, smelling the remains of his Kraft dinner. No matter how many recipes she showed him and how much he appreciated the results, he always cooked the same damn stuff, if cooking was the correct definition.

He tossed her a beer from the fridge. "Bad day?"

She sat at the table, her arms wrapped around the beer and looked at him over the top of the can, one eye closed as though sighting along a rifle barrel. "I had a run-in with Winky today about hauling dangerous loads. That fat little fart somehow managed to get bottles of propane along with oxygen, and acetylene onto my trailer of powder. Then to top it all off my trailer brakes failed on the return trip. Thank God the tractor brakes still worked because if I was loaded I might not be here now. I really blew up at him in the office; called him an obese little weasel with the morals of a rattlesnake. One of the secretaries had to go to the bathroom she was laughing so hard. I didn't make any friends today but I sure as hell know I made an enemy. If looks could kill, I'd be post-mortem material right now." She took a long swig from her beer and gave a small belch, and leaned back in a rickety kitchen chair with a sigh of relief. "So, how was your day?"

He told her about the accident but decided not to tell her about the picture sent to the newspaper. He talked instead about the measures being taken concerning the missing explosives. The more she listened, the more she calmed down. After finishing her beer she got up from the table and walked into the bathroom. She never ceased to surprise him, showing up on his doorstep, begging for a beer, still in her work clothes. Then, she walked into the shower as though she owned the place. He enjoyed her company, he just wasn't sure he wanted to sacrifice his privacy. How anyone managed to look sexy in greasy coveralls was beyond him, but she managed without effort.

The bathroom door opened. A whiff of steam and the aroma of shampoo came from within.

"Oh waiter, could I have another beer please?" crooned her voice as she extended one bare, wet arm around the door with the empty can in a freshly-scrubbed hand.

As he handed the hand another beer, her pink face peered impishly around the door, water dripping from her nose and his last clean bath towel wrapped around her. Damn, he thought, now I have to do another load of laundry. She handed him her car keys from the coveralls crumpled on the bathroom floor.

"Be a dear and get the bag from the back seat of my car with my spare clothes?" Her voice had a musical quality which had not been there while she had been talking about her woes at work.

It was amazing what her shower had done for the morale of them both. He whistled as he went to her car and noticed an object hanging from the interior rear-view mirror as he retrieved the bag. The object was a small leather pouch, adorned with a row of beads, suspended by a length of rawhide, similar to the one he had seen around the neck of the mysterious old man at the edge of the pond.

The bathroom door was open when he returned and he could hear Teresa's voice singing softly from his bedroom. He knocked softly and she opened the door a crack to allow her to receive the bag, and himself to glimpse surprisingly large breasts showing over the top of the towel she was gripping with one hand across her chest. He turned quickly, embarrassed that he had taken her by surprise.

"What's that leather bag hanging from your mirror? he called through the door. There was a sudden silence from the other side.

"Oh just something Joe gave me the other day after seeing his dad. His dad gave it to him to give to me. Guess it's some kind of good luck medicine. Supposed to keep it with me wherever I go to protect me from the evil spirits."

"What's in it?"

"I don't know, I never asked and thought it might be bad luck to peek."

"Do you really believe in that stuff?" Another long silence followed as he could hear her zipping up the fly on her jeans.

"I don't know what to believe anymore, but I thought it could do no harm. Besides, I didn't want to offend Joe by refusing it. You know I was brought up a Catholic and haven't been to church for years but it never seemed to do me any good, so..I see no harm in that little bag. At least I don't have to confess my sins to it. I'm just supposed to wear it..

The bedroom door opened and she appeared, dark curly hair freshly combed, skin pink from scrubbing, and even a small sheen of lip gloss on her wide sensuous mouth. Her dark eyes had a glint of humour in them as she assumed the pose of a high-fashion model in the doorway.

He wished at that instant he had his camera. It was the kind of image that spoke of the essence of this strange woman who could be a truck driver one instant and a model the next.

"You know, your bedroom is almost as interesting as your bathroom. The next time can I take a bath instead of a shower, I'd love to play with your bath-tubbies. That little panda bear looks really cute. What does it do?"

"It does the backstroke." replied Bardman with a little embarrassment that she was scrutinizing the most personal of his living quarters. He wished he had cleaned the dust-bunnies from under his bed and dresser drawer. Too late now. Can't make excuses for being a bachelor. Take me as I am and all that crap, he thought to himself.

She saw him blush and realized she had trod on his private domain, forgetting how protective she was of her own. "Don't worry about not having the place spotless, my place is a pig-stye by comparison. I just needed someone to talk to as badly as I needed that shower. You want me to go?" She stood before him in fresh blue jeans and T-shirt.

He didn't know how to react to her obvious need for his company. The fact that she seemed truly attracted to him was a surprise, for he had always considered himself low on the scale of 1 to 10 in which people were often measured in their attractiveness. He felt like a 2 being pursued by a 9 and his confusion was increasing.

She moved close to him, putting both hands on his shoulders. He automatically put his hands on her slim waist as her hips came in contact with his. For a moment they just looked at each other, standing in the middle of the kitchen, next to a sink full of dirty dishes. He glanced self-consciously at the stack of dishes and was kissed simultaneously, and quickly on the cheek.

"And I don't care how much you sweet talk me, I'm not going to do your dishes," she giggled and held him at arm's length, studying his face. "I've gotta go. I'm beginning to get confused."

She quickly gathered her dirty clothing, stuffed them into the bag and turned to face him. "I confess, I tried to sneak a peek in your closet because I know your birthday is coming up. I wanted to get you a shirt or something and wanted to check the size, but the door was locked tight. Maybe you got a skeleton in there or another woman?"

"Nothing like that," he said with a smile as he walked her up the flight of stairs from the basement apartment. "As a kid I used to have bad nightmares and they were sometimes about monsters coming out of the closet. I've kept the closet door locked ever since and won't even live in a place without closet doors." He smiled as he spoke but knew the explanation was a weak one. He hoped she would never learn the true nature of what lay behind the closet of clothing, stacked in more than forty boxes which had formerly held 250 sheets of photographic printing paper. With any luck, he felt tomorrow might be the last time he would have to carry any of the full boxes from the company premises, and hoped the security people would never ask to look inside one. He knew the warning about being opened only in total darkness might not carry any weight with a determined searcher and the consequences for him personally would be devastating.

He woke with a start as his alarm clock emitted its electronic shriek. He felt as though he had not slept at all, the remnants of a dream about lightning and shattered beer bottles in a cemetery clung to the recesses of his mind like cob webs in a rat-infested attic. The dream had come again and with it, a bed drenched in his sweat. He staggered bleary-eyed to the bathroom to relieve himself and shave with a razor which badly needed a replacement blade. He knew he was late and would have to grab a quick coffee at the doughnut shop on the way. The phone rang as he locked his door and he decided not to answer it. Probably from work anyway, he thought to himself.

It took all his will power not to buy several doughnuts for breakfast at Hazel's Hangout, but was determined that his pants which had become looser around his waist should become more so. He had actually begun to lose weight, thanks to the benign influence of Teresa and her vegetarian recipes.

As he waited in line to order his coffee he noticed someone reading the early delivery of the Winnipeg newspaper. The front page carried his shot of the workers looking down in horror where their friend had fallen. As he looked closer at the picture, the horror became his own when he saw his name in the bottom right hand corner of the shot. The newspaper had credited him with the shot when he had specifically asked that they not. His mouth became dry as he stared at the shot, bending low to get a better look and didn't realize that the person reading the paper was looking at him over the top of the page. He looked up quickly into the cold eyes of Roger Jenkins, the company president and felt a cold lump develop in the pit of his stomach. All desire for the doughnuts disappeared.

"We're going to have to have a little talk later Mr. Bardman," said Jenkins very quietly from a mouth that was a horizontal slit. "About this picture on the front page, and your future with this company."

He got his coffee to take out and went quietly from the dingy coffee shop. It was the kind of grunge place he never expected to see his immaculate boss, unless Jenkins had planned on encountering him there.

Later, still shaken from the encounter with the company president, he collected his photography gear and made his way to the 800 foot level. He had found a note tacked to his door to get some pictures of an area where a diamond drill crew had succeeded in pulling a heavy airline from the drift wall and photos were needed to establish liability for repair costs to the exploration company. He remembered it was also an area where blasting had been conducted earlier at the rock face nearby and decided to take a look at the debris that was left. He hoped that with any luck he would find some useful items for his own little project which was taking shape in his mind. It was a project he had spoken to no one about and had not been completely formulated.

His locked closet was stacked high with the materials for which he was beginning to formulate a plan, but he wasn't sure why he had embarked on this course. He hadn't done it consciously. It had been like watching a dream of himself carrying the stuff secretively from the mine. He seemed to float above it all, not judging or questioning the motive, simply acting for the sake of the act.

He used one of the small yellow electric locomotives from the siding to travel the half mile to the diamond drill site. It had sat untended, the property of some foreman who might have been in the lunchroom at that instant. Bardman claimed it for his own. He really didn't give a damn who it belonged to. It would save him a long walk with all his gear. As he approached the drill site, he could see the movement of lights in the distance ahead of him. He slowed the engine, hearing voices of the men ahead. He could see a small red-suited man moving jerkily around a toppled diamond drill, waving his arms. Every third word seemed to be a curse, and the men following his barked commands were the same ones he had talked to on a previous level. All

215

the hat lights turned toward him as he brought the motor to a halt, its headlight still shining on the scene.

"What the fuck now?" said the small red-suited man standing like a tiny, western gunfighter at high noon, short legs spread apart, tiny hands on his hips. His eyes were tiny blue marbles rimmed with hangover pink. He spat what appeared to be tobacco juice onto the track floor. "What the hell you need pictures of this for?" spat Wild Bill as the two drillers watched him with suspicion.

"Orders from on high," replied Bardman as he slung his camera and prepared the flash heads for maximum light coverage. He saw the short driller with the French accent remove his hard hat and begin combing his hair in anticipation of having his picture taken. The tall, gangly one simply stared and grinned.

The work to raise the drill was suspended as he concentrated on getting shots of the ruptured and distorted airline. Working automatically, his thoughts were at the rock face a hundred yards down the drift. For the next half hour he moved from one angle to the next to document the damage done to the airline by the drill crew. Between barked orders and curses from the foreman, he could sense the little man's eyes on his back and occasionally, when their eyes met, he could see a genuine hostility.

Frenchy and Pilson were disappointed to see the photographer finish at their site and move off down the drift to the rock face. Neither one knew what was of interest at the end of the dark tunnel. They had been glad for another person to divert the wrath of the snarling little foreman who had come just short of physical violence with them. He was more upset with the fact that his personal red locomotive was stranded on the other side of the toppled drill rig than with the damage to the airline which had curtailed the drilling operation.

"Boss, I don' t'ink dis anchor gonna 'old," said Rivest, critically surveying the thin strand of cable hooked to the rock bolt in the ceiling and connected with the Come-Along to the lifting eyelet on the top of the drill rig.

"Don't argue, just do it. You guys are standing around with your thumbs up your asses instead of earning your pay. In fact I'm gonna dock you both a days pay for the time you're takin' here and I might even dock the cost of the air line repairs. You guys could end up workin' here free for the next six months. If you hadn't screwed up so bad we could be usin' the air-winch on the drill to lift it instead of this puny piece of crap."

Pilson and Rivest looked briefly at each other. Rivest rolled his eyes and mouthed a French obscenity under his breath. In silence and under the baleful glare of Wild Bill, they began tightening the tension on the thin cable between the drill and anchor point in the rock ceiling. Rivest stood next to the drill head which was nearly as tall as he, working the ratchet handle which shortened the cable and gradually began to lift the drill from the track floor. The base made a metallic grinding sound as it moved by fractions of an inch across the rails, the result of the drill head being lifted with each pull on the handle. "Better stand back partner, dis t'ing might shift real quick." His voice came in short gasps as he pulled with all his weight on the ratchet handle.

Pilson moved away from the rig, his eyes shifting quickly from the drill to the anchoring bolt and back to his diminutive partner who had sweat now running from his forehead into his eyes.

"Get the hell in there and help him," yelled Wild Bill, trying to shove Pilson from the rear, to where Frenchy was working feverishly.

"No, stay out, too dangerous," came Frenchy's gasp as he reached and pulled with both hands and all his weight on the shiny handle. The drill rig had raised to the point where it was supported on only one side of the base of the metal frame. It had to be raised high enough to roll a flatcar under the frame to take the weight. The clicking sequence of the Come-Along slowed as the tension grew on the cable and he found it necessary to climb part way onto the steel frame to reach the handle. Finally the whole rig swung clear of the track floor and swayed slowly back and forth as Pilson and wild Bill attempted to stop the pendulum motion using the weight of their bodies. The rig had to be raised another six inches before the flatcar could be moved underneath, and Frenchy groaned with the extra effort as he kneeled directly on top of the drill head.

Pilson ran for the flatcar a short way down the track and had his back turned when he heard the suspending cable snap and the drill crash back to the track floor and topple once more onto its side. A single shout came, either from Wild Bill or Frenchy, he never knew which, and then all the shouting was being done by Wild Bill as he danced like a lilliputian madman around the figure of Rivest, pinned beneath the heavy drill.

He ran back, his hat falling from his head and nearly tripped on his light cord. He stopped to retrieve it and ran forward again toward the foreman who was now standing and looking down at the reclining drill. His mouth fell open and his breath came in a moan of mixed horror and sorrow at the sight of his friend and partner, trapped and still under the ton of steel. He knelt down and shone his hat light on the upturned face of his partner. His stomach lurched when he saw that the control valve of the drill had impacted with Frenchy's head, shattering the skull, forcing the eyes from their sockets to dangle like grotesque hard-boiled eggs on the cheeks by their muscle tissue and optic nerve. Blood and grey matter had been forced out the mouth and nose to rest on the upper part of his crushed chest. Pilson, on both knees began to sob, unable to take his eyes from Frenchy, aware of the stench of feces, not knowing if it was from himself or his dead friend, and not caring. A pair of red coveralls came next to his face.

"Well don't sit there doin' nothin', git this fuckin' thing off of him," came the raspy voice of Wild Bill as he rapped with his gloved hand on the top of Pilson's hard hat.

His hand touched the short hatchet, used for cutting burlap, which had fallen from the tool kit attached to the side of the drill frame. He stood slowly, like a man in a dream and looked down with utter hatred into the eyes of the foreman who took a step backward against the drift wall. His eyes were huge behind the thick lenses of his glasses, almost protruding to the point that the eyeballs came in contact with the glasses themselves. His Adam's apple was no longer moving, but the neck muscles stood out like cords. His next step brought him to within striking distance of the foreman.

Bardman had been glad to leave the diamond drill crew to their labours, especially the small hyperactive foreman who watched him with such malevolence while he had shot pictures of the damaged air line. He noticed small orange granules on the track floor, evidence of spilled Amex explosives.

He had heard the story of Jenkins running into the explosives-laden flatcar and surmised that had been the reason for the small orange particles between the railroad ties. His light showed the jagged rock at the base of the rock face. The mechanical mucker called a scoop tram had removed most of the loose rock, and it had not been deemed necessary to muck out the rest by hand. It was along the sides of the drift where the highballers would have prepared their charges, tying the fuse into the network of detonating cord to which the blasting caps were attached. The blasting caps were inserted into pentomex primers which were then gently inserted into each drill hole which had previously been pumped full of the granular explosive. The stability of the Amex required a multiple stage detonation and tremendous concussion to detonate it.

He searched slowly along the track with his hat light held in one hand. His eyes caught the reflection a small, shiny tubular form under a rail. He bent down and gently retrieved it, putting it into a plastic film container stuffed with cotton batting. A few feet further on he found another which he also put into the container, being careful to keep them separated. The second blasting cap was of the electric type. He smiled to himself when he came across a two foot length of yellow detonating cord, looking like an innocent piece of electrical wire, coiled and hidden under a piece of loose rock.

Thank you highballers for being so damned careless, thought Bardman as he coiled the B-line and put it into a separate film container. As expected, there was nothing as large as a Pentomex primer laying around. It would have been criminally negligent to have left one unaccounted for, because it had the explosive power of a hand grenade. He continued to search the track floor and was in the process of photographing the spilled explosive on the track when he heard the crash from the direction of the diamond drill crew.

He began walking in the direction of the drill-site, his camera bouncing on his chest with the added weight of the flash. He could hear someone shouting and the convergence of two hat lights near the side of the drift. Suddenly one light sank to the edge of the drift, and he could see its beam shining on the ceiling. The other light was moving up and down quickly and he could hear a sound as if someone was chopping open a watermelon. As he neared the moving light, he saw the drill rig once more on its side and could barely make out the still form of a human being beneath it. The moving light stopped its motion and shone in his direction, holding on his face for several seconds. With an unearthly howl, the owner of the light rose to his feet and Bardman could see the face of the tall gangly driller with a hatchet dripping blood in his right hand. Without focussing or even raising the camera to his eye, he triggered the shutter and camera flash into the driller's eyes.

The bizarre and bloody figure of Pilson turned and continued to howl He ran to Bardman's yellow locomotive and disappeared with it down the track, the electric motor whining at full speed.

With a cold lump forming in his stomach, he moved closer to the drill. He saw the body of the small driller, his lifeless, disconnected eyes laying on his chest, connected by thin bloody strings of matter. Near him was an equally small body in red coveralls. The red extended in a dark pool around the body and, he realized the blood had come from the foreman's head which had been hacked vertically in two. A large, bloody wedge separating the man's still-open eyes, stopping at the bridge of his nose. Bardman's stomach lurched and he fell to his knees and became sick. Finally, he was able to stand and focused the camera on the still-shining hat lights of the dead men before him. He took several exposures from different angles of the gory scene.

As he walked the half mile to the main shaft, his knees felt watery and his stomach churned with a gurgling sound. He could hear the snap and rumble of blasting on a level above. He looked nervously behind him, his common sense telling him there was no one there but sensing the departed souls of those who had died so violently behind in the darkness. Somewhere in the mine, he knew, there was a madman, driven by hatred and grief.

Arriving at the main shaft, he saw no evidence of his stolen locomotive and knew it had been taken further into the older network of drifts and stopes. It was the area where miners followed the path of a seam of ore, using the jack-leg drills and explosives to carve away the rock to expose the high grade minerals. He picked up the emergency phone near the opening to the shaft and called the Day-shift Foreman's office where it was answered by a high, uncertain voice, like that of a school boy being queried on a dreaded question in class. He related what had happened and was told the cage was on its way down as soon as they could get together members of the mine rescue crew.

"You don't need mine rescue," shouted Bardman. "There's nothing here to rescue, they're both dead. What you do need is somebody to find a lunatic running around down here with a motor, waving a bloody hatchet."

"It's standard operating procedure," squeaked the voice from the other end. "It's not up to us to determine who's dead and who isn't. Just stay there and wait for the men to come to you."

He hung up the phone in disgust. What's the point in sticking around here, he thought, then realised the foreman had neglected to ask who had called him. Rather than wait for the cage to come down full of men asking questions, he moved to a red door with a sign which said MANWAY. He opened the door and started up the wooden ladder, his light showing him the way. After one hundred rungs, he came to a small landing from which the rungs continued to another small landing further up. He knew there was two hundred feet between producing levels and that another length of rungs would bring him up to the 600 foot level. As he watched his footing in the beam of his light, he noticed dark marks on the rungs in front of him. Bending closer to study them he realised they were drops of blood, which had also smeared his hands, and they were still fresh.

He must have left the motor further down the drift and doubled back this way. He could be anywhere in this mine and he knows I saw him, might even have a picture of him. He's probably too crazy to care who saw him but he might kill the first person he sees. Sure hope it isn't me. He heard a faint giggle from somewhere above him and the echo of footsteps growing more distant. He stopped and held his breath, watching the darkness above him. For an instant, a brighter light glimmered far above and disappeared, accompanied by the sound of a closing door. Slowly, he moved up, making as little sound as possible, watching around the corners for movement. The wooden manway vibrated as the cage dropped through the shaft nearby. *Probably the mine rescue team going for the bodies If that lunatic gets me in here, they might not find me for months.* As he came to the last landing, slivers of cold florescent light could be seen around the doorway to the 600 foot level. He approached it cautiously and tried the handle. The door swung open to reveal a deserted loading area of track floor, and a couple of small flatcars waiting on sidings. The hum of the large overhead tubes sounded like a hive of angry bees. One was flickering with an intensity that made him blink. He glanced at the thick cables from which the cage was suspended. He could see through the latticework of the upward sliding doors that they had begun to move quietly past each other. He couldn't tell if the cage was ascending or descending because he wasn't able to decipher the constant bell signals to the topman by the cage-tender. On the wall next to the shaft doors was a red box with a suspended chain and a wooden red handle attached. Next to it was a list of the codes for the various levels. He read on the sheet that six quick rings indicated he was on the 600 foot level, three rings indicated he wished to ascend. If he had wanted to go to the 200 foot level, there would be a pause after the first six and three rings, before adding two more. Since he wanted to ascend to the surface, he would add no further bell signals. To acknowledge, the topman would ring back the identical signals in a quick staccato which only the most practiced ears could read with ease.

"Why not just use the phone if you're goin' topside?" said a voice behind him.

Bardman swung violently around, causing the miner in the greasy yellow slicker to jump back suddenly.

"You look like you seen a ghost partner. I may be ugly but I'm a real decent guy inside, so no need to be so nervous." The miner had lit a cigarette and was studying him from behind water-spattered safety glasses. The miner eyed his boots. "You get nose bleeds too from goin' up and down here all day?"

He looked questioningly at the man, not understanding the question.

The miner pointed at hiss boots. "Blood. You get that blood on your boots from a nosebleed?"

He nodded, remembering the blood on the rungs of the manway. He realised he must have also been standing in a pool of it as he surveyed the horrible scene at the drill. Both he and the lunatic had left tracks on the rungs of the manway. When he looked up he realised the cage had stopped at their level and held several grim-faced men. He and the miner joined them silently and the cage-tender rapped out the signal for surface delivery.

"Worst damn mess I ever seen," said one burly miner to his boots.

Another nodded without speaking, shuffling his feet. "We should have brought them up."

"No way," said another."That was no accident an' I don't want no responsibility for movin' em until the cops say so."

The miner who had just spoken turned and looked at him for the first time. "You been to the eight hundred level with that camera of yours?" The man's eyes were accusatory as he watched Bardman at the back of the cage, then when he shook his head, he turned back to face the front in silence.

He had forgotten the camera and flash were still around his neck. As the cage approached the surface, he hurriedly rewound the film in the camera and inserted another roll. The exposed roll went into a pocket of his shirt as they came to a halt. While the others walked to the change house, he moved to a small water hose near the wall and quickly washed the blood from his boots and hands. On his way to the locker, he passed the office of the underground foreman and saw the company president waving his arms and speaking with feeling to a pink faced man whose jowls quivered in response. He hoped that with the discovery of the bodies, Jenkins would have forgotten about the picture on the front page of the newspaper. He was disappointed when he saw the note pinned to his door from Zenon to report to Jenkins' office as soon as he returned. In the equipment room he placed the two film containers with the blasting caps into his half empty thermos of tea and placed it back in his lunch kit.

As he entered Jenkins' office, the secretary picked up the phone to announce his arrival. She motioned him to the office door and nervously returned to whatever she was doing before her head down in concentration as though preparing for flying objects.

"Mr. Bardman, come in, sit down," said Jenkins, standing against the front of his desk as he motioned him to a chair facing him. Zenon sat in another to the side with the expression of someone who had just had a tooth pulled.

"We would like to hear from you personally how one of your shots appeared on the front page of that Winnipeg rag." Jenkins was leaning forward from the waist, his behind resting on the edge of his expansive desk. His legs were crossed and his hands worked busily at something in his pockets. His smile was as cold as his eyes and the beginning of a five o'clock shadow made him appear like a mafia hit man.

"It was a spur of the moment thing for a friend who's camera had jammed," lied Bardman, feeling Mikeluk's eyes boring into him from the side.

"And what's the name of this friend of yours?"

"If I reveal it, it might get him fired. Besides I saw no harm in them using the picture as long as they didn't use my name. I also asked for no payment because I knew it would be a conflict of interest." He was beginning to sweat in the warm office and wished he had changed his shirt before coming up.

"This just might get you both fired Mr. Bardman and as far as conflict is concerned, you have no idea what kind of crap is going to hit the fan with the hydro people when or if they find out it was one of my employees who took that picture. They happen to be the major supplier of power for our smelter operation and I don't think they would be a happy supplier and give us the preferred status we enjoy now if they find out." Jenkins leaned forward, his minty breath washed over Bardman's face along with the occasional fleck of spittle.

He sat, trying to look as repentant as possible while noticing with some surprise that Jenkins' black dress shoes were tied with green laces.

Jenkins continued. "We also have another serious problem. What level were you shooting on this morning and what was your assignment?

He turned to Mikeluk, then back to Jenkins. "Eight hundred level to survey the damage done to an air line by a drilling crew."

"And you did that? Describe what you saw there."

He described the damage to the airline and the men working but said nothing of hearing the accident and ensuing carnage. He couldn't understand why he didn't volunteer the other information other than a subtle sense of mistrust of the two people before him. This was not a friendly chat It was an interrogation and he wanted desperately to get up, walk out, and leave the oppressive atmosphere of the company forever. While listening subconsciously to Jenkins ramble on about his lack of positive attitude toward the job, he noticed the mans tie was also a mismatch. As were his socks for the grey pin-striped suit. The tie was rust coloured and his socks a sombre tartan. Perhaps he's colour-blind he thought. If so, then he's not physically fit to work for the very company of which he's president. Every employee, whether they work underground or not, go through a rigorous physical examination in the event that if for whatever reason they have to go into another work area, they at least meet the physical standards.

"So you're saying that when you left the drill-site, everything was alright?"

"Yeah, they were just working. Where is this going anyway?"

He leaned even further forward to emphasize his words. "Because two of them are dead, and another is missing. The Underground Foreman got a call from the rescue team to call the police to investigate. They're on the way and a medical examiner is catching a plane from Winnipeg as we speak. Did you take any pictures of the men at the work site at all?

"No, none, only of the damage caused to the air line and the area further down the drift where the blasting was taking place. I also got some shots of the track floor where some granular explosives were spilled due to an accident between a motor and the flatcar they were on."

Jenkins straightened up, his face blushing slightly, stealing a glance at Mikeluk who was now inspecting his pink fingernails for tiny flaws.

"The police will want to see the film you shot, so go develop it right now. Consider yourself on extended probation due to that newspaper picture. Mr. Bardman, your future here is in serious jeopardy and still under consideration. As long as the police need your observations about what happened down there, you will remain on the payroll. You are expressly forbidden to talk to any member of the press about this, and if we get calls from any media about this, your ass will be in a sling. Now get the hell out."

He was happy to oblige. He longed for the soothing darkness of the photo-lab, away from prying questions and insinuations. Thirty minutes later the film was hanging in the dryer. He removed it and placed the short strip on the light table. He used the magnifying loupe to inspect each frame closely, skimming over those of the track floor and the damaged air line. The image of the insane driller caught his breath. The wide angle lens had enabled him to capture a full length shot of him. Miraculously the frame was in focus. He could clearly see the bulging eyes behind the thick eyeglasses and the hand clutching the blood-spattered hatchet. On one edge of the frame he could see only a portion of the body of the driller trapped under the drill rig, but it was easily identifiable as a body. The next frame was of the two bodies. Without really rationalizing his actions, he clipped the frames from the strip and inserted them in a clear plastic holder for protection and slipped it into a section of his wallet between some business cards. He knew withholding the shots was against the law and obstructing an investigation, but it gave him a sense of security to know he was the only one in possession of it. Somehow, it was insurance but it was still unclear in what way. It was probably the most dramatic shot he had ever taken and might one day be worth a lot of money but he knew that publishing it would probably get him thrown in jail for withholding evidence. With these thoughts occupying him, he locked the darkroom door and went home with the two film containers safely concealed in the thermos.

As he walked down his basement apartment steps into the aromas of stale coffee, unwashed dishes, and piled dirty laundry, his phone rang.

"Brady, I'm really sorry, I told them not to use your name, but the dolts went ahead and did it anyway. I wouldn't blame you if you wanted to come here and shoot me. God I'm sorry. After my promises, I'm probably going to get you fired." Samantha's voice was hurried and speaking with a jerky cadence. She truly sounded repentant and waited a long few seconds for a reply. "Please Brady speak to me."

"I'm here, and yes I'm in it up to my armpits," he said quietly, no anger in his voice, but a sadness that was obvious to the reporter on the other end. "I'm also forbidden to talk to any media or they could throw me out of here lock, stock and tripod."

"What can I do to make up for this? I mean these jerk editors don't give a crap about the position they've put you in. All they cared about was getting the picture. Maybe I can negotiate a really good fee for the shot, at least you'd get something out of it."

"No, that's the only thing that didn't get me fired, was the fact I did it for no fee. I said I gave the shot to another photographer whose camera seized up on him." He was enjoying listening to her voice. She had calmed down and he could hear a musical quality in it. "There are other things going on here that I've been forbidden to talk about, but if a single phone call from any of the media reaches the administration here, then I'm history. I mean they'll punt me out of here with glee."

"What other things are you talking about?"

He rolled his eyes, regretting he had mentioned other developments. "I can't mention it right now, but if things change and somehow word gets out, just remember one thing that only you and not your editors should know."

"Am I going to have to beat you with a stick? Tell me, tell me," chortled Paige on the other end. "You can't say something like that to Winnipeg's best investigative reporter and then leave her dangling."

He took a slow deep breath and spoke quietly. "Whatever you might hear, I have a photograph of it and I've suppressed it. It could get me thrown in jail if it gets in the wrong hands, so I'm going to put it somewhere safe. It might never get published if it means keeping me out of jail. I don't think we should talk on our personal phones anymore. If we have to talk, we use pay phones and a pocketful of change. I'm going to send you a letter with instructions how to retrieve this shot if anything happens to me, so when you get it, keep it somewhere safe. I'll also include the numbers of some of the pay phones in the town and each will have a corresponding address beside it. If need be, we'll set up a calling schedule if things start to heat up here."

"You're starting to scare me Brady. This is all starting to sound cloak and dagger-ish. Maybe you should call the police."

"Not now. I'm just trying to build a little insurance for myself and this picture is all I have. We'll talk later, but wait until you get my letter."

"Is it something to do with the hydro project? Because if it is, you should know that I've been doing some digging around at the Department of Workplace Health and Safety. I asked them about the safety record of the hydro project and they refused to turn over details of accidents and fatalities since it started.

"No, it has nothing to do with that, but it might open the door to what is going on here without implicating me. Suppose you broaden your investigation to include Quesnel Minerals and see what you turn up? Then, if both companies as well as the workplace people won't tell you anything, you might have a reason to do a story on the fact the information is being withheld." There was silence on the other end for several seconds, then: "I don't know Brady. I did some digging through our own newspaper archives and found reports of three deaths at the project since it started over a year ago. The reports were attributed to the project's Public Relations Department, but when I called earlier, I met the same dead end."

"Listen closely Samantha. If you can run a story about a possible coverup of unsafe work conditions at the site, then you could legitimately question the safety standards of any other company you wish. So why not Quesnel? It could attract other media to what's happening here and they wouldn't be able to connect me with it." It sounded plausible to him as he spoke the words, but a tiny voice in his sub-conscience was beginning to push the panic button. Maybe this was a very stupid thing to do, the little voice said to him. "You know that shot you ran on the front page? Take a close look at it, you'll see there's no safety barrier around that opening where the worker fell. Anybody who works in an area like that should have had somewhere he could have hooked up a safety line to his belt."

"That's a great tip, I'll see where it gets me. In the meantime, send me the shot and I promise, promise that I'll keep it safe until I hear from you. I've gotta go now, my editor's waving at me and looks like he could kill. Take care Brady and send that stuff by courier, expressly to me. That way I know I'm the only one who can receive it."

For the next hour he drove to several areas of town where there were pay phones situated alone and out of earshot of bystanders. He wrote down the number of each and allotted each a number. If he needed to talk to her, he would call and when either she or her answering machine replied, he would simply say a number. She would consult the list he sent her and call back in one-half hour exactly, to the pay phone where he would be waiting. He was actually beginning to enjoy the cloak and dagger aspect of his efforts and wondered how he would look in a slouch hat and a Humphrey Bogart coat with a cigarette stuck in his mouth. He thought, probably pretty ridiculous.

When he got home, a police car was parked at the front of his apartment with a constable behind the wheel. As he parked behind the cruiser, the constable got out and walked back to his car. He recognized the outlandish moustache of Constable Pusch. The last time he had seen him was on the ski trail with Teresa. Without his skis, he appeared a lot more coordinated, actually seemed to have nearly all his faculties in working order.

"Well, Mr. Bardman I presume. May I see your driver's licence?"

227

"Why? You already know who I am. Why do you need to see my driver's licence?"

"Because it's all standard procedure. Would you step out of the car please? "Constable Pusch drew himself up to his full height by gripping his large belt with both hands and yanking upwards. His large moustache travelled about the space above his upper lip like a small rodent searching for prey.

"Am I under arrest?"

"Oh no, nothing like that, just a few questions if you don't mind."

"What if I do mind? Then am I under arrest?"

"No...no, I have no reason to arrest you, at least not yet. However you were placed at the scene of a murder and that gives us every right to consider you a suspect if not a witness." The rodent appeared to drag its' imaginary prey to the other side of his face where it twitched with anticipation. Pusch leaned forward and fixed him with his black close-set eyes from either side of his large nose. His nostrils were beginning to flair and the internal hairs were protruding like brown shrubbery

Bardman decided he would run, if it seemed the man was about to sneeze. "Well, okay, ask away."

The questioning was only preliminary and thankfully quite informal. He related to Constable Pusch the same lies he had told Roger Jenkins, all the while wishing the negatives of the incriminating photo weren't sitting in his wallet, right next to the driver's licence. He resolved to find a safe haven for them as quickly as possible. While he spoke, sitting in the passenger seat of the cruiser car,

Pusch wrote quickly in a notebook.

Bardman was surprised he was using Pitman shorthand with its' squiggles and swirls to indicate sounds. He had a ridiculous image of Pusch sitting on the sergeant's knee, taking dictation. He could feel the corners of his mouth beginning to curl in an uncontrollable grin.

"Is something humorous in all this?"

He quickly erased the image with a mental effort and saw Pusch leaning toward him again. He hated people who leaned. Jenkins had done it in his office and now Pusch. It was their way of intimidation. He leaned toward the cop who abruptly pulled away and cast a startled glance back at him, a blush beginning to show on his cheeks.

"I think that just about does it Mr. Bardman. It's a shame you couldn't give a physical description of the other driller other than he was tall. We know his name and where he lived, but when we got there, most of his personal belongings were gone, if in fact he had any at all. A really strange fellow all in all. It seems no one has a picture of him. The only other people who could identify him are dead. By the way, we're serving a search warrant to your company so we can peruse the negatives you've shot underground in hopes we can I.D. the other driller, so please don't leave town for the next few days because we'll need your help."

He walked from the cruiser to his apartment door with a cold lump in his gut. If the police saw the discrepancy in the numbering of the negatives, he would have to do some creative explaining why they were missing.

After a hurried dinner, he moved all the heavy, yellow Kodak paper boxes from his closet, loaded them in the rear of his Volkswagen and drove ten minutes out of town to an old road which led to the bank of the Black Wood River. There, amongst an onslaught of voracious mosquitoes, he dug a hole and buried the boxes, wrapped in plastic garbage bags. Along with them went one of the two blasting caps he had found. He kept the other one along with a couple of pounds of the granular explosive sealed in two aluminum film cans which normally held one-hundred feet of bulk film. He put a tiny scratch on the side of each can to tell it apart from the others that were stored in the refrigerator and, still contained film .

He stood and quietly watched the river from the bank. Sweat from the exertion trickled down his back as the mosquitoes buzzed around his face. The sky was clear and a partial moon was slowly rising in the east. Overhead, he could hear the buzzing call of a nighthawk as it dove after insects in the darkening sky. He loved the summer here because the days lasted so long and twilight fought to stay a few moments longer. There was no breeze and the surface of the river was smooth as glass. The pale peach colour of the horizon shaded to a dark blue above, reflecting from the water's surface. The guttural warble of a raven floated to him from the far bank of the river. He could barely see its outline against the failing light, sitting high in a dead spruce tree. For several moments the two watched each other. With a final squawk, the raven flew away. He went to the car, wishing he had brought his tent and sleeping bag. The last place he felt like being was his stifling apartment, ripe with the aromas of his unwashed laundry and dishes.

CHAPTER 13

Teresa sat slumped in the jump seat of the truck cab and watched the baleful glow of the dashboard lights as they illuminated Joe McKay's face. A song about heaven by the dashboard lights by Meatloaf cycled over and over through her mind as she regarded him through half-closed eyelids. She had been trying to sleep, but the constant jolting of the cab's hard suspension would not allow it. His face had changed subtly; the lines of worry had smoothed. When they spoke, his eyes seemed to see past her as though there was something in the distance capturing his attention. The harsh exchange they had both had with their boss, Winky Winkwell, had not removed that facade of serenity which she had never seen before. Her partner was an enigma. She never knew what he was thinking behind those quiet, intelligent eyes, but there had been times while she was driving that during a quick glance she could see pain in his expression. Once, she was sure she had seen tears at the corners of his eyes, just before he had dropped off to sleep.

"What are you thinking Joe? Doesn't all that crap from Winky bother you even a little?"

His reply was directed to the windshield. "Should it bother me more now than before? He's been sending' me on trips with bad brakes ever since I started here. The first time I complained he said if I didn't like it I could go somewhere else to work. He knew if I did, the other company would ask for references and he would give me a lousy one. I got a wife and kid to support an' I'll be damned if they'll starve because of Winky." He had rolled his side window down and the warm night air filled the cab with fecund aromas of new growth in the ditches, still wet from a recent rain.

"We could call the Department of Transport and tell them what's going on here."

He turned to her, his eyes serious. "And then what? He repairs the brakes and fires us both? We have no union to back us up and we'd both be out on our butts. He could replace us both with one phone call."

The serenity was gone from his face as he stared into the night, his brow furrowed in thought.

They had picked up the trailer at midnight from the locked explosives blockhouse, the trailer doors sealed and a copy of the load manifest sitting on the lip of the loading dock. It said they were carrying thirty-thousand pounds of Amex and five-thousand pounds of Cil-gel and primers. She wondered what other little goodies had been included by Winky without her or Joe knowing.

The croaking of leopard frogs from the nearby marsh had been wet accompaniment, rising and falling in a chorus of croaks and quacks, their songs of courtship in full flight, while they had prepared the trailer for the journey. It had become routine for one of them to crawl under the trailer with a wrench and while the other operated the foot treadle, adjust the trailer brakes. It was greasy work and doing it in the dark with mosquitoes flying into their noses and mouths created dark smears of blood mixed with grease on any exposed skin which was scratched. And it was impossible not to scratch the countless, itching welts.

"I went to a sweat lodge a couple of days ago," said McKay, quietly, once more to the windshield.

She saw his features soften with a subtle smile, as he recalled the experience.

"Can you tell me about it?"

"Sure. It was hot." He smiled slowly at her as she sipped from a thermos-cup of coffee. He watched one of her eyebrows form a sceptical arc.

"I really can't say more about it because I'm not sure I understand what went on there, but it felt good."

"I thought you looked different. You look more... content with yourself."

"That's what Sadie said. She said I'm startin' to look like an Indian again."

"So she's glad you went?"

"She's the one who suggested it. Said I should go visit my old man once in a while. She said I needed time by myself." He sat, wrapped in contemplation as he drove, the warm night air with its perfumes caressing his face through the open window. "Real smart woman that wife of mine," he said quietly, almost to himself.

"Your dad was there?"

"Yeah. When I was waitin' for him at the cabin, he appeared like out of thin air, right in front of me. Well, I guess I fell asleep and the next thing I know, there he is sitting across from me. I remember when I was real young he would do these magic tricks with his hands. Make things disappear or appear out of thin air. I used to ask him where he learned that and he said he was learnin' his trade from the Master."

"The master?" She sat straighter in her seat, her full attention turned to her partner.

"Yeah, he was real close with the local shaman, Angus. I guess that's where he learned those things. He said they were just tricks though. Said the real hard stuff was somethin' nobody ever saw. Like an owl flyin' in the dark he said. Only the owl knows where it's goin', and only the owl's prey knows when it's arrived...usually too late."

"Sounds kind of spooky." She touched the small medicine bag around her neck which Joes' father had made for her. She hadn't taken it off except to shower and wondered why Joe never commented on it. *He never talks about the bag around his own neck,* she thought, *maybe we aren't supposed to talk about it, it's just supposed to be there.*

"Have you ever met my friend, Brady?" she asked, wanting to change the subject.

"Nope, but you've talked about him a couple of times. Is he still doin' his kayakin'?"

"Not lately. I think he's having a hard time at work, just like us. Why are there so many bosses who are absolute jerks?"

"It's like nature. Survival of the fittest. Look at Winky, he doesn't look very fit does he? But, he was given the job through his family, right?"

She could only nod, wondering where this twisted logic was going.

"Now he's in the position where if anyone who seems more qualified comes along, he can make their job so rough that they quit or they give him reason to fire them. He's protectin' his own position by gettin' rid of the competition. Just like young birds in a nest, the strongest one gets all the food while the others starve... survival of the fittest."

"The man's a turkey."

"More like a vulture,"

"A turkey vulture," they chorused, laughing in unison.

The air in the cab cooled as they dipped into a pocket of ground fog. Mckay rolled his side window up.

The rattle of the diesel engine finally lulled D'Amico to near-sleep. She pulled her jacket from the rear of her seat and placed it in a ball against the window. Laying her head on the jacket she closed her eyes listening to the sounds of the engine and release of the air pressure overload valve.

"Do you think your dad would make one of those medicine bags for Brady?"

"It's already finished. He was just waitin' for you to mention it. It's in my bag here." He motioned to the small nylon handbag between the seats. "Said to give it to you when the time was right."

"Give it to me later okay? I'm tired and need some sleep. Wake me when you need me to take over Joe. Say thanks to your dad for me, okay?"

In seconds she was asleep, leaving Joe alone with his thoughts and that strange smile on his lips.

Friday morning, Bardman went to work only to find the darkroom door sealed and small poster on the outside telling everyone to keep out due to a police investigation. Stuck to the poster was small note from Zenon Mikeluk asking him to come to Jenkins' office. When he arrived, he was introduced by Jenkins to two men, one of whom was constable Pusch who was in uniform and another man in plainclothes, introduced as detective-sergeant Warren from the RCMP headquarters in Winnipeg. All three men were standing as he was motioned to a chair in the middle of the floor, facing them. Another interrogation, he thought as he sat in the plain wooden chair.

"Mr. Bardman, I have the notes of constable Pusch here and I wonder if you could enlarge on a couple of things? Detective Warren licked a nicotine-stained thumb and flicked through several pages, grimacing with the foul taste that came from his fingers. He then looked with frustration at Pusch who watched with anticipation. "Constable did you have to write absolutely *everything* down in shorthand?"

Pusch nodded and began to blush as Warren held the notebook out to him in an accusing manner. "Er, um yessir, I assumed you could read shorthand sir."

"Constable, we're not all trained to be secretaries. Would you be so kind as to decipher what it is I'm reading on this page?"

"Well, er, that's my grocery list sir," replied Pusch blushing furiously. "Bread, milk, Cheerios..."

"Dammit man I don't need to know what the hell you eat, I need to know what the hell he said."

"Who?"

"Him." said Warren stabbing a finger at Bardman who was sitting back, feeling a lot more comfortable in the knowledge that rank in the police force didn't disqualify anyone from the effects of feeble-mindedness.

Pusch took the pad from Warren who hunched his heavy shoulders inside his grey suit and shortened his thick neck, like a snapping turtle preparing to strike. The man had a drinker's nose, bright red and laced with tiny, ruptured veins. His small red-rimmed eyes said that he had probably enjoyed more than a few drinks the night before. He glared intently at the sheet of scribbled symbols in his hand. Warren had difficulty averting his eyes from Pusch's moustache. He was offended by the luxuriant lip hair. He flinched as he saw the moustache approach his left ear.

Pusch whispered into Warren's ear while pointing at scratches on one page. Warren was trying to follow the finger while tilting his head away from the intruding nostril hairs and garlic- laden breath of the constable.

"Ah! said Warren victoriously. "Mr. Bardman could you explain why several of the frames from your strip of negatives are missing?"

"Which ones are missing?" asked Bardman with as much innocence as he could muster. A cold lump began to form in the pit of his stomach.

Warren turned and retrieved a negative file page from Jenkins' desktop and squinted at it using the light from the window. "The numbering on the negatives goes to forty-seven and then starts again at number one. Can you explain where the rest are?"

"I don't think there are anymore," Shit, he thought to himself, I was afraid they would find those gaps. "All the film used here is bought in bulk, in one-hundred foot rolls and the numbering has, as far as I know consistently reached the forties and then returned to number one. If you look at any other file pages, you will see a lack of numbering sequence for that reason and also because the beginning and end segments of the film are usually clipped and thrown away due to being fogged during the loading process."

"I thought that was always done in the dark?" Detective Warren was leaning against Jenkins' desk, pinching his lips together with a thumb and forefinger from the side, making them pucker as though preparing to spit an olive pit for a distance record.

Bardman continued: "Loading the film onto the film reels for processing is done in total darkness, but loading of film cassettes is done with a loader which allows it to be done in room light. It's at this time the film-ends are fogged." He watched detective Warren nod knowingly.

Pusch also nodded, trying to imitate his superior's expression and stance, in case he would one day have to conduct an investigation himself.

Warren was satisfied with the answer, having seen remnants of film in the garbage can and had routinely studied the reject strips on the light table.

"Excuse me," asked Pusch suddenly. "What exactly does fogged mean?"

Detective Warren held the bridge of his nose and leaned forward shaking his head slowly from side to side. There was silence as the other three observed this mannerism with some alarm.   "It means this session is now at an end," said Warren in a whisper. He leaned toward Bardman, fixing him with his small red eyes. "Don't plan on leaving town Mr. Bardman, there are a lot of unanswered questions concerning this case."

"I said that too," blurted Pusch, his moustache wriggling with self-satisfaction.

He started to rise from his chair and caught a glimpse of a strip of negatives on Jenkins' desk. The negative page was titled 'Rock-face blast site', and he recalled the other shots taken near where the drillers had been working.

"One other thing Mr. Bardman," said detective Warren, observing Bardman's interest in the negatives. "I believe part of your assignment was also to document areas where spilled explosives were noticed. There's an explosives investigator trying to find where several hundred pounds of granular explosive has gone over the past six months. So far as we know, it's all disappeared from underground from various sites. In your travels down there, have you seen or heard anything that might shed some light on this?" Warren watched him closely for reaction, noting that his upper lip was beginning to perspire.

For a second he had difficulty catching his breath. *My God, I didn't realize it was that much!* "No, I can't think of anything, but there are a lot of unhappy people who work down there. I mean miners bitch and complain like everyone else in a job that's dangerous and dirty. A lot of them also have access to explosives and they know how to use it." He was uncomfortable under the steady gaze of Warren and Pusch who had gone through his negative files and seen a correlation with the areas he photographed and where explosives had gone missing. Jenkins was also looking at him with a strange expression; a combination of shock and suspicion.

"I think we can consider calling it quits for today gentlemen," said Warren, nodding toward Jenkins and Pusch. The two police officers left the office, leaving Jenkins and Bardman alone.

Jenkins silently observed Bardman standing beside the chair where he had been questioned. "Ever since you arrived, things have become very complicated Mr. Bardman. Explosives start disappearing, people are getting killed underground and you seem to have pictures from every one of those areas. Is there something you haven't told us Mr. Bardman?"

He bristled at the question. "Am I a suspect here Mr. Jenkins? Because if so I would like to know why. I'm not the only person who comes and goes down there. There are foremen, drillers going on and off shift, geologists, mine surveyors, mechanics...." He was beginning to wave his arms, causing Jenkins to take a step back.

Jenkins mistook the fake indignation as the real thing and regretted having asked, wishing the police had asked instead.

"Everyone who was down there has to be considered a suspect Mr. Bardman, that includes you as well as the madman who murdered his foreman. I'm frustrated and frightened by what occurred down there. We don't even know what this guy looks like. Remember the shots you did of that crew several months ago? Well, every shot of the guy named Pilson didn't show his face. It appears he turned his face every time he saw the camera."

"So you've gone through all the negatives?"

"Yes we went through them all. Not a single face-on shot of the guy. The head office can't even identify him. The only people who know... or knew him on sight are in the morgue waiting for the medical examiner to come up from Winnipeg. Of course, you've seen him and we'll need your description, along with some of the patrons at the bar where he drank, but descriptions from people who are drunk most of the time are hardly reliable. The police also saw the families of the two men last night. They took it really hard from what I hear. I guess the wife of the one, Rivest broke down on the spot. Thank God the cops had taken a close friend of the family with them." Jenkins studied the floor, then looked back up at Bardman, his eyes glistening with the beginning of a tear. "If you can recall *anything*, you let us know. Okay?"

He started for the door.

"And Bardman, I still haven't forgotten about that newspaper episode," he said with the customary coldness returned to his voice.

He nodded and left the office, glad to be alone again. He went to the darkroom where the police barricade tape had been removed, and let himself in. The negative files were still stacked on the counter next to the enlarger, others spread in individual pages on the light table. He noticed some pages had individual negative strips missing and surmised the police had reason for keeping some. The pages were labelled 'Diamond drill site', and each page had a different date. He made himself busy cleaning up the mess and re-filing the pages while he mentally attempted to assess his situation. Perhaps it hadn't been such a good idea to make prints of the missing driller and then keep the negatives. *I could turn the negatives over to the police, saying I'd misplaced them. Then what? They'd keep them for evidence, I'd never get them back, and I'd still get fired for turning that shot over to the newspaper. Probably go to jail anyway. No. They don't get the negative.*

The phone rang. It was Mikeluk with an assignment for him to back underground. A new drill called a jumbo with multiple drill heads and operated by one man was to be tested. He was to go down with the Day Shift Foreman and Roger Jenkins. He hung up with a quiet curse and began gathering his equipment to meet the two men at the shaft entrance in fifteen minutes.

A half-hour later, one thousand feet below the surface, Roger Jenkins, Hank Aikins, and Bardman, watched a drill crew hook up the airlines to the huge pneumatically controlled drill rig. Jenkins and Aikins were both unsettled to see the miner who had introduced himself once before as the Czar of Russia was the man operating the drill.

Bardman had been amused on the trip down in the cage when he saw the change in facial colour of 'Upchuck' Aikins. He noticed Jenkins was equally observant, allowing plenty of room between himself and Aikins. The foreman refused to look up at his boss, electing instead to give his toes an immaculate inspection.

"Aha, iss underground racing driver and lackey. Come to watch how real men work eh?" The Slovak miner displayed an unfriendly smile of steel-filled incisors to the onlookers. The other miners, making the final hook-ups to the airlines, listened to the exchange and snickered to themselves.

"Iss new reinforced toilet over there in case of em-ay-rgency," he said, pointing with the beam of his hat light.

Neither Jenkins nor Aikins responded to the verbal jab as they watched the driller settle into a seat with hand controls in front of him.

With a loud hiss of air, the drill heads moved one by one to the rock ceiling. A water valve was opened and water spurted in small high-pressure streams from the ends of the hollow, four ten-foot lengths of drill rod. The rods were eased to the rock surface and with a roar the drills began to operate, each boring into the hard rock. Even with the yellow ear protectors, the noise was shattering. Each man could feel his internal organs vibrate with the tremendous level of sound contained within the rock walls.

Bardman took shots from various angles, the only evidence of the camera's operation being the brilliance of the flash. Using hand movements, he signalled Jenkins and Aikins to move closer to the operating rig to include them with the piece of equipment. Neither one wanted to smile or even appear the least bit interested. The driller had an uncanny ability to turn and smile a metal-laden smile at the camera each time the shutter was clicked. He finished the roll of film and went back to the electric locomotive they had arrived on, to get another roll from his camera bag. The instant he turned back toward the huge drill, the locomotive lurched and began moving away from him at increasing speed. He could see a figure with a red hard hat in the driver's seat and tried to shout but his voice was drowned out. He flashed his light at the figure as it receded and at the last minute the figure turned to look at him. There was just enough light to make out the magnified eyes behind the thick-glassed lenses. The face that looked back at him had no expression as it disappeared into the darkness.

"What do you mean someone stole the motor?" shouted Jenkins, his ears still ringing from the now silent drills. "Why would someone steal it? What in hell is going on around here?" His hands were on his hips, staring into the blackness of the drift, where the locomotive had disappeared.

The driller had climbed off the drill and was studying something along the side of the drift, near where the vehicle had been parked. He uttered what sounded like curses in his Slovak language and looked up at the others with hurt and surprise in his eyes. "Son em bitch, steal my lunch. No... steal everybody lunch."

There was a collective sound of shock and surprise from the others.

"Stole my camera bag," said Bardman to the unsympathetic gathering.

"Stole my motor," Mumbled Aikins, his fat cheeks quivering with indignation, his eyes peering into the darkness.

"Oh shut up," said Jenkins. "If I find that joker I'll thrash him.

"I saw who it was," said Bardman quietly. "It was Pilson, he's still down here."

"Madman who kill foreman on eight-hundred level?" The driller was also looking nervously down the drift as were his colleagues.

"We have to go back and report this," said Jenkins walking into the darkness with Aikins reluctantly on his heels.

"We come too, not stay down here with crazy man running around."

"How do you know he's crazy," asked Bardman of the driller.

"He steal my wife's cooking twice in two days. Must be crazy."

The others laughed nervously, staying huddled close together as they walked cautiously down the drift, their hat lights shining nervously into every nook and cranny as they made their way to the main shaft.

When Bardman woke Saturday morning, his head pounded from the intensity of the nightmare. He had dreamed he was back in the mine, his light burned out, and feeling the crazy driller was watching from nearby. He had jerked awake with the image of huge magnified eyes staring at him with unblinking reptilian intensity.

From the window at the top of the staircase he could see blue sky of early morning and realised he was late in preparations to go kayaking with Teresa. At least the coffee will be ready when she gets here, he thought as he quickly cleared the table of old crumbs with a sweep of his arm. After work, the day before, he had dragged out his seldom-used vacuum cleaner and did the bedroom and kitchen, after which, he wet-mopped. He was proud of the fresh pine aroma of the cleaner and wished he had done it much sooner.

The door at the landing opened and he heard Teresa's yoo-hoo float musically down the stairs. She bounced into the room, looked quickly around and began sniffing like a dog trying to unearth a bone. "You cleaned. Not for my sake I hope. But I'm glad you did. I have to admit it smelled a bit like petroleum in here the last time, when I showered."

"Glad you like it, I did it just for you," he said with a smile, thankful he had moved the boxes from the closet. He handed her a coffee while attempting to intercept an airborne slice of toast from his toaster. He missed, and it fell with a dry thump into the kitchen sink.

"You should get that thing fixed, it could be dangerous," giggled Teresa, sipping her coffee as she leaned against the counter.

"It keeps my reflexes sharp in the morning. Usually it lands on the floor; at least this time I managed to deflect it into the sink." He smeared strawberry jam onto the slice. "Can I make you some?"

"Naw, I had breakfast. Besides, I don't think my reflexes are up to it.

She was wearing baggy sweat pants much to Brady's disappointment with an equally baggy sweatshirt."So, where do you want to go paddling today?"

"You know those control gates on the Black Wood River? Why don't we go upstream from there? I'm curious to see how high the water is and how it's affected the wildlife."

"So this is a paddle with a purpose? I hoped we could just go out and have fun, hopefully without me falling in like last time."

He ate the toast in two gulps along with a slurp of coffee, part of which dribbled down his chin.

She reached over with a napkin and daintily dabbed his chin with an exaggerated motherly look. "What am I going to do with you Mr. Bardman? Am I going to have to teach you how to eat in a civilized manner or should I just join you in your obvious love of eating with noisy gusto?" She smiled at him as he searched for a reply and giggled again as he looked at her with embarrassment. "Don't you worry none," she said patting his cheek. "It's too late to change you and I wouldn't want to if I could. Are we going paddling or not?"

They quickly tied the kayaks onto the Volkswagen and with a packed lunch, drove north to where the Black Wood river was held back by the control gates.

On the way, they each talked about their work. Teresa had been shocked to hear of the deaths at the mine and the fact they had not been reported in the media. Brady had also considered this strange, since Jenkins had told him the next of kin had been informed. An investigation should not prohibit media coverage unless there was some aspect of the case they didn't want made public. He told her about seeing the suspect in the drift and describing him to her.

With the windows down and the sun warming them, they soon tired of discussing work. Instead, they each quietly watched the spruce trees dotting the Precambrian shield. The morning light reflected pinks, whites and greys from the granite surface as they followed the dusty road north. An hour later, they reached the long downhill toward the control gates which spanned the Black Wood River.

At the top of the hill he stopped the car and stepped out with his camera. He shot several frames with the wide angle lens and several more with a telephoto of the control gate structure.

She watched with interest, glad that he was at ease with himself as he worked. They got back in the car and started down the hill.

Brady watched for an access road which led near the shoreline. From the large oily stains on the ground, they guessed the area had at one time been used as an oil-change area during construction of the gates. The smell of oil was still strong from the packed soil, months after its abandonment, but at least it offered a short walk to the shoreline, upriver from the gates.

They stowed the gear inside the kayak hulls, behind the seats and pushed off into the river. There wasn't much current due to the amount of water being held back, and he surprised Teresa by paddling toward the control structure. He raised his camera again and took more shots from water level, then, using a sweep-stroke, spun the kayak upriver.

She followed, paddling hard to keep up but then decided to go her own pace and enjoy the scenery. To the west, a yellow and brown helicopter skimmed the tops of the high tension power lines. She watched it disappear over the horizon and looked back upriver. He was nearly out of sight around one bend and she decided to put on speed to keep him in sight.

Bardman stopped paddling and watched a beaver cut a smooth wake in the water from the shore across his path. The kayak continued to drift and suddenly the beaver lifted its tail and slapped the water as it submerged. He looked over his shoulder and saw Teresa smiling.

"How far up do you want to go?" she asked, pulling alongside and gripping the edge of his cockpit with her hand.

"We have all morning and most of the afternoon. Lets see if we can make it to the junction of the Muskrat river. That should be about another two hours paddle from here. We can have lunch at the junction and start back." He watched her strip off her sweatshirt, down to a blue sleeveless T-shirt. She then took some sun-screen from a small bum-bag and spread it liberally over her face and shoulders. She held the tube out to him.

"No thanks, it will only attract the bugs later on." No sooner had he said that, when a large horsefly, sometimes referred to as a bulldog began buzzing around his head. It landed on his arm and with his hand he swatted it into the water where it lay on its' back, helpless, legs scrabbling like some dangerous wind-up toy. He brought the flat of his kayak paddle down on the struggling insect. It made the same sound as the beaver, with its tail. He had a reverence for living creatures, but he couldn't seem to extend it to any of the biting insects.

As they paddled, they could see where the beaver had begun gnawing at the birch and poplar trees along the bank. Sections of other trees protruded from the water where the river bank had once been, but was now flooded.

The beaver were being forced to rebuild their homes to replace those underwater.

The overhanging branches groped for their heads like feathery fingertips as they paddled in their shade. Further up, on the opposite side of the river, a kingfisher swooped to the water after small fish. In many places there was a strong smell of plant decay where other trees had simply fallen into the water or their root systems had failed to keep them anchored to the bank.

"This isn't good is it?" said Teresa quietly surveying the rotting trees.

"No this is not good," he replied, shooting more film with the wide-angle lens. "I think the fishing and trapping on these river systems has been ruined for years."

"I think this is where Joe's dad had his trapline. He said there are all kinds of small lakes through here, so many, they don't even have names."

They paddled on, going from one bank to the other. Wherever something caught their attention, they investigated. In one case a majestic spruce had toppled into the river, its branches reaching upward from the half submerged trunk like arms raised in supplication. The beaver had attacked it voraciously, stripping the bark from the smaller exposed branches until it resembled a multi-limbed skeleton, its' bare wood showing white like bleached bones. A large painted turtle reclined on the naked trunk, warming itself in the sun.

He drifted close and with the 400 millimetre mirror lens, shot several close-up shots before drifting away to leave the turtle, its' neck extended in curiosity, but not so disturbed to make it return to the water.

Frequently they saw small tributaries, some of which apperared to dwindle to dead-end channels. Others beckoned them to be explored. On a couple of occasions they nosed the kayaks up the narrow channels until they could touch either side of the bank with the double blades of the paddles. They appeared to eventually open out into one of the many small lakes or wetlands that dotted the area by the thousands, but their time was limited and decided to press on to the junction of the Muskrat River.

As they exited from one such tributary and turned once more upriver, a small dot appeared ahead of them, just above the water. It quickly grew larger and they could hear the concussion of the blades as the helicopter approached, its landing skids nearly skimming the water. Brady paddled quickly for shore as the helicopter pulled its nose up at the last instant. Two faces with aviator sunglasses grinned back at them as the craft twisted and turned, following the course of the river.

"Stupid bastard," he shouted, shaking his fist at the departing aircraft. "Either he didn't see us or he didn't give a shit."

"I think they saw us alright," said Teresa, her kayak turned the direction which the helicopter had gone. "I think he was trying to send us a message."

Watching the treetops and listening for the sound of rotor blades, they cautiously paddled another half-hour until they reached the junction of the Black Wood and Muskrat River systems. It was obvious the Muskrat River was as affected by the back-flooding as the Black Wood. Uprooted trees floated like corpses along the river bank as they came ashore for lunch. He retrieved a bag of sandwiches, a couple or oranges and a bag of GORP, Good Old Raisins and Peanuts from the hull of the kayak. As they sat in the shade of the trees eating, a grey jay landed at their feet, watching for dropped food. He flicked a couple of crumbs from his sandwich toward it and watched it retrieve them, then flit to a branch nearby to watch for more offerings.

Teresa watched him study the riverbank as they sat on the long grass. She had pulled one long strand of grass and was slowly chewing the succulent lower end. "You don't like what's happening to the river do you? Is it all because of the hydro project?"

He picked up a small rock and flung it into the water. "What we see is only a small part of the impact. There are animals, maybe whole eco-systems being destroyed here; all in the name of development. There are also human lives being ruined." He thought of the small native reserve and the clapboard shacks. Those people were very poor, with only the hunting, trapping and fishing to help sustain them. That too was being taken from them.

"What's that strange smell?" She was wrinkled her nose, sniffing the air.

"That's methane from all the rotting plants caused by the flooding. I read in a magazine that all that methane is another form of pollution maybe as bad as what a large city produces. Look...look over there!" He was pointing to the far bank.

She leaned on his shoulder and sighted along his extended arm. She saw the subtle movement of a great blue heron wading into the water, watching for fish or frogs to spear with its long bill. It stood completely still for moments on end, then walked gracefully along the bank. Finally it spread its huge wings and gracefully took to the air, skimming the water as it flew downstream.

"Guess the hunting wasn't too good eh? She kept her head on his shoulder although he had lowered his arm. She enjoyed the aroma of him, the combination of his shaving cream and his freshly laundered shirt.

Brady gently turned his head and looked down at her.

She tilted her head up slightly and grinned, lopsidedly at him. "I think I'm becoming a real nature-lover, and I put all the blame on you." She turned and bit him on the shoulder, her eyes watching his to see his reaction.

He promptly offered a piece of orange with his other hand. "If you're still hungry, bite this." She opened her mouth and he inserted the segment. He watched juice dribble down her chin.

She gulped noisily, her eyes watching the river.

"I think I'm going to be fired from my job pretty soon."

She sat up and looked at him, her eyes questioning.

"I've done a couple of really stupid things lately. One of them was that picture in the newspaper. The other was a picture I took at the scene of the murder underground."

"I thought you told them all that happened after you had left."

"I lied. I have a picture that could have me thrown in jail if the cops find out and I need a place to hide it in case they search my place."

"Why would they want to search your place if you said you weren't there when it happened? Is this why you've been acting strange lately? I thought maybe I'd said something wrong and you were pissed off at me."

"Teresa, I don't know if I should tell you more than I already have, because then you might be implicated."

She put her head back on his shoulder and studied the branches of the surrounding trees. "You know, that's one of the few times you said my name, you can do it more often if you like, it won't wear out."

He gently leaned down and kissed her on the lips, tasting the orange.

"God, it's about time," she whispered as she opened her lips slightly to welcome his. "Why is it some guys just can't take a hint?"

For the next ten minutes they sat close, their heads touching, watching the water slip by and hearing the wind rustling the branches above them. The grey jay had moved to the hull of one kayak and regarded them with ill-concealed impatience. They both sensed but could not put into words the feeling that they were being pulled along by events over which they had little control.

"So what are you going to do if you get fired? There's not a hell of a lot to do in this town unless you work in the mine or construction."

"I suppose I'll just have to wait and see what they decide. In the meantime I'm going to explore the possibilities of selling some freelance work in the event I am fired. At least it might give me a little monetary insurance to help keep my options open."

"What kind of options do you have in mind?" She had taken his hand in hers and was entwining her fingers with his.

I have a feeling there's going to be an inquiry into workplace safety, both at the hydro project and in the mine. I've been taking a lot of pictures down there for the magazine and what they don't know is that I've also been documenting some very unsafe situations. That shot the newspaper used of the hydro project also shows their negligence. If that inquiry starts and I get canned, I'll at least be able to sell some of these shots to the highest bidder."

"Is that ethical? I mean you're working for them and they might see you as some kind of traitor."

"What kind of employer puts their workers lives at risk for the sake of profits?" He had removed his hand from hers and began breaking a small twig in pieces as he spoke. "I was talking to the reporter from the newspaper and she said she was refused statistics on the accident rate of the hydro project. She thinks the withholding of this information is a cover-up and expects to have the same results with the Quesnel Minerals records. If both these companies go on record of refusing this information, every media hound in the province if not the country will perk up their ears and start asking questions. That's when the feces will hit the fan for me. I was warned by the boss that if any media showed an interest in anything in the mine, my ass would be out flapping in the breeze."

"What proof would they have that it was you that caused the media to call?"

"They don't need proof, all they need is suspicion and I've already provided that because of some retarded editor on the night desk who used my name on the front page photo, after I had expressly asked them not to." He had a small pile of twigs between his outstretched legs, the results of his nervous energy while talking.

She watched his actions with the twigs as she listened, realizing the stresses he was under. "Planning on building a fire? Maybe stay the night on this lonely shore?"

"It's not so lonely," he said, pointing to the river. "Look."

Silently their eyes followed the passage of an aluminum canoe with a lone paddler. "That looks like a Brigden," whispered Brady. "And that's the old guy who showed up at my tent site and insulted my pancakes."

"What do you mean a Brigden?" she whispered back at him as the craft drifted past, the occupant sitting completely still, the paddle laid across the gunwales. The old man seemed to be searching for something.

"What? Oh, the canoe, made by an old guy in Winnipeg. He's made them for years and sold them all over the province if not the country. He' sort of a guru of the canoeing society.

She could barely make out an object hanging around the old man's neck, partially obscured by the buckskin jacket. "That reminds me, Joe gave me this to give you." She rummaged through her small tote bag and extracted a small leather bag on a rawhide string. "He said his dad made it for you."

"Why would he do that? He doesn't even know me." He took the small bag in his hand. *But then again, maybe he does.* He raised it to his nose and sniffed, detecting a faint scent of wood smoke. He had always loved the smell of wood smoke.

"I don't know," she replied. "I guess he figured you needed it. You know I hardly even know I have mine on. There's obviously something in it but it seems light as a feather."

"Can I look inside?"

"No, don't," she said, quickly putting her hand over his. "Don't ask me why, I just don't think we're supposed to know."

They both looked back to the far bank of the river. The old man and the canoe had nearly drifted out of sight, but not before they saw him turn and look their direction. They saw him smile before turning away and finally begin paddling with long powerful strokes that soon took him out of sight around the bend.

"I wonder who he is?" she said, still watching the ripples of the canoe, as they spread silently toward the shoreline.

Brady said nothing for a few seconds, and felt a strange chill come over him. "I think we should start back, it'll be almost dark by the time we reach the car and the bugs will be bad." He walked to the edge of the river and bent down, pulling at small fern-like leaves and rolling them in the palm of his hand. "Take some of this and spread the juice on your skin, it's a natural insect repellant."

Teresa sniffed the palm of his hand, enjoying the spicy aroma from the leaves. "What is it? Does it really work?"

"It's called yarrow, and yes it really works, at least for a while. You have to replenish it from time to time, but at least it's better for the environment than that crap in the cans and bottles." He showed her a small white head of flower petals clustered together at the top of the slender plant, so she could recognize it. They picked up their orange peels and placed them in a small plastic bag, leaving the site as clean as they had found it except for the tamped down grass where they had sat. As they pushed off into the river, a lone raven landed in a tall tree near the river bank and watched them silently. Had they turned and looked back at it, they would have noticed with some alarm that it appeared to be smiling.

CHAPTER 14

Francine Rivest sat in the last pew of the Catholic church. The hymnal was clutched in her hands, the perspiration dripping from her hands onto her lap. It wasn't unusual for her to come to church alone. Many of the congregation had become accustomed to her husband's absence as well as that of some of the other husbands who worked in the mine. Many of the wives understood that jobs which are dangerous can take a toll on a person and the occasional binge at the bar was not encouraged, but not unexpected. She had difficulty making eye contact with some of the others since she had been notified of Frenchy's death three days before.

The young police officer had fled from her apartment doorstep, his blurted words of sympathy as much comfort as cold snow on frostbite. She had stood facing the door, a dish cloth in one hand and an unwashed pot in the other, watching the police officer shaking his head, not knowing what to say or how to say whatever it was that would somehow make this meeting easier for both of them.

The next few days had gone by as if in a dream. She couldn't remember having eaten nor being hungry. Nor could she remember how the pot's handle had been broken, or how the large gouge had been taken out of the wall in the hallway.

A representative from Deep Core had come with more news. They said there was an investigation into another death at the time, that of his foreman, at the same site. She would have to delay funeral arrangements until some questions were answered. Frenchy's body would have to remain in the mortuary while a postmortem was done on each of the bodies.

"You mean they're going to cut Frenchy open and poke around inside and I can't even see my own husband?" She looked squarely into the eyes of the company's general manager who sat on the edge of her sofa, his hands trapped uncomfortably between his knees.

"I'm sorry. We had a call from the police and the medical examiner. They said that because of the suspicious nature of the death of the foreman, they have to complete the examination of both bodies before they can release them."

In his twenty years with the company, Kent Hoffburg had never had to bear such bad tidings as today. Other drillers in other mines had died, not frequently thank God, but often enough to remind them they were working in a hazardous environment.

Francine sat on the other end of the sofa, her body half-turned his direction as though reluctant to face both him and the reality of her situation. She was short and compact like her husband, with an adolescent chubbiness which made her appear younger than her thirty years. She had large blue eyes, now red-rimmed and moist with tears. Despite the grief, her small mouth held a look of determination. She was determined she wasn't going to break down in front of this man. She had dressed in dark slacks and white blouse, items she had not had occasion to wear for months. Everything else she had in her wardrobe was colourful, not appropriate she thought to discuss the death of her husband. She had been notified of her husband's death, of the need to delay her husband's burial due to the investigation. Her husband no longer seemed to have a name. It was as though death had taken that from him too, as if speaking his name would be too painful. "He's my husband, all I want to do is see him once more. Is there any harm in that?"

Hoffburg squirmed and adjusted a small cushion near his elbow. He thumped it twice to make it stay in place, needing a few seconds to formulate his reply.

"You know Mrs. Rivest, undertakers can really work miracles these days. I mean they can rebuild and reform parts of the human anatomy so they look good as new." His quick smile had come involuntarily, a reaction to a tense situation. At this moment he decided would rather be undergoing root canal work than be on this sofa facing eyes of cool inquisition.

"You mean he's been badly disfigured?"

"It was an industrial accident, a large drill fell on him. It was very heavy."

I always told Maurice he was too small to work down there."

"Maurice?"

"My God, he worked all these years for you people and you never knew his first name? Don't you people take any interest in your employees other than to get maximum production out of them? He came home dead tired day after day, grease all over him, cuts, scratches, and bruises from whatever it was he did down there, and now he's not just dead tired, he's dead, and you didn't even know his name?"

Hoffburg retreated to the extreme end of the sofa, his arms now folded in front as if in protection from her anger. He was shocked how this small, woman with kind eyes could suddenly speak with a snarl, bringing back unpleasant memories of his days as a paperboy facing down a customer's dog on collection day.

"Oh, it's in our files obviously. I just never had a chance to go through the whole thing, but I know his full name's there. Actually there's something else about those files I needed to talk to you about. Did you know your husband never subscribed to our life insurance plan? Our payroll department asked several times if he wanted deductions taken off his cheque to go into the company policy, but he never agreed."

Her mouth opened in surprise, then closed quickly, her body stiffening with surprise. "No insurance? He kept saying he would do it. He always said that if anything happened I would at least have something. *Oh Maurice, how can you disappoint me in death as well as in life?* "My God I can't even afford to have a funeral for him! What happens when you can't afford to bury someone?"

Hoffburg watched the young widow transform before his eyes from someone with at least a modicum of poise and inner strength to a woman drained of emotion and hope; almost deflate physically. He had no answers for her and quietly left, catching a last glimpse of her as she sat unmoving on the sofa, her eyes cast to the floor. He closed the door quietly and tip-toed down the dingy hall of the apartment building, thankful for the bright sunlight beckoning at the far end.

She looked up from her memory of that meeting and realised the Sunday service had ended. The congregation was moving past her to the door. Some nodded without speaking, others avoided her eyes, not knowing what to say. She sensed someone sliding onto the pew beside her but still sat, watching the people as they filed out. People she had come to know as friends and fellow-worshippers. She knew they were searching for words of solace, for despite the blanket of silence imposed by the mine administration, word had travelled fast that deaths had occurred.

When Frenchy was late coming home for dinner she thought he had gone for a beer as was the case often in the past. On those evenings he would peek around the apartment door and say: "You want to t'row some'ting at me?" If she didn't reply he would sneak up behind her, wrap his short muscular arms around her waist and hug her, nibbling her earlobe at the same time. She would smell the beer on his breath and the smoke from the bar, but was confused by the occasional aroma of a woman's perfume. She never asked where it came from, but the question haunted her. *God, he can't be gone. There's nothing for me to go back to.*

"Franny, some of us are going over to Frank and Jeannie's place for tea. Why don't you come with me? I could use the company," said Patty Watson, a small bird-like woman who had a voice like a lumberjack and was known to swear like one. Her dark hair stuck up in uncontrollable patches of frizziness which rebelled against all attempts to be controlled. She never wore makeup and her large dark eyes were sheltered by eyebrows which seemed to move independently of each other. She would have been considered attractive were it not for her hair and a mouth that rested on a thirty degree slant from the rest of her facial features. Ever since she was a teenager she had shocked her parents and friends following a bout of whooping cough. Her voice had changed from a musical bell-like pitch to male baritone and she was able to project it like a drill sergeant. "C'mon Franny, my car's out front," she whispered in a low rumble, like that of an approaching thunderstorm.

Francine nodded and they moved to the door, the last ones to leave. She noticed Patty nod to the priest as they left, and the priest nod back with a small smile as he began to remove his sacraments.

There were seven of them at Frank and Jeannie's place. She recognized the Smileys, Wanda and her husband Jake, who managed to brighten a room with his smile despite not having a single tooth in his head. With them was a huge quiet blonde man who appeared very ill-at-ease and was introduced to her as Big Don Bunkerfort. She felt her hand disappear up to her wrist in his hand when they shook hands, and was surprised at the gentleness of it. He nodded and mumbled something bashfully down at her, only briefly meeting her eyes with his glance.

"Frenchy was a friend. Anythin' I can do you let me know. Okay?"

She nodded and smiled up at him, sensing the gayness of the surrounding conversation was of a forced nature for her benefit. Jake Smiley was talking with Patty and they both cast quick glances in her direction, cups of tea balanced in their hands. Both Jake and Big Don appeared to wish they had something more potent to sip

The living room was barely big enough to contain the group, so natural reaction was to gravitate to the kitchen, where they could stand and lean on the counter or table, feeling much more comfortable than the formal atmosphere of the living room with its over-stuffed sofa and chair.

251

Jeannie had made coffee which Toothless Jake and Patty accepted gratefully in large mugs. With a wink to each of them Jeannie poured a liberal amount of orange liqueur into each mug. Patty and Jake smiled hugely back at her.

"Get Franny in here," rumbled patty under her breath. "If there's one thing that girl needs, it's a drink. She's been holdin' too much inside."

While Jake went to extricate Franny from Big Don, Patty and Jeannie prepared her spiked coffee. They were beginning to feel the effects of their first sips of the potent brew and began to giggle.

"Have some of this Fran m'dear," boomed Patty as she thrust the mug at her, the liqueur bottle on the counter, blocked from view by her small frame. Others had gravitated to the kitchen and the aroma of fresh coffee, the last being Big Don who's head collided with the hanging light fixture from the ceiling, creating a sound like a Chinese gong.

"Need a hard hat to drink coffee in this place," he mumbled to no one in particular as he reached up to steady the swinging fixture.

"My God Don, you've only been here twenty minutes and already you're wreckin' the place." Patty handed a mug up to him, wriggling her eyebrows at him, soliciting a slow crooked smile from a face that showed quiet humour and intelligence.

Franny was halfway through her coffee already, enjoying the taste and subtle light-headed feeling it gave her. "Patty, how come you never married? A single girl in her late twenties up here would have men stumbling over each other to get a date."

"I'm picky Franny. I seen so many men and their private parts as a nurse in that hydro project nursing station that the novelty was gone in the first three months. Besides, gettin' endless proposals from men you've just treated for the clap or mechanized dandruff didn't exactly make for optimum conditions for romance."

"Mechanized dandruff?" asked Franny, her coffee now gone and wishing for more.

"Crabs m'dear, crabs. Somethin' I learned from a fella I knew in the army reserves. Wish I coulda skipped that part of my education, because he gave 'em to me. Hey, anyone here know how you stone crabs to death?" She was met with confused silence. "Take a handful of sand and rub like hell."

The kitchen rocked with laughter as Patty promptly broke into song with her tuneless baritone, swinging her coffee cup back and forth.

Get out that old green ointment
The crab's disappointment
And we'll kill the bastards where they lay.

"That's all I remember. Had a record by Oscar Brand who sang all kinds of bawdy western songs. Nearly peed my pants I laughed so hard."

Jeannie had managed to brew more coffee and was trying to distribute it but realised there was competition from two bottles of whiskey which had materialized on the counter. She cast a questioning glance at Frank, who tilted his head toward Toothless Jake. Jake exposed his gums in a parody of an innocent grin. Some were drinking it straight, others with mix, but all were drinking. With a sigh she accepted a glass from Big Don and poured one for herself.

"Wait a minute, wait a minute," mumbled Big Don, bending down to everyone else's altitude. "Gotta make a toast."

Everyone became quiet as the huge man turned and faced Franny who had her back against the counter. She straightened, fearing what was about to happen, not knowing how she would react.

"Here's to Frenchy," he said quietly.

Everyone raised their glass and sipped, echoing the toast, if not verbally, at least in their hearts. Patty had moved close to Franny and draped an arm over her shoulder. The sudden quiet was embarrassing and Franny didn't know how to reply nor even if she should.

"Who the hell is Dorothy anyway?" she blurted. "I mean Frenchy talks in his sleep and he said her name twice one night. I felt like rolling him out of bed and asking him to his face if he was fooling around on me."

The men's eyes studied the floor as though searching for food scraps. The women appeared as confused as she.

"Waitress at the Stagger Inn," said Big Don in a slow drawl. "Nothin' to worry about Franny. You know how Frenchy was after a few beers, he'd go through the motions of chasin' anythin' in a skirt just to see how they reacted."

"Big boobf," volunteered Toothless Jake, cupping his hands over his chest to indicate the size, grinning in drunken delight at the recollection. His wife jabbed him sharply in the ribs, making him spill his drink down the front of his last clean shirt.

"At least she had 'em," exclaimed Patty with a voice that rattled the windows. "When I was a teenager I used to stuff Kleenex down my bra 'cause I was flat as a board. Went on a date once and had a bad nose cold, forgot my tissues so had to sneak 'em out of my bra just to blow my nose. By the time the date was over I only had one boob, and that one had my date's teeth marks all over it. He was so drunk he didn't know he was chewin' paper"

Franny laughed with the rest of them, thankful for Patty's ribald intervention. "I was starting to think he never took me to the bar because I would meet his girlfriend, and would feel uncomfortable if I held his hand at the table."

Toothless Jake and Big Don regarded her with serious expressions.

"You ever meet his partner Franny?

"You mean Pilson? That tall skinny guy? Yeah he came over for dinner one time after work with Frenchy. He gave me the creeps, kept watching me with his big googly eyes."

"Maybe he found you attractive Franny," replied Patty, working on another drink and beginning to list to one side.

"No, he looked jealous, you know like two women who wear identical dresses to the same function. It was like having a lizard to lunch, sitting there, never blinking, his throat bobbing up and down. It wouldn't have surprised me to see his tongue flicking out. I felt like putting turtle food or a live mouse in front of him to see if he would eat it. When he left I told Frenchy to never bring him back."

"Copf are lookin' for him now," said Toothless Jake quietly. "They fink he killed the foreman becauf Frenfy got killed. Went crafy down there. Thopped him to piefes."

"You mean chopped," corrected Big Don.

"Thath what I thaid," repeated Jake irritably. "Thopped."

"So where is he now and why are you guys looking so strange?"

"Well Franny, it's a little sensitive, an' I don't quite know how to put this," said Big Don, seeing the impatience on her face. "You see, me an Jake saw Frenchy an' Pilson holdin' hands in the bar the night before the accident. Frenchy looked real uncomfortable like he was tryin' to get his hand away, but Pilson looked insane."

Her mouth had opened involuntarily. She finally understood the malevolent stares Pilson had been giving her. A chill ran through her body. "Did they...?"

"I don't think so Franny, Frenchy wasn't like that. He looked scared an' just wanted out of there." Big Don was blushing at being the centre of attention and the object of her direct stare. "He finally got up and scooted outa there like he'd sat on somethin' hot, left Pilson sittin' there lookin real jilted. Funny thing was, nobody had the nerve to look at him, probably because one time he near beat a guy to a pulp in the bar last year. He never even changed his expression, just pounded away on the guy, eyes all bugged out behind those thick glasses. As a matter of fact it was a guy Frenchy had been talkin' to." Big Don stopped, embarrassed at how he had run-on about Pilson's bizarre nature.

Despite the alcohol, the mood in the kitchen became sober as everyone marshalled their own quiet thoughts of a man they were beginning to miss.

"Franny, have you made any funeral plans yet?" It was the first time Frank had addressed her. "If there's anything we can do you just holler. Okay?" Jeannie moved beside him and slipped her arm through his and nodded, affirming what he said.

She thought a few seconds, recalling how Frenchy and she had on rare occasions discussed what they should do in the event either of them should die.

"Don't wanna be no worm food. Lemme go wit de wind in smoke," he had once said as they lay in bed.

"Well, Frenchy didn't have any life insurance. Never got around to taking any out, so I guess that leaves out a formal funeral. Said he didn't want to be buried anyway. Couldn't stand the thought of being underground for eternity. Said he spent most of his life there and wasn't going to spend anymore than he had to." She spoke quietly, almost whispering, her eyes studying the floor. "Drilling was his life, it was all he knew. I remember him telling me once about a tour we had through the smelter. We watched the big furnaces and all the liquid metal. Late that night Frenchy said it would be a great way to meet his maker. Clean, everything into the air, no more underground, no fuss, no muss."

Frank studied her with a curious stare. "You sure that's what he said? Because if that's what you really want for him, I think we can help you out there." All eyes had turned toward him, some accusing, others thankful for a solution.

"I believe Frenchy'd really appreciate the gesture," said Big Don, his hands deep in his pockets, glancing to Toothless Jake for support.

"Out in a blafe of glory!" shouted Jake as he downed the last of his whiskey and displayed his pink gums in a huge grin to the others whose sense of adventure had been equally distorted by the alcohol.

Patty leaned close and spoke in a low voice. "Franny, your signature can release his body, but it's the funeral parlour that usually picks it up. You can't just waltz in there and stuff Frenchy in the trunk of your car and not expect some pointed questions." The deepness of her voice was picked up by Toothless Jake's over-sized ears.

He interjected,"No problem. I got thif black fuit an' bowtie. Borrow my brofer in lawf black stafion wagon an have him picked up fafter than you could order a piffa."

Wanda turned sharply toward her husband and saw he was searching the counter for another bottle of anything to drink. "Jake how the hell can you compare Frenchy to a pizza for God's sake? His poor widow is standing right there and you say something like that."

"Speakin' a which, I'm a might hungry with all this drinkin' an' talkin'," declared Big Don, eyeing the refrigerator door where Patty was helping herself to a cold bottle of Coke to go with her whiskey. "Why don't we order out fer a pizza, since we're already on the subject?"

"Don, you humungous hyperthyroidal excuse for a human," honked patty in her deep voice. "We're not talking about food, we're talking about Frenchy."

"Okay then let's call a French restaurant an' order out from them. I'm sure Frenchy wouldn't object to that." Big Don was becoming glassy-eyed and beginning to salivate at the thought of food. He had a penchant for staying with one thought, and the combination of hunger and booze and his eyes were unwaveringly on the refrigerator.

"Oh fit, don't let him near the food in there or you'll never get him out of here." Toothless Jake was standing in front of Big Don who was smiling, his eyes becoming more glassy as he saw his diminutive, toothless partner assume a defensive stance as though he was a football player.

Big Don saw the challenge and charged his small partner in slow motion, stumbling over his feet as he lurched forward. The room shook as he crashed to the floor, the men and women alike jumping aside to allow his huge bulk to land. A small figurine toppled from a shelf, shattering beside him, as well as a flurry of notepaper which had been attached to the refrigerator door by magnets.

"Quick, put fomething in hif mouf, food, food," shouted Jake with glee as he sat on the wide expanse of his friends back.

Jeannie grabbed a box of cookies from a shelf and went down on her hands and knees to shove them one at a time into Big Don's mouth as he worked his jaws like the primary crusher at the bottom of Q-1 shaft Crumbs fanned out before him on the floor as he tried to chew and breath at the same time.

Patty and Frank had maneuvered Franny toward the front door. She was beginning to look a bit pale and was in need of fresh air.

"Don't you worry about anything Franny," said Patty. "Frank here is the Smelter Foreman and if Jake can be sober enough to act like an undertaker, you can have your own cremation service for Frenchy with the biggest darn furnace you ever saw.

She saw Frank nod in agreement and watched his mouth move, but never heard the words that came. The next thing she saw was the ground fast approaching and a pair of large hands reaching for her. She had forgotten she had no tolerance for alcohol.

The next day, in a combined fog of grief and hang over, she signed the papers for the release of Frenchy's body to T.J. Smiley's Funeral Emporium, and told the hospital administration the body would be picked up that day.

Toothless Jake Smiley showed up on time, dressed in his only black suit, white shirt and bow tie. He had borrowed his brother-in-law's black station wagon, washed, waxed it, and hurriedly vacuumed the interior. His demeanour was appropriately severe, the result of his own alcohol withdrawal symptoms from the day before, and despite the occasional curious glances at his reddened eyes and pink gums, no one questioned his credentials.

They probably figured that anyone who could walk around looking half-dead, driving a hearse was unquestionably a bonafide undertaker.

From the hospital he quickly drove to the explosives compound where he and Big Don in the privacy of the air-conditioned explosives magazine, tightly wrapped Frenchy's body in a new linen sheet. They transferred Frenchy's body to an elongated wooden crate with a fake packing slip to Frank Wyman, Day Shift Foreman of the smelter.

An hour later, Teresa D'Amico and her partner Joe Mckay showed up with a five ton truck to pick up a small load of explosives for Q-1 headframe, with instructions to deliver the wooden crate to the smelter area after unloading the explosives. Their questions as to the contents of the box went unanswered from a sombre Big Don and the red-eyed Toothless Jake, now wearing coveralls over his black suit. Neither Joe nor Teresa asked why he was wearing a bow tie.

By 2 pm, Frank Wyman had signed for the box and promptly burned his copy of the packing slip. Joe and Teresa did likewise as per their instructions from Toothless Jake.

They watched the smelter foreman place the box on a small flatcar and roll it to a siding just inside the huge doors of the smelter area. Neither of them desired to stay long in the area due to the choking levels of sulphur dioxide coming from the roasters, where the refined copper ore was being heated with the aid of oxygen to burn off the sulphur and produce calcine.

"God, how could anyone want to work in a place like this?" D'Amico's throat was becoming irritated by the burning sulphur fumes and her eyes watered. She could hear the roar of the high temperature reverberating furnaces. The eleven-hundred degree Celsius flames melted the ore where it was mixed with the calcine and silica reagents known as fluxes to aid the separation of the ore and allow the reject slag to float to the top of the glowing molten mass. *This must be what hell smells like and the people who work here are getting a taste of it.*

They returned to the trucking terminal, wondering what their slightly crazy friends at the explosives depot were up to. Joe burned the packing slip and flushed the ashes down the terminal toilet.

Earlier that day, Patty Watson had called the Quesnel Public Relations Department, identifying herself as a member of the local environmental action group, requesting a tour of the smelter operation and asked if it would be possible to schedule it for 3:30 pm. The P.R. spokes- person hummed and hawed and at her insistence, called the day shift foreman of the smelter to see if they could be accommodated. As luck would have it, they could be because one of the converter furnaces was to be shut down today for maintenance and they could watch the final batch of ore being poured off. Patty quickly called the others and told them to appear at the Public Relations office where they were to pick up their hard hats for the guided tour. She made arrangements to pick up Franny Rivest.

Peter Elvers of the P.R. Department had never seen such a well-dressed tour come through since the Japanese contingent two weeks before. He was struck by their serious nature and was surprised and relieved they didn't ask any pointed questions about the extent of sulphur dioxide emissions fouling the air in the immediate area and hundreds of miles downwind.

Elvers, followed by the silent entourage, explained the smelting processes and stressed how the flue gases were passed through electrostatic precipitators to collect up to 95% of the dust and return it for reprocessing. He also told them how the sulphur dioxide was submitted to catalytic oxidation, producing sulphur trioxide which was used to make sulphuric acid, a by-product which they sold on the market. None of the tour group seemed interested in the information he was giving them.

They walked slowly, a couple of them holding hands with their spouses, others with their hands gripped together in front of them. They neither smiled nor showed any curiosity about the processes the tour guide had explained.

"I hope you folks don't mind, I've asked our company photographer to join us to get a few shots of this tour to update some of our file material." He pointed to the thickset and rather bored photographer who had just joined the group and was moving from one angle to another while taking shots.

"Now folks, we're coming to one of the final phases of the refining process. the slag from the blast furnace has been scraped or topped off and the remaining molten matte has been poured into this converter. It will be mixed with blown air as well as fluxes and reducing agents, the resulting 99% pure copper will then be cast into forms called anodes.

"My God," said Franny, "Frenchy's going to be an anode!"

"I beg you pardon?" said Elvers, turning to study the woman whose eyes were red and beginning to stream with tears. *Sulphur dioxide levels must be going up.*

For the first time, she became really aware of her surroundings, seeing themselves in a huge industrial cathedral-like area, a huge crane moving on twin gantries high above from where they stood on the track floor. Facing them was a row of six huge furnaces which were the converters where they could see their glowing mouths lit by the molten ore within. The roar of high pressure air was constant as the overhead crane moved silently above them, its huge steel bucket suspended on winch cables. She watched, now fascinated as the bucket approached one converter which had rolled on its horizontal axis to present a white hot open mouth. The crane's bucket tipped its contents into the hungry maw from which sparks and flame shot upon receiving its' load of flux and reducing agents. Another converter slowly rolled forward and poured a white hot stream of ore into a waiting ladle which would be hauled quickly away to be poured into waiting moulds. There was a cacophony of sounds mixed with sharp stinging odours and the glowing heat of the furnaces.

They stopped at the last converter where Elvers looked up to the sound of a warning siren. The huge crane was sliding along the gantry, its' huge bucket coming ponderously toward them. He recognized Frank Wyman at the controls. The others followed his gaze and also recognized Frank, dressed in a suit and tie. Elvers waved to Wyman who waved back. The rest of the group returned the wave and diverted their eyes to the bucket approaching them.

"My God, it's Frenchy," whispered Franny, clutching Patty's hand. She could see a bundle, wrapped in white cloth protruding from the bucket. Frenchy's body looked like a small, freshly-wrapped Egyptian mummy. Looking closer, she saw he had been placed head-up as though trying to get one last peek over the bucket's brim at the world, and those he had known and loved.

The bucket stopped in front of them and to the confusion of their tour guide, each of the group moved slowly forward and placed their hands on the top of the wrapped object resting in the bucket.

Elvers, the tour guide was confused. *What in hell is going on here, and why is Wyman up there in the cab crying?* He could see each member of the group's lips moving as though in prayer.

The photographer, sensing something extraordinary was occurring, shot frantically from every angle possible. No one paid him any attention.

Slowly, the bucket ascended to the accompaniment of the smelter's chorus of sounds. It moved laterally toward the molten mouth of the converter and tipped majestically, sliding the wrapped bundle into the roaring furnace. The red-hot mouth hungrily accepted the offering and belched a shower of smoke and sparks.

Franny screamed when she saw Frenchy's body disappear and the flash of sparks and flame from the converter's mouth as his small body came in contact with the molten mass. She buried her head in patty's shoulder and whispered his name over and over, trying to imagine his remains wafting in a cloud from the high stack to spread over the countryside, his elements mingling once more with those of nature.

Two smelter workers going off shift had moved closer to the group and unwittingly observed the cremation of Frenchy Rivest.

"Must be somethin' new," said one worker to the other. "Never seen flux used in lump- form before."

Patty held Franny close by the waist as the others moved around to console her.

They became conscious of a continued howling above them from a catwalk high above. Their eyes caught sight of a thin form with magnified eyes behind thick glasses. Except for his hard hat, he was stark naked. They stared as he clutched the railing of the catwalk, his mouth open, creating the ungodly wail of a man in mental agony. Off to the side, they were barely aware of the photographer shooting pictures with a telephoto lens of the figure high above them.

Bardman had been so surprised by the bizarre nature of the scene he was witnessing that he nearly forgot to use his camera. The sight of an obviously human form, wrapped in white cloth in view over the edge of the large steel ladle had unnerved him. He could also see it had unnerved Elvers, whose mouth hung open in dismay. No one else appeared surprised at the scene and it was then he realised he was witnessing a cremation. He worked frantically, shooting from every conceivable angle, no longer shooting for the company but for himself. He knew the company would order the negatives destroyed to avoid a public relations disaster. The howl at first had sounded like a warning siren to signal some smelter operation about to proceed. Glancing high above him, he saw movement on a narrow catwalk which ran the length of the building, near the ceiling. At several sections there were junctions where other catwalks joined among the latticework of steel supports and high intensity sodium-vapour lights.

With the 300 millimetre lens, he could recognize Pilson's face, the eyes bulging behind the huge lenses, his mouth open like a howler monkey, and what appeared to be a small stream of drool running from his cheek. Setting the shutter speed to one-sixtieth of a second and the lens aperture to f3.5, he had barely enough light to expose for his face. As the motor-driven Olympus exposed four quick frames in less than a second, Bardman sensed something different. He realised his subject was stark naked except for a hard hat and a pair of steel-toed gumboots. Three frames later, the naked apparition turned and ran along a short catwalk. A cloud of reddish sulphur dust billowed up behind him from the walkway. His gangly, white frame loped like a starved naked ape through a deafening, sulphur-stinking steel jungle to disappear into a darkened corner of pipes and steel braces.

Elvers' face was a mask of profound confusion, a subject Bardman could not resist. With the 24mm lens on the other camera body, Elvers never heard the clicking of the shutter over the tympanic symphony surrounding them.

Wordlessly, the group turned and started back down the track floor from whence they had come. One small woman with dark hair turned frequently to gaze back where the small body had been immolated, then with shoulders hunched and head lowered, walked arm in arm with a friend to a side door into the surrealistic brightness of a warm summer day. Brady Bardman was very confused.

"Bardman, did you get any pictures of all this?"

He turned to Elvers who was still glancing to the dark areas above. "Pictures of what?" he replied innocently.

"Of all of it. The thing in the ladle...looked like a body, and... and, that thing on the catwalk above. Didn't you see it?"

"What are you talking about Elvers? he replied, hoping to confuse the man even more. "Two smelter workers were standing right here. Said flux in lump form is being used all the time. And what's so special about some guy using the catwalk to get to the roaster section?"

Elvers looked hard at him, then blinked in slow motion as though awaking from a bad dream. "So, what did you get pictures of?"

"Oh I got shots of the group as you explained things to them. I concentrated on their looks of confusion. Sort of the expression you have on your face right now." He saw Elvers' expression become hostile. "Then I got a shot of the sparks flying from the mouth of the converter after the flux was dumped in. Zenon always tells me to get the parks because it's dramatic. I also got a shot of you pointing your finger at the crane, like this..." He duplicated the gesture for Elvers' benefit, enjoying the man's discomfort.

"Wrong finger Bardman." said Elvers with a hard voice. "Try this one next time," as he extended his middle finger toward him. There was hatred in his eyes. "You always were a smart-ass, and smart-asses don't go very far in this company."

"That's right," he said, facing Elvers, his arms hanging at his sides, but prepared to drop the camera bag in a hurry if need be. "We'd rather move aside and let the ass-kissers have the top jobs. We refuse to be wipers of other people's dirty little bottoms."

Elvers turned on his heel and stalked off.

Bardman hurried to the darkroom and quickly prepared the C-41 colour chemicals for the film. As the chemicals were warming to the desired temperature in the stainless steel water jacket, he closeted himself in the film-loading room and in total darkness, with a small bottle opener, began popping the tops from each of the four canisters of exposed film. Each 36 exposure roll was loaded by hand onto a spiral stainless steel reel and slid into a stainless steel, light-tight developing tank. The process of development, followed by a combined bleach-fixing step, and wash, took only twelve minutes. The film was hung in a drying cabinet and the temperature and fan turned to high.

Ten minutes later, he was looking at each individual frame as the negative strips lay on the long light table, using a magnifying loup close to his eye. With low grunts of approval he quickly clipped segments from the strips, placing them in clear sleeve-pages for storage. Other strips were transferred to sleeves which he folded and secured together with a paper clip. These folded strips were inserted into the neck of his unused thermos bottle and, placed in his lunch kit. The darkroom clock said four-fifteen and he quickly gathered his equipment, locked the darkroom door and headed for the exit. As he walked in the sunshine toward the parking lot, he became aware of shouts of displeasure from the security gate.

A long line of freshly showered miners and mill workers were in line, having each personal item, including their identification badges checked by the rent-a-cops. The contents of one man's lunch kit was spread on a table outside the security shack, and the guard, a three-hundred pound hulk with a scowling dark complexion was dumping the remains of the man's thermos bottle onto the ground, to the howls and protests of those still waiting in line.

Even more troubling was the presence of an RCMP squad car with two officers sitting inside. Another officer stood by the table with a leash in one hand, a sad-eyed, floppy-eared beagle straining at the end of it.

The beagle sat slightly ahead of the officer, sniffing each worker as he passed. Suddenly the beagle emitted a long howl, bouncing up and down its forelegs, ears flopping as it pointed its muzzle accusingly at the miner with the green garbage bag in one hand.

The officer motioned the man to the side as the two other officers exited from the car.

"You train that damn dog to sniff out dirty laundry? This where our tax dollars go to put you yahoos in those fancy monkey suits? The miner was flinging the filthy work clothing from the bag to the ground as the beagle became more agitated with each item. Finally, the miner flung a pair of thoroughly soiled long, red, underwear at the dog, which backed away, shaking its head to divest itself of this new and unappreciated adornment.

A tall constable stepped forward and with his back ramrod stiff and in his best parade ground voice shouted, "You there sir, stop throwing your underwear."

The crowd of miners in line broke up in laughter as the now blushing constable turned and silently threatened them with his unruly moustache. This elicited even more laughter amid the howls of the beagle which promptly lifted its leg and relieved itself on the formerly immaculate trouser leg of Constable Pusch.

A small bespectacled man in a suit and apologetic expression stepped forward and spoke quietly with the miner, then turned to Pusch. "I told you this wouldn't work, this man is a blaster. He handles explosives all day; the stuff is even in his skin. This dog is trained to sniff out explosives in luggage, not in an environment where the place reeks of it." The small man turned to the officer holding the leash. Constable, take Proboscis to the car and give him a biscuit. Have one yourself, you look like you could use something hard to chew on." The small man leaned toward Pusch, who visibly flinched, perhaps fearing a bite to his kneecap. "And you constable, from now on keep your *own proboscis* and that *hairy thing beneath it*, out of my investigation."

The constable strode ignominiously to the squad car where Proboscis continued to howl in the back seat. The car turned and with a spray of gravel, sped away, but not before the line of workers witnessed him remove his cap and fling it at the dog in the rear seat.

Bardman had watched the abortive attempt by the beagle and had the presence of mind to take his camera from the bag on his shoulder. He was thankful he had the habit of taking the telephoto lens wherever he went with his equipment. It allowed him to record events from a distance when he might otherwise be confronted.

He took mental stock of all the images he had made concerning the mysterious happenings underground. He knew that the images he had captured, as well as being the witness to much of it, that it would one day make one hell of a story. But who would buy it? It was almost too incredible to believe, and no credible publication would take it without rigorous corroboration.

In his apartment he retrieved the negative strips from within the thermos with the aid of a pair of long-nosed pliers. He gently grasped the edge of the folded file pages and drew the material gently to the opening where he could retrieve it with his fingers. The page was lovingly unfolded and placed between the pages of a large coffee table book about A Day in The Life of Australia. He replaced the book with others he had collected over the years and changed clothes in preparation to return to the sight where he had buried the explosives.

As he rummaged through his dresser-drawer in search of a clean T-shirt, he had the feeling something was different about his surroundings. He looked back at the collection of large photo books and saw they were in fact arranged in the opposite order he usually kept them. Looking back at his dresser drawer, he remembered that because the handles were missing from the top drawer, he usually kept it partially open so he could pull it out by hooking his fingers over the top lip. When he had opened it this time, he found it necessary to pry open with a pair of scissors. Somebody's been snooping through my stuff! He quickly changed, retrieved the negatives from the book and left the apartment, with the kayak on the roof-rack of his Volkswagen, taking with him, the phone number of Samantha Paige. With a pocketful of change, he dialled her work number from a pay phone and was put through to the editorial department by the switchboard. "It's me, call pay phone number three in exactly twenty minutes." He didn't giver her time to reply, once he was sure it was really her on the other end. He checked his watch and drove to the other side of town where he parked at a drive-in A&W There was a pay phone mounted on the outside of the building's wall. As he drank a root beer, the phone rang at the correct time and he answered after two rings.

"Are you okay?" Her voice sounded worried and he could hear other voices and a police scanner in the background.

"Yeah I'm okay. Are you alone?"

"You're never alone in a newsroom, but don't worry nobody can hear this conversation over the noise. Tell me what's happening?

"Do you have a safe place to store some sensitive negatives?

"How sensitive?"

"Enough to get us thrown in jail or make us moderately rich, depending on how they're used. I need a place that only you and I know about. Wait a minute. Why are you calling from the newsroom? I said use a pay phone.

"This is a pay phone, it's right next to the newsroom for public use, so give me a break with all this cloak and dagger stuff. Okay?"

"Sorry, I'm a little upset. Someone broke into my place today while I was at work and snooped around. I thought I was getting a little paranoid, but now I'm sure. You still there Sam?"

"Yes, I'm going to give you an address. It's my grandmother's. She's in the hospital and I'm collecting her mail. How are you going to send it?"

"Express Post," said Bardman as he wrote the address on the back of a business card. "Then what are you going to do with it?"

"She has a stack of photo albums, separate ones for each member of the family. The negs will be in the one with my name on it. Don't worry, they'll be safe. You still haven't told me what's going on. Before I run out of quarters, I'd appreciate a little reciprocity for my efforts here."

He realised he had called her at the end of the day and she was on deadline. It was the daily pressure-cooker environment which he was thankful at times to have escaped, but still missed the excitement of a breaking story.

"It's really bizarre and it would take more time than we have here. Please trust me on this Sam, because it's a story I want you to write to go with the photographs."

"Okay send it," said her voice, all business. "But I hope you're keeping notes because a story that can't be substantiated is worth nothing."

She abruptly hung up and he went to his car and transferred the address onto a large orange envelope for which he had paid several dollars for quick delivery through the mail. He had put the sheet of negatives between two cardboard stiffeners for extra protection and sealed it. He drove to the post office minutes before closing time and gave the envelope to the girl behind the wicket, who wrote the address in a large ledger. His next stop was a sporting goods store where he bought a box of twelve gauge shotgun shells. Thus equipped, he drove to the small road which led where he had buried the explosives, near the riverbank. The grass was longer, but the site was easy to find, equidistant between two distinctive birch trees. He recovered one box which had formerly held photographic paper and removed from it the heavy black plastic material containing the granular explosive. Re-covering the small excavation, he stowed the materials in the rear hull of the kayak and pushed off upstream. He stopped periodically to scratch and slap at the insects that had attacked him while on the riverbank. The horseflies in particular droned around his head and landed on his arms, sometimes flying off with what felt like small chunks of his skin in their jaws. He paddled for a half hour and turned into a small tributary which after five minutes of paddling, came to a dead end in a small pond surrounded by Precambrian shield. The granite was covered with patches of lichen and moss, living in their symbiotic relationship.

He sat a few minutes, listening to the sounds around him, breathing in the clean smells of nature. He flushed the stench of the smelter from his memory as he sat, eyes closed, the kayak rocking gently beneath him.

He regretted what he was about to do, but deemed it necessary for the required culmination of his plans. His plan, though still vague, was taking shape in his mind and he surprised himself that he had not seriously thought of the consequences. *Consequences result from inaction as well as action and only history can be the judge their worth.*

He eased the kayak to shore and removed the bag of explosives from the rear hull, along with a small plastic film canister from which he took a blasting cap. From another bag he took a length of fuse which he had made from smaller pieces recovered from the track floor while on his many assignments underground. With care he had spliced the segments together, except for one piece which he lay on a flat rock and ignited. As it burned, sputtering and smoking, he timed the duration of burn, then calculated the estimated burn-time for the longer fuse.

Taking one of the shotgun shells, he pried open the end and removed the pellets and the plastic wadding. From another shell casing, he poured the black powder contents into the first cartridge and re-crimped the end shut. The cartridge now contained twice as much powder but no pellets, and would act as the primer, or second stage of the detonation. He attached the blasting cap to the fuse and with a small piece of child's plasticine, attached the cap to the rear of the shotgun shell where the pin strikes the primer. The plasticine completely covered the cap to direct the force of the detonation against the cartridge primer. Cutting a small circular hole the size of the shot shell into the bag of explosives, he inserted the cartridge until only the fuse remained. More plasticine was flattened around the edges of the incision to seal the hole. He then partially filled two large orange heavy-duty garbage bags with water, tying the tops to contain the water. These were placed over the explosive package which was sitting next to a large moss-covered boulder. He took a lighter from his life jacket pocket and applied the flame to the end of the fuse, his hand shaking slightly from anticipation. He held the flame to the fuse for several minutes without results and realised a much hotter flame was needed to take the place of the usual fuse igniter-strip. He opened another shot shell and poured the black powder over the end of the fuse resting on the rock, to form a small mound of bitter smelling grains. Once more he applied the lighter flame and jumped back as the powder burned with a quick, white intensity. A prolonged hissing sound told him the fuse was burning and he quickly walked to the kayak and pushed off.

He estimated a time of ten minutes for the fuse to reach the charge and took note of the time as he paddled from the small tributary. Out in the main river channel, he paddled several more minutes and took cover under an overhang of rock. As he sat in the kayak, watching the minute hand of his watch, he felt the familiar paranoia of being watched sweep over him. Looking quickly around, he saw nothing unusual but could not shake the feeling of being observed. Another glance at the watch showed the blast should have occurred over a minute ago. He dreaded the thought of a misfire, as did the miners who had to flush the unexploded grains out of the bootleg holes before drilling could begin again. He knew that whenever a charge did not go off, it was given a half hour before someone braved a look to see what had gone wrong.

The air shook with the blast and echoed from the rock outcropping. A panicked raven flew from a nearby tree, squawking in protest.

He quickly paddled to the site to inspect the results. Shreds of orange garbage bag littered the ground where the boulder used to be. In its' place was a gouge from the underlying rock and fragments of stone fanned out from the point of detonation.

He was pleased the bags of water had directed the blast in mostly one direction, against the boulder, shattering it, and spreading it like shrapnel. He gathered up as much of the shredded plastic as possible, his ears still ringing from the report. He could detect the slight petroleum aroma of the explosive. With the sun lowering in the sky, he paddled downstream to where his car was parked thinking perhaps he should have used a little less explosive.

CHAPTER 15

He awoke amidst the roar of fans. Ever since that day when his arms and legs moved of their own accord, while his mind and eyes had watched in a dream-like state as his body brutally and systematically bludgeoned the small, squirming red object to a pulp. His brain had twisted like a trapped rat in a fleshy cage, unable to escape He had ceased to be in control with himself, if in fact he had ever been in control of what he considered to be himself. He had become more than one, perhaps several. *No, this is me. This is the true essence of my being. Now I'm FREE.* The voices had begun then.

The huge ventilator fans shook the metal building. Their blades mounted in the walls sucked in the fresh, cool air in chunks of flickering stroboscopic light which transformed the interior into a collage of flashes, shadows, and ceaseless noise. He could no longer hear the noise, but the voices still spoke to him. The little one, his partner was gone, killed by the little evil one in the red suit. His one reason for going each day into that hellish hole had been taken from him, but still he went back. There was a reason for going back, but the voices had not revealed his purpose.

We will.

They spoke to him and he obeyed. He could smell dust and grease combined with the sharp ozone smell created by electric motors. His hand crept from under the layers of rough burlap to search for his glasses, his long, nobby fingers walking across the rough wood like some blind, albino spider. They touched something soft and furry. Recoiling in surprise, the hand touched again, recognizing the carcass of a dead rodent. The glasses were found and placed on the face where the eyes finally blinked as though seeing whirling, deafening world for the first time. The hand found the shrivelled rat and held it to his nose. It was rancid and stiff, the meat gone from its rear haunches and tiny underbelly. He moved over the metal-grill floor through which the outside air passed to the depths, to a corner of the roaring building, squatted, and defecated, finally wiping himself with a corner of the pile of burlap which had been his bed.

You must go down again. There are things you must acquire to survive, to avenge the passing of the little one. I'LL BE WITH YOU. I WILL GUIDE YOU.

He reached for his ragged coveralls hanging from a nail and pulled them over his scrawny white body, slipping into the gumboots, the hard hat settling over his ears. He no longer had a light but he had his guides peering from behind his eyes and they had never led him astray, especially the one who shouted. His voice made his head ache with its intensity. Bending down, he opened a trapdoor in the floor which showed a vertical ladder, leading down into the depths of the ventilation shaft, and further into the bowels of the rock where there were things he needed. Unerringly and without hesitation he descended into the cool, inky blackness where the darkness was complete and his soul felt at home.

Joe and Teresa were on the last leg home from the powder run. They had taken a load of forty-thousand pounds of explosives to the hydro project, unloaded quickly and just as quickly, made the return trip. During the past six hours, Joe had barely spoken to her, his glance usually out the window, at the tree line.

"Watching for more raven farts Joe?" asked Teresa, disappointed in his lack of response. She saw his eyes move frequently from the road to the trees along the roadside. He chewed his lower lip in thought. At that moment, the only thing Teresa felt they had in common was the small leather medicine bag each wore around their neck. "You know, you've been really quiet since you've started spending more time with your dad. How come you don't take Sadie and Josh with you on those visits?"

"How do you know I don't?" he replied, impatience in his voice, his eyes straight ahead.

"Because I know that's where you go on your days off and sometimes when I go shopping I see Sadie shopping by herself. You used to always go with her and now she does it all." There was a tone of accusation in her voice which finally caused Joe to look at her. His eyes disturbed her. His expression was one of uncertainty and confusion.

"Not your business partner. My business."

She was taken aback by his abruptness, feeling a near hostility she felt she didn't deserve. "Just asking," she said quietly, now afraid to look at him. Instead, she watched the sun lowering in the west.

"Sorry," he said finally after several moments.

"No, it's okay, you were right It really wasn't my business. I didn't mean to snoop."

"It's just that I'm learnin' things that are turnin' my whole world upside down. Things about my dad, who he is, and who I am."

She said no more, happy to have elicited at least some response from him. Over the last month she had seen the changes in him and she knew they must be affecting his personal life. She knew these changes were none of her business, but knew mutual trust was important considering the cargo they were hauling. The cargo. She had been disturbed to see how Joe worked until sweating profusely to off-load the bags of explosives. He picked up each 50 pound bag and slammed it down onto the aluminum rollers that lead to the blockhouse and propelled them with an audible grunt of exertion into the waiting arms of the receivers. The rollers clattered and whirred as the bags passed over them, and on rare occasions, one would flip from the rollers to land with a thump on the ground, six feet below. There had been an audible intake of breath despite the stability of the explosive. *He seems to have a hatred for what we're hauling. Maybe it's more a hatred for what it does or at least represents.*

The sound of the explosion snapped their heads to the left. It had been a sharp crack of sound and quickly became an echo in the distance.

Joe quickly brought the truck to a stop on the side of the road and shut the engine off. Besides the groaning of the air brakes and tinkling of the cooling engine, there was no other sound. The air was dead still in the early summer warmth and the dust from the road hung in the air like brown fog. Gradually, the croaking of mating leopard frogs floated from the wet areas where they had been silenced by the blast. They sat several more minutes, listening, wondering why someone was blasting out there, wondering where it had come from. He restarted the truck and continued toward the Bailey bridge that spanned the Black Wood River. When they finally reached the bridge, he slowed the Kenworth to a crawl and as they crept across the swollen river, they both looked upriver toward the now-disappearing sun which had coloured the river's water a vivid orange.

As they neared the far end, Teresa caught a glimpse of a lone figure paddling a kayak, rounding the far bend. The double-bladed paddle was moving quickly, the water cutting a graceful wake behind the craft. She couldn't make out the features of the paddler but knew it was Brady.

Joe turned to her, a question forming on his lips but said nothing.

She simply shrugged her shoulders in reply and continued to stare at the paddler as the kayak disappeared among the darkness of the shoreline trees, only the wake of the craft remaining and spreading like a gentle fan on the sun-orange waters. *Why are people acting so strange these days, or am I the one who is acting strange?*

When Bardman got home, he immediately removed his clothing and threw them into the washing machine. As the laundry was being done, he showered to remove any possible traces of the explosive from his skin. The last thing he wanted was Proboscis the beagle sniffing around his ankles. As he dried his hair with a towel, he sat in his bathrobe at the small kitchen table studying the prints of the control gates which had swollen the waters of the river. A plan was taking form in his mind, but he was reluctant to put anything down on paper since he was convinced someone had searched his apartment.

With a beer in-hand, he turned on the television to catch the news and immediately saw a file photo of the hydro project. He quickly turned up the volume and caught a portion of the narration about another death being reported at the site. The camera cut to a man identified as the union representative, who was calling for an inquiry into the safety practices of the workforce. He knew Samantha Paige would be watching this and hoping to convince her editors of the need to pursue the issue. He sipped his beer, reclining on the ratty old sofa as the weather man came on, waving his hands at a weather map and audibly gulping his excess saliva between breathless explanations of fronts and lows. The announcer traded pre-planned, banal quips with the newscaster whose eyebrows moved up and down like a blow-dried puppet. The more banal the quip, the higher the eyebrows went.

A pounding came from the door at the top of the landing. He barely had time to check that his bathrobe belt was secured before hearing footsteps coming down the steps. He heard Teresa's yoo-hoo's just as he flung the shots of the control gate into a drawer and slammed it shut.

"Are you decent?" she said as she poked her head around the door frame, smiling at the sight of a slightly flustered Bardman, still checking the status of his robe.

"Always decent when you're around. I'm just having a beer. Would you like one?"

"I thought I could treat you, maybe go to the Stagger-Inn, take in some of the atmosphere and maybe go for dinner later. My treat." She watched with quiet amusement, the reaction of a man who was not used to being invited out by a woman. No matter how liberated he pretended to be, his chauvinistic inhibitions showed through.

"Yeah, sure, why not, sounds good," he replied without enthusiasm as he backed into the bedroom area and pulled the dividing curtain across for some privacy to change.

She could hear him rummaging through his dresser-drawers, heard him snap- test the elastic on a pair shorts and rattle hangers in the closet as he rummaged for a clean shirt.

"I saw you paddling on the river today. Were you out with your camera?" The sound of rummaging stopped abruptly, followed by a silence.

"Uh, yeah, didn't see anything though," he lied as he continued his hunt for fresh socks. He finally resorted to retrieving a recent pair from the laundry basket, sniffed, and deemed them barely suitable. He quickly smeared some Old Spice under his armpits and exited to the kitchenette where Teresa had made herself comfortable, her feet propped on the table. He was uneasy by the searching glance she gave him, knowing that for some reason she didn't quite believe what he was saying.

She wore a white blouse tucked into a pair of faded jeans and a pair of tattered running shoes on her feet. Her hands were folded across her flat belly, her thumbs twiddling as she studied him with an intensity that was troubling.

"Shall we go then? I can't wait for the aroma of second-hand smoke," he offered, grateful to break her studied silence.

She bounced from the chair, nearly toppling it to the floor and jogged up the stairs ahead of him.

Bardman knew he would never get tired of watching her pert derriere in tight jeans but had the discretion not to say so.

The stench of stale beer and cigarette smoke issued from the neon-lit entrance in a visible miasma, mingled with the sounds of shouts, laughter, and the constant moaning from the juke box, where Randy Travis groaned on about exhuming bones or something.

A pert blonde woman with a huge tray of beer balanced on one hand negotiated herself between a crush of patrons toward their table against the wall. "You vant beer peoples?"

Brady held up two fingers and she promptly plopped two glasses of draught in front of him.

Teresa ordered a rye and ginger-ale.

"You vant drink right now, you drink beer, oddervise you vait. Iss not cocktail lounge," said the waitress, her fist resting on her hip, sizing Teresa up and down with a critical stare.

273

"Alright, gimme the damn beer," she muttered under her breath, reaching for her purse.

With their backs to the wall, they were able to take in the semi-controlled chaos of the Stagger-Inn and watch in amazement as the two waitresses negotiated the crowded tables with the ease of surly ballerinas, pirouetting between the gantlet of grasping hands, delivering drinks, scooping up money and tips while verbally countering a litany of usually indecent proposals. That they could also remember what most people drank was equally amazing to Teresa and Brady, sitting quietly, sipping their beer, each thinking maybe this wasn't such a great idea.

A burly, bearded man wearing a white shirt and name tag on the pocket had approached a table near them and could be seen having a word with an obviously drunk patron.

Teresa elbowed Brady gently in the ribs. "This should be good, watch this."

The patron grinned drunkenly up at the bouncer, his hat on sideways, his tongue protruding from between pink gums where there were once teeth. At the same table sat a huge blonde man watching the bouncer with interest. The bouncer was obviously ill-at-ease with the stares of the big man but was determined to eject the drunken patron with the offensive tongue.

The patrons at the surrounding tables were also observing with interest. Finally, the bouncer reached for the small toothless man to bodily remove him only to have his wrist seized in the vice-like grip of the huge blonde friend. No words were spoken between them but the pain in the bouncer's wrist spoke volumes as he released Toothless Jake. The blonde waitress quickly intervened, shouldering the bouncer aside and gripping the earlobe of Toothless, pulled him slowly from the chair. With his earlobe still firmly in her grip, she quickly walked him like some errant school boy to the door as he imploringly slurred her name. "Aw Natafa, aw Natafa..."

Big Don gave a slow wink of recognition to Teresa and with surprising grace for a man of his size, rose from his chair to join them.

Brady had no intention of objecting and was surprised to see Teresa greet him with a pat on the cheek. He was quickly introduced and had his hand engulfed in a handshake.

Big Don shook his hand as though pumping water from a well. He then sat and leaned across the small round table, both elbows hanging over the edges, the eyes in his huge pink face squinting in the semi-

274

darkened room. He made a brief visual appraisal of Brady who had involuntarily leaned back in a defensive posture.

"Yer that photography fella ain't ya?"

Brady nodded.

"I heard ya took some interestin' pictures in the smelter the other day." Big Don smiled lethargically from one side of his mouth as he tipped his baseball cap back on his head. His chin was nearly resting on his arms on the table, but his eyes were alert. His right leg was pumping a rapid rhythm, making the beer glasses wobble on the table top.

"How did you hear that ?"

"Oh word gets around real quick about interestin' things in the mine, even to us 'boom-boys' out in the boonies." He glanced ponderously to the side at Teresa who was quietly sipping her beer and listening closely. "You got any special plans for those pictures of our friend, or do you plan on sittin' on 'em for the rest of your life?"

"I'm not sure I know which pictures you mean," replied Brady, defensively, feeling very uncomfortable with the direct stare from the huge man. "I take all kinds of shots every day."

Big Don leaned back in his chair, pursing his lips as though trying to whistle, then smiled at the ceiling. Finally he leaned back onto the table, causing it to shift closer to Brady and Teresa, nearly trapping them both in their seats against the wall. "Ya see that little blonde waitress there? The one full-a piss an' vinegar?" he said, gesturing with a thumb over his shoulder. "Some of the powder Teri here delivers goes to her husband underground. He comes home with all kinds a interestin' stories of things goin' on down there, like people gettin' killed, an' others disappearin'. He also says he seen a photographer lots of times takin' pictures where there don't seem to be a helluva lot of reason to take pictures."

He sat quietly, his beer glass cradled in both hands, warily watching the blonde giant's unsmiling face. For long seconds the two men looked at each other. Teresa did not saying anything. He turned to her and spoke quietly. "Is this why you wanted me to come here for a beer ?"

"I'm sorry Brady," she said quietly. "Things have been happening that have been upsetting to a lot of people, myself included. Big Don and Jake lost a friend a while ago and his partner underground has disappeared. There's also a lot of explosives missing from underground and nobody seems to know anything about that either." She watched him closely, hoping a trust had not been betrayed between them but knowing he had not been completely forthcoming with her either.

Brady watched her back, wondering if she suspected him of anything. "Did you guys have anything to do with whoever broke into my apartment and rummaged around in the dresser drawers?"

Big Don and Teresa looked with surprise at each other, then back at Brady who was becoming upset at this informal interrogation.

"We had nothing to do with that, we swear," said Teresa, putting her hand gently on his arm in reassurance. "Is anything missing?"

"Not that I can see, but you know how organized I am. I might look for something I haven't used for months and realize it's gone."

The three of them sat in thought for several minutes, finishing their beer. The noise of the bar had increased with a dispute at the pool table, attracting attention where two men were heatedly discussing a rule of the game.

Natasha quickly walked to the table and pulled the electrical connection, rendering the table inoperable.Both men, swaying on their feet, still clutching their pool cues watched her in amazement. She pointed at their table and they quickly reclaimed their seats without objection. The pert blonde waitress gave them a threatening smile over her shoulder, making it clear to the men their table had been cut off from service. The patrons were quickly learning that no one fooled with Natasha.

"I could eat the back end out of a mule," rumbled Big Don. "You two goin' anywhere to eat?"

"Why don't you join us," said Brady, hoping it was alright with Teresa, and hoping the gesture would alleviate some of the suspicion that seemed to be directed his way. He turned to see her reaction and was relieved she was smiling back at him. They finally decided to walk across the street to a Chinese restaurant fondly referred to as the Ptomaine Palace, where the atmosphere was more conducive to conversation.

In the absolute darkness, the sounds of his footsteps on the track floor echoed faintly from the nearby rock walls of the drift. In some places the high-pressure air line hissed above his head like a warning from some invisible snake. Infrequently, the snap and rumble of explosives being set off could be heard as the sound was first transmitted through the dense rock. The air was cool and smelled of rusty water from the water lines that seemed to leak incessantly. Occasionally his boot struck a piece of jagged loose that had fallen from the ceiling or from an ore car. The darkness no longer bothered him. It was a comfort to him not to have people look at him, stare at his eyes, watch his throat move in its manic nervousness. Nor did he sweat profusely anymore, something that he knew repelled people when he was in public. He remembered in high school how old Kroeker, the teacher had sent him home to change his shirt because of his sweating. Rather than tell him he didn't have another shirt, he left and didn't come back that day. *Yeah, old Kroeker, we croaked you alright. Made fun of us in front of the class and you became our guest at a barbecue. Town of Kneejerk didn't miss you. Nobody missed you, and nobody screwed with us after that. Not even sweet little Janice Brown. Too bad.* His stomach grumbled with hunger as he came to the turn in the drift that led to the lift station on the eight-hundred foot level. He slowly shouldered aside one of the huge orange swinging blast doors and peeked into the cavernous area. It was lit with the cold light of overhead fluorescent tubes, hurting his eyes. The only sign of activity was a small flatcar on a siding, stacked with bags of explosives. The mouth of the shaft entrance was blocked by the heavy steel lattice door, the steel cables barely visible beyond, quivering under the tension of the cage being raised or lowered. His ears caught the familiar sound of the ore-skip in an adjacent shaft, moving at blurring speed, lifting twenty tonnes of ore in a huge counter-weighted bucket from the primary crusher to the surface. His magnified eyes fell on the red door next to the cage entrance. He knew it was the lunchroom where the drillers, working two kilometres down the drift came for safe refuge during blasting. He quickly moved toward the red door and listened with his ear against it, hearing nothing from inside. Slowly, he opened the door and saw long benches and tables where several lunch kits and rucksacks lay in disarray. He opened each lunch box, removing an item from each, but took nothing from the fourth one. When he opened it, it stank of kilbasa with its spiced greasiness. Previously he had plundered this lunch kit because it was the only one available and the reaction of his stomach and bowels from the spiced sausage had been enough to shock his own insensitive nose. He quickly rummaged through two of the bags and found a change of clothing, a shirt and jeans. He rolled the jeans into the shirt and tied the arms together for easier carrying. Inside the bag was also a rolled magazine. He opened it hoping it would be a girly magazine and was disappointed to see it was the company magazine with the company logo, QM in the upper corner. Inside he saw pictures of areas he recognized and when he turned the page he held his breath, his eyes growing larger. He was staring at a shot of Frenchy as he worked on their drill rig. He saw himself with his face turned away from the camera. He had always hated seeing pictures of himself and had avoided cameras as others might avoid violence. The photographic image always mutilated the way he saw himself and he tried to avoid it at all cost.

Except the day we dealt with Frenchy's murderer. The bright light in our eyes, blinding us. He saw us. He knows who we are. We have to find him. He comes down here a lot. What's his name? It's inside the cover...there, Bardman. We've seen him, always snooping around. We'll wait for him. No, that might be too late, we have to FIND HIM. The voices inside his head had come to agreement, they had to find him.

The signal bell at the side of the cage entrance rang in a quick staccato, snapping his thoughts back to the present. He quickly stuffed the food inside his coveralls along with the magazine and ran in a loping gait to the door. He opened it cautiously and peered out. No one was there, but he could no longer hear the rattle of the drills from the drift. He moved to the door marked MANWAY and went through it to the steep set of rungs which he could take to any level of the mine. The image of the explosives car and its deadly cargo remained in the dark, worm-eaten recesses of his mind, where his voices gnawed with the persistence of termites.

As soon as Bardman came into work that morning he found a note on the darkroom door summoning him to the President's office. With his guts beginning to tighten again, he walked the distance up the two flights of stairs and presented himself to the receptionist. She watched him with silent disapproval as he waited to be summoned. He was disturbed to hear the whining voice of constable Pusch come from within the other office. He was motioned into the office by the receptionist and he entered to see Jenkins in his customary position of standing against the front of his desk with his hands deep in his pockets. Sitting to one side with his cap on his knee was Pusch, a notebook in one hand, his huge moustache wriggling in anticipation.

No introductions were deemed necessary and Jenkins came straight to the point. "Mr. Bardman, we thought it prudent to inform you that a search warrant was issued for your residence last week on the basis of substantial amounts of explosives missing from areas where you had frequently been seen taking photographs. According to constable Pusch here, a sniffing dog was used for the search, but considering that you frequented areas where it's possible your clothing could be exposed to the chemicals, the dog's reaction can't be considered incriminating, It seems every second worker here stinks of the stuff. Some more than others obviously"

He looked from Jenkins to Pusch, who twirled his cap on the forefinger of his right hand, an embarrassed grin on his face. "Am I still a suspect in this fiasco or can I assume my privacy will be respected from now on?"

"Unfortunately, you're still a suspect Mr. Bardman and we have the prerogative to search your premises with or without your permission," whined Pusch. "What we would really like to know is what has become of many rolls of film unaccounted for over the past seven months."

"I thought we had clarified this before at our latest interrogation." He tried but failed to keep the impatience from his voice. "I don't file every shot. There are many negatives that are rejected and not of any use."

"For instance?" replied Pusch, leaning forward in his chair.

"For instance, cases where the flash hasn't fired, camera or subject movement, causing blurring of the image, developing marks, all kinds of things that get a negative chucked out."

"Any of it for personal use perhaps? For instance for sale to a newspaper?"

He squirmed as he stood before the two men. "Yeah, that was bad judgment and I've already promised it won't happen again. I've replaced the film I used, at my own expense."

"Well, actually that's of no worry to us at the detachment, but something strictly between you and your employer. However, we've moved all your negative files to our detachment for a closer look at all the images you've shot since you've been here in the hopes of finding one of this Pilson fellow who, is still missing. We've found his residence and searched it. It was a pig stye," continued the constable, wrinkling his large nose in distaste at the recollection. His moustache reacted to the extent that it nearly crawled off the side of his face.

Both Jenkins and Bardman stared, transfixed by the sight.

"There's been no sign of him?" asked Jenkins.

"None, but we send a patrol car around on a regular basis to check for signs of life. He continued in a fake British accent." Seems he's gone to ground."

"More like underground," volunteered Bardman.

"Unlikely," continued the fake British voice. "Where would he live, eat, and so on?"

"There are all kinds of nooks and crannies down there, not to mention sections of the mine that aren't producing anymore and are waiting to be back-filled. There are pillar raises, old stopes, manways and even old ore chutes no longer being used." He watched the expressions of Pusch and Jenkins as they came to the realization that a murderer might be living in the maze of tunnels below them, literally free to come and go at will.

"But how does he eat?"

"I think I have the answer to that," said Jenkins, now walking in small circles in front of his desk, like a dog trying to decide where to lay down "I've heard from the Day Shift Underground Foreman that some drillers have had items go missing from their lunch boxes as well as from other containers."

There was a long silence as the three of them considered the possibilities.

"Mr. Bardman," said Jenkins. "I think you can go now. Mr. Mikeluk wants to see you in his office. If Constable Pusch needs to see you later, he can make arrangements through this office.

He walked down the hall to Zenon Mikeluk's office and found him standing in front of his desk in exactly the stance Jenkins had used. *My God, he wants to be clone of Jenkins, but ends up looking like a clown.*

Within twenty minutes, he was back underground, weighted down with his gear sent down to get more shots of men and equipment on the producing levels where the pneumatic hammering of the jack-legs filled the air with dust and vibration. *All he wants to do is fill holes with pictures where he has nothing to write. Some editor.*

The scoop-tram ran back and forth on the rails, its operator standing on a small running board on one side, operating the machine with small levers. The front-mounted bucket drove into the loose rock at the face with a metallic roar, then slam-dunked the bucket load of ore-bearing rock with an ear shattering clatter into its hopper. All around, the semi-darkness was etched with the yellow beams from the hat lights through the dust-permeated air.

He looked in vain for somewhere to set up his lights and tripod where they wouldn't get crushed by man or machine. *I can't get a shot in air full of this crap. Mikeluk is treating me like a mushroom, keeping me in the dark and giving me nothing but shit. Ever since that fiasco with the newspaper shot, they've had it in for me. I think they want me to quit. Well screw them, they'll have to fire me first.*

He finally secured a couple of flash heads with gaffer's tape to the air line along the upper side of the drift, pointing one of them to where the scoop-tram was working and the other directed to the rock face to help light the drillers. Another flash with a slave-cell for remote triggering of the other flash was set among the rock, near the bottom of the drift to provide side lighting to the rock face. He placed the camera with a 24millimetre lens on a tripod and attached a cable release to the shutter button. Using various lens openings he took several time exposures, at the same time triggering one flash head manually, which then activated the slave cells of the other two. He was trying for what was usually referred to as an artsy-fartsy shot, the lights of the miners represented on the film as yellow, wavy bands of light, and the rest of the scene frozen by the flashes. Each time the flashes triggered, the miners glanced at the nearest light source, their eyes forced to readjust again to their own low-level illumination. He knew the lights were a distraction to the men and decided to take only a couple more exposures.

With the triggering of the flash this time, the light of the scoop-tram operator abruptly pointed to the ceiling of the drift and remained there, shining from the track floor. The machine lurched to a halt, the bucket still in the dump position but without the operator in sight.

Bardman moved to the far side of the now stationary machine and saw the operator laying face up, a gash on his forehead. His hat lay beside him, the light still shining at the ceiling. He quickly bent down to the man in an attempt to feel for any breathing and could feel his warm breath on the back of his hand. With the racket of the drills, he knew it would be impossible to get the attention of the drillers. He quickly ran to the rock face and by while waving his light in the man's face, gestured to one of the men who was stabilizing the pneumatic leg of his drill. He saw the man's expression questioning him and with more gesturing, the driller looked where he was pointing.   The driller quickly waved his hat light beam to the two other drillers, who shut down their drills. The relative quiet, broken only by the water pumps and hissing air lines allowed normal voice communication.

"Man hurt," was all Bardman said, pointing where the scoop-tram operator lay, still not moving. They all moved to the fallen man's side as he resumed checking his vital signs, first his breathing, then his carotid pulse. He was relieved to find a strong, even pulse along with deep respirations.

"Oh shit, is Alf. Vat you do to him, hit him with camera?" said the stocky miner, leaning over his friend. He extended his hand as

281

though to pat the mans face in an attempt to wake him when Bardman grabbed the man's wrist from the side.

"Don't move his head, you might paralyse him."

"I paralyse you if not take hand away." The miner yanked his hand from his grip and stared him down with his light.

Bardman squinted into the light. "Please, I can help him, but we can't move him. He might have a neck injury. Somebody has to go for help."

"Vat you know how to help? You make picture, flashy lights, hurt eyes, probably cause accident. Vat you know Mr. picture-taker?"

"I know how to give CPR if he stops breathing. Do you know what to do if he stops breathing?" He watched the man lift his hard hat and scratch his thinning scalp in thought.

"Okay, this man go for help. You stay. I stay too. No more work. No more noise now."

Grateful, he once again bent over the man and made sure he was still breathing, then proceeded to check that he wasn't bleeding elsewhere, chastising himself for not doing it before summoning help. He was trying to remember his ski patrol first-aid training for doing the primary and secondary surveys and knew he could at least remember the basics. He kneeled next to the man's head and using the man's hat light, gently lifted his eyelids, shining the beam first in one, then the other. He noticed the pupil of the right eye was dilated and refused to come to a pinpoint like the left one when the light was trained on it. He knew the man had a concussion and would have to be immobilized on a backboard.

"Vat you do now picture-taker?"

"I have to write down his pulse and respiration along with the time. I'll check it frequently until the mine rescue guys come. Do you know any first-aid?"

The miner scratched his head again. "Naw, jump up and down on Annie love-doll vonce a year. I forget."

He knew there wouldn't be much help there for two man CPR if the need arose and decided to sit next to the man's head to stabilize the spine and monitor the breathing as closely as possible.

Twenty minutes later, four men of the mine-rescue team arrived with a small locomotive, pulling a smaller flatcar. One of the men was the cage-tender. They arrived with a wooden backboard onto which the man was secured using a system of straps and a cervical collar, and slowly placed onto the flatcar. Within minutes they were gone from sight toward a waiting ambulance on the surface.

"Good job picture-man," said the miner, patting Bardman on the cheek with a greasy hand. "You come anytime, take picture."

"What do you think hit him?" asked Bardman.

"Pah, rock from bucket, bounce off edge, onto head, boom. Happen all the time. Must have hard head."

And balls like grapefruit, thought Bardman. He admired the fatalistic attitude these men took toward the everyday hazards of their jobs, their misshapen fingers and hands, mute testimony to working with steel and hard rock.

Resolving to re-read his old ski patrol first-aid manual, he removed his equipment and packed it away into their cases. As he walked, equipment-laden back along the track to the lift station, the hair on the back of his neck began to stand on end. He quickly whirled around to face the darkness behind him. He saw nothing in the beam of his light. The tingling progressed down his back to the base of his spine, a cold lump developing in his stomach. He could see the two faint squares of light in the distance of the small windows set in the huge blast doors, two eyes of cold light coming from the lift station. A faint giggle came from his right and his heart leapt as he turned his head so quickly his neck twinged with pain.

His light, with its narrow beam showed where a pillar-raise, now unused had been blasted out of the side of the drift to accommodate a diamond drill rig. He remembered the site as one where he had taken pictures of the two diamond drillers, the one now dead, the other unaccounted for. The giggle came again, this time from within the high dome of the raise. "Who's there?" he said in a strangled voice. He stood still, reluctant to go closer to the dark opening, his whole body feeling cold now. His hands began to shake and his breath came in short gasps. His sweaty palms began to lose their grip on the heavy metal cases, and the light stand and tripod bundled together by straps that hung from his shoulder pulled him to one side. With a clatter, he put everything down to dry his hands and regain purchase on them. He shone his light back into the pillar-raise and could see under the rock lip of the opening that the wooden scaffolding was still in place.

He had seen such scaffolding ascend high into the darkness above so that long sections of drill rods could be pulled from the hole and stored side-by-side. He had, in the past, considered climbing the connecting series of ladders to their small platforms for the sake of a different perspective to his shots, but his fear of heights forbade it.

The high-pitched giggle echoed from the top of the darkened raise. Then it giggled his name, *"Bardman"*.

Without claiming his equipment on the track floor, he sprinted for the beckoning lights of the lift station. His breath came in ragged gasps as he tried to will his heavy boots to move faster and panicked when one flew from his foot, sending him stumbling, his hands outstretched to break his fall on the sharp rock of the track floor. As pain shot through his scraped and bleeding hands, the giggle from the raise became a demonic laugh, building to a howl. It ended abruptly with what sounded like a sob.

The florescent lighting of the lift station was cold comfort to him as he stood, gasping for breath, his heart pounding in his ears, mucous draining from his sinuses, making him gag. He spat a gob of phlegm against the rock wall, his eyes refusing to focus until he realised his eye glasses were fogged up from the effort. Clearing them on his shirt-tail, he looked around the cavernous area. He was alone, no sound or sign of life. Not even the lift cables were moving, nor the usually constant clanging of the cage-tender's bell.

With sudden embarrassment he remembered his photography equipment, still back on the dark track floor where he had dropped it in his panic. How would he explain the loss of the expensive equipment to Mikeluk or Jenkins, when they seemed to be searching for any possibility to give him the boot. He knew he had to go back. His search for some kind of weapon was nearly fruitless except for a broken axe handle, laying near the wall. He hefted it, feeling its comforting weight, a jagged end where the blade had broken away. With his hands shaking once again, and his breath coming in short gasps, he limped with only one boot through the huge swinging blast doors to where his equipment lay.

He became even more aware of the dankness of the drift. With his hat light the only illumination, he swung his head, directing the beam as far down the blackness as possible, and then against the drift wall from where the sounds of his steps echoed back to him. He forced himself not to look behind, knowing that if he did, he might imagine things that were not there. But what if something is there and I don't turn around? *Will I hear him if he comes up behind me? He'll see me first because I have a light on. He's crazy...and he knows my name.*

He estimated he had been walking nearly ten minutes. *I don't remember coming so far. Could I have gone past it and not seen it in the dark? No, I would have tripped over my equipment...unless he took it after I ran. Maybe I ran a lot farther than I thought I had.* He saw a dim reflection ahead on the track floor and stopped abruptly, setting his light beam to a narrow setting. It didn't improve his vision so he slowly walked closer.

His light was now able to pick out the dark, vertical edge of the pillar-raise where the voice had giggled his name. With relief he saw the lost boot in the middle of the track and returned it to his foot. He walked slower, almost on tip-toes, now turning his head and the light from side to side and frequently turning completely to the rear. He gripped the axe handle with both hands, determined to swing it at anything that moved. The photography equipment seemed to lay where it had fallen, one camera on the track where it had tumbled from the bag, now on its side. The tripod lay closer to the wall, below the large air line that ran along the top of the drift wall. He quickly shone the light into the opening of the pillar-raise where he could see the bottom section of the scaffolding. He quietly edged closer the entrance, unclipping the light from his hat to hold in one hand. That way he could swing the beam quickly in any direction. He edged fully into the vertical cavern and pointed the beam up through the scaffolding where the railway ties were suspended from rock bolts mounted at ten foot intervals up the sides of the rock walls. Heavy planks were laid across the ties to form a platform, each platform connected by a wooden ladder. The beam illuminated only the bottoms of the first two platforms and he could barely make out the third. He knew there was one more above that where the drill rods were disconnected from the plug which was used to pull them up by winch. At the base of the scaffolding, the light showed a multi-coloured array of candy bar wrappers and old sandwich bags, some still laying where they had been thrown, with remnants of mouldy food inside. Swatches of old greasy burlap lay everywhere, a fabric that was universally used underground to clean hands, grip greasy tools, and painfully wipe dirty bottoms when there was no paper to be had.

He knew some miners even used the large rolls of burlap as a sleeping bag, rolling themselves in the itching, dusty material to sleep. The stench of feces and body odour came to his nostrils. It hadn't been there before, and suddenly it was, surrounding him like a fetid mist. He whirled around to the entrance from whence he had come and his light reflected from the thick lenses of Pilson's eye-glasses.

Pilson smiled like a reptile. "I knew you'd come back. Couldn't leave this stuff behind." He giggled as he looked at the heap of camera

285

equipment near his boots, then back at Bardman, the smile now gone, his eyes magnified and unblinking behind the lenses.

"That's all I came for, nothing more. I just want to retrieve it and go, no trouble, no hassle. Okay? Bardman spoke while trying to hold his breath, his voice coming out in weak gasps. He watched Pilson, seeing the tattered coveralls covered with stains, some of which were assaulting his sense of smell. He nearly gagged. He kept the axe handle in his right hand behind his back.

"Don't shine that light in my eyes," replied Pilson in the voice of of a hissing viper

"Sorry. How's that?" said Bardman pointing it at the ground realizing Pilson didn't have a light. *He's getting around down here with no light. That's unbelievable! He has no access to charged batteries. But how does he see where he's going?*

"Are you okay? Is there anything I can get you?"

"Why would you or anybody care if I'm okay? Nobody ever cared before. Why now? I know why you're down here. Lookin' for more powder eh?" Pilson took a step closer.

He stepped back in response. " I was just taking pictures."

"Pictures of what? Of people bein' burned? Of Frenchy bein' burned? Ya know whose gonna burn next? This whole fuckin' place is gonna burn next, just like old man Kroeker. Teach 'im ta make a fool a me." Pilson smiled to himself and giggled again, then, with his mouth hanging open in a half-smile, looked at Bardman. "Frenchy's gone an' all that's left is pictures."

"I can bring you some. Would you like some pictures of Frenchy?" he asked nervously, attempting to mollify the clearly unstable apparition before him. "Who's Kroeker?"

"Never you fuckin' mind. You tryin' to make a fool a me?" Pilson had taken another step toward Bardman. "You think I'm dumb an' ugly too? Why you lookin' at me like that?"

Bardman took another step back, bringing himself up short against the drift wall. His knuckles turned white on the hand that gripped the axe handle. His light was still in his left hand, pointing at the ground. The man before him took the shape of a tall dark shadow which seemed to be coming closer, the thick eye glasses reflecting twin circles of yellow light from a darkened face.

"It's okay partner," he said, forcing himself to speak slowly. "Anybody who can get around down here with no light isn't dumb. Yeah I'm not kidding, you got my admiration man..." He realised he was

286

blathering senselessly on when he saw Pilson's form move with a dark fluid motion toward him. Before he could raise the axe handle, a hand had gripped the light in his left hand, wrenching it from his grip. With the sound of glass crunching, darkness overwhelmed them both as Pilson jammed a sharp piece of rock into the lens with his other hand, crushing the bulb of the hat light. He was nearly overcome by the repulsive stench coming from the amazingly strong body which had pinned him to the wall. Pilson's breath smelled as though the very inside of his mouth was rotting out and he fought the urge to vomit.

"Don't you move until you count to fifty," he giggled, then he kissed Bardman on the cheek.

Holding his breath in the blackness, his light now useless, he counted as he heard Pilson's footsteps diminish in the distance, punctuated by a high-pitched giggle. Finally, he stepped carefully forward, one slow step at a time until he could feel the steel rail of the track. He slowly slid his feet along the track in the direction where he remembered seeing the camera bag, finally touching it with his toe. He bent down and felt for the strap and lifted it to his shoulder. Moving slowly to the side he felt for the tripod until his foot touched it also. Encumbered once more with his precious equipment, he walked carefully forward, one hand extended in front, in what he thought was the direction of the lift station, and met with the drift wall. He stepped back, feeling for the rail once again and began walking slowly, keeping one foot in contact with the inside of the rail at all times. In this manner, he made his way back to the lift station, arriving a half hour later, bathed in a cold sweat, hands shaking, still gripping the broken axe handle which no longer gave any comfort whatsoever.

In the harsh overhead lights of the lift station, he noticed something in the pocket of his camera bag which had not been there previously. It was a copy of the company magazine, and as he pulled it from the pocket, he noticed some copy had been circled in ink. The circle was around his name on the masthead, and printed next to it were the words, I know your address. A terrible smell came from within the pocket and he carefully tipped the complete bag, firmly holding the flap over the camera pouches, and saw a rat in a state of advanced decomposition fall to the floor. A small blue ribbon bow was tied around its neck.

The sound of the cage bell made him jump. He had become used to the quiet and realised he had been listening to his own thoughts as one would listen to a normal conversation. In a few moments the cage appeared with the cage-tender grinning at him.

"In all the hullaballoo we completely forgot about you down here. The other guy's gonna be okay, nasty bump on the head is all. His partner wants to thank you for all the help you gave and... Say you okay partner? You don't look too good. Ya know nobody should stay down here too long alone, come outa here talkin' to yerself, seein' things nobody else believes. Hell, lookit me, up an down all day. The things I could tell ya. One guy I picked up swore on a stack of bibles he seen some guy sittin' on top of this cage near the pulleys, just ridin' up an down with this dumb smile on his face. Said this guy looked at him, didn't say nothin', just smiled with these big Coke bottle eyeglasses. Every time I hear a thump from up there I wonder if sombody's there. But hell sombody'd have to be crazy to do that, eh?"

During the swift ascent, while his ears popped with the changes of pressure, Bardman thought of what Pilson had said about burning the place. He remembered the small flatcar of explosives still down there, unused due to the delay caused by the accident. He would have to tell someone what Pilson had said.

What if they don't believe me? They already suspect a connection between me and the areas where the explosives are disappearing. If I tell them about Pilson without any evidence to back up my story, they'll think I did it just to cover my tracks. And what if he steals some explosives for himself? I was the last guy anybody saw down there. If anything's missing they'll come looking for me again, only this time they'll do a thorough job.

Cold windows of light flashed on their faces as the cage swiftly ascended past the other mine levels. Finally the square of light which was the surface station slid into view from above as the cage slowed and stopped.

"Last stop. Soap-up, wash-off, and bugger-off," chortled the cage-tender as he prepared to go off shift. "Partner, I thought it was just the light down there, but it really does look like you seen a ghost. You gonna be okay?

Before he could answer, the man touched his cheek with his finger. "Funny grease smear you got there, looks almost like a lip print. You hidin' a girl down there that uses grease for lipstick?"

He touched his cheek, feeling his face blush, then rubbed the spot vigorously without replying. He could still smell the stench of Pilson's body and felt his body grow cold, the bile beginning to rise in his throat. Feeling dirtier than he had ever felt in his life, he replaced his belt battery in its charging slot and turned in his lamp to the repair window where the laconic employee took it, shook it, and slapped a replacement in front of him without speaking a word.

Before going to the showers, he took the camera gear back to the darkroom. It was there he discovered one camera lens was shattered and a large dent in one camera body. He was going to have to explain these damages to Mikeluk, who would pass it along to Jenkins. No doubt it would come right back to him and he would have to explain the circumstances. Who would believe there is some filth-covered homicidal maniac with homosexual tendencies running around in the dark down there, kissing people on the cheek?

Better just to say I tripped and broke the stuff myself. If I told them the truth, they'd think I was crazier than a shithouse rat.

With a sigh of frustration, he locked the equipment room door and walked wearily to the showers where the hot water and soap would remove the ugly stain from his cheek. He was concerned that Pilson's repulsive stench had permeated his clothing and decided to take his coveralls to the laundromat that evening.

CHAPTER 16

The waters of the Muskrat River had risen further up the bank. Beaver lodges used for generations, had disappeared beneath the surface, forcing the beaver to seek more stands of trees with which to rebuild.

Joe McKay sat in the stern of his father's Brigden canoe. He had watched the changes over the past weeks and felt a cold rage building within himself. He had removed the small kicker-motor and paddled quietly upstream, keeping near one shoreline, watching for other signs of wildlife. The visit from his wife, Sadie, with little Joshua in tow had been like a splash of cold water on his face. It was as though he had awakened from a dream where he had been alternating between half-sleep and wakefulness. He could barely recall events which even now seemed unreal to him, the many sessions spent in the sweat lodge under the watchful eyes of his father and Angus Spence. He didn't believe in visions. At least he hadn't, until near-comatose with the heat, when everything seemed distorted and surreal.

When outside in the cool air, Angus and his father stood quietly, smiling at him as though he had passed some kind of test. Perhaps he had, but the realities of life imposed themselves on this dream-like state in the form of caustic comments from his wife.

"You had two weeks holidays and take em out here." she said. "Are you plannin' on comin' back or are we gonna drive back without you?"

Joe shrugged wordlessly, studying the patterns his boot was making in the dirt driveway of his father's shack. "I just needed time to think," he finally said quietly. I haven't forgotten you, I was just havin' a hard time livin' with myself."

"I'm your wife and this is your son. Were you havin' a hard time livin' with us too? Don't do to us what your old man did to you." She saw Joe's eyes flash with anger. "Before you start yellin' just listen eh. You never learned nothin' about how to be a father in that school down south, and your dad never learned nothin' about it either. Now the same thing's happenin' between you an' Josh. It's an evil circle. It has to be broken."

He moved to a stump near the woodpile and sat in thought while Sadie remained where she stood, hands in the pockets of her jeans, shirt hanging loose in the warm summer sun.

Josh released the grip he had on her leg and walked on stubby legs to his father, kicking at a daddy-long-leg spider which scurried out of his way. The kick sent him sprawling face first into the wood chips and dry earth surrounding the woodpile, forcing some dirt into his mouth. As he wailed in frustration, Joe's large gentle hands lifted him and placed him on his knee, wiping the dirt away from his son's mouth. He made quiet shushing sounds to soothe his son. He looked up and saw her steady gaze. He knew that look and knew it was useless to argue. "I realize now I've been takin' the wrong fork in the path. I look around me here an' I see somethin' I helped cause. The fish are dyin', the trappin' is dyin', an' I think it's killin' my dad."

She moved and sat in front of him, legs crossed, breaking a small stick into pieces with her hands as she searched for words. "You can't blame yourself for that. You had a family to support an' you did it ...at least up until now."

Josh squirmed off Joe's lap and toddled over to her, smearing the dirt from his grubby little hands on her shirt.

"Since you started comin' here, that's all changed. I don't know if I'm comin' or goin' no more, an' I don't know if you're stayin' or leavin', so what's it gonna be?"

"Da," said little Josh, now squirming in his mother's lap. "Da, home."

Sadie looked hard at Joe.

He was unable to match her gaze and kicked at the wood chips near his feet. "I'll be home day after tomorrow. I have to be back at work the next day. I need you to understand that I'm goin' through somethin' that might change our whole lives, but I'm still learnin' about it. The problem is, the more I learn, the more questions I have, an' that's one circle I don't wanna break."

"How are you gettin' back? I have the car."

"Every week, one of the company trucks stops here with stuff for the store. It'll be here day after tomorrow. I'll hitch a ride back."

She simply nodded and stood with Josh in her arms. Saying nothing more, she walked toward the car and drove from sight as he sat on the stump, feeling a sense of emptiness and confusion within. He thought a paddle on the river might help clear his thoughts.

As he slid the canoe into the river current, he heard the ratcheting cry of a kingfisher. It swooped from one branch to the next, sat still and studied the water below, then suddenly dived to the river surface and scooped a small fish into its mouth. A sharp pain made him slap the back

291

of his hand where a horsefly bit him. Others buzzed his face and neck, attracted by the light reflecting from the beads of sweat on his skin. The sun was beginning to go down and he knew the mosquitoes and black flies would be soon out in the cooler air, attacking warm-blooded creatures, driving some to the point of insanity. He had once seen a moose crashing through the bush in a blind charge, shaking its head, and colliding with trees in an attempt to dislodge thousands of black flies lodged greedily in its nostrils. for an instant he heard the subtle flutter of large wings, but upon looking around, saw no bird. Rounding a bend, he smelled wood smoke and at once saw the blue vapours wafting from the far shoreline. Paddling closer, he saw his father sitting near the small fire, swatting at the countless insects that were coming alive in the cool of the shade.

"Are they gone?"

"Who?"

"Your wife and boy. Did they go home?"

Joe nudged the bow of the canoe into the shoreline and still sitting in the stern, watched his father use one leathery brown hand to pull the smoke toward him. "What are you doin' out here, an' how did you know Sadie an' Josh came out?"

His father gave him a wide one-toothed grin and shrugged. Rising to his feet slowly, he came toward the canoe and gestured for the small plastic bailing bucket. Receiving it from Joe, he filled it with water from the riverbank and poured it over the smoking embers. He then returned and gently stepped into the bow of the canoe, placing his feet in the exact middle of the hull, both hands on the gunwales to steady it, and sat on the bow seat, facing his son. "Gonna give me a ride home?"

"How did you get here? " replied Joe with exasperation.

"Got a ride with someone."

"I didn't see any other boats on the river. Where did your friend go?"

"Didn't say it was a boat." Abe sat, still facing his son who was shaking his head and back-paddling away from the shore. "Didn't say it was a friend either."

"Why don't you turn around an' face the front? At least you'll be able to see where we're goin'."

"You know where you're goin' don't you? You have the only paddle. I'll just sit here an' watch you."

He paddled the hand-made Brigden downstream, uneasy under the watchful eyes of his father who sat with his arms folded, legs outstretched in front of him. In the calm of the late summer afternoon, the trees and grass took on a yellow hue from the lowering sun. He could feel the bite of the mosquitoes as they lined up by the score on his long-sleeved shirt, searching for his warm blood. He could feel them bouncing off his bare neck then settling, their wings whining like tiny electric motors as they maneuvered for space on his skin. He stopped frequently and slapped, drawing his hand away smeared with his own blood, mingled with the squashed carcasses of his tiny antagonists. "What are you smilin' at, you enjoyin' watchin' me get eaten alive?"

Abe stopped smiling, still watching his son's eyes. "They're doin' it from the outside, you're doin' it from the inside. How do you scratch the inside?"

"You're talkin' in riddles again. What am I doin' from the inside?"

"You're goin' back to Sadie eh?"

"What's that got to do with bugs suckin' me dry? I think you been out in the sun too long old man."

"She told you to make a choice today," replied Abe with sadness. "Be a good father to your son, eh? When I put you in that school, I didn't have a choice an' neither did you. Well, now you have a choice an' the fight is inside you. You fight too long an' it'll dry you up from inside just like those bugs are doin' from the outside, an' a man dried up inside is just a shell, no good to nobody."

He paddled automatically, trying to understand what his father was saying, wishing he would turn around so he wouldn't have to face his steady gaze. It was strange to have his own father stare at him, his black eyes bright from within the brown wrinkles of his face. It was a challenge, silent, powerful, but without malice.

"You're comin' back," said his father quietly.

He concentrated on his J-stroke as he paddled toward home, wondering why not a single mosquito had landed on his father, while he was literally being eaten alive. They hovered near his father but never seemed to land, tiny winged drillers, pushed away by some invisible barrier. As he glanced occasionally at his father's steady eyes, his breathing slowed and the motion of the canoe gave him the sense of floating through air rather than water. He saw his father's eyes crinkle in humour each time he mentally willed himself back to the confines of the canoe. He felt his tenuous connection to the immediate time and space he occupied at that instant could have been severed, allowing him to somehow drift away like a feather on the wind.

293

Teresa was happy for the change. The twice-weekly explosives run to the north was becoming mundane. She had mentally calculated the amount of explosives being used and found the amount staggering. With each visit to the site she had seen an increase in the structure. Because Joe had taken holidays with little notice, she had been stuck with doing the run alone and the hours behind the wheel had taken their toll. There were bags under her eyes and her face had an unhealthy palour. The weekly grocery run to the store at Hudson House reserve required only the five-ton straight truck, referred to as the pick-up, and she was enjoying the feel of a vehicle with acceleration. The split-axle five-speed transmission let her climb the hills like a sports car, and the tape player didn't distort the singer's voice to an electronic squeal. In the side mirror she could see a thick plume of dust rising from the rear of the truck as she sped along the smooth dirt road. Her left arm, hanging out the window had the typical trucker's tan, the other one being considerably lighter in colour. In the ditch on either side, was the yellow slash of goldenrod with an occasional tiger lily where pools of water lay. The windshield had a haze of dust mingled with countless bug strikes, most of the biting variety. She prayed not to have a flat tire because she knew the insects would make the work of changing it pure torture. In the distance she could see the lone church spire of the reserve.

"Hey partner, come sit in the shade an' let those guys earn their pay." It was Joe McKay's voice as he presented her with a cold bottle of pop. "You look like you should have taken the holiday instead of me."

She accepted it gratefully and drained the contents, some drops escaping from the sides of her mouth to dribble onto her chest. She handed it back with an audible sigh and small belch, smiling back at him.

"Always the delicate lady eh?" He watched her wipe her mouth with the back of her hand.

"It appears life has been agreeing with you, Joe. Do you suppose if I came out here for two weeks holiday I could look as rested as you?"

"Depends if you like sittin' naked in a sweat lodge every second day. How come you're on this run? Thought you'd still be doin' the powder run."

She sat on the front bumper of the truck where she had backed it into the loading dock at the rear of the building. She could hear thumps and bangs from the enclosed truck box, mingled with curses of those doing the unloading.

"No need this week," she replied wearily. "I suggested to Winky that he get the trailer brakes fixed on the explosives trailer while it wasn't needed and all he did was fart in my general direction and tell me to revise my logbook. Said I had too many hours in case some guy from the Ministry Of Transport came nosing around. I don't see how he can get off saying we're only driving ten hours per day when the run takes sixteen or eighteen, round-trip."

Joe sat on the shaded bumper beside her with his head back against the grill.

"Winky doesn't know it, but I've been sneakin' over sometimes an' tryin' to adjust them before we go out with it. I don't think that helps anymore, an' if we're smart, we'll tell him we won't take it if the brakes aren't fixed."

"Aw hell, he'll just pass gas and tell us to either drive or go looking for another job. I could probably find something else to do, but you've got wife and kid to support. Your hands are tied and he knows it."

A huge crash followed by a startled shout made them both sit up abruptly. "God, it's hard to find good help," groaned D'Amico as she stood and walked to the rear of the truck from whence the noise had come.

Two teenagers, one still holding a two-wheeled hand cart were staring at a huge red smear where a case of bottled ketchup had toppled from the cart. One began to giggle, which encouraged the other to join in, and soon the whole crew, including those receiving the goods in the store began to laugh. "Hey lady, your truck's bleedin'" said the one with the handcart, unaffected by the unsmiling stare from her around the side of the box.

Finally the store manager appeared with a shovel and push broom which he presented to the boy using the cart. The manager's expression advised the boy to say nothing, but to take the tools and begin the clean-up. For the rest of the unloading there were no more giggles and the remainder of the goods were received in good order.

"So what are you gonna do Teri, you gonna quit?" He had moved with her to the side of the truck and absently kicked one of the rear dual tires.

He leaned against the truck box, savouring the aroma of the wild flowers growing in colourful swathes around the reserve. An underfed dog wandered over to the truck, sniffed the tires and then with an upraised leg, peed on the tread.

"I feel like that dog," said D'Amico. "I feel like pissing on the whole thing. Winky gives us equipment that's starting to fall apart. He's too cheap to fix it, and all he's worried about is his own fat ass. I've even had dreams about the brakes failing with a full load of powder."

He watched her closely. "How does it end?"

"A big yellow flash, no noise, just a flash that makes my eyes hurt. It's really weird, I sometimes sit straight up in bed covered in sweat and can see little purple dots floating in front of my eyes. You know the kind that happen when someone takes your picture with a flash-camera?"

"That's pretty realistic. Have you talked to anybody else about these dreams?"

"No, I figure they'll just pass. My mom used to say a glass of warm milk cured nightmares when I was a kid, but all it did was make me go to the bathroom in the middle of the night. I tried it last night and I nearly wet the bed."

"So how often are you havin' these dreams?"

"Almost every night."

"Can I tell you somethin' without makin' it sound like a joke?" Joe saw she was biting her lower lip, unaware of how close she was to tears, concerned that she might be on the verge of a breakdown. "I don't think those are just dreams, I think they're a message. No, don't look at me like that. There's more happenin' around us and inside us than we are ever aware of...at least usually."

She listened with a sullen expression, her arms folded across her chest. "What do you mean usually?"

He studied the ground at his feet as he searched for words, seeing a lone red ant dragging a small moth many times its' own size backward toward an unseen mound. When he spoke, his voice was lower, so that she had to strain to hear him.

"I've had dreams too, but I've had 'em when I'm awake. You know what I told you about the sweat lodge? Well sometimes, not all the times though, I see things. My eyes are closed but it's as if they were open. The strange thing is I can smell too, an' feel the wind, all while I'm sittin' in there."

"You mean the heat was making you hallucinate?"

"Nope, I'm used to the heat. Took a while, but now I can sometimes sit down in the dark an' instead of feelin' heat, I feel a coolness come over my skin. It doesn't even feel like my own skin anymore."

"Joe, you're starting to scare me. I think I'd rather talk about something else."

"Yeah, that's okay, we'll talk about somethin' else. I see you're not wearin' the medicine bag pop made for you. How come?"

She gave a wordless shrug and an embarrassed smile.

"Do me a favour eh? Start wearin' it again. Is your boyfriend wearin' his?"

"I felt kind of silly having that thing around my neck all the time. Winky saw it once and asked me if I was starting to chew tobacco. As far as Brady is concerned, well, he's been acting strangely too. He's been taking off right after work with his kayak and I don't think he comes back until after dark."

"You didn't answer my question. I bet he ain't wearin' it, but he better start."

"Let me smell that thing," she said reaching across with alarming swiftness to Joe's throat.

Before he could react, she had taken a couple of loud sniffs with the small leather sack against her nostrils as he remained still, surprised at her sudden movement.

"Sorry," she laughed. "That must have looked really strange. Yours and mine smell the same, sort of spicy mixed with wood smoke and leather. I wonder if Brady's smells the same?"

He replaced the bag behind the top button of his shirt from which it dangled on the rawhide around his neck. "Why? Does his smell different?"

"I don't know, but something smells different. I went over to his place a few nights ago just to see how he was doing. His outer door, the one that leads down to his apartment was open. There were no lights on at his place but I poked my head part way down the stairs and a smell like I've never smelled almost made me sick. I backed out of there like a skunk had sprayed me."

"Can you describe the smell?"

"You know what a hockey dressing room smells like?"

Joe nodded, his mind flashing back to the days he played hockey at the residential school, slightly resentful that she had helped trigger the memories. "Maybe he just had a basket of dirty laundry down there."

"No, this was worse. Much worse. Imagine mixing in rotting meat, shit and vomit all together and you'll get some idea of the smell. She shivered involuntarily at the thought. "Ever since then I have the

297

feeling that someone was down there watching me, and if I had taken one more step down there, it would have been one step too many."

The store manager approached, his beefy hand holding the manifest for the groceries that had been off-loaded. He still wore a blood-spattered apron which he used while cutting meat, and was wiping his hands on a small white section remaining at one corner. "I marked down here that one case of ketchup was broken on delivery. I signed it and here's your copy," he said in a wheezing voice.

"Wait a minute, your employee broke that case," protested D'Amico. "Why should we pay for the loss?"

"Because honey it happened on your truck and you're responsible for how it's unloaded. You were goofing off out here while we were working our butts off in there, so take it or leave it." The manager's jowly face was beginning to quiver as he thrust the paper at her.

She snatched it from his hand and immediately applied the bill of lading to the still-wet dog urine on the rear tire. She held the paper daintily by one dry corner and said, "I'll put this under Winky's nose. This is the kind of business he understands." She started for the driver's door when Joe intercepted her by hooking one finger in the rear belt loop of her jeans. She turned with a questioning glance.

"Did I forget to tell you that I was catchin' a ride home with you? An' I'm drivin' 'cause   I think you'll fall asleep."

She nodded gratefully and went to the passenger side, glad for the chance to rest. By the time Joe had moved the truck away from the loading dock and closed the rear doors, she was sound asleep with her head on the back of the seat, her mouth open, snoring with enthusiasm. Joe drove into the setting sun and plumes of dust kicked up by traffic coming the other way, looking occasionally at his partner with concern. He was beginning to trust his other senses, including the one that caused the hair to stand up on the back of his neck, and her description of the smell in the doorway had done exactly that.

From high above, the canopy of the forest stretched, punctuated by the countless lakes and rock of the Precambrian shield.

For years it had been thus, without the hand of civilization gnawing greedily at the earth, spitting it out in a filthy phlegm of tailings and oily chemical spittle to defile everything it touched. Narrow dusty ribbons carried the vehicles that spread this scourge, creating a network of arteries like that of a cancerous tumour feeding on its host-body.

The other birds had instinctively given a wide birth to this one, their small brains unable to rationalize reasons why the strange one never came down to tear at the carcasses they fed upon. As they sat and squabbled over which of them had dominance over the carrion before them, the lone one rode the winds aloft in wide circles, its head swivelling, watching for something the others would never understand. On occasion, the feeding ravens would cock their heads sideways and watch the other one in flight, always in flight, seldom landing. Their eye-sight was nearly as sharp as a hawk's to be able to see the tiny carcass of a mouse from high above, and it was this sight they had used to observe something they would never understand, but deep within their tiny feathered heads, knew instinctively, that this bird was not of their world.

"Mr. *Bardman,* I'm so glad you could spare us some of your valuable time," said Roger Jenkins, his voice coated with oily venom. "It seems that the newspaper in Winnipeg is sending a reporter and photographer here today to do another story." He waited a few breaths, expecting some reply, but getting none, continued. "It seems they want to do a story on the environmental impact we're having on the area. The people at hydro tell me they've also been asked some very pointed questions about workplace safety. Mr. Bardman, I trust you will have *no contact of any kind with these people,* because what I said about your future or possible lack of it here, still stands."

Off to the side of the desk, near one wall, sat Zenon Mikeluk, his curly hair arranged to appear as though he had just removed his finger from the light socket. His pudgy face showed no expression, but his whole body seemed at ease in the high-backed chair, as though his position with the company magazine had become more consolidated. He finally gave Bardman a cold smile of recognition and folded his hands across the front of his rumpled shirt.

This must be what a hyperthyroidal six year old looks like, Bardman thought to himself.

"However Mr. Bardman, I do have some good news of which you *will* be a part of. Next weekend is the wedding of my daughter to Zenon here, and it is my and their *sincere* wish that you take the wedding photographs."

"I don't do weddings," he said quietly.

"Consider this an overtime assignment for which you will be paid overtime or be able to take time off in lieu of pay, which ever you like," continued Jenkins with an expansive smile.

"I don't do weddings" he reiterated.

"You'll do this one and you'll do it well," said Jenkins, his voice striking him like an early frost. "Or you'll never work here again and possibly never work in this line of work in the province. On the subject of photography Mr. Bardman, Zenon here has requested that you show the layout of the darkroom to his cousin who is up from Winnipeg for the summer. He's a student in photographic arts at the community college there and this would be a perfect chance for him to get some work experience."

He glanced back to Mikeluk who now beamed with a smile and appeared to be studying a flaw in the ceiling, refusing to meet his eyes. He nodded assent, feeling like a whipped dog, but one that still had teeth. Being backed into a corner like this was distasteful for him, and in the back of his mind, a low mental snarl began to develop.

Jenkins spoke quiet venom. *"You may get out Mr. Bardman."*

As he passed into the receptionist's area, he saw Samantha Paige and her photographer, sitting in the waiting area.

They had obviously arrived during his meeting with Jenkins. *He timed this so I would meet her here.*

Turning back to Jenkins' door, he saw the man standing, watching, with a smile. He turned back to Paige and subtly shook his head, thankful that she had deemed it wise to not acknowledge him. When he left Jenkins' office, it was with the same sense of relief that he got when exiting the house of reptiles at the zoo.

On the way past the large bulletin board, one item stood out from all the other personal detritus of ads selling cars, snowmobiles, and pleas for daycare. It was a photograph of a large black motorcycle with high handlebars and a stepped-seat.

On the gas tank was the word Norton, and on a small panel to the rear, the numbers 850. He had always wanted to own a motorcycle but had never had the chance to learn, despite riding with many friends, on the backs of theirs. He mentally took down the phone number, resolving to call, also noting the seller described it as immaculate at a sacrifice price. He knew some of the miners who were members of the local bike gang, who wore their colours on sleeveless jean-jackets and spread their throaty rumble wherever they rode. This wasn't a Harley, but it looked more manageable than a hog, and maybe...

When he got home that evening, he carefully checked the stairwell from his outer door. That evening several days ago, he had taken his laundry to the coin laundromat after being greasily bussed by Pilson and had returned with the dried clothing only to detect the very stench he had experienced underground. His first reaction was to drop the clothing and run, but there was barely enough light in the stairwell to confirm there was no one else there. He had carefully tried the lower door, finding it still locked but wondering if someone had got in and locked it from the inside. To his relief he discovered there had been no forced entry, but with a large kitchen knife in hand, he checked the few dark areas such as his closet and even behind his ratty old sofa. He figured anyone who would hide there amongst all the dust and hair balls had to be crazy. Since then, he had bought and installed a sliding bolt to lock the door from inside and sometimes even kept the lights off at night, so no one could peer through the flimsy curtains over the ground-level windows. His own home was beginning to feel like a prison and the only sense of escape was with the kayak.

Without really thinking, he picked up the phone and dialled the number of the person selling the motorcycle. After making an appointment with the seller for that evening, he called the Stagger Inn and learned a room had been booked by Samantha Paige, and another by the photographer. He left a note with the hotel receptionist, asking her to call his number as soon as she returned.

Her call came a half hour later as he was finishing a beer in his favourite position, semi-immersed in the bathtub, the beer perched on his stomach between his large hands.

He reached with soapy fingers to the extension phone on the floor, only to have it slip from his grasp. Leaning over the edge of the tub, he retrieved the handset while keeping the cold beer bottle clenched between his legs. The soapy bath water threatened to contaminate the remainder of its contents.

"That boss of yours is a *real sweety* Brady. I felt like I should have been wearing hockey pads for that interview. Does he know I'm the one you were talking to at the hydro project? No, that's a dumb question, of course he knows. Why else would he treat me just like a turd in a toilet bowl? Are you there?"

"I'm here. Can I say hello now?"

"I'm sorry, hello, hello, hello."

"I was supposed to say that but you said it for both of us. Thanks for not throwing your arms around me and kissing me in front of Jenkins today, I'm sure it would have got me fired. So tell me about this story you're on."

She told him how they planned to be there for the next week or more to talk to the local environmental group and the resident experts concerning contamination of the small waterways surrounding the mine. They would also be back at the hydro project where they were originally told they were personae non-grata, until the newspaper publisher convinced them it would be in the companies best interests to appear forthcoming, even though they probably weren't, about the number of deaths and injuries on-site over the last several months.

She talked breathlessly on until he realized his bath had grown cold and his beer warm. When she finally hung up a half hour later, he climbed from the tub like some wrinkled amphibian and poured the remainder of his beer down the toilet, wishing there was more in the cupboards to eat than Kraft dinner.

His appointment with the seller of the motorcycle was in a half hour, so he rummaged some dried crusts of bread from the refrigerator and spread some long-ignored cheese spread on it. It seemed his desire to cook anything for himself was declining in direct proportion to the amount of enjoyment he was getting out of his job. He also realized he hadn't seen Teresa in nearly two weeks and felt guilty of lavishing himself with self-pity and dealing with it by retreating in the kayak.

"Yeah man, I hate to let her go for this price, but I gotta blow town an' I gotta use my car to take all my stuff," said the seller of the motorcyle, a slim young man with shoulder length blonde hair that most women would have killed for.

"She's got Amal carbs, just gotta trickle the fuel into 'em like this, see before you start 'er up. This is yer choke on the left handle bar, an' all ya do is...this. The motorcycle sprang to life with a roar as he jumped on the kick-start and as it idled, the young man cranked the throttle, making the exhaust crackle. "They don't call 'em Snortin' Nortons for nothin' man. Climb on."

Bardman swung a leg over the Norton which was sitting on it's side stand, and put his weight on the machine. He could feel the power of the vibrations from the long stroke, two cylinder engine as the valve lifters sang their metallic song. He gently twisted the accelerator on the right handle bar and felt the machine talk to him. It was a song of freedom and speed.

He shifted the bike off the side-stand and gripped the western bars that reached back toward him. It was a comfortable stance, with one foot resting on a forward chrome peg on a small roll bar bolted to the frame. Each time he twisted the grip he saw the tachometer to his front twitch, its needle swinging to the right.

"Time to show me a test drive?"

The young man looked at him with incredulity. "You don't know how to ride man? I mean I'll sell it to ya man, but this is a bit big to start on don't-cha think?"

"Just show me." The tone of his voice discouraged any disagreement.

They went.

He was sold on it. It had more 'jam' than any of the bikes he had ridden with his friends and seemed to handle, at least in the hands of the young man, with the nimbleness of a thoroughbred. He understood then why they were sometimes referred to as 'crotch rockets'. After the ride, he gave the man a deposit of $50, got a receipt, and drove home with the realization that he had never before wanted to do anything so much in his life. He couldn't explain the sudden compulsion. It was as though it had been suppressed by all the peripheral events of his life and now there was a new focus. But if there was anything he hated, it was running away from unfinished business.

His telephone started to ring as he entered the upper door to his apartment, and he managed to answer it on the fourth ring. The plaster fell to the floor where the lower door had been slammed against the kitchen wall in his haste.

"Coffee at the coffee shop?" said Paige's voice.

"Nope. Meet me at the Stagger-Inn. None of the admin. cronies ever go there. Too many blue collars. The place scares the shit out of them."

"Well hell, that place makes me nervous too," she said with a pleading tone in her voice. "I'll be the only woman in the place and probably the only sober one. If you're not there within five minutes of the meeting time, I'm gone. I don't want a bunch of drunks hitting on me."

He agreed to the 8 pm meeting with apprehension that someone might recognize her as a reporter, and the word get back to Jenkins that he had been seen talking with her.

When he entered, he saw her in a dark corner, as far from the pool table as she could possibly get. She was nursing a drink and taking nervous puffs from a cigarette. She looked up as he approached and slid over to make room for him beside her on the bench seat.

"Thank god, I was about to pack my goodies and go. I know of a few bars like this in Winnipeg but I'd never go there."

303

He smiled at her concern as she nervously surveyed the smoke-filled room. "Fortunately for you this is the cocktail lounge, otherwise you'd be really nervous."

"Why? And how can you tell the difference?

"Oh, that's easy, in here they spit on the floor. In the bar they spit at each other."

She grimaced. "I feel like a nun at a wet T-shirt contest. Well, at least nobody tried to hit on me."

"I knew they wouldn't. You've got city girl written all over you. You'd intimidate the hell out of most of the guys here. Some of these guys have come out of the bush where the only thing female near them for the past month have been mosquitos."

"Does it always smell this bad?"

He sniffed the air delicately, including his own armpits. "Well my deodorant has wilted, but there does seem to be a definitely fishy aroma tonight."

He thanked Natasha effusively for the beer as she managed to spill a few drops in his lap. The possibility occurred to him that Samantha hadn't tipped her for her Coke. He surmised this might be the only beer he'd get this evening unless he made amends.

"So, all small talk aside, why did you want to meet tonight?"

She was obviously nervous about more than her surroundings by the way she chewed on her lower lip between sips from her glass. "You know those prints you wanted me to put in safe-keeping for you?"

He nodded, his expression a mixture of curiosity and anger.

"Well, I made black and white photocopies of them and sent them to a newspaper in Los Angeles, called The Comet. It's a tabloid with huge circulation and... Why are you looking at me like that?"

He leaned close, his elbows resting in a puddle of beer, the knuckles of his hand on the beer glass turning white. His face was openly hostile which made her lean back against the dingy wall in an attempt to distance herself from him.

"I told you, nobody, and I mean nobody sees those shots until I'm ready. Lady, you are playing with my life here and I don't like it. Those shots could get me thrown in jail for withholding evidence of a murder investigation and you send them off to some rag of a newspaper that prints stories of aliens impregnating grandmothers."

"Ah, so you've read it?"

"No I haven't read it. And what the hell are you smiling about?"

"I told them there are more and they asked if I would do the story to go with them. Don't you want to know how much they're offering for the package?"

"Whatever the amount, it couldn't be enough to compensate me for losing my job and facing criminal charges."

"You're really paranoid about these criminal charges aren't you? How does $10,000 sound?" She was leaning back, her arms folded and smiling smugly.

He stopped in the middle of an attempted rebuttal, his mouth hanging open in disbelief.

"Each."

"Each?" His mouth opened even more and spilled some of his beer on the table top. He absently took his handkerchief from his pocket and began mopping up the spilled beer. His mouth was still open and was shaking his head slowly from side to side in dismay.

She continued: "And that isn't all. That paper is just one of many owned by the publisher and they said that if the story ran in the broadsheets which have more credibility, then each publication means additional fees for us."

"What do you mean us?" Bardman's jaw had snapped shut like a fish taking bait, trying to take a sip from his quivering beer glass.

"I mean they want me to write the story. They said it sounds so bizarre, it might even make a movie. But, and it's a big but, the story has to be corroborated. Police reports, coroner reports, eye-witnesses, that kind of thing."

"Since when does a rag like that need corroboration? They don't get it from their little green men screwin' the grannies. Why do they want it from us?"

"Because they know that if it's true, then it's even more marketable, and that's the bottom line; it has to be marketable. My God it really does stink like fish in here and...wait a minute, that is a fish," she said pointing to the opposite wall where a large northern pike could be seen moving slowly from hand to hand along a line of drinkers.

They watched, incredulous, as the fish reached the end of the table where two men retrieved it and then stood unsteadily, the shorter of the two cradling the large fish in his arms like a baby.

It was toothless Jake and Big Don, and they were weaving their way toward them.

"Hey photographer, take a picture of this, it's a king-p-pike," slurred Big Don as Jake held it the way a proud father would carry a newborn.

Samantha held her nose and made a face when the fish was brought to table level by Jake as if presenting a tray of canapes. "It smells. And why is it bent in the middle like that?"

"Special lure 'n fishin' technique," volunteered Big Don, now leaning on their table with one hand, producing a pronounced slant to the surface. "Call it the warbler."

"The warbler?" she asked, not so overcome by the stench that the reporter instinct wouldn't kick-in.

"Yep, C.I.L. warbler. Short fuse, big bang, an' the fishies just all come a-floatin' to the top to be scooped up. 'Cept this time the fuse was dang near too short an' had Jake an' me paddlin' fer our lives."

"Dang near made it too," cackled Jake, now holding the fish by its tail at arms length. "Whew! It ith gettin' a might high ain't it?"

"You mean you blew your boat up while fishing?" Her stomach was beginning to feel queasy at the sight of the rotting fish which had been articulated at mid-body by the blast.

"Yeah, sorta," volunteered Big Don, trying to find his hat, which had slipped to the back of his head. "Motor wouldn't start an' the current took us right over the blast. Picked us up like bathtub toys an' dumped us upside down, fish everywhere. Jake here started swimmin aroun' lookin' for the biggest one an' he rescued this here fella. Hell he even tried to give it mouth to gill resus.. resuscit..."

"Resuscitation?"

"That's it. Yer a real smart li'l gal. I'm gonna recommend toothless Jake here fer a life-savin' award. That ought-ta look real good along side the Master Angler award."

Big Don searched through the pockets of his dirty coveralls and finally retrieved a greasy hanky. He blew his nose with a honk, causing his hat to fall from the back of his head.

Toothless Jake lunged for the hat with his free hand, missed and lost his balance. As Jake spun out of control to the floor like a stringless puppet, the fish slipped from his fingers and flopped onto their table with a wet slap.

Samantha shrieked and cowered against the back of the seat while Bardman covered his beer with one hand, trying to avoid the slimy tail which draped near his lap.

Big Don looked down at his diminutive friend sitting on the floor, then looked toward the bar. "Oh, oh, better git up li'l buddy, here comes Natasha. Let's git the fish outa here, 'cause she looks mad enough ta punch us in the kneecaps."

The two of them scurried unsteadily to the door with the fish between them and as they approached the exit, leaned in opposite directions to steady themselves. The fish tore into two reeking pieces, Big Don with the head and toothless Jake with the tail, as they left the premises with alacrity, they argued as to who had the larger piece.

"Is forst time Jake get piece of tail in here." said Natasha to Bardman and Paige, her hands on hips, watching the two explosives employees. "Vat I'm going to do? Iss dronks here, iss dronks d'ere. Vy you two not getting dronk? Iss lovers?"

Before they could reply, she walked toward the bar, automatically slapping a drunken, groping hand without looking to which drunk it was connected to.

Bardman could see she was disconsolate about something because she hadn't tossed any of the countless drunks out of the bar and seemed not to relish the possibility.

With the departure of Natasha, a relative sense of privacy returned to their table; relative in that nearly everyone near enough to hear their conversation were beyond comprehension of sober discussion.

"I need names and addresses," said Paige, leaning close enough that Bardman could tell she wasn't wearing a bra. "I need not only to have your version of events as you saw and experienced them, but also what the others saw. You said you had more pictures. Can you tell me what they were of and how they affect the story?"

He told her of the cremation of Frenchy Rivest and how it had been held under the auspices of a tour through the smelter. He watched her mouth open progressively wider as he described the demented howls of Pilson from the catwalk above them. Upon relating to her of the photos of Pilson and that he was naked, Paige had quaffed her beer, belched and waved her arms like a cheer-leader at Natasha for another.

"Shit, that'sh great! You got this all on film?" She sat back against the seat in thought that was becoming less sober despite having consumed only one beer. "This is so bizarre, it's almost unbelievable. Maybe the broadsheets won't take it because it sounds so sensational...but I bet the tabs will eat it up and come crawling for more. Where the hell is that Natalia or whatever her name is?

307

She waved her arms again to the far side of the bar, encouraging at least three tables of drunks to wave back. She looked at him and began to giggle. "Don't look so surprised. I should have told you I'm a cheap drunk. After I've had three I pass out, so this is my last one. If I start to slur my words, it's because my retainer's too damn tight, just had it adjusted before coming here and it hurts like hell." To prove her story, she leaned toward him and pulled her lower lip down with her finger so he could see the thin metal wire that curved around her lower teeth.

A patron behind Bardman shouted drunkenly, "Give the lady a beer, can't ya see she's thirsty?"

Two full glasses of beer struck the table as though dropped from considerable height.   They looked up abruptly to see Natasha, hands on hips glaring down at them.

"You inspect woman like peasant inspect horse Mr. photographer. Iss no vonder you not have girl friend."

"How do you know I'm a photographer?" queried Bardman, handing her some bills.

"My husband know you. Iss sitting at table over there," she said flinging a thumb over her shoulder as though disposing of a dead rodent. "Iss one waving hardest at this one who keeps waving arms like vindmill. Iss not good to en-courage single men who drink, except my husband not single and I do not like woman who wave at him."

With the last words, Natasha leaned forward, one hand on the wet table and stared hard at Samantha who sat docilely with her hands in her lap, her eyes cast down.

Bardman squinted through the haze of the room, barely able to make out the men's faces who had by now tired of waving their arms at Paige. He recognized the face of one of he miners who had been near when Frenchy had been killed, and had complained of having his lunch stolen a couple of times while underground. "Another piece of your puzzle is winking at you from that table, Sam. Take a look over there."

She leaned closer to him and sighted unsteadily along his forearm to see where his finger was pointing.

"Whish one? They all look blurry. An' stop movin' your finger." She returned to her beer, tipping it far enough to produce a large moustache of foam along her upper lip. She wiped the foam with the back of her hand, flicking some of the wetness at Bardman's glasses. She belched and then giggled apologetically. "My god, look at the time. I gotta get up early an' drive out to that damn hydro project." She struggled to her feet. "No, no, don' get up, might look suspicious. An' you get me those namesh Mr. Bar..Bardy Brademan, or whatever yer name ish."

He watched her leave for her room, weaving, occasionally bracing herself on the backs and sometimes head of other patrons as she swerved unsteadily between the tables.

The patron who had shouted for him to give her a beer, watched him with a sullen expression. His stubbly chin was on his chest, a greasy hand clenching a half-full glass which hadn't moved in the last half-hour. He shook his head in silent disapproval at Bardman's lack of manners, then turned his gaze back to the smoke-enshrouded crowd.

Bardman left the bar, thankful for the fresh air, needing some time to think by himself. Walking along the sidewalk, he could see the last vestiges of the sunset leaving a yellow and orange horizontal band above the treetops. Somewhere above him came the sound of a nighthawk and its buzzing cry as it dived after the myriad of night insects. Cars whistled past on the street, their exhausts mingling with that of the grass and wild flowers which thrived even along the boulevards of the town. He appeared to be the only one on foot, all others electing to take motorized transport, regardless of how short the journey. He walked without direction, allowing his body to follow a path of its own without influence of conscious thought. It was his way of clearing all the clutter and tensions from his mind.

The past confrontation with Jenkins and the assignment for his daughter's wedding had made his guts burn with resentment, but the threat of dismissal if he associated with anyone of the press turned that resentment to a pure white anger. *I'm trapped. I don't have any control over my own life. My job and my boss, and his cronies can tell me where to go, what to do, who I can talk to, even where to take a crap if need be. Take deep breaths. Stop clenching your fists. So many strange things are happening and somehow you end up in the middle of it, almost by design than chance.*

For the next hour, he walked side streets and on one occasion a narrow grass path between new developments. He stopped and admired the stars from his path of darkness which wound through the undisturbed grass. A small animal, perhaps a mouse made a startled squeak nearby, and rustled the grass in panicked flight.

I know how you feel little one. There are times I'd like to find a hole and crawl in too, except some snake will follow you and you become part of its digestive system and eventually rejected as a piece of shit.

He felt revulsion that he had sunk back into himself in self-pity. He had read articles about depression and recognized his own fears and symptoms in the things he read. It had taken him years to reconcile the fact that he suffered from depression, perhaps more frequently than others, but he had always been able to drag himself out of it, usually through action rather than introspection. He looked around and realized he was standing in front of a large truck. He had walked aimlessly and come face-to-bumper with a huge machine that smelled of diesel and grease. Its large headlights stared balefully back at him like some metallic accuser. It was the truck Teresa drove, minus the trailer. His subconscious had brought him here to her apartment but he felt no surprise at his arrival. It was evident she had brought the truck home with her.

It was a small apartment block with moths bouncing suicidally off the single entrance-way bulb. As he opened the outer door his nose was assailed with the smells of other people's cooking mingled with body odours. The aroma of freshly laundered clothing came to him from a stairwell to his left where the dryer made thumping and clanking sounds. Someone forgot to take the change out of their pockets, he thought to himself. The sound of a television came from the far end of the hallway and the raised voice of man, resulting in the wail of a small child. He checked the mailbox and found her name on the one with the number seven written in pencil above it. He went up the stairs toward the crying child and to the apartment near the fire exit sign. As he approached the door, he unconsciously walked softly. He stopped at the door, listening for sounds from the other side, hoping none of her neighbours would come into the hall and see him standing there. He heard no sounds and knocked softly. He thought he had detected a soft rustling sound from behind the door and knocked again, this time louder.

"Who is it?" came a muffled query from within.

"It's me, Brady." he answered in a near-whisper. A door across the hall made a soft clicking sound and he turned to see an older woman peering from the barely opened door.

Teresa let him in with a look of mild surprise.

"Well stranger. Come here often?"

"Maybe not as often as I should. Sorry I just dropped out of sight. I was going through some things that needed to be thought through. I just felt like dropping in and saying hello. Is it a bad time?"

"No, I was just sitting, reading. You look like you could use a coffee and you really smell of smoke. Been at the bar?"

310

He nodded, scratching at mosquito bites on the back of his hands. During his walk he had been unaware of the mosquitos and the scores of bites they'd inflicted on him. He still didn't know why he was here but took a chair at the kitchen table and watched her in her red jogging suit as she filled the kettle.

She looked back with a hint of curiosity. "I thought I'd done something to piss you off Brady. It's been nearly two weeks."

He sat without replying, searching for words that didn't want to come. "Things started getting weird at work, I don't know, maybe they're just getting weird everywhere."

She set a cup of instant coffee in front of him, then sat across the table from him, her chin resting in her hands, elbows on the table. She watched him thoughtfully as he took a couple of exploratory sips of the coffee. "Sorry, all I had was instant. It's pretty bad isn't it?"

He stared at the mug, refusing to meet her eyes. "Yeah, things are pretty bad all over."

"I meant the coffee, but now that you mention it, things are getting pretty bad aren't they? Do you want to talk about it or do you want to keep it bottled up inside the rest of your life?"

For the next hour she sat patiently, listening to him relate the problems with his boss, the unusual occurrences underground, and his general disgust with the way his career was souring like curdled milk.

He hated to admit it, but the way he related to his superiors was evidently the root problem with his inability to hold onto a job for any length of time. The last straw had been Jenkins ordering him to photograph his daughter's wedding this coming weekend. While voicing his resentment at being made Jenkins' personal photographer, he was unaware that she had re-filled his cup and laced it with a sweet, orange-flavoured liqueur. Halfway through the cup, his eyebrows arched in approval in conjunction with her smile upon seeing his reaction.

"Nothing like a little Cointreau to loosen the lips,eh?

"God, I'm sorry Teri, I've been sitting here feeling sorry for myself, bumming coffee and booze from you and whining like a jilted cat in heat."

"Well, you don't sound like any cat I've heard, but it does sound as though you have an acute case of Optical Rectalitis. You know what that is, eh?" She leaned across the table, her fists stacked atop each other, her chin resting on the top fist.

He shook his head. "Do you think it's something I can get workman's comp. for?"

"Don't you just wish. Actually it's a result of kissing someone's ass so much that you end up with a permanently shitty outlook on life. It's also closely related the Black Tongue Disease, due to licking your bosses boots. Show me your tongue. No, it looks okay, now show me your belly-button. Just kidding," she giggled. "I've seen more than my share of belly-button lint, and stop looking at me like that because I'm not going to show you mine."

His spirits had risen considerably, the injection of liqueur being a factor.

"Hey, I almost forgot to tell you the news, I bought a motorcycle today, at least put a deposit down on it. It's a '74, 850 Norton Commando, black, with saddlebags, the works."

"I didn't know you rode."

"I don't, but I intend to learn."

"You mean you intend to kill yourself. Brady, you can't teach yourself how to ride on something that size, you'll be a hazard to everything else on the road, including yourself. Now don't pout, I'm almost out of liqueur and I don't feel like making more coffee.

She was afraid she'd hurt his feelings, suggesting he wasn't competent to ride something that size, but knew he would kill or maim himself very quickly without some instruction.

"I never told you this before, but my ex-husband and I used to ride. We had a Suzuki 750 GT, called it the water buffalo because it was liquid cooled. It was also a two-stroke engine and shot blue smoke out the exhaust like some kind of mosquito abatement program; drove the neighbours nuts. However, I digress. What I was going to say was I will give you some pointers on how to ride that thing because I don't want to see you get bent. You may be a little warped as it is, but believe me, being bent is no fun. I've got to kick you out now Brady, but walk with me to the laundry room, my stuff has been in the dryer too long."

He stood and stretched. "Thanks again Teri, I appreciate your sitting and listening to my whining."

"It's nothing, one day I'll come to your place and whine. Then you'll really know pain.

"I'll supply the booze and the shoulder," he replied as they walked shoulder to shoulder down the dingy hallway toward the now silent laundry room.

She flicked on the light and went to one of four dryer units, wrinkling her nose at the unusual odour from inside the room. She had smelled it before but was unable to remember where.

"Shit, somebody stole my laundry, my new jeans and a blouse." She opened the dryer door, inserting her head for a better look.

Bardman went to check the other units. "Nothing in these either," he related to a visibly very pissed-off D'Amico.

She stamped her foot, silently mouthing obscenities, then bent down for another look, this time inserting her shoulders as well. "Wel-l-l-l, shit," echoed her voice from inside the dryer.

There was little consolation he could offer other than shake his head and make sympathetic sounds.

She appeared ready to start spitting nails but he could also see tears beginning at the corner of her eyes. "Aw hell, more shopping tomorrow. Next time I'll bring a book to the laundry room and stand guard. If you see some broad wearing a pair of jeans with leather strips on the pockets and a short-sleeved blouse with Mickey Mouse on the shoulder, let me know, okay? I'll give her a right-cross to the left jaw."

He left with a reluctant smile on his lips, savouring the sight of her standing with her fist clenched in anticipation of doing battle with the laundry thief.

It was a long walk home, but the amazing sight of the Milky Way galaxy wheeling above, kept him glancing upward frequently, unaware of the mosquitos massing on his bare arms and hands. He decided to go to the bank tomorrow and finalize the deal on the Norton. He was still considering her offer but felt he could learn a few things on his own. The thought didn't scare him, but he knew it should.

Samantha Paige woke the next morning with a pounding headache, part of the price of being hypersensitive to any kind of alcohol. As a high school student she had suffered through many, simply due to her efforts to become accepted as one of the group of girls in her class that drank and tried to smoke. She quickly found it was difficult to appear sophisticated while staggering and simultaneously puking her guts out. She felt fortunate that her physical reaction overcame peer pressure to continue these habits, resulting in her gradual gravitation to the track and field team. She came to excel in the high jump until her senior year when her breasts decided to catch up with the rest of her body, adding several inches to her bust line, not to mention the added interest of her fellow male students.

Hers was the only school in the division where the high jump became a highly attended event, mostly by the male student population. However, the girlfriends of these highly attentive spectators were chagrined at all this attention to her upper body development, and began referring to her as the three-headed jumper due to her breasts, without benefit of restraint, bouncing above her shoulders as she approached the bar.

It was also speculated by the competitors whom she defeated on a regular basis, that she had an unfair advantage due to the added momentum offered by her much-ogled and sometimes vilified mammaries.

To settle the momentum question, the science teacher argued with his colleagues of the competing schools that her breasts were actually a hindrance due to their weight.

Luckily for Samantha, the school year ended. The great boob debate never reached the stage where the various science teachers proposed a scientific study, including weighing and measuring her 'two friends'. The male students voted unanimously to make it a class study, each with his own innovative and usually licentious methods known only to themselves. Ever since then she had worn an athletic bra which considerably reduced her profile but increased her discomfort, for her breasts were like un-rehabilitated convicts, always trying to escape their confines.

The two Tylenol tablets had decreased the pain in her head as she brushed her long red hair, then tied it back in a bun.

She realized that some people she interviewed tended not to take her seriously because the shoulder length hair combined with a freckled nose and eyeglasses made her appear younger than her late twenties. The bun worked, although it made her appear like a school marm. The effect slightly intimidated most men and she was finally taken seriously as a conscientious reporter.

A soft knock came to her door as she was tying her running shoes. She quickly joined the staff photographer, Leif (Corny) Kernell in the hallway, his camera bag dragging one shoulder lower than the other and a cigarette slanting insolently from the corner of his tiny mouth.

"You going to coat your lenses with second hand smoke again Corny? Don't you ever worry about your health or for that of the people around you?"

"Yep an nope," replied Corny with his usual efficiency of words, tilting his head back to blow a stream of smoke at the ceiling. With his camera bag, Corny looked like an overladen anorexic, his pimply face framed by shoulder length black hair that flopped greasily with the strides of his long legs.

The fare in the hotel coffee shop was the standard grease-laden breakfast-special of eggs, home fries, and a choice of bacon, sausage, or ham. A paper-thin slice of tomato cringed on the side of the plate, a shrivelled token to a healthy diet.

She ate her unbuttered toast and jam, repulsed at the sight of her photographer shovelling the combined saturated fats into his mouth.

At an adjacent booth, two still-inebriated patrons in baseball caps and foul coveralls belched and snickered in her direction as she silently willed Corny to finish his coffee so they could leave.

As they paid the bill, she could feel the eyes of the two drunks on her, and she nearly pushed Corny from behind as they went out into the morning sunshine.

They were on the way to the hydro project, crossing over the Black Wood River at the outskirts of town, past clouds of insects rising in clouds from the dew-laden foliage of the ditches.

"Jeez Corny, I think this is the same rental car I had last time. See that hand print in the dust on the dashboard? That's mine. They haven't even cleaned this thing."

Corny sat back in the passenger seat, his feet propped on his side of the dashboard, his window down and elbow hanging out. His hair blew around his face as he studiously picked his nose and flicked the findings into the wind. He was the picture of boredom but he was trembling inside with anticipation at the assignment. When the front page shot of the shocked workers went to press, it had been he who persuaded his buddy on the news desk to include a photo credit. Although he was envious of the shot, wishing he had been there to take it instead, he had argued that any shot worthy of being included in a portfolio, must be credited. His arguments finally won out as did his pleadings to be sent to the project if the opportunity arose again. He was determined to get some good stuff and it didn't matter how gory it got. He just wanted front page portfolio stuff so he could eventually move on to somewhere more mainstream with bigger stories, higher profile and more money.

He removed his camera from the bag in the back seat, and attached the 300 millimetre lens to the Nikon FE body. He fiddled with the settings a few seconds, made sure it was loaded and then focused out the window.

The quick click and whir of the motor-drive caught her attention and she could see Corny focussing on a lone raven flying parallel with their car. She watched the raven as it veered to the right and landed in a tall spruce tree. The tree disappeared behind the plume of dust.

Corny turned to her with a puzzled expression.

"Something wrong with your camera? Did you get a picture of it?"

"Strange bird," mumbled Corny. "I think it smiled at me."

"Lay off the cigarettes, it reduces the oxygen to your brain, causes hallucinations." She smiled at him, hoping to initiate some conversation, anything to alleviate the boredom of the three hour drive. Instead, she watched him light another cigarette and keep his face turned to the tree line as though expecting another photo opportunity.

The three years she had worked at the newspaper, she found Corny to be one of the strangest people on a staff that had more than its share of eccentrics. Of the six photographers on staff, one had violent tendencies, one never stopped talking, even while shooting, and the others appeared relatively normal. Despite Corny's strangeness, she enjoyed working with him because in the past, his shots had transformed a mundane piece into something eye-catching. She liked to think that her talents as a writer transcended the need for photographs, but soon learned that good photo-art used intelligently improved the over-all quality of the story. She could suffer a few idiosyncrasies if the final product helped make her look good.

"Truck ahead," said Corny, his pinched face squinting through the dusty windshield, his camera still held in his lap.

She could make out the tail end of a semi-trailer at the side of the road and a figure moving at the side of the truck, shimmering through the heat haze from the road. She slowed and eased the car past the truck which had the words North Haul stencilled on the door and decided to stop and see if there was anything she could do. The driver was bouncing on a long bar on the end a lug wrench, trying to loosen the nuts on one of the huge tractor tires.

"Anything I can do to help?" She asked, half expecting a curt reply to move on down the road. All she could see was the short, curly dark hair as the driver continued to bounce on the bar, hands braced against the trailer's side for balance, the face turned away from her.

"Yeah. How heavy are you?" replied a woman's voice.

She jumped in surprise at hearing the feminine voice and was surprised when the driver turned and looked at her, her attractive face smeared with a streak of grease. "I weigh about 120 pounds. Why?"

"Want to come up here and bounce on this bar with me? I can't get these lug-nuts loose and I have to change this flat tire. I've been here almost two hours and got 'em all off except these two. The liquid rust remover doesn't work worth a shit and I'm almost out of bounce."

She climbed up on the long bar with the other woman, bracing herself against the trailer as she had seen her do and began gently jumping up and down on command.

The nut let out an agonized squeal as it loosened with the extra weight. The second and last required more bouncing and a few curses from both of them, but finally succumbed with a similar squeal as Corny stood at the corner of the truck photographing their exertions.

Seeing their success with the reluctant lug-nuts, he lit a cigarette in vicarious celebration, intrigued with the sinewy musculature of the tall woman-driver.

"Put that damn thing out!" yelled Teresa at the gangly man with the camera around his neck. "Can't you read? Look at the signs you dumb jerk."

Corny glanced at the large placard at the back of the trailer and quickly threw his cigarette to the ground and stomped on it as though keeping time to country music. He had never been this close to explosives before and knew from the size of the trailer that there was more than enough here to entirely ruin his day.

"Sorry," was all he said, his face reddening from the chastisement.

D'Amico didn't hear nor was she very interested in his mumbled apology as she rummaged for the jack. She placed it under the tractor axle and began pumping the jack handle to lift the drive wheels clear of the road. She then climbed on the rear deck of the tractor and unchained the spare tire.

"Stand clear, this is gonna bounce. Any traffic coming?"

Paige indicated there was no traffic and watched nervously as the driver rolled the tire to the edge of the deck and let it drop. It landed with a dull thump, bounced twice and wobbled to the side of the road to fall on its side in a cloud of dust, like a Saturday night patron of the Stagger Inn.

"I'd give you a hand changing that, but I'd get filthy and I don't have a change of clothes."

I can appreciate that," said D'Amico as she dragged a pair of greasy coveralls from the cab and handed them to Paige. Don't worry, they're only greasy on the outside. I could use some help getting this flat tire back onto the back of the tractor. Last time I did this I nearly got a

317

hernia. By the way, I'm Teri D'Amico, and I really appreciate you stopping."

"Samantha Paige, and this is Corny, Corny Kernell. He's a photographer and I'm a reporter from Winnipeg. We're doing a story on the hydro project." She donned the coveralls, finding the legs and sleeves several inches too long. "Somehow I don't feel like a reporter right now."

"It's you," said D'Amico gesturing with her hands like a merchant of haute couture. "If you had a moustache, you could be Charlie Chaplin in Modern Times. All you need is a wrench. Doesn't Corny there believe in lending a hand?"

"Not in my contract," replied Corny as he turned and walked down the road, still determined to have a cigarette, even if it meant being a half-mile from the truck, swatting mosquitos.

"Yeah, that's what I thought," mumbled D'Amico, seeing a look of embarrassment on Samantha's face.

They wrestled the tire off the road and onto the tractor deck, then placed the spare on the studs, finally tightening the nuts down with the use of the long bar. D'Amico retrieved her coveralls from a flush-faced Paige who appeared satisfied with the work they'd completed.

"Thank you Samantha Paige, but no thanks to your lazy friend there. If I see you again, I'll buy the beer."

The Kenworth rattled to life and as Paige and Corny stood by the side of the road, she gave an appreciative blast on the air horn as she pulled past their car.

Within minutes the truck was out of sight in the dust and a gritty silence descended around them, broken only by the hum of insects.

Paige looked accusingly at Corny who was chain-smoking another cigarette.

"Hey, I hurt these, I don't work," he said defiantly, holding both slim, delicate hands aloft. "Besides, trucking is woman's work." He smiled at her, glad to get a smile in return.

"Maybe more than you could ever realize, Corny."

She wondered what it would be like to drive something the size of the Kenworth. She thought if she ever met D'Amico again, she might ask to be given a chance to try it. She looked at her hands and saw they were filthy from the grease and dust of the tire, and gave off a strong smell of rubber. She used her whole stock of Kleenex and some stagnant ditch water to clean them, disrupting hordes of mosquitos trying to avoid the heat of the sun. She threw the car keys to Corny. "Here, I worked, you drive, I sleep."

He took them without argument and in minutes, she had her eyes closed and mouth open in a healthy snore, the pungent aroma of diesel fuel insinuating itself into her dreams of rattling engines and air horns.

As she drove, D'Amico thought about the reporter who had helped with the tire. She had seen the front page photo of the accident at the power project and had seen Brady's name under it. She had never asked him about the shot and wondered if the reporter for that story had been Samantha Paige. The newspaper was among a large stack which she was planning to throw out eventually. She decided to satisfy her curiosity by digging through the pile and discover who the reporter was, afraid that she might feel a twinge of jealousy if in fact Brady had given her the picture. At present though, that was the least of her worries. She hoped the flat tire wasn't a harbinger of things to come, because she could now feel the trailer brakes becoming soft each time she used them, despite taking the precaution of gearing down frequently to slow the truck. She had suggested the trucks be equipped with Jake brakes, an engine retarder device that used the engine compression to slow the vehicle, saving the brakes. Winky had refused, saying it was illegal to use such equipment within town limits and walked away, passing the usual gassy flatulent retort to all within earshot.

Maybe Brady's idea of a motorcycle isn't so bad. Maybe I should buy one too and go with him. Go anywhere, just get the hell out of here, no more assholes for bosses, nobody to answer to but the road. The least I can do is show him how not to kill himself. I wonder how well he knows that little reporter with the big boobs. Maybe that's why he's dropped out of sight, got a long distance thing going with her. None of my business. If he wants to tell me he will, but I think things are going to start changing around here, I can feel it.

For D'Amico, some changes came on a regular but unwelcome schedule. At the moment she could feel a creeping wetness between her legs. She had disregarded the cramps and general discomfort she had been experiencing over the past few days; too busy to recognize the onset of her period. She swore under her breath, preparing to pull the truck once more to the side of the road and fix the monthly problem, first checking her side mirror for traffic. The sight of the police car made her curse out loud and pound her fist on the steering wheel. The car's headlights were flashing as well as the blue and red emergency flashers on the top. Stopped once again, she began to wonder if she would ever get to the dam site. As she watched in the mirror, Constable Pusch walked nonchalantly to one of the rear trailer tires and gave it a swift kick with one of his highly polished size-fourteen boots. His right hand appeared to be twirling one end of his huge moustache as he quick-marched to the cab where she rested her elbow on the window, her head cradled against her hand.

"And how are we today miss D'Amico? Off to the project again are we? Looks like one of your rear tires may a be a bit low. Care to have a peek? And, um, bring the vehicle registration with you if you don't mind." Pusch wheeled as though on parade and marched back to the rear of the truck as she climbed down with the required documents. Thangyew," he said as he accepted the documents from her. "Yes everything seems okay here, just wanted to make sure the insurance was up to date and all that."

A pained howl emitted from the interior of the car, making D'Amico jump in surprise.   "Your car seems to be calling you constable. Is this one of those new talking models that tells you your door's open and the ash-tray needs emptying?"

"Actually no, it's the passenger saying he needs to go to the bathroom, and by the way, it's corporal now." He went to the passenger door and opened it. "Come on then Proboscis, do your business and back inside lickety-split."

Proboscis leaped from the car, ears flapping like furry wings, short legs scrabbling for traction on the loose gravel as he ran twice around the car. He stopped at the front of the car, sniffed and began howling again, this time at D'Amico, who was watching with amusement. Proboscis moved to the back doors of the truck and began howling with enthusiasm, his short front legs coming off the ground each time he threw his head back.

"He's trained to sniff out explosives," explained Pusch as he snapped a leash on the dog's collar.

She squatted on her haunches, beckoning to Proboscis.

The dog lunged, pulling the leash from Pusch's hand and promptly buried his nose in her crotch, sniffing and licking simultaneously.

"Proboscis, bad dog, yelled Pusch. *Lucky little bastard, I'd give my corporal's stripes to be able to do that.*

She tried to discreetly repel the snuffling beagle and still give the impression she was merely petting him. "Down Proboscis. Is this what they teach you in RCMP doggy school? The explosives are over there. There's nothing explosive here." She held one large ear in each hand, staring straight into his nose and slathering tongue, praying there were still some tampons in the glove box of the Kenworth.

Corporal Pusch watched, the urge to howl nearly overpowering him also, but his superior training and discipline overcame the urge. *Not explosive, my ass. I'd light your fuse anytime and screw the consequences.* He blinked in surprise, not sure if corporals were supposed to think like that, then considered that if he continued to do so, he might make sergeant very quickly.

D'Amico stood as Pusch restrained the dog and himself. She had become self-conscious of her womanly predicament, and wished she could get back to the truck and secure the leak. "Is there anything else corporal, or can I go now?"

"Well there is the matter of that tire," said Pusch, kicking the offending tread once again.   Proboscis sniffed where he had kicked and promptly lifted a leg and peed on the same spot.

"If you think I'm going to change it now, you're nuts. Besides, I've already used my other spare on another flat. Don't you want to look at the load like last time?"

"No, not necessary. *I just wanted to look at the driver.* It was just this tire that concerned me." He kicked the tire once again as though it was his duty and began twirling the end of his mustache while Proboscis strained against his leash once again in the direction of her crotch, his tongue slathering drool on the ground

Typical male, she thought.

"Well, there is one other thing actually." Pusch had inserted one hand into his trouser pocket and began fidgeting with the loose change. "I've, um been asked to attend a wedding this Saturday and well, er, I was wondering if you'd care to be my guest. Nothing big, just a little thing, don't have to stay long if you don't want." He could feel his face blush, and became more embarrassed when he realised he was getting an erection. He was tempted to hit it with his baton but thought the action might jeopardize his chances of a date.

She was slightly stunned at the proposition. Her first reaction was to reject the invitation, but she held her tongue. *What the hell, where's the harm? I haven't had a date in weeks and Brady seems to have something going with that little reporter.*

"What the hell, why not?"

Pusch's moustache nearly leapt off his face with delight, as it was, it wriggled hyperactively under his nose as he related the time and place, his erection growing in direct proportion with his optimism. He was reasonably sure he would have to discipline it with the baton before he could get back in the car. He was also made nervous by Proboscis who now stared at his crotch. He deposited him in the car as quickly as possible.

She got back in the truck under the watchful eyes of the mounty, wondering if she would regret her decision. She had made her decision and thought, what the hell, it's only one night, not the rest of her life.

Corporal Pusch turned his car around in a spray of gravel and dust, the tape deck howling a tune by Willy Nelson, accompanied in full vocal flight by himself and Proboscis. He discovered their voices were strangely compatible.

Corny Kernell found the visitor's parking lot at the hydro project, waking Samantha as the rented Dodge jerked to a stop. A city boy, he had never driven so long before on gravel road and his hands were cramped from gripping the steering wheel. There had been a couple of times when he had to move over to allow oncoming large trucks past, nearly throwing the car into a skid in the loose gravel of the shoulder. He was amazed how she could sleep through the whole ordeal, but her head rested against her jacket near the open window, a small trickle of drool coming from the side of her mouth.

"Time to go to work," he said as she looked back with reddened eyes, smacking the lips of her dry mouth.

"Blah, my mouth feels like crap. I've got to stop drinking beer, it always plugs up my sinuses."

"You went to the bar last night? Corny was incredulous. "I wouldn't have gone in there unarmed or at least without a bodyguard."

"That's your problem Corny, you have no spirit of adventure," she replied, slipping a Cert into her mouth. "You want to get the true flavour of a place, you go for a beer in the local pub. It can be very educational."

"So what did you learn last night?"

"Never to do it again," she groaned as she climbed stiffly from the car, shading her eyes with one hand from the harshness of the late morning sun.

Corny lit another cigarette and smiled to himself as he swung the heavy camera bag to his shoulder, thankful he didn't drink. Being brought up in a family dominated by an alcoholic father had given him a taste of the dark side and he rejected it as profoundly as those who would try to dominate him.

They were met at the security shack by the same bespectacled public relations person that she had asked some hard questions of the first time there. The man obviously remembered her, for he handed them their visitor hard hats with barely a smile, as they signed the log book.

She introduced Corny, who had placed the hard hat backwards on his head so he would be able to use the camera easier. She had seen the P.R. man look disapprovingly at Corny and his hat, but he said nothing. It was going to be tour by company truck around the site to show the overall construction and she hoped to relax their tour guide with some banal questions before springing anything about worker safety on him.

She only half-listened as the P.R. guy drove them through and around the site, his arm occasionally making a sweeping gesture over the expanse of concrete dotted with workers and crawled over by huge ore trucks. The scale of the site made the ore trucks look like hunch-backed beetles as they hauled away the rock which had been blasted out of the shield. The air was filled with dust, making her wish she had not worn her contact lenses today. The air vibrated with pneumatic drills as they bore into the rock where explosives would be poured and eventually detonated, shearing away another section of rock.

In the rear of the crew-cab, Corny busied himself, loading colour film into one camera body and black and white into another. He had taken a few shots from the lowered window, hoping the fast shutter speed froze the image despite the bouncing of the truck.

"They're drilling the last patterns for the spillway," said their guide, as he stopped the truck and stepped out. They were on a ledge over-looking the half-dozen drills working within 50 metres of each other, their two-man crews hard-hatted and ear-muffed to protect against the noise. Although they were nearly 100 metres away from the drills, they had to shout to hear each other.

Corny shot with a 200 millimetre lens and a wide angle lens to capture as much a panorama as possible. He knew the lens would never do justice to the true scope of the site. Sunlight back-lit the drillers and their rigs and he isolated one crew with the telephoto lens, underexposing to create a silhouette of the men against the cloud of rock dust the drill was producing. He made several exposures, varying the aperture each time although still under exposed according to the internal light meter. As he pressed the shutter for a series of final frames, the drill and men lifted from the surface of the rock at the same time his ears were rocked with a sharp concussion. He flinched with the sound and whirring of rock particles, but kept his finger on the button of the motor-drive.

A dusty stillness filled the air, combined with the ringing in their ears. The other drills had shut down, some of the drillers laying, writhing on the ground.

The drill where the blast had occurred, lay on it's side, the airline parted and twitching violently like a beheaded snake. The two drillers lay several feet away, not moving.

The P.R. man scrabbled down the steep embankment toward the men, Samantha and Corny sliding on their bottoms, following close behind. "Oh my God, oh my God," muttered the guide. "A bootleg, they must have been near a bootleg hole." He stared at the two unmoving men who now had blood seeping through their coveralls, puddling beneath them. He ran to one, briefly touching his clothing then the next, unsure what to do next, unaware of the moan of the siren in the distance.

"Can't we do something for these guys?" asked Paige as she watched him stare at the bodies. She could see the men's faces were white due to the rock dust mingled with their sweat, but the whiteness was mottled with the streams of blood running from their eyes, ears, noses and mouths. Their eyes were wide open and fixed, glazed over in a surprised stare. Suddenly the air was still as Corny bent down and shut off the valve on the air hose, finally stilling the twitching appendage. She had a vague recollection of Corny using his camera as the P.R. man stumbled from body to body.

Two ambulances came into view, raising huge plumes of dust. One stopped where the drillers lay still, the other stopping where the nearest drill crew still stumbled around holding their ears, faces grimacing in pain. The attendants quickly checked the breathing of the men and immediately attached oxygen masks. One attendant called for a helicopter for evacuation while the other prepared to do CPR on one of the men. An attendant from the other ambulance ran over, confident his partner could handle the other casualties, and inserted an airway in the one man, then attached a squeeze bag to force the oxygen into the lungs while the other did chest compressions.

The attendants had to make a difficult decision, one of triage, the practice of judging which man might survive, which patient had the priority. They picked the man who was bleeding the least from the facial orifices, leaving the other where he fell. They were both well experienced in their craft and knew that they would later question themselves and their judgment, especially if the person they picked also died. Critical

324

incident stress was part of their job and thankfully the company kept a psychologist on call to be flown in from Winnipeg on short notice.

The helicopter arrived and whisked both injured men away along with the ambulance attendants who had by then set an intravenous drip in the man's arm. The other injured men were driven by ambulance to the first aid station, most of their injuries being lacerations from flying rock chips and damaged ear drums.

"So what is a bootleg hole?" she asked of the guide. She stared him straight in the eyes but he didn't seem to realize she had spoken to him. She reached out and poked him gently on the arm and asked again. He jumped this time and recoiled from her touch.

"What? What did you say?"

"A bootleg hole. What is it?"

"Oh...it's a hole that has undetonated explosives in it. Sometimes faulty fusing won't detonate the cap and primer.

"Why was it there?" She was cradling her small tape recorder in her hand, keeping the microphone turned toward him, but partially obscured by a sweater she'd removed.

The guide tilted his hardhat back, wiping sweat from his brow with the back of his other hand. "They're not supposed to be. They're supposed to be flushed out with water before more drilling takes place. Otherwise the vibrations from a drill nearby could detonate the cap and the explosives. That's what happened here. These guys were trying to make big bonuses by circumventing their own safety rules."

They looked around them silently at the mangled drill and blackened spots of blood where the men had lain. To Samantha it had a dream-like quality almost as though she expected to awake at any moment to a more pleasant reality. Finally she spoke.

"Can I ask you some rather difficult questions back at the truck?" She watched the man nod and turn toward the incline they'd slid down and move like a man dream-walking. For the next hour they sat on the hot running board of the truck while the man answered her questions about the bonus program, wages and safety conditions. By the end of the hour she had gone through two tape cassettes and felt she had a story.

As they were signing out at the security shack, the phone rang and moments later the guard personnel had confiscated all of Corny's exposed film, including that in the cameras. He had made a scene, swearing, stamping his feet, and nearly physically refusing to hand it over until the guard simply referred to as 'sarge', extended a huge hand into which Corny dropped several rolls of film.

It wasn't until a half hour later while Paige was driving, that Corny pulled up his trouser cuffs and displayed the elastic of each sock bulging with film cassettes of the actual incident. She would have hugged him except his acne had broken out and his face was beginning to resemble an under-cooked pizza.

CHAPTER 17

His ears roared with the music of the fans, their huge blades carving the sunlight into swiftly moving wedges of light against the building's wall. The light transformed his face and the interior of the building into a kaleidoscope of brilliant light and dark shadows moving with hallucinogenic speed. Like the interior of the building, his mind was a roar of thoughts bouncing from one side to the other, some making perfect sense. But others, like the flashes of light and dark about him, conveyed a blurring cycle of dread and enlightenment. The thoughts came so quickly, like mental knives that excised his innermost, darkest thoughts They urged him into action.

Over the last couple of weeks he had ventured out of the dark, familiar maze of underground tunnels and into the town in search of food and clothing. It was always at night that he went, gaining comfort from the night because no one saw him and he saw everyone. His night vision, although myopic, along with an acute sense of hearing equipped him to be nocturnal. His body moved with the rhythm of his instincts and reactions to hunger and cold, but it jerked into uncontrollable directions with the commands of the voices.

Go to the home of the photographer and find what is rightfully yours. He has your image which belongs to you alone. If he possesses your image, he possesses you. No one can possess you.

No, you're wrong, someone has and always will.

But that was so long ago and a secret love should stay a secret.

That was rape.

But it became love.

It became fear disguised as love, a secret smelling of unwashed bodies and uncleansed souls, renewed until the film of filth was like a second skin, like armour, yet vulnerable.

He told him he was like a woman.

He used him like a woman.

His mother never knew?

How could she? He was raping her too.

He is his mother's son with his mother's torment.

The voices faded, driven away by the fans.

The sun had lowered in the sky, turning the wedges of light to orange, then red. He had sat for hours on the floor with the litter of food wrappers and rotting remnants of their contents. Rats scurried along the base of the building, casting quick glances toward him, sniffing the air, then the crumbs about them.

The rats never questioned why one of their profligate number would disappear, only to be found again, the head gone, the tiny ribs and haunches devoid of meat, the remains thrown on a pile of other headless bodies, mingled with human feces. The stinking mound of furry bodies and feces grew like a black cancer in one corner of the building, the fans sucking the foul stench into the bowels of the earth where on an upper level of the mine, men toiled and caught the occasional scent of his existence. Each man's nose would twitch and his skin crawl as though insects had been let loose upon him. The roar of the fans continued into the gathering darkness and still, he sat. Finally the rumblings of his much neglected stomach urged him to the outer darkness and onto a barely visible path through the trees toward the outskirts of town.

He moved slowly at first, listening and sniffing the air. Small animals scurried away from him through the rustling grass, having smelled his presence and recognized the smell of death.

The town lights glowed like a glittering oasis from beyond the tree line. It was an oasis that attracted and repelled at the same time. He could see and be seen there, compelling him to keep to the shadows of the back lanes and their buffet of cans containing discarded food. It was through these cans he had rummaged quietly, sometimes eating what he found immediately. Other times, filling his pockets with the previously gnawed fare, to be eaten later in his rancid nest. He knew where the dogs were and could smell them nearly as soon as they smelled him. Their growls of initial ferocity often became infected with fear, once the full impact of his odours reached them, but he habitually avoided them.

Several days previous, he had detected the aroma of freshly washed laundry. Sniffing the air like a fox, he followed the scent to a small apartment building where clothing tumbled in a dryer, the sounds and smells coming to him from a ground level window where he lay on the cool grass, still as a snake, away from the light from within.

He stepped from the shadows of the tree line, skirting the pools of cold light painted on the ground by the street lights. Traffic was light but he waited long minutes before crossing the street to avoid being caught in the headlights. When he did finally cross, his form was a stringy shadow flitting over the pavement, the only light flickering briefly from his thick eyeglasses. His hair, now nearly shoulder length and matted with filth, flapped around his face like some ragged animal gripping his scalp to keep from falling off. He was close. He could smell the laundry room and within minutes was able to crouch amongst the shrubbery and watch a tall dark haired woman loading wet clothing into one of the dryers. He lay there motionless, knowing the cycle would be long and that his stomach would not wait. He slowly rose and quietly moved to the back lane and the large trash cans. It was time to eat.

Teresa returned a half hour later for her laundry, still wondering if she would regret the date with Corporal Pusch tonight. Luckily it was only a wedding reception they were attending, no one she knew... she hoped, and as Pusch had said, there was no need to stay long. As she removed the clothing, she detected a strange smell, one she had smelled before in the confined landing of Brady's apartment. The sensation of being watched came over her and she glanced quickly up at the ground-level window over her head. It had been swung inward on the hinges along the top of its frame and she could see nothing but blackness beyond. She quickly gathered her laundry and left the room, looking behind her once as she hurried down the hallway to her apartment.

He waited under the shrubs, his stomach growling like one of the neighbourhood mongrels that he avoided. The trash cans had been recently emptied. There had been nothing in them except the miasma of smells from food that had once been there. Several streets away he had come to the rear of a building where the aromas of cooking had nearly driven him wild. The open door had afforded him a glimpse of steaming pots on stoves and mounds of food that made his mouth salivate until his scrawny chest was soaked with saliva. A large woman in a white apron moved among the other workers in the kitchen like a general, issuing orders.

It was to this building that he returned, crouching in the darkness between two vehicles parked in the lane, watching, waiting to pounce on any scraps being thrown into the large dumpster near the open door.

Bardman hated weddings. Over the years he had photographed many out of sheer economic necessity, but he still hated them. It had been contrary to his own instincts as a news photographer to try and show the attractive side of his subjects rather than the opposite, which was often what the paper expected.

Jenkins' daughter was an unattractive waif of a girl with poorly concealed acne and rebellious hair. Her mother had used ill-judgment in choosing her wedding gown with a low bodice and off the shoulder style which proved to all that she had practically no shoulders and absolutely no breasts. As a result she had to hunch her shoulders just to prevent the entire gown from dropping to her ankles, giving her the appearance of someone flinching from a blow.

Such were the shots Brady took of her in the Jenkins home, under the slightly inebriated but watchful eyes of his boss. He had used the soft-focus lens almost exclusively to reduce some of the acne on her face, but not with a great deal of success.

The ceremony was mercifully short, with the father of the bride staggering as he accompanied her down the aisle to a waiting and pallid Zenon Mikeluk. Bardman watched Mikeluk closely, half-expecting him to faint at any moment. He considered fainting a viable alternative to purgatory with such over-bearing in-laws.

The group photos with the family and wedding party had been taken at a small park where everyone including himself spent most of the time swatting mosquitoes and waving in what is known as the Australian Salute, at the marauding horseflies.

Bardman breathed a sigh of relief as the soothing beer went down his parched throat. There was a lull in activities until the dinner and reception two hours hence, and the darkness of the lounge in the Stag Inn let him unwind from the stress of being under the critical eyes of Jenkins and his wife. He had removed his tie, intending to keep it off for the duration of the day, when the familiar form of Samantha Paige entered, accompanied by a tall gangly young man with long, greasy hair. He waved them over and was pleased that she gave him a big smile and sat beside him as she introduced her photographer, Corny Kernell.

Samantha did all the talking, relating the previous day's events at the hydro project. Corny looked smug, puffing endlessly on a series of cigarettes as she gushed of how he had smuggled the film past the guards.

He was pleased to see her again but became uncomfortable under the watchful, silent gaze of Corny from across the table. It appeared that Corny might consider him some kind of adversary. He became aware of her perfume and the fact that when she leaned near to speak, her ample left breast pushed invitingly into his arm. To his relief, Corny felt out of place and excused himself, begging a need for sleep. When he had gone, she stayed near his side, moving even closer to the extent that his hand was beginning to sweat in anticipation.

"You know Brady, I think you and I could become real friends. We seem to have a lot in common and our work complements each others."

She was sipping from a glass of beer, seemingly becoming tipsy on the fumes alone. "It's too bad you have that wedding to shoot, we could talk more before we go back to Winnipeg tomorrow."

He reassured her he wouldn't be long at the reception and dance and they arranged to meet for coffee at ten o'clock, after he had finished his work.

Back at the reception, members of the wedding party and family had relieved their own tensions at the cash bar and were about to take their places at the various assigned tables. As the guests drifted to their places, he was surprised to see Teresa exit from the lady's room and sit beside a tall gentleman who appeared to be mopping something from his lap. His surprise multiplied when he realised it was Constable Pusch. A pang of jealousy swept through him when he saw her put her hand on his as she spoke to him. He saw the constable laugh in reply and it became evident they enjoyed each other's company.

He began to feel supremely sorry for himself, almost deceived, but realised he had no claim on Teresa and he had neglected to even call her the last couple of weeks. She has a right to a social life, he thought to himself. The sudden thought that perhaps their budding relationship might be at an end, caused a profound sense of regret and recrimination. He realised how much he had come to rely on her friendship, even take it for granted that they might one day be more than friends. The alternative made him feel very lonely, especially so in the midst of the drunken, noisy crowd of revellers.

"*Mr. Bardman,* would you mind *terribly* going from table to table and get shots of all the people? Just candid stuff please, for record's sake only. That's a good fellow," finished Jenkins who wandered unsteadily off, glass-in-hand toward the bar for a refill.

Might as well get it over with, he thought to himself, walking toward the table where Teresa and Pusch sat.

Teresa glanced up as the flash went off and opened her mouth to speak, but said nothing when she saw him. She saw him smile and focus for another shot. "Get my good side Brady," she finally said with forced cheerfulness.

Pusch leaned close to her to be in the frame and he took another. He had never seen her in a skirt before and its shortness showed her long legs to good advantage. He had forgotten what a striking woman she was and he could see that as the two tallest people in the room, she and Pusch made a handsome couple.

Dinner was served by staff from the kitchen, a local catering company which delivered steaming hot turkey, cabbage rolls, mashed potatoes, with gravy to each hungry and slightly be-sotted guest, some moreso than others. In fact a few were completely blotto, the bride's father being the most blotto of all.

Brady sat at a table with a group who spoke in heavy Slavic accents and cast wary glances in his direction between bites. Their clothing was of dark sturdy material and they ate with the urgency of those who might be in a hurry to return to the fields.

"You vant coffee Mr. photographer?" came the voice from behind him.

Turning, he saw Natasha from the Stag Inn with pot in hand smiling down at him.

"You sit with good pipples, not sit with uppity-ups eh?" She continued around the table with the coffee, pleasantly surprising the rest of the group with an understanding of their language. As she left, she gave him a good-natured wink and returned to the kitchen.

Just the presence of a familiar face made him more at ease, but he could see from the corner of his eye, Teresa looking his way from the far side of the room, occasionally nodding automatically to whatever it was Pusch was whispering in her ear.

"Ladiesh n' genelmen, I think itsh appro-priate to toasht the bride. Don' you?" Roger Jenkins was leaning drunkenly on the podium, wine glass in one hand, the other gripping the microphone as though trying to prevent it from escaping. "An to the young man who hash her...actually I think he'sh had her, hic, several time-sh before thish." He smiled crookedly at the audience, waving his glass in their general direction, slopping some on the floor.

The audience responded with a polite murmur of uncomfortable laughter as the newly-weds blushed in unison.

Mrs. Jenkins, at the nearby table was gesturing madly with white, puffy hands toward the podium, trying to attract her husband's attention.

Jenkins instead, leered at the maid of honour, whom he had previously surprised in a state of semi-undress when he had stumbled into her room by mistake at the home while his daughter was getting ready. He had misinterpreted her blushing smile as encouragement and had been trying to catch her eye ever since. To his impending misfortune he had caught his wife's eye instead, as well as most of those of the dinner guests.

"I've watched my li'l girl grow from diapersh to...whatever it ish they wear now, God forbid I should peek." He looked around with unfocussed eyes, expecting laughter of approval, hearing none. He took a slow sip from his wine glass, one arm supported on the podium.

"But look at 'er now. Ishn't she b'ooful? An' lookit 'er maid of honour. Ain't she a dish too?" He gave a long wink to the maid of honour who reciprocated with an embarrassed blush while closely studying the remnants of her dinner plate.

His daughter, the once-blushing, now-livid bride, glared at her cutlery, her shoulders hunched to prevent the decline and fall of her wedding gown.

Bardman rose from his chair from the nearby table, camera in hand. It had been one of the requirements that he photograph all the toasts as well as candid shots of friends and family having a good time. He took up a position slightly to the side of the podium and pre-focussed on his sozzled boss.

"To my daughter," blurted Jerkins, raising an empty wine glass in her general direction. "An' to my new sh-on in-law whom I intend to work mersh-ilessly to keep her in the manner to whish sh-she hash become acc-ushtomed. He smiled with drunken malevolence toward Zenon Mikeluk.

Mikeluk cowered behind a champagne bottle, forcing a smile toward the podium, wishing he had applied a more efficient anti-perspirant.

Jerkins raised his glass to drink, then lowered it realizing it was empty. Losing his balance, he put his hand out once more for the podium and leaned his full weight upon it. The casters on the bottom of the podium responded by allowing the podium to roll, thus allowing Jerkins and his glass to topple full-length to the floor.

The table of Slavic guests roared their approval at this North American custom and eagerly awaited their individual turn at the podium.

Mrs Jerkins moved across the floor like a multi-coloured ship of state and lifted her husband bodily by the armpits. His one hand still clutched the empty wine glass, while smiling stupidly at the maid of honour.

The maid of honour fought to control her bladder as well as her embarrassment. The evening became a blur of noise, smoke, lurching guests and ceaseless polka music played by an overzealous music man who introduced each song with a fake radio voice.

The music man needed all the practice he could get. He was the new disc-jockey and news reader for the local radio station, and he was told by his empoyer that his diction needed some work. The purchase of a dictionary to discover the meaning of diction had been his first tentative step to self-improvement. Unfortunately his reading ability hadn't progressed beyond grade six level and he was having difficulty reading the musical requests of the guests. Until he was able to decipher these requests, he simply kept playing polkas.

He crouched under the delivery truck, one hand resting on the suspension near the front tire. As he watched through the open receiving door. He saw the heavy-set woman and a younger blonde woman sitting and eating at one of the work counters. Between them was a green bottle from which they toasted each other frequently. It appeared the blonde woman was making sandwiches, placing them in a large paper bag as she sipped from her glass. Saliva dripped from his chin onto his shirt-front as he saw the mouth-watering food being consumed. None was being discarded into the large bin and the aromas coming from the kitchen were driving him wild. He wasn't sure if it was his stomach growling with particular ferocity or one of his voices saying eat, now, but, with a sinuous movement he came from beneath the truck and crouched at the edge of the open door. The aromas were unbearable as he watched the two women begin the task of cleaning their work areas. Other young women moved in and out with desserts, returning with tubs full of dirty dishes, laden with uneaten food. At knee level he poked his head around the door frame. The two women had moved to another table where he could hear the sound of running water. He kept his head down and crept quietly along one table where a large plate was still heaped with sliced turkey and drumsticks. He slowly reached up, his fingers feeling for the edge of the plate like a filthy, blind spider, finally encountering the soft delectable mound of meat. His hand came away with a large drumstick and he impulsively shoved the large end of the drumstick completely into his mouth.

Natasha was in dishwater up to her elbows when the foul stench came to her nostrils. She had smelled similar odours on the occasion someone had become sick in the bar, but this was different, much worse. This was a stench of vomit, feces, and rotting meat combined, and even the strength of the dish detergent could not overcome it. She turned and searched the kitchen, realizing her workmate had gone into the dining area, possibly to supervise the girls bussing the tables. A slight movement on one of the counters near the rear door caught her eye. The large brown paper bag which she had stocked with sandwiches for her husband's midnight shift was beginning to move. It moved slowly along the counter and then slowly lowered from sight beyond the edge. She watched incredulous, as the bag disappeared from view. She shifted her gaze to an array of large spoons hanging from a bracket above the counter. She could see movement reflected in the shiny surfaces of the utensils. With her hands still soapy, she moved slowly to the end of the kitchen. She knew the intruder was also moving to avoid detection.

"You vant food you ask, not steal," she shouted, trying to keep the nervousness from her voice. "You come out now an' everyt'ing okay. Okay?"

She moved toward the rear door, cutting off the intruder's escape route, forcing the intruder deeper into the kitchen and away from a rack of razor-sharp carving knives. She worried that someone would enter the kitchen and surprise the person still crouched out of sight. In a state of semi-panic she picked up a container of flour and heaved it toward the counter where the intruder crouched. The metal container landed on the top of the counter, spilling its contents over the side and onto the matted hair of Pilson who still had the turkey leg jammed into his mouth, the bone protruding like some long, obscene tongue.

He jumped upright, his tangled mass of hair throwing off flour in white clouds, his face caked with it, eyes bulging in panic from behind his thick and dusty eyeglasses. His Adam's apple moved vertically as though trying to force its way out his mouth, causing the protruding end of the turkey leg to move vertically in a corresponding manner.

Natasha let out a shriek as the flour-covered, stinking apparition ran in blind panic for the only escape, the door to the dining area. She saw her husband's lunch grasped tightly in one large grungy hand as the intruder bolted through the swinging door.

Bardman was getting perverse gratification from photographing the gutter behaviour of some of the so-called the town elites. The only ones who seemed able to hold their alcohol were the relatives with the Slavic accents as they toasted each other and practised knocking over the podium. Zenon Mikeluk was having beer poured down his throat by his best man and two ushers while, Roger Jerkins, having escaped the wrath of his wife, had cornered the maid of honour and, with one hand leaning on the wall beside her head, had tried to plant a poorly aimed kiss on her mouth. He took a photo just as she ducked, and Jerkins subsequently kissed the wall beside his hand. The wet stain on the wall indicated it was to be a French kiss.

The music man had finally deciphered one of the musical requests and began playing the Bird Dance in which the participants bob around, flapping their arms like chickens with perspiration problems.

Bardman turned as he heard a clang and shriek from the kitchen. The swinging door flew open, colliding with a heavy-set kitchen worker, laden with a tub of plates and cutlery. The woman landed with a crash amidst the cutlery and screamed upon seeing the countenance of a thoroughly panicked and flour-encrusted Pilson standing over her, the turkey leg still protruding from his mouth. He looked like a large, repugnant pastry in a blind panic.

Pilson tried to push his way through the mass of drunken humanity, taking a wrong turn which positioned him in the midst of a large group of dancers just as the Bird Dance reached a crescendo. One of the dancers, a tall dark-haired woman, lunged with both arms still flapping. She screamed a gurgling cry and pointed at him. He turned and ran blindly for an exit, shoving people aside, others backing away with looks of horror. He ran into the comforting night and its protective shadows. Finally, he removed the offending turkey leg from his mouth as he listened to the family of voices inhabiting his mind. The consensus seemed to be that the people in the hall were absolutely crazy. The voices were unanimous. They didn't want to go back.

"Brady did you see that? He was wearing them." Teresa was looking open-mouthed at the door where Pilson had fled.

He looked at her, wondering what she was talking about.

"My blouse and my new jeans, you dolt, he was wearing them. He had my Mickey Mouse blouse on too. He's the thief, and you know what really hurts?"

"No, what really hurts my dear?" replied Pusch, arriving with a drink in each hand.

She turned back to Bardman, agitated at Pusch's interruption. "Those clothes fit him better than they fit me. *That really pisses me off!*"

He didn't know how to respond to her outburst, relieved to see Pusch walk unsteadily to the men's room. He packed away his camera gear and headed for the self-serve bar. He was dying for a beer, wishing for a quiet corner in which to drink it. He felt a hand pluck his sleeve.

"Brady, bring your beer back here and talk with me for a while...please?"

He saw a pleading expression in her eyes and joined her, glad that Pusch had either locked himself in the men's room or been discrete enough to give them some privacy.

Later, while packing his equipment into the Volkswagen, he was relieved that Teresa was not upset with him, but there was still a pang of jealousy as he saw her leave with Pusch.

The corporal was giving her more attention than he'd given anything in his life and she appeared to bask in the glow of that attention.

Samantha Paige heard the soft knock on her hotel room door. She realised he had knocked softly, not wishing to have Corny, in the next room, see him at the door.

"I came straight here. I'm afraid I smell like smoke and booze."

"I'm used to the smell of a newsroom, it makes me feel comfortable. Besides I don't trust men who mask themselves with perfumes and gunk." She wore a short, silky shift with a floral print, belted at the waist, contrasted by dark pantyhose. Her auburn hair had been let down to flow over her shoulders and drape over the generous mounds of her breasts.

Push-up bra thought Bardman to himself, a tingling sensation beginning in his genitals, his breath becoming shallow.

"How do you like your coffee?" She moved near a chair next to a writing table and poured coffee from a thermos bottle into two mugs. On the counter was a bottle of Cointreau and one of Bailey's.

He smiled and pointed to the Bailey's.

She came close and handed him the glass. "I guess the only place we can sit is on the bed. Why don't we prop the pillows up on the end and lean on those?" She had put her own glass on a night table and was busily re-arranging the pillows, unaware that he was furtively appraising her pert bottom. She thumped the pillows decisively with a fist.

"There, have a seat," she said as she slid onto one side of the bed and propped herself against the pillows.

He eased himself alongside her, still clutching his cup of coffee and cursing under his breath as some dribbled onto his slacks. He leaned back against the pillows, aware that she had shifted her position so her bare shoulder touched his.

For several seconds they sat without speaking, sipping from their cups. Bardman felt himself blush when he realised the toe of his left foot was poking through a hole in his sock. He discreetly covered his bare toe with the other foot.

She watched his efforts and giggled over the lip of her cup. "You should try wearing pantyhose. Sometimes the whole end rips out or a seam creeps up the entire length." To illustrate the problem she lifted her right leg high in the air, running one hand along its length.

337

His breath quickened and he spilled more coffee, this time in the crotch of his pants which was beginning to manifest a life of its own. He held his breath as she put her cup on her night table and proceeded to gently trace the contours of her still up-raised leg, oblivious to the fact he had held his breath, and his face was beginning to turn slightly red.

"I think it would look better on you than me," he replied in a strangled voice which came to a slight quaver at the end. His mouth was open in wonder as she again raised the leg straight in the air with her toes pointed like a synchronized swimmer.

"So, how was the wedding?"

His jaw clamped shut with an audible click as he turned and saw her expression of amusement. "Oh... it was okay. The usual drunk in-laws, nervous groom, obnoxious guests. The kitchen got raided by that maniac from underground, wearing women's clothing with a turkey drumstick stuck in his mouth. Nothing special."

Both of her feet came back on the bed as she abruptly sat up. "Did you get pictures of him doing all this?"

"Some, not all of it."

She rolled over, straddling him with her legs across his hips, taking the coffee cup from his hands and placed it on the table next to the bed.

"This all happened and you never even gave a hint? This is all good stuff for the story we're doing about him. So tell me, tell me, tell me, what shots did you get of him?" Her fists were beating on his chest as punctuation to each question.

"I got him running around the dining area with a turkey leg stuck in his mouth. He stank like a rat that had been dead for weeks."

She shrieked with delight at his description, bouncing up and down on his pelvic area, straining his dress-shirt to the point that a couple of buttons popped. The bed springs groaned and the headboard hit the wall loud enough to signal the surrounding guests that their sleep might be interrupted. She was either unaware that the hard mound forming under his pants didn't exist, or was a phenomena of little importance.

"Fantastic, great, this is big, really big. Don't you just love it?"

"Love what?"

"The fact that it's all coming together! This story, your pictures, the...oh sorry. Did I do that?" She had finally become aware of his state of arousal and the fact she was inadvertently pounding it into submission with each bounce of her well endowed body. She leaned forward giving him a full view down the front of her blouse as she studied something on his shirtfront, where the buttons had popped over his belly. She bent closer and giggled with one hand over her mouth.

"What? What's so funny down there?"

"You have this big ball of lint in your navel. It looks like a humming bird nest."

His erection deflated to the consistency of over-cooked linguini as he strained to sit up. He was pushed back down by both her hands on his shoulders.

She deftly plucked the lint, holding it up to the light between her thumb and forefinger for inspection, like an entomologist with a new specimen. "Biggest one I've ever seen."

"Well it's mine and I want it back," he replied, straining to reach her hand.

"Under the bed with the rest of the dust bunnies," she cried as she shifted herself to the edge of the bed and disposed of the furry blob.

"My god look at the time! We have to drive back this morning and I haven't even let you finish your coffee. I have to kick you out so I can get some sleep."

"There's a lot we never finished," he said wistfully, watching her breasts strain above him against the fabric of her dress.

"Why sir, I only invited you for coffee. Did you have other things in mind?" She rolled off the bed and walked slowly toward the door.

He reluctantly got to his feet, the frustration in him growing. "I guess I did misinterpret your invitation, but at least the coffee was good."

She pecked him on the cheek, and as his hands touched her waist, planted her lips on his, throwing her arms around his neck. Her hips strained against his and she could feel his hands moving to her buttocks.

"Uh, uh, you have to go now." She gently shoved him out the door into the hallway.

"I don't know if I'm coming or going with you."

"Right now you're going, but don't worry," she said with a wink, "You'll know when you're coming."

She maneuvered him out of the room, aware of his frustration, feeling a pang of guilt. "Keep on the story Brady, and let me know if anything new comes up."

He didn't smile at the double-entendre as he headed for the lobby in a complete state of sexual confusion.

The door to the adjacent room opened and Corny Kernell poked his dishevelled head into the light, a malicious smile on his lips. "Biggest one I've ever seen!" he whispered loudly from his doorway.

339

"What did you do, hold a drinking glass to the wall?" He was angered that the pimply cretin had probably overheard their entire conversation.

"Didn't have to, these walls are like paper. Do you know you're missing two buttons off your shirt? Sweet dreams."

Bardman bit the inside of his cheek, his fists clenched in anger at the sight of the greasy haired photographer mocking him. The floor of the hallway thundered with the impact of his heels as he took his frustration home.

It seemed he had only been asleep minutes when the phone woke him. He answered groggily but slowly came to life when he realised it was Teresa on the other end.

"I'm coming over to show you how to ride that thing."

"What thing?"

"That dumb motorcycle. What did you do last night after the wedding? I tried to call you when I got home, but there was no answer."

"Coffee with a friend, got home late," he replied, rolling his tongue around inside his mouth in an attempt to relieve the dryness. His breath was foul from the combination of alcohol and coffee. He hung up without saying goodbye and glanced at his watch. He cursed when he saw it was only six in the morning and immediately called her number to beg for a couple of hours more sleep. There was no answer and knew she would be at his door in ten minutes. With a sigh of resignation he got up and went to the bathroom to shave and gargle with mouthwash.

When she knocked on the door, he was dressed and ready to go. The sun was burning off the early morning fog that rolled in from the Black Wood river.

The Norton sat on its centre stand, at the rear of the building, covered with fine dew.

"Okay, let's take a look at this beast," said Teresa under her breath as she walked slowly around the motorcycle. "Ooooh, Western bars, roll bars and foot pegs. All the goodies." She checked out the bolt-on luggage at the rear. "Cute saddle bags Brady. You could do some travelling with this baby. Do you know how to start it?"

"Not really, the guy showed me once but I'm not sure I could do it myself now." He handed her the key and watched as she slipped it into the slot on the left side below the seat.

He committed her moves to memory as she leaned down, turned the fuel cocks on and depressed the trickle button on each Amal carburettor to allow fuel to drain into the bowl. She then moved the choke on the left handlebar to full. She turned the ignition key one click clockwise and with the clutch lever depressed, slowly moved the kick-start lever to the bottom of its range of travel and allowed it to return part way. She pushed down on it again to feel whether one of the two pistons might be at top dead center of the ignition stroke. When she judged that a piston was at the top, she propelled herself upwards and came down with all her weight on the kick-start lever.

The Norton gave a short bark, followed by a mechanical gasp and was quiet.

"I've never been able to start one of these things cold on the first kick. Why didn't you buy something with an electric start?

"I thought it had one. I figured the kick-lever was just optional."

She rolled her eyes and repeated the process three more times, cursing each time under her breath. On the fifth try the Norton roared to life with a sound that startled Bardman.

She kept some throttle on while it warmed up in the cool morning air and worked the shifter to check it's smoothness. The small green light in the center of the headset which also housed the speedometer and tachometer, glowed brightly to indicate the transmission was in neutral. She also showed him the horn button and high beam switch on the left grip as well as the red kill-switch on the right hand-grip.

"If you ever think you're going to crash and you want to kill the ignition in a hurry, just hit this," she said, indicating the red button. She then explained the shift pattern, one up and three down, opposite the Japanese bikes which also had their shifters on the left side instead of the right.

"Put on your helmet, I'll get us out of town and then you can drive it." She revved the engine a couple of times, popped the shifter up into first-gear and gradually let the clutch handle out. When the Norton started to move, she increased throttle slowly, gently letting the clutch out all the way.

He was amazed at the acceleration as she moved smoothly through the gears, each increase of speed threatened to pull him from the back of the seat. This was a new experience for him, the rush of fresh air around his face and the tight grip he had on her waist.

At the outskirts of town they came to a gentle curve to the left and she cranked it open as they leaned into the turn. He could hear her whoop in delight as the motorcycle surged ahead with a throaty roar from the twin exhaust just below him. He glanced quickly down and saw the road surface blurring beneath his feet, only inches away. A few minutes later they slowed and came to a stop at the side of the road where she turned the bike off and they dismounted, leaving the bike resting on its side stand.

"Your turn to start it and ride it," she said, her face pink, and eyes watering slightly from the rush of the cool air from around the windshield.

He followed her previous moves and the bike started on the first kick. She got on behind him and calmly talked him through the gears. His first attempt resulted in stalling the motor, but his second try had them moving slowly but steadily along the road.

She rested her chin on his left shoulder, watching his progress. "Okay, shift into second and remember to let the clutch out gently."

He depressed the clutch lever with his left hand and popped the shifter down into second with his right foot, simultaneously giving more throttle. He forgot about the clutch and released it and allowed it to snap open on the return spring. The front wheel of the motorcycle raised into the air causing him to hold on tighter. Unfortunately it also made him twist instinctively harder on the throttle. The front wheel rose a foot off the ground as they accelerated at an alarming rate.

"Back off, back off!" screamed Teresa as they hurtled along the road, beginning to zig-zag due to the lack of steering. "The kill switch, hit it, hit it!"

Bardman was oblivious to the shouts in his ear, every molecule of his brain was intent on this surging mechanical monster under him and his lack of control of it. He could hear Teresa hollering in his ear, something that sounded like 'kill'. Finally he remembered the kill-switch she had showed him and he jabbed it with his right thumb. For the next few seconds they coasted silently and finally jerked to a stop with the motorcycle still in second gear.

They dismounted in silence.

Teresa walked to the shoulder of the road, head down, muttering under her breath."Gently I said, gently with the clutch. You want to do wheelies, do it on your own but don't kill me okay?" This thing has more power than you've ever handled. If it doesn't kill you in the first year, maybe you'll survive, but you have to do everything slowly. "EVERYTHING ," she screamed at him.

He kicked the gravel on the shoulder of the road, embarrassed that he had endangered her life as well as his own.

"Brady, I'll be dead honest with you. I expect that in the first year of riding you will either kill yourself or have a couple of accidents with this thing. After that you might have learned enough to stay alive. I would feel really bad if I contributed to your death by doing this but I figured you'd kill yourself a lot sooner if I didn't. So, you listen and listen like your life depends on it, because it does."

He listened.

He then climbed back on the machine, this time by himself and started it. He was soon moving once again, concentrating on his hand and foot actions, shifting and accelerating as smoothly as possible. There were a couple of jerky shifts, but no wheelies and within minutes he was able to enjoy the sensation of speed and power under him. He practised slowing by down-shifting, applying both the front brake with his right hand and the rear brake with his left foot to come to a smooth stop. For the next five miles he stopped and started until he felt comfortable, then turned the motorcycle around and returned to his starting point. So far not a single vehicle had come along the road, for which he was thankful. He realised that teaching himself to ride would have been like trying to solo in an aircraft without instruction.

He found her sitting in the warm morning sun on the shoulder of the road, throwing rocks at insects in the water laying in the ditch. The aroma of goldenrod and fire weed was strong in the still air. A patch of brilliant orange tiger lilies stood on their tall stalks, their petals adorned with dew. He wished he had brought his camera. It was the time of day he loved best. The light was clear and pure, the morning dew hanging from the grass and leaves.

"Want a lift lady or ya wanna kill bugs all day?"

She stood up, replacing her helmet on her head and smiled as she sat behind him. She leaned over his shoulder and yelled over the engine noise.

"Now don't you do something stupid or I'll rip your navel out." Her hands had a firm grip around his middle and she added a little pressure to punctuate her words.

He smiled nervously over his shoulder and then pulled onto the highway for town. *My navel seems to be getting more action than any other part of my body.* The thought disturbed him.

CHAPTER 18

Pilson sat naked on a large patch of newspaper, part of a stack of which was also stuck to the walls of the ventilator shaft housing. He used the newspapers to cover himself at night from the cold and wipe himself when his bodily functions made their demands. The walls became papered with images of politicians, sports heroes, and coloured comics, stuck there with the foul glue of his bowels. He liked the comics best because as far as he was concerned, it was the way the world should be. The violence depicted in some of them seemed innocent enough, albeit frequent. Hours ago he had eaten the food stolen from the kitchen, but his face and hair were still matted in places with the flour which had been thrown at him. It streaked his shoulder-length hair and covered his thick eyeglasses with a white dusting. He sat in a lotus position, his head nodding, eyes open but not really seeing.

The images came from inside, along with the voices. They played on the backdrop of his brain like some jerky movie, consisting of grainy images, as those in old-time movies. But these weren't silent movies.

You're no nephew of mine, you're more like a niece. Why don't you dress in little girl's clothes?

But I don't want to dress like that uncle, why are you making me do this?

This will be our little secret Sammy. If you tell anyone, you'll be taken away from home and never see your ma or pa again.

Pa hits me, but I want to see ma. Please don't do that it hurts uncle, please don't.

You want to be my little girl don't you Sammy? Didn't I tell you? Your folks invited me to stay with them so there'd be someone to watch over you while they work. Wouldn't you like that?

NO...NO...Noooo. His screams were muffled by the fetid, brown lining of the walls as he ripped the paper around him and flung it about. Anyone on the outside might have barely heard the screams over the fans, but inside his mind, the screams echoed without end, as did the other voices, some of which he recognized, others complete strangers. They all fought for authority over him, from time to time one or another taking control as he went off to fulfil their wishes.

From a green garbage bag he extracted a variety of women's clothes which he had stolen from the laundry late at night, especially from the one in the small apartment block. He had a selection of blouses and a couple of denim skirts along with an assortment of women's underwear. He held them in front of his face, studying them. *Uncle would like these, he always liked to see me in things like these.* His face contorted in rage as he flung the clothing against the wall, standing in his nakedness, his fists clenched at his sides. He struck out against the dried feces on the wall with his fists raising clouds of brown choking dust to mingle with the sweat-clotted flour in his hair and on his face. His breaths came in ragged gasps as he pummelled the wall. "Kill you, kill you," was all he said over and over under his breath. Quickly, he cleared the old newspapers from over the trapdoor and descended into the darkness of the mine.

Joe McKay's mental turmoil was such that he felt his brain was going to fly apart. He was being pulled in at least three directions at once. In a couple of years his son Joshua wold be going to school and Sadie had been making subtle hints that it might be a good idea to start putting away some money for his later education. On the other hand his father had helped open a door into a world of knowledge which the white men had no idea existed, or if they did, society would not acknowledge its existence. To do so would call into question all the values that had formed their society. The strongest glue holding their society together was slowly unravelling, that of the family unit. He hadn't realized that until his reunion with his father. He had been just like them, struggling to pay the bills, hoping for acceptance and approval from his peers as well as his superiors. *Superiors, they sign my cheques and tell me where and when to work, when to sleep, when to punch the clock, take a crap...*

He realized Teresa had spoken. "Sorry, I wasn't listening. What did you say?"

"I said he's going to kill himself with that damn motorcycle," She down-shifted to make it up a hill. "He has lousy hand-foot co-ordination, poor balance, and no mechanical aptitude."

"Too late now, you got him started."

She looked at Joe with his baseball cap down over his eyes, slumped in his seat, feet propped on the dust-covered dash. "Yeah, and too late for a lot of other things I think."

"Things aren't always what they seem partner. Sometimes to see somethin' clearly, you have to look at it sideways."

"That's how you've been looking at me lately, so what do you see?"

"I see an unhappy woman, unhappy with what she's doin' an' where she is."

"So what do you think I should do about it?"

"Get out before it's too damn late."

345

"You ever think of taking your own advice"

"Yep."

"So what are you waiting for?"

"I'm waiting for a sign."

"A sign."

"Yep, a sign...an' there it is, slow down."

"What?"

"This is our turn-off right here, right by that orange marker on the stake."

She made the turn, nearly jack-knifing the trailer onto the small access road. In low gear they crawled along a barely cleared road, the trailer dollies scraping against rock out-croppings as they neared the construction site.

The site was near the Black Wood River where trees had been cut or bull-dozed down. They were directed to the site of a small blockhouse to be unloaded where a work crew had been assembled and waited, unsmiling. Fortunately they didn't have to help unload and had a chance to stretch their legs by the river bank.

Joe swore quietly under his breath as he approached the water.

"What's the matter? You've been grouchy all day."

Joe pointed at the river bank. "They don't have any outhouses, they're crappin' straight into the river. This crap flows to Hudson House, an' my people have to drink this."

She could see the remnants of soiled toilet paper in the grass and felt revulsion. She wanted to get out of there, leave the desecration behind. It was on a tiny scale compared to the hydro project, but the scale was becoming less important.

Joe said no more and walked back to sit in the cab of the tractor, his hat down over his eyes as the work crew sweated and cursed while unloading the explosives.

D'Amico climbed into the driver's seat, leaning her head against her arms on the steering wheel and closed her eyes. The thumping sounds from the crew in the trailer continued to shake the tractor as the fifty pound sacks of Amex were pushed along the roller system, out to the waiting arms of those in the blockhouse. *Don't drop the caps and fuses or we'll all be hanging in pieces from the trees.*

"I don't know how much longer I can hack this shit Joe. We can't keep hauling mixed loads of three different classes of explosives just because Winky orders us to do it." Her face was still down on her arms, her voice muffled by the fabric of her shirt. She could smell the sweat from her armpits mingled with the dusty grease of the cab, and Joe's feet which were propped on the dashboard.

"Wanna write a letter to MOT?"

"We'd need proof to back it up."

He reached to the floor and retrieved a clipboard with several yellow coloured pages secured to it. "Easy partner, we just photocopy the manifest before we take it back to the office. Then we send a copy to MOT, but we don't sign it. That oughta get their attention."

"That's one of the things I like about you Joe, you have a devious mind. Let's see what Winky has done to incriminate himself." She took the manifest from his hand and studied the variety of explosives listed on the two pages. She flipped the pages back and forth a couple of times, comparing items listed. "Wait a minute, what's the date today?"

McKay glanced at the little date window on his watch. It said July 23rd.

"Strange," said D'Amico "Only one sheet has the right date, the other one is dated two days before that." She handed the clipboard back to his outstretched hand.

He had pushed his cap to the back of his head, his long black hair hanging in twin braids over his shoulders. "You think I'm sneaky eh? You know what Winky's up to here? He knows these mixed loads are illegal, so he put all the Amex and the primers on one page an' the caps and fuses on the other. This makes it look like they were shipped on different days."

She slapped the steering column with her hand and sat up. "Well that porker! He's been doing that with every mixed load and these guys at the other end don't give a shit as long as they get their stuff."

"We show 'em this," replied McKay holding his driver's log book. "If the dates and places on this book don't match the manifest, then they know somethin' is screwy. What's wrong, why are you shakin' your head?"

"How many times have you written pure fiction in this thing when you've driven more than ten hours a day?"

"Almost every trip we make up here, why?"

"And who told us to do that, promising us double-time instead of time and a half over ten hours?" She watched his face as he studied the log book. Finally he dropped it to the floor with a thoughtful frown.

"He made us lie to cover his ass."

"You bet yer boots. So if we lied on our log books, who at Ministry Of Transport will believe us about the mixed loads? They could even charge us with falsifying our log books."

He said nothing, resuming his former position, hat over his eyes and feet on the dash now liberally covered with his dusty boot prints, his arms folded across his chest. They sat immersed in their own thoughts for ten minutes and were startled when a fist banged twice on the driver's door.

"All done back there. Wadda ya want me to sign?" The crew foreman's extended arm was lean and sinewy, with the colour and texture of beef-jerky. He reached up with a brown, gristly hand to receive the clipboard and signed each page with a flourish, barely checking to make sure each item was there.

"Oh yeah, thought you might like to see this. Found it in the trailer, on the floor." He reached into his shirt pocket and extracted a misshaped lump of metal. "Think you guys better start usin' armour plate on this thing, 'cause somebody roun' here don't like you." He flipped the spent bullet to D'Amico who quickly showed it to her partner, who was now visibly more alert. They climbed from the cab and walked slowly along the length of the trailer looking for holes. They found nothing on two visual sweeps until McKay climbed on the rear of the tractor and reached up to remove the warning placard from its bracket on the upper front area of the trailer. It was an area that was visible over the cab when viewed from head-on. He lifted the battered piece of plywood which had the words EXPLOSIVES in red on a white background. There was a hole drilled neatly through the O and another through the corrugated metal of the trailer, directly behind where the O was located.

She watched silently, chewing the inside of her cheek as he reversed the sign and replaced it with the letters facing inward. He climbed down and went around the trailer repeating the process with each of the other placards on the sides and rear doors.

"At least he's a lousy shot." Her voice was nearly a whisper and she had trouble catching her breath after speaking. Her eyes met McKay's and she could see he was more troubled than tbe previous time they'd found such evidence.

"I'll drive," was all he said, climbing behind the wheel.

As the engine rattled to life, they waited for the air pressure to build so the brakes could be released. Finally the warning buzzer stopped and he reached to the dashboard, pushing on the coloured plastic squares, releasing the trailer and tractor brakes. He glanced through the windshield, lowering his head so he was nearly resting his chin on the top of the steering wheel. D'Amico leaned forward too, following his gaze.

From a low branch of a spruce tree, a lone raven observed them, not moving, making no sound. Each of them found it unnerving to have those sharp eyes watch them impassionately. They glanced at each other, each wondering if the other creatures of the forest harboured a strange feeling about the watchful eyes of the bird. When they glanced back, the bird was no longer there.

She looked at McKay. She prepared to say something, but a subtle shake of his head clipped the unspoken words from her tongue.

An hour from town, he finally spoke. "I've been thinkin' about Winky, I know how we can get him, but I need your help."

She listened to his idea while watching thunderheads build to the south. His idea was brilliant but it required her to have a discreet liaison with someone she was reluctant to use in this matter. With trepidation, she agreed to do it, mainly because, like the towering cumulonimbus clouds threatening to piss rain down on them, they were tired of being pissed upon by their boss.

Bardman squinted through the magnifying loupe, smiling with satisfaction at the negatives on the light table. His idea of wedding photography was to say the least, unconventional. He delighted in the shot of the bride's father, his boss, Roger Jenkins attempting to plant a drunken kiss on the reluctant lips of the maid of honour. He quickly counted five frames on either side of the incriminating shot and clipped the two strips of five, leaving the other free. Then he mounted the single frame in a slide-mount along with the one of Pilson crashing the party. There were a couple of shots of Teresa dancing with corporal Pusch. He didn't know what he was going to do with those. His immediate intention was to toss them in the trash. With the rest of the negatives clipped and inserted in clear pages, he spent the next hour producing contact sheets at the behest of his boss whom he feared may suspect he had taken more shots than he had been mandated to provide.

He had been ordered to have them delivered to Jenkins' office before lunch and a quick glance at his watch showed he would have only minutes to spare. Whenever Jenkins asked for something brought from the photo department, it was always "Have them delivered," instead of being told to bring them personally. It was as though the man refused to acknowledge Bardman's personal presence by inferring that another person might bring them. *I should call Walter the janitor and have him take them up in his dust cart. Sprinkle a few dust bunnies on them, that'll get his attention.*

The phone rang. "Yessir, on the way with them now, nossir I'm not asleep down here. Nossir I wouldn't want you to miss your lunch. My regards to your lovely daughter. May her zits never heal. Oh nossir, no sarcasm intended, I'm on my way.

Roger Jenkins stood before his desk holding a large magnifying glass in his right hand as though preparing to return a ping pong volley.

Bardman handed him the contact sheets and watched as Jenkins quietly turned to the window and peered with one eye through the large glass all the while saying "Hmmmm, hmmm." A couple of times

Jenkins straightened and looked over his shoulder to see if Bardman was still there, then took a black grease pencil from his desk and began making X marks on various sections of the contact sheet. There were six different contact sheets, each with 36 exposures.

He was apprehensive to see Jenkins making marks with the zealous energy of a driving examiner preparing to flunk a student.

"I need these by day after tomorrow, all eight-by-tens please Mr. Bardman. Have them delivered when they're done won't you? There's a good chap. Ah Mr. Aikins. Come in."

Bardman turned on his heels and saw a large man with a pink face full of quivering jowls standing, holding his hard hat with both hands over his groin as though expecting a swift kick to that area.

He wore grey coveralls with sharp creases and shiny black steel-toed rubber boots. The day shift underground foreman looked like any newly hired employee preparing to venture underground for the first time in his life. It was nearly the truth, for Bardman was familiar with Hank 'Upchuck' Aikins' reputation for fearing the darkness of the drifts and stopes, as well as his reputation to barf every time he got in the cage.

"Mr. Aikins, you know Mr. Bardman I believe. No? Well no matter, he'll be going underground with you in the event you find the origin of those strange smells. Might be worth documenting you know. Make sure you talk to that diamond drill crew who have noticed the smells, whatever it is may be in that area."

Aikins gave a little bow and gurgled something which Bardman couldn't understand.

"Don't worry about that, *just go, look... find.*" Jenkins waved a well manicured finger in their general direction as though adjourning royal court and turned his back on them, then quickly spun around on his heel. "Oh Bardman, don't forget these." He thrust the contact sheets at him and proceeded to scratch his back with the large magnifying glass. "Don't forget to put film in your camera eh?"

"How am I supposed to take pictures of a smell?" asked Bardman as he and Aikins returned to the photo department for his camera gear.

"I don't wanna talk about it. Let's just go do what he says." said Aikins as they walked shoulder to shoulder along the hall. Shit."

"Probably," replied Bardman

"What?"

"It's probably nothing but shit," he said again as he stocked his shoulder bag with film and accessories. "Half the drill crews down there don't use a pail, they just squat and drop in any little alcove they can find within easy reach."

"Naw, this crew says it smells as though something has died down there but none of them have the balls to look around for it. Stories have been goin' around about that driller who went nuts down there and they think he might have did himself in. They don't want to find his body is all."

"Well neither do I for that matter, so why don't we just not go and say we did?"

"Because we'd both have our asses in a sling is why and I have three mouths to feed."

"You got a kid?" asked Bardman.

"Naw, but my wife eats enough for two."

Ten minutes later they were hurtling down in the cage. The cage-tender apprehensively watched Hank Aikins' face with every lurch as the cage shifted on the twin steel vertical rails. The air roared through the latticework of the floor and exited out the top, making the cuffs of their coveralls flutter. The cage began to slow as they neared the twenty-five hundred foot level and all three occupants were praying for a smooth stop for the same reason. The cage lurched to a stop a half second before it should have and Aikins erupted as predictably as Old Faithful in Yellowstone Park.

The cage-tender ducked to the back of the cage to avoid the projectile vomitus. "Aww shit, fuckin' trainee hoistmen." The cage-tender swore even more vehemently when he realize his hard hat had fallen from his head, landing open end up to collect a large portion of Aikins' stomach.

Bardman gestured to a water hose near the cage entrance. "Want to flush it out?"

"Nope," replied the man with a strange smile. "Come the end of this shift, I have to pick that trainee topman up and when I do, he's gonna wear this hat an' everythin' in it. I got a spare hard hat at surface, an' for you Upchuck, I got some plastic bags you can tape to your face before you get on next time."

Aikins glared at the cage-tender while wiping his mouth with his hanky which he then threw into a trash barrel. His once pink jowls were the colour of chalk and there was a sheen of perspiration on his upper lip. His dark-rimmed safety glasses had slipped down his nose so that he looked like a nauseated version of Winston Churchill.

Bardman and Aikins turned on their hat lights and pushed through the huge swinging blast doors and onto the track. They stopped and adjusted their lights to narrow beams for distance vision and allowed their eyes to adjust to the gloom.

"You gonna be okay?"

"Don't you worry 'bout me," replied the foreman with an aggressiveness that belied his appearance. "You're gonna have to be my nose now, all I can smell right now is my own barf." He took a fresh blue polka-dot hanky from his coverall pocket and blew his nose with a honk that echoed from the walls. "Well, now everybody knows we're comin', if they can't hear us, at least they'll smell us."

They walked along the track for nearly twenty minutes, listening to the steadily increasing howl of the diamond drill as they approached. They could see the eery blue illumination emitted by the air-driven generator of the mercury vapour light. Shadows flitted against the opposite wall of the drift as the men moved about their station. They passed a large ore chute which had once conveyed ore dumped from one level of the producing mine, down to waiting ore cars where they then took the ore to the primary-crusher. The jaws of the crusher broke the large chunks of ore down for the skip tram to haul it quickly to the surface. The large steel door of the Ore chute and its operating mechanism were rusty with disuse.

Bardman had heard horror stories of large pieces of ore getting hung up in these chutes and of the efforts to clear them. Men had to jab with scaling bars at the offending mass, prepared to jump out of harms way, should it suddenly let go. Some men failed to move quickly enough and were crushed under the tons of rock that surged down the chute. The only worse job was picking away with the scaling bar at 'loose' on the ceiling of the shift. There was no telling how large a piece might come down and squash a man like a bug. Nobody liked the eight foot long scaling bar and it was usually the new guys who got stuck with it because the veterans knew how to look very busy at something else when it had to be used.

The howling stopped as they approached the drill station. Bardman recognized it as the same one where the little Frenchman had been killed. He was surprised there was still a crew working there. He asked the driller and his helper why they had been there so long.

"Break-downs man, nothing but break-downs," said the driller who was a young man with long blonde hair pulled back in a ponytail. "We've been gittin' cut airlines, missin' drillbits, tools disappearin', you name it, nothin' seems to let us finish this hole. Hell we got another five-hundred feet to go an' at this rate, it'll take another two weeks. I think we're jinxed man."

He dragged the word man out as maaaan the way Bardman had heard hippies talk when they were high on grass. In fact the guy probably was a hippy, he thought. It appeared he was even wearing love beads around his neck.

"Not natural," was all his partner said. "Or else somebody's tryin' to pull a bad joke on us is all I can say." He was an older man who appeared used to hard work and Bardman surmised he might be a farmer who had things go wrong and lost everything on the surface. The man removed his hard hat and scratched a greying brushcut with callous-covered hands and then said: "I'm Frank, and this here is my son Gordon. He's tryin' to make some money to go back to university this fall, but if we can't make any bonus on this site 'cause of breakdowns, it's gonna be touch an' go for him."

"Yeah maaaaan, like everytime somethin' happens down here, there's this horrible stench like somethin's died. Like, we've heard the stories of this nut that's supposed to be around but we never seen him."

"What are you majoring in at university Gordon?" asked Aikins.

"English literature, maaan."

They all looked around the heavy wooden staging on which the drill rig rested, trying to find some clue to the origin of the smells.

Bardman leaned down to pull on a piece of wire protruding from under one plank and was surprised that it was in fact the tail of a dead rat.

"We'll, I think we've found the answer," said Aikins with obvious relief in his voice.

Bardman held the rat up to his light for a closer look, glad that he'd put his gloves on previously. "I don't think so," he said quietly. This rat's been dead a long time and it's as dry as dead leaves. It doesn't seem to smell at all, but look at it's body, the meat seems to have been stripped away from the ribs and back legs, leaving the just the tail and head.

"Gross maaan, it looks like somebody's bin chewin' on it."

"I think this somebody has left you a calling card," said Bardman as he tossed the rat onto the track.

Frank grunted agreement and pointed to a stack of old greasy burlap used to aid in the pulling of drill rods. "Not the first one. There's three more under that, done the same way."

For several minutes no one spoke until Bardman related the story of the driller's death at this site and the disappearance of his partner. The two drillers were obviously agitated that they had not been told this historical gem before being sent to the site.

Frank said, "I don't believe in ghosts or nothin', but I don't want no double-nut fruitcake around here when we're tryin' to work." He shuffled his feet and looked at his son who was looking back.

Gradually, a smell insinuated itself on them, like a rancid mist from a meat rendering plant. The stench was enough to make their eyes water as they peered down the drift into the blackness from where the gas seemed to emanate.

"What's down there? " asked Bardman.

"Ventilation shaft," answered Aikins. He looked back at Bardman and checked his watch. "Shit, I guess we got time to go check it out, it's only a fifteen minute walk, but it's a long climb up a manway to the fan housing. At least we can check the housing from the surface another time." He gave a deep sigh which shook his jowls which had returned to their normal colour, turned in the direction of the ventilation shaft and walked like a man with a date with a firing squad.

Their boots echoed off the dark walls of the drift as they walked side by side along the track, trying to avoid stepping in the gaps between the sleepers upon which the rails rested. Behind them, they heard the laboured chugging of the air-driven winch as the drill rods were hoisted from the hole. It stopped and then began again momentarily as each rod was disconnected and placed beside its predecessor.

Bardman didn't envy the drillers their work, it was dark, dirty, noisy, and sometimes dangerous to the point of deadly. A chill ran over him as he recalled the crushed body of the little Frenchman with the drill rig on top of him. He switched his camera bag to the other shoulder to relieve the pressure. "Y'know Hank, the more I come down here the less I like it. The place feels like a wet tomb."

"I've always hated it down here," replied Aikins with a wheezy voice. "Sometimes I wish I'd never got this job, but now it's the only thing I know how to do. I look at Frank there and see myself twenty years from now. Ya see his face? White as chalk, never been in the sun. I seen him drink beer all night in the pub an' never talk to nobody but himself. You could see his lips moving, havin' these little conversations with himself. Then he'd git up an walk out, sober as a judge."

"I hope his son writes a lot better than he speaks, it doesn't say much for the university system when an English major talks like a pothead," replied Bardman.

Aikins reached up and widened the beam on his hat light. "You watch. If he's down here for more'n a year he'll be here the rest of his life, just a taste of good bonus an' he's hooked. Buy a car, find a girlfriend, maybe take out a loan an' goodbye university. Whadda ya get then? Another driller that sits an' talks to himself in the bar. Shit half of 'em are deaf as posts from not wearin' their ear protectors anyway, so they might as well talk to themselves because they can't hear nobody else."

They walked the last ten minutes wrapped in their own thoughts, joined only by the sound of their footsteps. They stopped suddenly when they saw sudden movement along the side of the drift. It scurried away, a darker shadow amongst the shadows with a squeak of panic.

The rat was huge, nearly as large as a house cat. Nearby, where they had first seen the movement were the remains of another rat nearly as large, its rib cage stripped flesh and fur. The other rat had stopped, turned and was watching them with bright, wary eyes. It's nose twitched as it took in their scent. Then it scurried away from them.

"There's the manway." Aikins narrowed his hat beam once more and they both directed their lights along the drift. They were at the end and they could feel the current of air from the huge fans as they pushed the air down from above. Riding along with the air was the stench from above. "No wonder the guys on the upper levels were bitchin' about the smell because it's...what the hell is that?"

They both swung their lights in unison. Their beams picked up tiny reflections from the rungs of the ladder near the first landing at the hundred foot mark. Anyone having to climb the manway would need the landings for a place to rest and they were obviously being used.

"Rats," said Bardman with a note of awe in his voice. "A whole shitload of 'em, and there's no way I'm going up there." He shone his light down, toward the base of the ladder. "More rats here, but they look dead. There must be thirty at least."

"More," said Aikins in a wheezing whisper, as he surveyed the sides of the drifts. "A lot more. Take some pictures and let's get the hell out of here."

He worked quickly to connect the Vivitar flash and Quantum battery to the camera. The first few shots were with the 135mm lens, and the flash set on maximum distance. He didn't want to get too close to the furry mess, but realized he would have to move in for more detail. The last thing he wanted was to be sent back down for a re-shoot. He moved closer and focused up the darkness of the manway but with his hard hat tilted back on his head to focus, his light was pointed in the wrong direction. "Hank, come here and shine your light up there so I can see to focus."

Aikins moved to his side and with his hat light unclipped and held in his hand directed it to the first landing. The foreman's mouth opened with wonder as he saw the edge of the landing move as though the whole structure had grown fur. "My God, they're everywhere, there's no room for them up there." He could see the rats maneuvering for position on the four foot square platform, hundreds of shiny eyes looking back down at him, their squeaks becoming louder with the agitation of being discovered.

Bardman focused and made an exposure. The flash seemed brilliant, set on full power and the flash capacitors whined in an effort to recharge. The rats shrieked in fright, some of them momentarily blinded. Something landed at their feet with the sound of a bag of water dropped from a great height. It was huge rat that had fallen off the landing or was pushed in the squirming panic. Something landed with a hollow THUNK beside him and Aikins gave a yell of terror, dropping the light from his hand and then began a macabre dance upon the rat that had landed on his hat, knocking it from his head.

The rat, injured from the fall tried to fight for it's life by turning on it's back and baring it's teeth, growling like a small dog. Aikins stepped back and with a swift soccer kick, booted the snarling rat against the rock face, near the manway where it lay still.

"He kicks, he scores," shouted Bardman, his voice quivering with excitement. His hands were shaking as he replaced the telephoto lens with the 24mm wide angle. In his excitement he nearly dropped it on the tracks.

"It ain't funny, let's get the fuck outa here. I seen enough and you couldn't pay me enough to stay. Are you comin' or not?" Aikin's face was sweaty and pale, his breath coming in ragged gasps. His heavy jowls quivered with his efforts to breath.

"In a sec," yelled Bardman as he shot several exposures of the dead rats heaped at the base of the ladder and those lining the sides of the drift. His hands were sweaty and shaking as he shot, focussing carefully in the dim light. He heard Aikins begin to run back the way they had come and then heard him gasp after only a few steps. He saw Aikins' light fall to the track floor accompanied by a dull thud and a gurgling sound. He jogged toward the fallen foreman, the camera gear bouncing against his body.

Aikins was face-up on the track floor between the rails, clutching his chest, his face was bathed in sweat and pale as chalk. There was a puddle of vomit on his chest and more in his mouth.

He rolled Aikins on his side and scooped the vomit from his mouth with a finger, tilting the head back to open the airway. He put his ear and cheek to Aikins' reeking face and listened, hearing and feeling nothing. *Not here, not now, I can't remember this CPR shit, Christ don't do this to me Aikins.* He screamed down the drift toward the drill station, knowing it was useless. They were too far away and he could hear the sound of their drill working again. They have the rods down again. There's no way they're going to hear me.

He took a deep breath and placed his mouth over Aikins', pinching the nostrils together with one hand, the other under the chin, tilting the head back. He gave two long breaths, watching the chest inflate. He could find no pulse on the neck but the neck was fat, he doubted he could find it even if he was breathing. He reached down and checked his radial pulse on the wrist, finding nothing. He screamed for help again. At least it makes me feel better to scream. He unzipped Aikins' coveralls to the navel, smearing the vomit on his hands. He found the big man's sternum and xiphoid process and began compressions. *Shit, I should have stayed in the ski patrol, at least I'd remember what the hell I'm supposed to do.* After doing a series of a dozen or more compressions and two breaths, he searched once again for a pulse. There was none. He kneeled over Aikins with coldness creeping into the pit of his stomach, his head feeling dizzy. *Don't get sick, for Christ's sake don't get sick. Put my head down, right down to the ground. That's better, starting to feel better now.*

A light was shining in his eyes. It was Aikins' hat light laying beside him, illuminating the far cheek of his face and his dead staring eyes locked on the top of the drift. A movement caught his eyes near the light. He gently raised his head and peered over the foreman's chalky features into the face of rat staring boldly back.

The rat bared it's teeth and snarled.

Bardman jumped back, hearing a squeak of pain from under his right boot, feeling the sensation of a struggling rat. In the meagre beam of his light he could see movement along the drift wall. *The place is crawling! I've gotta get outta here, gotta warn somebody.* He was up and running, still clutching the bouncing camera equipment, unable to see clearly due to the movement of his light, unable to get his breath. He could feel the damp rock walls closing in on him. He aimed for the dim light of the diamond drill station and forced himself to jog instead of run. *I'm sorry Hank, aw God I'm sorry, sorry...*

The father/son diamond drill crew looked up in alarm at the apparition of Bardman, his mouth open nearly as wide as his eyes. They shut down the drill.

"...get outa here, gotta outta here! Rats all over the place! He's dead! They're gonna eat him! His arms were waving like an Italian traffic cop until Frank walked over and gripped his shoulders firmly with both muscular hands.

"Whoa partner, slowly, deep breaths. That's better. Now, slowly, tell us what happened."

He related the story to the best of his ability as the two drillers listened intently. "Don't go down there, there's thousands of them and they're all hungry."

"Son, the only place we're goin' is up an' your comin' with us. Grab your stuff Gordon, we're scootin'."

"Like none too soon maaan, like this place is a real drag, bummer. Think I'll apply to clean sewers the rest of the summer. Like shit maaaan you can tell those honchos to stuff their job up their wazoos."

Glassy-eyed, Bardman listened to the exchange between them. "What year of English are you in at university?"

"Third year m'maaan, gonna go for my masters too. Why d'ya ask?"

Bardman blinked and shook his head, turning wordlessly with glazed eyes toward the lift area a half hour away.

"You gotta take care maaaan, like I think yer goin' inta shock."

At the lift station, Frank used an emergency telephone to call the surface where a mine rescue team was dispatched.

The team was made up of miners who were both on and off-shift and, carried pagers on their belts wherever they went. Trained in advanced first-aid and underground rescue techniques, each member took pride in being a member of an elite and highly trained team. None of them really looked forward to having to use it in real life but constant training gave them confidence they could do the job when called upon. The rescue team raced to the mine to be briefed by the rescue coordinator who was having a hard time believing what was being reported from the twenty-five hundred foot level.

The coordinator, a small wiry man with thinning hair and large false teeth that clicked every second word, counted the team members and was glad to see a couple of men who had been called upon for actual rescues. A couple of experienced people always helped the others keep their heads.

Jim Schute had been an Emergency Medical Technician prior to being hired by Quesnel as part of the safety division. His experience with auto-accident victims had been good experience for the unpredictable and sometimes grisly nature of industrial accidents. "Gentlemen I have only one question before we begin. Is anyone here afraid of rats?"

There was a stunned silence between the six men dressed in red coveralls.

"No? Well that's good because you have a body, possibly a dead one to recover from the twenty-five hundred foot level just below the ventilation shaft at Q-3." He pulled down a map of that level and showed them exactly where they had to go.

One man held up his hand. "Shooter, just how many rats are we talkin' about down there?"

"From what I understand, there could be thousands according to a man who was at the scene. He claims the other man had a heart attack and when the guy collapsed he tried to do CPR. It seems the rats intervened. He also says they're big as cats."

"Hey, I hate cats...but I don't mind rats," quipped one man, eliciting nervous laughter from the group. "Why don't we just send a bunch of cats trained in CPR down there?"

"Where do you propose to find that many cats Watkins?" asked Schute. He could sense these guys really were nervous about going down there, as was he, because he intended to go down with them.

Watkins replied: "We could get'em at the Pussy Parlour on Mudhen Bay, hell they seem to have enough for the whole town on a Saturday night."

The room cracked up, relieving some of the tension.

"Who is it down there Shooter?"

"It's Upchuck Aikins."

The men looked at each other with disbelief. They all knew Aikins hated to be underground despite being the day shift underground foreman. Their mutterings of disbelief filled the room.

Schute looked over their heads at his assistant who had appeared in the door and given him a nod. "Okay listen up. Your equipment has been taken to the cage along with your Scott Packs, although I don't think you'll need an emergency air supply. But, what you don't have, you can't use, right? One other thing. There's a box of railroad flares with the sharp ends mounted on long wood handles. If the rats are as bad as they sound, light those flares and burn the whiskers off their nasty little faces. Watkins, don't forget the scoop stretcher this time, okay? "

"Wasn't my fault boss, I was supposed to trade with Nelson."

"I don't care whose fault it is, lets just get it done. I'm comin' with you."

They quickly loaded their gear on the cage and were dropping like a rock to the lowest level. No one spoke. The cage tender informed them on the way down that a small electric locomotive and a flatcar had been moved to the lift station from an adjacent drift system. They were all relieved they weren't going to have to walk. Someone in the cage began to sing the Mighty Mouse theme song. Heeere we come to save the daaay! Before long they had all joined in and were in full vocal flight by the time they stopped at their level.

Three astounded men awaited them at the station, one with a pudgy white face and cameras draped on one shoulder.

"You Bardman?" asked Schute.

Bardman nodded.

"You have to come with us to the site, you're the only witness."

"I don't want to come with you to the site, replied Bardman under his breath, moving nose to nose with the coordinator who was slightly shorter and fifty pounds lighter than he. "And," he said with a whisper, "If you try to make me, I'll feed you this camera."

The rescue team watched in uncomfortable silence as the two men stood nose to nose.

"Okay, Bardman that's cool, I'm not that hungry, but I want to hear from you personally what you saw down there, and then I want you to go talk to the doc. You've been through a lot, he can help you. Let him, okay?"

He told them of the rats without embellishment and that scared the team even more, because embellishment was a possible sign things weren't as bad as they seemed. No one felt like singing the Mighty Mouse song anymore. One of the rescuers said, "Meow." A couple of others laughed nervously.

The next day the mine was buzzing with the story of what they had found, or rather didn't find. They didn't find the body, nor any live rats, but lots of dead ones under the manway and along the sides of the drift. In the report one man smelled a terrible stench from an old ore chute as they passed on the way to the scene. When he attempted to open the chute it seemed to be jammed shut from the other side. He claimed he could hear a human or near-human voice giggling from behind it and the sounds of chewing. Under the ore chute were scraps of burlap. When they tried collectively to force the chute open, they heard a scrabbling noise which finally diminished into the distance. It wasn't until three days later that

360

someone decided to check the large metal shack that housed the huge ventilation fans above Q-3.

"We don't have to get out here very often unless one of these bearings burn out," said the maintenance man to Corporal Pusch who was standing behind him, watching as he fumbled with the large padlock. The hot, late-summer sun reflected off the silver-coloured corrugated metal sides of the building. Large circular holes covered with metal screening housed the three huge fans with blades over a meter long. The building seemed to shudder with sympathetic vibrations as the air was sucked from the surface and driven underground through a maze of large duct-work.

The door swung open with a creak, revealing a brownish-grey wall matter obscuring the complete doorway from top to bottom. The doorway appeared to have been stuccoed shut with brown, stinking mud, embedded with small, grimacing skulls, feet, and black tails.

Both men stood open-mouthed, while the police beagle, Proboscis whined and strained at his leash to escape the terrible smell.

"What'n hell," muttered the maintenance man. "Never seen nothin' like this before." He leaned forward for a closer look, then flinched, taking a quick step back. "Gawd-a-mighty, those are rats, an' what a stink!"

Pusch was holding his breath, hardly able to believe the sight of the rat heads and tails protruding from the reeking mass. He could see the wall of human feces mixed with old newspaper and rodent remnants was a couple of inches thick. His large nose wrinkled in distaste causing the huge moustache to climb his face, perhaps in an escape attempt. "Proboscis, let up. I know it smells bad but it's time to earn your dog biscuits, now heel." He yanked on the leash eliciting a prolonged howl from Proboscis, still straining to leave this terrible place. It reminded him of his master's offensive socks, several of which he had managed to bury in the backyard.

Pusch removed his baton from his belt and pushed it against the brown wall. The wall stretched inward slightly, the sightless eyes of several rats fixed on his efforts. He pushed harder. The wall fell apart in several large chunks at his feet, raising a cloud of grey dust. The contrasting darkness of the interior made him squint. He thought he saw a movement in the semi-darkness and leaned cautiously closer.

The apparition sitting before him looked like a human sewer rat with severe myopia. The shoulder length hair was brown and matted, the wiry body, naked and covered with sores mingled with blobs of feces. The man's mouth was open, howling accompaniment to the roar of the fans, his eyes squinting at the sudden invasion of light. He was surrounded by a nest

361

of crumpled newspaper, food containers, soiled clothing, and rat carcasses with the meat and fur missing from the ribs and hindquarters. Countless live rats scurried along the base of the interior walls, disappearing through any available crevice. With his eyes huge behind the thick eyeglasses, blinking from the invasion of brilliant light, he lifted the manway trapdoor and scurried down the ladder into the darkness.

"Don't go in there officer, you'll catch a disease for sure. Shit I ain't goin' nowhere's near that, so don't ask me, I ain't goin'." The maintenance man had moved back several steps, failing to see Pilson make his exit down, through the hatch.

Pusch stood, dumbfounded at the sight, while Proboscis was the epitome of action, his efforts aimed at rapid departure. The beagle howled and strained away from the doorway and the hand that held the leash. When he finally gave a mighty tug of frustration on the leash, Proboscis promptly turned and bit him on the ankle. In pain and surprise, he released the leash and Proboscis dashed, ears flapping wildly, still howling for the security of the squad car.

Proboscis watched from under the car while his newly-bitten master limped into the reeking building.

He entered slowly, flashlight in hand, shining the beam where he had seen the filthy apparition. The roar of the fans slowed then stopped. A cloud of flies had risen from the feces and began covering any exposed skin on his hands and face, seeking moisture. He brushed them away only to have them come back with endless persistence.

"Found the master switch," called the maintenance man from the outside.

The air buzzed with insect life and the stucco of human and rat waste crawled with wriggling new life as fly eggs hatched into maggots.

Pusch prodded an object near the trapdoor with his baton, removing a wrapping of coloured Saturday comics. A human foot lay before him, connected to the lower leg which appeared to have been gnawed by human or rodent life. Perhaps both. "We found Aikins," he said quietly. "At least part of him."

"Mother of God," breathed the maintenance man from the doorway, refusing to come any closer. "How could he be here? He was missin' underground three days ago. Nobody could find him. This ain't natural. This is just pure evil."

Pusch raised the trapdoor and aimed his light down into the darkness. The eyes of countless rats reflected back at him from the rungs of the ladder. He began to realize the being who lived here had a symbiotic relationship with the rats. He helped feed them, their bodies helped feed him, and each gave the other free rein to move at will down the manway and into the darkness.

CHAPTER 19

Abe Mckay could see the subtle changes taking place on Two Island Lake. The water had risen along the shoreline, engulfing several large beaver lodges. There were far fewer trees with fresh tooth marks, and fewer trees still being felled by the quietly industrious animals. Where he had at one time seen the splayed hoof prints of moose along the shoreline, there was now only rotting vegetation. And the fishing was lousy. The nets he had set previously had given up only a fraction of the pickerel and whitefish of prior years.

Two Island Lake had also been a major source of wild rice, the tall stems like a fragile forest thrusting from the clear waters, yielding their grains to those who harvested from large canoes. They would gently bend the stalks over the gunwales and knock the grains loose with sticks until they sat ankle-deep in the long, dark kernels. Although harvest season was two months away, the crop was diminishing. The higher water levels covered the young plants, forcing them to grow even higher to reach the sun.

His brown gnarled fingers gently plucked the fish from the net, placing each species in a separate plastic box. He could feel the warm sun on his back as the anchored boat rocked gently under him.

His thoughts were of his son, Joe.

He knows he's helpin' do this. He don't know how to quit an' he ain't seein' the warnin' signs. This place used to talk to me like my father. It used to say it would take care of me, of all of us if we respected it but now the white men are emptyin' their bowels into it, pissin' their hatred for it's beauty into it's open mouth. They're forcin' its children to do the same, sayin' that if they don't, they will starve an' won't be educated. What good is their education if they're ignorant about their own people. But now their bellies are full but their spirit is starvin'. When the spirit goes, the people will wither up an' blow away like leaves in the fall.

Old Abe shook his thoughts back to the fishnet. His thoughts surprised him. He had never had such thoughts before and was sometimes startled by the words forming in his mind. He had never spoken these words to anyone and didn't always understand what they meant. A visceral feeling in his guts told him they were truth. *Truth.*

He recalled years ago giving a lift to the United Church minister, a serene white-haired man who had at one time spent thirty years in China as a missionary. All he talked about was the quest for truth and he sensed a pure spirituality in the minister that he had seldom experienced in any white man. He realised it wasn't conventional religion the Reverend Harris was discussing, but rather the bare essence of his soul. The desire to know the truth. The representatives of the hydro project had come to Hudson House with their own version of it to allay the population's fears. The town's-people questioned it but were overwhelmed by reams of statistics on overhead projectors. *Plastic lies.* Everyone had their own version of the truth and those who screamed it loudest, were most often heard and unfortunately, believed.

He pulled the last of the net into the boat without being aware of it. His short legs shifted as the boat rocked with a gust of wind on the beam. The leaves of the aspen and birch rattled delicately in the fresh breeze as he started the 30 horsepower Johnson outboard motor. He had borrowed the boat from Angus Spence who accepted a percentage of the sold catch. He sadly watched the blue smoke from the two stroke-engine waft away in the wind and leave a rainbow sheen on the water. He knew he shouldn't be casting the first stone at those who desecrated nature, because in some ways, he was one of them, but the temptation was very strong. There were a lot of fine targets.

As the sun's rays lengthened he knew he might be a little late to meet his son who was driving out alone to see him that evening. He had sensed an urgency in his son's voice over the telephone. *Maybe he's beginnin' to see the truth, maybe it ain't too late.*

Joe McKay had arrived early. He was sitting at the old table, leaning back in a chair with his feet propped on the edge. In his hands he lovingly cradled an old rifle with an octagonal barrel. It was a Remington pump-action 44-40. On the table was a box of cartridges that appeared to be generations old, the brass grown dull, the label on the box nearly illegible. They were short, squat, flat-nosed cartridges, sometimes referred to as bush-cutters. In dense bush the 44-40 could be used effectively on deer at close range because the smaller tree branches wouldn't deflect the slug like that of a high velocity, sharp-nosed slug. He worked the well-oiled action several times and was surprised to see one cartridge eject from the side port and clatter loudly to the floor. It was unlike his father to keep the rifle loaded. He sniffed the barrel and the breech. He could smell the sharp tang of gunpowder. It had been fired recently, possibly to sight it in for deer season, but then any day was deer season around here. Their aboriginal rights allowing them to put meat on the table whenever needed.

He looked up and saw his father sitting across from him. "Jesus I wish you wouldn't do that!" he said, nearly falling backward off the chair.

"Didn' want you to shoot me as I came through the door. You lookin' to do some huntin eh?"

Joe watched his father's dark eyes beneath the shadows of his cap. The eyes glittered from the yellow light of the hissing gas lantern above them.

"No, just thinkin' of this old rifle an' how we used to hunt with it."

His father grunted in reply and remained silent, watchful.

"It's been fired lately. You been doin' any huntin'?

"A little. Didn't get much, but I think I scared it."

Joe regarded his father closely, seeing wariness combined with sadness in his eyes. The once straight back was now becoming bent and the muscular hands beginning to show the hideous signs of arthritis. He seldom smiled, but when he did, it was more a toothless grimace. One of the first things that go are the teeth, he thought. Too much junk food from the store, not enough of the natural diet. Little out there to hunt or catch now, he thought. "You still as good a shot as you used to be?"

His father nodded, as though about to fall asleep, then placed both hands on the table in front of him, palms together as if praying. He looked at his son's accusing expression. *He looks like his mom. I wish he could have known her. I hope she forgives me.* "You wanna know why I was shootin' at your truck?"

Joe leaned back in his chair, arms folded in front of him, sucking in a deep breath with a shocked, audible gasp coming from his mouth. His mouth was set in a grim line as he waited for his father to answer his own question.

"You needed wakin' up. You're walkin' around in a bad dream, an' your makin' that dream come true."

"What does that mean?"

"You're makin' other people's dreams come true. Our people have always listened to their dreams because they know they mean somethin'. Now it's like this television, somebody keeps changin' the channel. Too much noise. You can't hear the message for the noise."

"I got a wife an' kid to feed, an' Josh starts kindergarten next year. My dream is he won't ever have to go on welfare. I want him to get an education."

"An' learn what? How to be a white man, look like one, think like one? Don't you know what I been tryin' to teach you here? There's somethin' deep inside you that will never be white. Look around, see what white man thinkin' has done for us. It made us beggars, an' we don't beg."

Joe's eyes widened in surprise at the strength in his father's voice.

The soft melodious tone was gone and sitting before him he saw for the first time was a man filled with quiet rage and determination. He watched his father's large hands, fingers interlocked, the tendons standing out, as though trying to crush a walnut. Their eyes were locked together for what seemed long minutes. Finally Abe McKay lowered his eyes to his own hands.

Joe followed his gaze and watched as his father's hands opened to reveal an egg. It was a raven's egg. His father made a swift upward motion with both hands and the egg was gone.

"Sometimes what you think is a dream is real, an' what you think is real is only a dream," said his father rising to his feet. "I'm hungry. You wanna stay for supper? I got some Kraft dinner an' fresh carrots from the garden."

"You got a beer?" replied Joe, watching his father with new respect.

"Only if you help do the dishes after." he smiled a huge gap-toothed grin at his son, who smiled back with a confused expression.

After his son had gone, he sat back in his old easy chair with the cigarette burns on the arm, watching the warm flickering of the gas lantern over the kitchen table. He had stoked the wood burning stove because the late summer evenings were becoming cool, and his old joints were less pliable in the morning than they used to be. The aroma of wood smoke wafted throughout the shack. Despite his aches and pains, he was looking forward to the pristine quiet of the forest in winter. Slowly, his eyes closed and he slept in the chair.

The sky was a brilliant blue and the blazing colours of autumn unrolled far below. Between the golden and red leaves, the river wound like a silver serpent, carrying the life blood of the land to the countless lakes and marshes. The air was cool in contrast to the warmth of the sun on the feathers of the large wingspan. The sharp eyes scanned the landscape below, seeing the river turn from silver to a sickly brownish green.

Dead fish and trees floated together in death on its surface, the plants along the shoreline wilting with illness. An alien shape that shone like the skin of a fish lay on the river, the centre of the desecration.

The raven watched with interest as a two-legged creature climbed slowly from the shoreline of the river and onto the large shining shape. The smaller creature pointed something at the reclining form upon which it stood. The raven uttered a croak of alarm and flapped its wings to gain altitude. The sky all around turned red, then shook as though Hell itself had opened up. The heat seared its underbelly, the force flipping it over, the wings refusing to support it any longer. It could smell a sharp odour as its sharp eyes widened in panic to see the face of a man rushing up to meet it. It was the face of the old trapper and he was shouting a joyous, toothless laugh.

Teresa noticed the pleasant surprise in the voice of Corporal Pusch when she invited him to join her for coffee at one of the local hangouts. She had called a half hour before she knew his shift was scheduled to end, hoping to catch him writing up the daily reports of the day's activities. He had mumbled and hummed and haw-ed with genuine embarrassment when she made the proposition. *Why corporal*, she thought to herself with amusement, *I do believe you're a virgin.*

She smiled as she remembered the evening of the wedding reception and how attentive he had been. He hadn't cracked any bad jokes and he managed to keep the moustache movement to a minimum. He had shaken her hand rather than try and kiss her goodnight although she wouldn't have refused the kiss either. A frown slowly took the place of a smile as she recalled seeing Brady glancing their way. Perhaps she had played it a little too strong with the intention of making him jealous, only to have him find solace somewhere else.

She knew the woman reporter, Samantha Paige had been in town that evening, working on a story about the hydro project. There had been a hint of strange perfume in his apartment when she picked him up the next morning for the motorcycle lesson. *I do believe Brady's found himself a bimbo. I don't know if I should be happy or disappointed.*

She looked up from her table in the coffee shop to see Pusch enter, tall, straight, and the crease of his uniform pants sharp enough to endanger nearby patrons.

He gave her a nod and a slanted smile that threatened to slide the moustache clear off his face. He approached with two large take-out coffees and leaned over from the waist to whisper in her ear. "Why don't we take these out to the car where we can talk in private," he said with a subtle smile.

"Why officer are you arresting me, and if so, what's the charge?"

"It's two dollars and fifty-cents because I didn't bring any money and you're going to have to pay for this coffee," he replied, beginning to blush. He motioned over his shoulder where a dour woman with a scarf over her hair watched with a scowl of disapproval. Teresa rummaged through the pockets of her jeans and paid for the coffee, still feeling the woman's eyes on her back.

As they entered the cruiser car, two large ears and a muzzle poked up from behind the front seats, smiling a patent beagle smile, black gums exposed, ears flapping, and tongue panting in anticipation.

"This is Proboscis, police dog tres-ordinaire," said Pusch, introducing the two, both of whom were a mystery to him.

"Yes, he certainly is a nose, and an impressive one at that." She reached between the seats and scratched the beagle behind the ears, receiving an approving wet tongue along the full length of her lower arm in reciprocation. The dog's tail beat the seat-back in pleasure, raising small clouds of dust.

"I got the impression there was something you wanted to discuss, that is if I can tear you two apart for a few moments." He threatened Proboscis with his moustache when the dog tried to climb over the seats and into Teresa's lap.

Proboscis gave him a forlorn look, licked his chops a couple of times and retreated to the back seat where he lay down, dignity injured.

She told him of the situation at North Haul and the mixed loads of explosives they were being ordered to carry. She watched his face change from serious to angry when she mentioned the falsified manifests. She then proposed the plan she and Joe had discussed to have Walter (Winky) Winkwell finally pay the consequences of his actions. The smile returned to the corporal's face and she turned to see Proboscis once again poke his head over the front seat. They both reached over and scratched his floppy ears as their wrists were each anointed with his tongue. The back seat became a virtual dust storm from his scrabbling hind feet and flailing tail.

The waters of the Muskrat River burbled from the stern of the River Runner kayak. Bardman's double-bladed paddle strokes were long and slow, his entire upper body twisting from side to side as he drove the craft against the current. He had been surprised to see several large trees bearing down on him in the river, their branches reaching imploringly, the leaves beginning to turn yellowish. The early morning air cleansed his soul as he watched the last of the mist dissipate under the rays of the rising sun. Two startled mallards thrashed in panic from the shoreline and took flight, quacking their displeasure. He watched them skim the surface of the water and disappear from sight. He wondered where the young ducklings were, there should have been scores of them with their parents, but none were in sight.

The small tributary appeared to his left and he dug the paddle blade in near the bow, pivoting the kayak around toward the opening. A canopy of leaves created a cave-like environment as the kayak moved silently over the clear, still water. The smell of rotting vegetation was strong along the bank and he realised the water level had crept up nearly a foot since his last visit. The canopy soon opened and he was surrounded by a cathedral of towering spruce, interspersed with aspen and birch near the water's edge. The leaves rustled a soft greeting with the morning breeze.

A kingfisher swooped from branch to branch, peering into the water, hoping for an unwary minnow for breakfast.

He sat still, letting the kayak quietly drift forward as the silence enveloped him. This was his retreat and he had been away too long. His very essence, both physical and spiritual drank in the life-giving nature around him. He closed his eyes, the paddle resting across the cockpit coaming, the kayak now stationary in the glass-flat water. His breaths became deeper and slower as he sank into a near sleep. A soft splash to his right made him open his eyes.

A hundred yards away was a young bull moose, partially turned away from him, up to his belly in water along the shoreline. The moose stole a glance over its shoulder at him while slowly chewing, then dipped its large head under water to rip up more succulent water plants.

With painful slowness, he reached to the waterproof camera bag strapped in front of him on the kayak. He withdrew the camera body with the four-hundred millimetre mirror lens and slowly turned his torso toward the hungry moose. The moose looked back at him and waggled its ears. He quietly made several exposures, holding his breath for each. The light was only marginal in the shade of the trees as he shot at one-sixtieth of a second. With a final waggle of its ears, the moose leisurely moved up the bank and out of sight amongst the trees.

He slowly paddled across the large pond and through bull rushes that gently explored his shoulders. He approached the site where he had made camp in the past. He could see the water had risen on the rock shelf, considerably decreasing the campsite area. He pulled sideways in a draw-stroke to the shelf and exited onto the rock, pulling his craft after him.

With a pair of small Pentax binoculars he scanned the far shoreline, washed in the yellow rays of the early morning sun. The trees reflected the light with the clarity of a surrealistic painting, sparkles of dew hanging from the bent grasses. He changed lenses for a shot of the shoreline. Focussing through the telephoto lens, he could see the beaver house on the far side. It appeared unusual, so he slid back into the kayak and slowly paddled to the site. It was then he realised there were no young branches stacked around the area, necessary food for a thriving beaver population. He eased along the shoreline and saw no newly-felled or gnawed trees. Those which had been previously gnawed were turning brown, their material unused by the beaver. The beaver family had gone.

He had looked forward to hearing their groans in the morning like some reluctant wage-earner trudging off to work each day. There was only silence but this time it was an unnatural silence. It was a silence imposed by industrial progress, a precursor of silent decay, away from human eyes which might protest but within full view of the powerless. He could see that some of the trees along the shore had become inundated by the rise in water level, the leaves turning prematurely yellow.

A thumping sound approached from the east, growing quickly louder. He looked up as the yellow and brown helicopter roared over at treetop level, making the branches sway. He recognized it as having the same colours as the one that had buzzed him and Teresa on the river. This time the helicopter continued unerringly on its business, the buzz of its tail rotor finally fading.

"Enough to wake the dead," said the voice quietly from the tree line.

He turned quickly, alarmed, and looked in the direction of the voice, nearly upsetting the kayak with his sudden movement. He heard a soft chuckle from between two trees. It was a soft sound, as though the wind itself had chuckled. He peered closer and saw the toothless grin of the old trapper. He was sitting with his legs crossed on a blanket of spruce needles "Hello Abe. Is this your second home?" *How does he do that? He seems to appear from nowhere!*

"This is my home. It's everybody's home, but we're the only ones who know the way." Abe worked his mouth, rolling something around from cheek to cheek, finally swallowing with an audible gulp. "You want some pemmican? Too hard for me, all my teeth is gone." He held out a small plastic bag to Bardman who crawled from the kayak and walked over to join him.

He took a pull on the piece of hard smokey meat and chewed it appreciatively as Abe watched silently. "You're an unusual man Abe, sometimes I feel you're nothing more than a dream and I'll wake up snug in my bed."

"You'll wake up my young friend, but you won't be in bed, an' you won't be snug."

He stopped chewing, seeing the anger in the old man's eyes.

"This...is a crime," said Abe quietly, sweeping his arm toward the still water before them. "The people who do this, an' others that sit an' watch it bein' done are the criminals. Sometimes doin' the wrong thing is better'n doin' nothin'. It makes other people act an' all it takes is one to show the way."

"Why are you looking at me like that? Am I supposed to know the way? I'm just a photographer, I don't know anything about showing anybody the way. Hell I get lost in supermarkets, somebody has to show me the way out of them." *He knows what I've buried near the river bank. Shit, that stuff might be flooded by now, I've got to dig it up before it's ruined.*

Abe smiled and wagged a deformed finger at him. "I know what you been doin', but you been doin' it in a dream. Somethin' inside of you has told you to act before it's too late but because you're alone, you're afraid."

"What am I afraid of?"

"You're afraid of what you will become."

"And what's that?"

"You're afraid of changin' as a human bein', an' not knowin' what those changes will be. Your actions are the signs of those changes an' you know it's time to act. Look around you. It is almost too late." Abe's accusing glance swept from his face to the beginning desolation of the shoreline.

He had been brought to this place fifty years ago by his father who patiently explained the workings of nature and his reverence for it to his son. They had trapped beaver from the pond, hunted moose and water fowl, always thanking the Creator and the spirits of their prey for allowing them to use their meat to survive. They sprinkled tobacco on the pristine water as an offering to the spirits.

It was on the very shoreline where he had found the photographer camping, that he had spent his wedding night with his young bride, wrapped in blankets under a canvas tarp, the brilliant stars of the universe wheeling above them. With the songs of the wolves echoing among the still forest, he and his bride conceived their son, Joe. Nine months later she died giving birth. His desire to join her in death was overwhelming and would have been realised had it not been for his squirming infant who looked so much like her. Now his son was changing and spiritually fighting tooth and nail against the forces of change. His son was being torn between two worlds. *The thread that connects him to me is weakening. He has not been completely open to the teachings. He must be made to see instead of just looking. This man before me is beginning to see but I must show him where to look...inside himself where the only true answers can be found.*

They had been sitting in silence without a sense of time.

"Got any more of them apple pancakes?" He asked with a slow smile.

"You know I'm getting hungry too," replied Bardman rising to his feet and walking to the kayak. He reached behind the movable seat and extracted the bag of supplies from which he took the container of pre-made powder mix and one of dried apples. He also retrieved his Peak-1 cook stove with it's wind baffle and under the watchful gaze of the old trapper, added water to the mix in a pot into which he put a handful of dried apple slices. He had made the pancakes for friends on occasion and suffered their comments of how the finished, cinnamon-sprinkled product resembled a fresh cow-pie.

The aesthetics of the dish didn't affect the old trapper in the least, as the food was wolfed down past toothless gums, followed by a healthy belch.

"It appears I have a convert," said Bardman, smiling at the way old Abe used his tongue to lick his lips clean of maple syrup.

"Me too," replied Abe quietly, not meeting his questioning glance.

He took the dishes to the shoreline to fill with water. He turned to suggest that his guest could help with the duties and realised the old man was no longer there. He stood quietly for a moment in the silence, peering into the darkness between the trees. There was no sign of him. As he bent down to pick up his small cook stove, he looked at the thick grass where they had been sitting. There was only one portion of grass depressed to indicate anyone had been there. The grass on the side where the old trapper had been, appeared never to have been disturbed. He glanced at the utensils to be sure two sets had been used, and was reassured by their presence. *At least I didn't dream this. What did he mean by 'me too'? How the hell does he disappear like that? Wish I could get out of doing dishes that easily.*

The sweet aroma of wood smoke came to his nostrils making him look around, half-expecting to see a campfire. He was just beginning to realize how much he loved the smell of wood smoke.

Without knowing why, nor questioning his own actions, Bardman did not set up camp on the far shoreline where the old trapper had stared so wistfully during their prolonged silence. Glancing at his wrist watch for the first time that day, he was surprised to see it was late afternoon. *My God, we've been sitting there for hours! How is that possible? It feels like I've only just arrived.* As he climbed into the kayak, he could see the lower angle of the sun to confirm the time of day. With strong silent strokes, he propelled the kayak toward the small, tree-sheltered tributary that would lead back onto the Muskrat river.

There was a note taped to his apartment door when he arrived in the warmth of the early dusk. It was from Teresa, asking him to meet her for coffee. He was glad today was Friday and he wouldn't have to go into work the next day. *One of these days, Mikeluk's going to tell me to take a flying leap if I ask for another Friday off.*

He quickly unloaded the VW Rabbit and stored the kayak in the shed along with the other one. *I bought this one for Teresa, hoping it would give us something in common. She hasn't used it since that time we went paddling together. Spending all her spare time with that cop with the moustache. He was ashamed to feel jealousy.* He knew he had no right.

He took his helmet from the apartment and walked to the Norton. As he opened the fuel cocks to each carburettor, and trickled fuel slowly into the bowls, a plan took form in his mind.   He moved the choke on his left handle grip to the right and bent down to turn the ignition two clicks to the right so the headlight would also come on. Surprisingly, the motorcycle fired on the first kick of the starter. The handlebars vibrated as the Norton idled, then ceased to shiver as he cracked the throttle briefly, creating a throaty roar, combined with the mechanical clatter of the valve lifters. He could tell a British bike from the sound its engine made. By the time he had shifted smoothly through the gears, feeling the warm air against his face, the spark of his plan became clear. He knew what to do with the buried explosives, but he was afraid the rising waters might have covered the place where he had buried it. He dreaded rising early on a Saturday unless he was going paddling, but was resigned to his actions.

What did the old trapper say about being afraid of your own actions? Well, all of a sudden I don't feel afraid anymore. Maybe that's a sign I'm going crazy. Whatever happened today didn't seem normal, but I feel more relaxed than I have in months.

He stayed to the perimeter road around the town, taking the long way, revelling in the power and agility of the motorcycle. His down-shifting had become smoother, without the jerkiness he had first experienced when he eased the clutch out. He had learned the hard way that you never come to a complete stop while part way through a turn. The motorcycle had flopped over on its side, taking him with it onto the gravel parking lot of Hazel's Hangout where he was going to meet Teresa now. He had thought he was going to give himself a hernia as he grasped the handlebars to lean the motorcycle back onto its kick-stand. He hoped some of the regulars who had observed his prior, graceless arrival of a few days before weren't there now.

Hazel, the short, frizzy-haired proprietress, had refused payment for the coffee, saying, "Anybody with the guts to do that in my parking lot deserves a free coffee."

He had blushed in embarrassment at her comment and even more when a couple of the regulars asked him if they could go out and flop the Norton over for a free coffee too. He had learned a valuable lesson, that just when you start feeling cocky about your abilities, something happens to bring you swiftly back to reality.

Teresa was sitting quietly at a corner table in the non-smoking section, smiling as he came through the door and he smiled back. He noticed how good she looked in tight jeans, taking a couple of extra seconds to appreciate her long athletic legs.

"You buyin' or just window shoppin'?" said Hazel, her head and shoulders barely emerging from above the glass counter-top.

He turned his eyes from Teresa, to the diminutive woman peering disapprovingly at him through rhinestone encrusted eyeglasses. She was squinting as though trying to bring him into focus, her frizzy hair poking rebelliously out from under her paper cap. He ordered a coffee and moved to Teresa's table, but not before hearing Hazel mutter something about somebody having more men than the Queen of Sheba.

"Looking good on that scooter there Brady. I hear you put on a bit of a show a few days back."

He tried to smile, but only grimaced. "I wish I could forget that, the only thing I got out of it was a bruised ego and a free coffee." He sat across from her, watching her smile back as though harbouring some humorous secret. "So, I got your note. It sounded kind of urgent."

"Well not really. Partly, I just wanted to have coffee with you. It's been a while since we've done this and I got the impression you might be avoiding me, so..."

"Take the bull by the horns, that sort of thing?"

Teresa laughed. "Yeah, only to find out I'm grabbing the wrong end.

"Well, don't worry, I'll let you know if you grab the wrong end."

They both gave a hearty laugh and immediately felt more comfortable with each other despite the glares from Hazel from behind the counter.

"Hazel muttered something about the queen of Sheba when I came in. Any idea what she was talking about? "

"Oh I had coffee this morning with Hans and now because I'm with you, Hazel thinks I'm a loose woman. It seems she worries about the welfare of any single woman who comes in here."

"Well she should. Have you noticed how the regulars leer at anything in a skirt that walks in here? Hell I think a couple of them have started leering at me, and I'm not even wearing a skirt. Who's Hans?"

"Oh, Constable Hans Pusch, actually it's corporal now, and speaking of men who wear women's clothing..."

"You mean he wears women's clothing? A cop?"

"No, no, no, let me finish and for shit's sake don't speak so loud. What I was trying to say was that the guy who stole my jeans and then showed up at the wedding was found in some structure over a ventilation shaft."

"So how long have you been on a first name basis with this Corporal Pusch?" He was leaning over the table, his coffee mug clenched in both hands.

"Not long...well, since the wedding, but it hasn't been long. Actually his full name is Hansupp."

"Hansupp?"

"Yeah, I guess he came over from Germany with his parents as an infant and an immigration official made some kind of mistake in spelling on his birth certificate. His parents never saw the mistake until he started school and never bothered changing it."

"Hansupp?" repeated Bardman incredulously.

"Yeah." giggled Teresa. "You know those 'knock-knock' games kids play? Well, they play them at the detachment and Hans' favourite is to say knock-knock, they say who's there and he says Hansupp. So, here are all these cops, the sergeant included, standing around with their hands in the air, laughing like idiots. It sounds like they never get tired of it."

"Sounds to me like they're all a bit short of a posting. I hope I never get arrested by one of them. Wait a minute, who did they find?"

"I was trying to tell you when you interrupted, that guy who crashed the wedding party."

"Pilson?"

"Yeah, him. Hans and Proboscis found him. I guess the whole place was covered in shit and dead rats, but he got away through some trapdoor into the mine. I thought I should warn you, Hans wants to talk to you. It seems they found a company magazine and this Pilson had circled your name on that section where the editor's name and staff are listed."

"On the masthead. Who the hell is Proboscis?"

"Yeah, the masthead I guess. That's his dog. Anyhow, he had written your address there too and I was just wondering if maybe you keep anything at home that has my address, like maybe an address book?"

He nodded. "So he's been calling on us when we're away. That explains some of the terrible smells that are around there sometimes."

She became serious. "It gives me the creeps to think he's been stealing my underwear and stuff from the dryer. I mean the only way he can do that is to watch for when I leave. Ewww, yuk, it just gives me the shivers when I even think of it." She stuck her tongue out as though having just swallowed cough medicine. "I shouldn't tell you this because it isn't public yet, so keep it under your hat, okay? They found the remains of a human leg, partly eaten in that shack, along with thousands of partly eaten rats."

"Hank Aikins?" he replied in a whisper of disbelief. "Christ, I've been having nightmares about that day." He was beginning to feel his gorge rising in his throat along with a repugnant taste of bile.

"You want to know what's really sick?" continued Teresa.

"There's more?"

"Hans says they're listing the official cause of death as consumption, I mean who's going to write that in the obituary?"

He snorted in derision. "That wouldn't surprise me after seeing them run the front page photograph upside down."

"Well how were they to know a cat could stand on its head."

He shook his head as though trying to clear ear wax, amazed at how the conversation had degenerated. He could see Hazel approaching them with a fresh pot of coffee held at eye level, as though checking for foreign objects in the dark brew. There was a crooked cigarette protruding from the side of her lipstick-smeared mouth, the smoke wisping up between under her glasses, making her eyes water. The long ash appeared ready to fall down the front of her blouse.

"Hey biker, you an' Sheba want refills?"

They both declined.

"Y'know," continued Hazel sagely, "I wouldn't spread it around if I was you that one of our local cops was wearin' women's clothes. Know what I mean?" She turned her squat body and thundered back behind the counter, digging her slippered heels into the linoleum like a storm trooper on parade.

They smiled at the bucolic advice offered by Hazel. She was sometimes referred to as the Ann Slanders of the north by the regulars who had heard her dole out advice like food at a soup kitchen. It didn't always hit the mark and those nearby often got splashed.

"So, tell me," said Brady leaning closer and speaking with a quiet uncertainty. "I mean you can tell me it's none of my business, but I was wondering if you and the cop had a thing going, y'know? Well I know it's none of my business, but I was just wondering."

She leaned back in her chair as though to keep the same distance between them and although she smiled, there was a sadness in her eyes. "Is that what you thought when you saw us at the wedding? Hell, that invitation came right out of the blue. I hadn't seen hide nor hair of you for at least two weeks and I was getting a little tired of taking the initiative in this relationship...if that's what it is. It's hard to tell where I stand with you Brady. It seems we're great friends one day and it cools right off the next. I've had better success forecasting the weather."

He studied the patterns on the table where former patrons had spilled their coffee, rings intersecting with smeared crumbs, nodding slowly, not looking up at her. He spoke to the crumbs. "I know. I've had a lot on my mind lately and things aren't that great at work."

She snorted a half-laugh. "That's an understatement. Shit, if I had people dying around me and getting eaten at work I wouldn't be happy either. That isn't a mine, it's an abattoir. It's like that hydro project, people are getting eaten up and the scale is so great, nobody misses them. It's like the preying mantis. They eat their own children and breed the need for more."

He looked up quickly, surprised at the analogy she had described. He could hear the words of the old trapper, almost feel the wizened old eyes upon him. His memories twitched and sniffed the aroma of wood smoke like stale perfume wafting from a steamer trunk, long unopened.

"Do you ever get the feeling that time's running out, Teresa? I don't mean between you and me, but time to make a difference in this world. I'm afraid that one day I'll look around me and realize I've grown old and haven't done anything of value, just treading water, always on the verge of going under. The stream keeps moving on and I'm still stuck in a back-eddy, paddling like mad and going nowhere."

She regarded him the way a mailman watches a dog, wary of the next move but afraid to initiate it. She forced a smile with her mouth but her eyes refused to reflect it. "You know Brady, I think this is probably the first serious conversation this establishment has ever heard. Maybe you're going through male menopause a little early with all this soul-searching, but I'll answer your first question. The answer is you're right, it is none of your business and secondly, I've been studying my navel just like you're doing now, for every day of my life ever since I made the mistake of getting married to a man who thought the word wife was synonymous with servant. And yes time is running out for all of us, it's called entropy, but it's an even greater waste of time to sit around worrying about it. God, just talking like this is making my head ache. Let's talk about hockey scores or something, okay?"

"Sorry Teri, I just remembered something I have to do. I promise I'll call and stay in touch more often. Why don't we go out for dinner like we did that last time?"

"Actually, that was our first time Mr..Bardman, and yes let's do it again." She smiled again, hoping it would lighten his mood but, was disappointed as he walked unsmiling toward the Norton.

"Don't fall off that thing, biker," hollered Hazel from behind the counter, a haze of blue cigarette smoke swirling about her like an approaching storm front.

He blushed as he heard her cackling laughter from behind the slowly closing door. It was nearly dark, a thin band of peach coloured light along the western horizon which wouldn't disappear until nearly midnight.

The sky immediately above the horizon was azure, turning quickly royal blue, then black directly above. The cloudless sky revealed the countless stars in the clear blackness as he accelerated away, catching a last glimpse of Teresa still at her table. He thought he saw tears in her eyes but she turned her head quickly away when she saw him looking back.

An hour later, he reassured himself that the explosives he had buried near the riverbank were alright despite the rising waters. He didn't want to have to dig another hole because the sight of anyone working with a shovel in this remote area would raise suspicion, and the last thing he wanted was a carload of teenagers with bootlegged beer looking for somewhere to party. He was glad he had parked the motorcycle at home and brought the VW because the bugs were getting bad and he wanted to think as he drove, something the Norton wouldn't tolerate if he wanted to stay on the road.

When he reached his apartment, he went immediately to his equipment closet where he kept his personal camera gear and extracted a small flash which housed a nine volt battery. With a small jeweller's screwdriver he removed the plastic housing of the small flash, exposing the small circuit board along with its capacitors. He switched the flash on and heard the high-pitched whine as the capacitors charged. The small ready-light flashed, signalling that the capacitors were ready to be discharged. He pressed the tiny red test button and the flash tube discharged with an audible poof. The capacitors began to whine as they recharged and he timed the process, using the sweep hand of his watch. It took ten seconds, indicating that the battery had plenty of charge under load. From a small drawer, he removed a tiny electric soldering gun and a roll of soldering wire. He applied the hot tip of the soldering iron to the connection between the capacitors and the flash tube, holding the hot tip on the small blob of silvery solder. With gentle pressure he finally removed the flash tube from the fine wire, leaving only a remnant of solder, shining like a silver tear drop on the end. Smoke swirled around him with an acrid stench like that of an overheated electric motor.

A sharp screaming made him jump, nearly upending the hot equipment before him. He quickly picked up a section of newspaper which was on the arm of the chesterfield and ran to vigorously wave it back and forth under the shrieking smoke alarm on the ceiling. He was thankful the neighbours had grown accustomed to the sound of his smoke alarm when he cooked. Several had suggested he learn to boil more food rather than fry it. They said his cooking was giving them ulcers without the hazards of eating it. Thus was born his culinary compromise of Kraft dinner. So far it had only set the smoke alarm off once and thankfully the neighbours had gone out.

Once more in the smoke-laden quiet, he retrieved the soldering iron and with the guts of the flash propped in front of him, he soldered a longer copper wire to the end which had previously been attached to the flash tube. He reinserted the small nine volt battery against the contact points which were no longer housed by the plastic, and taped the battery in place with black electrical tape. He flicked the switch to ON and heard the capacitors begin to whine again until the ready light glowed. Placing the longer copper wire against a metal fork on the table, he pressed the test button and watched a small blue spark jump to the fork. With satisfaction he turned the unit off and took from a box a brand new compact travel alarm clock, also powered by a nine volt battery. He removed the plastic shell from the back, exposing the small contacts where the alarm was turned on and off. Leaving the switch for the flash turned on, he removed the flash's battery to prevent the capacitors charging. He carefully soldered a long thin copper wire to a point on the alarm contact of the clock and another where the circuit was completed when the alarm contacts met. There were now two thin copper wires exiting from the guts of the alarm clock and to be connected to the circuitry of the electronic flash. One of the two copper wires was soldered to the battery lead of the flash and the other to the ON side of the switch. This made the nine volt battery of the alarm clock the sole power source to the flash unit as well as to the clock. There was now no need for a battery in the circuitry of the flash. He set the alarm to trigger in fifteen minutes and sat back to watch the results from the copper wire where the flash tube had been. He suddenly saw an oversight. He had forgotten to tape down the tiny test button on the flash to close the circuit, leaving the alarm contacts the only break in the circuit. As the time approached, he held his breath and watched silently. Simultaneously, the contacts of the small travel alarm clock closed with a click and the capacitors began to whine. When the capacitors became fully charged, a spark flashed from the copper wire to the fork. The alarm made a series of shrill beeping sounds in groups of three. It was a sound he had learned to hate. He smiled in anticipation as he thought of the two blasting caps he had found on the track floor. He hadn't realised until later that one of them was electrically detonated and , the other by the heat of a fuse. He was thankful for the careless ways of the highballers. The heat-activated cap had been used as a test to be sure the powder could be detonated, when he had blown up the rock on the riverbed.

He was finally beginning to feel that time was not standing still for him. His stomach grumbled and he realised he hadn't eaten for hours. All he had in the cupboard was the omnipresent Kraft dinner and a couple of beers in the fridge. The late-night news would be on in a half hour and he planned to watch it while eating, the only time he ever turned the set on and find out about the outside world. A world he was planning on seeing soon.

He went to bed later that night, his mind still seeing images of the story on the hydro project. The project had eaten another of its worker-children and a major work-safety inquiry was being called for by concerned citizens and families of the workers in Winnipeg.

In the background of the t.v. camera shot, he had seen a placard being waved by a member of an environmental group, protesting the rising waters of the lakes and rivers. Behind the environmentalists were a half-dozen natives with placards of their own protesting the loss of hunting and trapping areas. As the camera had panned back, he had seen the dome of the legislature building with its naked representation of a young man carrying a torch, perched in the centre of the structure. It was said that the torch was the only defence the Golden Boy had against a host of pigeons whose sole aim in life seemed to be defecation upon the world below.

Now we're being shit upon by the turkeys of industry and politics. Bigger birds need bigger controls. If the Golden Boy could piss in frustration, he'd flood Memorial Boulevard. Thought Bardman, half asleep, finally drifting off, his last thoughts a jumble of images of Teresa crying, and a jumble of wires connected to a small alarm clock that kept going beep, beep, beeep...

CHAPTER 20

The search teams knew from the evidence found in the fan-shed that all they might expect to find of Hank Aikins would be bones and various body parts. His lower left leg with the boot still attached now resided in the freezer of the evidence room of the local constabulary until a qualified forensic investigator could examine it. All the officers who had seen the leg were of the consensus that the marks around the partially eaten calf muscle were human teeth marks mingled with those of rats. They had wrapped the leg in plastic, refusing to look at it again. Many of them without telling their colleagues had become devout vegetarians, unable to again look at meat on their plates without becoming sick.

The mine rescue team had split up, each member with a member of the RCMP. Each man was dressed in orange coveralls, with hard hat and light. The officers each carried a can of mace and a pistol on his belt. There were eight teams of two men each, one man armed, both very nervous. Each team had a section of the labyrinth to search. The twenty-five hundred foot level was the lower-most producing level, but there were four other lower levels used only for exploration drilling and these lower levels had quickly been sealed off and searched first, due to the only access being the main shaft and the single hoist. From there they had worked their way toward the surface, twenty-four hour watch on all the openings, including the shit-covered trapdoor at the top of Q-3, the ventilation shaft where evidence was still being gathered in plastic bags by officers gagging into face masks. The Vicks Vaporub each had smeared under his and her nose, did little to diminish the gag reflex.

Many of them wished they had never been transferred up from Winnipeg. Several large green garbage bags were filled with the carcasses of partially eaten rats, others with dried feces from both the walls and the floor. In another bag was an assortment of women's clothing, including underwear. There were stacks of newspaper which had been used as bum-wipe, and most curious of all, a company news magazine kept in pristine condition by a plastic freezer-bag. The magazine had been opened at a story about two diamond drillers. The photograph showed a partial profile of a very shy Sam Pilson and a smiling image of Frenchy Rivest. The photo credit to Brady Bardman, was circled by pen. The magazine was kept apart from the rest of the evidence with the intention of having a long talk with this Mr. Bardman, foremost in the minds of the investigators.

Pilson, entirely swaddled in dusty burlap, tied together with lengths of twine, had seen some of his escape routes cut off. The ore chute near his last drill site had been spot-welded shut, removing one alternative mode of travel between the level above. His hair was shoulder length with the beginnings of a patchy beard and moustache. Ever since adolescence he had tried to grow facial hair, an attempt to hide the pimply skin of his sallow cheeks. His thick-lensed eye glasses were nearly useless because nearly all his time was spent in either near or complete darkness. His eyes had become hyper-sensitive to daylight as well as the light from the miner's lamps. His body odours were a repulsive mixture of vomit, feces, and natural human body aromas of one who hadn't bathed in weeks. He carried with him a slender wooden rod, the type which was used at blasting sites to push stick-explosives into a drill hole without causing a spark. The rod allowed him to probe ahead in total darkness for obstructions, but over the last few weeks he had been able to rely more on the echoes the rod produced when he tapped the end on the rocky environment around him. The speed of the return echoes had indicated to him any large objects in his path and more importantly the presence of depressions and holes into which he might fall as he negotiated his way along the track floor between the steel rails. When he walked, it was with a shuffling gait in over-sized rubber boots, rod tapping in front of him, preceded by his stench. His visage presented the apparition of a tall, gangly, slightly hunched biblical figure in dire need of immersion baptism with generous quantities of soap. Whenever he saw the blinding headlight of a locomotive pulling an ore car, he lay prone, face down beside the track, as close to the wall as possible. He pulled his feet up under the burlap and stayed motionless as the driver of the locomotive regarded the mass of burlap as simply more discarded material from another drill crew. The fabric deposits were seen on all levels of the mine, some were cleaned up, others left in place for months. Had the motor operator seen the resurrection and tentative movement of the mass of fabric after passing, his future in mining would have been in doubt as would his sanity in the eyes of his fellow workers.

The cage began to slow its descent.

Pilson rose from his fetal position around the pulley system atop the cage and faced the rear wall of the shaft. As the cage slowed to a crawl, he stepped from the roof onto a large, horizontal steel beam at the back of the shaft. He deftly turned himself around on the beam and watched the light through the lattice work of the cage as several men debarked. The cage-tender's bell rapped out it's typical staccato of sounds, and the large greased cables tightened before his eyes, pulling the suspended vehicle past him

383

missing his face by mere inches. He watched it from beneath as the floor of the cage diminished with distance into the darkness above. At regular and ever-diminishing intensities, there were the lights of cage stations at higher levels, appearing like cold blue windows suspended in a pillar of blackness.

He listened for the sounds of the men to move off. When he was satisfied they had all left, he edged his way around the periphery of the shaft on the beam, his back straight against the wall. He held the long stick in one hand as the other gripped the edge of a beam above. He positioned himself slightly above and to one side of the steel lattice gate through which the fluorescent lights illuminated the interior of the shaft. Hundreds of feet below, he could hear the faint clangour of equipment on other levels, drifting up to him from the dark abyss. He slowly lowered his wooden rod through an opening of the lattice-work and allowed it to slide into the well-lit track floor area of the lift station. The rod clanked and rattled with a hollow sound before coming to rest. He held his breath during the silence then slowly lowered himself with both hands until he was spread-eagled against the framework of the door, suspended only by the strength of his sinewy arms and hands. He resembled a scrawny, furry creature which had been stretched over a stretching-board after being skinned. He lowered himself slowly, his feet searching for the ledge of the rock opening. Finding the ledge, he reached down with first one hand then the other and heaved upward. The door moved upward on its rollers and he ducked under it into the glaring bluish light as gravity took over and re-lowered the door once more to the ledge. With his eyes nearly screwed shut against the harsh light, he felt for his rod and upon finding it, shuffled quickly toward the huge orange blast doors which led out onto the darkened drifts. He stopped suddenly, his nose twitching. His improved sense of smell, immune to his own aromas, had picked up the scent of food emanating from the adjacent lunchroom near the lift station. He moved quietly and quickly to the red door and listened. With care, he opened the door and peered inside. The lights were off but the smell of the food was even stronger. *Ham and cheese! And apple pie! What's that? Somebody breathing! Somebody here!* He looked further into the depths of the lunchroom and slithered in sideways, not turning on the lights. The door was left open a crack to allow a modicum of light to spill along the cement floor. Two tables in, he could see a human arm hanging to the floor from one of the benches which accompanied each of the long tables. The sound of a snore came to him as he moved slowly on hands and knees into the room, closing the door behind him. Slowly, and in complete darkness, he moved toward the sounds of the breathing. Using his sense of hearing and smell, he positioned himself at the head of the sleeping man and slightly below the level of the bench. He reached slowly to the top of the table and let his fingers explore, like some blind, foraging insect. The hand came in contact with the miner's hard hat and light as well as the belt battery laying beside them. Next to that was the lunch kit, which the hand opened deftly and without sound.

The aromas of the food made his head swim with ecstasy. The urge to stuff it all into his mouth was only barely overcome by the need for caution. He carefully put the hard hat on his head. It was several sizes too large but he had no time to make adjustments. He had to adjust the belt for the battery to prevent it falling noisily to the floor over his non-existent hips. He cradled the lunch kit under his arm and this time, slowly walked toward the place where his memory told the door was.

The miner gave a loud snort, then coughed in mid-snore. Pilson jumped in alarm, nearly dropping the lunch box. He reached the door, opened it a crack and looked out. The area was deserted. Once more and with food and a fresh light, he shuffled beyond the swinging blast doors. He giggled and made a right turn-signal with his arm and disappeared into the darkness toward the site where he and Frenchy had last worked together. He didn't turn on the hat light, but relished the darkness and the blanket of security it gave him. The hat and light were for something else, something he had been accumulating, objects of appropriate size and content where he could sit for hours and think and, try to remember.

After a half-hour of walking in the dark, he detected a hollow quality to the echo of the rod as he tapped it in front of him. The deeper echo came from his left and he slowly swept the long end of the rod into the pillar raise where their drill had once sat. Now there was only a platform of large railway ties and a wooden ladder attached to the still-present wooden staging from which he had once helped pull the drill rods. He felt for the ladder and made his way up by feel, past the first two small platforms, high into the heights of the pillar raise where the highest platform was suspended near the rock ceiling. It was from here that he had disconnected the thirty foot lengths of rod while looking lovingly down on the diminutive form of his friend, Frenchy.

Frenchy is not gone, he still lives here, you can feel his soul in these rocks. You can still be with him. The voices had been speaking less frequently to him and one voice seemed to dominate the others which on occasion whimpered their way into his thoughts. A mental shouting match would ensue, causing him to cover both ears with his hands and shut his eyes tightly in the darkness as though it would make the voices go away. He had sometimes stood like that for hours in a state of near catatonia until one voice managed

385

to out-shout the rest. By that time he was exhausted by the battle within his brain, his head pounding with a dull pain that seldom abated. He thought he might have screamed, but he couldn't discern the internal screams from the external.

With loving care and by sense of feel alone, he began to arrange the objects he had collected. The hat and light were placed on the skull which had been placed on a two-by-four plank, with another plank nailed across at right angles to form a crude cross. At the ends of the horizontal ends of the cross, Frenchy's old work gloves dangled. The battery and belt, he tied around the vertical portion of the cross, but the heavy objects slid to the platform with a thump. His shrine to Frenchy had been a long time in the making, but now that he had begun, the voices in his head were less insistent, although the dominant voice would sometimes ring out like a shout, causing him to stop in mid-stride.

It had the same grating tone as his father, like a metal bar being rubbed across concrete, hard and emotionless. *You must join him soon. He wants you to be with him.* It was like a bad radio commercial that he couldn't tune out nor reduce in volume, over and over in the echoing recesses of his ephemeral thoughts.

He sat cross-legged on the platform for what seemed in his mind to be minutes but was actually hours. His primal urges awoke him from his stupor, rumbling of his stomach like another voice from his visceral regions. As he shifted in the dark to descend the ladder, a sudden sharp snap sounded through the rock, followed by a deep rumble as explosives were detonated at a rock-face one level above him. A whispering coherent thought told him it must be one-o'clock in the morning, the time when the drifts are deserted on the levels where charges are set off.

As though in a dream-state he stood in a fluid motion and descended the ladder. The mental image of a loaded explosives car appeared in his mind. He knew what Frenchy's shrine needed to be complete. Its colour was like a bright gift, it's aroma a deadly perfume.

Bardman sat on a ridge of the Precambrian shield, twisting fine strands of copper wire together, connecting the electric blasting cap to it's power source and then to the small travel alarm clock.

When he had left work that afternoon he was glad to have escaped the presence of his editor. Mikeluk had come into the photo department under the auspices of discussing an upcoming assignment but the way his eyes wandered the shelves of photo supplies, he appeared to Bardman to be taking stock.

Now, having paddled nearly an hour upriver, he was prepared to test his homemade detonating apparatus, using the one extra blasting cap. He played out about fifteen feet of the fine, insulated wire and made the final connections to the contact points on the detonator itself. Lastly, he set the timer for the alarm at what he estimated to be about ten minutes hence. He then walked a dozen paces away and crouched behind a ridge of rock, not trusting the accuracy of the timer. Five minutes later he was startled by a loud report like that of a high-powered rifle. Several ducks flew up in alarm from the river bank and he could hear their continuous panicky quacks as they flew low over the trees. There was a small white scuff-mark gouged into the rock where the tiny explosive device had been. The white material was powdered granite where some of the blast had been directed downward, although most of it had been directed away from the rock. He sat next to the spot and collected the remainder of the apparatus, the air around him warm from the heat of the day radiating from the hard granite. The lowering sun reflected like diamonds from tiny facets of rock in subtle shades of pink and white. His thoughts returned to the strange behaviour of his editor, the way his eyes seemed to be searching for something.

The next morning while walking down the hallway to the photo department, he heard a strange guttural wailing sound. It came from the open doorway to his office and he could hear two voices, one unrecognizable at first, the other, Mikeluk's. As he entered the film storage area he saw his editor saying something and pointing to a shelf.

The beagle caught his scent and careened around the corner, skidding to a stop before him and began howling a canine dirge, all the while hopping up and down stiffly on it's front legs, ears flapping in unison.

Mikeluk looked at him accusingly. "Come on in Brady, Proboscis won't bite but his nose can be dangerous." His mouth smiled, showing tiny crooked teeth, his eyes wary, refusing to meet Bardman's gaze.

Corporal Pusch looked around the doorway at him, preceded by his moustache which waggled bushily with the silly smile on the officer's face
.

"What's going on here?" he asked, seeing the way the two men glanced at each other conspiratorially.

Mikeluk had jammed both hands deep into the pockets of his baggy slacks and blushed slightly. "We had a phone tip that we might find something interesting here, you know about the explosives that have gone missing from underground."

He could feel the blood flow from his face and a cold knot begin in his stomach. He forced himself to look directly at both men. " And what have you found so far?"

"Well nothing really," replied Pusch, speaking for the first time, "But with the reaction from Proboscis, there seems to have been explosives in here at one time."

"Does Proboscis think I'm hiding explosives in my crotch, or does he do this with everyone?" The beagle had moved closer, its nose snuffling, buried between his thighs his tail moving back and forth with joyful anticipation.

"Mr. Bardman I must inform you that we have a search warrant for your apartment and at this moment an officer is going through your belongings looking for residue of explosives. We have also taken your rubber boots from this office for analysis of any residue of explosives."

"Am I under arrest?'

"No sir, but you are a suspect in the disappearance of nearly four-hundred pounds of explosives, much of it the granular type known as Amex. You know about Amex don't you Mr. Bardman? You seem to keep turning up in areas where it's being used all the time."

"Is that an accusation officer? Because if it is, I'd sure as hell like to see some evidence to corroborate it." *Like hell I would.* "And would you mind getting this dog's nose out of my groin, he's making me look like I've wet my pants."

Pusch gave a yank on the dog's leash, eliciting a howl of indignation but the dog finally returned to it's master's side where it looked up at the officer with large baleful eyes.

"So who made this so-called phone-tip?"

"Sorry, I can't tell you that because it was anonymous but we have to follow all leads in this matter and you're one of the common denominators in your frequency of visits to these sites."

Bardman reached for his assignment log which contained the written assignments from either Mikeluk or Jenkins. He waved them under Pusch's moustache which appeared to recoil at the movement. *"I was assigned to go down there by Mr. pocket pool here or the president of this company."*

Mikeluk quickly extracted his hands from his deep pockets, blushing furiously and startled at Bardman's outburst.

"Corporal I suggest you either charge me or get that moustache the hell out of my face and your dog out of my groin. You guys have set yourselves up for a wrongful search lawsuit and believe me, it'll cost you if you don't get out of here and out of my apartment now."

"We're finished here anyway Mr .Bardman and we'll certainly let you know of our results of our little peek through your apartment. If charges are pending, It'll be my pleasure to come and inform you personally. And by the way, without trying to sound melodramatic, please don't leave town." Pusch lead Proboscis down the hall, the beagle glancing wistfully back at Bardman's groin.

"I should press charges of sexual assault against your perverted beagle, have his nose amputated or nostrils permanently plugged with cat shit. How would you like that you flop-eared throw rug?

The dog howled in response as Pusch pulled Proboscis into the beginning heat of the late- August day.

He stood in thought for a minute, disregarding Mikeluk's silent, brooding form. *What did he mean most of it was Amex? All I took was Amex and I didn't swipe the detonators, they had already been lost by the blasters. Could someone else be raiding the powder car?*

He returned to the photo department, seeing equipment on the shelves where it hadn't been before. He could see that all the chemical jugs, full and empty alike had been moved and probably peered into. There were dark smears on the usually clean linoleum floor, evidence that the refrigerator containing the film stock had been moved. Well bwana, he said to himself, what do you think of all the crap that's coming down around here? Do you think it would be paranoid delusion to feel that somebody is out to get me?

Mikeluk's face, previously blushing pink was now quite pale, his eyes still refusing to meet his. His soft paunchy body seemed to be sinking in on itself, like a human balloon suffering a slow leak. "You're not very happy with this job are you Brady?"

"Whatever gave you that idea, and what's that got to do with anything that's going on here?"

"You don't have to be confrontational with me. I didn't have anything to do with this."

"Then why are you still here?"

"Don't forget I'm still your immediate superior and I don't have to put up with this attitude from you."

"You're my immediate boss, Zenon old boy, but I don't think the word superior applies."

"You're always looking for an argument Bardman. Why not just do your job and try to look like you 're enjoying it once in a while?" Mikeluk was holding out a piece of yellow assignment paper toward him. He could see his hand shaking as it held the paper, and perspiration marks where he was gripping it.

"What's this, more administrative toilet paper?" He took it and began unfolding it, seeing that it had been folded several times into the size of a book of matches. He saw Jenkins' signature on the bottom before reading the assignment. "What is this some kind of joke? He wants occupational portraits of the stope crew on the two-thousand foot level?" His face grimaced with disbelief, his eyeglasses sliding partway down his nose. He looked back at Mikeluk who was now watching him the way a postman watches a dog. With his back to the equipment room wall, he appeared ready to either run, duck, or fight.

"It's a pet project, says he wants capture the personalities and character of the type of person who works underground."

"For God's sake, let's be realistic. These guys work on bonus. To stand still to have their picture taken means money to them. They won't agree to this." He re-folded the paper back into a tiny square and handed it back to Mikeluk.

"They'll do it, you just have to show them Mr. Jenkins' signature on the bottom. He wants to see contacts by five this afternoon, in colour."

Bardman shook his head slowly back and forth the way a bull moose does when it meets an interloper.

Mikeluk exited hurriedly and scurried down the hall, back to the sanctuary of his office.   "Give my thanks to your father in-law Zenon."

"One of these days you're going to say too much Bardman," came the high-pitched and slightly strangulated voice of his editor.

He smiled as he watched the editor walk with a distinctive swish of his ample hips. *You can bet your fat ass on that Zenon old fart.*

He hurriedly packed his gear, two camera bodies, several lenses, flashes, light stands and umbrellas. He loaded it all on a small collapsible luggage cart, the type the constantly hurrying air travellers dragged along behind them. He fantasized how great it would be to be pulling this equipment behind him on the way to some foreign news assignment, instead of the damp, greasy depths of this mine. Plopping his hard hat on his head and donning his steel-toed rubber boots, he trudged, cart in-tow to pick up his light and battery from the charging rack near the main shaft cage.

He leaned resignedly against the cage wall as it plummeted to the lowest producing level of the mine. The cage-tender stood near the door facing the image of the grey hard wall streaking past, worrying at the brownish-wet remains of his hand-rolled cigarette. *His life consists of going up and down in this hole. A fitting testament to a wasted life. HE WENT UP AND DOWN A LOT.* He giggled aloud to himself, then realised the cage tender had turned and was watching him.

When he exited the cage, he could feel the man's eyes on his back and imagine him during his lunch break, relating his encounter with a crazy photographer. He smelled the dankness of the air and heard the buzz of the overhead fluorescent lights hanging from the rock ceiling. He was alone there and felt a chill come over his body. With both large hands he hitched up his sagging work pants and the very act seemed to buoy his spirits. His boots galumphed along the track floor as he pushed through the huge swinging blast doors and into the darkened drift. *Hi, the boss sent me to take your portrait, wanna stand still for a second? I'm the company photographer, and I'm supposed to take your picture. My names Brady, and I'll be your photographer for the day. Just stand the fuck still for a minute while I take your fuckin' picture.* He giggled again, still not sure how the folded piece of paper in his pocket would convince the stope miners to give up their time. He felt that just the confined environment of the stope, the low-ceilinged tunnel which followed the ore seam, created a surly nature in the men who worked there. He had seen miners follow a seam of ore, nearly crawling on their bellies to operate their pneumatic jack-legs, fighting for another foot of bonus that shift, before the seam disappeared entirely. Sometimes they moved around under the low rock in a full crouch for the full shift. At the end of the day they appeared like silent, filthy young men with premature dowager humps.

The sound of his luggage cart went bump, bump, bump along the track floor as he surveyed the track ahead with his light, barely able to hear the echo of the drills at the end of the drift. He wished there had been a flatcar available to push his gear, but he was glad for the relative quiet of the two-wheeler behind him. He found he relied as much on his sense of hearing and smell as much as sight down here, fully aware of what it was like when a light went dead. He passed the pillar raise where the Frenchman had been killed and recognized the welded-shut ore chute where the remains of Hank Aikins had been found, gnawed upon by rodent and human teeth alike. *Died of consumption, died of consumption...* he realised he had giggled again, hardly aware of his own actions. *Wait a minute! I didn't giggle, somebody else did. Oh shit!* The luggage cart went bump, bump, bump much faster as he nearly jogged the final distance to the stope, his light alternately lighting the floor and ceiling of the drift.

He was slightly out of breath when he reached the stope area where an electric powered scoop-tram sat on the track, a large flatcar of explosives

391

attached to it. Usually the explosives were kept further away, but with the disappearance of even more powder, the miners were keeping it under close scrutiny.

He scrambled up the incline of loose, jagged rock, following several snaking air and water lines into the low, dark confines where the loose rock came closer to the ceiling. Over the lip of the rock he could barely see the silhouettes of the miners, their hat lights flashing briefly against the rock face where they were drilling, then back to their equipment. He could taste the fine rock dust that permeated the air and smell the grease and hot steel of the bits. A water pump hammered nearby, forcing cooling water to the drill bits, obviously inadequate due to the dust in the air. The drills rattled like machine guns, boring into the rock.

He cursed as he slipped and skinned one knee on a sharp piece of rock. In an ever-lowering crouch, he approached the four miners, their backs to him, watching the progress of the drill rods. A light flicked toward him, then waved frantically at the other three lights beside it. All four lights quickly turned toward him and held him like four suspended yellow eyes in an unblinking stare. The drills went quiet, only the hiss of air and the water pump remaining. Soon the water pump was silenced and the four lights approached cautiously.

"Hey, it's only me, the photographer. You know, the fat guy with the camera?" The lights drew closer, then stopped, fixing him in their collective beam.

"Shit, iss picture-taker. Vat the fuck you doink here Mr. picture-taker?" said one of the lights.

Bardman stared up into the lights from a kneeling position, trying to make out the features of the men behind them, only able to see the red colour of the fronts of the hard hats. "The boss sent me down, said he wants portraits of the drillers, said to show you this," he said, waving the yellow assignment sheet in front of them.

A hand came out of the darkness and took the paper from him. The beam scanned the paper and said, "Good, more bum-wipe."

"Yah", said the other light, you vant picture, take picture of my butt, I sign it for Mr. president."

"Well really guys it won't take long, only a couple of shots each. It's not like it was a wedding or anything."

"Veddink? You at boss's daughter veddink?"

"Yeah. So vat, er what?"

"My vife t'ink you cute, nice to sit wit pipple from old country. Natasha, she say you point camera at everybody doink stoopid t'ings. Best kind of pictures. Yah?"

"Yah, er sure whatever you say, so what do you say about these pictures here?" He waited while the four hat lights huddled and whispered to each other. One of the lights chuckled. "Hokay, but we make pose for group shot," said one light, blinding him with it's beam.

He had the four of them come to the more open confines of the drift where he set up his lights and reflector umbrellas. With the flash units indicating they were fully charged, Bardman fitted the camera with a wide angle lens and plugged in the synch-cord for the flashes.

"Vait, you turn round for moment, hokay?"

"Why, what are you going to do?"

"No, iss hokay, really, tr'ost me. I say ven to turn back."

He turned around reluctantly, hearing a series of chuckles and the subtle clinking of equipment combined with a rustle of clothing.

"Hokay, ready!"

He turned back to see a display of four pair of long red underwear, still topped by the lights the coveralls of each man down around his ankles. Around each mans waist was the belt holding the lamp battery. "Oh no guys, I can't give something like this to the boss, he'd fire me...and maybe you too."

"Ve let you take two picutres only or you not valk out of here on two fat legs, so stop talk, take picture now."

He took one exposure with the dual umbrella flashes, the brief view through the lens showing the red-clad miners grinning idiotically. He groaned audibly, hoping to elicit some empathy from the miners but actually looking forward to seeing the results.

"Vait, vait, one more picture, den you finish." The lights turned away and with a single movement all four beams pointed to the track floor.

Bardman could make out the image of four bare buttocks peering back at him from the opened rear flaps of the long red underwear.

"Quick, you take, can't stand like dis all day, bad for hemorrhoid."

He managed to take three exposures, hearing guffaws of laughter each time the flash was triggered. He found himself laughing along with them, not really caring what Jenkins thought of the results. It was the most fun he'd had underground in a long time and possibly his last, but he realised he was beyond caring and the realisation was like a tangible weight lifted from his shoulders.

A giggle echoed down the drift from which he had come.

All five hatlights stopped moving and listened. All sounds of their breathing stopped.

"What duh fuck?"

"Ssssh!"

The giggle came again, only from further down the drift in the inky blackness.

"Oooh shit," said one of the lights. "He's baaack." The three other lights turned and nodded, their beams making small patches of light moving up and down on the drift wall. The rustle of clothing became frantic as the miners pulled their coveralls into place and re-donned their yellow waterproof slickers.

The giggle from the darkness quickly became a demented laugh and finally a plaintive wail, ending in a sob. "Frencheeee," wailed the voice over and over, echoing down the drift.

"Screw the bonus, this shift is over, I'm outta here right now," said one of the miners as he climbed onto the electric locomotive.

Another miner stopped half way onto the locomotive and sniffed the air. "God, I can smell him, he stinks like a sewer."

"Never mind that, look," said another as his hat light illuminated the small flat car where they had their explosives stacked. The other lights turned to the car where they could see that one fifty pound sack of Amex was missing as well as several sticks of Cil-Gel. The small wooden cask which contained the caps and fuses had also been opened, the fuses appeared like thick black wire coiled around the inside circumference of the cask.

"You stand with mouth open Mr. photographer or you comink?"

"My lights, I have to take them down..." he stopped and stared at the track floor near his feet. Another blasting cap lay beside his right boot, an electrical one. He couldn't believe his luck as he quickly plucked it up and put in his pocket.

"Start dis fuckin' t'ing, ve go now, you valk if you vant."

The battery-powered motor hummed and the transmission clunked into reverse as Bardman shouldered his camera bag, the camera still around his neck. He abandoned the umbrellas and flashes on their stands, as he clambered aboard the motor. As they moved, he took a small flash from a pocket of the bag and clipped it to the hot-shoe of the camera. The motor's hum increased to a high whine as they accelerated down the track, the vehicle making sharp jerks to either side as it crossed the occasionally misaligned piece of track.

"I see a light on the right," said one miner, almost breathless. "Slow down." They all looked at a glow coming from the high confines of the pillar raise, a hard, flickering light like that of an electrical wire short-circuiting. The vehicle came slowly to a stop as the five of them leaned over to peer into the upper reaches of the raise. A single light flicked on and peered back at them, the second flickering light slightly below it.

"Frencheee," screamed the figure above them, hurling an object down at them.

The four miners and one photographer were paralysed in place on the locomotive as a human skull bounced and then rolled to the edge of the track.

With their eyes wide in surprise, they saw the apparition of Sam Pilson, dressed in the coveralls of the late and recently eaten Hank Aikins, descend the wooden ladder from the upper staging of the pillar raise.

"He's gained weight," said one miner with quiet awe.

The apparition appeared decidedly plump as it came hand over hand down the ladder, emitting a strange giggle as it descended. A yellowish sand trickled from the ankles of the figure, making tiny pattering sounds on the bare planks below. The harsh flickering light came from his waist, producing a curl of white smoke.

"Oh shit, that's a lit fuse!" said a voice beside Bardman. "And he's got his coveralls stuffed with Amex and Cil-Gel." They could now see Pilson's face, caked with filth, bearded, and hair hanging to his shoulders. His eyes without the thick lenses were dark orbs that didn't blink, fixing them with a hypnotic stare. His mouth opened and with an ungodly wail, he screamed Frenchy's name again as he began to move stiff-legged toward them, like an insane, explosive scarecrow. "Go,go,go," screamed a miner. The locomotive clunked into gear and lurched along the track as the apparition advanced on them, the burning fuse at its waist growing shorter. By now all the miners were exhorting the driver to greater speeds as the approaching human bomb began to lurch hurriedly after them.

Bardman finally remembered the camera around his neck and attempted to focus on the lurching figure as the car picked up speed. He managed to get off a couple of exposures before switching to a slower shutter speed, hoping to compensate for the increasing distance and the lack of light. In the low light he could only guess what the shutter was set at and he didn't want to take his eyes off the now-receding form behind them.

The others were still shouting encouragement and expletives at the driver, knowing that the remaining fuse gave them only seconds before reaching the explosives contained in the coveralls.

Bardman propped his camera on the back of the moving locomotive and pointed the camera, lens open, down the drift, at the barely-visible figure still pursuing them.

"Frencheeee," came the final wail, followed by a brilliant flash behind them.

They were instantly rocked by a roaring concussion that blew the hats from their heads and made their heads feel like they were being squeezed in a vice. Loose pieces of rock fell around them, shaken from the ceiling as their ears rang from the blast and their nostrils filled with a combination of rock dust and residual fumes from the explosive chemicals.

The locomotive slowly came to a halt, its brakes shrieking with the sound of metal on metal. All heads were turned back to where the running figure had self-detonated, turning himself into unrecognizable bits of bone, flesh, clothing, and a spray of blood, all now spread for twenty paces along all surfaces of the drift.

He saw one of the miners move his mouth, the man's light shining directly into his eyes. "What?" said Bardman, his voice sounding as though it came from within his head. The other mans mouth moved again, this time closer to his ear which was still ringing with a shrill frequency.

"Do you think we should go back?" said the barely-audible voice.

He looked down the track, seeing nothing through the dust and fumes. He shook his head. The others agreed with nods of their hat lights.

The locomotive began moving again, pushing its carload of plundered explosives in front of it. They all knew that if the human bomb had been close enough, the blast could have detonated the whole carload of a dozen bags, each weighing 50 pounds, along with another 50 pounds of sticks of Cil-Gel.

Gradually, Bardman's hearing began to return and he could again hear the hum of the electric motor. No one spoke until they eased the vehicle onto a siding near the lift station.

"I t'ink I find anodder line of vork to do," said one miner. "Maybe join vife in catering business, vatch pipple act like fools at veddinks.

The five men climbed from the locomotive in stiff, jerky motions as though they had been sitting for hours. Each seemed slightly unstable on his feet, due to the abuse the inner ears had suffered.

The Czech miner walked as though in waist-deep water to a telephone mounted near the lift doors and spoke briefly to someone on the other end. "Rescue crew comink down. I say nobody left to rescue, iss now little bits. D'ey say vait here. Where d'ey expect us to go?" His eyes seemed to have sunk into his head and his face was a grey tinge, partly from the

396

rock dust, mostly from fatigue.   They stood watching the large cables vibrating as they lowered the cage to their level. Four men in red coveralls, respirators on their faces and air tanks on their backs stepped from the cage. One of the red-clad men took notes as the others related what happened. Between them they had brought down a scoop stretcher, the type made of tubular aluminum and splits open along it's length, to be scissored closed under a victim. Each of the miners was examined by the members of the mine-rescue team for any injuries. Bones were palpated, eyes peered into to check pupil response, pulses and breathing rates noted. Two men were found to have a ruptured eardrum and another a nose bleed due to the concussion of the blast.

    The leader of the rescue team turned to Bardman, the camera still around his neck. "You the photographer?"

    The miner who had summoned them rolled his eyes as Bardman stared at them slack-jawed, wishing he could think of an appropriate answer rather than the "Yes," he croaked back.

    "You have to come with us, we have to document the scene before we touch anything."

    "I'm not going back down there", he replied feeling a chill come over his body. "I've seen enough for today thank you and I don't want to see anymore." The overhead lights began to darken and spin and he found it difficult to keep his balance.

    "These weren't my orders, they came from your boss and he said....oh shit."

    Bardman was caught in mid-fall by one of the miners at his side. He felt like he was at the bottom of a large barrel and he was seeing several heads peeking over a darkened rim, looking down at him. Their voices echoed unintelligibly as the scene began to darken. He was vaguely aware of his feet, feeling as though they were floating. Gradually his vision returned and he saw the concerned expressions on the faces around him. His feet were propped at an angle on a tool chest while his body remained flat on the track floor.

    "On second thought partner, you don't have to go anywhere, said the rescue team leader. We're the ones who call the shots down here, and you don't have to go anywhere but up."

    He was gradually helped to his feet by the other miners and eased into the cage. The signal bell clanged several times and they began to move swiftly and silently up the shaft. He still felt weak-kneed and slightly sick to his stomach.

"Got to be better vay to make livink," said one miner. Four heads nodded wordless agreement as they made their way to the surface and the welcome light of the sun.

He had been in the darkroom several minutes, unloading the film from his camera before he realised the phone was ringing. Zenon Mikeluk's voice was on the other end, calling for an immediate meeting in Roger Jenkins' office. He put the film in his pocket, removed his coveralls, and like someone trying to walk underwater, went to the president's office.

Five minutes later he exited the office, newly relieved of his job, told to clear his belongings out of the building and be off the premises within the hour. To his surprise as well as Jenkins and Mikeluk, he smiled and left without saying a word to either of them. Suddenly he felt he could breath again and despite his considerable girth, there was a spring in his step. On his way back to the photo department he could feel the roll of film still in his pocket and decided it was going to come with him. There wouldn't be time to process it but he could have the one-hour lab in the mall do it and give him negatives only. He didn't want some technician seeing images that might set tongues wagging and people looking for him.

The security rent-a-cops met him at the gate through which all plant and underground employees must pass, subject to having to show their pass and possibly have their lunch boxes searched.

The sergeant was a dour bear of a man with a permanent tan and eyes that never smiled. His huge hand was extended. "Your pass Mr. Bardman if you please." It was handed over and put in an envelope. "Now your lunch box." The box was opened and the remains of old sandwiches inspected with distaste. The thermos bottle was shaken, opened and sniffed. The sergeant wrinkled his nose and returned it. "Now please step inside and empty all your pockets on the counter. Don't look at me like that. Just do it or I'll do it for you."

Bardman could feel a cold knot in his gut as he emptied his pockets of old change, a wallet and a dirty handkerchief. Finally he was allowed to pass and as he straddled the Norton motorcycle, he grimaced slightly in discomfort as the film canister wrapped in plastic was pushed a little further up his rectum. He wasn't looking forward to fishing it out.

The ride home was fast but supremely uncomfortable. Two hours later in Hazel's Hangout, he was looking through a magnifying loupe at colour negatives, fresh from the one-hour lab. Two were out of focus, but two others showed Pilson clearly, running after the locomotive, the ankles of his coveralls tied shut to contain the granular explosives. The burning fuse at his crotch was clearly visible, as were the tears of insane grief running down his cheeks. The last frame was a complete surprise. He had only hoped that the opened shutter of the camera would catch something. The walls of the drift were illuminated by the flash of the explosion in the distance to mark the instant when Pilson had finally gone to join his friend Frenchy Rivest. In the dark he had turned the shutter speed to the 'bulb' setting which held the shutter open a long as finger pressure held the button down. The light from the blast had done the work of an electronic flash, even to illuminating the tops of the steel rails. The two previous frames showed the four miners in their long red underwear, their bare buttocks in an appropriate salute to management. He smiled at the image.

"Brady you finally look happy about something. Is it something you can share or do I have to dig it out of you as usual?"

He looked up in surprise at the sound of Teresa's voice. Coffee in hand, she looked like a fashion model in a silk blouse and dark slacks. A pair of medium heel shoes had added another inch or more to her considerable height. Her hair was newly-permed, framing a face that never seemed to need makeup. "Wow! Where are you off to, a social function this time of day?"

"Do you always answer a question with a question Brady? No wonder you're so hard to read. Well I might as well start with the answers otherwise this conversation will go nowhere." She sat across the table from him studying his features for a moment. "This is the most content I've seen you look in a long time. Is this the sign of an improved love life? Sorry, sorry as usual, none of my business. Actually...I'm going for a job interview."

He had forgotten how much he enjoyed the aroma of her perfume, realising he wasn't the only one who looked content. "I was about to say the same for you Teri. So you finally decided to do something else with your life. What kind of job around here could possibly get you dressed up looking so good?"

"I'm going to try to be a horse person."

"A what?"

A female RCMP officer, you know they're sometimes referred to as horsemen, well I'm gonna be a horse person," she replied, leaning back on the rear leg of her chair, wiggling her eyebrows at him. "At least I'm seeing a recruiter today. They sometimes go to places where members of the detachment have told headquarters of interested persons who might fit their needs. Hans has already put in a good word for me and his word seems to carry some weight."

"Shave off his moustache and you could cut that weight in half."

"Now don't be harsh with Hans, he's really not a bad guy under all that facial and nasal hair and fake British accent. I think he's actually very shy and that's how he deals with it. Anyway, he thinks I have potential, and I'm really due for a change. God, one more week of that truck and I should know if I'm accepted or not. Luckily the doctor at the hospital has done medicals for the RCMP before and I don't even have to go to Regina to know if I meet the physical standards."

"I don't think you have to worry Teri, Corporal Pusch has been admiring your physical attributes so much he's beginning to get eyestrain. But I'm glad for you, you needed a change just like I do. I just don't know where I'm heading yet."

"That certainly sounds final. So tell me what happened."

He related the day's events, omitting the part about the film in his possession. He watched her face cloud with doubt as he told her about meeting Pusch and Proboscis in the darkroom where they were searching. She appeared to be gnawing on her lower lip when he told her of Pilson blowing himself up in the mine, as well as the search of his apartment and the warning not to leave town.

She leaned close in a conspiratorial manner, avoiding the coffee spilled on the table top. "But don't you see Brady, it looks like this guy has been stealing explosives and squirrelling them away somewhere in the mine. I think Hans has been under pressure from that ferret-faced little investigator to find someone to pin it on. You always seemed in the wrong place at the wrong time, but now there's evidence and even witnesses that he stole explosives. If I were you, I'd get a lawyer right now, tell him the whole story and get him to tell the cops to back off. I don't think they would have grounds to keep you under travel restrictions."

"More coffee folks? My, your lookin' real nice today dear. Where'd ya park ya truck?"

Bardman and D'Amico looked up to see Hazel, pot in hand standing next to their table. Her greying hair was awry as though just having come in from a high wind, her glasses were half way down her nose and the ever-present cigarette hung with a long ash from the side of her lipstick-smeared mouth. The lipstick appeared to have been applied with a paint roller.

"No more for us, thanks Hazel," replied D'Amico. "By the way Hazel, I thought you were turning this into a non-smoking place."

"It is, but I own it an I can do what I want. So, what are ya gonna do, fire me?" She squinted disapprovingly through her rhinestone glasses at her and then at Bardman who was leaning back in his chair, enjoying the encounter. She turned away, coffee pot still held at the ready, looking for other victims, emitting a dry cackle which ended in a hacking cough.

"I got fired today," said Bardman abruptly, watching her reaction.

"I thought you'd quit first. I could see you weren't happy. I'm actually glad for you. Who was it that said each ending is the start of a new beginning?"

"I don't know, probably the same guy who said that even the longest journey begins with a single step... or was it, shit happens."

"So what are you going to do now?"

"I have a few plans, nothing concrete." *No plans! Maybe just go out and blow up something that really is concrete.*

"Well, the way you're smiling, I'd say you must have something up your sleeve Mr. Bardman. You know, you've always been rather secretive. You're a hard person to get to know."

"So now you want to be a cop and investigate me through official channels?"

"That's not such a bad idea. I could show up on your door in my spanking new uniform, put you in handcuffs and have you take me out for dinner. Of course you'd pay."

"Of course." He was surprised to see they had easily slipped back into the familiar way of speaking which they had so enjoyed when they had first met. He wondered who had changed to create the invisible rift that now seemed between them. Perhaps they both had; growing in different directions at different speeds.

She looked at her watch. "My God, I've got ten minutes to get to my interview. Gotta run, I'll call you later. Will you be home later?" She left the table and started for the door.

"Yeah, and I hope you get rejected."

She smiled sadly back. "I know you do, but you know I won't. Don't you?"

He watched her run to her car in the parking lot. Her beauty and athleticism was magnetic and he knew she would be accepted. It was difficult to watch someone he cared for, suddenly see a clear path for their future, especially when his own seemed so murky. It was like trying to see to the bottom of a muddy pool of water, knowing that others had seen their way, but he was being denied that sight.

"Where's Cleopatra off to in such a hurry," asked Hazel, her head barely visible above the counter top, smoke curling around her squinting features.

"She's going to become a pig," he replied as he moved toward the door.

Hazel's eyes widened slightly behind the filthy glasses before returning to the normal squint. "I dunno about you sometimes," was all she said.

"I don't know either Hazel, see ya." He picked up his helmet and started out the door toward the motorcycle.

"Don't you fall off that damn thing. Y' hear?" called Hazel after him. Her voice had the quality of rusted metal scraping on rock.

With his back to her, he simply gave a wave of his hand, his mind on what he was going to do next. To his chagrin he was destined to spend the next half hour sitting in an RCMP cruiser car in front of his apartment, giving a statement to a newly arrived officer, concerning the bizarre events underground that morning. He was equally surprised that despite being searched, his apartment was not a shambles as he had expected it to be. The fact they had not arrested him was a positive sign. Perhaps Pilson had diverted their attention away from him. He hoped so. He needed as much privacy as possible for the next step of his plans.

CHAPTER 21

Abe McKay was asleep. He had been sitting on the bank of the Muskrat River, fishing rod in hand, trying for a nice fat pickerel for dinner when the autumn sun lulled him into slumber. He lay back in the high, lush grass, mouth wide open in a full volume snore, still gripping the rod, its lure dangling in the water at the river's edge.

He was in a canoe, floating on a surface which seemed to have no boundaries, no shoreline or sky. Everything except the water was a white, hazy mist which at times changed in density as though something was trying to break through the whiteness. His paddle made gentle swirls in the water's surface as he propelled the canoe aimlessly through the mist. Leaning slowly over the gunwale of the craft, he saw his reflection looking back with a quizzical expression. In the reflection he could also see a distant inverted tree line and lying upon the shore, a large shiny creature with an aura of evil about it. He knew the creature was helpless as long as it lay on its side. He also sensed that he had been sent there to prevent the creature from ever returning to its natural element. Using only the reflection in the water to guide him, he paddled closer to the creature. He looked up once from the surface of the water and his head swam in confusion. He saw nothing but whiteness around him, no tree line, no sky, not even a breath of wind. His world had become inverted, but his mind was still oriented to the former. He knew that to truly understand what was happening, he must succumb to it, accept it as the new reality no matter how confusing the images. He glanced back into the water and as though watching from another body, saw his reflected image climb from the canoe onto the shoreline next to the creature. In his hand was his old 44-40 rifle. His reflection climbed carefully upon the shining creature which dwarfed him with its immensity. He appeared to be searching for something, as he bent closer to look at the shiny white skin. He saw his inverted image carefully raise the rifle to its shoulder and put the muzzle to the shiny skin of the creature. He wanted to cry out a warning but no sound came from his mouth. He raised his paddle and hit the water with a loud SMACK, destroying the reflected image. The water splashed from the surface and onto his face causing him to lose his balance and fall back into the canoe.

He lay there looking at the flawless blue of the sky. His hand holding the fishing rod jerked again and nearly tore from his grasp. The tail of the large pickerel broke the surface in a frenzy, splashing more water on him. He quickly sat upright and played the fish, letting it tire itself on the line before bringing it to shore. With the fish safely in his sack, he took some tobacco from a small pouch in his pocket and sprinkled some on the water, and quietly thanked the Creator for providing his dinner.

His thoughts went back to the dream. Its inverted realism troubled him. Normally he was able to find a message in his dreams but this time the answer escaped him. While walking back to his cabin through the warm late afternoon sun, he dwelt upon the images that swirled in his mind like wisps of smoke, first creating recognizable forms, then dissolving into the fog of barely un-recalled dreams.

His son's car was parked on the dirt driveway next to his cabin. He could see that the paint job was beginning to peel badly, with more rust showing through the door panels. He realised Joe, who once had a reverence for mechanical things, was now less attentive to them. He opened the door to the cabin, expecting to see his son sitting with his feet up on the kitchen table, beer in hand. No one was there. He called his name once, softly and getting no answer, called again, louder.

"Out here," came a muffled voice from behind the cabin.

He went around behind the cabin. "Where are you?"

"Here," came the muffled voice from the decrepit outhouse. "Will you do me a favour an' go get me some toilet paper?"

"Forgot to buy some but I might have somethin' in the cabin." He chuckled quietly as he went to the cabin and returned with the weekend coloured comics from the Winnipeg newspaper. An extra had come to the Hudson's Bay store and he used the pages to set his dirty boots upon the sheets inside the door. He couldn't read very well but he enjoyed the cartoons just the same. "Here," he said as he slipped the paper under the door, "Use the page with the penguin on it. I never understood that one anyway."

Joe's voice gave a groan from within the hot stinky confines amid ripping sounds of paper. "Is this the best you can do?"

Abe laughed aloud.

"I suppose you think this is funny eh pa?"

"You should be glad I like to read the comics. You can't do this with t.v."

The door opened and his son came out, still tucking in his shirt and smiled at his father who returned a toothless grin. " I left some for you for later."

"Never use it, I got paper towel under the kitchen sink." He laughed as his son gave him a gentle kick in the behind and laughed with him. "You forgot to do up your fly. Won't catch nothin' with that around here."

They filetted and fried the pickerel in a batter of flour sprinkled with black pepper. They ate quietly and appreciatively, each sipping a warm beer from a six pack which Joe had brought with him He knew the reserve was considered a 'dry' one, but he knew the risk was small of being disciplined for bringing in a small quantity of alcohol for personal consumption.

"I've been thinkin' of comin' back to the reserve. Sadie an' I have been talkin' an we think that as long as Josh can go to school here, it'll be better'n livin' in town."

Abe stopped eating and looked up from his plate." What changed your mind?"

Joe shrugged his shoulders and spoke between bites. "I dunno. Things haven't been that good at work, an' I thought there might be somethin' I could do around here. I'm pretty handy with tools an Sadie thought she might find work at the store here, she has experience." Joe was uncomfortable with the lack of response from his father who had stopped eating and sat looking at him. "What?"

"It's a big change. You sure you want to do that?"

"I thought you wanted us to come back here. Why are you actin' like we should stay away now?"

"I want you to be sure. You're not just changin' houses, you're changin' your life. Your family's too."

"We talked about it. I told you. There's that house next to the nursin' station. We could live there."

"First you have to talk to the band council, they have to agree, an' they'll want to talk with Sadie too."

"You're on the band council, can't you talk to them?"

"They have to vote, an' they have to do it without me. I can't show favourites."

Joe heaved a sigh as he pushed his plate away from him. "I didn't think it would be that hard. You didn't have any trouble gettin' rid of me when I was a kid. Do you want me to come back or not?"

Abe sat silently, his head lowered and eyes closed, his breaths came in long slow gasps. Finally he looked up, tears beginning to form in the corners of his eyes. "Havin' you come back will be a lot easier than lettin' you go the first time. I just don't want to see you go again without givin' it a chance here. Sadie an' Josh might find it harder than you an' want to leave." He sat quietly, his hands clasped in front of him on the table. The orange early evening light of the setting sun through the window painted a golden hue over the interior. Old masonry jars on the window ledge, surrounded by the dried bodies of long-dead flies, projected colours of the rainbow on the opposite wall.

"I'll talk to the band council tonight an' let you know when they want to talk to you." *One of my dreams is comin' true, but I can't see the end of it, only the beginnin'.*

Joe rose from his chair with his plate in hand and moved to the enamelled sink. "I'll wash, why don't you dry?"

Teresa was ebullient. Her interview with the RCMP recruiting officer had gone well. She had sat in the detachment waiting room while two others, a local boy and a young native man from a nearby reserve had walked nervously into the interview room, references, school marks, and anything else in hand which they thought might improve their chances of acceptance. She hadn't realised Corporal Pusch had written a glowing personal reference based on what he had referred to as his 'observances.' She realised that most of the times he had observed her, the stares were more of a sexual nature than objective.

The two young men returned from the interview with sombre expressions, their school marks as well as their motives for wanting to join the force being questioned.

When she was finally asked why she wanted to join, she was afraid her emotions might have showed through too clearly when she replied that she felt her life had been going nowhere and finally wanted some direction and stability.

The interviewer, his uniform pressed to knife-edge perfection, had smiled to himself and made a couple of notations on a large sheet in front of him. "Well miss D'Amico, so far you appear to be living an interesting life, and I guarantee you this one won't be boring." He pushed a paper across the table to her. "Take this form to the hospital here and see Dr. Ainsley. He is certified to do the medicals for the RCMP for this region. I'll be in town until tomorrow afternoon, so drop off the results in the sealed envelope to this office, and no peeking. If that envelope has been opened by anyone but me, you're automatically disqualified."

She had the sealed envelope in her hand. The doctor had given her the most complete physical, lasting nearly two hours and at the end of it as he wrote out his report, she watched with apprehension.

He looked up, winked and said, "I don't think you have anything to worry about."

Her heart leapt, but soon after, a gnawing doubt formed in her guts as she wondered what she had got herself into. She dropped the medical report off at the detachment, hoping the interviewer would be there. He wasn't and since the day was getting late, decided to go home for dinner and maybe a celebratory glass of wine along with the meal.

Her phone rang half way through the first glass of wine as a rice casserole baked in the oven. Walter Winkwell's whiny voice was on the other end, sounding like some underpowered electric drill, moaning that he needed her at work early tomorrow morning.

"How early Winky?" she replied, the irritation obvious in her voice.

"Five o'clock sharp dear. I've also called McKay and he'll meet you at the yard with the tractor. The explosives crew has been working late loading your trailer so all you have to do is unlock the gate, hook-up and be on your way. So get your buns in gear deary."

She slammed the phone down in disgust at the man's chauvinistic attitude. The taste of the wine had soured in her mouth and her appetite had diminished. *Please God let me be accepted by the horsemen, I promise I'll make a good horsewoman.* She leaned back in her chair at the kitchen table, staring at the cracks in ceiling when the phone rang again.

It was Joe McKay calling to tell her not to come to work early.

"Joe the little fart just got off the phone after telling me to be there at five in the fucking morning and now you're telling me to sleep in. What's going on?"

"Big Don called me at home, said it was another mixed load, caps, fuses, the works, and said Winky told him he wanted it on the road before the cops go on shift. Big Don says he called the cops' an they're gonna be waitin' for us somewhere on the road. If we get busted, we're down the tubes, 'cause the driver signs the manifest takin' responsibility for the load."

She felt her skin grow cold, knowing what would happen to her chances in the RCMP if they were apprehended with such a load. "So what do you want me to do?"

"Go to Hazel's Hangout for an early coffee. Just don't be at home tomorrow morning before eight o'clock. That's all I'm gonna tell you. The less you know the better." Joe had hung up before she could ask more. She settled the phone thoughtfully onto the cradle, her hand resting on the white plastic, now slippery from the perspiration from her hand. The phone rang again. "What?" she shouted into the handset.

"Bad timing miss D'Amico? Should I call back another time?"

She recognized the RCMP interviewer's voice. "No, no, please don't hang up, sorry, just caught me with the oven door down. Just let me put this hot dish down." She thumped the half empty wine bottle on the counter a couple of times near the phone and then opened and slammed shut the oven door, receiving a hot blast of air along with the unmistakable smell of burnt casserole. "Oh shit, that's all I need." She reached into the oven using dish towels over her hands and extracted the burnt dinner, plopping it in the sink where a small portion of water hissed when it came into contact with the hot dish. "Damn." She reached for the phone. "Sorry, bad day in the kitchen. You still there?"

"Yes miss D'Amico I'm still here. Luckily the force doesn't need kitchen workers, however we do need constables and your medical report says you're fit. You'll get a notice in the mail, but I wanted to let you know before I leave town tomorrow that you'll be required to report for basic training at Regina, Saskatchewan in three weeks time from today. You still there miss D'Amico?"

"What? Yes, I'm still here." She let out a whoop of delight. "Sorry, I couldn't control that."

"That's quite alright miss D'Amico, we're pleased that you're pleased. I hope you enjoy your dinner, such as it is, or at least what it sounds like."

She hung up the phone and whooped a couple more times as she poured more wine into her glass. She glanced at the blackened casserole. "Shit, I didn't feel like pizza again tonight."

Joe had not slept soundly that night, his plan going over and over in his mind. He didn't want to implicate Teresa in case anything went wrong. As he drove the Kenworth tractor toward the isolated explosives depot on the far side of the mine, he forced himself to breath deeply until he gradually relaxed. False dawn began to show in the east, the bottoms of the clouds on the horizon glowing pink from the yet-unseen sun. A couple of startled ravens rose in a flurry from the road where they had been picking at some recently run-over animal. The private company road was devoid of traffic, the headlights illuminating the aromatic goldenrod plants along the roadside as the tractor bob-tailed without a trailer to the depot. The plants along with the smell of dust and diesel mingled in his nostrils, a contradictory perfume that he found not entirely unpleasant. He slowed and stopped at the large outer gate to the depot, climbed down from the cab and unlocked the large padlock. After swinging the gates open, he followed the winding, dirt road to the depot where he saw the fully loaded trailer. It was still backed up to the loading dock, resting on its dollies, the rear doors locked and sealed. He had a key for the padlock at the rear of the trailer, but the numbered seal wasn't to be broken for any other reason than unloading at the destination or official inspection. He wheeled the tractor around in the yard and slowly backed the fifth wheel at the rear of the tractor under the trailer. The dogging pin on the trailer locked in with a satisfying

CLUNK. He climbed down from the cab to hook up the air and electrical lines to the trailer. Finally, he used the exterior crank to raise the dollies which the trailer had been resting upon. Instead of climbing back into the tractor's cab, he walked to a telephone mounted on the outside of the small unoccupied shack where outgoing loads were checked during normal working hours. He called Walter Winkwell's home number. "Winky? I can't go I'm sick."

"What the hell do you mean you can't go, where the hell's D'Amico? Let me talk to her, she can drive while you goof off."

"I dunno, she hasn't showed up yet, but I feel like shit an I just barfed."

"You hung over McKay? Cause if you are, you can drive anyway. Hell you've driven sick before, you can do it again."

He could hear a pleading note in Winky's voice. "I don't get drunk, you know that. I think I got the flu."

"More like self-inflicted flu. I'll call D'Amico and see where she is."

"I already did. There was no answer, dunno where she is." He heard a muted conversation on the other end of the phone and a couple of muffled curses in a female voice. There was the sound of bed springs and tired groans.

"Okay," said Winky's voice full of resignation. "Can you at least bring the truck to the yard here so I can find another driver?"

"Nope, if I get sick while driving I might hit the ditch, an' I don't wanna do that with a load of powder on." More muffled curses came from the phone, male and female combined.

"Okay, okay, shit stay there, I'll be there in ten minutes.

He hung up the phone, not looking forward to what he had to do next. From his lunch kit he took out a small plastic bottle of fluid and a tiny plastic bag of red powder. He delicately took a pinch of the cayenne powder and while looking up, carefully sprinkled a few grains into each eye. He cried in pain as his eyeballs felt like they were on fire, the tears streaming in torrents down his cheeks. He then removed the cap from the small bottle and forced himself to drink deeply. After two gulps, the mixture of warm water, salt, and raw egg came back up his throat along with the mornings breakfast. He allowed a smear of the vomit to collect on his shirtfront. He threw the bottle as far a possible into the bush at the edge of the depot and then sat on the running board, his head in his hands to wait for his boss to show up.

"Christ, you look like shit and smell worse," said Winkwell, studying Joe's face in the lights of his car. "Can you take my car back to the yard without puking all over the inside?

He nodded silently, not looking up in case Winky saw the smile in contrast to his tear-filled eyes.

Winky climbed into the still-running Kenworth, looked around for a few seconds to find the paddles on the dashboard to release the air brakes and looked out the window at his employee who was still sitting on the running board. His short stature made it difficult for him to look over the window sill. He struggled with the air-powered adjustment to the driver's seat and soon found his head pushed against the ceiling of the cab. With some effort, he lowered the seat to where his short legs could finally touch the pedals.

"You didn't sign the manifest," he bleated with exasperation as he waved the clipboard out the window at the top of Mckay's head. "Never mind, I'll sign it." He signed his name with a flourish and waved a copy out the window as though trying to ward off the stench coming from McKay.

"Boy I'll tell ya, you an' D'Amico are in real deep shit, you hear? We got some real serious things to discuss back at the office, so you both better be there. Here take this copy of the manifest and put it in the box over by the shack there." He dropped the paper and Mckay picked it up where it landed at his feet.

Joe slowly walked to the depository and shoved a copy of the manifest into the slot. The vision finally returning to his eyes.

The Kenworth growled past in first gear as Winky leaned out the window and yelled at him to lock the outer gate when he left.

He waved acknowledgment without looking up and took his time getting to Winky's car, wanting the load of explosives to be well ahead of him before he left the area. Ten minutes later he left the depot and idled the car at near-walking speed toward the yard of North Haul Trucking. His lips moved in silent prayer as he neared the intersection where the company road ended at the highway to town. He saw two sets of flashing red and blue lights in the distance as he came nearer.

The truck was stopped with a police cruiser blocking it at the front and rear. He could see the officers peering into the trailer with flashlights as Winky stood beside them, his arms gesturing wildly while an officer studied the load manifest which his boss had just signed. There was a look of pure desperation on his boss's face as he drove past, combined with a glance of hatred in his direction when he realised he had been set up.

With three classes of explosives making up the forty-thousand pound load, and Winky not in possession of a class 1 driver's licence, he knew there was enough evidence against his boss to have a huge fine thrown at him as well as the company. He drove the car to the yard, left a note inside that simply said, I quit, and took his own vehicle to find Teresa.He hoped she was still sipping coffee at Hazel's Hangout. He would go find her but he first had to get into fresh clothing. The smell of his vomit on the shirtfront was starting to really make him sick.

The sun came over the horizon as he drove home to change his shirt and reassure Sadie that all had gone as planned. He was accompanied by a chorus of birdsong through the open car window. Dew shone like diamonds from the leafs of plants. The air brushing his face was crystal clear and fresh... fresh with the possibility of a new beginning for Joe McKay.

It was nearly 8:30 in the morning when Bardman's phone rang, waking him from a sound sleep. He answered as though his mouth was stuffed full of cotton , his tongue refusing to form the words properly.

"Hello Brady, I need a photographer and I want it to be you." Samantha Paige's voice was entirely too cheerful for that time of day.

He took several deep breaths, trying to recognize the voice and finally grunted something unintelligible at the phone as he realised who it was.

"You're such a conversationalist Brady. You've swept me off my feet already. You available for some freelance work this Saturday?"

He gulped once, running his hand through a mop of tangled hair and sat up in bed. "Yup, I can work any day of the week if you like, 'cause I just got fired."

"Oh Brady, I'm sorry. Well actually I'm not, it's probably the best thing that could have happened for you. Listen, Corny's sick and my plane arrives there Saturday around nine in the morning. Can you pick me up? We'll take a rented car up to the hydro project. We're doing one last story before they start to flood the forebay."

"Flood the what?"

"The forebay, the area behind the dam that's going to turn into a man-made lake. Don't you read the newspapers up there?"

"Actually I don't very often," he replied as he scratched an armpit and yawned, except maybe the comics.

"Well you should. I thought you were a fan of mine and read all my stuff as though it was gospel. I'm hurt, truly hurt. So... are you picking me up or what?"

"Yeah, sure."

"Well don't act over-enthused about the whole thing. Jeez."

"I'll be there Sam, with bells on, hopping from one foot to the other in excitement."

"Maybe that's not such a good idea, you'll look like you have to go to the bathroom."

"I probably will. In fact I have to right now.

"Brady?"

"What?"

"Remember me telling you about that publication down south? Hearing no reply from him she continued cautiously. "Well, I showed them some of your shots and they really flipped, said it was great stuff and want more if you have it."

"Are you talking about...?"

"Yeah, I sent them a rough draft of the story and they said the shots alone would pay you $,1000 per shot, and with the story they..

"Sam, Sam, remember what we talked about? I'll call you back, stay there."

"Oh yeah, I forgot, sorry Brady, I'll be here."

He jumped from his bed to get his clothing, knowing he would have to shave later. He cursed under his breath as he realised she had completely forgotten that she wasn't to call his number about any of the photographs he had taken and smuggled out of the mine. The last ones just prior to his dismissal, he had mailed to her aunt's address where he hoped they were in safe-keeping. He was becoming paranoid about any conversations on his phone after the police admitted they had searched his apartment. With his shirttail flapping, he went to his car and headed for Hazel's Hangout, and the pay phone next to the bathroom.

The RCMP officer in the nondescript van parked on the street several buildings down from Bardman's apartment block, played the tape back and quickly made a copy. He then picked up a cellular phone and called the detachment. "Corporal Pusch? Yeah, I've got something. No, it came from out of town but we didn't have time to trace it. I don't think we need to, it sounded like a woman reporter with the name of Sam. Yeah, I know it's a strange name for a woman...no it wasn't some guy with a high voice. Believe me corporal I know the difference between a man's and woman's voice."

The officer hung up with a sigh of exasperation and continued to monitor the tiny electronic bug which had been placed in Bardman's telephone. When he glanced up through the one way window in the side of the van, he barely had time to see Bardman's Volkswagen Rabbit disappear around the corner, leaving a cloud of blue smoke in its wake. He quickly picked up a radio mike and simply said, "On the move." He was reluctant to use the radio at all in case Bardman still used a police scanner such as the type used by news photographers and reporters, enabling them to monitor all the police and ambulance calls.

The officer hadn't been told why he had been brought in from Winnipeg to monitor the man's telephone. He only knew that the man rarely spoke on the telephone and the court order had allowed only the one listening device, so there was little need for him to follow the car.

It was a small town and a small police force, so by the time the surveillance man's message came through, Corporal Pusch could only guess where Bardman might go. It was fifteen minutes later, due to a message from the surveillance van that he saw him in the coffee shop, hanging up the phone and sitting down alone to a cup of coffee. Pusch was reluctant to move too close with the unmarked cruiser car, nor did he wish to enter the coffee shop. He not only didn't want to frighten Bardman, he had grown weary of Hazel's constant haranguing about cops taking up valuable space at the counter. He had taken it as a joke, but she never smiled when she said it, always blowing smoke in his face, squinting all the while daring him to arrest her.

Despite the demise of the psychopathic driller called Pilson and evidence that he had stolen explosives prior to blowing himself up, there was far more explosives missing than could be accounted for, and Bardman had shown a talent for showing up in areas that had found itself short of the dangerous material.

Proboscis sat in the passenger seat, noisily licking his chops after his own hurried breakfast. His eyes followed those of his reluctant master, occasionally glancing at him or rather his moustache which reminded him of a particularly fat caterpillar he had caught as a puppy. He sneezed due to the dust in the car, huge ears threatening to make him airborne with the sudden movement of his head. His master's hideous cologne turned his stomach, creating considerable gastrointestinal distress which manifested itself in a silent but most effective manner. He watched his master with apprehension, wondering when his over-sized, under-sensitive nose would detect his latest gaseous emission.

Pusch's nose quivered, making his moustache come alive. "Proboscis you stinky little baloney loaf, if you have to fart, do it outside the car." The beagle's tail wagged manically, slapping against the car seat. Pusch reached across and opened the door, reaching for the leash at the same

413

time, but too late. With a howl the beagle dashed across the street toward the coffee shop, narrowly missing an oncoming car.

Bardman had hung up the phone after his conversation with Samantha Paige and was halfway out the door when he heard the screech of tires.

Coming directly toward him at full beagle-gallop was Proboscis, ears flapping, tail wagging, and mouth wide open to allow a slathering tongue to dampen anything within spray-range. He had the foresight to catch the beagle with both hands before the large nose could impact with his groin. The dog's hind legs continued to pump, the tail moving at full-wag.

He held Proboscis at bay and looked across the street. He saw corporal Pusch attempting to slump down in the unmarked car, the profile of his nose unmistakable, like part of an ice-berg jutting over the ledge of the window. He walked across, feeling the indignation rising within him. "Out for a little exercise corporal? Just follow the local citizenry around and generally harassing them a little eh?"

"Why, no Mr. Bardman, I come here for coffee too on occasion you know, and Proboscis just wanted to say a friendly hello."

"If his friendliness was any more friendly I could have him convicted of sexual assault. You make a good pair corporal, because both your noses are sniffing in the wrong direction and if it continues, I'll start screaming police harassment. Is that clear?" He was gratified to see Pusch blush with irritation.

The officer's eyes then became distinctly harder as his skin lightened in colour. He was like a chameleon, his skin changing colour to suit his mood. "If noses are your concern Mr. Bardman, then I suggest you keep yours clean around here. There's something about you that smells and I'll find out what it is."

He leaned close to the window, within inches of Pusch's face. "If you have a charge to make corporal, make it now or stay away. I'm getting a lawyer today to represent me and he'll be dropping around to the detachment with an order to cease and desist any surveillance you might have on me. Your suspicions are groundless and your actions are nothing less than paranoid."

A howl came from the far side of the car. Pusch leaned over and opened the door for Proboscis who leapt up and sat with morose eyes, watching the conversation. Without saying more, Pusch started the car, smiled coldly at Bardman and accelerated away in a spray of dust and gravel.

By ten o'clock that morning, Bardman had one of the two kayaks on the roof-rack of the Volkswagen. To any casual observer it would appear he was simply going for a paddle, but for the fact he didn't take a paddle, nor a life jacket.

He was not aware that the van which had been parked down the street was no longer there. His half-hour meeting to retain legal counsel had been more effective than he realised, the lawyer going immediately to the detachment to lodge a protest on his behalf. He had become suspicious of an electronic listening device in his telephone but didn't search for it, thinking it may be a way of diverting them.

As he drove north of town with the kayak, he was filled with self-doubts about his plans. He wasn't even sure how the plans had come about; it was as though something was guiding him or at least pushing him gently in a direction he wasn't sure he wanted to go. He remembered the old trapper's words as they had sat by the river bank, something about the wrong action being better at times than inaction. If this was better than inaction, what could it possibly achieve? Probably land him in jail, he thought. A gesture, he thought. Nothing more than a gesture, but someone has to make it or no one pays attention. No one will get hurt and no real damage will be done. He decided he would leave a warning with the people operating the gates so they would stop all traffic over it and evacuate the area. That idea made him feel better, no one would get hurt and his gesture would be anonymous, but it would get attention, he was sure of that.

An hour out of town he found the turn he was looking for. The only way he was able to see the old track to a former diamond drill site was an old winch from the rig, sitting abandoned about ten paces off the side of the road, rusting atop a flat section of the rock shelf. A long section of rusted wire rope was still attached to the winch drum, a ragged snake, gradually oxidizing into the air.

The track dipped steeply off the side of the road between a copse of aspen trees, their roundish, trembling leaves beginning to turn yellow, a sign of an early autumn. The old Volkswagen bounced and creaked as it crept over the track, branches scraping along it's side like dry, probing fingers as it neared the river. He stopped the car and stepped out into the silence. A gentle breeze caressed his face and he could smell the stench of newly rotted vegetation. The river was much higher than it had been before, nearly reaching the spot where he had re-buried the plastic containers of explosives. He unstrapped the kayak from the car and laid it in the high grass and reeds. With a small spade he dug carefully next to a tree he had marked with a knife and quickly found the cache of explosives, along with the alarm clock, electronic flash capacitor and detonating cap. In a separate bag were two 12 gauge shotgun shells, the pellets removed, but the wadding still in place.

Opening several of the heavy, black plastic bags, usually used to contain photographic paper, he was pleased to see that the orange granules of Amex were still dry. The bags gave off an unmistakable smell of petroleum. As he removed each bag and checked it for moisture, he carefully re-sealed it and inserted it down inside the hull of the River Runner kayak. Using a long piece of dead branch, he managed to gently shove 15 of the black bags into each side of the hull, front and rear, being careful not to break the flaps closed with fibreglass tape. The last item, the timer and capacitor, were wrapped in a black bag of their own and set behind the cockpit seat. A large green garbage bag was put over the cockpit and sealed around the rim with more fibreglass tape. He felt there was no way moisture could get inside. With considerable effort he dragged the kayak near a tree and with a bicycle cable and lock, secured it to the tree. He then covered the hull with a camouflage material like that used by hunters to construct hunting blinds. Several paces into the bush, he cut a half-dozen small saplings at their base and jammed them into the muddy river bank, near the camouflaged kayak, hoping their leaves would obscure it even more from view. He stepped back to admire his work, hoping the grass that had been packed down by the car's tires would eventually straighten enough to hide the fact he had been there.

He estimated the distance from here to the control gates over the Black Wood River at about 10 kilometres each way. In one week's time there would be a full moon. He prayed for clear skies. A movement caught his eye and he turned quickly. Twenty paces away sat a raven, still as a piece of black sculpture, except for the eyes which observed him with a frightening intelligence. He hadn't realised he had been holding his breath for some time and finally released it with a whoosh.

The raven cocked its head toward him, emitted a guttural croak, opened its beak as though about to speak, and flew lazily to the other side of the river.

He lost sight of the bird and moved as if in a dream to his car. He managed to turn the car around in the tight confines of the bush and approached the main road slowly, listening for any on-coming traffic. Hearing none, he eased onto the road and as he turned for town, he re-set the trip odometer of the car so he would know the exact distance to the turn-off when he had to return in the dark, one week later. He saw a discarded drink can by the roadside, stopped, filled it with gravel and placed it on the rocky outcropping, next to the turn-off. It would be a secondary means of finding the site in the dark, should he misread the odometer.

He could feel the momentum increasing. He was no longer in stasis. His thoughts had generated actions and his actions would precipitate consequences. It was the consequences that concerned him. A hundred pounds of explosives being detonated was bound to create considerable consequences, to say nothing of the noise. He noted the exact distance he had come as he approached the Bailey bridge on the outskirts of town.

With that errand done, he put his mind to the task of preparing his camera equipment for the freelance job with Samantha Paige. He remembered the way she had looked that night in her hotel room, her shapely legs and large breasts under her blouse. He began to get an erection in the car until he recalled her comment on finding the lint in his belly-button. The erection deflated quickly and no matter how he tried mentally, it wouldn't return. As he drove, his right hand unconsciously explored his navel for lint.

Later that Friday afternoon, he sat alone at a table in the 'Stagger Inn'. His beer had hardly been touched in front of him and he was oblivious of the generally drunken chaos around him. He had customarily chosen a table where he could sit with his back to the wall, able to observe any kind of behaviour that might jeopardize his health, such as hastily thrown ashtrays or pool cues.

"How come you look so sad an' everybody else looks so happy?" Big Don Bunkerfort from the explosives depot stood like a large, blonde tree, looking down at him. He had a benign, slightly curious drunken grin on his face. "I hear ya got canned, an' from what I hear, that's reason to celebrate." He sat down across from Bardman and leaned forward over the table, his hands in his lap, nearly resting his huge chin on the table top. "You gonna drink that or just stare at it?" he said in his typical soft drawl.

He smiled and took a sip of his warm beer. "Just thinking Don. Sometimes it gets the better of me."

"This is a drinkin' establishment Mr. photographer, thinkin' is not allowed, it just gits in the way of the drinkin', so drink up an' turn off that over-heated brain of yours." He removed his baseball cap from a huge partially bald blond head and waved it toward the bar as though trying to drive off a horde of mosquitoes.

Seconds later Natasha arrived with a huge tray of beer that dwarfed her tiny frame.   Bardman had been amazed at the strength of the tiny blonde woman, not only physical, but mental. She worked every evening until closing, serving patrons, mostly men who were trying to relieve boredom, perhaps escape from the stresses of the job, domestic life, or perhaps the sense of living in a community which was a long way from everywhere else.

She saw them drinking their lives away, wasting a freedom she and her husband had to fight for before escaping their homeland. The fact she was helping feed the hunger that ate the souls of these men depressed her and the only way she could reconcile herself to it, was to offer a bit of humanity in a place that served dehumanizing beverages.

"Mr. photographer, how do I make tip when you don't drink beer?" She stood with one hand on a hip, the heavy tray resting on Big Don's shoulder, supported by the other hand beneath it. She managed to wink at both of them at the same time. "Good veddink for boss's daughter eh? Good idea to bring crazy man. Friend of yours?"

Bardman shook his head without telling her the crazy man was now scattered in pieces in a dingy drift underground. He realised her husband who had been on the electric locomotive that day had said nothing about the incident to her. He watched her put another beer in front of him and a couple for Big Don, all of which Big Don paid for. He gave her his customary pat on the bottom as she left, to which she customarily slapped his hand and gave them another wink before disappearing into the jangling smokiness of the room.

Big Don had his hat tipped to the back of his head where it threatened to fall off. His chair was also tipped back while he cradled his beer glass between massive hands resting it on his stomach. He watched Bardman, squinting through eyes that were beginning to water from the dense cigarette smoke. In the smoky background near the wall, two men, unsteady on their feet were having a heated argument at the pool table. He hoped there wouldn't be a fight. He hated violence and was glad that his imposing size was usually enough to deter anyone from fighting him. One of the men stumbled against the juke box and Randy Travis briefly sang in an uncustomary warble. He tipped his chair back onto the front legs and slowly slid his huge torso part way onto the table. His hands pushed the beer glass across the small, circular surface, until it reached the centre. His eyes, nearly at the same level as the glass, appeared to the amber liquid for impurities as he spoke. "Ya hear about the boss at North Haul?"

"Winky?" Bardman's wandering attention came back to Big Don.

"Yep, the cops bust his butt the other day fer illegal and unsafe loads. They caught him with a mixed load of powder and found out he wasn't even qualified to drive the rig. They impounded the rig after they unloaded it back at the depot and now he's probably sittin', sweatin' bullets back at his office."

He could envision the fat, pasty-faced little man in a near-panic. "Teri said he made them carry mixed loads all the time. How come you guys never reported it before?"

Big Don shrugged his shoulders. "We had our orders from the bosses too, they just said load' em an' look the other way, because if we didn't, they said another explosives supplier could be found real easy, an' we'd all be out of a job."

"Who gave you these orders?"

"Our bosses. But you know who their bosses are don't-cha?"

"Who?"

"The hydro people. Hell they're usin' hundreds of tons of the stuff up there now with plans for a couple more dams in the next five years. We got the contract for this one but there's no guarantee we'll get the next one. We piss 'em off, we're toast, so we were told to just load 'em an' look the other way."

"So Winky got nailed. How did the cops find out?"

Big Don leaned forward again, a quiet malevolence in his eyes.

The closer the big man's face came, the farther Bardman leaned back in his chair.

"I called 'em. Found out the fat little turd was gonna load cylinders of oxygen an' acetylene on the back-end to drop off at the control gate project on the way out. I like that girl that drives for 'em an' that partner of hers, Joe. Their asses have been out flappin' in the breeze too long, an' it's time somebody gave 'em a break."

"Anybody else know about this phone call?"

"The cops don't know it was me but I'm sure they'd know my voice. Don't matter, I'm gettin' sick of this place. Too many chiefs an' not enough Indians. An' I know you got somethin' up your sleeve too Mr. photographer. Oh, don't look so surprised an' innocent. We know how much powder is missin', an' I know how ya feel about the rivers and lakes here. That lady friend of yours says a few things while we load her truck an' she thinks you're up to somethin' too. An' ya know what?" Big Don's face was nearly halfway across the small table, his chin nearly resting in a small puddle of spilled beer from his glass inches from his nose.

"What?" asked Bardman, who nervously slid his chair backwards a few more inches.

"I don't give a fiddler's fuck what happens to that powder, just as long somethin' is done to show certain people who think they run this world that other people might have somethin' to say about it. An that's all I have to say on that."

Big Don had returned to a normal sitting position and promptly downed his beer in two long gulps. Without saying more, he rose ponderously from the table, belched once and walked unsteadily to the exit.

He sat, slightly stunned, unaware that his thoughts and actions were so obvious to those whom he thought were not perceptive of his intentions. What surprised him was their apparent approval that something, anything be done. He realised his actions were not going be a statement of just one man, but possibly the actions of a spokesman for many, for those who felt helpless against the momentum of government and big business. *God, I'm becoming an eco-terrorist.* The thought scared him as he watched the receding back of the huge man. He looked around the dingy room to see if anyone had been watching the exchange between them. He realised the bar had been the ideal place to meet, so many others creating noise and drunken disruption, that it would have been impossible to overhear their conversation.

He could see one man asleep or passed out at an adjacent table. His drinking partners simply saw it as an opportunity to drink the man's untouched beer. A heated argument was in progress at the pool table between several men, each with cue in hand, pointing accusingly at a ball on the table, yelling at the top of their lungs, as though admonishing the ball for some wrongful action. They were in competition with the juke box, and the moans of Hank Williams Junior complaining about tears in his beer overpowered them with a twanging clangour. The noise, stench of stale beer, and smoke became too much for him and he quickly departed the scene of alcohol-induced insanity. He left the bar feeling dirty, badly in need of a shower to be rid of the stench of cigarette smoke. He thought it might be a good way to clear his mind before organizing his camera gear before picking up Samantha at the airport the next morning.

He woke early Saturday morning, electing to have coffee and some breakfast at the airport coffee counter. He always enjoyed the activity of the arriving and departing aircraft. When he had been fourteen years old, he joined the Royal Canadian Air Cadets due to his interest in aircraft. He hadn't realised that most of what 320 Squadron would teach was drill and how to spit-shine his high topped shoes. He gradually came to enjoy the demands of marching in formation, obeying instantly the shouted commands of the skinny Warrant Officer Second Class, whose rimless glasses tended to slide down his nose every time he bellowed an order. Most of all he enjoyed the sounds of the aircraft at the joint air training centre where pilots from the air force and navy were learning basic and advanced flying.

From inside the large aircraft hangar number 5, where their inspection parades were held, the whine of jet and piston engines could be heard as they roared on take-off, did a circuit and landed again. It added a sense of purpose to their stomping around, sometimes referred to as "Looking like ruptured crabs," by the Warrant Officer who often shook his head in disgust and in frustration turned the rabble over to his huge Flight Sergeant.

An ear-splitting bellow made Bardman turn his head as he drove to the airport. To his right was the float-plane base where the newly risen sun painted the water a rippled orange.

The morning mist swirled behind the twin-engine Beechcraft 18 as it moved up onto the step of its floats, the twin Lycoming engines battering the air with the sound of its propellers and exhaust.

He slowed the car and watched it lift off, perhaps on its way to supply some bush camp or haul a load of fish from one of the many fish camps, further north. It was at times like this he wished he had taken advantage of the flying scholarship available through the air cadets. The inherent rebellious nature and raging hormones of a teenager often overpowered any discipline to apply it to flying, although his interest had always manifested itself in the many balsa-wood models he had built.

Perhaps he had subconsciously realised the futility of endeavouring to learn to fly, since not one of his models ever achieved anything resembling prolonged flight. Instead, a schoolmate and he took great delight in producing their own home made gunpowder and, blowing some of the models to smithereens, after being launched by hand, on a short trajectory from the roof of the house in Quick Ville.

Neighbours had complained of loud explosions, followed by smoking tatters of balsa wood and paper, wafting with the wind onto their yards. The fact that an occasional grass fire had resulted in the calling out of the volunteer fire department soon squelched any further plans for demolition of more of the semi-flying models. It had also become a spectator sport with kids from all over town passing the word that another model was about to meet its demise in a blaze of glory. He felt it had been divine intervention that he never fell off the roof of his parent's house, much to the regret of some of his neighbours.

As he walked from the parking lot to the small air terminal, he watched an old, oil-streaked DC-3, sitting on the tarmac as the pilot checked the magnetos. The engines revved in turn, then dropped back to an idle as it sat on the approach ramp to the one runway. Not far away sat a red and white Twin Otter as well as a couple of single-engine otters, the workhorses of bush flying and the largest single-engine aircraft in the world. Parked inside one hangar was a huge Canadair CL-215, a water bomber renowned and used all over the world to drop water on forest fires. It resembled a huge red and yellow boat with wings, squatting on over-sized tires that folded out from its boat-shaped belly.

One stool was available at the counter where he ordered fried eggs, hash browns and toast, along with coffee. An easy banter was going on between the patrons, many of them pilots, and the waitress.

The waitress was a fresh-faced and full-figured young girl who had made it clear that she would do almost anything to get a ride in plane. As a result, a majority of the salivating done by the pilots had nothing to do with the food.

Some of the pilots were unshaven and bleary-eyed, the result of 5 am take-offs, preceded by the pre-flight activities. Many of them had been up since 3 am and the breakfast was more like lunch to them. Some were grumbling about having to make several more trips before the day was finished and not wanting to use the autopilot. The joke was that none of the small aircraft had autopilots, but rather the pilot simply trimmed his aircraft for the most stable flight, pointed it in the right direction, and dozed-off for several minutes at a time. Had they been equipped with transponders and on anyone's radar scope, the radar operator would have been aghast to see various aircraft wandering around the sky, losing or gaining altitude at random, suddenly to be jerked back on course by its fatigued pilot. Most air services up there were referred to as the 'white knuckle' variety, and only the most brave or desperate chartered them for anything other than hauling cargo.

The airport Public Address system crackled to life with the sound like a needle being poorly placed on a scratchy record. Every third word was interrupted by an electronic crackle and hum. "Flight 03 fr...humm, crackle, ..peg, now arriving. All...crackle crackle, needing ass...hum...your boarding pass to the...hummm, crackle..attendant.

"Lori, you got a real sexy voice. Ya ever thought of bein' one of those stewardi?" said one of the older pilots at the counter.

"Oh you..." giggled Lori from the far end of the counter where she held the microphone in one hand and the pot of coffee in the other. Her finger still depressed the transmit button on the microphone, and her giggled reply crackled over the speakers.

"Can I say hi to my mom? She's sittin' right over there. She said I should always be on radio," asked another of the now blushing waitress.

"You guys keep giving me a hard time, I'm not gonna give you refills." she walked the length of the counter, hands on hips, daring them to continue the teasing.

"What's 'Panic Air' flying in today Lori, another one of them little Japanese YS-11's that won't allow passengers over five feet to fly in them?" came a query from the far end of the counter. He was a large man with a propeller insignia on the front of his greasy baseball cap.

"I dunno, Ralph, all I know is it's got two wings an' a little, bitty tail."

"Well Lori, if you need a little-bit-a tail, you just put down that microphone there, an' we'll fly to heaven together."

The entire length of patrons at the counter broke out in laughter, a couple of them with mouths full of coffee, sprayed the liquid on their neighbours in their attempts to laugh and swallow at the same time.

One man had got up and was peering out the main window of the terminal. "Kamikaze on final," was all he said, prompting the entire counter-line of patrons to get to their feet and join their colleague.

"Wonder who's flyin' it today?" said one.

"We'll soon see," replied Ralph, his hat now turned backwards so he could put his nose on the glass, watching the twin-engine turbo-prop aircraft, it's landing gear lowered and beginning to settle gently to the runway.

Half-way down the runway the aircraft became airborne again and proceeded to bounce twice more on tires that screeched each time they met the surface. A couple of the onlookers said, "Boing, boing, boing," in unison.

Almost in one voice, the men let out a long whooping sound. "It's Boing Weger, Christ, they let him fly again." said one man with awe in his voice.

"Musta gone on a diet," said another. "Hell they suspended him because he was so fat he couldn't haul the controls back far enough to flare out on final, damn near flew straight into the ground a couple of times."

Bardman moved with the others outside the terminal, into the warm morning sunshine. He caught the aroma of jet exhaust as the aircraft taxied toward them, its engines making the high-pitched sound like that of smooth metal surfaces being rubbed together at high speed.

The left side cockpit window slid open and a huge arm extended and waved at the group. The group laughed in unison at seeing the salutation of their overweight friend at the controls. The propellers, twin shining discs reflecting the sunlight, slowed and stopped.

He watched the passengers debark from the exit, down the mobile steps which had been rolled to the fuselage of the aircraft. He finally saw the red hair of Samantha Paige, partially obscured by a large man in a buckskin jacket who appeared to stagger slightly as he descended.

"Looks like Boing is still gittin' his passengers drunk to keep 'em calm," said the big man with the propeller on his cap.

"Well, it worked for Boing, it's the only way he'd get behind the controls anymore." The man who spoke wore the dirty coveralls of a mechanic and his face held no humour when he spoke.

The others didn't reply, but cast wary glances at the man and then back at the aircraft, wondering if he spoke the truth.

Bardman had seen the landing on the uneven runway. At the halfway point, the aircraft had encountered the small rise in the hard surface where permafrost, the permanently frozen muskeg had begun to thaw, creating the mound. The pilots referred to it as Holy Shit Hill because the first time a pilot encountered it and realised his aircraft was airborne again, his first reaction was to say "Holy shit!"

"Hey, how's my favourite photographer?" Sam stood before him, her hair pulled back in a ponytail, a bag slung from her shoulder, containing her notepads and tape recorder.

"Hello Sam. The usual, under exposed and over developed. How was the flight?"

"It's no wonder they refer to it as Panic Air. You know what the pilot said over the intercom just before we took off from Winnipeg?"

"I can't imagine, I avoid this airline like anthrax."

She rummaged through her shoulder bag as they walked into the terminal.

He became aware that every male gaze was fixed on the young reporter and the shortness of her skirt.

She was blissfully unaware as she continued to rummage. "He called back and asked if anyone had today's newspaper, and if so, would they give it to the flight attendant. So I had one from work and gave it to her and she hustles up to the cockpit with it. I asked her what she did with it when she came back and she said the pilot wanted to check the weather."

Bardman laughed.

"Hey, it's not funny and she didn't crack a smile when she said it. Aha, found it." She waved a receipt with the car rental logo in the air as though driving away flies. "I got the Winnipeg office to reserve a car for us."

They walked to the rental desk where a blackboard serving as a message centre had written upon it in chalk, 'It never hurts to rent a Hertz'.

"Shit, it's the same piece of junk I had last time, full of dust and...cripes, look, my old chewing gum wrappers are still on the floor." She looked around the car rental lot, realising theirs was the only car there. "What do they have, just one car to rent?" It was the same old Plymouth with a newly cracked windshield, the ashtray was full and beer bottle caps lay on the rear floor mats.

Bardman drove as she settled in and watched the scenery. She seemed genuinely glad to be there, perhaps, he hoped, glad to see him as much as getting out of the city.

"Pull over here, I think it's safe now." She waved her hand toward the shoulder of the gravel road.

"Safe for what?"

"This, "she replied, reaching into her shoulder bag and extracting an envelope. "Open it."

He saw the smile in her eyes as he opened the envelope. His jaw dropped when he saw the cheque. He had to look twice to confirm the amount. He looked at Sam and she giggled at his expression of disbelief.

"And that's just for starters partner, I got a cheque for $5,000 too. Look at the covering letter. They say that we each get another five-thousand on completion of the story along with the last shots you took underground of that guy blowing himself up. Your shots alone are going to get a double-page spread in full colour and they may even use it in more than one issue." She leaned over and kissed him on the cheek. "Stick with me big guy, we're gonna be rich! "

He continued to stare at the cheque from World Wide Publishing Corp. He noticed the address from Los Angeles. "You should have told me Sam. At least we should have talked about it, I mean these are my shots, in fact it's my story too and I should have some say how it's used."

They sat quietly in the car, each trying to read the other's thoughts.

"I know Brady," she replied quietly. "But I followed a hunch and I knew I had to do it quickly. This tabloid isn't even carried in Winnipeg as far as I know, but it has affiliates all over the world and the market is endless. I have the contacts and I know you don't so I became your marketing department. I just assumed a split down the middle would be okay. It is isn't it?"

He saw the apprehension in her eyes and reached to squeeze her hand. "Yeah, it's okay. I guess I just like to have more sense of control over my work and my life in general. Honestly Sam, I'm really thankful for what you've done, and the split is fine. Hell ten-thousand dollars isn't rich is it? But at it's a lot more than I have now."

She smiled again but with a hint of sadness, remembering he had just been fired and undergone a traumatic experience recently. "Brady, the potential of this story is much more than you realize. World Wide is paying us just for one-time publication rights. Look it's right there in the letter. That constitutes a contract. After that, if any of their affiliates want to pick up the story, they will pay us the same rates as the first payment. They have offices on three different continents and the Features Editor, that's his name at the top is going to courier a copy of this to each of their head offices there. If they pick it up, bingo, another cheque for the full amount will be re-issued or deposited in a bank of your choice before publication. Brady, we could each come out of this with forty or fifty-thousand dollars yet. So, now what do you say, partner?"

He stared at the cheque. "Do you believe these people are going to do all this for us? For god's sake Sam, they're way down there and we're up here. What's to stop them from just running the stories with fake names and not paying us a cent?"

She reached across and poked the cheque with a long, manicured fingernail. "Mine didn't bounce, I don't expect yours will either. I know what you're saying because I cashed mine the instant I got it. That was a week ago."

"All the same, I'm going to do a bounce test on this as soon a we get back."

"You're a cautious man Bardman and I don't blame you. But consider that those people use almost exclusively freelance stuff from all over the world. If they failed to pay for a story like this, how many writers and photographers would continue to send them stuff? They'd be goosing their own golden egg."

He shrugged with resignation and turned the car back onto the gravel road, tasting the dust kicked up by passing trucks as he spoke. "I wasn't born a sceptic y'know, it was forced on me by this business."

She nodded in silent agreement as she admired the wildness of the forest passing on each side of them, feeling the warm sunshine on her bare arm as it rested on the edge of the window. She had begun to envy Brady and his proximity to the nature he loved, the lack of rush hour, and fresh clean air to breathe. At least, she thought, as fresh as the refinery smelter stack would allow with the tons of particulate spewing from its three-hundred foot height. On previous visits she had caught whiffs of the sulphur-dioxide that originated in the roasters and when an inversion layer moved into the area, the colder, heavier air sat over the warm lower one, arching the fumes toward the ground like a river of airborne acid. Her nasal passages and eyes would burn, exposed skin itched, and birds were seen to drop from the sky as though shot. Sometimes they were even dead before they hit the ground. She knew the previous stack had been half the height of the current one, creating the terrible conditions on a regular basis until the populace began to complain. Now, the extra height simply allowed the gases and dust to travel much further, coming to rest where the town couldn't see the damage done to the lakes and trees hundred of miles downwind.

Now that he no longer worked for the 'Company', she had considered enlisting his help in doing an environmental story on the effects of all the effluents insinuating themselves into the eco-system.

She realised it wasn't just his talent with a camera that attracted her. She was attracted by his lack of verbosity. He didn't speak unless he had something to say. It was a refreshing change from the gibbering office workers that frequented the bars in the Old Market section of Winnipeg. Suits with drunken attitudes was the way she saw them, always on the make, whether it was for money or a bimbo.

She had stopped going with her co-workers for the customary Friday Beer & Leer as her licentious managing editor liked to refer to it. God knows, he had leered at her enough to the point where she dreaded being called into his office for some trivial news-related conversation, only to endure his searching eyes. She knew he was undressing her in his imagination by the way his face flushed and he squirmed in his chair behind his desk. She breathed deeply and pushed the thoughts from her mind, revelling in the aroma of the flowers along the roadside. Within minutes she was sound asleep, her head bouncing gently against the doorpost as images of blue sky and green forests crept into fitful sleep.

Bardman had watched her fall asleep. He sensed her watching him, wondering what was going through her mind. He was glad he didn't have to talk while driving, preferring to watch the beauty of the countryside. With sadness he realised his days here were numbered. There was no way for an unemployed photographer to make a living here unless it was within one of the mining or transportation industries. He was going to miss the early-morning and evening paddles with the kayak. There had been few places that had cleansed his soul so completely of the mental and emotional filth he accumulated from the industrial nature of his employment.

Two hours later, Samantha woke, bleary-eyed and stiff as the car jounced over the rough road which skirted the edge of the planned forebay. She stared down the incline at the stumps where the trees had been clear-cut logged from the area to be flooded. The air was full of blue wood smoke where the remnants of unmarketable trees had been burned. She had never seen a war zone but thought it might look something like this, instead of human bodies, the bodies of trees were disposed of like so many corpses from a death camp.

"Ugly."

"Yeah, that's the beauty of progress isn't it? They can hide all this under water and in a few years time it'll seem as if it never existed." Bardman watched the desolation as he guided the car around a large pothole. The smell of ashes was strong in the air. He sneezed a couple of times. His eyes began to water from the smoke as he stopped the car and retrieved a camera from his bag in the back seat. He could see there was much more water in the forebay than the last time they had been here. He felt a sense of urgency, as though the rising waters measured the time remaining in which he could act. He took several exposures, the stumps silhouetted trough the blue smoke. A huge tractor-trailer with a load of logs loomed around a bend and blasted its air horn at him as it covered them in yellow dust that settled on the windshield. He had to turn on the windshield wipers as he and Samantha simultaneously rolled up their side windows. The interior was soon hot as an oven, but he didn't want the talcum-like dust to invade his cameras, or they would seize up and cost a fortune to clean.

At the company parking lot, their feet sank into the spongy black asphalt, radiating the heat of the sun through the soles of their feet, sticking like bunker oil to their shoes.

She appeared horrified at the black muck on her flat-heeled shoes, afraid to touch them with her hands. "This must be how the dinosaurs felt when they fell into the tar pits," she said, trying to scrape the black ooze away with a stick. She made a face as she flung the stick away.

They walked to the guard shack where the rent-a-cop regarded them with a mixture of mirth and suspicion.

He recognized them as media people and knew how his bosses barely concealed their hostility toward those with prying questions and watchful eyes. It was one of the few pleasures he had in this job to use his officialdom to the limit. He asked for several kinds of identification and media credentials, all the while looking from behind his sunglasses down the front of the young woman's blouse. The silent, direct stare from the heavy-set man with the dark curly hair and camera bag unnerved him. There was obvious hostility here and the man's stance with feet wide apart and large hands clenched into fists signalled that his delaying tactics had been played to the limit.

The information officer finally arrived with hard hats and visitor's badges. The rent-a-cop watched appreciatively as the young woman's pert behind moved under the tight skirt. With nothing further to do, he went back to his Louise L'Amour western novel, wishing he could have at least been issued a gun of his own. He was sure he wouldn't have to look too hard to find something to shoot around here.

It had been an un-noteworthy tour, except for the palpable tension from the information officer. He looked unfamiliar to Brady, the other he surmised had been either transferred or fired due to the pictures he had taken when the worker fell to his death.

The pouring of the reinforced concrete was finished, the workers now running electrical cables to and from the huge generators.

Every time he raised his camera, the tour guide flinched visibly, his eyes darting to where he was focused, possibly prepared to jump in front of the lens. He began to make a game of it, raising the camera, then suddenly lowering it, then just as suddenly raising it again. He could hear Samantha giggle quietly, realising how he was toying with the man. By the time the tour was over, the information officer's white shirt was plastered to his back with sweat and his reddened face glanced with open hostility at him.

"You know, you can really be cruel Bardman. I saw what you were doing with that poor flunky. You had him scared shitless." She smiled as she chastised him, trying to fill in her notes as the car bumped over the road.

"He was probably the most useless information officer I've ever seen," he replied. "It's obvious he was told to give us a tour but say nothing. Did you notice he didn't take us anywhere there was important work going on? Just people running around, cleaning up, trying to look busy for our benefit."

"I think we've worn out our welcome. I hope you managed to get at least something visual."

He was disappointed with the blandness of the subject matter presented to them. They hadn't been taken to the exterior of the upper structure for overall shots for what the tour guide referred to as safety reasons. He knew the desolation created by the logging around the forebay area would be the strongest image, one he was sure the tour guide and his superiors would prefer not to see published.

On the drive home they crossed over the control gates downstream from where the Black Wood and Muskrat Rivers joined. From the roadway over the gates, they could see the sun lowering over the brackish water which was backing into both of the tributaries, inundating even more of the river bank. For miles the waters backed up, eventually to be freed by the gates in a controlled flow to flood the forebay of the hydro project and create that patented insult to nature, the man-made lake.

He could see the reflection of the sun from a solitary canoe in the quiet waters. He slowed the car and saw the lone paddler sitting still as a statue. On the bow of the canoe sat the form of a raven, facing the paddler. He thought he could see the beak of the bird moving as though speaking to the man holding the paddle across his lap. As they neared the far end of the control gate road, he thought he caught a glimpse of each of the canoe's occupants turn in his direction. He wondered why he didn't seem surprised to see a raven perched on the canoe's bow. He also knew without doubt that the lone canoeist was the old trapper, Abe McKay.

"You know, sometimes I think I come way up here just for the sunsets." Samantha had spoken with her nose pressed against the glass of the passenger-side window. She had rolled it up to block the clouds of dust from oncoming traffic, mostly, huge transport and gravel trucks which often forced them onto the shoulder of the road.

He quietly chastised himself for not stopping to get a shot of Abe Mckay in his canoe. How often do you see a canoeist with a raven perched on the bow? he asked himself. He slowed the car suddenly and began to turn in the middle of the road. He saw Sam glance questioningly at him. "That canoe with the raven would have made a great shot. I'm going to go back and get it now. I must be getting lazy," he said more to himself than his passenger.

"I didn't see any canoe."

"You didn't? Hell, it was right there on the bend, right in line with the setting sun. It'll make a great shot, especially with that raven sitting on the bow." The car was fast approaching the control gate structure again, encountering its own cloud of dust from the previous crossing.

"Brady I was looking at the sun as we came across and all I saw was sunset. There was no canoe."

"Sure there was, right on the bend, I'll show you where in a minute."

"You poor man. I've been working you too hard haven't I? Tell you what, after we get back, I'll buy the beer. My tongue feels like one of these trucks ran over it."

He stopped the car in the middle of the bridge and stared. There was no canoe and couldn't see how it might have been paddled out of visual range so quickly. The water was an orange mirror reflecting the colour from the sky, the trees and bull rushes along the flooded bank like dark sentinels, motionless in the still water. "What the..." he stared in disbelief. "It was there...right there." He pointed, nearly poking her in the nose in his haste to verify his sighting.

She studied where he pointed and shrugged her shoulders. "Well it isn't there now. How could you see something out there when you should have been watching the road? Why don't you let me drive Brady? I've been sitting here like a lump making you do all the work."

"No that's okay, I don't mind driving."

"You mean you don't trust women drivers."

"I didn't say that, it's just that I don't mind driving."

"You didn't have to say that. The fact is, I'm an excellent driver and you don't trust me because I'm a woman. Right?" Her voice had become hard as she stared directly at his face. She watched his expression turn to one of exasperation, wondering if she had pressed the issue too far. Screw it, she thought, let's get this out in the open, hoping this guy wasn't as chauvinistic as so many others she had known.

"It's just that you're not familiar with these roads and the conditions,' he replied, a sheen of sweat developing on his upper lip. The car was moving slowly to the far end of the structure where he planned to turn around to head home.

"Hey, it's just another road, except is has a few more rocks than normal. So what's the big deal?"

"Okay, okay, but I'll turn us around first, okay?"

"Fine, you turn us around Mr. Expert."

He had the car partway across the roadway when he saw the tractor-trailer unit approaching from the far end of the control gate. The truck's air horn was blasting and a cloud of dust from the trailer had obscured the road from where it had come. He pressed on the accelerator and it was at that moment the old Plymouth chose to stall with a gasping clunk.

"Brady, for Christ's sake!" Samantha had both hands placed on the dashboard as she heard the car's starter whine. The engine caught and the car spun it's tires in a spray of gravel, giving the now-braking semi barely enough room to avoid a collision.

As the truck roared past he became aware of two things: first was the driver giving him the finger, the second was the large sign on the side of the trailer which said, EXPLOSIVES.

"Brady!"

"Okay, okay, show me what an excellent driver you are, it's all yours."

She quickly slid over behind the wheel as he walked around to the passenger side, glancing quickly upriver. The canoe was there again, but without the raven. He suddenly felt his bladder lose control and he quickly unzipped and urinated into the dust of the shoulder.

The car horn sounded, resulting in him getting a wet right hand. He got back in the car, discreetly wiping his hand on the seat cover near the door.

"It's not fair, I've been wanting to go for the last half hour and you just hop out and write your name in the dust whenever you feel like it," declared Sam with an injured whine.

"I like to think of it as poetic justice," he grumbled, continuing to dry his hand secretly on the seat-cover. He returned the silent gesture of her Protruding tongue with his own, and to their mutual surprise they broke out in laughter. It also came to his surprise that she really was an excellent driver and it wasn't long before the sound of the road lulled him to sleep.

"God, this road's even got Sunday drivers now. Why can't they stay in town and go to church or something?" Teresa clutched the truck's wheel tightly, her pulse still racing at the close call on the control gate.

"Shoulda hit' im," muttered Joe. "That way we mighta got a new truck." His cowboy boots were propped on the dusty dashboard as usual, his peaked cap pulled down over his eyes, nearly resting on his prominent nose. He had grown his black hair even longer, and it hung in two braids, one over each shoulder, nearly reaching his waist. His hands rested on his stomach, playing with his belt buckle, a huge, tarnished brass shield depicting a slavering trucker, half out of the vehicle's window. Around the perimeter of the buckle were the words, If you ain't truckin' you ain't shit.

"Yeah, and we could be tuning harps on a cloud if we had," replied D'Amico.

"I always wondered how they got those damn things up there."

"Same way with people, Joe, give 'em wings."

"Flyin' harps, sounds too dangerous, think I'll stay right here."

She chuckled. She was glad that next week was her last trip before taking a week's holidays before reporting to the RCMP training facility at Regina. "You know Joe, I'm really going to miss our talks. You have a knack for seeing the humorous side of things. I'm also glad you got rid of the note to Winky about quitting so we could do this last trip together."

"That's because sometimes the humorous side is the only one worth seein', an I didn't think it would be funny if you had to do it alone." He had watched the river as they had crossed the control gates, seeing his father's canoe resting on the water. His only defence against crushing depression had been his sense of humour, able to crack dry jokes about most things which were painful to him. It prevented others from seeing his pain, but he was having difficulty hiding the pain that had resulted from the plight of his people, and more personally that of his father.

Three nights ago he stood before the elders of the Band Council. Each of them had listened quietly as he expressed his desire to return to the reserve. Because he had been so long away, his Cree was inadequate. A result of the dictates of the Catholic Brothers who prohibited the use of their native tongue. He retained the scars, mental and physical over the battle of wills between his culture and their religion. He realised the battle wasn't over, possibly never would be, but it was a battle worth fighting.

He knew that most of the reserve's people were on welfare, their traditional hunting, trapping and fishing destroyed by the hydro project. He had been surprised when his idea to start his own trucking company, based in Hudson House rolled off his tongue. He had no idea where the thought had originated, but the more he improvised his plans to the elders, the more they appeared to nod and confer in low voices between themselves. It would be a company financed with hydro flood compensation money, after the white lawyer received his ten percent commission, and it would haul all freight destined for the reserves. The other reserves would hopefully boycott the other companies in favour of their own. The only condition was that no materials, explosive or otherwise would be carried for the hydro project, no matter how lucrative.

They all seemed to agree on that matter of principle. In fact it was all an agreement in principle, grandiose plans that proposed some form of hope where hope had been profoundly absent.

That evening his father sat and smoked quietly beside him, sitting on the wooden steps of the school. They had heard voices muttering from inside, the occasional raised voice, and the scrape of a chair on the wooden floor as someone stood to speak.

"I thought it would be easier than this," he said to his father.

"They don't know you. They only know you been comin' here for healin', that's what Angus is sayin' to 'em right now."

"Your hearin's that good?"

"Nope, but that's what I'd be sayin' right now if I was him."

433

Joe watched his father's leathery hands as they rolled another cigarette while the limp remains of the other one hung from the side his father's mouth like a smoldering brown flap of skin. "You an' Angus go way back."

Abe nodded, staring at the sky where northern lights were beginning to flicker above the treetops. The twilight was dying quickly, the days visibly growing shorter. He had already seen formations of Canada geese winging south, their calls haunting him with a message to join them in their travels. "Gonna be an early winter," he said to the northern lights. The wispy green curtain shimmered and flickered as if in reply.

From the edge of the forest a raven warbled, its song echoing into the darkness. A dog barked several houses away and soon the whole neighbourhood was treated to a canine chorus. An hour later they had been summoned into the school house and told that Joe's application had been accepted.

The next day Abe had taken the canoe and fishing rod, hoping to hook a nice pickerel or white fish for his supper. He had spent the first several hours in the early morning with no result except a half-hearted nibble that made his lure bob and weave for a few seconds. At dusk he headed back out with the canoe onto the Black Wood River and sat in the glow of the lowering sun as his line lay in the water.

Even the prime wild rice areas had been flooded, depriving him of the tasty grain which dropped from its tall stalks into the canoe at harvest time. For as long as he could remember there was wild rice to eat with the fish, now it too was gone, if not severely depleted. With his leg bracing the fishing rod against the gunwale of the canoe, he closed his eyes and slept.

The mist still swirled about the canoe as he paddled toward the shore but now the shoreline was barely visible.   A strange framework was there, like the red skeleton of a long house, without a roof. Inside the skeleton rested the body of the white creature, massive and still.

As he paddled closer he could see that this time the image was not just reflected in the water, but could also be seen in reality as well as in reflection. He wondered which was real, the reflection or the original image. The mist was cold and damp on the nape of his neck, like a wet cloth. He shivered.

He climbed upon the shiny creature where it lay still, his rifle in his hand. The creature exuded a strange pungent smell, an alien stench as though rotting everything it touched. He raised the rifle, pointing it down at the unmoving side of the creature. He heard a voice shout his name. In the distance he saw his son running toward him, his mouth open. . He smiled and waved at his son, trying to reply but the words refused to

come. He pumped the slide of the rifle to chamber a round and pointed it between his feet
at the skin of the creature, feeling his finger tighten on the trigger.

The blast of the horn jolted him awake, nearly making him capsize the canoe. He could see the tractor-trailer barrelling across the control gate, swerving at the last minute to avoid the car. He smiled to himself when he saw the truck driver raise a finger to the car's occupants who were obviously shaken by the experience. A movement caught his eye and he turned to see a large raven perched on the bow of his canoe. It too had been watching the truck. The raven turned its large head and prominent beak toward him. Its intelligent eyes regarded him quietly, unblinking, and with the sound of dry feathers, flew away into the darkening sky.

He reeled in his line, the bait untouched. He was filled with an inner peace the likes of which he had seldom experienced except for the rare occasion in the sweat lodge. His stomach would not be full this evening but his mind was filled with quiet anticipation.

As he paddled the few miles upriver he watched the orange upper fringe of the sun as it settled behind the trees.

Far overhead a jet at high altitude traced white condensation trails arrow straight against the dark velvet blue of the sky. The sun glinted in a sudden, final flash from its underbelly.

Turning gently in the canoe toward the east, he could see over his shoulder, the moon beginning to rise. The dark splotches of the craters littered its silvery surface. Almost a full moon, he thought to himself, something for the wolves and coyotes to howl at.

He could remember the many evenings he had paddled upon the silvered waters of the river in the spring, hearing the croaks and whistles of the mating frogs. He could recall the occasions when at last light, a bullfrog would let forth with a loud woonk, one after the other as the smaller leopard frogs hesitated in their calls to appreciate the voice of a true maestro.

An object cut across the water in front of him, leaving a smooth wake on the glassy surface. As he approached, the flat tail of the beaver rose up and slapped the water in warning, then disappeared beneath the surface.

He had left instructions with Angus Spence that all his meagre possessions were to be left with his son, in the event of his death.

Angus had written it down, knowing his lifelong friend had never learned to read or write well, but was able to make his personal mark on the paper with a pen. He didn't ask the reason for the request, knowing that everyone at a certain stage of their life becomes more aware of their own mortality. He had seen a change in his friend ever since his son had asked to return to the reserve. He watched the river more, as did the whole community with a sense of trepidation and impotence. The whole reserve knew Joe drove a truck that supplied explosives to the project that was killing them. Better to have him here than there they thought. If they could have enough young people stay they might even find another teacher for the school. Maybes, mights and ifs were the only words of hope for them.

CHAPTER 22

Bardman dropped Samantha Paige off at the airport. The small building was packed with people who were either arriving, departing or just watching aircraft. It was a microcosm of a large international airport. Languages from all over the world could be heard, Greek, Spanish, Portuguese, French, and English, often in an unmistakable Newfoundland dialect.

To his surprise, Samantha gave him a hug and kiss on the cheek before boarding. It made him blush but his face quickly went pallid when he saw the malevolent glare of his former boss, Roger Jenkins. He was holding a shoulder bag belonging to his daughter, who was also boarding the plane. His daughter beside him was pallid for a different reason, fear of flying. Her acne stood out on her paper-white cheeks like splotches from a blue felt-tip pen. He saw Jenkins watching Samantha, suspecting they had been working together on a story. The fact it was no longer Jenkins' business was of small comfort due to the hostility of the man's stare.

When he arrived home there was a message on his answering machine in reply to his ad to sell his diesel Rabbit. For the last week he had been divesting himself of anything he couldn't pack on the motorcycle. He didn't think he would ever become attached to a car but the old Volkswagen had given years of trouble free use, seemingly developing a personality all its own. Luckily the apartment had come meagrely furnished, so there was no furniture to be rid of. His cookware and utensils went to a local church for distribution to the needy. All he kept were a knife and fork, one bowl, and a cup. All that remained was another kayak which he intended to give to Teresa. He soon wouldn't need it and thought it might be a nice going away present for her. He was amazed how a cheque for five-thousand dollars could make him feel benevolent.

The next day, Monday, he went to the bank, deposited the cheque, withdrew a thousand dollars in cash and traveller's cheques, then promptly had the account transferred to a branch in Winnipeg. The cashier regarded him with a hint of suspicion and reminded him that the newly deposited cheque may take a week to clear. That was okay with him, he figured there was about one week left before he was ready to head south. *I'm not just burning my bridges behind me, I'm going to blow them up!* With the promise of another warm fall day ahead of him, he had an urge to take one last paddle to the quiet tributary that he had come to love so much. He looked forward to again seeing that quiet pond where the trees seemed to talk to him. He knew it might be the last time he would ever see it.

Corporal Pusch sat in the brown Chevy van, watching the dust from the vehicle in front. The driver was the same RCMP officer from Winnipeg who had carried out the initial surveillance on the Bardman residence. Both the officers had been chagrined at the order to remove the electronic listening devices, restricting them to human surveillance. They had changed vehicles often, sometimes with a vehicle in front. Luckily, Bardman's habits had been regular and predictable, allowing them to plan a schedule which gave them both several hours sleep each night.

"Don't lose him in this dust Frank, I want to see where he goes with that kayak of his; at least I want to know where he turns off."

The driver grunted a reply as the wipers cleared the talcum-like powder from the windshield. "Don't worry, there's only a couple of places along this road for him to go. There, his brake lights are coming on. See, he's turning right, just past that large rock." The driver passed the Volkswagen as it turned onto a barely visible track. He slowed the van as Pusch, dressed in a brand new plaid shirt and fishing vest topped by a floppy hat, craned his long neck to the rear to get a better view. The hat was festooned with a myriad of fishing-flies and spoon lures which jangled each time he moved his head. He had neglected to return the points of the lures back to the outside of the hat, having them instead, lurking perilously close to his scalp, on the inside of the hat.

"Got 'im," said Pusch. "I can just see the car through the trees by the river's edge. Good thing his kayak's red or he might be hard to see." He brought a pair of small binoculars to his eyes, leaning out the passenger window, his moustache twitched with anticipation.

Frank watched, hoping his insufferable partner would fall out onto the ground and at least get some dirt on his sparkling-new disguise. He had seen Pusch's ill-concealed disgust when he realized his undercover partner from Winnipeg looked like a street punk from Portage and Main. In fact, that's exactly what he was supposed to have been. He had been pulled quickly out of an undercover job within a motorcycle gang when his cover appeared to be blown. His long unkempt hair, poor complexion and slim muscularity gave him the aura of being half-starved and slightly feral. The poor tattoo on the back of his hand, similar to those given in prison added to his persona, belying the fact he was a highly disciplined officer with years of martial arts training.

"You keep gawking and he's going to get suspicious."

"I'm the officer in charge here Frank, you just drive," said Pusch, trying to wipe the dust from the rear elements of the binoculars. "He's in the water and paddling upstream, too bad we don't have something to follow him with."

"How about the forces big spanking motorboat?"

"Very funny Frank, obviously you have a lot to learn about surveillance work. By the way, how did you manage to get accepted by the force at the ripe age of fourteen?"

"Strictly on I.Q. corporal. It seems it's double that of the average thirty year old."

"You don't say," replied Pusch, turning and looking at him with eyes that had become ringed with dust from the binocular eye-pieces. He looked slightly like a racoon with a red nose. "And what rank are you by the way?"

"In plain clothes we disregard rank. It could get you killed. Do you plan on sitting here all day or would you rather we push weeds up our bums and try and sneak up on him through the grass when he returns?"

"I'm sure you'd enjoy that Frank. Since we can't follow him, why don't we go for a pizza and stake out his place for the evening?" He waggled his moustache at him, wishing his pseudo-teenage partner would be less cynical and try and at least look like an RCMP officer. He didn't even drive like one, spinning gravel from the tires and neglecting to make directional signals. Had he any choice, he would have gladly flunked him on the basis of his driving skills alone to say nothing of his general lack of professionalism

Bardman paddled slowly, savouring the sunshine on his back. He could see the leaves of the ash and aspens beginning to turn yellow along the progressively flooding riverbank. Without conscious thought he made his way along the gentle curves of the river, seeing the drowning foliage along with the carcasses of several dead fish, their white bellies contrasting with the dark water. The kayak cut quietly through the water, gently shoving aside weeds and foliage which had at one time been on dry ground. It was a bit like paddling through a grave yard, the dry branches reaching for him like the hands of corpses, imploring him to bring them back to life.

I could just leave it all, walk away and do nothing. What point is there to making some dangerous gesture that might not achieve anything? I managed to get myself fired, maybe lost a good friend in Teri. Ah Teri, to think of the things that might have been if only the times had been different. There's a kayak full of explosives sitting under the grass up the road. I can't leave it there. Why not just wash it all down the river and blow this place? No, that would be pollution, what I plan to do is cleanse a place that's been defiled already. What did the old trapper say? Inaction is sometimes worse than the wrong action?

He glided quietly beneath the overhanging branches that formed an archway above him as the kayak slipped along the narrow tributary. It soon opened up onto the quiet waters of the pond where he had once camped and where he had learned the old trapper had spent his wedding night with his new bride. *Memories like that don't die, they linger like sweet mist between the trees.*

The bank where he had previously set up his tent on the rock shelf was nearly covered with the encroaching waters. The tall bull rushes on the other side were nearly covered, their dark heads now grey from wet and rot, like rotten fruit floating on the surface. There was a smell of decay, a rancid mustiness hung in the air, the malevolent stench of plant life that had been reduced to dark husks emitting methane and other swamp gases. He saw movement amongst the trees and realized he was looking at a moose which was staring back at him. It waggled its ears a couple of times, snorted and quietly walked away.

He quickly turned the kayak back toward the entrance, distraught at the changes he saw, when the sound of a sob made him stop. He turned back toward the tree line where the moose had been. He paddled quietly toward the shade of the trees. The sob came again, sounding like a sigh on the wind. The aroma of wood smoke and rawhide came to him. He felt like he had inhaled the ghost of a memory which was not his to breath. For the first time he felt like an interloper.

"Abe, is that you?" he said, barely above whisper. There was no reply except the trees rustling in a fresh breeze. He sat for long minutes, listening, hoping to see the old man but finally paddled disconsolately from the once beautiful pond. He knew he would never see it again and knew his personal world would be poorer for its loss.

By the time he arrived home it was nearly dark and didn't feel like cooking anything, least of all the usual Kraft dinner. Sometimes he poured it over toast and called it Kraft on a raft, chuckling at his own sense of humour as he ate it, sipping on a beer. This time he just had the beer, electing to order out for a pizza instead. He sat at the small kitchen table, feet propped on the table edge and chair tilted back. The lone bulb suspended over the table from the ceiling where the salmon coloured paint was cracking, barely illuminated the room. He mentally went over his preparations for the control gate. There was no longer any doubt in his mind what he was going to do.

The door buzzer startled him. He went up the stairs and saw a skinny pizza delivery boy balancing a flat cardboard box in one hand. He ate it with the help of another beer and then went outside to the rear of the building where his kayak rested against the back wall.

He had caught a glimpse of the Chevy van parked several houses away and wondered why he had never seen anyone come or go from the adjoining house. He was sure he had seen the van somewhere before and wasn't sure why it's presence was making him nervous. In one hand he carried a large can of matte-black spray paint. He checked to see that the top of he red kayak was

440

dry, then shook the spray can vigorously. In minutes the upper and lower surfaces of the kayak was a matte black, barely visible against the dark wall. He did the same thing with his double ended paddle, then covered it all with a large piece of black plastic. He then went over to the Norton motorcycle, checking that the fuel cocks were turned off and it was secure on its centre stand. That done, he went inside, ready for sleep although it was only nine o'clock, thoughts of explosions and the stench of dead rats infiltrated his mind.

He had the nightmare again. Pilson was chasing him down the darkened drift, the explosives covering his body, coming closer, his mouth open, screaming not Frenchy's name, but his own, *Bardman, Bardman*. He woke several times, gasping for air, his body covered in a cold sweat. He could recall only snatches of the dreams, sometimes nothing at all, but one recurring image of a man with a rifle came back to him. In the dream, he hadn't seen the man's face but his posture was familiar. The man had been pointing the rifle downwards at something and in the dream at the instant the trigger was pulled, he woke, choking for air.

His alarm clock went off with a shriek and his legs jumped in reaction, making him nearly cry out as the calf muscles knotted in spasm. For several minutes he sat in the dark bedroom, massaging his leg muscles. The time was one o'clock in the morning and he realized he was about to do something that might effect the rest of his life. He quickly shaved and dressed, then quietly went out to the car which he had previously loaded with the kayak. During that time he had also disconnected the brake and taillights, a reaction to a slightly paranoid feeling of being watched. He started the car, quietly cursing the noise of the cold diesel engine, and without headlights, drove toward the bridge over the Black Wood River north of town.

Corporal Pusch had fallen asleep at the wheel. His head was thrown back against the seat rest, his mouth wide open and snoring within the eighty decibel range. His young partner was in the back of the van, asleep on a thick pad of foam rubber covered by a sleeping bag. Frank had finished his four hour shift at midnight, allowing a bleary-eyed Pusch to relieve him, hoping the obnoxious corporal could stay awake for his own four hour shift, while they watched Bardman's residence.

"For Christ's sake wake up." Frank slapped Pusch's shoulder from behind the driver's seat.

He came awake in mid-snore, lurching toward the steering wheel. " I wasn't asleep, I was just resting my eyes."

"Like hell you were, you were rattling the windows with your snores. Shit, you've only been on watch for an hour and a half and you fall asleep. Have some more coffee."

"Can't, I finished it. I have to take a leak."

"Good, while you do it, why don't you do a quick perimeter check of that guy's place. The fresh air will do you good, besides you really stink. When's the last time you took a bath?"

"That's not the problem," replied Pusch, scratching his crotch. "I don't have any more fisherman-type clothes for my cover, and I haven't had time to wash these." He yawned like a hippo, his arms stretched over his head, pushing on the roof of the van. The roof of the van bulged outward and gave a loud *poing*.

"Good, now you're at least starting to smell like a fisherman. Forget what I said, forget the bath, I'll stick some Vicks Vapour-rub up my nose or something."

"Yeah, well you can stick more than that up your nose as far as I'm concerned Franky m'boy. Don't start thinking you can give me orders, I'm still the leader of this operation and I'll decide what I'm going to do."

"So what are you going to do corporal?"

"I'm going to go take a pee and check out the area. I'm getting sick and tired of using that little chemical piss-pot in the van."

"It wouldn't be so bad if your aim was better. You ever consider getting glasses?"

The van door creaked open as he exited to the cold damp air, making him even more desperate to relieve himself.

"Don't get your leg wet," whispered Frank.

Pusch gave him the middle finger while desperately fumbling with his fly with the other hand. Thirty seconds later he was back, scrambling into the driver's seat. "It's gone," he shouted at the top of his lungs.

"What's gone?"

"His car, it isn't there. He must have just left because I can still smell the diesel fumes. Damn." He hunted through his fishing vest for the ignition keys. "Shit, why do they put so many pockets in these damn things?"

"Oh sure, blame the disguise. I hope you include the fact you fell asleep while on duty in your report. This detachment needs a good laugh, and I think you're it."

He finally found the keys and backed the van onto the street with a screech of tires. He snapped both their necks with acceleration as they sped toward the river.

442

"Where do you think he's gone?" asked Frank, watching Pusch's jaw muscles clenching and his moustache threatening to abandon his features entirely.

Pusch held the steering wheel at the three and nine o'clock positions, just as the driving manual said he should. His knuckles turned white with tension as the vehicle careened toward the bridge. He didn't answer his partner's question, more concerned with how he was going to write his report. He was beginning to see his career take a turn for the worse, perhaps lose his corporal's stripes. The sergeant had even threatened to make him shave off his moustache. In the pit of his hungry stomach, he felt things might get a lot worse before they got better. He didn't know what he wanted least to lose, his corporal rank or his moustache, because he had come to consider his facial hairy appendage with as much status as anything sewn to his sleeve. Besides, without his uniform he was simply another naked man. His moustache gave him consistent status, even naked, or so he thought. He wriggled it under his nose to reassure himself it was still there.

"Shit, it rained during the night," said Frank, squinting into the darkness.

"Well at least it helps keep the dust down."

"That's the problem, we don't even have dust to show how far he might be ahead of us. Can you recognize the place where he turned off before with the kayak?"

Pusch nodded, his face illuminated a dull green by the dashboard lights. "I know the exact distance on the trip odometer, we're only five clicks from there now."

"Good thinking corporal, don't forget to include that bit of brilliance in your report." Frank saw his partner's jaw clench even tighter and decided he had chastised his partner enough. He didn't appear all that stable under stress, and the way he was driving did nothing to relax either of them. He reached for the radio and began to key the transmitter.

"Do you think that's wise?" said Pusch, trying to do up his seat belt with one hand. "We know Bardman has a police scanner in his car, he might hear us,"

"I don't think it makes much difference now, I think he's been aware of us all along. Keep watching ahead for any taillights, there aren't many vehicles on the road this time of night, so it shouldn't be hard to spot him." Frank keyed the mike. "Base this is watchdog."

The constable on radio duty answered with a howl which he had learned from Proboscis, then replied. "What are you puppies doing up so late?"

"We lost him."

"Who?"

"Who the hell do you think? Is there more than one stake-out going on in this pimple of a place?"

"Ooooh, bad dogs, bad dogs," replied the constable. "Somebody's going to have to use a rolled up newspaper on you. Are you in hot pursuit?"

Frank shook his head and replaced the mike on the dashboard. "I think there's a major flaw in the recruiting department, and what dim-bulb dreamed up a call-sign like watchdog? You okay?"

Pusch nodded again, watching the side of the road, glancing frequently at the odometer. "There's the turn-off." He slowed the van as they approached the spot where they had previously seen Bardman take the kayak. He carefully nosed the van down the rough track, his headlights on high beams, shining against the white trunks of the aspen and willows as they neared the river. They both sat quietly as he brought the van to a halt in a small clearing. The Volkswagen was nowhere in sight.

Frank looked at Pusch with a sad smile. "We're screwed partner."

Pusch nodded, his features folded into a worried expression and slowly turned the van back toward the road. He knew their chances of finding Bardman were now almost nil. "Get on the horn and see if we can get an air search at first light."

Frank shrugged, reaching for the radio. "It might be too late, but I reckon that's all we can do. Some poor charter pilot is going to get a very early phone call this morning and I don't want to be the one to talk to him."

The van came to the main road and stopped.

"Any ideas?"

"That way," replied Frank, jabbing his finger to the north.

"Brilliant," replied Pusch.

Joe McKay worked his way through the thirteen speeds of the Kenworth's transmission, the tractor straining each time the next gear took the full weight of the loaded trailer. The smell of diesel fumes was thick in the cab, along with that of grease and accumulated dust on nearly every surface of the cab's interior.

"Well partner, we didn't really need this rain tonight, gonna make parts of this road like grease." He glanced over at D'Amico as she tried to sip coffee from her Thermos cup without spilling it down her shirtfront.

"Go slow Joe, there's no rush. No matter what time we get to the project they still have to unload us. It's too dangerous to have us sit around with our thumbs up our bums. At least they've reduced our gross weight to seventy-thousand pounds."

"Big deal, thirty-thousand pounds of Amex, one-thousand pounds, a hundred pounds, makes no difference. I'm glad this is my last week haulin' this crap with equipment that should be on the scrap heap. Winky gettin' fired didn't change a hell of a lot did it partner? Now his uncle's here from Winnipeg an' he's just as much a jerk."

"It still worked Joe, you got him out of here, but we're still hauling mixed loads."

"It's a legal load. Amex and primers is okay as long as we don't haul caps and fuse with it, but I hear what you're sayin'. Are you gonna miss me after this trip? Glad it's your last day?"

She smiled to herself in the dark. "Miss this? God no, it's been like a vacuum in my life. All the time I was working here, something in the back of my head kept telling me I was supposed to be doing something else."

"You too eh? It took me a long time to see that too. I still have a hard time seein' you as a cop though. I mean how are you gonna make a hat fit over that hair?"

"Maybe I'll just get a brush cut like all the other guys, speak with a deep voice, swagger like I got balls. I mean wouldn't you be intimidated if you saw me coming to give you a ticket?"

"I'd just give ya big hug back partner."

"Not while I'm in uniform, you wouldn't, that would be obstruction."

"Guess you'd just have to take the uniform off, eh. Then I could really give you a hug. Would you still give me a ticket then?"

"Bet your boots, one for speeding and one for failure to negotiate the curves."

Joe laughed along with her, afraid she would see how much he would really miss her. She had become a good friend, probably his best friend and he found he could talk to her about things he had never tried to discuss with his wife. "Sadie's not comin' you know."

"Why not? I thought she wanted to go back to the reserve with you."

"She does but there's no school for Josh, an' he starts grade one here in two weeks. Says she's not gonna have an uneducated kid. I'll get started at Hudson House an' send her money until we can get another school teacher, maybe even one who can speak Cree."

"That could take time."

"Time is like a river, an' I've spent too long tryin' to swim upstream. This time we're all gonna swim or drown tryin'."

She finished her coffee, wiping her chin with her shirt sleeve. "How far until the control gate?"

He checked his watch. Thirty minutes, an' I'm not lookin' forward to that steep hill just before the gate. It'll be slippery as snot to get down, especially with these brakes feelin' as soft as they are."

She sat up, leaning across from her seat to look at the air pressure gauge. "We've only got 90 pounds of pressure, much less than that and the brakes will start to drag. They could burn out before we realize it. I don't want to get to that hill without brakes, Joe, let's stop and adjust them here."

" We can't. The road's too narrow here, no room for other traffic to pass safely. We'll have to wait until the wider area at the top, before the downgrade, won't be long now." He leaned forward, peering upward through the windshield. "At least the rain's stopped, an' I can see the moon between the clouds. Might be sunny this mornin'."

"You should be a weather forecaster. Well folks, it'll be dark tonight and maybe a little brighter in the day." She smiled at him but got nothing back.

The full moon slid from behind the swiftly moving clouds, pushed by a high pressure front from the north, although the early morning air was warm and humid, the cloud movement said there was a change coming. The spruce and pine were like tall, straight sentinels, bathed in silver light. On the horizon, the aurora borealis flickered, diluted green in the ionosphere, slowly writhing toward to top of the sky, the countless streaks showing the path of highly charged particles from the sun to the earth.

"I'll miss this," she said, watching the lights from her side window. She spoke quietly, almost to herself, her eyes following the magnificent display.

McKay said nothing, understanding the conflict that she was experiencing. He realized he had missed it every day of his life when he had been away at the residential school. He vowed never to be taken from it again.

"Joe, we're here!"

"Shit," was all he said as he applied the brakes to slow the truck before they reached the top escarpment of the river valley. "Brakes aren't workin' right." He pulled gently on the trailer-brake lever and pumped the tractor brakes, but the air pressure buzzer sounded the warning that pressure was dangerously low.

"Shift down," she shouted, smelling the stench of burnt brake linings.

He quickly began gearing down as they passed the lip of the escarpment, keeping the rpm up so the gears would mesh properly with their forward speed, progressively slowing them down with the higher torque. The tractor and trailer began fish-tailing on the wet mud of the road. There was a grinding sound as he tried to go to a lower gear, his back pressed tightly against the back of the seat, foot on the brake pedal which had gone all the way to the floor.

"Blew the shift," he screamed. "I'm gonna compound the brakes." He reached for the flat coloured plastic square on the dashboard in front of him which applied the full force of the trailer brakes, prepared to pull it toward him and engage it.

"You'll blow a hose and lose all the brakes Joe." Her voice went up a couple of octaves.

"Too late now, an' screw the hose, I'm worried about blowin' what's sittin' behind us." He yanked on the square of plastic and the tractor and trailer lurched in unison with a blast of air, the tractor beginning to slew sideways from the force of the trailer pushing from behind. Their speed dropped, but the brakes were gone, reminded by the shrill warning of the buzzer. The only thing restraining the whole unit from free-wheeling down the incline was the tractor being pushed sideways in slow motion toward the control gates and its narrow crossing. The trees, illuminated by the headlights, swept past the front of the truck like a slow-motion film

"No good. We're gonna have to jump, I can't hold it." McKay had opened his driver's door on the upward side of the unit. "Come out this side, you'll get run over if you go out that side." He dove from sight, leaving the truck driverless.

Teresa lunged across the gearshift, landing on the vacant driver's seat. Without hesitation she leapt from the door ledge as far into the night with all her strength. She landed flat on her stomach, knocking the wind from her lungs and was barely conscious of the tires of the rear bogies on the trailer brushing past her face. She tasted a combination of mud and blood in her mouth and possibly a fragment of a broken tooth. *Shit, if I have another big dentist bill, I'll scream.* The air stank of burned rubber. She was barely aware of where she was when the tractor and trailer reached the control gate.

The crossing over the control gate was only wide enough to accommodate one vehicle at a time. Control lights were installed at each end to regulate traffic.

The runaway unit reached the narrow opening, tractor, still sideways, but jack-knifed at an acute angle to face back along the trailer. It barely cleared the steel girders on either side. Suddenly the front bumper snagged something, wrenching the tractor backwards, detaching the fifth wheel away from the connecting trailer pin. The trailer flipped onto its side riding up on the back of the tractor and skidded another fifty feet onto the crossing. The unit lay quietly, like a deadly beached whale, wedged tightly between the girders. The tractor's engine rattled on, the headlights shining toward the blackness of the river.

"Joe, where are you?" She had barely enough air to speak. She heard a groan to her right. She staggered to her feet, spitting the mud from her mouth, her knees shaking. A groan came from the ditch. She found him sitting up, holding his head, blood running between his fingers from a cut over the left eye, appearing in the moonlight like black ink oozing onto the skin.

"I don't believe it, we're alive," he groaned rocking from side to side.

"Don't try to move yet. Joe, let me check you over." She began running her hands over his limbs, checking for other bleeding and broken bones.

"Now she wants to run her hands over my body. Does blood excite you or somethin'?"

"Shut up and don't move. Where do you hurt?"

"Everywhere, but I don't think nothin's broke. Where's the truck?"

"On the control gate, stuck tighter than my uncle's hemorrhoid."

He groaned again, rising slowly to his feet and looked the quarter mile toward the control gates. "Holy shit. What are we gonna do?"

She pulled him to his feet, steadying him with an arm around his waist. "We have to keep anyone else from coming near here; that means we need all the road flares and reflectors from the cab. That means we have to put them before the tops of the inclines so traffic will have time to stop. If somebody can't stop...we're all gone."

McKay groaned in reply as they walked toward the shining headlights, the sound of the engine like a mechanical death rattle. Still holding his head, his fingers stuck together from the blood which had slowed to a trickle, He turned stiffly toward his partner. "Still glad it's your last day?"

"Ain't over yet," was all she replied.

Bardman drove slowly, never over 50 kph, relying on the light of the full moon to show the way. If he saw oncoming traffic, he planned to pull over, stop, and slouch down in the seat, making the car appear abandoned. If someone stopped and tried to cannibalize the car, he would have no choice but to turn on the headlights and drive on. His eyes flicked constantly to the rear view mirror, searching for headlights, possibly those of the van which had been parked several houses away. At one time he thought he had seen a flicker of light behind him, but it disappeared and didn't reappear. With a small flashlight he checked the odometer reading. Thirty kilometers to go. The sound of mud and gravel rattled against the underside of the wheel-wells, the smell of the wet road and grass came through the open window, along with the cool air which helped keep him awake.

It's a half-hour paddle, can't waste time, have to go like hell and get back. This is crazy. What the hell am I doing? People could get hurt if they're near when it blows, don't want anybody to get hurt. Have to call the radio station from the emergency phone on the highway and tell them about the bomb. They'll call the cops and have the construction camp

448

evacuated and road blocked before the 6 am explosion. I have to be back in town by then. Shit, it's going to be tight. Why the hell am I doing this?

He flicked the headlights on for the next few kilometres and managed to see the marker on the rock, showing the turn-off. His watch showed 2:15 am. He had to be in the water in fifteen minutes and back here an hour later. His neck hurt from tension and his eyes felt scratchy from lack of sleep. The vision of the old man with the rifle in his dreams kept coming back to him. Without knowing why, he slipped the string of the small medicine bag he had been given by the old trapper over his head. It hung beneath his shirt, its aromas of dried flowers and strange plants soothing his tense nerves.

Amongst the moon-shadowed trees he pulled the explosive-laden kayak from beneath the high grass and dragged it to the river. With muscles straining, he slipped it slowly into the water and tied a length of rope to its bow ring. Leaning into the cockpit, he carefully unwrapped the heavy plastic from around the small travel alarm clock which he had previously connected to the capacitor of the electronic flash. The connections appeared good and the electrical cap was still attached to the metal primer of the 12 gauge shotgun shell. The small bag of Amex surrounding the shell was still dry, as was the inside of the plastic kayak. The plastic afforded no danger of static electricity setting off the detonator by accident. He inserted a new nine volt battery into the electronic flash, as well as one in the alarm clock, then set the timer on the clock. He quickly tied the bow rope of the laden kayak to the stern of his own. He climbed into his kayak and carefully pulled away from shore. He paddled in a dream-like state, downstream toward the control gates.

The trees were a black jagged line against the sky. The lowering moon still highlighted parts of the dark water and the occasional fallen tree, appeared like sleeping giants, their bark reflecting the moonlight. The current burbled around the partially immersed branches of the fallen trees, allowing him to hear them in time to avoid them. His eyes had adapted well to the near-darkness as he watched the dark shoreline pass. His back began to sweat with the exertion of pulling the heavily laden kayak. It had a tendency to swerve to the left, pulling the bow of his own kayak to the right and nearly into the grasping branches of a sweeper, a fallen spruce, connected to the flooded shore by only a few root tendrils. He compensated by staying more in midstream, in the baleful light of the moon which bounced highlights from the wakes of the two craft. A sharp splash made him jump, a beaver in the shadows signalling alarm at his presence. He shivered as the clammy hand of low-lying mist slid along his face, forming tiny water droplets on his glasses. He stopped to wipe the lenses clear. The following kayak pulled nearly alongside, jerking the rope taut, swerving his own boat hard to the right. He cursed quietly as he replaced the glasses and did a hard sweep stroke to the left to avoid hitting debris. The water exploded close to his right with the panicked quacks of two mallard ducks as they skimmed the shiny water surface, flapping and quacking in panic downstream.

Downstream, I'm being carried along on currents that I seem to have no control over. I could stop paddling now turn back, but the current will fight me. The current! There wasn't this much current before. Why didn't I notice it before? This water used to be still, but now it's moving me faster than I've ever seen it. I'm almost there, but it'll take more time to get back. I have to get back in time to make the phone call.

Around the next bend he could see the gantry and the sodium-vapour lights of the control gates reflecting like yellow jewels from the water. He didn't see any traffic moving over the structure. A wave of relief came over him. He was confused by a large light coloured object on he roadway of the structure. Construction? Perhaps some kind of worker's shelter? To his right he could see the glow of the construction camp through the trees. They would all have to be warned and evacuated in time. Doubts were beginning to crowd in on him. Maybe this wasn't such a great idea. How could he possibly ensure everyone was evacuated in time? He knew that he couldn't be sure.

"Screw it, this is stupid," he said out loud, preparing to turn the kayaks about and return to his launching point. It was then he heard the voices. One voice was obviously female and sounded familiar, except for its tone of alarm. A male voice answered and as he drew closer to the lights, staying in the shadows of the shoreline, he realized the large object on the roadway was a truck and trailer. The lights he had not identified were those of the tractor's marker lights, still shining on part of the structure. He saw the explosives warning placard on the front of the trailer and was aware that the trailer was on its side, resting on part of the tractor. The female voice called again, this time from further up the far incline of the road, from the far side of the river. As he searched the area, a bright red flare burst to life and he saw the person jamming the sharp end of the road flare into the road. Teresa! She was suffused with a surreal red light as she moved away and further up the slope, gradually over the lip and out of sight. Momentarily, another red glow lit the horizon. The same was happening on the opposite ridge, a person scrambling, stopping and setting up reflectors. It was her partner, moving with unmistakable urgency.

He sat enthralled by the sight. His mind was slow taking in the scope of the danger that was present, until his elbow felt a nudge. Turning, he saw the trailing kayak had drifted ahead to the limit of its rope and was caressing his arm like some deadly plastic pet. *The timer! It can't go off with this truck on the bridge, it'll destroy things for miles!*

He quickly paddled for shore and dismounted onto the shore where he pulled the other kayak close so he could reach the cockpit. He removed the plastic-wrapped detonator bundle, extricating the alarm clock and flash unit. He hurriedly, with shaking hands, removed the batteries from each item and threw them into the water. No time to worry about polluting now. The shotgun shell and detonator cap followed. With his Swiss army knife, he slashed the small bag of explosives, spilling the contents into the water. He then began removing the larger plastic bags from inside the hull of the boat, slashing them open and dumping their contents also into the water. He was sweating with exertion, his hands covered with the petroleum smell of the explosive mixture. He washed his hands in the water, throwing some quickly over his face. A fierce buzzing made him realize mosquitoes had been feeding off him the whole time he had been on the river. He pulled the emptied kayak from the water, onto the shore, re-entered his own craft and began paddling with urgency, back to his car. Not only did he not want to be anywhere near the load of explosives that lay on the gates, he had more reason to call in a warning. *The construction camp. I can go there and warn them. People will start asking why I'm out here at this time of night. Screw it, first warn them, then worry about the explanation.*

He turned the kayak back toward the control gate complex, searching for a landing site close to the structure where he could get to the road. He saw a large tree trunk protruding from the shore. He paddled alongside, and braced his double-bladed paddle on it, then pulled himself slowly from the cockpit, onto the cold wood. As he crawled along the trunk, he pulled the kayak to shore and left it on the riverbank. The area around him was bathed in yellow light as he clambered up the crushed rock which formed the approach roadway to the control gates. He reached the top gasping, the smell of burned rubber and diesel heavy on the humid night air. His eyeglasses had slid partway down his perspiring nose. He heard footsteps running from behind and he turned to see a quickly approaching silhouette.

"What the...who the hell..Brady? What in hell are you doing here?"

"Later Teri, just later. Okay? Have you warned the construction camp?"

Her shoulders moved up and down with each laboured breath as she tried to get the word out. "Next...that's next, warnings are out, both ends, Joe's up there." She pointed to the crest of the other escarpment.

He looked back at the truck on its side. "How...?"

"Don't ask. Later...okay?"

He moved around so the gantry lighting shone on her face. "You alright? your face is all covered with mud, maybe a little blood too."

"Too late for appearances; got to warn the camp."

They jogged south from where the truck had come, toward the access road to the construction camp. There were over a hundred men and women sleeping soundly nearly two kilometres away, unaware of the danger.

"Had to jump. The brakes went, couldn't stop on the hill, trailer jack-knifed."

"Not now, save your breath for the camp. I see a light in one of the trailers, let's try that one."

"Cook shack," she gasped as they approached. "Making breakfast. You hungry?"

"Starved, but after this is over, I'll buy you breakfast. Okay?"

"Deal," she agreed, grinning through the mud. She reached for the handle of the screen door to the cook shack and they entered into a world of delicious aromas.

"Hey folks, you're a few hours early for breakfast, but the coffee's on," called a rotund man garbed in white, with a high white, floppy hat. His face and hands were covered in flour, beads of sweat making damp streaks over pink, quivering jowls.

"Girl have you bin mud-wrestlin'?"

Teresa blurted out what had happened, watching the expression on the baker's face grow more serious. The baker picked up a phone and spoke quickly, then hung up.

"Called the night foreman, he has to stay ready to change the gate level in case of a change in run-off from the diversion. Ah, there we go." A low moan soon grew into the howl of a fire siren, causing lights all over camp to come on. People could be heard running to fire-fighting equipment, where the foreman met them and passed the word to evacuate.

"Damn, this is bad timing," said the baker as he went from oven to oven, turning them off. "Not a complete loss. Before you two bugger off, here, these will just go to waste." The baker quickly bagged a half dozen fresh cinnamon buns and tossed them to a surprised Bardman, who snagged them with one hand.

On the stoop, they watched organized chaos as workers started vehicles to move people out, some in various states of undress, eyes bleary with fatigue. One large pickup truck moved past the cook shack just as the baker came out with a huge tray of fresh cinnamon buns. The people in the backs of the trucks shouted their appreciation as he hurled the buns at the surprised occupants of the departing trucks.

They looked at each other in disbelief, then began jogging back to the main road and the slumbering load of explosives.

He handed a cinnamon bun to D'Amico, wishing there was some hot coffee to go with it.

She stuffed into her mouth in three gulps, hardly swallowing. "This doesn't get you of the hook from buying me breakfast y'know."

He shoved another bun into her filthy hands in reply.

They met Joe, watching the exodus of vehicles turning onto the main road and scurrying southward. Someone from the pick-up truck hit him in the face with a cinnamon bun, which he retrieved from the road and studied with a confused expression.

"Eat it, don't look at it," she said she and Bardman approached.

"How'd he get here?" mumbled McKay, crumbs of bun spraying from his mouth.

"Later," was their simultaneous reply.

McKay shrugged and finished the bun, then belched.

A yellow pickup truck with the hydro symbol on the door pulled up, blinding them with its headlights on high beam. A heavy-set man in coveralls struggled out from behind the wheel and looked at the obstruction laying on the control gate roadway, then at them. "Holy moly, would ya look at that. How much powder is on that thing?"

"Thirty-thousand pounds, Amex and primers," said McKay, wishing there were more buns, eyeing Bardman's paper bag suspiciously.

"Well, it ought to be pretty stable there. Don't ya think? Hell, takes a lot to set that stuff off don't it? Hell, I seen guys take that Amex an throw it in a fire to watch it burn."

"You want to go down and check it out for stability?" asked D'Amico

"Oh, no, nope, that's okay," replied the man who was lifting his hard hat and scratching a bald spot. He took a couple of steps backwards towards his truck. "I radioed the project downstream. They're evacuatin', just in case, an' the cops too. they said they're gonna set up road blocks both sides of the gates, long ways back I hope. But, that stuff's pretty stable like that ain't it? Well, think I'll git the hell outa here. Oh, here, you can use these." He hurriedly handed over a handful of road flares to D'Amico. "You folks need a ride somewhere?"

The three of them shook their heads without speaking and the nervous foreman reversed the truck and turned around in a spray of gravel.

"Don't know what his hurry is." muttered McKay, "That stuff is stable."

They laughed as the truck departed into the darkness and they turned to look silently at the shiny trailer wedged across the roadway in the cold yellow lights.

"Another bun?" said Bardman holding out the bag.

McKay quickly reached in for another. "Thought you'd never ask," he grunted between bites.

Abe McKay was awakened by the same dream, but more vivid. This time he could hear the water of the river and smell flowers on the shoreline. In the dream he stood again upon the dead creature, the rifle in his hands. *My hands, I saw my hands. That's never happened in a dream before.* He remembered part of the dream when he had held one hand in front of his face and studied it as though seeing it for the first time, like an infant developing self-awareness.

Without knowing why, he dressed in warm clothing and took his canoe paddle from behind the door. It was still dark outside, with a hint of false dawn like a white mist beyond the horizon. His stomach grumbled with hunger, but he felt it appropriate not to eat. He couldn't rationalize to himself why he felt that way, rather, he obeyed the subliminal nudges his mind was receiving, moving without conscious thought or purpose. Before closing the door to his shack from the outside, he stopped and looked for long seconds at the dark interior where he had lived most of his more than seventy years. His eyes swept over the linoleum covered table with its rickety chairs, reinforced with baling wire, the unwashed dishes in the porcelain sink, and his old rifle on the wall. As if in a dream, he went back inside and retrieved the old pump action 44-40 Remington. He checked to see if there were cartridges in a drawer, putting a half dozen in a shirt pocket. Without looking back, he left the old cabin, locking the door, something he had never done before.

He sniffed the air as the canoe moved silently through the water. A kingfisher dived from a branch into the still water on the opposite shore and flew off with a small fish in its beak. The grass along the river was bowed with dew, in some places spider webs hanging between plants like freshly-strung strings of pearls. Somewhere in the darkness of the trees, a blue jay traded insults with an indignant squirrel. He smiled at the sounds of nature's domestic disputes, the conversations of the forest, unchanged for millenniums and yet somehow different. He watched the river pass more as an observer than a participant. He felt removed from its vital life force, the current moving him inexorably towards something he didn't understand. He wasn't sure he wanted to understand, but felt compelled to seek an answer.

The early morning mist lay on the river's surface like a ghostly grey blanket. Everywhere he looked from the canoe, appeared out of focus as though a film had lowered itself over his eyes. The only thing that seemed real was the canoe and the water which parted quietly to let it pass. His hands and shoulders ached from the exertion of paddling, and his posterior had grown numb from sitting on the small webbed seat. He wished he was young again so his legs would allow him to kneel in the bottom of the hull, the way his father had taught him when he was a boy. The orange ball of the sun began to peek through the tall spruce, bathing the trees of the opposite shoreline in golden light. He stopped paddling and took a deep breath, savouring the aroma of the water and plant life. Tiny bluebells bowed with droplets of dew on their petals, amongst the tall goldenrod on the shoreline. A male goldfinch flitted from plant to plant, its wings tucked to its body between beats, giving its repetitive call as it swooped through the air. Even the lichen and moss in their symbiosis seemed to glow with life, more vibrant than he had ever been aware of before. He smiled a toothless grin and resumed paddling, arms grateful for the short rest.

In the distance, the control gates appeared like a yellow latticework emerging from the river mist, as though buoyed up by the mist itself. A fresh morning breeze came up and slowly the mists swirled and parted to reveal a strange silvery object on the roadway. He caught his breath and stopped paddling, allowing the canoe to drift silently toward the structure. *The dream. Is this just another dream?* He dipped his hand into the water and splashed some on his face. *If this is a dream, this'll wake me up.* The object was still there, partially obscured by the mist. He sat and lifted his cap to scratch. In the distance he could hear voices and the sounds of vehicles. To his right and near the top of the valley escarpment he could barely discern several people standing around a yellow truck, dark paint strokes around a splash of yellow. The dark blobs moved, one of them moving downhill toward the object. Without knowing why, he paddled with urgency toward the structure and finally stared up at the object, seeing it for what it really was, recognizing the red and white danger signs. He pushed the bow of the canoe onto rocks at the shoreline and cautiously, with is rifle in hand, slowly climbed the bank near the structure. He knew it was no time to be careless, a fall now could be disastrous. He reached the metal corrugated sides of the trailer, running his hand along the cool surface, smelling faint odours of the brakes that had burned out and failed. The tractor remained upright but peering back at him along the length of the trailer like some protective overseer, its engine no longer rattling. He saw where the trailer had detached from the trailer, the airlines still intact but now useless. With care he climbed onto the rear of the tractor, his coveralls becoming smeared with grease from the effort. He then climbed onto the trailer's side and walked its length, hearing the metal make creaking sounds as his weight pushed it downwards. He sat on the metal surface, forcing his legs to cross in front of him like he had done in the sweat lodge. The effort made him grunt with pain, but it was a posture he refused to forfeit to age. He cradled the rifle across his lap, facing the direction from which the figure was approaching down the road. He recognized the walk and smiled inwardly.

"You the driver of this thing?" he said softly to the figure approaching through the mist.

The figure stopped, then continued forward slowly, slightly hunched at the shoulders, head thrust forward as if to see better.

"I think your parkin' needs a little work."

"Dad...what are you doin' here, an' why do you have your rifle?"

"I'm guardin' your property."

"It's not my property, it belongs to North Haul."

"I'm not talkin' about the truck, I'm talkin' about *this*." he swept his hand expansively toward the river and trees.

Joe got over his initial surprise quickly. He was no longer surprised at the strange places his father appeared with seeming ease. He squinted his eyes against the rising sun, seeing his father as a silhouette, rimmed by yellow fire. Mosquitoes and black flies hovered in clouds around his head and body, but didn't seem to land. "Why not give me your rifle. You know what you're sittin' on eh?"

Abe clutched the old rifle tighter in his hands, and worked the pump action to chamber a round. "This is your insurance I'm sittin' on, an' I'm gonna stay here until somebody who has somethin' to do with all this comes an' talks to me about it." He slowly swept his arm again to encompass his surroundings.

"An' if they don't come?" replied Joe, wondering if he could some way take the rifle from his father. *There's no way. He might be old but he's not weak.*

"Then one shot from this will finish everythin'"

"You mean it'll finish you."

"Nothin' left to live for."

"What about me... an' Josh? He's your grandson. Are we nothin' to you anymore?"

"I would be nothin' to him or you, if I didn't do everythin' I could to stop all this. Look aroun' you, they've killed our culture an' our spirit. We're trees without roots bein' cut down to make furniture. To do what? *So they can sit on us like they sit on their furniture!*

Joe stepped back involuntarily, never before hearing such anger in his father's voice. "What do you want me to do?"

"Go back up there an' tell 'em that I want to talk to somebody in charge of all this. They send me one of their indians and not a chief, I'll put a bullet right down into this thing." He looked at his son's direct gaze, and the injury above his eye covered with dried blood, feeling a combination of love and sorrow. "That's a bad cut. You get it from this?"

Joe nodded and began to turn away to deliver his father's message.

"Got anythin' to eat?"

Joe turned back, with a the hint of a smile. " Got a couple of cinnamon buns up there."

"Whole wheat?"

"Don't think so."

"Aaah, no time to be picky, eh? Bring me one when you come back with your answer, eh. Only you. No one else."

Joe saw his father smile, combined with a sly wink. He smiled sadly back and returned to the top where he saw a plain brown van parked behind the hydro truck.

Bardman and D'Amico saw the van skid to a stop behind the pickup truck and two men approach, one dressed like a street punk, the other like some fisherman who loathed his clothing. The fisherman had a self-conscious walk, pulling at his shirt collar which was buttoned to the top, and shooting his cuffs which were attached tightly around his wrists The man's large nose and mobile moustache gave away his identity immediately.

"Ooooh My God," muttered D'Amico under her breath. "Why Corporal Pusch, what a surprise. Out to do a little fishing are you?"

Pusch approached, his hands clasped behind his back, head thrust forward, the way he had seen Prince Philip walk, when he inspected troops. He looked like a poorly dressed fisherman at parade-rest. He stared at them, his close-set eyes sparkling as though he had caught them corpus-indelecto at a drive-in movie. His floppy hat with the lures imbedded was being mobbed by various blood-sucking insects, like children to a circus ride.

"Well, well, well. What have we here?" he said, leaning forward at an acute angle toward the control gate, sniffing as though various aromas would supply the answer. His partner stood back near the van, reluctant to be seen in his company. "Mr. Bardman, we've been wondering where you had gotten to. Where did you get to by the way?"

"I'm right here corporal," replied Bardman, smiling innocently.

"I know that," said the corporal, leaning toward him until their noses nearly touched. "But where were you before here?"

"I went for a paddle."

"At night?"

"There was a moon. I like to paddle in the moonlight."

Pusch snorted like a horse ejecting snuff. "A likely story. Where's your boat?"

"It's down there by the river,"

"And why is it down there Mr. Bardman?"

"Well...I didn't feel like carrying it all the way up here."

The entire group who had been listening, broke into laughter, including Pusch's partner who was still leaning against the van, shaking his head in disbelief.

Pusch punished them with a hauty glare and turned back toward the control gates. "Who is that? Is that someone sitting on top of that trailer down there? And who is this walking back from there?"

Joe had heard Pusch's question concerning himself and replied: "I'm Joe, and that's my dad. He wants to talk to somebody about the river and the hydro project. He don't want to talk to some jigaboo, he wants to talk to a big-wig."

"Or what?" queried Pusch, sniffing in the direction of the brown paper bag in Bardman's possession."

'Or he's gonna blow it up, along with everythin' within a few miles of here." Joe was looking at Pusch's gaze fixed on the brown paper bag, seeing his nose twitch in recognition of the aromas it gave off. "He also sent me for this," he continued, reaching for the paper bag.

"And is that, what I think it is?" his eyes had narrowed as his olfactory senses homed in on the bag. "And how does he intend to do that, blow it up I mean?"

"He has a rifle."

"I thought that stuff was stable."

"It is, but a bullet isn't."

"Doesn't sound like he is either," sniffed Pusch in the direction of Joe's father.

"You don't smell so stable yourself constable." Joe had turned downhill, then turned back to the hydro employee, still sitting in his cab. "You called anybody at your head office about this?"

"Yup," replied the man behind the wheel, called the project on the radio so they could evacuate in case that gate blows. Don't think they need to though, 'cause they're already startin' to flood the forebay in front of the dam. All it'll do is fill it a lot faster, but won't do no damage."

"That's not what I asked. Is there a big-wig comin' or not. If not...you can kiss your gates goodbye."

"Ah, yup, they said they was gonna call head office in Winnipeg an' git somebody up here right away. They got a private jet down there, an' he can git a chopper from town to here."

Joe nodded and started back down toward his father with the cinnamon buns, eating one on the way, feeling pleased that he had denied Corporal Pusch the pleasure of tasting them. He delivered the bag to his father who appeared asleep, still in the sitting position, the rifle still across his lap.

"What did they say?" asked his father, his eyes still closed, basking in the warmth of the rising sun.

Joe handed the bag up. "They're sendin' somebody from Winnipeg. Be here in a few hours." He watched his father's eyes flicker beneath his eyelids, as though seeing something within. His face was lifted toward the rising sun, a slight smile on his lips.

Abe slowly reached with both hands toward his neck and removed the small leather bag which had been suspended by a length of rawhide. He handed it to Joe in his outstretched palm, his eyes still closed. "Give this to Josh when he gets older,eh?

Joe took it in his hand just as his father suddenly opened his eyes, watching him with a hint of humour. "Don't teach him to drive, eh. You set a bad example."

Joe smiled back and winked, turning back toward the top, leaving his father with his thoughts or dreams or whatever it was he saw behind those closed eyes. When he arrived at the top, he saw Pusch, notebook in hand, taking some kind of statement from D'Amico. She turned to him with a look of exasperation.

Pusch also turned and smiled coldly. "Well Mr. McKay, I understand you were driving that vee-hicle down there. Is that correct?"

McKay nodded.

"Brake failure you said.That's a good one."

"It's the truth."

"Just a coincidence then how your dad happens by and comes and sits on it with his gun, hmm?"

"I can't explain that."

"Seems there's a lot you can't explain Mr. McKay. Is there anything more about this scenario I should know before I charge you with careless driving as well as aiding and abetting someone in the act of committing a crime?"

"What aid?"

"The buns, you gave him the buns." Pusch was nearly hopping up and down in anger, his hands straight by side. "You gave him energy to resist any attempt to overcome him before he can do something serious. Besides, *I was hungry too."*

"Aaaah, so that's it."

"Yes that's it. You aided him before you aided the lawful authorities on the scene."

"I don't think your law applies to what he has in mind, besides, he's my dad."

Pusch threw up his arms in frustration. He turned toward his partner who was observing the control gates through a pair of binoculars. "You're not being much help."

459

Frank lowered the binoculars, and looked at his red-faced partner. "How large a blast area do you think thirty-thousand pounds of explosives would affect?"

Pusch shrugged. "Give me a hint. Is this twenty questions we're playing?"

"I figure about two miles radius, and we're about three-hundred yards away right now. Do you think we'd survive if he started shooting into that trailer?"

He pondered the question, chewing on his lower lip, making it appear his moustache was trying to eat his chin from the top down.

"I radioed for back-up to set roadblocks a minimum of four miles from the gates, that's why you haven't seen any traffic this way, it's all backed up for miles either way. The airport has been called and they've restricted any low-level flights in this area. No point in making that old gentleman down there any more upset than he is. We just have to tell him the big-wig he wants to see will be here in about two hours, he's already airborne in a Lear jet and there's a helicopter waiting for him at the airport."

He continued to chew his lip, then said, "For a new constable, you're not doing so badly." His tone of condescension was unmistakable.

"Try detective-sergeant, corporal, and I'm thirty years old under this long hair and fake acne."

Pusch gulped, not knowing whether to salute or pee his pants. Instead, he simply turned and stared at the unmoving form, still sitting on the explosives-laden trailer. Heat waves from the increasing heat of the day created a shimmering effect in the low part of the river valley. He took his partner's binoculars from him and focused them on the trailer.

"There's something down there with him."

All eyes strained through the wavering air to see where Pusch was looking.

"The raven," said Joe quietly, as he could see the large black bird standing on the metal of the trailer, facing his father who still did not move.

Pusch removed the binoculars, looking questioningly at Joe.

He was back in the canoe, paddling through familiar, quiet waters. The branches hung over like a protective canopy as he negotiated the narrow channel. He could see the narrow pathways between the grasses where the muskrats had created their burrows beneath the bank. A deer came to the water's edge ahead of him and he stopped paddling. The deer look warily around, sniffing the air and waggling its ears before finally bending to drink. He admired the sheen of its coat and the large watchful eyes. As the deer moved off, he heard a sob, as soft as a sigh on the wind, the leaves moving gently at its passing. He paddled further, troubled by what he sensed around him, the changes, things that would never be the same. He felt eyes upon him with a watchfulness that could read his soul.

Abe McKay opened his eyes and saw the raven before him. The bird's eyes regarded him with a cool intelligence, unblinking, perhaps with a bit of humour. "What you want with me bird?" His back and legs hurt, and his tongue was dry from thirst. As sweat dripped from his forehead into his eyes he saw the bird cock its head to one side and peer at the metal skin of the trailer. With an awkward waddle the raven then moved toward the muzzle of the old rifle still across his lap. For a long moment it gazed into the darkness of the muzzle, then back down at the trailer. He watched the bird with a mixture of curiosity and fear. "You're sayin' it's my choice now eh? But what good will it do? The damage is done."

Time appeared to stand still for him until he realized he was talking to himself. The raven was no longer there and he thought he might have imagined its presence. The sun had moved across the sky and was beginning its torturous descent toward the west. Through eyes stinging with sweat he saw two figures approaching down the road from the crest of the ridge. They wavered through the layers of heat as though walking through moving water, one dark, the other light, side by side, like the forces of good and evil sharing the same path.

"Dad, you okay?" Joe watched his father with concern, seeing his unsteady gaze, and his laboured breathing. He handed up a plastic bottle. "Brought you some water."

Abe grunted in thanks, then said, "Who's the white man in the tie?"

Standing before him was Jim Thompkins Chief Executive Officer of the Hydro Corporation. Sweat was trickling down his back and prickly heat rash was developing under his armpits. He extended an immaculately manicured hand and said, "Mr. McKay I'm sure we can resolve this little dispute quickly for the good of all concerned." He removed his hand, unshaken, and wiped the sweaty palm on his charcoal grey dress pants.

"Nice shirt," replied Abe, wiping a droplet of sweat away from the tip of his nose, then taking a drink of cool water from the bottle. He removed his cap and poured some over his thinning hair. The water ran down his face, his long, sparse hair plastered to the side of his head and his forehead. He replaced the cap on his head, seeing the executive look self-consciously at his shirt, then back at him.

"I could get you a dozen like this if you wanted," replied Thompkins, holding out one studded cuff for Abe's cursory inspection. "Finest silk, you'd be the best-dressed man in town." He was a thin, balding man with the pasty complexion of one who spends his days inside. His narrow face was pinched with unfriendly, myopic blue eyes, corrected by rimless spectacles. A large

461

garish tie was knotted at the throat of a scrawny neck which appeared inadequate to support his head which tended to jerk from side to side as he spoke.

"Wampum," snorted Abe. "You bring some beads to trade too? Maybe a couple of treaties to have signed? You think I'm some kinda dumb injun, white man?"

"Not at all, gracious me no," said Thompkins, a nervous quiver in his voice. "We know you people have valid concerns and I'm here to address them, with you, like equals, but I can't do that while you have a gun in your hand."

"You've had a gun to our heads ever since you started this project, an' this makes us equal now, so let's talk."

Thompkins eyed the plastic water bottle next to Mckay, licking his lips. "Say, do you mind if I have a drink of that? Damn hot down here, wish there was some wind."

Abe swept his hand upstream from the control gate complex. "You flooded all this, drink some of it yourself an' see how it tastes."

Thompkins turned to Joe who was standing to the side, silently imploring him for something to drink.

Joe slowly shook his head, averting his glance toward the swollen river. It had become so hot that even the insects had taken refuge in the cool shade of the trees and grasses. The occasional horsefly landed lethargically on exposed skin in attempt to drink the beads of sweat. They often finished by taking a painful bite of skin from the human flesh, before either being squashed or escaped to try again. Several flew around the heads of each person, loud, insectile dive-bombers, fraying nerves.

While the two men tried to find common ground, he walked slowly around the trailer, looking for any signs of external damage. He saw near the front, a section of steel railing from the walkway had been peeled away by the tractor and had pierced the front of the trailer, extending an unknown distance into the load of explosives. He peered over the railing, seeing that the flow of water had been increased through the gates. He knew the dam downstream was virtually complete and that his father's actions were merely academic. This could not be reversed but he couldn't think of anything else that could be done. At least his father had got the attention of the big-wigs, a term he found humorous, considering the man's lack of hair. He distrusted anyone who wore a tie and smiled too much.

"Politicians have brain damage," said his father once, as they sat at the small table in his cabin. "Those ties cut off circulation to the brain, an' the brain starts to die, little by little. These are the men who are makin' all the decisions for you an' me, an' they're brain damaged."

Joe had considered the logic of it then but wasn't sure if his father had been joking, since he usually smiled or chuckled whenever the topic of politics came up. The anaemic looking man talking with his father appeared to be a manifestation of his theory, with his sweaty pallor and uncoordinated movements as he spoke.

He walked slowly toward the rear of the trailer, seeing obvious frustration on the executive's face and carved-in-stone determination on his father's. It was clear who had won the fist round of discussions.

"But you're not being reasonable, we can't tear all this down, it won't go away," said Thompkins, his arms flapping and swatting at the horseflies which had seen his shirt as a some type of resort. Nearly a dozen of them sat unmoving as they contemplated where they wanted to chew into the man's flesh, sending him into a paroxysm of anger whenever they made their decision. "Damn, how do you live in this place with these things, why don't they bother you?"

"Didn't wear my aftershave this mornin'" replied Abe, enjoying the man's discomfort. "Those flies are like my people, we can bite when we have to, an' flappin' your arms won't make us go away. It's their nature to bite, an' it's our nature to live with nature."

"Mr. McKay, this conversation is going in circles."

"But the circles are gettin' smaller chief, an' pretty soon one of us will come to the point. What happens if this truck blows up, eh? I'll tell you. This thing disappears an' the water returns where it should. Can that dam work without this piece-a steel sittin' here?"

"Sir, you'd kill yourself in the process."

"You started my death a long time ago, but I'll be the one who says how it's gonna end, not you. All you people do is talk, hopin' nobody will act. The time for talkin' is past an' all you're doin' is passin' gas from the wrong end Mr. executive."

I think we have nothing more to say to each other Mr. McKay. I'm going to put this in the hands of the proper authorities and let them handle it the way they would handle any criminal activity." Thompkins turned and began walking up the dusty road, waving both arms at the flies as they attempted to use his bald spot as a landing pad.

"My people are the proper authorities, chief," he called to the man's receding back. He turned to Joe who was standing quietly nearby, studying the horizon. Seeing him in profile brought back the images of his son's mother when she was young. She had been nearly his son's age when she had died giving birth to him. He saw strength in his straight nose and high cheekbones. His wide-set eyes held an honesty of expression and intelligence. When he

463

smiled, it was his wife's smile he saw, just like their wedding night at the quiet pool where the trees conversed in whispers.

"Gonna rain," said his son, watching cumulo-nimbus clouds as they towered on the horizon. Their anvil heads reached like white monsters to the sky, reflecting the pastel yellows and pinks of the descending sun.

"Good," grunted Abe. "I need a bath."

"You need anythin' else?" Joe's voice showed concern for his father, knowing the heat must have taken its toll. He had always been amazed how his father had been able to sit motionless in all kinds of weather, especially when they had gone hunting together.

Abe shook his head, watching his son turn to walk back up the road. "Goodbye son," he said quietly.

Joe turned. There were tears in his eyes. "Bye dad."

"What the hell do you mean there's nothing you can do? You're the police and that man is threatening to blow up a load of explosives, if that isn't against the law I don't know what is." Thompkins had finally removed his tie and unbuttoned a top shirt button to reveal the beginnings of a white, freckled chest. His whole skin was fish-belly white, except for his bald spot which had become hot-pink from sunburn and beginning to be painful.

"What would you have me do sir, go down there and ask him for his rifle? We both know he wouldn't give it to me. He'd rather die than give it to me," said Pusch, thankful for a cooling breeze from the west.

Thompkins paced in circles, kicking at rocks, bouncing them off the hubcaps of the surveillance van. "He just wants to go out in a blaze of glory and you're going to sit here and let him do it."

"I don't intend to go out with him Mr. Thompkins. I'm hoping this heat will put him to sleep so we can sneak down there and disarm him. So far he hasn't told us what he plans to do and what you're saying is pure speculation."

He stopped walking in circles and looked for a long moment toward the control gates. "How far is that, about three-hundred yards? Don't you people have anyone trained to shoot that distance?"

"He sitting on a load of explosives. We'd all be blown to shreds from this distance if the shot missed, or he decided to do it himself. I don't think you realize the power of what he's sitting on down there, sir."

"I'm beginning to," he said quietly, to no one in particular. "Too bad he ruined your fishing trip," he added.

"What?"

"Weren't you going fishing with your son here?"

464

"My son?" Pusch glanced quickly at his partner, Frank, and then down at his malodorous fishing disguise.

"I was actually born to him out of wedlock," interjected Frank, smiling hugely.

"So legally that makes you a bastard."

"That's right Mr. Thompkins, and I'll show you what a mean bastard I can really be if you don't drop the idea of shooting people. Before you wear out your welcome completely, why don't you get on the horn to your people down south and see what they're prepared to do to help settle this little dispute?" Frank had moved nose to nose with the executive until the man returned to his rented helicopter squatting on the road in the distance.

Ten minutes later, the turbine of the helicopter began spooling up and took off in a flurry of noise and dust as it rushed the hydro executive back to the airport. The two RCMP officers were relieved to see the man go, preferring to play the waiting game rather than try the old trapper's patience any further.

"By the way dad, next Thursday is my birthday. Are you going to get me a nice present?"

"You know Frank," said Pusch with a weary voice, I'll bet you never had any parents at all." He sat on the hot running board of the van and watched the building wall of clouds in the west. "Why don't you do something useful and call in for a weather report." Pusch's moustache was beginning to wilt in the heat and humidity, an omen he had come to know bode ill for his safety. His fears were confirmed when his partner returned in moments with a prediction of severe thunderstorms with lightning and possibly hail. With trepidation he watched the towering clouds and their approaching dark underbellies where he could see occasional flickers of lightning and hear the muted muttering of thunder, as the sound arrived several minutes later. As the sun began to disappear behind the clouds, a fresh breeze came up, carrying with it the unmistakable smell of rain. He ordered the vehicles to move back further from the control gates, to join the long line of traffic at the roadblock. Before they departed, he took one last look through the binoculars at the old trapper, still sitting with the rifle on his lap, appearing to be asleep. High in the sky, he saw many birds, wheeling on the rivers of air, between the towering white clouds.

The air was motionless as the dark wall approached, a surrealistic vision of lightning flashes on a backdrop of dark grey which changed to a near luminous green at times.

Bardman, McKay and D'Amico sat on a large rock on the side of the road when they saw the van approaching along the shoulder. It was white with the logo of the local television station emblazoned on the side.

465

Corporal Pusch waved the van down with his floppy fishing hat. A couple of poorly attached lures flew into the ditch. He had a short conversation with the driver, a young man with bushy hair and horn-rimmed glasses who could barely see over the edge of the window. He gesticulated, then appeared thoughtful, finally nodding, signalling some kind of agreement had been reached. The driver and another man, got out of the van and quickly began moving equipment from the rear door. The assistant, equally young, but chubby, was grinning from ear to ear of his chubby cheeks as he carried a large Betacam camera and tripod toward the silent trio.

"I'll be damned," said Bardman. "The local media talked their way past the roadblock."

The chubby assistant was sweating and breathing heavily under his load, closely followed by the driver, encumbered by a large spool of cable, his frizzy hair beginning to stick to the sides of his head.

"Don't you guys know what's down there?" asked Bardman.

The skinny driver stopped, looking like an ant lugging an over-sized prey home. "Remote camera," puffed the driver. "Gonna hook it up to a monitor in the van...record everything from there." His eyelids began to blink rapidly in an effort to dissipate the sweat which had run into them. Without saying more he jogged after his assistant who had reached the down slope and now waited, gesturing frantically with his hands.

He watched them from his rock, as they set the camera on the tripod in the ditch. The frizzy-haired cameraman focussed the camera at the figure on the trailer, then had his assistant hold a white card in front of the lens. He checked the contacts to the battery belt on the ground, and then unwound the spool of co-axial cable from the camera back toward the parked van. He could see the two technicians looking anxiously over their shoulders at the lowering sky, as the muttering of the thunder became louder.

Teresa glanced at Bardman with a look of concern, then back at Joe. McKay's face was a pasty colour and covered with sweat, his eyes open but with a glazed quality.

"Gonna be sick," mumbled Joe. He bent slowly from the waste and retched at the base of the rock, D'Amico gripped his shoulders as they heaved with the strain. Flies congregated within seconds around the rancid puddle. Joe began to shiver despite the heat.

Bardman leaned closer to McKay and looked at his eyes. He blocked the light from one eye with a hand, then removed it to check the way the pupil reacted to the change of light. He did the same to the other and noted that his left pupil barely reacted at all. "Joe has a concussion Teri, we have to get him to a hospital, right now."

"No...no hospital," moaned Joe as he tried to retch again. "Can't leave my dad...might need me."

"You can't help him the way you are Joe," replied D'Amico. Besides, I don't think he wants anybody's help now."

Bardman leaned close to McKay to be sure he would hear. "Listen to me Joe, I think you also have heat exhaustion. Your fluids have to be replaced but we can't give you anything by mouth, the only way they can do that is at the hospital. You have to let us help you."

McKay's eyes were shut has he shook his head.

"What's wrong with him?" asked the chubby assistant, his face red and sweaty.

"We need to get him out of this heat, and he needs to get to a hospital," replied D'Amico.

"We got room in the van, but only if he lays on the floor." The cameraman continued past, unreeling the cable. His assistant helped D'Amico hold Joe between them and half walk, half drag him to the van in the distance. Bardman followed close behind, prepared to catch him if he fell.

Corporal Pusch watched without helping as Joe was loaded onto the floor of the van where a blanket for padding equipment had been placed. He had been shoved gently against one side of the van, his face next to metal shelving which held electronic gear, including two Beta recorders.

"Just make sure there's room for me and my partner in there when you start to film, otherwise the deal's off and you won't be allowed to keep that camera there." He waggled his flaccid moustache at the camera man, expecting him to flinch from the bushy anomaly. He looked quickly around to see the accusing faces of Bardman and D'Amico. "Hey, I'm not kicking him out, at least not until the ambulance gets here."

His partner tapped him on the shoulder.

"What... what?"

"Sorry bwana, I just heard over the radio, no joy on that ambulance, it's over-heated about halfway here. They think they blew a radiator hose."

Pusch shook his head slowly in frustration, looking at Joe's semi-prone form on the floor of the van. "Alright, okay, you two will sit in the front seats, the rest of us will stay back here to watch the monitor. If it looks like the old guy is going to pack it in, we'll be able to go down there and take that rifle away from him before he does something stupid."

"He ain't that dumb," came Joe's shaky voice from the van floor. "You go near him, an' he'll shoot the beast."

"What beast?"

"He calls the trailer the beast, Pusch, an' all he's gotta do is smell you an' He'll start shootin'" Joe had rolled partway over so his one eye could focus on the corporal standing in the rear door of the van. "You got no choice but to wait for him to do whatever he's gonna do."

Large raindrops began to hit the metal top of the van like small pebbles, signalling the coming onslaught. Bardman and D'Amico sat in the front, D'Amico in the driver's seat, as the others, Pusch, his partner, Frank, and the two technicians crowded into the rear where the assistant worked hurriedly to hook up the cable to the recorder and remote control for the camera.

"My God, what's that smell?" said the assistant, looking around at the faces in the semi-dark interior.

All faces turned toward Pusch in silent accusation. He glared back, saying nothing, his eyes watching the monitor. Finally the monitor flickered to life, the image of Abe McKay clear on full tele-zoom as he sat in the downpour with his rifle still across his lap.

Abe McKay barely felt the harsh impact of the large drops of rain, nor was he aware of the howl of the wind as it bent the tops of the trees and whipped the waters into a froth. His eyes were closed but the harsh flashes of lightning created an image of pink, criss-crossed lines with a delicate lattice of red, the tiny veins in the skin of his eyelids. His breathing and heart rate had slowed until his entire body relaxed as though in a deep sleep. He had the sense of floating above the ground, time flowed through him, rather than he through it.

"Nobody in their right mind would sit out in a storm like this," said the camera man, sitting with his nose nearly against the screen of the monitor.

The others sat quietly, their faces reflecting the bluish glow from the screen, nearly shoulder to shoulder, watching and waiting. Each time the lightning flashed, the screen nearly went white, then the camera adjusted exposure for the figure illuminated by the sodium vapour lights of the control gate structure. Their eyes turned to the roof of the van as the sound of rain gave way to the more harsh rattle of hail. The van began to sway with each gust of wind, droplets forcing themselves around the gasket of the double rear doors.

Joe slowly rolled himself to a sitting position, his nose nearly level with the posteriors of the others as they watched the screen. With both hands he reached out and separated the buttocks of Pusch from that of his partner. Both turned inquiringly, and moved slightly aside so Joe could see the image of his father on the monitor.

"Finally, commercial-free t.v," he said, then turned and began to retch onto the floor of the van.

The others in the van shuffled their feet like a spastic dance troupe, trying to avoid the mess about their feet. Pusch opened the rear door, put his head outside and breathed deeply. Frank, seeing the opportunity, shoved him from behind, sending him sprawling face down on the muddy road. He then quickly closed and locked the doors. With the racket from the hail and lightning, they barely heard Pusch beating on the door with his fists. He appeared at the front of the van, screaming like a sodden demon at them through the windshield where Bardman and D'Amico had a first-hand view of his frenzy, refusing to open their doors.

"Don't let him in," called Pusch's partner. "Maybe the rain will wash some of that stink off him."

Pusch gave a final kick to the wheel of the van as he stalked off toward his own surveillance van.

Frank began to chuckle, his long hair beginning to smell like that of a wet dog. He saw the others questioning him with their eyes. "I have the keys to our van... and it's locked."

All eyes turned quietly back to the monitor.

"How much time on the tape?" asked Bardman from the front seat.

The cameraman indicated about fifteen minutes left. Everyone was surprised they had been watching for nearly two hours.

Abe felt the hail and heard it as it rattled off the corrugated metal sides of the trailer. There was another sound which he had never heard before. It began as a low hum as though a giant bass string was being plucked. Gradually, it fluctuated in tone and volume, coming from all around him. His skin began to tingle and the hairs on his arms and head began to stand away from his body. He opened his eyes as the humming reached a crescendo in time for him to see the tremendous arc of lightning as it leapt to the steel girders of the control gates. The bolt was so powerful that lightning rods on the structure couldn't divert the charge entirely through its ground wires. Part of the bolt flashed along the girder to the section of steel that had been embedded in the front of the trailer. The metal skin of the trailer itself conducted the thousands of volts over its surface toward the ground, passing through objects that even offered high resistance. One of those objects was Abe McKay.

Abe felt his muscles go into spasm and his blood begin to boil in his veins. An instant later, the bolt of electricity which had entered the trailer of explosives came in contact with a box of primers which had been ripped open due to the crash. The concussion and heat of the lightning charge detonated the primers along with the nearly 30,000 pounds of Amex.

The water was clear and cool as the canoe moved quietly through the water lilies. The tall trees rustled gently in the warm summer breeze, bringing with it the scent of wood smoke and sweet grass. He could see the figure on the shoreline where they had spent their wedding night. She tended the fire, her long black hair flowing over her shoulders, her dark eyes beckoning to him, her lips whispering his name like a wind through the trees. As the bow of the canoe scraped the rocky shoreline, she rose and walked to him, carefully entering the canoe, leaning over and kissed him on the lips.

"I knew you'd come, I've been waiting so long. We can go now."

Abe McKay smiled, his heart filled with an intensity of love he never thought could exist as he quietly paddled the canoe with his young bride toward the beckoning mists of the river. It looked as though it could go on forever.

Far above, a lone raven soared on the winds. It watched the young couple and seemed to smile as they paddled from its sight.

EPILOGUE

Bardman sat quietly, reading the newspaper, his eyes scanning the headline: *Control Gates Destroyed. Man becomes martyred hero.* He read on while massaging his severely bruised shoulder with his left hand. The front page picture was an image he had photographed from a television monitor at the local station, with the permission of the station manager, showing a grainy image of Abe McKay as he sat under the yellow lights, atop the explosives trailer. He appeared to be meditating, the lightning having struck only minutes after that last image had been made by the remote video camera.

"Hell of a story, eh?"

He looked up from the table in the dingy newspaper cafeteria.

Samantha Paige pulled out a chair and sat across from him, a coffee cup cradled in both hands. She slurped noisily from it, looking at him over the brim, her green eyes like emerald magnets. "You always do a good job, no matter what the story, Sam."

"Without your picture and your first-hand account, we'd have nothing, Brady. You should take most of the credit. Sorry for the lack of credit on the photo. The guys on the desk went wild when they heard there was art to go with the story, which I emphasised, you also supplied. Their jaws dropped and all they said was, Oh, him. They really black-balled you when they fired you from this paper didn't they? I mean you could shoot Pulitzer Prize stuff and they still wouldn't hire you back would they? What did you do, kick one of them in the gonads?"

Bardman smiled wanly, leaning back in his chair. "No, just expressed myself too profoundly for their liking. They had an old crony waiting in the wings doing freelance for them and getting good assignments while they shoved product shots and grip-and-grins at us staff shooters. I was the only single guy there, so...the most disposable."

"So they put a dead fish on your desk as a way of saying don't come back?"

"Something like that, only in the verbal sense. They wrote me a little acid-note saying I had a combative attitude and did mediocre work. I told them they wouldn't know a good photograph if it came up and bit them on their mediocre butts."

"Well, that doesn't sound too combative to me."

"Well there you go. But whoever said there's fairness in the workplace?"

"Sorry to hear about your car, that must have been a hell of an explosion to topple all those trees down on top of it."

He shrugged, trying to interpret the pattern of the grounds in his coffee cup. "Worked out better than I thought, really. The insurance people saw the tape of the lightning strike on t.v. and said it was an act of God. They wrote the car off and gave me a cash settlement, just like at least a dozen other claims from people who were on the road."

"How are the others after the media van was flipped onto its top?"

"I was the lucky one with just my shoulder, Teri got cuts to her face when the windshield blew in, and the two technicians both got electrical burns when the power surge hit the cable from the video camera. It arced right through the power-surge protector, burned the cable off and then sat and heated up a puddle of Joe McKay's vomit. God, what a stink!"

Samantha made a face.

"At least I managed to retrieve one kayak, the other was skewered by branches, thirty feet up in a tree."

" Why did you have two kayaks out there?"

He thought for a moment, carefully choosing his words. "It's something I might tell you about some day, all I can say is I changed my mind about something, and the possibilities of what might have been scare me silly."

"Sounds like it might make a good story some day. So, what are you going to do now?"

"Got my trusty Norton outside, all loaded up. I got a call from that trash paper in Los Angeles to stop in and talk about more publication rights for those shots. I guess you heard from them too eh?".

"Yeah, they're clambering for more about this latest story. Don't let them talk you down, Brady, make them make you rich." She reached across the table and gave his hand a maternal-like pat. "We made a good team. I wish you weren't leaving. How do prospects look in Central America?"

He unconsciously dug a plug of lint from his navel, then began to blush as he saw Samantha smiling at his unwitting gesture. "Wow, that sure is a big one," he said, holding the offensive fibre in front of his thick-lensed spectacles.

They laughed uncontrollably, gaining the attention of a tobacco-stained scribe, hunched over his own edition in the corner.

"Well, actually, Sam, the paper's editor called, the San Jose News I mean, and said they could use me freelance only, and pay me under the table. Costa Rican immigration laws won't allow them to hire a non-local, even though it is an English publication. However, they said that they'd love to hire another reporter who spoke Spanish and English. So, how's your Spanish?"

"Non-existent. How's yours?"

"It's going to get better, I've signed for a six week immersion class in Guatemala. School called Proyecto Linguistico, in the town of Antigua. They

472

billet students with local families. If I can't learn it down there, I can't learn it anywhere, because nobody speaks English there, not even the teachers, and there's one student per teacher. One minor problem is that I have to stop in San Francisco to get my visa, but after that, zoom, through Mexico, muchos cervezas con comeda caliente."

"What?"

"Hot food and cold beer m'dear," replied Bardman, eyeing the ceiling as he dreamed of the gastronomical delights, patting his substantial belly in anticipation.

"Just don't drink the water, Brady. The Aztec Two-Step isn't a fun dance, and can't be done slowly. All the same, I envy your freedom."

He stood up from the table, picking up his helmet, wedged it over his thick, curly hair. The attempt pushed his eyeglasses to the end of his nose, making him peer over them at Samantha in an avuncular manner. "I'm going to miss you Sam; wish me luck."

She gripped his helmet by each side, pulling his head down to her level. "Don't let this go to your head Brady," she said as she planted her lips fully on top of his helmet, leaving a large lipstick imprint.

He rolled his eyes heavenward as though trying to see the mark. "I swear Sam, I'll never wash this helmet again." He smiled, winked, and planted a kiss on her cheek, butting her forehead with the visor of the helmet, making tears come to her eyes from the pain. "Now, now, no tears. God I hate goodbyes." He moved deftly to escape the swift kick she aimed at his posterior, and went out to the warm sunshine and to his fully-loaded Norton. It looked like a beautiful day to travel.

473

ISBN 142510934-9